W9-BNR-928

L. A.
NOIR

Also by James Ellroy

My Dark Places
American Tabloid
Hollywood Nocturnes
White Jazz
L.A. Confidential
The Black Dahlia
Killer on the Road
Clandestine
Brown's Requiem

JAMES ELLROY

L. A. NOIR

THE MYSTERIOUS PRESS

Published by Warner Books

A Time Warner Company

Blood on the Moon © James Ellroy 1984
Because the Night © James Ellroy 1985
Suicide Hill © James Ellroy 1986

Copyright © 1998 by James Ellroy
All rights reserved.
This Mysterious Press edition published by arrangement with Arrow Books, Random House UK
Limited, 20 Vauxhall Bridge Road, London SW1V 2SA

 Mysterious Press books are published by Warner Books, Inc., 1271
Avenue of the Americas, New York, NY 10020.

Visit our Web Site at http://warnerbooks.com

 A Time Warner Company

The Mysterious Press name and logo are registered trademarks of Warner Books, Inc.
Printed in the United States of America
First Mysterious Press Printing: June 1998

10 9 8 7 6 5 4 3 2 1

Library of Congress Cataloging-in-Publication Data

Ellroy, James.
    L.A. noir / James Ellroy.
        p.   cm.
    Contents: Blood on the moon — Because the night — Suicide hill.
    ISBN 0-89296-686-6
    1. Detective and mystery stories, American—California—Los
Angeles.   2. Murder—California—Los Angeles—Fiction.   3. Police—
California—Los Angeles—Fiction.   4. Los Angeles (Calif.)—
Fiction.   I. Title.
PS3555.L6274A6   1998
813'.54—dc21   98-15470
                                                                    CIP

INTRODUCTION

I sat down to plot *Blood on the Moon* late in 1980. I'd written two previous novels, *Brown's Requiem* and *Clandestine*—a private eye story and a period cop book. I wanted to write a contemporarily set, contrapunctually structured novel about a sex obsessed cop tracking down a sexually motivated killer. I was not familiar with the term "serial killer." Thomas Harris's brilliant and ground-breaking novel *Red Dragon* was yet to be published. I didn't know that the mano-a-mano duels of cops and serial killers would soon become a big fat fucking cliché. *Red Dragon*—to my mind the greatest suspense novel ever written—spawned an entire sub-genre. It was explicit in a way that Lawrence Sanders's *The First Deadly Sin* wasn't. The killers' psychopathology scared the shit out of me—more than the killers' psychopathology in *Blood on the Moon*.

I wrote *Blood on the Moon*. I read *Red Dragon* and realized it was a far superior book. I carried the hero of *Blood on the Moon* on to a second and third novel—*Because the Night* and *Suicide Hill*. I hadn't planned to write a trilogy at first. I did not possess the long-range planning skills I possess today. I finished *Blood on the Moon*, read *Red Dragon* and wanted another shot at making Sergeant Lloyd Hopkins as great a character as Thomas Harris's Will Graham.

Hopkins was my antidote to the sensitive candy-assed philosophizing private eye. I wanted to create a recognizably racist and reactionary cop and make his racism and reactionary tendencies casual attributes rather than defining characteristics—wanted to build a complex monument to a basically shitty guy—and I didn't care whether my readers liked Lloyd Hopkins—as long as they liked the books he was in.

You can take Hopkins or leave him. You can dismiss him as a fascist fuckhead or dig him as a vessel of urban torment. I don't care what you think of Hopkins. I hope you dig the books.

James Ellroy

18 February 1997

Contents

BLOOD ON THE MOON

In Memory of
KENNETH MILLAR
1915–1983

The bay trees in our country are all withered,
and meteors fright the fixed stars of heaven;
the pale face moon looks bloody on the earth,
and lean look'd prophets whisper fearful change.

Shakespeare
Richard II

PART ONE
FIRST TASTES OF BLOOD

1

Friday, June 10, 1964, was the start of a KRLA golden oldie weekend. The two conspirators scouting the territory where the "kidnaping" would take place blasted their portable radio at full volume to drown out the sound of power saws, hammers and crowbars—the noise of the third-floor classroom renovation and the music of the Fleetwoods battling for audial supremacy.

Larry "Birdman" Craigie, the radio held close to his head, marveled at the irony of this construction work taking place a scant week before school was to close for the summer. Just then, Gary U. S. Bonds came over the airwaves, singing: "School is out at last, and I'm so glad I passed," and Larry fell to the sawdust covered linoleum floor, convulsed with laughter. School was maybe gonna be out, but he wasn't gonna pass, and his name was Chuck and he didn't give a fuck. He rolled on the floor, heedless of his recently swiped purple fuzzy Sir Guy shirt.

Delbert "Whitey" Haines started to get disgusted and mad. The Birdman was either psycho or faking it, which meant that his long time stooge was smarter than him, which meant that he was laughing *at* him. Whitey waited until Larry's laughter wound down and he propped himself into push-up position. He knew what was coming next: A series of lurid remarks about doing push-ups on Ruthie Rosenberg, how Larry was going to make her blow him while he hung from the rings in the girls' gym.

Larry's laughter trailed off, and he opened his mouth to speak. Whitey didn't let him get that far; he liked Ruthie and hated to hear nice girls blasphemed. He nuzzled the toe of his boot into Larry's shoulder blades, right where he knew the zits were really bad. Larry screeched and hopped to his feet, cradling the radio into his chest.

"You didn't have to do that."

"No," Whitey said, "but I did. I can read your mind, psycho. Phony psycho. So don't say no nasty things about nice girls. We got the punk to deal with, not nice girls."

Larry nodded; that he was included in such important plans took the sting out of the attack. He walked to the nearest window and looked out and thought of the punk in his saddle shoes and his argyle sweaters and his pretty-boy looks and his poetry review that he printed up in the camera shop on Aluarado where he lived, sweeping up the store in exchange for room and board.

The *Marshall High Poetry Review*—punk, sissy poems; gooey love stuff that everyone knew was dedicated to that stuck-up Irish parochial school transfer girl and the stuck-up snooty bitches in her poet crowd, and vicious fucking attacks on him and Whitey and all the *righteous* homeboys at Marshall. When Larry had gotten zonked on glue and cherry bombed the Folk Song Club, the *Review* had commemorated the occasion with line drawings of him in a storm trooper's outfit and maiming prose: "We now have a brownshirt named Birdman—illiterate, not much of a wordman. His weapons are stealth, and poor mental health; he's really much more like a turdman."

Whitey had fared even worse: after kicking Big John Kafesjian's ass in a fair fight in the Rotunda Court, the punk had devoted an entire copy of the *Review* to an "epic" poem detailing the event, calling Whitey a "white trash loser provocateur" and ending with a prediction of his fate, phrased like an epitaph:

"No autopsy can e'er reveal, what his darkest heart did most conceal; that shallow muscleman void, defined by terror and hate—Let that be the requiem for this light-weight."

Larry had volunteered to give Whitey a swift revenge, doing himself a favor in the process: The Boys' V.P. had said that he would be expelled for one more fight or cherry bomb episode, and the idea of no more school nearly made him cream in his jeans. But Whitey had nixed the notion of quick retribution, saying, "No, it's too easy. The punk has got to suffer like we did. He made us laughing stocks. We're gonna return the compliment, and then some."

So their plan of disrobing, beating, genital painting, and shaving was hatched. Now, if it all worked out, was the time. Larry watched Whitey trace swastikas in the sawdust with a two-by-four. The Del-Vikings' rendition of "Come Go with Me" ended and the news came on, meaning it was three o'clock. Larry heard the whoops a moment later, then watched as the workmen gathered up their hand tools and power equipment and bustled off down the main staircase, leaving them alone to wait for the poet.

Larry swallowed and nudged Whitey, afraid of upsetting his silent artwork.

"Are you sure he'll come? What if he figures out the note's a phony?"

Whitey looked up and kicked out at a half-open wall locker door, snapping it off at its hinges. "He'll be here. A note from that Irish cunt? He'll think it's some kind of fucking lovers' rendezvous. Just relax. My sister wrote the note. Pink stationery, a girl's handwriting. Only it ain't gonna be no lovers' rendezvous. You know what I mean, homeboy?"

Larry nodded; he knew.

The conspirators waited in silence, Larry daydreaming, Whitey rummaging through the abandoned lockers, looking for left-behinds. When they heard footsteps on the second-floor corridor below them, Larry grabbed a pair of jockey shorts from a brown paper bag and pulled a tube of acetate airplane glue from his pocket. He squeezed the tube's entire contents onto the shorts, then flattened himself against the row of lockers nearest to the stairwell. Whitey crouched beside him, homemade knuckle dusters coiled in his right fist.

"Sweetheart?"

The endearment, whispered hesitantly, preceded the sound of footsteps that seemed to grow bolder as they neared the third-story landing. Whitey counted to himself, and when he calculated that the poet was within grabbing range he pushed Larry out of the way and stationed himself next to the edge of the stairs.

"Darling?"

Larry started to laugh, and the poet froze in mid-step, his hand on the stair rail. Whitey grabbed the hand and jerked upwards, sending the poet sprawling over the last two steps. He yanked again, relieving the pressure at just the right angle to twist the poet into a kneeling position. When his adversary was staring up at him with impotent, beseeching eyes, Whitey kicked him in the stomach, then pulled him to his feet as he trembled uncontrollably.

"Now, Birdman!" Whitey screeched.

Larry wrapped the glue-streaked jockey shorts around the poet's mouth and nostrils and pushed until his tremors became gurgling sounds and the skin around his temples went from pink to red to blue and he started to gasp for breath.

Larry relinquished his grip and backed away, the jockey shorts falling to the floor. The poet writhed on his feet, then fell backward, crashing into a half-open locker door. Whitey stood his ground, both fists cocked, watching the poet retch for breath, whispering, "We killed him. We honest to fucking god killed him."

Larry was on his knees, praying and making the sign of the cross, when the poet's gasps finally caught oxygen and he expelled a huge ball of glue covered phlegm, followed by a screeching syllable, "sc-sc-sc."

"Scum!"

He got the word out in a rush of new breath, the color in his face returning to normal as he drew himself slowly to his knees. "Scum! Dirty white trash, low-life scum! Stupid, mean, ugly, wanton!"

Whitey Haines started to laugh as relief flooded through him. Larry Craigie began to dry-sob in relief and molded his prayer-forming hands into fists. Whitey's laughter became hysterical, and the poet, on his feet now, turned his fury on him: "Muscle-bound auto mechanic peckerwood trash! No woman would ever touch you! The girls I know all laugh at you and your two inch dick! No dick, no sex fool. No—"

Whitey went red, and started to shake. He pulled his foot back and sent it full force into the poet's genitals. The poet screamed and fell to his knees. Whitey yelled, "Turn the radio on, full blast!"

Larry obeyed, and the Beach Boys flooded the corridor as Whitey kicked and pummeled the poet, who drew himself into a fetal ball, muttering, "scum, scum" as the blows rained into him.

When the poet's face and bare arms were covered with blood, Whitey stepped back to savor his revenge. He pulled down his fly to deliver a warm liquid coup de grâce, and discovered he was hard. Larry noticed this, and looked to his leader for some clue to what was supposed to happen. Suddenly Whitey was terrified. He looked down at the poet, who moaned "scum," and spat out a stream of blood onto the steel-toed paratrooper boots. Now Whitey knew what his hardness meant, and he knelt beside the poet and pulled off his Levi cords and boxer shorts and spread his legs and blunderingly plunged himself into him. The poet screamed once as he entered; then his breathing settled into something strangely like ironic laughter. Whitey finished, withdrew and looked to his shock-stilled underling for support. To make it easy for him, he turned up the volume on the radio until Elvis Presley wailed into a garbled screech; then he watched as Larry delivered his ultimate acquiescence.

They left him there, bereft of tears or the will to feel anything beyond the hollowness of his devastation. As they walked away, "Cathy's Clown," by the Everly Brothers, came on the radio. They had both laughed, and Whitey had kicked him one last time.

He lay there until he was certain the quad would be deserted. He thought of his true love and imagined that she was with him, her head resting on his chest, telling him how much she loved the sonnets he composed for her.

Finally, he got to his feet. It was hard to walk; each step shot a rending pain through his bowels up into his chest. He felt at his face; it was covered with dried matter that had to be blood. He scrubbed his face furiously with his sleeve until the abrasions ran with fresh trickles of blood over smooth skin. This made him feel better, and the fact that he hadn't betrayed tears made him feel better still.

Except for a few odd groups of kids hanging out and playing catch, the quad was deserted, and the poet made his way across it in slow, painful steps. Gradually, he became aware of a warm liquid running down his legs. He pulled up his right trouser leg and saw that his sock was soaked in blood laced with white matter. Taking off his socks, he hobbled toward the "Arch of Fame," a marble inlaid walkway that commemorated the school's previous graduating classes. The poet wiped the bloody handfuls of cotton over mascots depicting the Athenians of '63 all the way back through the Delphians of '31, then strode barefoot, gaining strength and purpose with each step, out the school's south gate and onto Griffith Park Boulevard, his mind bursting with odd bits of poetry and sentimental rhymes; all for her.

When he saw the florist's shop at the corner of Griffith Park and Hyperion, he knew that this was his destination. He steeled himself for human contact and went in and purchased a dozen red roses, to be sent to an address he knew by heart but had never visited. He selected a blank card to go with them, and scribbled on the back some musings about love being etched in blood. He paid the florist, who smiled and assured him that the flowers would be delivered within the hour.

The poet walked outside, realizing that there were still two hours of daylight left, and that he had no place to go. This frightened him, and he tried composing an ode to waning daylight to keep his fear at bay. He tried, and tried, but his mind wouldn't click in and his fear became terror and he fell to his knees, sobbing for a word or phrase to make it right again.

2

When Watts burst into flames on August 23, 1965, Lloyd Hopkins was building sand castles on the beach at Malibu and inhabiting them with members of his family and fictional characters out of his own brilliant imagination.

A crowd of children had gathered around the gangly twenty-three-year-old, eager to be entertained, yet somehow deferential to the great mind that they sensed in the big young man whose hands so deftly molded drawbridges, moats, and parapets. Lloyd was at one with the children and with his own mind, which he viewed as a separate entity. The children watched, and he sensed their eagerness and desire to be with him and knew instinctively when to gift them with a smile or waggle his eyebrows so that they would be satisfied and he could return to his real play.

His Irish Protestant ancestors were fighting with his lunatic brother Tom for control of the castle. It was a battle between the good loyalists of the past and Tom and his rabble-rousing paramilitary cohorts who thought that Negroes should be shipped back to Africa and that all roadways should be privately owned. The loonies had the upper hand temporarily—Tom and his backyard arsenal of hand grenades and automatic weaponry were formidable—but the good loyalists were staunch-hearted where Tom and his band were craven, and led by about-to-be police officer Lloyd, the Irish band had surmounted technology and was now raining flaming arrows into the midst of Tom's hardware, causing it to explode. Lloyd envisioned flames in the sand in front of him, and wondered for the eight thousandth time that day what the academy would be like. Tougher than basic training? It would have to be, or the city of Los Angeles was in deep trouble.

Lloyd sighed. He and his loyalists had won the battle and his parents, inexplicably lucid, had come to praise the victorious son and heap scorn on the loser.

"You can't beat brains, Doris," his father told his mother. "I wish it weren't true, but they rule the world. Learn another language, Lloydy; Tom can commune with those lowlifes in that phone sales racket, but you solve puzzles and rule the world." His mother nodded mutely; the stroke had destroyed her ability to talk.

Tom just glowered in defeat.

Out of nowhere, Lloyd heard the music and very slowly, very consciously forced himself to turn in the direction from which the raucous sound was coming.

A little girl was holding a radio, cradled preciously into herself, attempting to sing along. When Lloyd saw the little girl, his heart melted. *She* didn't know how he hated music, how it undercut his thought processes. He would have to be gentle with her, as he was with women of all ages. He caught the little girl's attention, speaking softly, even as his headache grew: "Do you like my castle, sweetheart?"

"Y-yes," the little girl said.

"It's for you. The Good Loyalists fought the battle for a fair damsel, and that damsel is you."

The music was growing deafening; Lloyd thought briefly that the whole world could hear it. The little girl shook her head coquettishly, and Lloyd said, "Can you turn the radio off, sweetie? Then I'll take you on a tour of your castle." The child complied, and fumbled the volume switch the wrong way just as the music stopped and a stern-voiced announcer intoned: "And Governor Edmund G. Brown has just announced that the National Guard has been ordered into South Central Los Angeles in force to stop the two day reign of looting and terror that has already left four dead. All members of the following units are to report immediately . . ."

The little girl fiddled the radio off just as Lloyd's headache metamorphosed into a perfect stillness. "You ever read *Alice in Wonderland*, sweetheart?" he asked.

"My mommy read me from the picture book," the little girl said.

"Good. Then you know what it means to follow the rabbit down the hole?"

"Does it mean what Alice did when she went into Wonderland?"

"That's right; and that's what old Lloyd has to do now—the radio just said so."

"Are you 'Old Lloyd'?"

"Yes."

"Then what's going to happen to your castle?"

"You inherit it, fair damsel—it's yours to do with as you please."

"Really?"

"Really."

The little girl hopped into the air and came down square on top of the castle, obliterating it. Lloyd ran for his car and what he hoped would be his baptism by fire.

In the Armory, Staff Sergeant Beller took his prize cadre aside and told them that for a few bucks they could appreciably cut down the odds of getting eaten alive in niggerland and maybe have a few laughs, besides.

He motioned Lloyd Hopkins and two other P.F.C.s into the lavatory and displayed his wares and elaborated: ".45 automatic. Your classic officer's sidearm. Guaranteed to drop any fire-breathing nigger at thirty yards, regardless of where it hits him. Strictly illegal for E.M., and a valuable asset in its own right—but these babies are fully automatic—machine pistols, with my specially devised elephant clip—twenty shots, reload in five seconds flat. The piece overheats, but I throw in a glove. The piece, two elephant clips and the glove—an even C-note. Takers?" He proffered the sidearms around. The two motor pool P.F.C.s eyed them longingly and hefted them with love, but declined.

"I'm broke, Sarge," the first P.F.C. said.

"I'm staying behind at the command post with the half-tracks, Sergeant," the second P.F.C. said.

Beller sighed, and looked up at Lloyd Hopkins, who gave him the creeps. "The Brain," the guys in the company called him. "Hoppy, what about you?"

"I'll take them both," Lloyd said.

Dressed in Class C fatigues, leggings, full bandoliers and helmet liners, Co. A of the 2nd Battalion, 46th Division, California National Guard stood at parade rest in the main meeting hall of the Glendale Armory, waiting to be briefed. Their battalion commander, a forty-four-year-old Pasadena dentist who held the reserve rank of Lieutenant Colonel, formulated his thoughts and orders into what he hoped would be considered a fierce brevity and spoke into the microphone. "Gentlemen, we are going into the firestorm. The Los Angeles police have just informed us that a forty-eight square mile portion of South Central Los Angeles is engulfed in flames, and that entire commercial blocks have been pillaged and then set on fire. We are being sent in to protect the lives of the firemen battling those fires and to divert through our presence the looting and other criminal activity taking place. This is the sole regular infantry company in an otherwise armored division. You men, I'm sure, will be the spearhead of this peace-keeping force of civilian soldiers. You will be briefed further when we reach our objective. Good day, and God be with you!"

Nobody mentioned God as the convoy of armored half-tracks and personnel carriers rolled out of Glendale toward the Golden State Freeway southbound. The main topics of conversation were guns, sex, and Negroes, until P.F.C. Lloyd Hopkins, sweltering in the canvas covered half-track, took off his fatigue jacket and introduced fear and immortality:

"First of all, you have to say it to yourselves, get it out in the air, say it—'I'm afraid. I don't wanna die!' You got that? No, don't say it out loud, that takes the power out of it. Say it to yourselves. There. Two, say this, too—I'm a nice white boy going to college who joined the fucking National Guard to get out of two years' active duty, right?"

The civilian soldiers, whose average age was twenty, started to drift in to Lloyd's drift, and a few of them muttered, "Right."

"I can't hear you!" Lloyd bellowed, imitating Sergeant Beller.

"Right!" the guardsmen yelled in unison.

Lloyd laughed, and the others, relieved at the break in the tension, followed suit. Lloyd breathed out, letting his big frame go slack in an imitation of a Negro's shuffle. "And you all be afraid of de colored man?" he said in broad dialect.

Silence greeted the question, followed by a general breakout of hushed conversations. This angered Lloyd; he felt his momentum was drifting away, destroying this transcendent moment of his life.

He banged the butt end of his M-14 into the metal floorboard of the half-track. "Right!" he screamed. "Right, you dumb-fuck, pussy-whipped, nigger-scared, chicken-shit motherfuckers! Right?" He banged his rifle again. "Right? Right? Right? Right?"

"*Right!!!*" The half-track exploded with the word, the *feeling*, the new pride in candor, and the laughter that followed grew deafening in its freedom and bravado.

Lloyd slammed his rifle butt one last time, to call the group to order. "Then they can't hurt us. Do you know that?" He waited until he was rewarded by a nod of the head from every man present, then pulled his bayonet from its scabbard and cut a large hole in the canvas top of the half-track. Being tall, he was able to peer out the top with ease. In the distance he could see the flatlands of his beloved L.A. Basin awash in smog. Spirals of flame and smoke covered its southern perimeter. Lloyd thought it was the most beautiful thing he had ever seen.

The division bivouacked at McCallum Park on Florence and 90th Street, a mile from the heart of the firestorm. Trees were downed to provide space for the hundred-odd military vehicles that would cruise the streets of Watts that night, filled with men armed to the teeth, and C-rations were distributed from the back of a five ton truck while platoon leaders briefed their men on their assignments.

Rumors abounded, fed by a cadre of L.A.P.D. and Sheriff's liaison officers: The Black Muslims were coming out in force, in whiteface, bent on hitting the profusion of discount appliance stores near Vermont and Slauson; scores of Negro youth gangs on pep pills were stealing cars and forming "kamikaze" squads and heading for Beverly Hills and Bel-Air; Rob "Maga-wambi" Jones and his Afro-Americans for Goldwater had taken a distinct left turn and were demanding that Mayor Yorty grant them eight commercial blocks on Wilshire Boulevard as reparation for "L.A.P.D. Crimes Against Humanity." If their terms were not met within twenty-four hours, those eight blocks would be incinerated by firebombs hidden deep within the bowels of the LaBrea Tar Pits.

Lloyd Hopkins didn't believe a word of it. He understood the hyperbole of fear and understood further that his fellow civilian soldiers and cops were hyping themselves up to kill and that a lot of poor black bastards out to grab themselves a color TV and a case of booze were going to die.

Lloyd gobbled his C-rations and listened to his platoon leader, Lt. Campion, the night manager of a Bob's Big Boy restaurant, explain orders that had come down to him from several other higher echelon civilian soldiers: "Being infantry, we will provide foot patrol, walking point for the armored guys—checking out doorways, alleys, letting our presence be known; bayonets fixed, combat stance, that kind of shit. Look tough. The armored platoon we trained with last summer at camp will be the platoon we hang with tonight. Questions? Everyone know who their squad leader is? Any new men with questions?"

Sergeant Beller, stretched out on the grass at the back of the platoon, raised his hand and said: "Loot, you know that the platoon is hanging in at four men over strength? Fifty-four men?"

Campion cleared his throat. "Yes . . . uh . . . yes, Sergeant, I do."

"Sir, do you also know that we got three men who got special M.O.S.s? Three men who ain't regular grunts?"

"You mean . . ."

"I mean, *sir*, that myself, Hopkins, and Jensen are infantry scouts, and I'm sure you'll agree we could be of more value to this operation by running far point ahead of the armor. Right, *sir?*"

Lloyd saw the lieutenant start to waver, and suddenly realized that *he* wanted it as bad as Beller did. Raising his hand, he said, "Sir, Sergeant Beller is right; we can walk far point *and* protect the platoon better *and* make it more autonomous. The platoon is over strength, and . . ."

The lieutenant capitulated. "All right then," he said, "Beller, Hopkins and Jensen, you walk point two hundred yards ahead of the convoy. Be careful—stay sharp. No more questions? Platoon dismissed."

Lloyd and Beller found each other just as the tanks and half-tracks were starting their engines, flooding the twilight air with the sound of volatile combustion. Beller smiled; Lloyd smiled back in silent complicity.

"*Far* point, Sergeant?"

"*Far, far* point, Hoppy."

"What about Jensen?"

"He's just a kid. I'll tell him to hang back with the armor. *We're* covered. We've got carte blanche; that's the important thing."

"Opposite sides of the street?"

"Sounds right to me. Whistle twice if it gets hairy. Why do they call you 'The Brain'?"

"Because I'm very intelligent."

"Intelligent enough to know that the niggers are destroying the whole fucking country?"

"No, too intelligent for that shit. Anyone with half a brain knows that this is just a temporary blow-out and that when it's over it'll be business as usual. I'm here to see about saving innocent lives."

Beller said scornfully, "That's a crock. It just proves brains are overrated. Guts are what counts."

"Brains rule the world."

"But the world's all fucked up."

"I don't know. Let's see what it's like out there."

"Yeah, let's do that." Beller began to worry about his ass. Hoppy was starting to sound like a nigger lover.

*   *   *

They ditched the division completely, walking south toward where the flames rose the highest and the gunfire sounded its loudest echoes.

Lloyd took the north side of 93rd Street and Beller the south, rifles at high port with bayonets fixed and sharpened, eyes scanning row after row of cheap white clapboard houses where Negro families peered from lighted windows and sat on porches, drinking, smoking, chattering and waiting for something to *happen.*

They hit Central. Lloyd gulped and felt a trickle of sweat run down into his skivvies, which hung below his hipbones, weighted down by the two specially constructed automatics jammed into his waistband.

Beller whistled from across the street and pointed forward. Lloyd nodded as he felt a whiff of smoke hit his nostrils. They walked south, and it took long moments for Lloyd's head to click into place and assimilate the epiphanies, the perfect logic of the self-destruction he was viewing:

Liquor stores, night clubs, process parlors and storefront churches interspersed with vacant lots covered with abandoned cars burned out from the inside. Gutted storefront after gutted storefront spilling profusions of broken liquor bottles; broken glass everywhere; the gutters filled with cheap electric ware—non-hockable items obviously looted in haste and discarded when the looters realized they were valueless.

Lloyd poked his M-14 into smashed-in windows, squinting into the darkness, cocking his ears the way he had seen dogs do it, listening for the slightest sound or presence of movement. There was nothing—only the wail of sirens and the crack of gunshots in the distance.

Beller trotted across the street just as an L.A.P.D. black-and-white turned onto Central from 94th. Two flak-coated officers jumped out, the driver running up to Lloyd and demanding: "What the fuck are you *doing* here?"

Beller answered, startling the cops, who swiveled to face him, reaching for their .38s. "Far point, officer! My buddy and I been assigned to run ahead of our company and search out snipers. We're infantry scouts."

Lloyd knew that the cops didn't buy it and that he *had* to pursue the violent wonder of Watts without his low-life partner. He sent a sharp look Beller's way and said, "I think we're lost. We were only supposed to go out three blocks ahead, but we took a wrong turn somewhere. All the houses on these numbered streets look alike." He hesitated, trying to look bewildered.

Beller caught the drift and said, "Yeah. All these houses look alike. All these niggers on their steps sloppin' up juice look alike, too."

The older of the two cops nodded, then pointed south and said, "You guys with that artillery down near 102nd? The heavy-duty coon hunting?"

Lloyd and Beller looked at each other. Beller licked his lips to try to keep from laughing. "Yes," they said in unison.

"Then get in the car. You ain't lost no more."

As they highballed it southbound without lights or siren, Lloyd told the cops he was flagged for the October class at the academy and that he wanted the riot to be his *solo* training ground. The younger cop whooped and said, "Then this riot *is* a preordained training ground for you. How tall are you, six-four? Six-five? With your size, you're gonna get sent straight to 77th Street Division, Watts, these selfsame fucking streets we're cruising right now. After the smoke clears and the fucking liberals run off at the mouth about the niggers being victims of poverty, there's gonna be the job of maintaining order over some very agitated bad-ass niggers who've had a distinct taste of blood. What's your name, kid?"

"Hopkins."

"You ever kill anyone, Hopkins?"

"No, sir."

"Don't call me 'sir.' You ain't a cop yet, and I'm a plain old patrolman. Well, I killed lots of guys in Korea. Lots and *lots*, and it changed me. Things look different now. Real different. I've talked about it to other guys who've lost their cherry, and we all agree: You appreciate different things. You see innocent people, like little kids, and you want them to stay that way because you got no innocence yourself. Little things like little kids and their toys and pets get to you, 'cause you know they're heading straight into this big fucking shitstorm and you don't want them to. Then you see people who got no regard for gentle things, for decent things, and you gotta come down hard on them. You gotta protect what two cents' worth of innocence there is in the world. That's why I'm a cop. You look cherry to me, Hopkins. You look eager, too. You understand what I'm saying?"

Lloyd nodded, tingling with a pins and needles sensation. He smelled smoke through the open patrol car window, and the feeling began to numb as he realized the cop was talking instinctively about Lloyd's Irish Protestant ethos. "I understand exactly what you're saying," he said.

"Good, kid. Then it starts tonight. Pull over, partner."

The older cop braked and drew up to the curb.

"It's all yours, kid," the younger cop said, reaching over and banging

Lloyd's helmet. "We'll take your buddy back to your outfit. You see if you can stir up anything on your own."

Lloyd tumbled out of the patrol car so fast that he never got to thank his mentor. They hit the siren by way of farewell.

102nd and Central was a chaos of smoldering ruins, the hiss of fire hoses, the squeal of tires on the now wet pavement, all modulated by police helicopters that hovered overhead, casting broad searchlights into storefronts to give the firemen light to work by.

Lloyd walked into the maelstrom, grinning broadly, still suffused with the eloquent recapitulation of his philosophy. He watched an armored half-track move slowly down the street, a fifty caliber machine gun mounted in its bed. A guardsman in the cab barked into a powerful bullhorn: "Curfew in five minutes! This area is under martial law! Anyone found on the streets after nine o'clock will be arrested. Anyone attempting to cross official police barriers will be shot. Repeat, curfew in five minutes!"

The words, clearly enunciated with force and malice, echoed loudly down the street, resulting in a flurry of activity. Within seconds Lloyd saw dozens of young men dart from burned-out buildings, running full speed in any direction not caught by the searchlights. He rubbed his eyes and squinted to see if the men were carrying pilfered merchandise, only to discover they had disappeared before he could yell out or train his M-14 on them.

Lloyd shook his head and walked past a group of firemen milling around in front of a ravaged liquor store. They all noticed him, but no one seemed puzzled by the anomaly of a lone guardsman on foot patrol. Emboldened, Lloyd decided to check out life indoors.

He liked it. The darkness inside the burned-out store was soothing and Lloyd sensed that the shadow-shrouded silence was there to inform him with essential knowledge. He stopped and took a roll of friction tape from his fatigue jacket pocket and fixed his flashlight to the bottom edge of his bayonet. He swung his rifle in a figure eight arc and admired the results: wherever the M-14 pointed, there would be light.

Mounds of charred wood; piles of insulation stuffing; crushed booze bottles. Used condoms everywhere. Lloyd chuckled at the thought of subterranean liquor store coupling, then felt himself go dead cold as his chuckle was returned, followed by a hideous low moan.

He moved his M-14 around in a three hundred sixty degree arc, the muzzle at waist level. Once, then twice. On the third time around he was rewarded: an old man lay crumpled atop a mound of wadded up insulation fiber. Lloyd's heart melted. The old bastard was withered to prune dimensions and was obviously a threat to no one. He walked to the old man and handed him his canteen. The old man grasped it with shaking hands, raised it to his lips, then threw it to the ground, screeching:

"That not be what I need! I needs my Lucy! I gots to have my Lucy!"

Lloyd was befuddled. Was the old geezer crying out for his wife or some long lost love?

He removed the flashlight from his bayonet housing and shined it in the old man's face, then winced; the mouth and chin of that face were covered with congealed blood, from which glass shards stuck out like crystalline porcupine quills. Lloyd recoiled, then pointed his light into the old man's lap and recoiled further: the withered hands were cut to the bone, and three fingers of the right hand had been ground down to bloody stubs. The gnarled left hand held the shattered remnants of a bottle of Thunderbird wine.

"My Lucy! Gimme my Lucy!" the old man wailed, spitting globules of blood out with each word.

Lloyd took his flashlight and went crashing through the glass-strewn ruins, brushing tears from his eyes, searching for an intact bottle of liquid salvation. Finally he found one, partially hidden by an overturned ceiling beam—a pint of six-year-old Seagram's 7.

Lloyd carried the bottle over and fed the old man, holding his head by the short nap of his grey hair, keeping the bottle a few inches from his bloody lips lest he try to ingest the entire thing. Thoughts of going for medical attention crossed his mind, but he pushed them away. He knew that the old man wanted to die, that he deserved to die drunk and that this service he was performing was the wartime equivalent of the many hours he had spent talking to his mute, brain-damaged mother.

The old man made slurping sounds, sucking convulsively at the bottle each time it touched his lips. After a few minutes had passed and half the pint was consumed, his tremors subsided and he pushed Lloyd's hand away.

"Dis be de start of World War Three," he said.

Lloyd ignored the comment and said, "I'm P.F.C. Hopkins, California National Guard. Do you want medical attention?"

The old man laughed, coughing up huge wads of blood-streaked sputum.

"I think you're bleeding internally," Lloyd said. "I can get you to an ambulance. Do you think you can walk?"

"I can do anything I wants to," the old man shrieked, "but I wants to die! Ain't no place for me in this war—I gots to make the scene on de other side!"

The bloodshot, filmy old brown eyes importuned Lloyd as if he were an idiot child. He fed the old man again, watching some kind of liquid acceptance course through the ancient body. When the bottle was finished the old man said, "You gots to do me a favor, white boy."

"Name it," Lloyd said.

"I'm gonna die. You gots to go over to my room and get my books and maps and things out and sell dem so I can have a decent burial. Christian like, you dig?"

"Where's your room?"

"It in Long Beach."

"I can go there when the riot is over. Not until then."

The old man shook his head furiously, until his body shook with it, rag-doll like, all the way down to his toes. "You gots to! They gonna lock me out tomorrow 'cause I behind on the rent! Then de po-lice gonna throw me in de sewer with the rats! You gots to!"

"Hush," Lloyd said. "I can't go that far. Not now. Don't you have any friends here I can talk to? Someone who can go to Long Beach for you?"

The old man considered the offer. Lloyd watched his wheels turn slowly. "You goes to de mission on Avalon an' One hundred and sixth. De African church. You talk to Sister Sylvia. You tell her she got to go to Famous Johnson's crib and get his shit and sell it. She gots my birthday in de church records. I wants a nice headstone. You tells her I loves Jesus, but I loves sweet Lucy more."

Lloyd stood up. "How bad do you want to die?" he asked.

"Bad, man, bad."

"Why?"

"Ain't no place for me in dis war, man."

"What war?"

"World War Three, you dumb motherfucker!"

Lloyd thought of his mother and reached for his rifle, but couldn't do it.

Lloyd ran all the way to 106th and Avalon, composing epitaphs for Famous Johnson en route. His chest was heaving and his arms and shoulders ached from holding his rifle at high port, and when he saw the neon sign proclaiming the "United African Episcopal Methodist Church" he took in last gulps of air to bring his raging heartbeat down to a low ebb; he wanted to be the very picture of armed dignity on a mission of mercy.

The church was storefront, two stories high, with lights shining in violation of the curfew. Lloyd walked in, to be confronted by a pandemonium that was part prayer meeting, part coffee klatch. Large tables had been set up lengthwise between rows of wooden pews, and middle-aged and elderly Negroes were kneeling in prayer and helping themselves to coffee and donuts.

Lloyd moved slowly along the walls, which were festooned with paintings of a black Christ, weeping, blood dripping from his crown of thorns. He started looking to the faces of the kneelers for signs of holiness or compassion. All he saw was fear.

Until he noticed a fat black woman in a white robe who seemed to be smiling inwardly as she dispensed shoulder taps to the people who knelt by the pews nearest the aisle. When the woman noticed Lloyd she shouted, "Welcome, soldier," above the other hubbub and walked up to him, hand extended.

Startled, Lloyd shook the hand and said, "I'm P.F.C. Hopkins. I'm here on a mission of mercy for one of your parishioners."

The woman dropped Lloyd's hand and said, "I'm Sister Sylvia. This church is strictly for the Afro-American folk, but tonight is sort of special. Did you come to pray for the victims of this Armageddon? Do that be your mission?"

Lloyd shook his head. "No, I came to ask a favor. Famous Johnson is dead. Before he died, he asked me to come here and tell you to sell his belongings so he can have a proper burial. He told me you know the address of his place in Long Beach and his birthdate. He wants a nice headstone. He told me to tell you he loves Jesus." Lloyd was startled to see Sister Sylvia shaking her head ironically, a grin starting to form at the corners of her mouth. "I don't think it's funny," he said.

"You don't!" Sister Sylvia bellowed. "Well, I does! Famous Johnson was trash, young white man! He deserved to be called what he was—a nigger! And that room in Long Beach? That nothing but fantasy! Famous Johnson lived out of his car, with his sin things in the back seat! He used to come by this church for the donuts and coffee, but that all! Famous Johnson didn't have nothin' to sell!"

"But I . . ."

"You comes with me, young man. I shows you, so you forget all about Infamous Johnson with a clean conscience."

Lloyd decided not to protest; he wanted to see the fat woman's definition of sin.

It was a high-finned, chopped and lowered 1947 Cadillac, what Crazy Tom would have called a "Coon-Mobile."

Lloyd flashed his light into the back seat as Sister Sylvia stood triumphantly next to him, legs spread stolidly, her arms wrapped around her midsection in an "I told you so" attitude. He swung the door open. The tuck and roll upholstered seats were covered with empty soda pop bottles and pornographic photographs, most of them depicting Negro couples engaged in fellatio. Lloyd felt a sudden wave of pity; the sucker and suckee were overweight and middle-aged, and the tawdriness of the photos was a far cry from the *Playboy* magazines he had collected since high school. He didn't want it to be; it was too rotten a legacy for any human being.

"I told you so!" Sister Sylvia barked. "This is In-famous Johnson's house! You gonna sell them pictures and return them empties, and get you a fast dollar ninety-eight, which ain't gonna get you nothin' but two bottles o' T-Bird to pour over In-famous's pauper grave!"

Lloyd shook his head. Radio noise from a block away pounded him, causing the whole ugly moment to sway in his vision. "But you don't understand, ma'am," he said. "Famous entrusted this job to *me*. It's my *job*. It's my *duty*. It's my . . ."

"I don't wanna hear nothin' 'bout that sinner! You hears me? I wouldn't bury that trash in our cemetery for all the tea in China. You hears me?" Sister Sylvia didn't wait for an answer; she strode angrily back in the direction of her church, leaving Lloyd alone on the sidewalk, wishing the gunshots in the distance would escalate to the point where they drowned out the radio noise.

He sat down on the curb and thought of the two wretched people in the photographs, and of Janice who wouldn't blow him, but who did the final deed on their first date two weeks before high school graduation, leaving Lloyd Hopkins, Marshall High Class of '59, aglow with wonder at the love in his future. Now, six years later, Lloyd Hopkins, *summa cum laude* graduate of Stanford University, graduate of the Fort Polk Infantry School and the Evelyn Wood Speed Reading Class and six-year lover of Janice Marie Rice, sat on a curb in Watts wondering why he couldn't get what a fat Negro slob probably got all the time. Lloyd shined his light in the back seat window again. It was as he suspected: the guy's dick was at least two inches bigger than his. He decided it was God and commitment. The jerk in the photo had a low I.Q. and a bad build, so God threw him a big wang to slide through life on. It all worked out.

Janice would take him orally when he graduated the academy and they got married. The last thought made him sex-flushed and sad. Janice made him sad. Then he thought of the daughters they would create. Janice, five foot eleven barefoot, slender, but with a robust set to her hips, was made for bearing exceptional children. Daughters. They would have to be daughters, made to be nurtured by the love in his Irish Protestant credo . . .

Lloyd took his Janice-daughter fantasies to ends of fulfillment both good and bad, then shifted his mind to women in general—women pure, wanton, vulnerable, needy, strong; all the ambivalences of his mother, now silent in her strength, rendered dumb by years of giving shelter to her lunatic male brood, from which only he emerged sane and capable of providing solace himself.

Lloyd heard a burst of gunshots in the near distance. Automatic weapon fire. At first he thought it was the radio or TV, but it was too real, too right, and it was coming from the direction of the African Church. He picked up his M-14 and ran to the corner. As he rounded it he heard screams, and turned to look in the shattered storefront window. When he saw the devastation inside, he screamed himself. Sister Sylvia and three male parishioners lay on the linoleum floor in a mass of tangled flesh, melded together in a river of blood. From somewhere within the twisted mound of bodies a severed artery shot up a red geyser. Lloyd, transfixed, watched it die and felt his scream metamorphose into the single word, "What! What! What!"

He screeched it until he was able to will his eyes from the bodies to the rest of the cordite-reeking church. The tops of dark heads peered above pews. Dimly, Lloyd perceived that the people were terrified of him. Tears streaming down his face, he dropped his rifle to the pavement and screamed, "What? What? What?" only to be answered by a score of voices hurling, "Killer, killer, murderer!" in horror and outrage.

It was then that he heard it, faintly but plainly, back off to his left, clicking in so succinctly that he knew it was real, not electronic: "*Auf wiedersehen*, niggers. *Auf wiedersehen*, jungle bunnies. See ya in hell."

It was Beller.

Lloyd knew what he had to do. He tossed the Negroes huddled behind their pews his sternest resolve and went after him, leaving his rifle behind on the pavement, crouching his long frame low behind parked cars as he made his way toward the destroyer of innocence.

Beller was running slowly north, unaware that he was being followed. Lloyd could see him framed plainly in the glow of those streetlights not destroyed, turning every few moments to look back and savor his triumph. He checked the second hand on his watch and calculated. It was obvious: Beller's unconscious was telling him to turn around and scan his blind side every twenty seconds.

Lloyd sprinted full out, counting to himself, and hit the pavement prone just as Beller would turn and peer backward. He was within fifty yards of the killer when Beller ducked into an alleyway and started screaming, "Freeze, nigger, freeze!" A burst of shots followed, fully automatic. Lloyd knew it was the elephant clip .45.

He reached the alley and halted, catching his breath. There was a dark shape near the end of the cul-de-sac. Lloyd squinted and discerned that it was clad in fatigue green. He heard Beller's voice a moment later, spitting out garbled epithets.

Lloyd entered the alley, inching his way along a brick wall. He pulled one of his .45s from his waistband and flipped off the safety. He was almost within firing distance when his foot hit a tin can, the sound reverberating like hollow thunder.

He fired just as Beller did, and the flash from their gun barrels lit up the alley blindingly, illuminating Beller, crouched over a dead Negro man, the man headless, blown apart at the shoulders, his neck a massive cavity of bloody, charred tissue. Lloyd screamed as the recoil from his .45 lifted him into the air and slammed him back to the ground. A dozen shots tore into the wall above him, and he rolled frantically on the glass-strewn pavement as Beller fired another burst at the ground, causing glass and blacktop shrapnel to explode before his eyes.

Lloyd started to sob. He flung his arm over his eyes and prayed for courage and the chance to be a good husband to Janice. His prayers were interrupted by the sound of footsteps running away from him. His mind clicked in: Beller was out of ammo and was running for his life. Lloyd willed himself to stand upright. His legs wobbled, but his mind was steadfast. He was right: Beller's empty M-14 lay across the torso of the dead man, and the .45, spent and burning to the touch, lay a few feet away.

Lloyd deep breathed, reloaded and listened for sounds of flight. He caught them; off to his left he heard the scuffle of feet and strained breathing. He followed the sounds by the shortest possible route, scaling the cement alleyway wall and coming down into a weed-strewn backyard, where the breath-noise mixed with the sound of a radio playing jazz.

Lloyd blundered through the yard, mumbling prayers to engulf the music. He found a walkway leading to the street, and the light from the adjoining house let him pick out a trail of freshly spilled blood. He saw that the blood led into a huge vacant lot, pitch dark and eerily silent.

Lloyd listened, willing himself to assume the ears of a highly attuned animal. Just as his eyes became accustomed to the darkness and let him pick out objects in the lot, he heard it: a snapping of metal on metal, coming from the direction of a portable construction toilet. It was unmistakable: Beller was still armed with one of his evil customized .45s, and he knew Lloyd was near.

Lloyd hurled a rock at the outhouse. The door creaked open and three single shots rang out, followed by the sound of doors slamming all the way down the block.

Lloyd got an idea. He walked down the street, scanning front porches until he found what he was looking for, nestled among an evening's array of potato chip bags and empty beer cans—a portable radio. Steeling himself, he turned on the volume and was bombarded by rhythmic soul music. Despite his headache, he smiled, then turned the volume down. It was poetic justice for Staff Sergeant Richard A. Beller.

Lloyd carried the radio into the vacant lot and placed it on the ground ten yards in back of the construction toilet, then flipped the volume dial and ran in the opposite direction.

Beller burst out the door of the outhouse seconds later, screaming, "Nigger! Nigger! Nigger!" Blindly, he fired off a series of shots. The light from his muzzle bursts illuminated him perfectly. Lloyd raised his .45 and aimed slowly, pointing at Beller's feet to allow for recoil. He squeezed the trigger, the gun kicked and the elephant clip emptied. Beller screamed. Lloyd dug into the dirt, stifling his own screams. The radio blasted rhythm and blues, and Lloyd ran toward the sound, the butt end of his .45 extended. He stumbled in the darkness, then got down on his hands and knees and bludgeoned the music to death.

Lloyd stood up unsteadily, then walked to the remains of Richard Beller. He felt strangely calm as he carried first the entrails of the former civilian soldier to the outhouse, then the lower body, then the disembodied arms. Beller's head was nothing but splattered bone and brain debris, and Lloyd let them lie in the dirt.

Muttering, "God please, please, God, rabbit down the hole," Lloyd walked out to the street, noting with his animal antennae that there was no one about—the locals were either scared shitless by the gunfire or inured to it. He emptied his canteen into the gutter and found a length of surgical tubing in his bayonet case—good strangling cord, Beller had once told him. There was a '61 Ford Fairlane at the curb. Deftly manipulating the tubing and canteen, Lloyd managed to siphon a solid pint of gas from the tank. He walked back to the outhouse and doused what remained of Beller, then reloaded his .45 and paced off ten yards. He fired, and the outhouse exploded.

Lloyd walked back to Avalon Boulevard. When he turned around, the entire lot was engulfed in flames.

Two days later, the Watts Riot was over. Order had been restored to the devastated underbelly of South Central Los Angeles. Forty-two lives were lost—forty rioters, one deputy sheriff and one National Guardsman whose body was never found, but who was presumed dead.

The riot was attributed to many causes. The N.A.A.C.P. and the Urban League attributed it to racism and poverty. The Black Muslim Party attributed it to police brutality. Los Angeles Chief of Police William H. Parker attributed it to a "breakdown in moral values." Lloyd Hopkins considered all these theories fatuous nonsense. He attributed the Watts Riot to the death of the innocent heart, most specifically the heart of an old black wino named Famous Johnson.

When it was over, Lloyd retrieved his car from the parking lot of the Glendale Armory and drove to Janice's apartment. They made love, and Janice provided what comfort she could, but refused the oral comfort Lloyd begged for. He left her bed at three in the morning and went looking for it.

He found a Negro prostitute at the corner of Western and Adams who was willing to do the deed for ten dollars, and they drove to a side street and parked. Lloyd screamed when he came, frightening the hooker, who bolted out of the car before she could collect her money.

Lloyd cruised aimlessly until dawn, then drove to his parents' house in Silverlake. He could hear his father snoring as he unlocked the door, and he saw light coming from under the door to Tom's room. His mother was in her den, sitting in her bentwood rocker. All the lights in the room were off, except for the colored light from the fish tank. Lloyd sat down on the floor and told the mute, prematurely old woman his entire life story, ending with the killing of the killer of innocence and how he could now protect innocent people as never before. Absolved and fortified, he kissed his mother's cheek and wondered how he would kill the eight weeks before he entered the academy.

Tom was waiting for him outside the house, stationed firmly on the pathway leading to the sidewalk. When he saw Lloyd, he laughed and opened his mouth to speak. Lloyd didn't let him. He pulled a .45 automatic from his waistband and placed it against Tom's forehead. Tom started to tremble, and Lloyd said very softly, "If you ever mention niggers, commies, kikes, or any of that shit to me ever again, I'll kill you." Tom's florid face went pale, and Lloyd smiled and walked back to the shattered remains of his own innocence.

Part Two
Torch Songs

3

He cruised west on Ventura Boulevard, savoring the newness of daylight saving time, the clarity of the extra-long afternoons and the unseasonably warm spring weather that had the harlots dressed in tank tops and bare-midriff halters and the real women in a profusion of demure summer pastels: pink, light blue and green, pale yellow.

It had been many months since the last time, and he attributed this hiatus to the shifting weather patterns that had his head in a tizzy: warm one day, cold and rainy the next, you never knew how women were going to dress, so it was hard to get a fix on one to rescue—you couldn't feel the colors, the texture of what a woman was until you viewed her in a context of consistency. God knows that when the planning started the little fluxes of her life became all too evident; if he lost love for her then, the resultant pity reaffirmed the spiritual aspects of his purpose and gave him the detachment necessary to do the job.

But the planning was at *least* half of it, the part that edified, that cleansed *him*, that gave him abstention from minor chaos and precarious impunity from a world that gobbled up the refined and sensitive and spit them out like so much waste fluid.

Deciding to drive through Topanga Canyon on his way back to the city, he killed the air-conditioning and put a meditation tape on the cassette player, one that stressed his favorite theme: the silent mover, self-assured and accepting, armed with a compassionate purpose. He listened as the minister with the countrified voice spoke of the necessity of goals. "What sets the man of movement apart from the man dwelling in the netherworld of stasis is the road, both inward and outward bound, toward worthwhile goals. Traveling this road is both the journey and the destination, the gift both given and received. You can change your life forever if you will follow this simple thirty-day program. First, think of what you want most at this moment—it can be anything from spiritual enlightenment to a new car. Write that goal down on a piece of paper, and write today's date next to it. Now, for the next thirty days, I want you to concentrate on achieving that goal, and allow no thoughts of failure to enter your mind. If these thoughts intrude, banish them! Banish all but the good pure thoughts of achieving your goal, and miracles will happen!"

He believed it; he had made it work for him. There were now twenty pieces of carefully folded paper attesting to the fact that it worked.

He had first played the tape fifteen years before, in 1967, and was impressed. But he didn't know what he wanted. Three days later he saw her, and knew. Jane Wilhelm was her name. Grosse Point born and bred, she had fled Bennington in her senior year, hitching west in search of new values and friends. She had drifted, oxford shirt and penny loafer clad, to the dope scene on the Sunset Strip. He had first seen her outside the Whisky A Go-Go, talking to a bunch of hippie lowlifers, obviously trying to downplay her intelligence and good breeding. He picked her up and told her of his tape and piece of paper. She was touched, but laughed aloud for several moments. If he wanted to ball, why didn't he just ask? Romanticism was corny, and she was a liberated woman.

It was then, in his refusal, that he took his first moral stand. He now knew the exactitude of his immediate goal and all his future ones: the salvation of female innocence.

He kept Jane Wilhelm under loose surveillance until the end of the thirty-day period prescribed by the minister, watching her make the rounds of love-ins, crash pads and rock concerts. Shortly after midnight on the thirty-first day, Jane stumbled away alone from Gazzari's Disco. From his car, parked just south of Sunset, he watched her weave across the street. He turned on his high beams, catching her full in the face, committing to memory her drug-puffed features and dilated eyes. It was her final debasement. He strangled her right there on the sidewalk, then threw her body into the trunk of his car.

Three nights later he drove north to the farmland outside of Oxnard. After a roadside prayer service that featured his salvation tape, he buried Jane in the soft earth adjoining a rock quarry. So far as he knew, her body was never found.

He turned onto Topanga Canyon Road, recalling the methodology that had allowed him to save twenty women without the excitable mass media or fuzz ever seizing on him. It was simple. He became his women, spending months assimilating the details of their lives, savoring every nuance, cataloguing every perfection and imperfection before deciding on the method of elimination, which was then tailored to fit the persona, indeed the very soul, of his intended. Thus the planning was the courtship, and the killing the betrothal.

The thought of courtship brought forth a huge rush of ardent imagery, all revolving around prosaic detail, the small intimacies that only a lover could appreciate.

Elaine from 1969, who had loved baroque music; who, although pretty, had spent virtually all her free time listening to Bach and Vivaldi with the windows of her garage apartment open, even in the coldest weather—wanting to share the beauty she felt with a world dead set on ignoring her. Night after night he had listened with a boom receiver from a nearby rooftop, picking up muttered declarations of loneliness beneath the music; almost weeping as their hearts fused in the strains of the Brandenburg Concerti.

Twice he walked through the apartment, collating directions that would indicate the proper way to salvage Elaine's soul. He had decided to wait, to meditate on the end of this woman's life, when he found underneath her sweaters an application for a computer dating service. That Elaine had succumbed to that vulgarity was the final indicator.

He spent a month studying her handwriting, and a week composing a suicide note in that hand. One cold night after Thanksgiving he climbed in through a window and opened three grain and a half Seconal capsules into the bottle of orange juice that he knew Elaine drank from every night before retiring. Later, he watched through a telescope as she took death's communion, then gave her two hours of sleep before entering the apartment, leaving the note and turning on the gas. As a final act of love he put a Vivaldi flute concerto on the stereo to provide accompaniment to Elaine's departure.

Blinding memories of other lovers caused his eyes to well with tears as he pictured their moments of culmination: Karen the horse lover, whose house was a virtual testament to her equine passion; Karen who rode bareback in the hills above Malibu and who died astride her strawberry roan as he ran from cover and bludgeoned the horse over the edge of a cliff; Monica, of the exquisite taste in small things, who clad the polio-riddled body she hated in the finest of silk and wool. As he continued to steal glimpses of her diary and watched her loathing of her body grow, he knew that dismemberment would be the ultimate mercy. After strangling Monica in her Marina Del Rey apartment, he rent her with a power saw and dumped her plastic encased parts into the ocean near Manhattan Beach. Police attributed the death to the "Trashbag Killer."

He dashed tears from his eyes, feeling the memories snowball into yearning. It was time again.

He drove into Westwood Village, paid to park and went walking, deciding not to be hasty, yet also not unduly cautious. Late dusk was falling, bringing with it a corresponding drop in temperature, and the Village streets were bursting with female vitality: women everywhere; snuggling into sweaters, hugging close to storefronts as they waited to enter movie theaters, browsing through bookstores, walking around him, past him, almost through him, it seemed.

Late dusk became night, and with darkness the streets had thinned to the point where individual women stood out in all their uniqueness. It was then that he saw her, standing in front of Hunter's Books, peering into the window as if in search of a vision. She was tall and slender, wearing a minimum of makeup on a soft face that tried hard to project a no-nonsense air. Late twenties—a seeker—a good-natured artificer with a sense of humor, he decided; she would enter the bookstore, check out the best-sellers first, then the quality paperbacks, finally settling on a gothic romance or detective novel. She was lonely. She needed him.

The woman pulled her hair into a bun and slid a barrette over the loose ends. She sighed and pushed open the door of the bookstore, then strode purposefully to a display table covered with books on self-improvement. Everything from *Creative Divorce* to *Winning Through Dynamic Yoga* was represented, and the woman hesitated, then grabbed a copy of *Force Field Synergistics Can Save Your Life*, and carried it back to the cashier.

He was a discreet distance behind her all the way, and when she pulled out a checkbook to pay for her purchase, he memorized the name and address printed on her checks:

Linda Deverson
3583 Mentone Avenue
Culver City, Calif. 90408

He didn't wait to hear Linda Deverson converse with the cashier. He ran out of the store and all the way to his car, seized by love and the territorial imperative: the poet wanted to see the ground of his new courtship.

Linda Deverson was many things, he thought three weeks later as he developed the latest batch of photos. Pulling them out of the solution and hanging them up, he watched her spring to life in vivid black and white. There was Linda leaving the office where she worked as a real estate salesperson; Linda scowling as she attempted to pump her own gas; Linda jogging down San Vicente Boulevard; Linda staring out of her living room window, smoking a cigarette.

He locked the shop, took the photos and went upstairs to his apartment. As always when he walked through his darkened kingdom, he felt proud. Proud that he had had the patience to save and persevere and never relent in his determination to own this place that had given him the finest moments of his youth.

When his parents died and left him homeless at fourteen, the owner of Silverlake Camera had befriended him, giving him twenty dollars a week to sweep out the store at closing every night, and allowing him to sleep on the floor and study in the customers' bathroom. He studied hard and made the owner proud of him. The owner was a horse lover and gambler, and used the store as a bookie drop. He had always thought that his benefactor, who suffered from congestive heart disease and was familyless, would leave the store to him; but he was wrong—when he died the shop was taken over by the bookies to whom he owed money. They promptly ran it to hell—hiring nothing but incompetents, turning the quiet little shop into a low-life hangout—running football pools, booking horses, and selling dope.

When he realized what had been done to his sanctuary, he knew that he had to act to save it, whatever the price.

He had been making a good living as a free-lance photographer, shooting weddings and banquets and communions, and he had saved more than enough money to buy the store should it go on the market. But he knew that the scum who owned it would never sell—it was turning too great an illicit profit. This vexed him so much that he completely forgot about his fourth courtship and threw all his energy toward permanent ownership of his despoiled safe harbor.

Batteries of anonymous phone calls to the police and district attorney did no good; they would not act on the malfeasance at Silverlake Camera. Desperate now, he searched out other means.

Through surveillance, he knew that the new owner got drunk every night at a bar on Sunset. He knew that the man had to be poured into a cab at closing time, and that the cabbie who met him at the door of the bar each night at two A.M. was a compulsive horse player who was heavily in his debt. With the same diligence that marked his courtships, he went to work, first acquiring an ounce of uncut heroin, then approaching the cab driver and making him an offer. The cabbie accepted the offer, and left Los Angeles the following day.

Two nights later, *he* was the one behind the wheel of the cab in front of the Short Stop Bar at closing time. At precisely two A.M., the owner of Silverlake Camera staggered outside and flopped into the backseat, promptly passing out. He drove the man to Sunset and Alvarado, and stuffed a plastic bag bursting with heroin into his coat pocket. He then hauled the unconscious drunk over to Silverlake Camera and placed him in a sitting position, half in and half out of the front door, the key in his right hand.

He drove to a pay phone, called the Los Angeles Police Department and told them of a burglary in progress. They took care of the rest. Three patrol cars were dispatched to Sunset and Alvarado. As the first car screeched to a halt outside Silverlake Camera, the man in the doorway came awake, got to his feet and reached inside his coat pocket. Misinterpreting his gesture, the two patrolmen shot and killed him. Silverlake Camera went into receivership the following week and *he* picked it up for a song.

The camera shop and the three-room apartment above it became *his* song, and he renovated it into a symphony; a complete aesthetic statement of purpose, one steeped in his own past and the clandestine histories of the three people who had given him the terrible catharsis that set him free to salvage female innocence.

One whole wall was devoted to his attackers—a photographic collage that updated their warped progress in life: the musclebound one a Los Angeles County Deputy Sheriff, his sniveling lackey a male prostitute. Their brief, violent transit with him had shaped their lives for the negative—the acquisition of money and cheap one-on-one power the only balm for their spiritual emptiness. The candid snapshots on the wall spelled it out plainly: The Birdman, stationed at curbside on a "Boy's Town" street, hip outthrust, hungry eyes trawling for wretched lonely men to bring him a few dollars and ten minutes of selfhood; and Muscles, overweight and florid-faced, staring out the window of his patrol car at his West Hollywood constituency—the hip gays that he was sworn to protect, but who disdained his "protection" and ridiculed him as "Officer Pig."

The opposite wall held blown-up yearbook photographs of his original beloved; her innocence preserved forever by the extraordinary clarity of his art. He had clipped the photographs on graduation day 1964, and it wasn't until over a decade later, when he was a master photographer, that he felt confident enough to embark on a complex blow-up and reproduction process in an attempt to make them larger than life. Taped next to the blow-ups were gnarled, shriveled and twisted rose branches—twenty of them—the detritus of the floral tributes that he sent to his beloved after claiming a woman in her name.

He had set out to turn his sanctuary into a *total* sensory testament to the three, but for years the methodology had eluded him. He had claimed his visual access, but he wanted to hear these people *breathe*.

The solution came to him in a dream. Young women were tied to the spindle of a giant recording turntable. He sat at the control board of an elaborate electrical system, pushing buttons and flipping levers in a futile effort to make the women scream. Himself near the point of screaming, he had somehow willed the ability to quash his frustration by waving his arms in the simulation of flight. As his limbs treaded air, he ran out of breath and was close to suffocating when his hands touched free-floating streams of magnetic tape. He grabbed the tape and used it as ballast to return to the control board. All the lights on the panel had gone off during his flight, and when he began pushing buttons the lights switched on, then short-circuited and burst with blood. He began to stuff the bloody holes with tape. The tape slithered through the apertures, onto the turntable and around the spindle, crushing the young women who were held captive there. Their screams awoke him from his dream, dissolving into his own scream when he discovered that his groin had exploded into his clenched hands.

That morning he purchased two state-of-the-art transistorized tape recorders, two condensor microphones, three hundred feet of wire, and a transistor power pack. Within a week the apartments of both Officer Pig and his original beloved had been outfitted with brilliantly concealed listening devices; and his access to their lives was complete. He would make weekly runs to change the tapes, almost exploding as he returned home and looked at the pictures on the wall and listened to their breathing compliment, learning intimacies that not even the dearest of lovers would know.

Those intimacies validated his judgment straight down the line: His first beloved took her flesh lovers with caution—they were sensitive-sounding men who loved her and capitulated to her subtle will absolutely. He could tell that she was lonely beneath her sometimes strident feminist facade, but that was natural: she was a poet, one of growing local renown, and loneliness was the bane of all creative people. Officer Pig was, of course, corruption incarnate—an up-for-grabs cop who took bribes from the male prostitutes of Boy's Town, allowing them to ply their wicked craft while he and his sleazy cop buddies looked the other way. The Birdman was his liaison, and hours of listening to the two old high school buddies gloat over their picayune crime scams had convinced him that the wretchedness of their lives was *his* revenge.

His years of listening passed, long evenings where he would touch himself in total darkness as the tapes unfurled into his headphones. He grew even bolder in his desire to be in total sync with those who had brought about his rebirth, and on the anniversary of the beginning that he rarely thought of anymore, he staged betrothals artificed as suicides to celebrate his own act of submission in a sawdust covered high school corridor. Four times, twice in Officer Pig's veritable backyard, once in his own apartment building. The love he had felt in those moments of symbiotic reverie had made his clenched hand explosions magnify tenfold, and he knew that every gauntlet of camera art and breath and blood that he ran would only serve to make his song more inviolate.

Back in the present, he thought again of the many things Linda Deverson was, then felt his mind go blank as he tried to find a narrative line to impose on the welter of images that constituted his new love.

He sighed and locked the door of his apartment behind him, then took the photographs of Linda and taped them to the Tiffany glass window that fronted his writing desk. Sighing again, he wrote:

5–17–82

Three weeks into the courtship and as yet no access to her apartment, much less her heart—triple locks on the one door, it will take a bold gambit to get inside—I will have to risk it soon—Linda remains so elusive. Or maybe not; what has caught me so far is her sense of humor—the rueful smile that lights up her face as she pulls a cigarette out of her sweatsuit after jogging three miles down San Vicente; her firm but humorous refusals to go out with the obdurate young salesman who shares a cubicle with her at the real estate office; the way she talks to herself when she thinks no one is looking and the broad way she covers her mouth when a passerby catches her in the act. Two nights ago I followed her to the Force Field Synergistics seminar. That same rueful smile when she wrote the check for registration and again at the first "grouping" when they told her she couldn't smoke. I think that Linda possesses the same detachment I have noticed in writers—the desire to commune with humanity, to have a common ground or dream—yet the concurrent need to remain aloof, to hold her intrinsic truths (however universal) above those of the collective. Linda is a subtle woman. While the first grouping (ambiguous jive talk about unity and energy) was going on, I snuck back to the registration office and stole her application. I now know this about my beloved:

1. Name: Linda Holly Deverson
2. Birthdate: 4/29/52
3. Birthplace: Goleta, California
4. Education: High school 1 2 3④
    College 1②3 4
    Advanced degrees? No.
5. How did you find out about F.F.S.?—I read your book.
6. Which four of these words best describe you?
    1. Ambitious
    2. Athletic
    3. Aggressive
    ④ Enlightened
    ⑤ Tuned In
    6. Befuddled
    7. Inquisitive
    ⑧ Passive
    9. Angry
    ⑩ Sensitive
    11. Passionate
    12. Aesthetic
    13. Physical
    14. Moral
    15. Generous
7. Why did you come to the F.F.S. Institute?—I can't honestly say.

Some of the things in your book struck me as truthful things that could help me to better myself.

8. Do you think F.F.S. can change your life?—I don't know.

A subtle woman. I can change your life, Linda; I am the only one who can.

Three nights later he broke into her apartment.

It was carefully thought out and bold. He knew that she would be attending the second Synergistics Seminar, which was scheduled to last from eight o'clock until midnight. At seven forty-five he was stationed across the street from the F.F.S. Institute on 14th and Montana in Santa Monica, armed with a matchbook-size circuit breaker and wearing skin-tight rubber gloves.

He smiled as Linda pulled into the parking lot, exchanged guarded greetings with other arriving F.F.S.ers and wolfed down a last cigarette before running into the large red brick building. He waited ten minutes, then sprinted over to her '69 Camaro, opened the hood and attached the circuit breaker to the underside of the car's distributor housing. Should anyone attempt to start the Camaro, it would turn over once and die. Laughing at the small perfection of it, he slammed the hood and ran back to his own car, then drove to the home of his beloved.

It was a pitch-dark spring night, and warm winds gave added audial cover. Parking a block away, he padded over to 3583 Mentone Avenue, carrying a flat-handled lug wrench and a transistor radio in a brown paper bag. Just as a huge gust of wind came up, he placed the radio on the ground outside Linda's living room window and turned the volume up full blast. Punk rock bombarded the night, and he slammed the lug wrench full force into the window, grabbed the radio and ran back to his car.

He waited for twenty minutes, until he was certain that no one had heard the noise and no silent alarm had been sounded. Then he walked back and vaulted into the dark apartment.

Drawing curtains over the broken window, he deep-breathed and let his eyes become accustomed to the darkness, then followed his most urgent curiosity straight back toward where the bathroom had to be. He turned on a light and then rummaged through the medicine cabinet; checked out the makeup kit on top of the toilet; even went through the dirty clothes hamper. His soul sighed in relief. No contraceptive devices of any kind; his beloved was chaste.

He left the door ajar and walked into the bedroom. Quickly noting that there was no overhead light, he turned on the lamp next to the bed. Its diffused glow gave him light to work by, and he flung open the walk-in closet door, hungry to touch the fabric of his beloved's life.

The closet was packed with garments on hangers, and he swept them up in a giant armful and carried them into the bathroom. There were mostly dresses, in a variety of fabrics and styles. Trembling, he fondled polyester suits and cotton shifts, pseudo-silk culottes and businesslike tweed; stripes, plaids, tattersall checks—all feminine and all pointing to the subtle, searching nature of Linda Deverson. She doesn't know who she is, he said to himself; so she buys clothes to reflect all the different things she *could* be.

He carried the bundle of clothing back to the closet and arranged it as it had been, then went looking for further evidence of Linda's chastity. He found it on her telephone stand—all the phone numbers in her address book belonged to women. Heart leaping with joy, he went into the kitchen and rummaged beneath the sink until he found a can of black paint and a stiff paint brush. He pried the can open and drew out a big glob of paint and smeared "Clanton 14 St.—Culver City—Viva La Raza" on the kitchen wall. To make it look even better, he grabbed a toaster and portable cassette player and took them with him.

Fondling the toaster on the seat beside him, he drove back to the F.F.S. Institute and removed the circuit breaker from Linda Deverson's car, then went home to meditate on the subtlety of his woman.

The following Wednesday night was the first F.F.S. "Question and Answer" grouping. He had purchased his ticket two days before at the Ticketron outlet near his shop and was curious as to how Linda would query the F.F.S. programmers, who had thus far brooked no feedback from their trainees. He was certain his beloved would interpose intelligent, skeptical questions.

There was a cordon of religious zealots outside the institute, brandishing signs that read "Synergistics is sin! Jesus is the only way!" He laughed as he walked into them; he thought Jesus was vulgar. One of the zealots noticed the ironic smile on his face and asked him if he had been saved.

"Twenty times," he replied.

The zealot's jaw dropped; he had been on the butt end of many sacrilegious one-liners, but this was a new one. He stood aside and let the nondescript heretic enter the building.

Once inside, he gave his ticket to the security guard, who handed him a large cushion and pointed in the direction of the assembly room. He walked through a hallway adorned with photographs of celebrity F.F.S.ers and into a huge room where knots of people milled around anxiously, chattering and sizing up the new arrivals. At the back of the room he wadded his cushion up and sat down with his eyes glued to the door.

She came in a moment later, setting her cushion down just a few feet away from him. His heart shuddered and pounded so hard that he thought it would drown out all the excited psychobabble that was floating through the room. Staring into his lap, he assumed a meditation pose that he hoped would forestall any conversation she might attempt. He shut his eyes so hard and wrenched his hands so tightly that he felt like a shrapnel bomb about to explode.

Then the lights in the room were dimmed twice, indicating the session was about to begin. A hush came over the assembly as the lights went out completely and candles were lit and placed in strategic positions throughout the room. The sudden darkness gripped him and held him like a lover. He turned his head and caught a glance of Linda silhouetted in candlelight. Mine, he said to himself, mine.

Sitar chords came over the P.A. system, winding down into a soft male voice. "Feel the fields that separate you from your greater self start to dissipate. Feel your inner self mix with the synergy of other tuned-in force fields to produce true energy and union. Feel the synthesis of yourself and everything good in the cosmos."

The voice lowered itself to a whisper. "Today I am here to relate to you personally, to help you apply the principles of Force Field Synergistics to your personal lives. This is your third workshop; you have the ammunition necessary to change your lives forever, but I am sure you have many questions. That is why I am here. Lights, please!"

The lights went on, jarring him. Carefully modulating his breathing to keep his control at optimum, he watched a silver-haired young man in a blue blazer walk to a flower-draped lectern at the front of the room. He was greeted with wild applause and bliss-filled gazes.

"Thank you," the man said. "Questions?"

An elderly man at the front of the room raised his hand and said, "Yeah, I got a question. What are you gonna do about the niggers?"

The man at the lectern went beet red beneath his silver coiffure and said, "Well, I don't think that's germane to the issues at hand. I think—"

"Well, I do!" the old man bellowed. "You people took this building over from the Moose, and you got a civic responsibility to address yourself to the nigger problem!" The old man looked around for support and got nothing but embarrassed shrugs and hostile looks. The man at the lectern snapped his fingers and two burly, blazer-clad teenagers entered the room.

The old man ranted on. "I was a member of the Moose Lodge for thirty-eight years, and I rue the day we sold out to you bimbos! I'm gonna call for a meeting of the zoning board, and get an ordinance passed to keep all niggers and religious crackpots south of Wilshire. I'm a member in good . . ." The teenagers grabbed the old man by his arms and legs and carried him, kicking, biting, and screaming, out of the room.

The man at the lectern called for quiet, raising his hands in a supplicating gesture to quell the relieved hubbub that followed in the old man's wake. Running a hand through his silver hair, he said, "Now there's someone with a low karma synergy! Racism is low chakra! Now . . ."

Linda Deverson raised her hand forcefully and said, "I have a question. It relates to that old man. What if his inner self is bad and all his native force fields are so twisted with fear and anger that meanness is all he can relate to? What if he has just one germ of kindness, of curiosity, and that's what brought him here tonight? He *paid* to attend this meeting tonight, he—"

"His money will be refunded," the man at the lectern interjected.

"That's not what I'm talking about!" Linda shouted. "That's not what I mean! Don't you understand that that man can't be dismissed with a cheap crack about low chakra? Don't you . . ." Linda slammed her hands into her cushion, then got to her feet and rushed to the front door.

"Let her go!" the group leader said. "Her misery will be refunded if she leaves our program. Let her pay for her chakra!"

Barely containing his excitement, the poet got up to follow her and was almost knocked over by a tall buxom woman in a corduroy pantsuit. When he got outside to the parking lot, he found her conferring with Linda, who was smoking a cigarette and brushing angry tears out of her eyes. Shielded by a tall hedgerow, he could hear their conversation plainly.

"Shit, shit, shit," Linda was muttering.

"Just forget about it," the woman answered. "You win a few, you lose a few. I've been searching for a few years longer than you; listen to the voice of experience."

Linda laughed. "You're probably right. God, could I use a drink!"

"I wouldn't mind one myself," the woman said. "Do you mind scotch?"

"No, I love it!"

"Good. I've got a bottle of Chivas at home. I live in the Palisades. Did you bring your car?"

"Yes."

"Want to follow me?"

Linda nodded and ground out her cigarette. "Sure."

He was right behind them as they drove the twisting roads of Santa Monica Canyon up to a quiet block of large houses fronted by broad lawns. He watched as the first car hit its right-hand directional and pulled into a long circular driveway. Linda followed suit, parking directly behind. He drove on and parked at the corner, then walked casually over to the house the woman had entered.

The lawn extended around both sides of the house, with towering hibiscus plants forming its perimeters. He threaded his way along them, staying in the shadows, making a complete circuit of the house before catching sight of the two women sitting in adjoining easy chairs in a warmly appointed den. Crouching low, he watched Linda sip scotch and laugh in pantomime, imagining that she was being regaled by him, by his wit and the humorous verse that he wrote only for her. The other woman was laughing too, slapping her knee and freshening Linda's glass every few minutes from the bottle on the coffee table.

He was staring into the window, lost in Linda's laughter, when he suddenly became aware that something was drastically wrong. His instinct never failed him, and just as he was about to hit on the cause of his uneasiness, he saw the two women move toward each other very slowly and in perfect synchronization kiss on the lips, first tentatively, then hungrily, knocking over the bottle of scotch as they moved into a fierce embrace. He started to scream, then stifled the sound by jamming his hand into his mouth. He raised his other fist to smash the window, but reason took tenuous hold and he smashed the ground instead.

He looked in the window again. The women were nowhere to be seen. Frantically, he pressed his face to the glass and craned his neck almost off its axis, until he saw two pair of nude legs wrapped together, twisting and straining on the floor. Then he did scream, and the otherworldly sound of his own terrified voice propelled him out to the street. He ran until his lungs burned and his legs started to wobble. Then he fell to his knees and was perfectly still as comforting images of the twenty others washed over him. He thought of them at their moments of salvation, and of how much they looked like the ones who had betrayed his original true love so many years before.

Restored by the righteousness of his purpose, he got up and walked back to his car.

Performing the rituals of life allowed him to operate over the next week, keeping images of the betrayal from bludgeoning him into desperate action.

He minded the store from morning until late afternoon, then fielded calls that came in from his answering service. Wedding assignments were picking up, as they did each spring, and this year he could afford to be choosy, spending his early evenings interviewing the doting parents of engaged young couples who thought they were interviewing him. No uglies, he decided; no porkers. Only slender, good-looking young people would stand before his camera. He owed himself that.

After conducting business he would drive to the Palisades and watch Linda Deverson and Carol March make love. Dressed in black, he would scale a shadow-shrouded telephone pole and peer down through the upstairs bedroom window as the women coupled on a quilt-covered waterbed. At about midnight, when his arms were weary from hours of hugging the rough wood of the phone pole, he would watch the sated Linda get up from the bed and dress as Carol importuned her to spend the night. It was always the same; his brain, willfully shut off as he viewed the lovemaking, would snap to life with speculation as Linda took her leave. Why was Linda leaving? Was buried guilt coming to the surface? Regret at the way she had debased herself?

He would then jump down from the pole and run for his car, pulling up without lights behind Linda's Camaro just as she walked out the door. Then he would follow the glow of her taillights as she drove home via the most scenic route possible, almost as if she needed an injection of beauty after her night of debauchery. Keeping a safe distance behind, he would let her part at the intersection of Sunset and the Pacific Coast Highway, wondering how and when he could bring her salvation.

After two more weeks of extensive surveillance, he wrote in his diary:

6–7–82

Linda Deverson is a tragic victim of these times. Her sensuality is self-destructive, but indicative of strong parental need. The March woman capitalizes on this; she is a viper. Linda remains unsatisfied in both her sensuality and search for a mother (the March woman is at least fifteen years her senior!). Her midnight excursions through the most soulful parts of Pacific Palisades and Santa Monica speak volumes on her guilt and subtle searching nature. Her need for beauty is *so* strong in the aftermath of her self-destruction. I must take her at this moment—that must be the precise time of her salvation.

Emboldened by knowledge of the place, he put the time out of his mind, losing himself in his courtship. But the late nights were taking their toll in little portents of slippage in his work life—rolls of film clumsily shot, then stupidly exposed to sunlight; appointments forgotten, photo orders misplaced. The slippage had to stop, and he knew how to do it. He had to consummate his courtship of Linda Deverson.

He set the date: Tuesday, June 14th, three days hence. His tremors of expectation began to grow.

On Monday, June 13th, he went to an auto supply store in the Valley and bought a case of motor oil, then drove to a junkyard and told the owner he was looking for chrome hood ornaments. While the owner scurried about looking for them, he scraped up several huge handfuls of iron filings from the ground and loaded them into a paper bag. The junkman came running back a few minutes later, waving a chrome bulldog. Feeling generous, he offered the man ten dollars for it. The man accepted. Driving back over the Cahuenga Pass to his shop, he threw the bulldog out the window and laughed as it clattered over to the edge of the roadway.

His consummation day was carefully planned and honed down to the second. Upon rising he placed the "Closed Due to Illness" sign in the window, then returned to his apartment, where he played his meditation tape and stared at the photos of Linda Deverson. Next he destroyed the pages in his diary that pertained to her and took a long walk through the neighborhood, all the way over to Echo Park, where he spent hours rowing around the lake and feeding the ducks. At nightfall he packed his consummation tools into the trunk of his car and drove to his first and last rendezvous with his beloved.

At 8:45 he was parked four doors down from Carol March's house, alternately shifting his gaze from the darkened street to his dashboard clock. At 9:03 Linda Deverson pulled into the driveway. He swooned at the perfection of it; she was right on time.

He drove to Santa Monica Canyon, to the intersection of West Channel

Road and Biscayne, where West Channel bisected and the right fork led
into a small campground filled with picnic tables and swings. If his calculations were correct, Linda would be driving through at precisely ten minutes
of midnight. He pulled his car off to the side of the road on the edge of the
park proper, where it was shielded from street view by a row of sycamore
trees. Then he went for a long walk.

He returned at 11:40 and got his equipment out of the trunk, first donning his park ranger's outfit of Smokey the Bear hat, green wool shirt and
field belt, then assembling his sawhorse detour signs and carrying them over
to the intersection.

Next he hauled his five gallon can of motor oil and iron filings to the
middle of the street and poured them smoothly over the pavement, until
the blacktop just before the detour signs was a slippery purple ooze glinting
with sharp steel. Then all he could do was wait.

At 11:52 he heard her car approaching. As her headlights appeared, his
body shuddered and he had to will himself to contain his bowels and blad-
der.

The car slowed as it neared the detour signs, braking and going into a
right turn, then fishtailing and sliding into the sawhorses as it hit the pool
of oil. There was a crash of wood on metal, then two loud ka-plops! as the
rear tires blew out. The car came to a stop and Linda got out, slamming the
door and muttering, "Oh shit, oh fuck," then going around to the back of
the car to examine the damage.

Steeling himself with all the courtliness he could muster, he walked from
the trees and called out, "Are you okay, miss? That was a nasty slide you
took."

Linda called back, "Yes, I'm okay. But my car!"

He pulled a flashlight from his field belt and shined it into the darkness,
arcing it over the campground several times before letting the beam rest on
his beloved. Linda blinked against the glare, raising a hand to shield her
face. He walked toward her, pointing his light at the ground.

She smiled as she noticed his hat—Smokey the Bear to the rescue; it was
good that she had smoked her last cigarette at Carol's. "Oh God, I'm glad
you're here," she said. "I saw that detour sign and then skidded on something. I think two of my tires blew out."

"That's no problem," he said. "My service shack is right over here; we'll
call an all-night gas station."

"Oh God, what a pain in the ass," Linda said, fumbling in gratitude for the arm of her savior. "You don't know how glad I am to see you."

He faltered at her touch; joy consumed him and he said, "I've loved you for so long. Since we were kids. Since all tho . . ."

Linda gasped. "What the he . . ." she said. "Who the he . . ."

She started to back away, then tripped and fell to the ground. He reached out a hand to help her up. She hesitated. "No, please," she whimpered, moving backward. He fumbled at his field belt and unclipped a two-edged fire axe. He bent down again, grabbing Linda at the wrist and yanking her up just as he brought the axe down in a high, rail-splitting swing. Linda's skull crashed inward as his love went into slow motion and blood and brain fragments burst into the air, suspending the moment into a thousand eternities. He brought the axe down again and again until he was drenched in blood and blood had splattered onto his face and into his mouth and through his brain and his entire soul was a bright lover's red; the bright red of flowers he would send his true love tomorrow. For you, for you, all for you, the poet muttered as he left the remains of Linda Deverson and walked to his car; my soul, my life for you.

4

Detective Sergeant Lloyd Hopkins celebrated the seventeenth anniversary of his appointment to the Los Angeles Police Department in his usual manner, grabbing a computer printout of recent crimes and field interrogation reports filed by Rampart Division, then driving to the old neighborhood to breathe past and present from the vantage point of seventeen years of protecting innocence.

The October day was smoggy and just short of hot. Lloyd got his unmarked Matador from the lot at Parker Center and drove westbound on Sunset, reminiscing: over a decade and a half and the fulfillment of his major dreams—the job, the wife, and the three wonderful daughters. The job thrilling and sad in excess of fulfillment; the marriage strong in the sense of the strong people he and Janice had become; the daughters pure joy and reason for living in themselves. The exultant feelings were the only thing lacking, and in the magnanimity of nostalgia Lloyd chalked up their absence to maturity—he was forty now, not twenty-three; if his seventeen years as a policeman had taught him anything, it was that your expectations diminished as you realized how thoroughly fucked-up the bulk of humanity was, and that you had to go on a hundred seemingly contradictory discourses to keep the major dreams alive.

That the discourses were always women and in direct violation of his Presbyterian marriage vows was the ultimate irony, he thought, stopping for the light at Sunset and Echo Park and rolling up the windows to keep the street noise out. An irony that staunch, strong Janice would never understand. Feeling that his reverie was recklessly overstepping its bounds, Lloyd plunged ahead, anxious to voice it flat out, to himself and the vacant air around him: "It wouldn't work between us, Janice, if I couldn't cut loose like that. Little things would accumulate and I'd explode. And you'd hate me. The girls would hate me. That's why I do it. That's why I . . ." Lloyd couldn't bring himself to say the word "cheat."

He stopped his musings and pulled into the parking lot of a liquor store, then dug the computer sheets out of his pocket and settled in to think.

The streets were pale pink with black typescript, edged with seemingly random perforations. Lloyd fingered through them, arranging them in chronological order, starting with the ones dated 9–15–82. Beginning with the crime reports, he let his perfectly controlled blank mind drift through brief accounts of rapes, robberies, purse snatchings, shopliftings, and vandalism. Suspect descriptions and weaponry from shotguns to baseball bats were recounted in crisp, heavily abbreviated sentences. Lloyd read through the crime reports three times, feeling the disparate facts and figures sink in deeper with each reading, blessing Evelyn Wood and her method that allowed him to gobble up the printed word at the rate of three thousand per minute.

Next he turned to the field interrogation reports. These were accounts of people stopped on the street, briefly detained and questioned, then released. Lloyd read through the F.I.s four times, *knowing* with each reading that there was a connection to be made. He was about to give each stack of printouts another go around when he snapped to the buried ellipsis that was crying out to him. Furiously shuffling through the pink rolls of paper, he found his match-up: Crime Report #10691, 10–6–82. Armed robbery.

At approximately 11:30 P.M., Thursday, October 6, the Black Cat Bar on

Sunset and Vendome was held up by two male Mexicans. They were of un-
determined age, but presumed young. They wore silk stockings to disguise
their appearances, carried "large" revolvers, and ransacked the cash register
before making the proprietor lock up the bar. They then forced the patrons
to lie on the floor. While prone, the robbers relieved them of wallets, billfolds and jewelry. They fled a moment later, warning their victims that the
"back-up" would be outside with a shotgun for twenty minutes. They
slashed the two phone lines before they left. The bartender ran outside five
minutes later. There was no back-up.

Stupid fools, Lloyd thought, risking half a dime minimum for a thousand dollars tops. He read over the F.I. report, filed by a Rampart patrolman: 10–7–82, 1:05 A.M.—"Questioned two w.m. outside res. at 2269
Tracy. They were drinking vodka and sitting on top of late model Firebird,
lic. # HBS 027. Explained that car was not theirs, but that they lived in
house. Partner and I searched them—clean. Got hot call before we could
run warrant check." The officer's name was printed below.

Lloyd kicked the last bits of information around in his head, thinking it
sad that he should have greater intimate knowledge of a neighborhood than
the cops who patrolled it. 2269 Tracy Street was a low-life holdover from
his high school days over twenty years before, when it had been a halfway
house for ex-cons. The charismatic ex-gangster who had run the operation
on State funds had embezzled a bundle from local Welfare agencies before
selling the house to an old buddy from Folsom, then hightailing it to the
border, never to be seen again. The buddy promptly hired a good lawyer to
help him keep the house. He won his court battle and dealt quality dope
out of the old wood-framed dwelling. Lloyd recalled how his high school
pals had bought reefers there back in the late '50s. He knew that the house
had been sold to a succession of local hoods and had acquired the neighborhood nickname of "Gangster Manor."

Lloyd drove to the Black Cat Bar. The bartender immediately made him
for a cop. "Yes, officer?" he said. "No complaints, I hope."

"None," Lloyd said. "I'm here about the robbery of October 6th. Were
you tending bar that night?"

"Yeah, I was here. You got any leads? Two detectives came in the next
day, but that was it."

"No real leads yet. Do . . ."

Lloyd was distracted by the sound of the jukebox snapping on, beginning to spill out a disco tune. "Turn that off, will you?" he said. "I can't compete with an orchestra."

The barman laughed. "That's no orchestra, that's 'The Disco Doggies.' Don't you like them?"

Lloyd couldn't tell if the man was being pleasant or trying to vamp him; homosexuals were hard to read. "Maybe I'm behind the times. Just turn it off, okay? Do it now."

The bartender caught the edge in Lloyd's voice and complied, creating a small commotion as he yanked the cord on the jukebox. Returning to the bar he said warily, "Just what was it you wanted to know?"

Relieved by the music's termination, Lloyd said, "Only one thing. Are you certain the two robbers were Mexican?"

"No, I'm not certain."

"Didn't you . . ."

"They wore masks, officer. What I told the cops is that they talked English with Mexican accents. That's what I said."

"Thank you," Lloyd said, and ran out to his car.

He drove straight to 2269 Tracy Street—Gangster Manor. As he expected, the old house was deserted. Cobwebs, dust, and used condoms covered the warped wood floor, and sets of footprints that Lloyd knew had to be recent were clearly outlined. He followed them into the kitchen. All the fixtures were ripped out and the floor was covered with rodent droppings. Lloyd opened cabinets and drawers, finding only dust, spider webs, and mildewed, maggot-infested groceries. Then he opened a floral patterned bread basket and jumped into the air, dunking imaginary baskets and whooping when he saw what he found: a brand new box of Remington hollow point .38 shells and two pair of Sheer Energy pantyhose. Lloyd whooped again. "Thank you, o' nesting grounds of my youth!" he shouted.

Phone calls to the California Department of Motor Vehicles and L.A.P.D. Records and Information confirmed his thesis. A 1979 Pontiac Firebird, license number HBS 027 was registered to Richard Douglas Wilson of 11879 Saticoy Street, Van Nuys. R&I supplied the rest: Richard Douglas Wilson, white male, age thirty-four was a two-time convicted armed robber who had recently been paroled from San Quentin after serving three and a half years of a five-year sentence.

Heart bursting, and snug in his soundless phone booth, Lloyd dialed a third number, the home of his one-time mentor and current follower, Captain Arthur Peltz.

"Dutch? Lloyd. What are you doing?"

Peltz yawned into the mouthpiece. "I'm taking a nap, Lloyd. I'm off today. I'm an old man and I need a siesta in the afternoon. What's up? You sound jazzed."

Lloyd laughed. "I am jazzed. You want to take a couple of armed robbers?"

"All by ourselves?"

"Yeah. What's the matter? We've done it a million times."

"At least a million—more like a million and a half. Stake out?"

"Yeah, at the guy's pad in Van Nuys. Van Nuys Station in an hour?"

"I'll be there. You realize that if this thing is a washout, you're buying me dinner?"

"Anywhere you want," Lloyd said, and hung up the phone.

Arthur Peltz was the first Los Angeles policeman to recognize and herald Lloyd Hopkins's genius. It happened when Lloyd was a twenty-seven-year-old patrolman working Central Division. The year was 1969, and the hippie era of love and good vibes had dwindled out, leaving a backwash of indigent, drug-addicted youngsters floating through the poorer sections of Los Angeles, begging for spare change, shoplifting, sleeping in parks, back yards and doorways and generally contributing to a drastic rise in misdemeanor arrests and felony arrests for possession of narcotics.

Fear of hippie nomads was rife among solid citizen Angelenos, particularly after the Tate-LaBianca slayings were attributed to Charles Manson and his hirsute band. The L.A.P.D. was importuned to come down hard on the destitute minstrels of love; which it did—raiding hippie campgrounds, frequently stopping vehicles containing furtive-looking longhairs and generally letting them know that they were personae non gratas in Los Angeles. The results were satisfying—there was a general hippie move toward eschewing outdoor living and "cooling it." Then five longhaired young men were shot to death on the streets in Hollywood over a period of three weeks.

Sergeant Arthur "Dutch" Peltz, then a forty-one-year-old Homicide detective, was assigned to the case. He had very little to work on, except a strong instinct that the murders of the unacquainted young men were drug related and that the so-called "ritual markings" on their bodies—an xed out letter H—were put there as subterfuge.

Investigation into the recent pasts of the victims proved fruitless; they were transients existing in a subculture of transients. Dutch Peltz was baffled. He was also an intellectual given to contemplative pursuits, so he decided to take his two-week vacation smack in the middle of his case. He came back from fishing in Oregon clearheaded, spiritually renewed, and pleased to find that there were no new victims of the "Hippie Hunter," as the press had dubbed him. But dire things were happening in Los Angeles. The basin had been flooded with a particularly high-quality Mexican brown heroin, its source unknown. Instinct told Dutch Peltz that the heroin onslaught and the murders were connected. But he didn't have the slightest idea how.

On a cold night around this time, Officer Lloyd Hopkins told his partner he was hungry for sweets, and suggested they stop at a market or liquor store for cookies or cupcakes. His partner shook his head; nothing open this late except Donut Despair, he said. Lloyd weighed the pros and cons of a raging sweet tooth versus the world's worst donuts served up by either sullen or obsequious wetbacks.

His sweet tooth won, but there were no wetbacks. Lloyd's jaw dropped as he took a seat at the counter. Donut Despair (or Donut Deelite, open all nite!), as it was known to the world at large, hired nothing but illegal aliens at *all* its locations. It was the policy of the chain's owner, Morris Dreyfus, a former gangland czar, to employ illegals and pay them below the minimum wage, but make up the difference by providing them with flop-out space at his many Southside tenements. Now this!

Lloyd watched as a sullen hippie youth placed a cup of coffee and three glazed donuts in front of him, then retreated to a back room, leaving the counter untended. He then heard furtive whispers, followed by the slamming of a back door and the starting of a car engine. The hippie counterman reappeared a moment later and couldn't meet Lloyd's eyes; and Lloyd knew it was more than his blue uniform. He knew something was *wrong*.

The following day, armed with a copy of the Los Angeles Yellow Pages, Lloyd, in civilian clothes, made a circuit of over twenty Donut Despairs, to find the counters manned by longhaired white men at all locations. Twice he sat down and ordered coffee, letting the counterman see—as if by accident—his off-duty .38. In both instances the reaction was cold, stark terror.

Dope, Lloyd said to himself as he drove home that night. Dope. Dope. But. But any streetwise fool would know that anyone as big as I am, with my short haircut and square look, is a cop. Those two kids made me for one the second I walked in the door. But it was my *gun* that scared them.

It was then that Lloyd thought of the Hippie Hunter and the seemingly unrelated heroin influx. When he got home he called Hollywood Station, gave his name and badge number and asked to talk to a Homicide dick.

Dutch Peltz was more impressed with the huge young cop himself than he was with the fact that they had been thinking along almost identical lines. Now he had a hypothesis—that Big Mo Dreyfus was pushing smack out of his donut stands, and that somehow people were getting killed because of it. But it was young Hopkins himself, so undeniably infused with a brilliance of instinct for the darkness in life, that had him awestruck.

Peltz listened for hours as Lloyd told of his desire to protect innocence and how he had trained his mind to pick out conversations in crowded restaurants and how he could read lips and memorize with time and place any face that he glimpsed for only a second. When he went home, Dutch Peltz said to his wife, "I met a genius tonight. I don't think I'll ever be the same."

It was a prophetic remark.

The following day Peltz began an investigation into the financial dealings of Morris Dreyfus. He learned that Dreyfus had been converting his stocks and bonds into cash and that he was contacting former gangland associates with offers to sell the Donut Deelite chain dirt cheap. Further investigation showed that Dreyfus had recently applied for a passport and had sold his homes in Palm Springs and Lake Arrowhead.

Peltz began a surveillance of Dreyfus, watching him make steady rounds of his donut stands, where he would motion the longhaired counterman into the back room and depart a moment later. That night Peltz and a veteran narcotics detective tailed Dreyfus to the Benedict Canyon home of Reyes Medina, a Mexican reputed to be the liaison between poppy-growing combines in southern Mexico and scores of heavyweight stateside heroin dealers. Dreyfus was inside for two hours, and left looking distraught.

The following morning, Peltz drove to the Donut Deelite on 43rd and Normandie. He parked across the street and waited until the stand was empty of customers, then walked in and flashed his badge at the youth behind the counter, telling him he wanted information, and not on donut recipes. The youth tried running out the back way, but Peltz wrestled him to the floor, whispering, "Where's the smack? Where's the shit, you hippie fuck?" until the youth began to blubber out the story that he expected.

Mo Dreyfus was pushing Mexican brown heroin to medium-level local dealers, who were turning it over for a huge profit. What Peltz didn't expect was the news that Dreyfus was dying of cancer and was accruing capital to take exorbitantly expensive treatments by a Brazilian doctor-medicine man. The word had come down that all drug sales out of all Donut Deelite locations were to stop the following week, when the new owner took over. Big Mo would be on his way to Brazil by then, and all the countermen-pushers would be contacted by a "rich Mexican" who would give them their "going away" bonuses.

After uncovering three ounces of heroin underneath a meat locker, Peltz handcuffed the youth and took him downtown to the central jail, where he was booked as a material witness. Peltz then took the elevator to the eighth floor offices of the L.A.P.D.'s Narcotics Division.

Two hours later, after obtaining search and arrest warrants, four shotgun-wielding detectives burst into the home of Morris Dreyfus and arrested him for possession of heroin, possession with intent to sell, sales of dangerous drugs and criminal conspiracy. In his jail cell, against his attorney's advice, Morris Dreyfus made the connection that convinced Dutch Peltz beyond *any* doubt of Lloyd Hopkins's genius: In hushed tones, Dreyfus told how a "death squad" of militant illegal aliens was behind the killing of the five hippies and how they were now demanding $250,000 from him for firing his immigrant work force en masse. The hippies were killed as a terror tactic; their random selection a ruse to keep attention from being focused on the Donut Deelite chain.

The following morning a dozen black-and-whites cordoned off both sides of the 1100 block of Wabash Street in East Los Angeles. Flak-jacketed officers surrounded the building that housed the death squad. Armed with fully automatic AK-47s, they broke through the front door, firing warning bursts above the heads of four men and three women quietly eating breakfast. The seven stoically submitted to handcuffing and a search team was deployed to check the rest of the house. A total of eleven illegal aliens were arrested. After a gruelling series of interrogations, three men admitted to the Hollywood killings. They were indicted on five counts of first-degree murder and ultimately received life sentences.

The day after the confessions were secured, Dutch Peltz went looking for Lloyd Hopkins. He found him going off duty in the parking lot at Central Division. Unlocking his car, Lloyd felt a tap on his shoulder. He turned around and found Peltz shuffling his feet nervously, gazing up at him with a look that he could only think of as pure love.

"Thanks, kid," the older cop said. "You've made me. I was going to tell—"

"No one would believe you," Lloyd interrupted. "Let it go down the way it is."

"Don't you want—"

"You did the work, Sergeant. I just supplied the theory."

Peltz laughed until Lloyd thought he would keel over of a heart attack. As his laughter subsided, Peltz regained his breath and said, "Who are you?"

Lloyd flicked the antenna of his car and said softly, "I don't know. I Jesus fucking Christ don't know."

"I can teach you things," Dutch Peltz said. "I've been a Homicide dick for eleven years. I can give you a lot of solid, practical information, the benefit of a lot of experience."

"What do you want from me?" Lloyd asked.

Peltz took a moment to consider the question. "I think I just want to know you," he said.

The two men stared at each other in silence. Then Lloyd slowly extended his hand, sealing their fates.

It was Lloyd who was the teacher; almost from the start. Dutch would provide knowledge and experience in the form of anecdotes and Lloyd would find the hidden human truth and hold it up for magnification. Hundreds of hours were spent talking, rehashing old crimes and discussing topics as diverse as women's clothing and how it reflected character to dog-walking burglars who used their pets as subterfuge. The men discovered safe harbors in each other—Lloyd knew that he had found the one cop who would never look at him strangely when he retreated at the sound of a radio or begrudge him when he insisted on doing it *his* way; Dutch knew that he had found the supreme police intellect. When Lloyd passed the Sergeant's exam, it was Dutch who pulled strings to get him assigned to the Detective Division, calling in a career's worth of unreturned favors.

It was then that Lloyd Hopkins was able to manifest his intellect and produce astounding results—the greatest number of felony arrests and convictions of any Los Angeles police officer in the history of the department, all within a period of five years. Lloyd's reputation grew to the point where he asked for and was granted almost complete autonomy, deferred to by even the most stern-minded, traditionalist cops. And Dutch Peltz proudly watched it happen, content to play in the august light of genius provided by a man he loved more than his own life.

*   *   *

Lloyd found Dutch Peltz in the muster room at Van Nuys Station, pacing the walls and reading the crime reports tacked to the bulletin boards.
He cleared his throat and the older cop wheeled and threw up his hands in
mock surrender.

"Jesus, Lloyd," he said, "when in God's name will you learn not to tread
so softly among friends? A Kodiak bear with the tread of a cat. Jesus!"

Lloyd laughed at the expression of love; it made him happy. "You look
good, Dutch. Working a desk and losing weight! A fucking miracle."

Dutch gave Lloyd a warm, two-handed handshake. "It's no miracle, kid.
I quit smoking and lost weight too. What have we got?"

"A gunsel. Works with a partner. He's got a pad on Saticoy. I figured we'd
drive over and check if his car is around. If he's at home, we'll call for a couple of back-up units; if he's gone, we'll wait him out and take him ourselves.
You like it?"

"I like it. I brought my Ithaca pump. What's the joker's name?"

"Richard Douglas Wilson, white male, age thirty-four. Two-time loser
with a Quentin jacket."

"Sounds like a charming fellow."

"Yeah, a Renaissance lowlifer."

"You'll tell me about it in the car?"

"Yeah, let's go."

Richard Douglas Wilson was not at home. Having checked every street
space, driveway and parking lot on the 11800 block of Saticoy Street for a
'79 Firebird, Lloyd made a circuit of number 11879; a rundown, two-story
apartment house. The mailbox designated Wilson as living in Number 14.
Lloyd found the apartment at the rear of the building. A screen-covered,
sliding glass window was wide open. He looked inside, then walked back to
Dutch, who was parked across the street in the shadow of a freeway off-
ramp.

"No car, no Wilson, Dutch," Lloyd said. "I looked in his window—brand
new stereo, new TV, new clothes, *new money*."

Dutch laughed. "You happy, Lloyd?"

"Yeah, I am. Are you?"

"If you are, kid."

The two policemen settled in to wait. Dutch had brought a thermos of
coffee, and when twilight stifled the heat and smog, he poured two cups.
Handing one to Lloyd, he broke the long, comfortable silence. "I ran into
Janice the other day. I had to testify for an old snitch of mine in Santa Mon-

ica. He took a fall for a burglary one, so I went down to rap sadness to the
D.A. about how the poor bastard was strung out and would he talk to the
judge about diverting him to a drug program. Anyway, I stop at a coffee
shop, and there's Janice. She's got this fag with her, he's showing her fabrics
out of this binder, really giving her the hard sell. Anyway, the fag sashays
off and Janice invites me to sit down. We talk. She says the shop is doing
well, it's acquiring a reputation, the girls are fine. She says that you spend
too much time working, but that it's an old complaint and she can't change
you. She looks sort of disgusted, so I come to your aid. I say, 'Genius writes
its own rules, sweetie. Lloyd loves you. Lloyd will change in time.' Janice
screams at me, 'Lloyd is incapable of it, and his fucking love isn't enough!'
That was it, Lloyd. She wouldn't talk about it any more. I tried to change
the subject, but Janice keeps taking these cryptic little digs at you. Finally,
she jumps up and kisses me on the cheek and says, 'I'm sorry, Dutch. I'm just
being a bitch,' and runs out the door."

Dutch's voice trailed off as he searched for words to end his story. "I just
thought I'd tell you," he said. "I don't believe partners should keep secrets
from each other."

Lloyd sipped his coffee, his mind quietly turbulent, as it always was when
he felt cracks appearing in his major dreams. "So what's the upshot, partner?" he asked.

"The upshot?"

"The riddle, you dumb fucking krauthead! The undercurrents! Haven't I
taught you better than that? What was Janice *really* trying to tell you?"

Dutch swallowed his crushed pride and spat it out angrily. "I think she's
wise to your womanizing, brainboy. I think she knows that the finest of
L.A.'s finest is chasing cunt and shacking up with a bunch of sleazy bimbos
who can't hold the remotest candle to the woman he married. That's what
I think."

Lloyd went calm beneath his anger, and the cracks in his major dreams
became fissures. He shook his head slowly, searching for mortar to fill them
up. "You're wrong," he said, giving Dutch's shoulder a gentle squeeze. "I
think Janice would let *me* know. And Dutch? The other women in my life
aren't bimbos."

"Then what are they?"

"Just women. And I love them."

"You *love* them?"

Lloyd knew as he said the words that it was one of the proudest moments of his life. "Yes. I love all the women I sleep with, and I love my daughters and I love my wife."

After four hours of silent surveillance, Dutch had dozed off in the driver's seat, his head cradled into the half-opened front window. Lloyd remained alert, sipping coffee and keeping his eyes glued to the driveway of 11879 Saticoy Street. It was shortly after ten o'clock when he saw a late-model Firebird pull up in front of the building.

He nudged Dutch awake, placing a hand over his mouth. "Our friend is here, Dutch. He just pulled up, and he's still in the car. I think we should get out on my side and walk around and take him from the rear."

Dutch nodded and handed Lloyd his shotgun. Lloyd squeezed through the passenger door onto the sidewalk, keeping the shotgun pressed into his right leg. Dutch followed suit, slamming the door and throwing an arm around Lloyd, exclaiming, "God, am I smashed!" He went into an adept imitation of a weaving drunk, leaning against Lloyd and talking gibberish.

Lloyd kept his eyes on the black Firebird, waiting for the doors to open, wondering why Wilson was still inside. When they got to the end of the block, he handed Dutch the Ithaca pump and said, "You take the driver, I'll take the passenger." Dutch nodded and jacked a shell into the chamber. Lloyd whispered, "Now," and the men hunkered down and ran up behind the car, swooping down on it from opposite sides, Dutch jamming his shotgun into the driver's side window, whispering, "Police, don't move or you're dead"; Lloyd resting his .38 on the doorjamb and saying to the woman passenger, "Freeze, sweetheart. Put your hands on the dashboard. We want your boyfriend, not you."

The woman stifled a scream and slowly complied with Lloyd's orders. The driver started to jabber, "Look man, you got this wrong, I ain't done nothin'!"

Dutch tightened his finger on the trigger and rested the barrel on the man's nose and said, "Put your hands behind your head. I'm gonna open this car door real slow. You get out *real* slow or you're gonna be *real* dead."

The man nodded and wrapped shaky hands around his neck. Dutch pulled the shotgun back and started to open the car door. As his hand hit the latch, the man kicked out with both legs. The door swung into Dutch's midsection, knocking him backward, the shotgun exploding into the air as his finger reflexively yanked the trigger. The man jumped out of the car and stumbled into the street, then got up and started to run.

Lloyd relinquished his bead on the woman and fired a warning shot into the air, yelling, "Halt, halt!"

Dutch got to his feet and fired blindly. Lloyd saw the running figure starting to weave in anticipation of further volleys. He watched the rhythm of the man's swaying, then fired three times at shoulder level. The man buckled and fell to the pavement. Before Lloyd could approach cautiously, Dutch had run up and was slamming the man in the ribs with the butt of his shotgun. Lloyd ran over and pulled Dutch off, then cuffed the suspect's hands behind his back.

The man had been hit twice just below the collarbone. Clean, Lloyd noticed; two crisp exit wounds. He pulled the man roughly to his feet and said to Dutch, "Ambulance, back-up units." Looking around at the crowd that was starting to form on both sides of the street, he added: "And tell those people to back off onto the sidewalk."

Lloyd turned his attention to the suspect. "Richard Douglas Wilson, right?"

"I don't gotta tell you nothin'," the man answered.

"That's right, you don't. Okay, let's take care of the legalities. You have the right to remain silent. You have the right to have legal counsel present during questioning. If you cannot afford counsel, an attorney will be provided. You got anything to say, Wilson?"

"Yeah," the man said, twisting his wounded shoulder, "I say fuck your mother."

"A predictable response. Can't you guys come up with something original like 'Fuck your father'?"

"Fuck you, flatfoot."

"That's better; you're learning."

Dutch ran back over. "Ambulance and back-up are on their way."

"Good. Where's the girl?"

"She's still in the car."

"Good. Look after Mr. Wilson, will you? I want to talk to her."

Lloyd walked to the black Firebird. The young woman sat rigid in the passenger seat, her hands still clamped to the dashboard. She was crying, and her mascara had run all the way down to her chin. Lloyd knelt by the open door and placed a gentle hand on her shoulder. "Miss?"

The woman turned to face him, starting to weep openly. "I don't want to have a record!" she bawled. "I just met the guy. I'm not a bad person, I just wanted to get stoned and listen to some music!"

Lloyd smoothed an errant lock of her blonde hair. "What's your name?" he asked.

"Sarah."

"Sarah Bernhardt?"

"No."

"Sarah Vaughan?"

"No."

"Sarah Coventry?"

The woman laughed and wiped her sleeve across her face. "Sarah Smith," she said.

Lloyd took her hand. "Good. My name's Lloyd. Where do you live, Sarah?"

"In West L.A."

"I'll tell you what. You go over and wait in that crowd of people. I've got a few things to do here, then I'll drive you home. Okay?"

"Okay . . . and I won't have a record?"

"No one will ever even know that you were here. Okay?"

"Okay."

Lloyd watched Sarah Smith compose herself and move into the crowd of rubberneckers on the sidewalk. He walked over to Dutch and Richard Douglas Wilson, who were leaning against the unmarked Matador. Lloyd motioned Dutch to leave, and as he departed, fixed Wilson with a hard look and disgusted shake of the head.

"No honor among thieves, Richard," he said. "None at all. Especially the punks over at Gangster Manor." Wilson's jaw trembled at the last words, and Lloyd continued. "I found a box of shells and a pantyhose wrapper there with your prints on them. But that wasn't how we nailed you. Somebody snitched you off. Somebody sent the Rampart dicks an anonymous letter making you for the Black Cat stick-up. The letter said you only knocked off fruit bars because you got turned out by some bad-ass jockers at Quentin, and you liked it. You love queers and you hate them too, because of what they made you."

"That's a fucking lie!" Wilson screamed. "I took down liquor stores, markets, even a fucking disco! I done—"

Lloyd cut him off with a chopped hand gesture and went in for the kill. "The letter said that you were drinking outside Gangster Manor after the heist, and you were bragging about all the cunt you scored. Your buddy said he was cracking up because he knew you liked to take it up the ass."

Richard Douglas Wilson's pale, sweat-streaked face went purple. He shrieked. "That scumbag motherfucker! I *saved* his ass from getting porked by every nigger on the yard! I carried that punk through Quentin, now he—"

Lloyd put a hand on Wilson's shoulder and said quietly, "Richard, you're looking at a dime *minimum* this time. Ten bullets. You think you can handle that? You're tough, you're a stand-up guy; I know that. I'm tough too. But you know what? I couldn't do a dime up there. They got niggers up there who'd eat me for breakfast. Turn your partner over, Richard. He snitched you off. I'll go . . ." Wilson was shaking his head frantically in denial. Lloyd started to shake his head in pure loathing. "You dumb asshole," he said. "Go by the old code, let some piece of shit rat on you, facing five to life and you look a gift horse in the mouth. You dumb motherfucker." He turned and started to walk away.

He had gotten only a few feet when Wilson called out, "Wait. Wait. Look—"

Lloyd stifled the huge grin that was lighting up his face and said, "I'll go to the D.A., I'll talk to the judge, I'll see to it that you go to the protective custody tank while you're waiting for your trial."

Richard Douglas Wilson weighed the pros and cons a last time, then capitulated. "His name is John Gustodas. 'Johnny The Greek.' He lives in Hollywood. Franklin and Argylle. The red brick building on the corner."

Lloyd squeezed Wilson's undamaged shoulder. "Good fellow. My partner will take down your statement at the hospital, and I'll be in touch." He craned his head to look for Dutch, and spotted him on the sidewalk talking to two uniformed officers. He whistled twice, and Dutch walked over, warily. "You tired, Dutchman?" Lloyd asked.

"A little. Why?"

"Wilson confessed. He snitched off his partner. The guy lives in Hollywood. I want to go home. You want to take down Wilson's statement, then call Hollywood dicks and give them the info on the guy?"

Dutch hesitated. "Sure, Lloyd," he said.

"Great. John 'Johnny The Greek' Gustodas. Franklin and Argylle. Red brick apartment house on the corner. I'll write up *all* the reports, don't worry about that."

Lloyd heard the wail of an ambulance siren, and shook his head to combat the noise. "Fucking sirens ought to be outlawed," he said as the ambulance rounded the corner and ground to a halt. "There's your chariot. I gotta get out of here. I promised to take Janice out to dinner at eight. It's almost eleven now." The two policemen shook hands. "We did it again, partner," Lloyd said.

"Yeah. I'm sorry I barked at you, kid."

"You're on Janice's side. I don't blame you; she's better looking than I am."

Dutch laughed. "Talk to you tomorrow about Wilson's statement?"

"Right. I'll call you."

Lloyd found Sarah Smith with the remnants of the spectators, smoking a cigarette and shuffling her feet nervously on the pavement. "Hi, Sarah. How are you feeling?"

Sarah ground out the cigarette. "All right, I guess. What's going to happen to what's-his-name?"

Lloyd smiled at the sadness of the question. "He's going to prison for a long time. Don't you even remember his name?"

"I'm bad at names."

"Do you remember mine?"

"Floyd?"

"Close. Lloyd. Come on, I'll take you home."

They walked over to the unmarked Matador and got in. Lloyd scrutinized Sarah openly as she gave her address and fiddled with the contents of her purse. A good girl from a good family gone slightly loose, he decided. Twenty-eight or nine, the light blonde hair legit, the body beneath the black cotton pantsuit both slender and soft. A kind face trying to look tough. Probably a hard worker at her job.

Lloyd headed straight for the nearest westbound on-ramp, alternately savoring his anniversary triumph and picturing confrontations with Janice, who would doubtless give him one of her incredible slow burns—if not an outright battle for being so late. Feeling kindness well up in him for sparing Sarah Smith the harshness of the law, he tapped her shoulder and said, "It's going to be all right, you know."

Sarah dug into her purse looking for cigarettes and found only an empty pack. She muttered, "Shit" and threw it out the window, then sighed. "Yeah, maybe you're right. You really get off on being a cop, don't you?"

"It's my life. Where did you meet Wilson?"

"Is that his name? I met him at a country-western bar. Shit-kicker's paradise, but at least they treat women with respect. What did he do?"

"Held up a bar at gunpoint."

"Jesus! I figured he was just some kind of dope dealer."

Out of the mouths of babes, Lloyd thought. "I'm not lecturing you or any-thing like that," he said, "but you shouldn't hang out in dives. You could get hurt."

Sarah snorted. "Then where should I go to meet people?"

"You mean men?"

"Well . . . yeah."

"Try the continental approach. Drink coffee and read a book at some pic-turesque sidewalk café. Sooner or later some nice fellow will start a conver-sation with you about the book you're reading. You'll meet higher class people that way."

Sarah laughed wildly and clapped her hands, then poked Lloyd in the arm. When he took his eyes from the road and gave her a deadpan, her laughter became hysterical. "That's funny, that's so funny!" she squealed.

"It's not *that* funny."

"Yes, it is! You should be on TV!" Sarah's laughter subsided. She looked at Lloyd quizzically. "Is that how you met your wife?"

"I didn't tell you I was married."

"I saw your ring."

"Very observant. But I met my wife in high school." Sarah Smith laughed until she ached. Lloyd laughed along in a more sedate cadence, then dug in his pocket for a handkerchief and reached over and dabbed at Sarah's tear-mottled face. She leaned into his hand, rubbing her nose along his knuckles.

"You ever wonder why you keep on doing things even when you know they don't work?" she asked.

Lloyd ran a finger under her chin and tilted her head upward to face him. "It's because outside of the major dreams everything is always chang-ing, and even though you keep doing the same things, you're looking for new answers."

"I believe that," Sarah said. "Get off at the next exit and turn right."

Five minutes later he pulled to the curb in front of an apartment build-ing on Barrington. Sarah poked him in the arm and said, "Thanks."

"Good luck, Sarah. Try the book trick."

"Maybe I will. Thanks."

"Thank you."

"For what?"

"I don't know."

Sarah poked Lloyd's arm a last time and darted out of the car.

*   *   *

Janice Hopkins looked at the antique clock in her living room and felt her fearful slow burn leap ahead as the hour hand struck ten and she realized that this was her husband's "second major anniversary" and that she could not rationally fight with him over their missed dinner date, could not use that minor grievance to force confrontations on any of the disturbances that undercut their marriage, could do nothing but say, "Oh shit, Lloyd, where were you this time?" smile at his brilliant answer, and know how much he loved her. Tomorrow she would call her friend George, and he would come to the shop and they would commiserate at length about men.

"Oh God, George," she would say, "the life of a muse!"

And George would reply, "But you love him?"

"More than I know."

"Realizing that he's slightly off the deep end?"

"More than slightly, kiddo, what with his little phobias and all. But they just make him more human, more my baby."

And George would smile and talk of his lover, and they would laugh until the Waterford crystal rang and the bone china plates spun on their shelves.

Then George would take her hand and casually mention the brief affair they had had when George decided he needed to experience women to be more of one himself. It had lasted a week, when George accompanied her to San Francisco for a seminar on appraising antiques. In bed all he talked about was Lloyd. It disgusted her, but thrilled her too, and she went on to divulge the most intimate facts of her marriage.

When she realized that Lloyd would always be the unseen third party in bed with them, she broke it off. It was the only time she had cheated on her husband, and it was not for the standard reasons of neglect, abuse, or sexual boredom. It was to gain some kind of parity with him for the adventurous life he led. When Lloyd was frightened or angry and came to her with that look of his and she unhooked her bra and gave him her breasts, he was hers utterly. But when he read reports, or talked with Dutch Peltz and his other cop friends in the living room and she saw the wheels turning behind the pale gray eyes, she knew he was going to places that she never could. Her other parities—the success of the boutique, the book on Tiffany mirrors she had co-authored, her business acumen—all these satisfied only at the level of logic. Because Lloyd could fly and she couldn't; even after seventeen years of marriage, Janice Rice Hopkins did not possess a syllabus to explain why this was so. And inexplicably, her husband's capacity for flight began to frighten her.

Against the sum total of over twenty years of intimacy, Janice collated the recent evidences of Lloyd's strange behavior: his hour-long sojourns in front of the mirror, casting his eyes in circles as though trawling for flying insects; the increasingly long stints spent at his parents' house, talking to his mother, who had not uttered or comprehended a sound in nineteen years; the insanely sardonic set to his face when he talked to his brother on the telephone about their parents' care.

But the stories that he told the girls were the most disturbing: cop tales that Janice suspected to be half parable and half confession, lurid travelogues on the darkest Los Angeles streets, populated by hookers, junkies, and other sundry lowlifes and cops who were often as raunchy and brutal as the people they threw in jail. A year ago Janice had told Lloyd not to tell her the stories. He had agreed with a silent nod of his head and a cold look in his eyes, and took his parable/confessions to the girls, bringing them into adolescence with detailed accounts of sleaze and horror. Anne would shrug the stories off—she was fourteen and boy crazy; Caroline, thirteen and with a real talent for ballet, would brood over them and bring home true detective magazines and ask her father to discourse on the various articles inside. And Penny would listen and listen and listen, with pale gray eyes shining right through her father and her father's story to some distant termination point. When Lloyd concluded his parable, Penny would kiss him sternly on the cheek and go upstairs and knit the cashmere and madras plaid quilts that had already earned her feature coverage in five Sunday supplements.

Janice shivered. Was Penny's innocence blasted beyond redemption already? A master artisan and fledgling entrepreneur at twelve? She shivered again and looked at the clock. An hour of fearful speculation had passed, and Lloyd was still not home. Suddenly she realized that she missed him and wanted him beyond the limits of normal desire in a twenty-year-old love affair. She walked upstairs and undressed in the dark bedroom, lighting the scented candle that was Lloyd's signal to wake her up and love her. Crawling into bed, a last dark thought crossed her mind, like predator birds blackening a calm sky: As the girls grew older they looked more and more like Lloyd, especially in their eyes.

She heard Lloyd enter the house an hour later, his ritualistic sounds in the entrance hall: Lloyd sighing and yawning, unhooking his gunbelt and placing it on the telephone stand, the familiar shuffling noises he made as he slowly walked upstairs. Tensing herself for the moment when he would open the door and see her in amber light, Janice ran a teasing hand between her legs.

But the bedroom door didn't open; she heard Lloyd tiptoe past it and walk down the hall to Penny's room, then rap his knuckles lightly on her door and whisper, "Penguin? You want to hear a story?" The door creaked open a second later, and Janice heard father and child giggle in gleeful conspiracy.

She gave her husband half an hour, angrily chain-smoking. When her last remnants of ardor had fled and she started to cough from the half-dozen cigarettes, Janice threw on a robe and walked down the hall to listen.

Penny's bedroom door was ajar, and through it Janice could see her husband and youngest daughter sitting on the edge of the bed, holding hands. Lloyd was speaking very softly, in an awe-tinged storyteller's voice: ". . . after clearing the Haverhill/Jenkins homicide, I got assigned to a robbery deployment, a loan-out to the West L.A. squad room. There had been a series of nighttime burglaries of doctor's offices, all in large buildings in the Westwood area. Cash and saleable drugs were the burglar's meat; in shortly over a month he'd ripped off over five grand in cash and a shitload of pharmaceutical speed and heavyweight downers. The West L.A. dicks had his M.O. figured out this way: The bastard used to hide out in the building until nightfall, then hit his mark, then break into a second-floor office and jump out the window into the parking lot. There was evidence to point to this—chipped cement on the window ledges. The dicks figured him for a gymnast, a bullshit cat burglar type who could jump two stories without getting hurt. The commander of the squad was setting up parking lot surveillances to catch him. When the burglar hit an office building on Wilshire that two teams of detectives were staking out, it blew their thesis to hell and I was called in."

Lloyd paused. Penny nuzzled her head into his shoulder and said, "Tell me how you got the scumbag, Daddy."

Lloyd brought his storyteller's voice down to its lowest register: "Sweetheart, nobody jumps two stories repeatedly without getting hurt. I formed my own thesis: The burglar brazenly walked out of the buildings, waving to the security guards in the foyer as if everything were hunky-dory. Only one thing troubled me. Where was he carrying the dope he ripped off? I went back and checked with the guards on duty the nights of the robberies. Yes, both known and unknown men in business suits had walked out of the building in the early evening hours, but none were carrying bags or packages. The guards assumed them to be businessmen with offices in the building and didn't check them out. I heard that same statement six times before it all came together in my mind: The burglar dressed in drag, probably in the protective coloring of a nurse's uniform, carrying a large purse or shoulder bag. I checked with the guards again and, bingo! An unknown woman wearing a nurse's uniform and carrying a large shoulder bag was seen leaving the burglarized buildings at almost the exact time on all six burglary nights. The guards couldn't describe her, but said she was 'ugly,' 'a dog,' and so forth."

Penny fidgeted when Lloyd took in a deep breath and sighed. She took her head from his shoulder and poked him sharply in the arm. "Don't be a tease, Daddy!"

Lloyd laughed and said, "All right. I ran a computer cross-check on vice offenders and registered sex offenders with burglary convictions. Double bingo! Arthur Christiansen, a.k.a. 'Misty Christie,' a.k.a. 'Arlene the Queen' Christiansen. Specialties: giving cut-rate blow jobs to drunks who thought he was a woman and full-drag B&Es. I staked out his pad for thirty-six hours straight, determining that he was dealing uppers and Percodan—I heard his customers comment on the righteous quality of his stuff. This was solid corroboration, but I wanted to catch him-her in the act. The following afternoon old Arthur-Arlene left the pad with a giant quilted shoulder bag and drove to Westwood and walked into a big office building two blocks from the U.C.L.A. campus. Four hours later, an hour after dark, a very ugly creature in a nurse's uniform walks out, carrying the same shoulder bag. I whip out my badge, yell 'Police officer!' and rush Arthur-Arlene, who screams, 'Chauvinist!' and swings on me. The blows are ineffectual and I'm reaching for my handcuffs when Arthur-Arlene's falsies pop out of his blouse. I get him handcuffed and flag down a black-and-white. Arthur-Arlene is screaming 'sisterhood is powerful' and 'police brutality,' and a crowd of U.C.L.A. students start shouting obscenities at me. I barely managed to get into the black-and-white. The scene was almost L.A.'s first transvestite police riot."

Penny laughed hysterically, collapsing on the bed and pounding the covers with her fists. She burrowed her head into the pillow to wipe away her tears, then giggled, "More, Daddy, more. One more before you go to bed."

Lloyd reached over and ruffled Penny's hair. "Funny or serious?"

"Serious," Penny said. "Give me some dark stuff to sate my ghoulish curiosity. If you don't make it good, I'll stay up all night thinking of Arthur-Arlene's falsies."

Lloyd traced circles on the bedspread. "How about a knight story?"

Penny's face grew somber. She took her father's hand and scooted down the bed so that Lloyd could rest his head in her lap. When father and daughter were comfortable, Lloyd stared up at the tartan quilt suspended from the ceiling and said, "The knight was caught in a dilemma. He had two anniversaries in one day—one personal, one professional. The professional one took precedence and in the course of it he shot a man, wounding him. About an hour later, after the man was in custody, the knight started to shake like he always did after he fired his gun. All those delayed reaction questions hit him: What if his shots rendered the asshole for good? What if next time he gloms the wrong info and takes out the wrong guy? What if he starts seeing red all the time and his discretion goes haywire? It's a shitstorm out there. You know that, don't you, Penguin?"

"Yes," Penny whispered.

"You know that you've got to develop claws to fight it?"

"Sharp ones, Daddy."

"You know the weird thing about the knight? The more complicated his doubts and questions become, the stronger his resolve gets. It just gets weird sometimes. What would you do if things got really weird?"

Penny played with her father's hair. "Sharpen my claws," she said, digging her fingers into Lloyd's scalp.

Lloyd grimaced in mock pain. "Sometimes the knight wishes he weren't such a fucking Protestant. If he were a Catholic he'd be able to get formal absolution."

"I'll always absolve you, Daddy," Penny said as Lloyd got to his feet. "Like the song said, 'I'm easy.'"

Lloyd looked down at his daughter. "I love you," he said.

"I love you too. One question before you go: You think I'd be a good Robbery/Homicide dick?"

Lloyd laughed. "No, but you'd be a great Robbery/Homicide dickless."

Janice watched Penny squeal in delight, and suddenly she was violated at the womb. She walked back to the bedroom she shared with her husband and flung off her robe, preparing to do *her* battle in the nude. Lloyd walked through the door moments later, smelling the scented candle and whispering, "Jan? You ardent this late, sweetheart? It's after midnight."

As he reached for the light switch, Janice threw her overflowing ashtray at the opposite wall and hissed, "You sick, selfish, son-of-a-bitch, can't you see what you're doing to that little girl? You call spilling out that violence being a father?" Frozen in the ugliness of the moment, Lloyd pushed the light switch, illuminating Janice, shivering in the nude. "Do you, Lloyd, god-damn you?"

Lloyd moved toward his wife, arms extended in a supplicating gesture, hoping that physical contact would quell the storm.

"No!" Janice said as she backed away, "Not this time! This time I want a promise from you, an oath that you will not tell our children those ugly stories!"

Lloyd reached a long arm out and caught Janice's wrist. She twisted it free and knocked down the nightstand between them.

"Don't, Lloyd. Don't want me and don't placate me and don't touch me until you promise."

He ran a hand through his hair and started to tremble. Fighting an impulse to punch the wall, he bent over and picked up the nightstand. "Penny is a subtle child, Jan, possibly a genius," he said. "What should I do? Tell her about the three . . ."

Janice hurled her favorite porcelain lamp at the closet and shrieked, "She's just a little girl! A twelve-year-old little girl! Can't you understand that?"

Lloyd tripped across the bed and grabbed her around the waist, burying his head in her stomach, whispering, "She has to know, she had to know it, or she'll die. She has to know."

Janice raised her arms and molded her hands into fists. She started to bring them down, clublike, onto Lloyd's back but hesitated as a thousand instances of his erratic passion washed over her, combining to form an epigram whose words she was too terrified to speak.

She lowered her hands to her husband's face and gently pushed him away. "I want to see if the girls are all right," she said. "I'll have to tell them we were fighting. Then I think I want to sleep alone."

Lloyd got to his feet. "I'm sorry I was so late tonight."

Janice nodded dumbly and felt her sense of things confirmed. Then she put on a robe and went down the hall to check on her daughters.

Lloyd knew that he wouldn't be able to sleep. After saying good night to the girls, he prowled around downstairs looking for something to do. There was nothing to do but think of Janice and how he could not have her without giving up something dear to him and essential to his daughters. There was no place to go but backward in time.

Lloyd put on his gunbelt and drove to the old neighborhood.

He found it waiting for him in the pre-dawn stillness, as familiar as the sigh of an old lover. Lloyd drove down Sunset, feeling overwhelmed by the right-ness of his usurping of innocence via parable. Let them learn it slowly, he thought, not the way I did. Let them learn the beast by story—not repeated example. Let that be the new hallmark of my Irish Protestant irregulars.

With this surge of affirmation, Lloyd floored the gas pedal, watching night-bound Sunset Boulevard explode in peripheral flashes of neon, suck-ing him into the middle of a swirling jetstream. He looked at the speedome-ter: one hundred thirty-five miles per hour. It wasn't enough. He bore down on the wheel with his whole being, and the neon turned to burning white. Then he closed his eyes and decelerated until the car hit an upgrade and the laws of nature forced it to a gliding stop.

Lloyd opened his eyes to discover them flooded with tears, wondering for an awkwardly long moment where on earth he was. Finally, a thousand memories clicked in and he realized that chance had left him at the corner of Sunset and Silverlake—the heart of the old neighborhood. Propelled by a subservient fate, he went walking.

Terraced hillsides drew Lloyd into a fusion of past, present, and future.

He sprinted up the Vendome steps, noting with satisfaction that the earth on both sides of the cement stanchions was as soft as ever. The Sil-verlake hills were formed by God to nurture—let the poor Mexicans live hearty here and thrive; let the old people complain about the steepness yet never move away. Let the earthquake the scientific creeps predicted come . . . Silverlake, the defiant traditionalist anomaly, would sustain its havoc and stand proud while L.A. proper burst like an eggshell.

At the top of the hill, Lloyd let his imagination telescope in on the few houses still burning lights. He imagined great loneliness and sensed that the light burners were importuning him for love. He breathed in their love and exhaled it with every ounce of his own, then turned west to stare through the hillside that separated him from the very old house where his crazy brother tended their parents. Lloyd shuddered as discord entered his reverie. The one person he hated guarding his two beloved creators. His one conscious compromise. Unavoidable, but . . .

Lloyd recalled how it happened. It was the spring of 1971. He was working Hollywood Patrol and driving over to Silverlake twice a week to visit his parents while Tom was away at work. His father had settled into a quiet, oblivious state in his old age, spending whole days in his backyard shack, tinkering with the dozens of television sets and radios that eclipsed almost every square inch of its floor space; and his mother, then eight years mute, stared and dreamed in her silence, having to be steered to the kitchen thrice daily lest she forget to eat.

Tom lived with them, as he had all his life, waiting for them to die and leave him the house that had already been placed in his name. He cooked for his parents and cashed their Social Security checks and read to them from the lurid picture histories of Nazi Germany that lined the bookshelves of his bedroom. It was Morgan Hopkins's express wish to Lloyd that he and his wife live out their days in the old house on Griffith Park Boulevard. Lloyd reassured his father many times, "You'll always have the house, Dad. Let Tom pay the taxes, don't even worry about it. He's a sorry excuse for a man, but he makes money, and he's good at looking after you and Mother. Leave the house to him; I don't care. Just be happy and don't worry."

There was a silent agreement between Lloyd and his brother, then thirty-six and a phone sales entrepreneur operating at the edge of the law. Tom was to live at home and feed and care for their parents, and Lloyd was to look the other way at the cache of automatic weapons buried in the backyard of the Hopkins homestead. Lloyd laughed at the inequity of the bargain—Tom, craven beyond words, would never have the guts to use the weaponry, which would be rusted past redemption within a matter of months anyway.

But one day in April of '71, Lloyd got a phone call informing him that there was now a gaping hole at the periphery of his major dreams. An old buddy from the academy who worked Rampart Patrol had cruised by the Hopkins home, noticing a "For Sale" sign on the front lawn. Puzzled, since he had heard Lloyd often mention that his parents would rather die than give up the house, he called Lloyd at Hollywood Station to voice his puzzlement. Lloyd took the words in with a silent rage that had the locker room wobbling surreally before his eyes. Still wearing his uniform, he got his car from the parking lot and drove out to Tom's office in Glendale.

The "office" was a converted basement with four dozen small desks jammed together along the walls, and Lloyd walked into it oblivious to the salesmen shouting the panacea of aluminum siding and home bible-study classes into telephones.

Tom's desk was off by itself near the front of the room, next to a large urn filled with Benzedrine-laced coffee. Lloyd swung his lead-filled billy club into the urn, puncturing it and sending geysers of hot brown liquid into the air. Tom walked out of the men's room, saw the rage in his brother's eyes and the club, and backed into the wall. Lloyd advanced, and was arcing the club in a perfect roundhouse aimed at Tom's head when the terror in the pale gray eyes that so resembled his own halted him. He threw the billy down and ran to the first row of desks, startled phone salesmen darting out of his way, running for cover at the back of the basement.

Lloyd began jerking the telephone cords out of their wall mountings and hurling the phones across the room. One row; two rows; three rows. When the salesmen had all deserted the office, and the floor was littered with broken glass, scattered order forms, and inoperative telephones, he walked up to his quaking older brother and said, "You will take the house off the market today and never leave Mother and Dad alone."

Tom nodded mutely and fainted into a puddle of his dope-saturated coffee.

Lloyd deepened his gaze into the dark hillside. That was over ten years ago. His mother and father were still alive in their separate solitudes; Tom was still their custodian. It was his one unsatisfying holding action, but there was nothing he could do about it. He recalled his last conversation with Tom. He was visiting his parents and found Tom in the backyard, burying shotguns under cover of night.

"Talk to me," Lloyd said.

"About what, Lloydy?" Tom asked.

"Say something real. Insult me. Ask me a question. I won't hurt you."

Tom backed a few steps away. "Are you going to kill me when Mom and Dad are gone?"

Lloyd was thunderstruck. "Why on earth would I want to kill you?"

Tom retreated again. "Because of what happened on Christmas when you were eight."

Lloyd felt himself embraced by monsters, over thirty years dead in the wake of the strong man he had become. His eyes strayed to his father's radio shack, and he had to will himself to return to the present, the force of the horrific memory was so compelling. "You're crazy, Tom. You've always been crazy. I don't like you, but I would never kill you."

Lloyd watched dawn creep up on the eastern horizon, outlining the L.A. skyline with strands of gold. Suddenly he was lonely and wanted to be with a woman. He sat down on the steps and considered his options. There was Sybil, but she had probably gone back to her husband—she was considering it the last time they talked. There was Colleen, but she was probably on her mid-week sales run to Santa Barbara. Leah? Meg? It was over with them, to resurrect it in the fierceness of early morning need would only cause pain later. There was only the uncertainty of Sarah Smith.

Lloyd knocked on her door forty-five minutes later. She opened it bleary-eyed, dressed in a denim bathrobe. When her eyes focused in on him she started to laugh.

"I'm not that funny looking, am I?" Lloyd asked.

Sarah shook her head. "What's the matter, your wife kick you out?"

"Sort of. She found out that I'm really a vampire in disguise. I prowl the lonely dawn streets of Los Angeles looking for beautiful young women to give me transfusions. Take me to your wisest muse."

Sarah giggled. "I'm not beautiful."

"Yes you are. Do you have to go to work today?"

Sarah said, "Yeah, but I can call in sick. I've never been with a vampire."

Lloyd took her hand as she motioned him inside. "Then allow me to introduce myself," he said.

PART THREE
CONVERGENCE

5

Lloyd was seated in his office at Parker Center, his hands playing over papers on his desk, alternately forming steeples and hanging men. It was January 3, 1983, and from his sixth-story cubicle he could see dark storm clouds barrelling northward. He hoped for a pulverizing rainstorm. He felt warm and protective when foul weather raged.

The relative solitude of the office, situated between typewriter storage and Xeroxing rooms, was pleasing, but Lloyd's primary reason for acquiring it was its proximity to the dispatcher's office three doors down. Sooner or later, all homicides within the L.A.P.D.'s jurisdiction were reported over their phone lines, either by investigating officers requesting assistance or concerned parties screaming for help. Lloyd had rigged a special line to his own phone, and whenever an incoming call hit the switchboard a red light on his answering machine went on and he could pick up the receiver and listen in, often making him the first L.A.P.D. detective to gain crucial information on a murder. It was a surefire antidote to burdensome caseloads, dreary report writing, and court appearances; so when Lloyd saw the light on his machine blink, his heart gave a little lurch and he picked up the receiver to listen.

"Los Angeles Police Department, Robbery/Homicide Division," the woman at the switchboard said.

"Is this where you report a murder?" a man stammered in return.

"Yes, sir," the woman answered. "Are you in Los Angeles?"

"I'm in Hollyweird. Man, you wouldn't believe what I just seen . . ." Lloyd came alive with curiosity—the man sounded like he had witnessed a stoned visitation.

"Do you wish to report a homicide, sir?" The woman was brusque, even a little bullying.

"Man, I don't know if it was the real thing or a fuckin' hallucination. I've been doin' dust and reds for three days now."

"Where *are* you, sir?"

"I ain't *nowhere*. But you send the cops to the Aloha Apartments on Leland and Las Palmas. Room 406. There's something inside out of a fuckin' Peckinpah movie. I don't know, man, but either I gotta quit usin' dust or you got some heavy shit on your hands." The caller went into a coughing attack, then whispered, "Fuckin' Hollyweird, man; fuckin' weird," and slammed down his receiver.

Lloyd could almost feel the switchboard operator's befuddlement—she didn't know if the caller was for real or not. Muttering "Goddamned creep," she let her end of the line go dead. Lloyd jumped to his feet and threw on his sports jacket. *He* knew. He ran to his car and tore out for Hollywood.

The Aloha Regency was a four-story, moss-hung, Spanish-style apartment house painted a bright electric blue. Lloyd walked through the unkempt entrance foyer to the elevator, quickly grasping the building as a once grand Hollywood address gone to despair. He knew that the inhabitants of the Aloha Regency would be an uneasy mélange of illegal aliens, boozehounds, and welfare families. The sadness in the threadbare carpeted hallways was almost palpable.

He got into the elevator and pressed 4, then unholstered his .38, feeling his skin start to tingle as he sensed the nearness of death. The elevator jerked to a halt and Lloyd got out. He scanned the hallway, noting that the doors on the even-numbered side leading up to 406 bore jimmy marks. After 406 the jimmy marks stopped. The wood on the doorjambs was freshly splintered with no evidence of warping, which meant that the doors had probably been tried as recently as this morning. Feeling a thesis forming already, Lloyd pointed his .38 straight at the door of 406 and kicked it in.

Holding his gun in front of him as a directional finder, he walked into a small rectangular living room lined with bookshelves and tall potted plants. There was a desk wedged diagonally into one corner and three beanbag chairs on the floor, arranged in a semi-circle opened toward the front picture window. Lloyd walked through the room, savoring its feel. Slowly he swiveled to face the kitchenette off to the left. Freshly scrubbed tile and linoleum; dishes piled neatly by the sink. Which left the bedroom—separated from the rest of the apartment by a bright green door bearing a Rod Stewart poster.

Lloyd looked down at the floor and felt his stomach start to churn. In front of the crack below the door was a pile of dead cockroaches, melded together in a pool of congealed blood. He kicked in the door, murmuring, "Rabbit down the hole," closing his eyes until he assimilated the overwhelming stench of decomposing flesh. When he felt his tremors go internal and knew he wouldn't retch, he opened his eyes and said very softly, "Oh God, please no."

There was a nude woman hanging by one leg from a ceiling beam directly over a quilt-covered bed. Her stomach had been ripped open from pelvis to ribcage and her intestines were spilled out onto her upended torso, splaying out to cover her blood-matted face. Lloyd memorized the scene: the woman's free hanging leg swollen and purple and twisted out at a right angle, caked blood on her breasts, a bluish-white tint on what he could see of her unbloodied flesh, the bed coverlet drenched with so much blood that it crusted and peeled in layers, blood on the floor and walls and dresser and mirror, all framing the dead woman in a perfect symmetry of devastation.

Lloyd went into the living room and found the telephone. He called Dutch Peltz at the Hollywood Station, saying only, "6819 Leland, Apartment 106. Homicide, ambulance, Medical Examiner. I'll call you later and tell you about it."

Dutch said, "Okay, Lloyd," and hung up.

Lloyd walked through the apartment a second time, willing his mind blank so that things could come to him, moving his eyes over the living room until he noticed a leather purse lying next to a cactus plant. He reached down and grabbed it, then dumped its contents onto the floor. Makeup kit, Excedrin, loose change. He opened a handtooled wallet. The woman had been Julia Lynn Niemeyer. The photo and statistics on her driver's license made him ache: pretty, 5'5", 120 pounds. D.O.B. 2–2–54, making her a month short of twenty-nine.

Lloyd dropped the wallet and examined the bookshelves. Romances and popular novels predominated. He noticed that the books on the top shelves were covered with dust, while the books on the bottom shelf were clean.

He squatted down to examine them more closely. The bottom shelf contained volumes of poetry, from Shakespeare to Byron to feminist poets in soft cover. Lloyd pulled out three books at random and leafed through them, feeling his respect for Julia Lynn Niemeyer grow—she had been reading good stuff in the days before her death. He finished flipping through the classics and picked up an outsized paperback entitled *Rage in the Womb— An Anthology of Feminist Prose.* Opening to the "Contents," he went numb when he saw dark brown stains on the inside cover. Flipping forward, he found pages stuck together with congealed blood and bloody smatterings growing fainter as he worked toward the end of the book. When he reached the glossy finished back cover, he gasped. Perfectly outlined in white were two bloody partial fingerprints—an index and pinky; enough to run a make on.

Lloyd whooped and wrapped the book in his handkerchief and carefully placed it on one of the beanbag chairs. On impulse, he walked back over to the bookshelf and ran a hand in the narrow space between the bottom shelf and the floor. He came away with a handful of vending machine dispensed sex tabloids—the L.A. *Nite-Line,* L.A. *Grope,* and L.A. *Swinger.*

He carried them over to the chair and sat down and read, saddened by the lurid fantasy letters and desperate liaison ads. "Attractive divorcee, 40, seeks well-hung white men for afternoon love. Send erect photo and letter to P.O. Box 5816, Gardena, Calif. 90808."; "Good looking gay guy, 24, into giving head, seeks hunky young high school guys with no mustache. Call anytime—709-6404"; "Mr. Big Dick's my name, and fucking's my game! I give good lovin' to much acclaim! Let's get together for a swingin' nite, my dick is hard if your pussy's tight!—Send spread photo to P.O. Box 6969, L.A., Calif. 90069."

Lloyd was about to put the tabloids down and send up a mercy plea for the entire human race when his eyes caught an advertisement circled in red. "Your fantasy or mine? Let's get together and rap. Any and all sexually liberated people are invited to write to me at P.O. Box 7512, Hollywood, Calif. 90036 (I'm an attractive woman in her late 20s)." He put the paper down and dug through the other two. The identical ad was featured in both.

He stuck the papers into his jacket pocket, walked back into the bedroom, and opened the windows. Julia Lynn Niemeyer swayed from the draft, turning on her one-legged axis, the ceiling beam creaking against her weight. Lloyd held her arms gently. "Oh, sweetheart," he whispered, "oh, baby, what were you looking for? Did you fight? Did you scream?"

Almost as if in answer, the woman's cold left arm was caught by a gust of wind and flopped out of Lloyd's grasp. He grabbed it and held the hand tightly, his eyes moving to the large blue veins at the crook of the elbow. He gasped. A pair of needle marks were outlined clearly against the middle of the largest vein. He checked the other arm—nothing—then scraped away patches of dried blood from the ankles and backs of the knees. No other tracks; the woman had been professionally sedated at the time of her desecration.

Lloyd heard footsteps in the hallway, and seconds later a plainclothes cop and two patrolmen in uniform burst into the apartment. He walked into the living room to greet them, pointing a thumb over his shoulder and saying, "In there, guys." He was staring out the window at the black sky when he heard their first exclamations of horror, followed by the sound of retching.

The plainclothes cop was the first to recover, walking up to Lloyd and blurting out bluff-hearty, "Wow! That's some stiff! You're Lloyd Hopkins, aren't you? I'm Lundquist, Hollywood dicks."

Lloyd turned to face the tall, prematurely gray young man, ignoring his outstretched hand. He scrutinized him openly and decided he was stupid and inexperienced.

Lundquist fidgeted under Lloyd's stare. "I think we got a botched-up burglary, Sergeant," he said. "I saw B&E marks on the door here. I think we should start our investigation by hauling in burglars known to use viol—"

Lloyd shook his head, silencing the younger detective. "Wrong. Those jimmy marks are fresh. The edges would have rounded off from moisture if the attempted burglaries coincided with the murder. That woman has been dead for at least two days. No, the burglar was the guy who called in to report the body. Now listen, the woman's purse is on that chair over there. Positive I.D. There's also a paperback book with two bloodstained partial prints. Get them to the lab and have the technicians call me at home when they have something conclusive one way or the other. I want you to search the premises, then seal it—no reporters, no TV assholes. You got that?"

Lundquist nodded.

"Good. Now, I want you to call the M.E. and S.I.D., and have them bring in a fingerprint team and dust this place from top to bottom. I want a complete forensic work-up. Tell the M.E. to call me at home with the autopsy report. Who's the top dog at Hollywood dicks?"

"Lieutenant Perkins."

"Good. I'll call him. Tell him I'm handling this case for Robbery/Homicide."

"Right, Sergeant."

Lloyd walked back into the bedroom. The two patrolmen were staring at the corpse and cracking jokes. "I had a girlfriend once who looked like that," the older cop said. "Bloody Mary. I could only get together with her for two weeks outta the month, her period lasted so long."

"That's nothing," the younger cop said, "I knew an attendant at the morgue who fell in love with a corpse. He wouldn't let the coroner slice her—said it took the R out of romance."

The other cop laughed and lit a cigarette with shaking hands. "My wife takes the R out of romance every night, also the O and the M."

Lloyd cleared his throat; he knew that the men were joking to keep their horror at bay, but he was offended anyway, and didn't want Julia Lynn Niemeyer to hear such things. He rummaged through the bedroom closet until he found a terrycloth robe, then walked into the kitchen and found a serrated-edged steak knife. When he re-entered the bedroom and stood up on the blood-spattered bed, the younger cop said, "You'd better leave her like that for the coroner, Sergeant."

Lloyd said, "Shut the fuck up," and cut through the nylon cord that bound Julia Lynn Niemeyer at the ankle. He gathered her dangling limbs and violated torso into his arms and stepped off the bed, cradling her head into his shoulder. Tears filled his eyes. "Sleep, darling," he said. "Know that I'll find your killer." Lloyd lowered her to the floor and covered her with the robe. The three cops stared at him in disbelief.

"Seal the premises." Lloyd said.

Three days later, Lloyd was stationed at the main Hollywood post office with his eyes glued to the wall containing P.O. boxes 7500 through 7550, armed with the knowledge that Julia Lynn Niemeyer had placed her tabloid advertisements in the company of a tall, blonde woman of about forty. Office personnel at both the L.A. *Night-Line* and L.A. *Swinger* had positively identified the dead woman from her driver's license photograph, and distinctly remembered her female companion.

Lloyd fidgeted, keeping his anger and impatience at bay by recapitulating all the known physical evidence on the killing. Fact: Julia Lynn Neimeyer was killed by a massive dose of heroin, and was mutilated after her death. Fact: The coroner had placed the time of her murder as seventy-two hours before the discovery of her body. Fact: No one at the Aloha Regency had heard signs of a struggle or knew much about the victim, who lived on money from a trust fund set up by her parents, who had died in a car accident in 1978. This information had been supplied by the woman's uncle, who had read of the killing in the San Francisco newspapers and who went on to describe Julia Niemeyer as a "very deep, very quiet, very intelligent girl who didn't let people get close to her."

The killing had made the newspapers in a big way, and similarities to the Tate-LaBianca slayings of 1969 had been graphically pointed out. This caused a torrent of unsolicited information to flood the switchboards of the Los Angeles Police Department, and Lloyd had assigned three officers to interview all callers who didn't sound like outright cranks. The blood-stained fingerprints on the paperback book—the one *hard* piece of physical evidence—had been scrutinized by fingerprint experts, then computer fed and teletyped to every police agency in the continental United States, with astoundingly negative results: The partial index and pinky prints could not be attributed to anyone, anywhere, meaning that the killer had never been arrested, never been a member of the armed services or civil service, never been bonded, and had never applied for a driver's license in thirty-seven of the fifty United States.

Lloyd felt his thesis take on the form of what he called the "Black Dahlia Syndrome," a reference to the famous unsolved 1947 mutilation murder. He was certain that Julia Lynn Niemeyer had been killed by an intelligent middle-aged man who had never killed before, a man with a low sex drive who had somehow come in contact with Julia Niemeyer, whose persona somehow triggered his long dormant psychoses, and eventually led him to plan her murder carefully. He knew also that the man was physically strong and capable of maneuvering on a broad-based societal level: a solid citizen type who could also score heroin.

Lloyd was impressed with both killer and the challenge his capture presented. He surveyed the post office crowd at random, then shifted his gaze back to Box 7512. He felt his impatience grow. If the "tall blonde woman" didn't show by lunchtime, he would smash the box open and rip it off by the hinges.

She showed an hour later. Lloyd sensed that it was she as soon as she walked through the broad glass doors and nervously made for the aisles of boxes. A tall, strong-featured woman whose manner was like a barely controlled scream, he could almost feel her body tension as she looked fearfully in all directions, inserted her key and withdrew a handful of mail, then ran back outside.

Lloyd came up behind her as she was opening the door of a double-parked Pinto hatchback. She turned around as she heard his footsteps, her hand flying to her mouth when she saw the badge he was holding up at eye level. Transfixed by the badge, the woman flopped against the car and let the handful of mail drop to the street.

Lloyd bent down and picked it up. "Police officer," he said quietly.

"Oh, Jesus," she said, "Vice?"

Lloyd said, "No, Homicide. It's about Julia Niemeyer."

An angry flush came over the woman's face. "Jesus," she said, "that's a relief. I was going to call you. I suppose you want to talk?"

Lloyd smiled; the woman had a certain panache. "We can't talk here," he said, "and I don't want to subject you to a police station. Do you mind driving somewhere?"

"No," the woman said, adding "Officer" with the thinnest edge of contempt.

Lloyd told her to drive south to Hancock Park. En route he learned that she was Joanie Pratt, age 42, former dancer, singer, actress, waitress, Playboy Club Bunny, model, and kept woman.

"What are you doing *now?*" he asked as she pulled into the Hancock Park parking lot.

"It's illegal," Joanie Pratt said, smiling.

"I don't care," Lloyd said, smiling back.

"Okay, I deal Quaaludes and fuck for selected older guys who don't want to get involved."

Lloyd laughed and pointed to a collection of plaster dinosaurs standing on a grassy knoll a few yards from the tar pits. "Let's go talk," he said.

When they were seated on the grass, Lloyd bored in, describing Julia Niemeyer's corpse in hideously graphic detail. Joanie Pratt turned white, then red and started to sob. Lloyd made no move to comfort her. When her tears subsided, he said softly, "I want this animal. I know about the ads you and Julia placed in the sex papers. I don't care if the two of you have fucked half of L.A. or the kangaroos in the San Diego Zoo or each other. I don't give a fuck if you deal dope, snort dope, shoot dope, or turn little kids on to dope. I want to know everything that you know about Julia Niemeyer: her love life, her sex life, and why she put those ads in those papers. Have you got that?"

Joanie nodded mutely. Lloyd dug a handkerchief out of his coat pocket and handed it to her. She wiped her face and said, "All right, it's like this. I was in the Hollywood Library about three months ago, returning some books. I notice this good-looking chick standing in line next to me, checking out all these scholarly books on sex—Kraft-Ebbing, Kinsey, *The Hite Re-*

port. I crack a joke to the girl, who turns out to be Julia. Anyway, we go out-side and smoke a cigarette and talk—about sex. Julia tells me she's re-searching sexuality—that she wants to write a book about it. I share my racy past with her, and tell her I've got this gig going—floating swingers' parties. It's kind of a scam—I know some heavyweight real estate people, and I score dope for them in exchange for letting me sublet these really primo houses when the owners are out of town. Then I place ads in the sex pa-pers—high, *high* line sex parties. Two hundred dollars a couple—to keep the riffraff out. I provide good food and dope, music and a light show. Anyway, Julia—she's obsessed with sex, but she doesn't fuck—she's just a sex scholar . . ."

Joanie paused, and lit a cigarette. When Lloyd nervously blurted out, "Go on," she said, "Anyway, Julia wants to interview the people at my par-ties. I tell her 'fuck no! These people are paying *goood* money to come, and they don't want to be hassled by some sex-obsessed interviewer.' So Julia says, 'Look. I've got lots of money. I'll pay for people to come to the parties, and I'll interview them there, as their price for admission. That way, I can watch them have sex.' Anyway, that's why Julia placed those ads. People contacted her, and she offered to pay their way to the parties if they con-sented to interviews."

Lloyd was riveted, staring into Joanie Pratt's pale blue eyes until she started to wave a hand in front of his face. "Come back to earth there, Sergeant. You look like you just took a trip to Mars."

Lloyd felt vague instincts clicking into place. He brushed Joanie's hand away. "Go on."

"Okay, Mars Man. Anyway, Julia conducted her interviews and watched people fuck until she was blue in the face. She wrote out tons of notes and had the first draft of her book completed when her pad was burglarized and her manuscript and all her notes and files were stolen. She tol—"

"What!" Lloyd screamed.

Joanie leaped back, startled. "Whoa there, Sarge. Let me finish. This was about a month ago. The pad was ransacked. Her stereo and TV and a thou-sand dollars in cash were stolen. She . . ."

Lloyd interrupted. "Did she report it to the police?"

Joanie shook her head. "No, I told her not to. I told her she could always rewrite her book from memory and do some more interviews. I didn't want any cops nosing around us. Cops are notorious moralists, and they might have gotten wind of my scam. But listen. About a week before she died,

Julia told me she had the feeling she was being followed. There was this man that she used to see in all these odd places—on the street, in restaurants, in the market. He never stared at her or anything like that, but she had this feeling he was stalking her."

Lloyd went cold all over. "Did she recognize the man from the parties?"

"She said she couldn't be sure."

Lloyd was silent for a long moment. "Do you have any of the letters Julia received?"

Joanie shook her head. "No, just the ones I picked up today."

Lloyd stuck out his hand, and Joanie withdrew the letters from her purse. He stared at her, tapping the collection of envelopes against his leg. "When are you having your next party?"

Joanie lowered her eyes. "Tonight."

Lloyd said, "Good. I'm going to attend. You're going to be my date."

The party was in a three-story A-frame nestled at the end of a cul-de-sac on the Valley side of the Hollywood Hills. Lloyd wore cuffed chino pants, penny loafers, a striped polo shirt, and a crew-neck sweater over his .38 snubnose, prompting Joanie Pratt to exclaim, "Jesus, Sarge! This is a swing party, not a high school sock hop! Where's my corsage?"

"It's in my pants," he said.

Joanie laughed, then ran hooded eyes over his body. "Nice. You gonna fuck tonight? You'll get offers."

"No, I'm saving it for the senior prom. You want to show me around?"

They walked through the house. All the furniture in the living room and dining room had been moved up against the walls, and the carpets had been rolled up and wadded ceiling high next to a row of low tables where cold cuts, hors d'oeuvres, and canned cocktails in bowls of ice were arrayed. Joanie said, "Buffet and dance floor. There's a primo stereo system with a hook-up to speakers all over the house." She pointed to lighting fixtures hung from the ceiling. "The stereo is hooked up to the lights, so the music and the lights work together. It's wild." She took his hand and led him upstairs. The two upper floors contained bedrooms and dens on either side of a winding hallway. Red lights blinked on and off above the open doors, and Lloyd could see that inside the entire floor space of each room was covered by mattresses with pink silk sheets.

Joanie poked him in the ribs. "I hire these wetbacks from the slave market on Skid Row. They do all the heavy lifting. I give them ten bucks before the party, then twenty bucks and a bottle of tequila when they move all the furniture back. What's the matter, Sarge? You're scowling."

"I don't know," Lloyd said, "but it's funny. I'm here looking for a killer, this whole 'party' is probably against the law, and I think I'm happier than I've been in a long time."

The celebrants started to arrive half an hour later. Lloyd briefed Joanie on what he wanted—she was to circulate, and point out any people she recognized as having been interviewed by or having seemed interested in Julia Niemeyer. She was to report to him all men who even *mentioned* Julia or her recent demise. She was also to report anything that seemed darkly incongruous, anything that violated her self-described party ethos of "Good music, good dope, good fucking"; *no one* was to know that he was a police officer.

Lloyd stationed himself behind the two burly bouncers scrutinizing incoming guests and collecting their invitations. The partygoers, coupled off to insure an even ratio of partners, seemed to him to be the very microcosm of jaded money—the finest clothes in the latest styles over unfit, tension-ridden bodies, the men middle-aged and afraid of it, the women looking hard, competitive, and brassy in the worst camped-out faggot manner. As the bouncers locked and bolted the door behind the last arrivals, Lloyd felt that he had just viewed a perfect impressionist representation of hell. His left knee was twitching in reaction to it, and when he walked back to the buffet he knew that he would need every ounce of the love in his Irish Protestant ethos to keep from hating them.

He decided to play the jocular stud. As Joanie Pratt brushed by him, he whispered to her, "Make it look like we're together."

Joanie closed her eyes. Lloyd bent in slow motion to kiss her, his hands reaching out and grasping her waist and lifting her so that her feet dangled inches above the floor. Their lips and tongues met and played in perfect unison. Whistling and good-natured jibes drowned out Lloyd's furious heartbeat, and when he broke the kiss and lowered Joanie to the floor he felt he had conquered the jaded assembly with love.

"That's all, folks," he said with a mock humble twang, patting Joanie on the shoulder. "You folks all have a good time. I have to go upstairs and rest." Wild applause greeted this irony, and he ran for the staircase.

Lloyd found a bedroom at the far end of the third-story hallway. He locked himself in, feeling proud of his performance, yet ashamed of its ease and dumbfounded by the fact that he was starting to like the revelers down-

stairs. He sat down on the pink sheeted mattress and dug out the letters that
Joanie had given him—the last correspondence delivered to P.O. Box 7512.
He had planned to go over them later, aided by Joanie, but now he needed
work to keep his almost heart-stricken ambivalence at bay.

The first two envelopes contained underground junk mail, form letters
advertising king-size electric dildos and bondage attire. The third envelope
was hand-printed. Lloyd looked more closely and noticed that the letters in
the address were perfectly squared off, obviously formed by pen and ruler.
His mind clicked, and he held the envelope gently by the edges and slit it
open with a deft thrust of his fingernail. It contained a poem, block ruler
printed in maroon ink. Lloyd tilted the page sideways. Something about the
ink bothered him. Letting the paper wobble in front of his eyes, he realized
that the maroon ink was starting to flake, revealing a brighter shade underneath. He deliberately smudged a stanza, then smelled his finger and felt his
mind click a second time: The poem was written in blood.

Lloyd willed his mind to be still, using his method of deep breathing and
forcing himself to concentrate on the vertical lines in the plaid quilt Penny
had loomed for him two Christmases ago. When he had been blank for solid
minutes, he began to read the blood-formed words:

> I took you from
>   your grief;
> I stole you like
>   a thief;
> I rent my heart
>   to give you
>   mercy;
> You begged me to end
>   your strife
> And I gave you life.
> Your body was the
>   ellipsis,
> Your heart my
>   wife
> Your whorish studies
>   my burden;
> Your death, my
>   life.

I read your words,
  hell bound;
Sorrowed to the
  core by the dirt
  you found—
You grieved me more
Than all the rest—
You were the smartest,
The kindest, the worst
  and best—
And I faltered at the
  moment I put you
  to rest.

Tribute in anonymous
  transit,
Live life enclosed
  in a cancer
    cell,
Only the love in my
  knife grants it;
Reprieve from the gates
  of this blood-drenched
    hell.

Lloyd read the poem three more times, memorizing it, letting the permutations of the words enter him and regulate his heartbeat and the flow of his
blood and the thrust of his brainwaves. He walked over and sought his image
in the mirror that completely covered the back wall. He couldn't decide if
he was an Irish Protestant knight or a gargoyle, and he didn't care; he had
been placed in the vortex of divinely evil compulsions and he knew, at long
last, precisely why he had been granted genius.

As the poem engulfed him further it began to assume musical dimensions, cadences of the corny signature tunes of all the old TV programs that
Tom had made him . . .

The cadences grew, and "Live life enclosed in a cancer cell" became an
improvisation on the big band theme song of Texaco Star Theatre, and suddenly Milton Berle was there next to him, rotating a cigar against his wood-

chuck teeth. Lloyd screamed and fell to his knees, his hands cupped to his ears.

There was a screeching, and the music stopped. Lloyd tightened his grip on his ears. "Tell me a story rabbit down the hole," he whimpered beatifically until he heard the crackle of static coming from a large speaker mounted on the bedroom wall. His dry sobs trailed into relieved laughter. It was the radio.

Rational thoughts of combat entered Lloyd's mind. He could trash the central source of the music by yanking a few wires and twisting a few dials; let the revelers fuck *sans* accompaniment, the whole scene was illegal anyway.

Carefully placing the poem back in its envelope and securing it in his pocket, Lloyd walked downstairs, his hands clamped against his sides, twisted into his pants legs. He ignored the couples who were fornicating in standing positions in bedroom doorways and concentrated on the shimmering crimson lights that bathed the hallway. The lights were the reality, the benign antithesis of the music, and if he could let them guide him to the stereo system, he would be safe.

The first floor was a massive swirl of nude bodies moving with the music, heeding and heedless of the beat, rhythmic and abandoned limbs flung wildly into the air, brushing flesh, lingering in the briefest of caresses before being yanked back in seizure-like movements. Lloyd threaded his way through the swirl, feeling arms and hands twist and prod and pluck at him. He saw the stereo system at the opposite end of the living room, Joanie Pratt standing beside it, scrutinizing a stack of record albums. Fully clothed, she looked like a fixed beacon light in a world of insane noise.

"Joanie!"

The alarm in his own voice startled him, jolting him away from the music, into bodies that retreated as he cut a path through them. He crashed through the kitchen, down strobe-lighted hallways and out into a pitch black yard that was enveloped by shuddering silence. Falling to his knees, he let the silent night air and the scent of eucalyptus embrace him.

"Sarge?"

Joanie Pratt knelt by his side. She stroked his back and said, "Jesus, are you okay? The look on your face on that dance floor . . . I've never seen anything like it." Lloyd forced himself to laugh. "Don't worry about it. I can't stand loud noise or music. It's old stuff." Joanie pointed a finger at her head and twirled it. "You've got a few loose up there. You know that?"

"Don't talk to me that way."

"I'm sorry. Wife and kids?"

Lloyd nodded and got to his feet. Helping Joanie up, he said, "Seventeen years. Three daughters."

"Is it good?"

"Things are changing. My daughters are wonderful. I tell them stories, and my wife hates me for it."

"Why? What kind of stories?"

"Never mind. When I was eight years old my mother told *me* stories, and it saved my life."

"What kind of . . ."

Lloyd shook his head. "No, let's change the subject. Did you hear anything at the party? Did anyone mention Julia? Did you notice anything unusual?"

"No, no, and no. Julia used a phony name when she interviewed people, and that was a bad photo of her on the news. I don't think anyone even made the connection."

Lloyd considered this. "I buy it," he said. "My instinct tells me that the killer wouldn't come to a party like this; he'd consider it ugly. I want to cover all the angles, though. One of those letters you gave me contained a poem. It was written by the killer; I'm sure of that. The poem made a vague reference to other victims, so I'm certain that he's killed more than one woman." When Joanie responded with a blank face, he went on. "What I need from you is a list of your regular partygoers."

Joanie was already frantically shaking her head. Lloyd grabbed her shoulders and said softly, "Do you want this animal to kill again? What's more important, saving innocent lives or the anonymity of a bunch of horny assholes?"

Hysterical giggling from inside the house framed Joanie's answer. "It's not much of a choice, Sarge. Let's go over to my place; I've got a Rolodex file on all my regulars."

"What about your party?"

"The hell with it. I'll have the bouncers lock up. Your car or mine?"

"Mine. Is this an invitation?"

"No, it's a proposition."

*   *   *

Afterward, too full of each other to sleep, Lloyd played with Joanie's breasts, cupping and pushing and probing them into different shapes and running soft fingers around the edges of the nipples.

Joanie laughed and said *sotto voce*, "Do-wah, wah-wah, do-rann-rann." Lloyd asked her what the strange sounds meant and she said, "I forgot; you never listen to music.

"Okay. I came out here from Saint Paul, Minnesota, in 1958. I was eighteen. I had it all figured out—I was gonna be the first female rock and roll star. I was blonde, I had tits, and I thought I could sing. I get off the bus at Fountain and Vine and walk north. I see the Capitol Records Tower north of the Boulevard, and I figure it's gotta be a message, so I hotfoot it up there, lugging this cardboard suitcase, wearing a crinoline party dress and high heels on the coldest day of the year.

"Anyway, I sit down in the waiting room, eyeballing all these gold records they've got on the walls. I'm thinking, 'Someday' . . . Anyway, this guy comes up to me and says, 'I'm Pluto Maroon. I'm an agent. Capitol Records is not your gig. Let's splitsville.' I go, 'Huh?' and we splitsville— Pluto says a buddy-roo of his is making a movie-roo in Venice. We drive out there in this Cadillac soul wagon. Pluto's buddy is Orson Welles. No shit, Sarge; Orson fucking Welles. He's making *Touch of Evil*. Venice is doubling as this sleazy Mexican border town.

"Right off the bat I can tell that Orson baby is condescending to Pluto— that he digs him strictly as a sycophant, kind of an amusing picaresque buffoon. Anyway, Orson tells Pluto to dig him up some extras, locals who'd be willing to hang around all day for a few scoots and a jug. So Pluto and I go walking down Ocean Front Walk. What a revelation! Innocent Joanie from St. Paul hobnobbing with beatniks, junkies, and geniuses!

"Anyway, we go by this beatnik bookstore. A guy who looks like a werewolf is behind the counter. Pluto says, 'You wanna dig Orson Welles and make a five-spot?' The guy says, 'Crazy,' and we splitsville on down the boardwalk, picking up this incredible low-life entourage on the way.

"Anyway, the werewolf zeroes in on me. 'I'm Marty Mason,' he says, 'I'm a singer.' I think, 'Wowie zowie!' and I say, 'I'm Joanie Pratt—I'm a singer, too.' Marty says, 'Sing "do-wah, wah-wah, do-rann-rann" ten times.' I do it, and he says, 'I'm playing a gig in San Berdoo tonight. Wanna be my backup?' I said, 'What do I have to do?' Marty says, 'Sing "do-wah, wah-wah, do-rann-rann."'

"So that was it. I did it. I sang 'do-wah, wah-wah, do-rann-rann' for ten

years. I married Marty, and he became Marty 'Monster' Mason and cut the
'Monster Stomp,' capitalizing on his werewolf resemblance, and we were
biggg time for a couple of years, then Marty got strung out and we got di-
vorced, and now I'm sort of a business woman and Marty is on Methadone
Maintenance and working as a fry cook at a Burger King in the Valley, and
it's still 'do-wah, wah-wah, do-rann-rann.'"

Joanie sighed, lit a cigarette and blew smoke rings at Lloyd, who was trac-
ing patterns on her thighs and thinking that he had just heard existential-
ism in a nutshell. Wanting Joanie's interpretation, he asked, "What does it
mean?"

She said, "Whenever things are up in the air, or scary, or about to maybe
get good, I sing 'do-wah, wah-wah, do-rann-rann,' and they seem to fall into
place; or at least they're not so scary."

Lloyd felt a little piece of his heart work its way loose and drift back to
Venice in the winter of '58. "Can I sleep with you again?" he asked.

Joanie took his hand and kissed it. "Anytime, Sarge."

Lloyd got up and dressed, then picked up the Rolodex file and cradled it
to his chest. "I'll be very discreet about this," he said. "I'll have smart, competent officers do whatever questioning has to be done."

"I trust you," Joanie said.

Lloyd bent over and kissed her cheek. "I've memorized your phone number. I'll call you."

Joanie leaned into the kiss. "Take care, Sarge."

It was dawn. Lloyd drove downtown to Parker Center, feeling spellbound
with purpose. He took the elevator to the fourth-floor computer room.
There was a lone operator on duty. The man looked up from his science-
fiction novel as he saw Lloyd approach, wondering if there was a chance to
banter with the big detective the other cops called "The Brain." When he
saw the look on Lloyd's face, he decided against it.

Lloyd said brusquely, "Good morning. I want printouts on every unsolved
female homicide in Los Angeles County over the past fifteen years. I'll be
up in my office. Ring extension 1179 when you have the information."

Lloyd about-faced and walked the two flights of stairs up to his office.
The cubicle was dark and quiet and peaceful, and he flopped into his chair
and fell asleep immediately.

6

It was the poet's eleventh complete reading of the manuscript, his eleventh journey into his most recent beloved's shameful passion, his third since he consummated their love.

His hands shook as he turned the pages, and he knew that he would have to return to the repulsively fascinating third chapter, the words that tore and bit at him, that made him feel his organs and their functions, that made him sweat and tingle and drop things and laugh when nothing was funny.

The chapter was entitled "Straight Men—Gay Fantasies," and it reminded him of his early poetry writing days, the days before he became so obsessed with form, when stanzas didn't have to rhyme, when he trusted the thematic unity of his subconscious. In this chapter his beloved had gotten a disparate sampling of normal men to admit things like, "I would really like to take it up the ass just once. Just do it—and fuck the consequences, then go home and make love to my wife and wonder if it felt any different to her," and "I'm thirty-four now, and I've screwed every woman who'd let me for seventeen years and I still haven't quite found the nitty-gritty excitement that I thought I would. I drive down Santa Monica Boulevard sometimes and see the male hustlers and everything goes slightly haywire and I think and think and . . . (here Interviewee sighs disgustedly) . . . and then I think that a new woman will do it, and I think of coming here to these parties and before you know it I'm turning off Santa Monica and thinking of my wife and kids and then . . . oh, shit!"

He put the looseleaf binder down, feeling the little body flushes that had ruled his life since his consummation with Julia. She had been dead for two weeks and they were continuing unabated, undaunted by the courage he had shown in writing her anonymous tribute etched in his own blood, undaunted by his first sexual transit since . . .

*　　*　　*

He had read the third chapter beside Julia's body, savoring her nearness, wanting the completeness of her flesh and her words. The men who had told Julia their stories were so blighted in their dishonesty that he wanted to retch. Yet . . . he read the man's account of driving down Santa Monica Boulevard over and over, looking up only to watch Julia sway on her external axis. She was more *of* him than any of the first twenty-one, more even than Linda, who had moved him so deeply. She had given him *words* to keep—tangible love gifts that would grow in him. Yet . . . Santa Monica Boulevard . . . yet . . . the poor wretch so devastated by societal mores that he couldn't . . .

He walked into the living room. *Rage in the Womb*. A lesbian poet wrote of her lover's "multiunioned folds of wetness." Visions of muscular torsos, broad shoulders, and flat, hard backsides entered him, given to him by Julia, telling him to seek a further union with her by showing courage where the cowardly wretch had failed. He balked inside, searching frantically for *words*. He tried anagrams of Julia and Kathy, five letters each. It didn't work. Julia wanted more than the others. He walked back to the bedroom to view her corpse a last time. She sent him visions of sullen young men in macho poses. He obeyed. He drove to Santa Monica Boulevard.

He found them a few blocks west of La Brea, standing in front of taco stands, porno bookstores, and bars, outlined in neon tendrils that gave them the added enticements of halos, auras, and wispy appendages. The idea of looking for a specific image or body crossed his mind, but he killed the thought. It would give him time to retreat, and he wanted to impress Julia with his unquestioning compliance.

He pulled to the curb and rolled down the window, beckoning to the young man leaning against a newsrack with one hip thrust toward the street.

The young man walked over and leaned in through the window. "It's thirty; head only, pitch or catch," he said, getting an inward wave of the arm as his answer.

They drove around the corner and parked. He clenched his body until he thought his muscles would contract and suffocate him, then whispered, "Kathy," and let the young man unbutton his pants and lower his head into his lap. His contractions continued until he exploded, seeing colors when he came. He tossed a handful of cash at the young man, who vanished out the door. He was still seeing colors, and he saw them on his drive home and in his restive, but altogether wonderful, dreams that night.

His post-consummation ritual of sending flowers took up the following morning. Driving away from the florist's, he noticed that his usual valedictory feeling was missing. He spent the afternoon developing film and setting up shooting assignments for the following week, thoughts of Julia rendering his workday pursuits a treadmill of ugly boredom.

He read her manuscript again, staying up all night, seeing colors and feeling the weight of the young man's head. Then the terror began. He could feel foreign bodies within his body. Tiny melanomas and carcinomas that moved audibly through his bloodstream. Julia wanted more. She wanted written tribute; words to match her words. He severed an artery in his right forearm with a paring knife, then squeezed the gash until it yielded enough blood to fill completely the bottom of a small developing tray. After cauterizing the wound he took a pen quill and ruler and meticulously printed out his tribute. He slept well that night.

In the morning he mailed his poem to the post office address he had seen on the front page of Julia's manuscript. His feeling of normalcy solidified. But at night the terror returned. The carcinomas were inside him again. He started dropping things. He saw the colors, this time even more vividly. The Santa Monica Boulevard phantasmagoria flashed continually before his eyes. He knew that he had to do *something* or go insane.

The poet had now possessed the manuscript for the two weeks since Julia's death. He began to look on it as an evil talisman. The third chapter was particularly evil, inimical to the control that had been the hallmark of his life. That night he burned the manuscript in his kitchen sink. He doused the charred words with tap water and felt new purpose grip him. There was only one way to obliterate all memory of his twenty-second lover.

He had to find a new woman.

7

It had been seventeen days since the discovery of Julia Niemeyer's body, and Lloyd wondered for the first time if his Irish Protestant ethos had the juice to carry him through what was turning into the most vexing episode of his life, a crusade that portended some deep, massive loss of control.

For perhaps the thousandth time since securing the printouts, he recapitulated all the known physical evidence pertaining to Julia Niemeyer's murder and unsolved homicides of women in Los Angeles County: the blood that formed the words of the poem was O+. Julia Niemeyer's blood was AB. There were no fingerprints on the envelope or single piece of paper. Interviews with residents of the Aloha Regency Apartments had yielded nothing; no one knew much about the dead woman; no one knew her to have visitors; no one recalled any strange occurrences in the building near the time of her death. The surrounding area had been thoroughly searched for the double-bladed knife believed to have been used for the mutilations—nothing even closely resembling it had been found. Lloyd's vague hope that Julia's killer had been connected to her through the swing parties proved futile. Experienced detectives had interviewed all the people in Joanie Pratt's Rolodex and had come away with nothing but new insights into lust and sad knowledge of adultery. Two officers had been assigned to check bookshops specializing in poetry and feminist literature for weird male requests for *Rage in the Womb* and generally strange male behavior. All investigatory avenues were covered.

And the unsolved homicides: The twenty-three Los Angeles County police agencies whose feed-ins composed the central computer file listed 410 of them going back to January 1968. Discounting 143 vehicular homicides, this left 267 unsolved murders. Of these 267, 79 were of women between the ages of twenty and forty, what Lloyd considered to be his killer's perimeters of attraction—he was certain the monster liked them young.

He looked at the map of Los Angeles County adorning the back wall of his office. There were seventy-nine pins stuck into it, denoting the locations where seventy-nine young women met violent death. Lloyd scrutinized the territory represented and let his intimate knowledge of L.A. and its environs work in concert with his instincts. The pinpoints covered the whole of Los Angeles County, from the San Gabriel and San Fernando Valleys to the far-flung beach communities that formed her southern and western perimeters. Hundreds and hundreds of square miles. Yet of the seventy-nine, forty-eight were situated in what police referred to as "white trash" suburbs—low income, high crime areas where alcoholism and drug addiction were epidemic. Statistics and his own policeman's instinct told Lloyd that the bulk of these deaths were related to booze, dope, and infidelity. Which left thirty-one murders of young women, spread throughout middle, upper middle class, and wealthy L.A. County suburbs and municipalities; murders unsolved by nine police agencies.

Lloyd had groaned when he had taken his last available direct action of querying those agencies for Xeroxes of their complete case files, realizing that it might take them as long as two weeks to respond. He felt powerless and beset by forces far beyond his bailiwick, imagining a city of the dead coexisting with Los Angeles in another time warp, a city where beautiful women beseeched him with terrified eyes to find their killer.

Lloyd's feelings of powerlessness had peaked three days before, and he had personally telephoned the top interagency liaison officers at the nine departments, demanding that the files be delivered to Parker Center within forty-eight hours. The responses of the nine officers had varied, but in the end they had acquiesced to Lloyd Hopkins's reputation as a hot-shot Homicide dick and had promised the paperwork in seventy-two hours tops.

Lloyd looked at his watch, a Rolex chronometer marked in the twenty-four-hour military time method. Seventy hours and counting down. Adding two hours for bureaucratic delay, the paperwork should arrive by noon. He bolted from his office and ran down six flights of stairs to street level. Four hours of pounding pavement with no destination in mind and a willfully shut-off brain would put him at his optimal mental capabilities—which he was certain that he would need to devour the thirty-one homicide files.

*   *   *

Four hours later, his mind clear from a dozen brisk circuits of the Civic Center area, Lloyd returned to Parker Center and jogged up to his office. He could see that the door to his cubicle was open and that someone had turned on the light. A lieutenant in uniform passed him in the hallway and hastily explained, "Your paperwork arrived, Lloyd. It's in your office."

Lloyd nodded and peered in his doorway. His desk and both his chairs were covered with thick manila folders filled with papers still reeking of the photostatic process. He counted them, then moved his chairs, wastebasket, and filing cabinet out into the hallway, arraying the files on the floor in a circle and sitting down in the middle of them.

Each folder was marked on the front with the victim's last name, first name, and date of death. Lloyd divided them first into region, then into year, never looking at the photographs that he knew were clipped to the first page. Starting with Fullmer, Elaine D.; D.O.D. 3/9/68, Pasadena P.D., and ending with Deverson, Linda Holly; D.O.D. 6/14/82, Santa Monica P.D., he selected all the paperwork outside the L.A.P.D. and placed it to one side. This accounted for eighteen files. He looked at the thirteen L.A.P.D. files. Their front markings were slightly more detailed than those of the other departments; each victim's age and race were listed immediately below her name. Of the thirteen murdered women, seven were listed as black and Hispanic. Lloyd put these folders aside and double-checked his first instincts, letting his mind go blank for a full minute before returning to conscious thought. He decided he was right; his killer preferred white women. This left six L.A.P.D. files and eighteen from other agencies, twenty-four in total. Averting his eyes from the front page photos, Lloyd scanned the interagency files for mention of race. Eight of the victims were listed as being non-Caucasian.

Which left sixteen folders.

Lloyd decided to make a collage of photographs before reading the complete files. Again willing a blank mind, he slipped the snapshots out of their folders face down in chronological order. "Talk to me," he said aloud, turning the photographs over.

When six of the snapshots smiled up at him he felt his mind begin to lurch forward convulsively, grasping at the horrific knowledge that he was assimilating. He flipped over the remaining photos and felt the logic of terror grip him like a blood-spattered vice.

The dead women were all of a kind, almost kinlike in the Anglo-Saxon planes of their faces; all possessed demure, feminine hairstyles; all were wholesome-looking in the spirit of more traditional times. Lloyd whispered the single word that summed up his constituency of the dead, "Innocent, innocent, innocent." He surveyed the photographs a dozen more times, picking up details—strands of pearls and high school rings on chains, the absence of makeup, shoulders and necks clad in sweaters and anachronistic formal wear. That the women had been killed by one monster for the destruction of the innocence they heralded so splendidly was beyond question.

With trembling hands Lloyd read through the folders, partaking of death's communion served up by strangulation, gunshot, decapitation, forced ingestion of caustic fluids, bludgeoning, gas, drug overdose, poisoning, and suicide. Disparate methods that would eliminate police awareness of mass murder. The one common denominator: no clues. No physical evidence. Women chosen for slaughter because of the way they looked. Julia Niemeyer killed sixteen times over, and how many more in different places? Innocence was the epidemic of youth.

Lloyd read through the folders again, coming out of his trance with the realization that he had been sitting on the floor for three hours and that he was drenched in sweat. As he got to his feet and stretched his painfully cramped legs, he felt the *big* horror overtake him: The killer's genius was unfathomable. There were no clues. The Niemeyer trail was dead cold. The other trails were colder. There was *nothing* he could do.

There was *always* something he could do.

Lloyd got a roll of masking tape from his desk and began taping the photographs along the walls of his office. When the smiling faces of dead women stared down at him from all directions he said to himself, *"Finis. Morte. Cold City. Muerto. Dead."*

Then he closed his eyes and read the vital statistics page in each folder, forcing himself to think only *region*. This accomplished, he got out his notebook and pen and wrote:

Central Los Angeles:
1. Elaine Marburg, D.O.D. 11/24/69
2. Patricia Petrelli, D.O.D. 5/20/75
3. Karlen La Pelley, D.O.D. 2/14/71
4. Caroline Werner, D.O.D. 11/9/79
5. Cynthia Gilroy, D.O.D. 12/5/71

Valley and Foothill Communities:
1. Elaine Fullmer, D.O.D. 3/9/68
2. Jeanette Willkie, D.O.D. 4/15/73
3. Mary Wardell, D.O.D. 1/6/74

Hollywood–West Hollywood:
1. Laurette Powell, D.O.D. 6/10/78
2. Carla Castleberry, D.O.D. 6/10/80
3. Trudy Miller, D.O.D. 12/12/68
4. Angela Stimka, D.O.D. 6/10/77
5. Marcia Renwick, D.O.D. 6/10/81

Bev. Hills–Santa Monica–Beach Communities:
1. Monica Martin, D.O.D. 9/21/74
2. Jennifer Szabo, D.O.D. 9/3/72
3. Linda Deverson, D.O.D. 6/14/82

Willing himself to think only *modus operandi*, Lloyd read through the Vital Statistics page a second time, coming away with three bludgeonings, two dismemberments, one horseback riding accident that was seriously considered as a homicide, two deaths by gunshot, two stabbings, four suicides attributed to different means, one poisoning, and one drug overdose-gassing that was labeled "murder-suicide?" by a baffled records clerk.

Turning to *chronology*, Lloyd read over the dates of death that he had written next to his list of victims, gaining his first make on the killer's methodology. With the exception of a twenty-five month hiatus between Patricia Petrelli, D.O.D. 5/20/75 and Angela Stimka, D.O.D. 6/10/77, and a seventeen-month gap between Laurette Powell, D.O.D. 6/10/78 and Caroline Werner, D.O.D. 11/9/79, his killer performed his executions at intervals of between six months to fifteen months which, Lloyd concluded, was why he was able to elude capture for so long. The murders were undoubtedly brilliantly executed and based on intimate knowledge gleaned from long-term surveillance. And, he reasoned further, those longer hiatuses probably contained victims that could be attributed to lost files and computer errors—every police agency was susceptible to a large paperwork margin of error.

Lloyd closed his eyes and imagined time warps within time warps within time warps; wondering how far back the killings went—all police departments in Los Angeles County threw out their unsolved files after fifteen years, giving him *zero* access to information predating January 1968.

It was then that his mind pulsated into perfect focus, and as he whispered "The forest for the trees," Lloyd looked at his list of Hollywood–West Hollywood homicides and felt his skin start to tingle. Four "suicide" killings had taken place on the identical date of June 10th; in 1977, '78, '80 and '81. It was the one indicator that pointed to obsessive, pathological behavior out of his killer's ice-water restraint norm.

Lloyd grabbed the four folders and read them from cover to cover, once, then twice. When he finished, he turned off the light in his cubicle and sat back and *flew* with what he had learned.

On Thursday evening, June 10th, 1977, residents of the apartment building at 1167 Larrabee Avenue, West Hollywood, smelled gas coming from the upstairs unit rented by Angela Marie Stimka, a twenty-seven-year-old cocktail waitress. Said residents summoned a deputy sheriff who lived in the building, and the deputy kicked in Angela Stimka's door, turned off the wall heater from which the gas was emanating and discovered Angela Stimka, dead and bloated on her bedroom floor. He carried her body outside and called the West Hollywood Sheriff's substation, and within minutes a team of detectives had combed the apartment and had come up with a suicide note that cited the breakup of a long-term love affair as Angela Stimka's reason for wanting to die. Handwriting experts examined Angela Stimka's diary *and* the suicide note, and decided that both were written by the same person. The death was labeled a suicide, and the case was closed.

On June 10th of the following year, a sheriff's patrol car was summoned to a small house on Westbourne Drive in West Hollywood. Neighbors had complained of uncharacteristically loud stereo noise coming from the dwelling, and one old lady told the deputies that she was certain that something was "drastically wrong." When no one answered the officers' persistent knocking, they climbed in through a half opened window and discovered the owner of the house, thirty-one-year-old Laurette Powell, dead in a large wicker chair, the arms of the chair, her bathrobe, and the floor in front of her soaked with blood that had exploded out of the artery-deep gashes on both of her wrists. An empty prescription bottle of Nembutal lay on a nightstand a few feet away, and a razor-sharp kitchen cleaver was resting in the dead woman's lap. There was no suicide note, but homicide detectives, noting the hesitation marks on both wrists and the fact that

Laurette Powell was a long time holder of several Nembutal prescriptions, quickly classified her death as suicide. Case closed.

Lloyd's wheel turned silently. He knew that the Westbourne Drive and Larrabee Avenue addresses were a scant two blocks apart, and that the Tropicana Motel gun-in-mouth "suicide" of Carla Castleberry on 6/10/80 was less than a half mile from the first two crime scenes. He shook his head in disgust; any cop with half a brain and ten cents' worth of experience should know that women *never* kill themselves with guns—the statistics on female gunshot suicides were nonexistent.

The fourth "suicide," Marcia Renwick, 818 North Sycamore, was the non sequitur, Lloyd surmised; the most recent June 10th murder, four miles east of the first three, in the L.A.P.D.'s Hollywood Division. Occurring a full year after the Carla Castleberry homicide, the Renwick pill overdose had the feel of an unimaginative impulse killing.

Lloyd turned his attention to the file of the most recent victim before Julia Niemeyer. He winced as he read the coroner's report on Linda Deverson, D.O.D. 6/14/82; chopped to pieces with a two-edged fire axe. Blinding memories of Julia swaying from her bedroom ceiling beam combined with his new knowledge to convince him that somehow, for some god-awful, hellish reason, his killer's insanity was peaking.

Lloyd lowered his head and sent up a prayer to his seldom-sought lip-service God. "Please let me get him. Please let me get him before he hurts anyone else."

Thoughts of God were paramount in Lloyd's mind as he walked down the hall and knocked on the door of his immediate superior, Lieutenant Fred Gaffaney. Knowing that the lieutenant was a hard-ass, born-again Christian who held grandstanding, maverick cops in pious contempt, he decided to invoke the deity heavily in his plea for investigatory power. Gaffaney grudgingly had given him a free rein on his caseload, with the implicit proviso that he not beg favors; since he was about to plead for men, money, and media play, he wanted to pitch the lieutenant from a standpoint of mutual religiosity.

"Enter!" Gaffaney called out in answer to the knock.

Lloyd walked in the open door and sat down in a folding chair in front of the lieutenant's desk. Gaffaney looked up from the papers he was shuffling and fingered his cross-and-flag lapel pin.

"Yes, Sergeant?"

Lloyd cleared his throat and tried to affect a humble look. "Sir, as you know, I've been working full time on the Niemeyer killing."

"Yes. And?"

"And, sir, it's a stone cold washout."

"Then stick with it. I have faith in you."

"Thank you, sir. It's funny that you mentioned faith." Lloyd waited for Gaffaney to tell him to continue. When all he got was a silent deadpan, he went on. "This case has been a testing of my own faith, sir. I've never been much of a believer in God, but the way that I've been stumbling into evidence has me questioning my beliefs. I—"

The lieutenant cut him off with a chopped hand gesture. "I go to church on Sunday and to prayer meetings three times a week. I put God out of my mind when I clip on my holster. You want something. Tell me what it is, and we'll discuss it."

Lloyd went red and forced a stammer. "Sir, I . . . I . . ."

Gaffaney leaned back in his chair and ran his hands over his iron-gray crew cut. "Hopkins, you haven't called a superior officer 'Sir' since you were a rookie. You're the most notorious pussy hound in Robbery/Homicide, and you don't give a rat's ass about God. What do you *want?*"

Lloyd laughed. "Shall I cut the shit?"

"Please do."

"All right. In the course of my investigation into the Niemeyer killing I've come across solid, instinctive evidence that points to at least sixteen other murders of young women, dating back fifteen years. The M.O.s varied, but the victims were all of a certain physical type. I've gotten complete case files on these homicides, and chronological consistencies and other factors have convinced me that all sixteen women were killed by the same man, the man who killed Julia Niemeyer. The last two killings have been particularly brutal. I think we're dealing with a brilliant psychopathic intellect, and unless we direct a massive effort toward his capture he'll kill with impunity until the day he dies. I want a dozen experienced Homicide dicks full time; I want liaisons set up with every department in the county; I want permission to recruit uniformed officers for the shit work, and authority to grant them unlimited overtime. I want a full-scale media blitz— I've got a feeling that this animal is close to exploding, and I want to push him a little. I—"

Gaffaney raised both hands in interruption. "Do you have any *hard* physical evidence," he asked, "any *witnesses*, any notations from detectives within the L.A.P.D. or other department that lend credence to your mass murder theory?"

"No," Lloyd said.

"How many of these sixteen investigations are still open?"

"None."

"Are there any other officers within the L.A.P.D. who corroborate your hypothesis?"

"No."

"Other departments?"

"No."

Gaffaney slammed his desk top with two flattened palms, then fingered his lapel pin. "No. I won't trust you on this. It's too old, too vague, too costly, and too potentially embarrassing to the department. I trust you as a troubleshooter, as a very fine detective with a superb record—"

"With the best fucking arrest record in the department!" Lloyd shouted.

Gaffaney shouted back, "I trust your record, but I don't trust you! You're a showboat glory-hound womanizer, and you've got a wild hair up your ass about murdered women!" Lowering his voice, he added, "If you really care about God, ask him for help with your personal life. God will answer your prayers, and you won't be so disturbed by things out of your control. Look at how you're shaking. Forget this thing, Hopkins. Spend some time with your family; I'm sure they'd appreciate it."

Lloyd got to his feet, trembling, and walked to the door. His peripheral vision throbbed with red. He turned to look at Gaffaney, who smiled and said, "If you go to the media, I'll crucify you. I'll have you back in uniform rousting piss bums on skid row."

Lloyd smiled back and felt a strangely serene bravado course through him. "I'm going to get this animal, and I'm going to stick your words up your ass," he said.

Lloyd packed the sixteen homicide files into the trunk of his car and drove to the Hollywood Station, hoping to catch Dutch Peltz before he went off duty. He was in luck; Dutch was changing back into civilian clothes in the senior officers' locker room, knotting his necktie and staring at himself abstractedly in a full-length wall mirror.

Lloyd walked over, clearing his throat. Without taking his eyes from the mirror, Dutch said, "Fred Gaffaney called me. He told me that he figured you'd be coming my way. I saved your ass; he was going to blow the whistle on you to one of his born-again high brass buddies, but I told him not to.

He owes me favors, so he agreed. You're a sergeant, Lloyd. That means you can only act like an asshole with sergeants and below. Lieutenants and up are verboten. *Comprende*, brain-boy?"

Dutch turned around, and Lloyd saw that his abstracted look was glazed over with fear. "Did Gaffaney tell you all of it?" Lloyd asked.

Dutch nodded. "How sure are you?"

"All the way."

"Sixteen women?"

"At least that many."

"What are you going to do?"

"Flush him out, somehow. Probably by myself. The department will never authorize an investigation; it makes them look too inept. I was stupid to go to Gaffaney in the first place. If I go over his head and make a stink, I'll get yanked off the Niemeyer case and detached to some bumfuck robbery assignment. You know what this feels like, Dutchman?"

Dutch looked up at his huge genius-mentor, then turned away when he felt tears of pride welling in his eyes. "No, Lloyd."

"It feels like I was made for this one," Lloyd said, keeping eye contact with his own mirror image. "That I won't know what I am or what I can be until I get this bastard and find out why he's destroyed so much innocence."

Dutch put a hand on Lloyd's arm. "I'll help you," he said. "I can't give you any officers, but I'll help you myself, we can . . ." Dutch stopped when he saw that Lloyd wasn't listening; that he was transfixed by the light in his own eyes or some distant vision of redemption.

Dutch withdrew his hand. Lloyd stirred, jerked his gaze from the mirror and said, "When I had two years on the job, I got assigned to the junior high school lecture circuit. Telling the kids picaresque cop stories and warning them about dope and accepting rides from strangers. I loved the assignment, because I love children. One day a teacher told me about a seventh grade girl—she was twelve—who used to give blow jobs for a pack of cigarettes. The teacher asked me if I'd talk to her.

"I looked her up one day after school. She was a pretty little girl. Blonde. She had a black eye. I asked her how she got it. She wouldn't tell me. I checked out her home situation. It was typical—alcoholic mother on welfare, father doing three-to-five at Quentin. No money, no hope, no chance. But the little girl liked to read. I took her down to a bookstore on Sixth and Western and introduced her to the owner. I gave the owner a hundred bucks and told him that the little girl had that much credit there. I did the same thing at a liquor store down the block—a hundred bucks buys a lot of cigarettes.

"The girl was grateful and wanted to please me. She told me she got the black eye because her braces cut some guy she was sucking off. Then she asked me if I want some head. Of course I say 'No' and give her a big lecture. But I keep seeing her. She lives on my beat, and I see her all the time, always smoking and carrying a book. She looks happy.

"One day she stops me when I'm out cruising in my black-and-white alone. She says, 'I really like you and I really want to give you head.' I say 'No,' and she starts to cry. I can't bear that, so I grab her and hold her and tell her to study like a demon so she can learn how to tell stories herself."

Lloyd's voice faltered. He wiped his lips and tried to remember the point he wanted to make. "Oh yeah," he said finally. "I forgot to mention that the little girl is twenty-seven now, and she's got a Masters in English. She's going to have a good life. But . . . but there's this guy out there who wants to kill her. And your daughters and mine . . . and he's very smart . . . but I'm not going to let him hurt anyone else. I swear that to you. I swear it."

When he saw that Lloyd's pale gray eyes were shrouded with a sadness that he could never express with words, Dutch said, "Get him."

Lloyd said, "I will," and walked away, knowing that his old friend had given him a carte blanche absolution for whatever he had to do, whatever rules he had to break.

8

The following morning, after a restive night of assimilating the data in the sixteen files, Lloyd drove to the downtown public library, figuring out the shit work logistics in his mind en route, sorting minor details and bureaucratic cover your ass stratagems to one side so that he could come to his first day of legwork in an absolutely silent mental state.

With the car windows rolled up and the squawk box of his two-way radio disconnected to reinforce the silence, Lloyd pushed aside all the extraneous details regarding his investigation. He was covered up drum-tight with Fred

Gaffaney and the higher echelon Robbery/Homicide brass, having called the two detectives working under him on the Niemeyer case, learning that their bookstore canvass of the downtown/central L.A. area had thus far yielded nothing solid, telling them to pursue their instincts full time and on their own autonomy and to report to Gaffaney twice weekly, letting the Jesus freak that they both despised know that Sergeant Hopkins was working hard in the dark solitude that was the stalking ground of genius. Gaffaney would accept this as part of their silent agreement, and if he complained about Lloyd's absence at Parker Center, Dutch Peltz would intercede and kibosh his complaints with every ounce of his prestige. He was covered.

As for the investigation itself, there were no physical facts that Lloyd didn't already know from his first run-through of the files. *Stunning* silence underlined this; Janice and the girls had slept over at the Ocean Park apartment of her friend George, and Lloyd had had a big silent house in which to do his reading. In a desire to juxtapose the destruction of innocence via murder to his own efforts to diminish it through storytelling, he had gone over the hellish manila folders in Penny's bedroom, hoping that his youngest daughter's aura would give him the clarity to forge facts out of elliptical psychic labyrinths. No new facts emerged, but his psychological character study of the killer gained an added dimension infused with a coldly subtle verisimilitude.

Although he had no access to information on unsolved homicides before 1968, Lloyd was certain that the murders did not date back much further. He based this on his strongest character assessment/feeling—the killer was a homosexual. His whole genealogy of death was an attempt to hide the fact from himself. *He did not yet know.* The homicides prior to Linda Deverson and Julia Niemeyer, though often brutal, bespoke an effete satisfaction with a job well done and an almost refined love of anonymity. *He did not have an inkling of what he was.* Linda and Julia, hideously butchered, were the dividing points, the division irrevocable and based on the terror of an emergent sexuality so shamefully compelling that it had to be drowned in blood.

Lloyd traced instinctual links back in time. His killer had to live in Los Angeles. His killer was tremendously strong, capable of severing limbs with a single swipe of an axe. His killer was undoubtedly physically attractive and capable of maneuvering with grace in the gay world. He wanted it desperately, yet to submit to the vulnerability inherent in sexual interaction would destroy his urge to kill. Sexuality burgeons in adolescence. Assuming

that the killer was still in an ascendent sexual curve and assuming that the
murders began in or around January 1968, he allotted the monster a five-
year trauma incubation period and placed him as coming of age in the early
to middle '60s, making him now in his late thirties—forty at the oldest.

Exiting the freeway at Sixth and Figueroa, Lloyd whispered, "June 10th,
June 10th, June 10th." He parked illegally on the wrong side of the street
and stuck an "Official Police Vehicle" sign under his windshield wiper.
Running up the library steps, the epiphany slammed him like an axe handle between the eyes: the monster killed because he wanted to love.

Lloyd's microfilm time travel consumed four hours and traversed every
June 10th from 1960 to 1982. Starting with the *Los Angeles Times* and ending with the *Los Angeles Herald-Express* and its offshoot newspaper the *L.A.
Examiner*, he sifted through headlines, feature articles, and clipped
accounts detailing everything from major league baseball to foreign insur-
rections to previews of summer beach wear to primary election results.
Nothing in the parade of information caught his eyes as being a potential
contributing factor to murderous passion and nothing caused his mental
gears to snap forward and expand on his thesis at any level. June 10th was
his one crucial clue to the killer—but Los Angeles newspapers treated it
like just another day.

Although Lloyd had expected the negative results, he was still disap-
pointed and was glad that he had saved the film for the four "suicide" years
of 1977, '78, '80, and '81 for last.

His disappointment grew. The deaths of Angela Stimka, Laurette Powell, Carla Castleberry, and Marcia Renwick were relegated to quarter-
column obscurity. "Tragic" was the adjective both papers used to describe
all four "suicides"; "Funeral arrangements pending" and the names and addresses of the next of kin took up the bulk of the print space.

Lloyd rolled up the microfilm, placed it on the librarian's desk and
walked outside into the sunlight. Sidewalk glare and eyestrain from his
hours of squinting combined to send a pounding up his neck into his head.
Willing the pain down to a murmur, he considered his options. Interview
the next of kin? No, sad denials would be the common denominator. Visit
the death scenes? Look for indicators, chase hunches? "Legwork!" Lloyd
shouted out loud. He ran for his car, and the headache disappeared altogether.

*   *   *

Lloyd drove to West Hollywood and scouted the first three June 10th killing grounds.

Angela Stimka, D.O.D. 6/10/77, had lived in a mauve-colored ten-unit apartment house, fifties building-boom ugly, an obviously jerry-built structure whose one claim to prestige was its proximity to the gay bars on Santa Monica and the cross-sexual nightlife on the Sunset Strip.

Lloyd sat in his car and wrote down a description of the block, his eyes perking only once—when he noticed an "Illegal Nighttime Parking" sign across the street from the 1167 Larrabee address. His gears clicked twice. He was in the heart of the gay ghetto. His killer had *probably* chosen the Stimka woman for the location of her dwelling as well as for her physicality, somehow wanting to run a gauntlet of subconscious denial by choosing a victim in a largely homosexual neighborhood; and the West Hollywood sheriffs were demons on parking enforcement.

Lloyd smiled and drove two blocks to the small wood-framed house on Westbourne Drive where Laurette Powell had died of Nembutal ingestion and "self-inflicted" knife wounds. Another "Illegal Nighttime Parking" sign, another click, this one very soft.

The Tropicana Motel yielded a whole series of clicks, resounding gear-mashings that went off in Lloyd's mind like gunshots that tore ceaselessly at innocent bodies. Carla Castleberry, D.O.D. 6/10/80, the means of death a .38 slug through the roof of the mouth and up into the brain. Women never blew their brains out. Classic homosexual symbolism, perpetrated in a sleazy "Boy's Town" motel room.

Lloyd scanned the sidewalk in front of the Tropicana. Crushed amyl nitrate poppers on the ground, fruit hustler junkies holding up the walls of the coffee shop. His thesis exploded in his mind. When its symbiotic thrust dawned through the noise of the explosion, he was terrified. He ignored his terror and ran for a pay phone, dialing seven familiar digits with shaking hands. When an equally familiar voice came on the line, sighing, "Hollywood Station, Captain Peltz speaking," Lloyd whispered, "Dutch, I know why he kills."

An hour later, Lloyd sat in Dutch Peltz's office, sifting through negative information that had him slamming his best friend's desk top in frustration. Dutch stood by the door, watching Lloyd read through the teletypes that had just come in from both the L.A.P.D. and Sheriff's central computers. He wanted to stroke his son's hair or smooth his shirtfront, anything to ease the anguish that had Lloyd's features contorted in rage. Feeling meek in the wake of that rage, Dutch said, "It's going to be all right, kid."

Lloyd screamed, "No, it's not! He was assaulted, I'm certain of that, and it happened on a June 10th when he was a juvenile! Juvenile sex-offense records are never shredded! If it's not on the computer, then it didn't happen in L.A. County or it was never fucking reported! There's nothing on these fucking juvie vice printouts except fruit shakedown and backseat blow jobs, and you don't become a fucking mass murderer because you let some old man suck your cock in Griffith Park!"

Lloyd picked up a quartz bookend and hurled it across the room. It landed on the floor next to the window that overlooked the station parking lot. Dutch peered out at the nightwatch officers revving up their black-and-whites, wondering how he could love them all so much, yet not at all when compared to Lloyd. He placed the bookend back on his desk and ruffled Lloyd's hair.

"Feel better, kid?"

Lloyd gave Dutch a reflex smile that felt like a wince. "Better. I'm beginning to know this animal, and that's a start."

"What about the printout on the parking tickets? What about F.I. cards on the dates of the killings?"

"Negative. No parking tickets *at all* on the applicable dates and streets, and the only Sheriff's F.I. cards were filled out on women—hookers working the Strip. It was a long shot at best, and *our* department wasn't computerizing F.I.s when the Renwick woman was killed. I'm going to have to start from scratch again, send out sub-rosa queries to old-time juvie dicks, see if I can get some feedback on old assault cases that never made the files."

Dutch shook his head. "If this guy got molested or porked or whatever around twenty years ago, like you figure, most of the dicks who might know something would be retired by now."

"I know. You send out the feelers, will you? Pull some tails, call in some favors. I want to keep moving out on the street; that's where it feels right."

Dutch took a chair across from Lloyd, trying to gauge the light in his eyes. "O.K., kid. Remember my party Thursday night, and get some rest."

"I can't. I've got a date tonight. Janice and the girls are probably hanging out with their fag buddy, anyway. I want to keep moving."

Lloyd's eyes flickered; Dutch's eyes bored in. "Anything you feel like telling me, kid?"

Lloyd said, "Yeah. I love you. Now let me get out of here before you get sentimental about it."

On the street, without his paperwork to refer to and with three hours to kill before meeting Joanie Pratt, Lloyd recalled that his subordinates had yet to canvass the Hollywood area bookstores.

He drove to a pay phone and leafed through the yellow pages, finding listings for one poetry bookshop and one specializing in feminist literature: New Guard Poetry on La Brea near Fountain and the Feminist Bibliophile on Yucca and Highland.

Deciding on a circuit that would allow him to hit both stores and then head toward Joanie's house in the Hollywood Hills, Lloyd drove first to New Guard Poetry, where a bored, scholarly looking man in incongruous farmer overalls told him that no, there had been no suspicious browsers or sales of feminist prose collections to strongly built men in their middle to late thirties, for the simple reason that he did not stock feminist poetry—it was aberrantly anti-classicist. Most of his customers were academics of long standing who preferred to order from his catalog, and *that* was *that*.

Lloyd thanked the man and swung his unmarked Matador north, pulling up in front of the Feminist Bibliophile at precisely six o'clock, hoping that the small, converted-house bookstore would still be open. He trotted up the steps just as he heard the door being bolted from inside, and when he saw the lights in the windows going off he rapped on the doorjamb and called out, "Police. Open up, please."

The door swung open a moment later, and the woman who opened it stood silhouetted against the light in a challenging attitude. Lloyd's body gave a slight shudder as he felt the pride in her pose, and before she could voice any challenge out loud he said, "I'm Detective-Sergeant Hopkins, L.A.P.D. Could I talk to you for a moment?"

The woman remained silent. The silence was unnerving, so to keep himself from doing an embarrassed little foot-dance, Lloyd memorized her physicality, maintaining a probing eye contact that the woman returned without flinching. A rigid angularity trying to hold reign over a soft, strong body, he decided; thirty-four to thirty-six, the slight traces of make-up a concession to awareness of her age; the brown eyes, pale skin, and chestnut hair somehow denoting breeding; the severe tweed suit a coat of armor. Smart, contentious, and unhappy. An aesthete afraid of passion.

"Are you with the Intelligence Division?"

Lloyd gawked at both the non sequitur and the force in the woman's voice. Recovering, he shifted his feet and said, "No, why?"

The woman smiled mirthlessly and spat out her challenge: "The L.A.P.D. has a long history of trying to infiltrate causes they deem subversive, and my poetry has been published in feminist periodicals that have been highly critical of your department. This bookshop carries a list of titles that includes many volumes that explode myths surrounding the macho mentality."

The woman stopped when she saw that the big cop was beaming broadly. Aware that a parity of discomfiture had been achieved, Lloyd said, "If I wanted to infiltrate a feminist bookstore, I would have come in drag. May I come in, Miss—"

"My name is Kathleen McCarthy," the woman said. "I prefer Ms., and I won't let you in until you tell me what this is all about."

It was the question Lloyd was hoping for. "I'm the most honored homicide detective on the West Coast," he said softly. "I'm investigating the murders of close to twenty women. I discovered one of the bodies. I won't insult you by describing how it was mutilated. I found a blood-stained book at the crime scene, *Rage in the Womb*. I'm certain that the killer is interested in poetry—maybe feminist poetry in particular. That's why I came here."

Kathleen McCarthy had gone pale, and her challenging posture had slumped, then tensed up again as she grabbed the doorjamb for support. Lloyd moved in, showing her his badge and I.D. card. "Call the Hollywood Station," he said. "Ask for Captain Peltz. He'll verify what I've told you."

Kathleen McCarthy motioned Lloyd inside, then left him alone in a large room filled with bookshelves. When he heard the sound of a phone being dialed he slipped off his wedding band and examined the books that covered the four walls and spilled over onto chairs, tables, and revolving metal bookracks. His respect for the strident poet grew—she had placed her own published works in preeminent spots throughout the room, alongside volumes by Lessing, Plath, Millett and other feminist icons. An out-front ego, Lloyd decided. He started to like the woman.

"I apologize for judging you before I heard you out."

Lloyd turned around at the words. Kathleen McCarthy was not chagrined by her apology. He started to *feel* her, and threw out a line calculated to secure *her* respect. "I can understand your feelings. The Intelligence Division is overzealous, maybe even paranoid."

Kathleen smiled. "May I quote you on that?"

Lloyd smiled back. "No."

An embarrassed silence followed. Sensing the mutuality of the attraction deepen, Lloyd pointed to a book-strewn couch and said, "Could we sit down? I'll tell you about it."

In a low voice and with a deliberately cold deadpan stare, Lloyd told Kathleen McCarthy how he had discovered Julia Lynn Niemeyer's body and how a blood-smeared copy of *Rage in the Womb*, along with the poem sent to Julia's post office box, had convinced him that his assumed one-time killer was in reality a mass murderer. Ending with a recounting of his chronological work-up and the psychological profile he had deduced, he said, "He's brilliant beyond words, and going completely out of control. Poetry is a fixation with him. I think that he *wants* subconsciously to lose control, and that he may view poetry as his means to that end. I need your feedback on *Rage in the Womb*, and I need to know if any strange men— specifically men in their thirties—have been coming here to your store, buying feminist works, acting furtive or angry or in any way out of the ordinary."

Lloyd sat back and savored Kathleen's reaction of cold, hard, muscle-constricting rage. When she was silent for a full minute, he knew that she was mustering her thoughts into a severe brevity, and that when she spoke her response would be a perfect model of control, devoid of rhetoric or expressions of shock.

He was right. "*Rage in the Womb* is an angry book," Kathleen said softly. "A polemic, a broadside against many things, violence on women in specific. I haven't stocked it in years, and when I did, I doubt if I ever sold a copy to a man. Beyond that, the only male customers that I get are men who come in with their girlfriends and college students—young men in their late teens and twenties. I can't remember when I've had a single man in his thirties in the store. I own the store, and run it by myself, so I *see* all my customers. I—"

Lloyd cut Kathleen off with a wave of his hand. "What about mail orders? Do you do a catalog business?"

"No, I don't have the facilities for mailings. All my business is done here in the shop."

Lloyd muttered "Shit," and punched the arm of the couch. Kathleen said, "I'm sorry, but listen . . . I have a lot of friends in bookselling. Feminist literature, poetry, and otherwise. Private dealers you've probably overlooked. I'll call around. I'll be persistent. I want to help."

"Thank you," Lloyd said. "I could use your help." Feigning a yawn, he added, "Do you have any coffee? I'm running on empty."

Kathleen said, "One moment," and departed into the back room. Lloyd heard the sounds of cups and saucers being readied, followed by the electric crackle of a radio and the blare of some kind of symphony or concerto. When the music picked up tempo, he called out, "Would you turn that off, please?" Kathleen called back, "All right, but talk to me."

The music diminuendoed, then died altogether. Lloyd, relieved, blurted out, "What shall I talk about, police work?"

Kathleen came into the living room a moment later, bearing a tray with coffee cups and an assortment of cookies. "Talk about something nice," she said, clearing books from a low end table. "Talk about something dear to you." Scrutinizing Lloyd openly, she added, "You look pale. Are you feeling sick?"

Lloyd said, "No, I feel fine. Loud noise bothers me; that's why I asked you to turn off the radio." Kathleen handed him a cup of coffee. "That wasn't noise. That was music." Lloyd ignored the statement. "The things that are dear to me are hard to describe," he said. "I like poking around in sewers, seeing what I can do about justice, then getting the hell out and going someplace where it's gentle and warm."

Kathleen sipped coffee. "Are you talking about being with women?"

"Yes. Does that offend you?"

"No. Why should it?"

"This bookstore. Your poetry. 1983. Pick a reason."

"You should read my diaries before you judge me. I'm a good poet, but I'm a better diarist. Are you going to catch this killer?"

"Yes. Your reaction to my being here impresses me. I'd like to read your diaries, feel your intimate thoughts. How far do they date back?"

Kathleen flinched at the word "intimate." "A long time," she said, "since my days with the Marshall Clarion. I . . ." Kathleen stopped and stared. The big policeman was laughing and shaking his head delightedly. "What *is* wrong?" she asked.

"Nothing, except that we went to the same high school. I had you *all* wrong, Kathleen. I figured you for East Coast Irish money, and you turn out to be a mick from the old neighborhood. Lloyd Hopkins, Marshall High Class of '59 and cop of Irish Protestant grandparents meets Kathleen McCarthy, one-time Silverlake resident and Marshall High graduate, Class of . . ."

Kathleen's features brightened with her own delight. "Class of '64," she finished. "God, how funny. Do you remember the rotunda court?" Lloyd nodded. "And Mr. Juknavarian and his stories about Armenia?" Lloyd nodded again. "And Mrs. Cuthbertson and her stuffed dog? Remember, she called it her muse?" Lloyd doubled over, consumed with laughter. Kathleen continued, throwing nostalgia out between her own gleeful squeals. "And the Pachucos versus the Surfers, and Mr. Amster and those T-shirts he had made up? 'Amster's Hamsters'? When I was in tenth grade someone tied a dead rat to his car antenna and put a note under the wipers. The note said, 'Amster's Hamsters bite the big weenie!'"

Lloyd's laughter crescendoed into a coughing fit that had him in fear of spewing coffee and half-digested cookies all over the room. "No more, no more, please, or I'll die," he managed to get out between body-wracking coughs. "I don't want to die this way."

"How *do* you want to die?" Kathleen asked playfully.

As he wiped his tear-stained face, Lloyd sensed a probing intent behind the question. "I don't know," he said, "either very old or very romantically. You?"

"Very old and wise. Autumnal serenity long gone into deep winter, with my words carefully prepared for posterity."

Lloyd shook his head. "Jesus, I don't believe this conversation. Where did you live in Silverlake?"

"Tracy and Micheltorena. You?"

"Griffith Park and St. Elmo. I used to play 'chicken' on Micheltorena when I was a kid. *Rebel Without a Cause* had just come out and chicken was *in*. Being too young to drive, we had to play it on sleds with little rubber wheels attached. We started at the top of the hill above Sunset, at two-thirty every morning that summer; '55 I think it was. The object of the game was to sled all the way across Sunset against the light. At that time of the morning there was just enough traffic out to make it slightly risky. I did it once a night, all summer long. I never dragged my feet or hit the hand brakes. I never turned down a dare."

Kathleen sipped her coffee, wondering how bluntly she should phrase her next question. To hell with it, she decided and asked, "What were you trying to prove?"

"That's a provocative question, Kathleen," Lloyd said.

"You're a provocative man. But I believe in parity. You can ask me anything you like, and I'll answer."

Lloyd's face lit up at the possibilities for exploration. "I was trying to follow the rabbit down the hole," he said. "I was trying to light a fire under the world's ass. I wanted to be considered a tough guy so that Ginny Skakel would give me a hand job. I wanted to breathe pure white light. Good answer?"

Kathleen smiled and gave Lloyd a sedate round of applause. "Good answer, Sergeant. Why did you quit?"

"Two boys got killed. They were riding on one sled. A '53 Packard Caribbean smashed them to pieces. One of the boys was decapitated. My mother asked me to quit. She told me that there were safer ways to express courage. She told me stories to take the edge off my grief."

"Your *grief*? You mean you wanted to continue playing that insane game?"

Lloyd savored Kathleen's incredulous look and said, "Of course. Teenage romanticism dies hard. Turnabout, Kathleen?"

"Of course."

"Good. Are you a romantic?"

"Yes . . . In all the deepest essentials . . . I . . ."

Lloyd cut her off. "Good. May I see you tomorrow night?"

"What did you have in mind? Dinner?"

"Not really."

"A concert?"

"Very amusing. Actually, I thought we might be-bop around L.A. and check out urban romanticism."

"Is that a pass?"

"Absolutely not. I think we should do something that neither of us has ever done before, and that rules out *that*. You in?"

Kathleen took Lloyd's outstretched hand. "I'm in. Here at seven o'clock?"

Lloyd brought the hand to his lips and kissed it. "I'll be here," he said, walking out the door before anything could happen to defuse the power of the moment.

When Lloyd wasn't home by six o'clock, Janice went about preparing for her evening, feeling relief on all fronts. She was relieved that Lloyd's absences were becoming more frequent and predictable, relieved that the girls were so engrossed in their hobbies and social life that they didn't seem to mind their missing father, relieved that her own loving detachment seemed to be growing to the point where some time soon she would be able to tell her husband, "You have been the love of my life, but it is over. I cannot get through to you. I cannot stand any more of your obsessive behavior. It is over."

As Janice dressed for her night of dancing she recalled the episode that had first given her the impetus to consider leaving her husband forever. It was two weeks ago. Lloyd had been gone for three days. She missed him and wanted him physically, and was even ready to make concessions about his stories. She had gone to bed nude and had left her bedside candle burning, hoping to be awakened by Lloyd's hands on her breasts. When she finally did awaken, it was to the sight of Lloyd hovering above her in the nude, gently spreading her legs. She held back a scream as he entered her, her eyes transfixed by his hellishly contorted features. When he came and his limbs contracted spastically, she held him very tight and knew that she had finally been given the power to forge a new life.

Janice dressed in a silver lamé pantsuit, an outfit that would brilliantly reflect the swirling lights at Studio One. She felt little twinges of slavish loyalty, and reflexively defined her husband in coldly clinical terms: He is a disturbed, driven man. An anachronistic man. He is incapable of change, a man who never listened.

Janice rounded up her daughters and drove them over to George's apartment in Ocean Park. His lover Rob would look after them while she and George discoed the night away. He would tell them kind, gentle stories and cook them up a big vegetarian feast.

Studio One was crowded, bursting to the rafters with stylish men undulating toward and away from each other under the benevolent distortions of stereo-synched strobe lights. Janice and George tooted some coke in the parking lot and imagined their entrance as one of the grandest, most closely scrutinized promenades in history. The only woman on the dance floor, Janice knew that she was the most desired body under the lights—desired not in lust but in desperate yearning for transference—tall, regal, tanned, and graceful, every man there wanted to *be* her.

When she returned home late that night, Lloyd was waiting in bed for her. He was especially tender, and she returned his caresses with great sorrow. Her mind ran disconnected images together to keep her from succumbing to his love. She thought of many things, but never came close to guessing that he had made love to another woman just two hours earlier; a woman who considered herself "something of a businesswoman" and who once sang unintelligible rock and roll lyrics; and that with her, as well as now with his wife, his thoughts were of an Irish girl from the old neighborhood.

That night Kathleen wrote in her diary:

Today I met a man; a man whom I think fate put in my path for a reason. To me he represents a paradox and possibilities that I cannot begin to access; such is his incongruous force. Enormous physically, fiercely bright—yet of all things, a man content to go through life as a policeman! I know that he wants me (when we met I noticed him wearing a wedding band. Later, as his attraction to me grew more obvious, I saw that he had slipped it off—a roundabout and very endearing subterfuge). I think that he has a rapacious ego and will—ones to match his size and self-proclaimed brilliance. And I sense—I know—that he wants to change me, that he sees in me a kindred soul, one to touch deeply but also one to manipulate. I must watch my dialogue and my actions with this man. For the benefit of my growth, there must be a give and take. But I must keep my purest inner soul apart from him; my heart must remain inviolate.

9

Lloyd spent the morning at Parker Center, putting in a ritual appearance to appease Lieutenant Gaffaney and any other superior officers who might have noted his prolonged absence. Dutch Peltz called early; he had already initiated informal inquiries on old homosexual assault cases, delegating two desk officers the job of phoning the entire list of retired Juvenile detectives in the L.A.P.D.'s "private" retired personnel file. Dutch would be telephoning current Juvenile dicks with over twenty years on the job himself, and would call back as soon as he had gleaned a solid pile of information for evaluation. With Kathleen McCarthy checking out the bookstore angle, there was nothing Lloyd could do but chase paper—read the suicide files over and over again until something previously missed or overlooked or misunderstood jumped out at him.

It took two hours and digestion of thousands of words to make a connection, and when the number 408 appeared in the same context in two different files, Lloyd didn't know if it was a lead or a mere coincidence.

The body of Angela Stimka was discovered by her neighbor, L.A. County Deputy Sheriff Delbert Haines, badge #408, *other* neighbors having summoned the off-duty deputy when they smelled gas coming from the woman's apartment. A year to the day later, officers T. Rains, #408, and W. Vandervort, #691, were called to the scene of the Laurette Powell "suicide." Rains, Haines—a stupid spelling blunder; the identical badge numbers obviously denoted the same deputy.

Lloyd read over the file of the third West Hollywood "suicide"—Carla Castleberry, D.O.D. 6/10/80, the Tropicana Motel on Santa Monica Boulevard. Entirely different officers had filed this death report, and the names of residents of the motel who were interviewed at the scene— Duane Tucker, Lawrence Craigie, and Janet Mandarano—did not appear at all in any of the other files.

Lloyd picked up his phone and dialed the West Hollywood Sheriff's Substation. A bored voice answered. "Sheriff's. May I help you?"

Lloyd was brusque. "This is Detective Sergeant Hopkins, L.A.P.D. Do you have a Deputy Haines or Rains, badge 408, working out of your station?" The bored officer muttered, "Yessir, Big Whitey Haines. Day watch patrol."

"Is he on duty today?"

"Yessir."

"Good. Contact him on his radio. Tell him to meet me at the pizza joint on Fountain and La Cienega in one hour. It's urgent. You got that?"

"Yessir."

"Good. Do it now." Lloyd hung up. It was probably nothing—but at least it was movement.

Lloyd arrived at the restaurant early, ordering coffee and taking a booth with a view of the parking lot, the better to get a visual fix on Haines before their interview.

Five minutes later a sheriff's black-and-white pulled in and a uniformed deputy got out, squinting myopically against the sunlight. Lloyd sized the man up—big, blonde, a strong body going to flab. Middle thirties. Ridiculously sculpted hair, the sideburns too long for a fat face; the uniform encasing his musclebound upper torso and soft stomach like a sausage skin. Lloyd watched him don aviator sunglasses and hitch up his gunbelt. Not intelligent, but probably street-smart; play him easy.

The deputy walked directly to Lloyd's booth. "Sergeant?" he said, extending his hand.

Lloyd took the hand, squeezed it, and pointed across the table, waiting for the man to take off his sunglasses. When he sat down without removing them and picked nervously at an acne cluster on his chin, Lloyd thought: Speed. Play him hard.

Haines fidgeted under Lloyd's stare. "What can I do for you, sir?" he asked.

"How long have you been with the Sheriff's, Haines?"

"Nine years," Haines said.

"How long at the West Hollywood Station?"

"Eight years."

"You live on Larrabee?"

"That's right."

"I'm surprised. West Hollywood is a faggot sewer."

Haines flinched. "I think a good cop should live on his beat."

Lloyd smiled. "So do I. What do your friends call you? Delbert? Del?"

Haines tried to smile, involuntarily biting his lip. "Whitey. Wh-wh-what do you—"

"What am I here for? I'll tell you in a moment. Does your beat include Westbourne Drive?"

"Y-yeah."

"Have you worked the same car plan your whole time at the station?"

"S-sure. Except for some loan-out time to Vice. What's this all—"

Lloyd slammed the table top. Haines jolted backward in his seat, reaching up and straightening his sunglasses with both hands. The muscles around his eyes twitched and tics started at the corners of his mouth. Lloyd smiled. "Ever work Narco?"

Haines went flush and whispered "No" hoarsely, a network of veins throbbing in his neck. Lloyd said, "Just checking. Basically, I'm here to question you about a stiff you found back in '78. A wrist slash job. A woman on Westbourne. You remember that?"

Haines's whole body went lax. Lloyd watched his muscles unclench into an almost stuporous posture of relief. "Yeah. My partner and I got an unknown trouble squeal from the desk. The old bag who lived next door called in about the stiff's record player blasting. We found this good lookin' babe all bl—"

Lloyd cut him off. "You found another suicide in your own building the year before, didn't you, Whitey?"

"Yeah," Haines said, "I sure did. I got wasted from the gas, they had to detox me at the hospital. I got a commendation and my picture on the honor board at the station."

Leaning back and stretching out his legs beneath the table, Lloyd said, "Both those women killed themselves on June 10th. Don't you think that's a strange coincidence?"

Haines shook his head. "Maybe. Maybe not. I don't know."

Lloyd laughed. "I don't know, either. That's all, Haines. You can go."

After Haines had left, Lloyd drank coffee and thought. A transparently stupid cop strung out on speed. No guilty knowledge of the two murder-suicides, but undoubtedly involved in so much penny-ante illegality that a questioning on old homicides was like being spared the guillotine—he never asked *why* the interview was taking place. Coincidence that he discovered both bodies? He lived *and* patrolled the same area. *Logically*, it fit.

But instinctively it was somehow out of kilter. Lloyd weighed the pros and cons of a daylight breaking and entering. The pros won. He drove to 1167 Larrabee Avenue.

The mauve-colored apartment building was perfectly still, the doors of the ten units closed, no activity on the walkway leading back to the carport. Lloyd scanned the mailboxes at the front of the building. Haines lived in apartment 5. Running his eyes over the numbers embossed on the first-story doorways, he spotted his target—the rear apartment. No screen door, no heavy brass hardware indicating security locks.

Working a short bladed penknife and a plastic credit card in unison, Lloyd snapped the locking mechanism and pushed the door open. Flicking on a wall light, he shut the door and surveyed the tasteless living room he had expected to find: cheap Naugahyde couch and chairs, a Formica coffee table, a ratty "deep-pile" carpet going threadbare. The walls boasted velveteen landscape prints and the built-in bookcases held no books—only a pile of skin magazines.

He walked into the kitchen. Mildew on the chipped linoleum floor, dirty dishes in the sink, a thick layer of grease on the cabinets and ceiling. The bathroom was dirtier still—shaving gear scattered on a sidebar near the sink, congealed shaving cream on the walls and mirror, a clothes hamper spilling soiled uniforms.

In the bedroom, Lloyd found his first indicators pointing to character traits other than aesthetic bankruptcy and sloth. Above the unkempt bed was a glass-fronted mahogany gunrack holding a half dozen shotguns—one of them an illegal double barreled sawed-off. Lifting the mattress, he discovered a Browning .9 millimeter automatic and a rusted bayonet with a tag affixed to its handle: *"Genuine Viet Cong Execution Sword! Guaranteed Authentic!"* The drawers beside the bed yielded a large plastic baggie filled with marijuana and a bottle of Dexedrine.

After going through the closets and dressers and finding nothing except dirty civilian clothes, Lloyd walked back into the living room, relieved that his instincts about Haines had been validated, yet still troubled that nothing more had *spoken* to him. With a blank mind, he sat down on the couch and let his eyes circuit the room, trawling for anything that would perk his mental juices. One circuit; two circuits, three. Floor to ceiling, along the walls and back again.

On his fourth circuit, Lloyd noted an inconsistency in the color and shape of the wainscoting at the juncture of the two walls directly over the couch. He stood up on a chair and examined the area. The paint had been thinned, and some sort of quarter-dollar size circular object had been stuck to the wood, then lightly painted over. He squinted, and felt himself go cold all over. There were tiny perforations in the object, which was the exact size of a high-powered condenser microphone. Running a finger along the bottom ridge of the wainscoting, Lloyd felt the wire. The living room was bugged.

Standing on his tiptoes, he traced the wire along the walls to the front door, down the doorjamb and through a bored-out floor runner to a bush immediately adjacent to the steps of the apartment. Once outside, the wire was covered with a mauve-colored stucco spackling identical in hue to the whole building. Reaching behind the bush, Lloyd found the wire's terminus, an innocuous-looking metal box attached to the wall at just about ground level. He grabbed at the box with both hands, and wrenched with all his strength. The cover snapped off. Lloyd crouched, then looked down the walkway for witnesses. None. He held the bush and metal cover to one side and looked at his prize.

The box contained a state-of-the-art tape recorder. The tape spool was not running, which meant that whoever was doing the bugging had to turn the machine on himself or, more likely, there was a triggering device at work, probably one that Whitey Haines unconsciously activated himself.

Lloyd looked at the door, a scant three paces from where he stood. It *had* to be the trigger.

He walked to the door, unlocked it from the inside, then closed it again, and walked back to the recorder. No movement of the spools. He repeated the procedure, this time opening the door from the outside, then closing it. Squatting by the bush, he admired the results. A red light was glowing, and the tape spools spun silently. Whitey Haines worked day watch. Whoever was interested in his activities knew this and wanted his evenings recorded—the front-door-opening-inward trigger was proof of that.

Lloyd locked the door. Take the recorder with him, or stake out the apartment and wait for the bugger to come and pick up the tape? Was any of this even *connected* to his case? Again scanning the walkway for witnesses, Lloyd tried to make up his mind. When curiosity prickled up his spine and bludgeoned all his other considerations to death, he cut the wire with his penknife, picked up the tape machine, and ran for his car.

Back at Parker Center, Lloyd donned surgical thin rubber gloves and examined the tape recorder. The machine was identical to a prototype he had seen at an F.B.I. seminar on electronic surveillance equipment—a "deep dish" model that featured four separate twin spools stationed on either side of self-cleaning heads that snapped into place automatically as each eight-hour increment of tape was used up, making it possible to record for as long as thirty-two hours without coming near the machine.

Probing inside the recorder, Lloyd saw that the primary spools and the three auxiliary spools all held tape, and that the tape on the primary spool was half on the blank side and half on the recorded side, meaning that there was no more than approximately four hours of recorded material contained in the machine. Wanting to be certain of this, he checked the compartment that stored the finished spools. It was empty.

Lloyd removed the auxiliary tapes and placed them inside his top desk drawer, thinking that the small amount of "live" tape was a mixed blessing—there would probably be very little information to be gleaned from four hours of bugging time, but assuming that the bugger had a good fix on Whitey Haines's habits and some kind of shut-off device secreted inside his apartment to record only *x* number of hours per night, the absence of "live" tape would allow plenty of time to set up a stake-out to catch the bugger when he returned to put in fresh spools. Anyone clever enough to set up an electronic surveillance this complex would risk only a minimum number of tape pick-up forays.

Lloyd ran down the hall to the interrogation cubicle that bordered the sixth-floor briefing room. He grabbed a battered reel-to-reel recorder from atop a cigarette-scarred table and carried it back to his office. "Be good," he said as he placed the "live" tape on the spindle. "No music, no loud noise. Just be good."

The tape spun, and the built-in speaker hissed, then crackled with static. There was the sound of a door being locked, then a baritone grunt followed by a noise Lloyd recognized immediately—the thud of a gunbelt dropped on a couch or chair. Next came barely audible footsteps, then another grunt, this one octaves higher than the first. Lloyd smiled. There were at least two people in Haines's apartment.

Haines spoke. "You gotta feed me more, Bird; cut the coke with some of the bennies I glom from the narco guys, raise your prices, find some new fucking customers or some fucking thing. We got new fish coming in, and if I don't lay some bread on them, all my fuckin' juice ain't gonna keep you and your asshole buddies outta the queens' tank. You dig me, homeboy?"

A high-pitched male voice answered. "Whitey, you said you wouldn't raise my nut! I'm giving you six bills a month plus half the dope action, plus kickbacks from half the punks on the street! You said—"

Lloyd heard a whirring sound dissolve into a sharp crack. There was silence, then Haines's voice. "You start that shit again and I'll hit you for real. You listen, Bird—without me, you are shit. You are the king fucking dick of Boy's Town because I got you to lift weights and build up your puny body and because I get the fucking kiddy bulls to roust the pretty boy juvie's off your turf, and because I shoot you the dope and the protection that make you and your punk pals a class act. As long as I've got clout with Vice, you are safe. And that takes money. There's a transfer-happy new day watch commander, and if I don't grease his fucking palm I may end up busting nigger heads down in Compton. There's two new fish rotating into Vice, and I got no fucking idea if I can keep them off your tight little ass. My nut is two grand a month before I see a fucking dollar profit. *Your* nut is going up twenty percent as of today. You dig me, Bird?"

The high voiced man stammered, "Sh-sh-sure, Whitey." Haines chuckled, then spoke in a soft voice rich with insinuation. "I've always took good care of you. Keep your nose clean and I always will. You just gotta feed me more. Now c'mon in the back. I wanta feed you."

"I don't want to, Whitey."

"You got to, Birdy. It's part of your protection."

Lloyd listened as the sound of footsteps metamorphosed into a silence inhabited by pitiful monsters. The silence stretched into hours. It was broken by the sound of muted sobbing and the slamming of a door. Then the tape went dead.

Fruit hustler shakedowns, vice pay-offs, dope dealing and a corrupt, brutal cop unfit to wear a badge. But was it connected to mass murder? And *who* had bugged Whitey Haines's apartment, and *why*?

Lloyd made two quick phone calls, to the Internal Affairs Divisions of both the L.A.P.D. and Sheriff's Department. Using his reputation as a lever, he was able to get straight answers from the I.A.D. high brass. No, Deputy Delbert Haines, badge 408, was not under investigation by either division. Disturbed, Lloyd ran down a mental list of probable parties interested in the affairs of Whitey Haines: rival dope rings, rival male prostitution combines, a fellow deputy with a grudge. All were possible, but none of the choices rang any bells. Some sort of homosexual tie-in to his killer? Unlikely. It violated his theory of the murderer having been chaste for years, and Haines had no guilty knowledge of the two June 10th suicides he had discovered.

Lloyd took the concealed tape recorder down to the third-floor offices of the Scientific Identification Division and showed it to a data analyst who he knew was particularly enamored of bugging devices. The man whistled as Lloyd placed the machine on his desk, and reached over lovingly to touch it.

"Not yet, Artie," Lloyd said. "I want it run for latents." Artie whistled again, pushing back his chair and sending "Ooh la la" eyes heavenward. "It's gorgeous, Lloyd. It's perfection."

"Run it down for me, Artie. Omit nothing."

The analyst smiled and cleared his throat. "The Watanabe A.F.Z. 999 Recorder. Retail price around seven thousand clams. Available at only the very best stereo showrooms. Used primarily by two rather diverse groups of people: music lovers interested in recording rock festivals or lengthy operas in one fell swoop, and police agencies interested in long-term clandestine bugging. Every component of this machine is the finest that money can buy and Jap technology can produce. You are looking at absolute perfection."

Lloyd gave Artie a round of applause. "Bravo. One other question. Are there hidden serial numbers on the thing? Individual numbers or prototype numbers that can fix the date when the machine was sold?"

Artie shook his head. "The A.F.Z. 999 hit the market in the middle seventies. One prototype, no serial numbers, no different colors—just basic black. The Watanabe Corporation has a thing about tradition; they will not alter the design on these babies. I don't blame them. Who can improve on perfection?"

Lloyd looked down at the recorder. It was in perfect shape, not a scratch on it. "Shit," he said, "I was hoping to narrow down the list of possible buyers. Look, is this thing listed in one of S.I.D.'s Retailer Files?"

"Sure," Artie said. "Want me to compile a list?" Lloyd nodded. "Yeah. Do it now, will you? I'm going to take our baby down the hall and leave it for dusting. I'll be right back."

There was one fingerprint technician on duty at the S.I.D.'s Central Crime Lab. Lloyd handed him the tape recorder and said, "Latent prints, nationwide teletype. I want you to *personally* compare them to L.A.P.D. Homicide Bulletin 16222, Niemeyer, Julia L., 1/3/83, partial right index and pinky. Those prints were bloodstained; if you're in doubt about a match-up on the bulletin, roll the new prints in a blood sample, then recompare. You got that?"

The technician nodded assent, then asked, "Think we'll find prints?"

"It's doubtful, but we have to try. Be thorough; this is very important." The technician opened his mouth to offer assurances, but Lloyd was already running away.

"Eighteen retailers," Artie said as Lloyd burst through the door. "That's up to date, too. Didn't I tell you our baby was esoteric?" Lloyd took the printed list and put it in his pocket, looking reflexively at the clock above Artie's desk. 6:30—too late to begin calling the stereo supply stores. Remembering his date with Kathleen McCarthy, he said, "I have to run. Take care, Artie. Some day I may tell you the whole story."

Kathleen McCarthy closed the store early and went back to her living quarters to write and prepare for her evening with the big policeman. Her business day had been frustrating. No sales, and an endless series of browsers who had wanted to discuss feminist issues while she was on the phone trying to secure information toward the capture of a psychopathic woman-killer. The irony was both profound and cheap, and Kathleen felt a vague diminishing of selfhood in its aftermath. She had hated the police for so long that even though she was doing her moral duty in aiding them, the price was a piece of her ego. Bolstering herself with logic, Kathleen grabbed the ego fragment and killed it with words. Dialectic at the expense of helping others. Pride. Your intractable Irish heart. The rhetoric fell short of its mark, and Kathleen smiled at the *real* irony—sex. You want the cop, and you don't even know his first name.

Kathleen walked into the bathroom and stripped before the full length mirror. Strong flesh, satisfyingly lean; firm breasts, good legs. A tall, handsome woman. Thirty-six, yet looking . . . Kathleen's eyes clouded with tears, and she braced herself by maintaining eye contact with her image. It worked—the tears died, stillborn.

Throwing on a robe, Kathleen walked into her living room–study and arrayed pen, paper, and thesaurus on her desk, then went through her prewriting ritual of letting random prose patterns and thoughts of her dream lover battle for primacy of her mind. As always, her dream lover won, and Kathleen plucked absently at the crotch of her robe and relinquished herself to the smell of the flowers that always came just when she most needed them, when her life was almost to some brink. Then, anonymously and in perfect psychic sync the flowers would be at her doorstep and she would be overwhelmed and wonder who, and look to the faces of strange men for signs of kinship or commiseration or *special* interest.

She knew that he had to be tall and intelligent and about her age— eighteen years of floral tribute without a clue to his identity! Except that he had to have come from the old neighborhood, had to have seen her on the way to school with her court . . .

Thoughts of her court gave Kathleen a hook. She took up her pen and wrote:

> Bring back the dead
> Give them head
> Remember the songs they sang
> And the words they said.
> From protracted adolescence
> To premature senescence
> I do penance with regret;

For the epiphanies I never held
And the joy I never met.

Sighing, Kathleen settled back in her chair. Sighing again, she got out
her diary and wrote:

Good prose seems just about to burst out of me, so I'll do a little
tease number and sit back and collate the present again, from approximately my nine thousandth "good prose breakout" plateau.
Weird these days. Even good serviceable prose seems contrived. This
diary (which will probably never be published!) seems much more
real. I'm probably moving into a period where I'll just sit back and let
things happen, figure them out as they happen, then shut whatever is
happening out and sit down and grind out another book. The cop
seems to be evidence of this. O.K., he's compelling and attractive, but
even if he weren't I'd probably give his attentions a shot. Weirder yet:
Is this "Let it flow" attitude undertaken out of the desire for edifica-
tion or out of loneliness, horniness, and the desire to ultimately give
up that awful part of me that wants to stand apart from the whole
human race and exist through my words? Empirically speaking, who
knows? My solitude has given me brilliant words, as have my abysmal
relationships with men. Another (nine billionth?) meditation on the
identity of *him*? Not today, today is strictly the realm of things possible. All of a sudden I'm tired of words. I hope the cop isn't too right
wing. I hope he is capable of bending.

Kathleen placed her pen across her words, surprised that the combination of her dream lover and the policeman had inspired such somber sen-
timents. Smiling at the unpredictability of muses, she glanced at her
watch. 6:30. As she showered for her date, she wondered where those first
stanzas would take her and how she would react when her doorbell rang at
seven o'clock.

The bell rang precisely at seven. When Kathleen opened the door, Lloyd
was standing there, wearing beat-up cords and a pullover sweater. She saw
a holstered revolver outlined on his left hip and cursed herself; her Harris
tweed pantsuit was a definite overdress. To correct the mistake she said,
"Hi, Sergeant" and grabbed at the gun bulge and pulled Lloyd inside. He

let himself be led, and Kathleen cursed herself again when she saw him smile at the gesture.

Lloyd sat on the couch and spread out his long arms in a mock crucifixion pose. Kathleen stood over him self-consciously. "I made those phone calls," she said. "To over a dozen bookdealers. Nothing. None of my friends recall seeing or talking with a man like the one you described. It was bizarre. I was helping the police to find an insane woman-killer, and women kept interrupting me to ask questions about the Equal Rights Amendment."

"Thank you," Lloyd said. "I didn't really expect anything. Right now I'm just fishing. Badge 1114, homicide fisherman on the job."

Kathleen sat down. "Are you supervising this investigation?" she asked.

Lloyd shook his head. "No, right now I *am* this investigation. None of my superiors would authorize me to detach officers to work under me, because the idea of mass murderers killing with impunity makes them afraid for their careers and the Department's prestige. I *have* supervised homicide investigations, duties normally assigned to lieutenants and captains, but I'm—"

"But you're that good." Kathleen said it as a matter of fact.

Lloyd smiled. "I'm better."

"Can you read minds, Sergeant?"

"Call me Lloyd."

"All right, Lloyd."

"The answer is sometimes."

"Do you know what I'm thinking?"

Lloyd draped his arm over Kathleen's tweed shoulders. She buckled, but didn't resist. "I've got an idea," he said. "How's this for starters? Who is this guy? Is he a right-wing loony, like most cops? Does he spend hours cracking jokes about niggers and discussing pussy with his policeman buddies? Does he like to hurt people? To *kill* people? Does he think there's a Jew-commie-nigger-homo conspiracy to take over the world? Does . . ."

Kathleen put a gentle restraining hand on Lloyd's knee and said, "Touché. In basic theme you were correct on all counts." She smiled against her will, slowly withdrawing her hand.

Lloyd felt his blood start to race to the tempo of their banter. "Do you want my answers?" he asked.

"No. You've already given me them."

"Any other questions?"

"Yes. Two. Do you cheat on your wife?"

Lloyd laughed and dug into his pants pocket for his wedding band. He slipped it onto his ring finger and said, "Yes."

Kathleen's face was expressionless. "Have you ever killed anyone?" she asked.

"Yes."

Kathleen grimaced. "I shouldn't have asked. No more talk of death and woman-killers, please. Shall we leave?"

Lloyd nodded and took her hand as she locked the door behind them.

They drove aimlessly, ending up cruising the terraced hills of the old neighborhood. Lloyd steered the unmarked Matador through the topography of their mutual past, wondering what Kathleen was thinking.

"My parents are dead now," she said finally. "They were both so old when I was born, and they doted on me because they knew they'd only have me for twenty years or so. My father told me he moved to Silverlake because the hills reminded him of Dublin."

She looked at Lloyd, who sensed that she wanted to end her games of will and be gentle. He pulled to the curb at Vendome and Hyperion, hoping that the spectacular view would move her to divulge intimate things, things that would make him care for her. "Do you mind if we stop?" he asked.

"No," Kathleen said, "I like this place. I used to come here with my court. We read memorial poems for John Kennedy here on the night he was shot."

"Your court?"

"Yes. My court. The 'Kathy Kourt'—spelled with two Ks. I had my own little group of underlings in high school. We were all poets, and we all wore plaid skirts and cashmere sweaters, and we never dated, because there was not one boy at John Marshall High School worthy of us. We didn't date and we didn't neck. We were saving it for Mr. Right, who, we all figured, would make the scene when we were published poets of renown. We were unique. I was the smartest and the best-looking. I transferred from parochial school because the Mother Superior was always trying to get me to show her my breasts. I talked about it in hygiene class and attracted a following of lonely, bookish girls. They became my court. I gave them an identity. They became *women* because of me. Everyone left us alone; yet we had a following of equally lonely, bookish boys—'Kathy's

Klowns' they were called, because we never even deigned to speak to them. We . . . We . . ."

Kathleen's voice rose to a wail, and she batted off Lloyd's tentative hand on her shoulder. "We . . . We . . . loved and cared for each other, and I know it sounds pathetic, but we were strong. Strong! Strong . . ."

Lloyd waited a full minute before asking, "What happened to your court?"

Kathleen sighed, knowing that her answer was an anticlimax. "Oh, they drifted away. They found boyfriends. They decided not to save it for Mr. Right. They got prettier. They decided they didn't want to be poets. They . . . they just didn't need me anymore."

"And you?"

"I died, and my heart went underground and resurfaced looking for cheap kicks and true love. I slept with a lot of women, figuring I could find a new entourage that way. It didn't work. I screwed a lot of men—that got me the entourage, all right, but they were creeps. And I wrote and wrote and wrote and got published and bought a bookstore and here I am."

Lloyd was already shaking his head. "And what *really*," he said.

Kathleen spat out angrily, "And I am a damn good poet and a better diarist! And who the hell are you to question me? And? And? *And?*"

Lloyd touched her neck with gentle fingertips and said, "And you live in your head, and you're thirty-something, and you keep wondering if it's ever going to get better. Please say yes, Kathleen, or just shake your head." Kathleen shook her head. Lloyd said, "Good. That's why I'm here—because I want it to get better for you. Do you believe that?" Kathleen shook her head affirmatively and stared into her lap, clenching her hands. "I have a question for you," Lloyd said. "A rhetorical question. Did you know that the L.A.P.D. treats the undercarriage of all their unmarked cars with a special shock-proof, scrape-proof coating?"

Kathleen laughed politely at the non sequitur. "No," she said.

Lloyd reached over and secured the passenger safety harness around her shoulders. When she remained blank-faced he waggled his eyebrows and said, "Brace yourself," then hit the ignition and dropped into low gear, popping the emergency brake and flooring the gas pedal simultaneously, sending the car forward in an almost vertical wheel stand. Kathleen screamed. Lloyd waited until the car began its crashing downward momentum, then gently tapped the accelerator a half dozen times until the rear wheels caught friction and the car lurched ahead, straining to keep its front end airborne. Kathleen screamed again. Lloyd felt gravity fighting sheer engine power and winning. As the hood of the Matador swung down, he punched the gas pedal and the car nosed upward, holding its pattern until he saw an intersection coming up and hit the brakes, sending them into a tire squealing fishtail. The car was spinning out toward a row of trees when its front end finally smashed into the pavement. Lloyd and Kathleen bounced in their seats like spastic puppets. Dripping with nervous sweat, Lloyd rolled down his window and saw a group of Chicano teenagers giving him a wild ovation, stomping their feet and saluting the car with raised beer bottles.

He blew them a kiss and turned to Kathleen. She was crying, and he couldn't tell if in fear or joy. He unstrapped the harness and held her. He let her cry, and gradually felt the tears trail into laughter. When Kathleen finally raised her head from his chest, Lloyd saw the face of a delighted child. He kissed that face with the same tenderness as he kissed the faces of his daughters.

"Urban romanticism," Kathleen said. "Jesus. What next?"

Lloyd considered options and said, "I don't know. Let's stay mobile, though. All right?"

"Will you observe all traffic regulations?"

Lloyd said, "Scout's honor" and started up the car, waggling his eyebrows at Kathleen until she laughed and begged him to stop. The teenagers gave him another round of applause as he pulled out.

They cruised Sunset, the main artery of the old neighborhood. Lloyd editorialized as he drove, pointing out immortal locations of his past:

"There's Myron's Used Cars. Myron was a genius chemist gone wrong. He got strung out on heroin and kicked out of his teaching post at U.S.C. He developed a corrosive solution that would eat off the serial numbers on engine blocks. He stole hundreds of cars, lowered the blocks into his vat of solution and set himself up as the used car king of Silverlake. He used to be a nice guy. He was a big rooter for the Marshall football team, and he lent all the star players cars for hot dates. Then one day when he was fucked up on smack he fell into his vat. The solution ate off both his legs up to the knees. Now he's a cripple and the single most misanthropic individual I've ever known."

Kathleen joined in the travelogue, pointing across the street and saying, "Cathcart Drugs. I used to steal stationery there for my court. Scented purple stationery. One day I got caught. Old man Cathcart grabbed me and dug into my purse. He found some poems I had written on the same kind of stationery. He held me and read the poems aloud to everyone in the store. Intimate poems. I was so ashamed."

Lloyd felt a sadness intrude on their evening. Sunset Boulevard was too loud and garishly neon. Without saying a word he turned the car north on Echo Park Boulevard and drove past the Silverlake Reservoir. Soon they were in the shadow of the power plant, and he turned and looked at Kathleen for approval.

"Yes," she said, "it's perfect."

They walked uphill silently, holding hands. Dirt clods broke at their feet, and twice Lloyd had to pull Kathleen forward. When they reached the summit they sat in the dirt, heedless of their clothes, leaning into the wire fence that encircled the facility. Lloyd felt Kathleen pulling apart from him, regrouping against the momentum of her tears. To close the gap, he said, "I like you, Kathleen."

"I like you, too. And I like it here."

"It's quiet here."

"You love the quiet and you hate music. Where does your wife think you are?"

"I don't know. Lately she goes out dancing with this fag guy she knows. Her soul sister. They snort cocaine and go to a gay disco. *She* loves music, too."

"And it doesn't bother you?" Kathleen said.

"Well . . . more than anything else I just don't understand it. I understand why people rob banks and become thieves and get strung out on dope and sex and become cops and poets and killers, but I don't understand why people fart around in discos and listen to music when they could be goosing the world with an electric cattle prod. I can understand you and your court and your screwing all those dykes and creeps. I understand innocent little children and their love, and their trauma when they discover how cold it can get, but I don't understand how they cannot want to fight it. I tell my daughters stories so they'll fight. My youngest, Penny, is a genius. She's a fighter. My two older girls I'm not so sure about. Janice, my wife, isn't a fighter. I don't think she was ever innocent. She was born practical and stable and stayed that way. I think . . . I think maybe . . . that's why I married her. I think . . . I *knew* I didn't have any more innocence, and I wasn't quite sure that I was a fighter. Then I found out I *was* and got scared of the price and married Janice."

Lloyd's voice had assumed an almost disembodied monotone. Kathleen thought briefly that he was a ventriloquist's pawn, and that whoever was pulling his strings was really trying to get to *her*; laying clues in the strange barrage of confession she had just heard. Two words—"killers" and "price" stuck out, and in her haste to make sense of the story Kathleen said, "And so you became a policeman to prove you were a fighter, and then you killed in the line of duty and you knew."

Lloyd shook his head. "No, I killed a man—an evil man—first. Then I became a cop and married Janice. I lose track of chronology sometimes. Sometimes . . . not often . . . when I try to figure out my past I hear noise . . . music . . . awful noise . . . and I have to stop."

Kathleen felt Lloyd wavering in and out of control, and knew that she had broken through to his essence. She said, "I want to tell you a story. It's a true romantic story."

Lloyd shifted his head onto her lap and said, "Tell me."

"All right. There was once a quiet, bookish girl who wrote poetry. She didn't believe in God or her parents or the other girls who followed her. She tried very hard to believe in herself. It was easy, for a while. Then her followers left her. She was alone. But someone loved her. Some tender man sent her flowers. The first time there was an anonymous poem. A sad poem. The second time just the flowers. The dream lover continued to send the flowers, anonymously, for many years. Over eighteen years. Always when the lonely woman needed them most. The woman grew as a poet and diarist and kept the flowers dated and pressed in glass. She speculated on this man, but never tried to discover his identity. She took his anonymous tribute to her heart and decided that she would reciprocate his anonymity by keeping her diaries private until after her death. And so she lived and wrote and listened to music—a quiet mover. It almost makes you want to believe in God, doesn't it, Lloyd?"

Lloyd took his head from its soft tweed resting place, shaking it to bring the sad story into sharper focus. Then he stood up and helped Kathleen to her feet. "I think your dream lover is a very strange fighter," he said, "and I think he wants to own you, not inspire you. I think he doesn't know how strong you are. Come on, I'll take you home."

They stood in the doorway of Kathleen's bookstore-apartment, holding each other loosely. Kathleen burrowed into Lloyd's shoulder, and when she raised her head he thought that she wanted to be kissed. As he bent to her,

Kathleen pushed him gently away. "No. Not yet. Please don't force it, Lloyd."

"All right."

"It's just that the whole thing is so unexpected. You're so special, and it just . . ."

"You're special, too."

"I know, but I've got *no* idea of who you are, of your natural habitat. The *little* things. Do you understand?"

Lloyd pondered this. "I think so. Look, would you like to go to a dinner party tomorrow night? Policemen and their wives? It'll probably be dull, but illuminating for you."

Kathleen smiled. His offer was a major capitulation; he was willing to be bored to please her. "Yes. Be here at seven." She moved backward into her dark front room and closed the door behind her. When she heard Lloyd's departing footsteps she turned on the lights and got out her diary. Her mind rambled with profundities until she muttered, "Oh, fuck it," and wrote:

He is capable of bending. I am going to be his music.

Lloyd drove home. He pulled into the driveway to find Janice's car gone and all the lights in the house glowing brightly. He unlocked the door and walked inside, seeing the note immediately:

Lloyd, darling:

This is goodbye, for a while at least. The girls and I have gone to San Francisco to stay with a friend of George's. It is for the best, I know that, because I know that you and I have not communicated for a long, long time, and that our values are markedly different. Your behavior with the girls was the final straw. I have known almost since the beginning of our marriage of some deep disturbance in you—one you disguised (for the most part) very well. What I will not tolerate is your passing your disturbance on to them. Your stories are cancerous in their effect, and Anne, Caroline, and Penny must be free of them. A note on the girls—I am going to enroll them in a Montessori School in S.F., and I will have them call you at least once a week. George's roommate Rob will look after the shop in my absence. I will decide in the coming months whether or not I want a divorce. I care

for you deeply, but I cannot live with you. I am withholding our address in S.F. until I am certain you will not try to do something rash.
When I get settled, I'll call. Until then be well and don't worry.

Janice

Lloyd put down the note and walked through the empty house. Everything feminine had been cleared out. The girls' room had been picked clean
of personal belongings; the bedroom that he shared with Janice now contained only his solitary aura and the navy blue cashmere quilt that Penny
had crafted for his thirty-seventh birthday.

Lloyd drew the quilt around his shoulders and walked outside. He looked
up at the sky and hoped for an annihilating rainstorm. When he realized
that he couldn't will thunder and lightning, he fell to his knees and wept.

10

When the poet saw the empty metal box, he screamed. Cancer cells ma-
terialized out of the dawn sky and threw themselves at his eyes, hurling him
onto the cold pavement. He wrapped his arms around his head and drew
himself into a fetal ball to keep the tiny carcinogens from going for his
throat, then rocked back and forth until he had blunted all his senses and
his body started to cramp, then numb. When he felt self-asphyxiation coming on he breathed out, and familiar Larrabee Avenue came into focus. No
cancer cells in the air. His beautiful tape machine was gone, but Officer Pig
was still asleep and the early morning scene on Larrabee was normal. No
police cars, no suspicious vehicles, no trench-coated figures huddled behind
newspapers. He had changed the tape forty-eight hours ago, so the machine
was mostly likely discovered that day, when it was empty or running, or yesterday, when it contained a minimum of recorded material. If he hadn't
wanted to touch himself so badly he would never have risked the early pick-
up, but he needed the stimulus of Officer Pig and his lackey, who had been
doing things to each other on the couch for weeks now, things that Julia
had written about in her evil manu—

He couldn't complete the thought; it was too shameful.

He got to his feet and looked in all directions. No one had seen him. He bit at the skin of his forearms. The blood that trickled out was red and healthy looking. He opened his mouth to speak, wanting to be sure that the cancer cells hadn't severed his vocal cords. The word that came out was "safe." He said it a dozen times, each time with a more awed inflection. Finally he shouted it and ran for his car.

Thirty minutes later he had scaled the bookstore roof, a silenced .32 automatic in his windbreaker pocket, smiling when he saw that his Sanyo 6000 was still hidden underneath an outsized sheaf of tarred-over pipe insulation. He grabbed the two spools of finished tape from the machine's storage compartment. Safe. Safe. Safe. Safe. He said the word over and over again on his drive home, and he was still saying it as he put the first spool on the old machine in the living room, then sat back to listen, his eyes moving over the rose branches and photographs on the walls.

The sound of a switch being flipped; the porch light going on; the trigger activating the tape. His original beloved muttering to herself, then deep silence. He smiled and touched his thighs. She was writing.

The silence stretched. One hour. Two. Three. Four. Then the sound of yawning and the switch being flipped again.

He got to his feet, stretched and changed spools. Again the porch light trigger—his punctual darling, 6:55, like clockwork.

He sat down, wondering if he should make himself explode now while he could hear footsteps, or wait and take a chance on his original beloved talking to herself. Then a doorbell rang. Her voice: "Hi, Sergeant." The scuffle of feet. Her voice again: "I made those phone calls. To over a dozen bookdealers. Nothing. None of my friends recall seeing or talking with a man like the one you described. It was bizarre. I was helping the police to find an insane woman-killer, and women kept—"

At the last words he began to tremble. His body went ice cold, then turned burning hot. He punched the stop button and fell to his knees. He clawed at his face until he drew blood, whimpering safe, safe, safe. He crawled to the window and looked out at the passing parade on Alvarado. He took hope with every identifiable evidence of business as usual: traffic noise, Mexican women with children in tow, junkies waiting to score in front of the burrito stand. He started to say "safe," then hesitated and whispered "maybe." "Maybe" grew in his brain until he screamed it and stumbled back to the recorder.

He pushed the play button. His first beloved was saying something about women interrupting her. Then a man's voice: "Thank you. I didn't really expect anything. Right now I'm just fishing. Badge 1114, homicide fisherman on the job."

He forced himself to listen, gouging his genitals with both hands to keep from screaming. The horrific conversation continued, and words leaped out and made him gouge himself harder. "The idea of mass murderers killing with impunity makes them afraid . . . I *have* supervised homicide investigations . . . call me Lloyd."

When the door slammed and the tape spun in blessed silence he took his hands from between his legs. He could feel blood dripping down his thighs, and it reminded him of high school and poetry and the sanctity of his purpose. Mrs. Cuthbertson's eleventh grade honors English class. Logical fallacies: *post hoc, propter ergo hoc*—"After this, therefore because of this." Knowledge of crimes committed does *not* mean knowledge of the perpetrator. Policemen were not breaking down his door. "Lloyd," "Homicide fisherman badge 1114," had no idea that his original beloved's dwelling was bugged, and may have had nothing to do with the theft of his other tape recorder. "Lloyd" was "fishing" in shark-infested waters, and if he came near him he would eat the policeman alive. Conclusion: they had no idea who he was, and it was business as usual.

Tonight he would claim his twenty-third and most hurriedly courted beloved. No "maybe." It was a pure "yes," powerfully affirmed by his meditation tape and every one of his beloveds from Jane Wilhelm on up. Yes. Yes. The poet walked to the window and screamed it to the world at large.

11

His sleepless night in the empty house had been the precursor to a day of total bureaucratic frustration, and each negative feedback tore at Lloyd like a neon sign heralding the end of all the gentle restraining influences in his life. Janice and the girls were gone, and until his genius killer was captured, he was powerless to get them back.

As the day wound down into early evening, Lloyd recounted his dwindling options, wondering what on God's earth he would do if they died out and left him with only his mind and his will.

It had taken him six hours to call the eighteen stereo supply stores and secure a list of fifty-five people who had purchased Watanabe A.F.Z. 999 recorders over the last eight years. Twenty-four of the buyers had been women, leaving thirty-one male suspects, and Lloyd knew from experience that telephone interviews would be futile—experienced detectives would have to size up the buyers in person and determine guilt or innocence from the suspects' response to questioning. And if the recorder had been purchased outside L.A. County . . . and if the whole Haines angle had nothing to do with the killings . . . and he would need manpower for interviewing . . . and if Dutch turned him down at the party tonight . . .

The negative feedback continued, undercut with memories of Penny and her quilts and Caroline and Anne squealing with delight at his stories. Dutch had gotten nothing positive from his queries to both retired and long-term active juvenile detectives and the "monicker" files on "Bird" and "Birdy" had yielded only the names of a dozen ghetto blacks. Useless—the high-pitched voice in Whitey Haines's living room had obviously belonged to a white man.

But the greatest frustration had been the absence of a print make on the tape recorder. Lloyd had stalked the crime lab repeatedly, looking for the technician he had left the machine with, calling the man at home, only to find that his father had had a heart attack and that he had driven to San Bernardino, taking the recorder with him, intending to use the facilities of the San Bernardino Sheriff's Department for his dusting and comparison tests. "He said that you wanted him to do the tests *personally*, Sergeant," the technician's wife had said. "He'll call from San Bernardino in the morning with the results." Lloyd had hung up cursing semantics and his own authoritarian nature.

This left two last-ditch, one-man options: Interview the thirty-one buyers himself or cop some bennies and stake out Whitey Haines's apartment until the bugger showed up. Desperation tactics—and the only avenues he had left.

Lloyd got his car and headed west, toward Kathleen's bookstore-cottage. When he got off the freeway he realized he was bone weary and flesh hungry and pointed his Matador north, in the direction of Joanie Pratt's house in the Hollywood Hills. They could love and talk and maybe Joanie's body would smother his feeling of doomsday attrition coming from all sides.

Joanie jumped on Lloyd as he walked through the open front door, exclaiming, "Sarge, *wilkommen!* Romance on your mind? If so, the bedroom is immediately to your right." Lloyd laughed. Joanie's big carnal heart was the perfect spot to place his tenderness.

"Lead the way."

When they had loved and played and looked at the sunset from the bedroom balcony, Lloyd told Joanie that his wife and children were gone and that in the wake of his abandonment there was only himself and the killer. "I'm giving my investigation two more days," he said, "then I'm going public. I'm taking everything I have to Channel 7 News and flushing my career down the toilet. It hit me while we were lying in bed. If the leads I have now don't pan out I'm going to create such a fucking public stink that every police agency in L.A. County will *have* to go after this animal; if my reading of him is correct, the exposure will drive him to do something so rash that he'll blow it completely. I think he has an incredible ego that's screaming to be recognized, and when he screams it to the world I'll be there to get him."

Joanie shuddered, then put a comforting hand on Lloyd's shoulder. "You'll get him, Sarge. You'll give him the big one where it hurts the most."

Lloyd smiled at the imagery. "My options are narrowing down," he said. "It feels good." Remembering Kathleen, he added, "I've got to go."

"Hot date?" Joanie asked.

"Yeah. With a poetess."

"Do me a favor before you go?"

"Name it."

"I want a happy picture of the two of us."

"Who's going to take it?"

"Me. There's a ten-second delay on my Polaroid. Come on, get up."

"But I'm naked, Joanie!"

"So am I. Come on."

Joanie walked into the living room and came back with a camera affixed to a tripod. She pushed some buttons and ran to Lloyd's side. Blushing, he grabbed her around the waist and felt himself start to go hard. The flash cube popped. Joanie counted the seconds and pulled the film from the camera. The print was perfect: the nude Lloyd and Joanie, she smiling carnally, he blushing and semi-erect. Lloyd felt his tenderness explode as he looked at it. He took Joanie's face in his hands and said, "I love you."

Joanie said, "I love you too, Sarge. Now get dressed. We've both got dates tonight, and I'm late for mine."

Kathleen had spent her entire day in preparation for her evening; long hours in the women's departments of Brooks Brothers and Boshard-Doughty, searching for *the* romantic purist outfit that would speak eloquently of her past and flatter her in the present. It *took* hours, but she found it: pink Oxford cloth button down shirt, navy blue ankle socks and cordovan tassel loafers, a navy crew neck sweater and the pièce de résistance—a knee length, pleated, red tartan skirt.

Feeling both sated and expectant, Kathleen drove home to savor waiting for her romantic conspirator. She had four hours to kill, and prescribed getting mildly stoned and listening to music as the way to do it. Since tonight she would be juxtaposed iconoclastically against a staid gathering of policemen and their wives, she put a carefully selected medley of flower child revolution on the turntable and sat back in her robe to smoke dope and listen, filled with the knowledge that tonight she would teach the big policeman—wow him with her poetry, read classic excerpts from her diary, and maybe let him kiss her breasts.

As the Colombian gold took her over, Kathleen found herself playing out a new fantasy. Lloyd was her dream lover. He was the one who had sent the flowers all those years; he had waited for the terrible impetus of searching for a killer to bring them together—a casual meeting wouldn't have been romantic enough for him. The genesis of his attraction had to be Silverlake—they had grown up a scant six blocks apart.

Kathleen felt her fantasy drift apart with the diminishing of her high. To fortify it, she smoked her last Thai stick. Within minutes she was at one with the music and Lloyd was nude in front of her, admitting his deepening love of almost two decades, breathless in his desire to have her. Regal in her magnanimity, Kathleen accepted, watching him grow bigger and harder until she, Lloyd, and the deep bass guitar of the Jefferson Airplane exploded at once and her hand jerked from between her legs and she looked reflexively at the clock and saw that it was ten of seven.

Kathleen walked to the bathroom and turned on the shower, then dropped her robe and let the stream of water run alternately hot and cold over her until she felt her sober self tenuously emerge. She dressed and appreciated her image in the full-length mirror: She was perfect, and pleased to note that dressing in such nostalgic garments caused her not a hint of remorse.

The bell range at seven. Kathleen turned off the stereo and threw open the door. Seeing Lloyd standing there, huge and somehow graceful, jerked her back to her fantasy. When he smiled and said, "Jesus, are you stoned," she returned to the present, laughed guiltily and said, "I'm sorry. Weird thoughts. Do you like my outfit?"

Lloyd said, "You're beautiful. Traditional clothes become you. I didn't think you were a doper. Come on, let's get out of here."

Dutch Peltz and his wife Estelle lived in Glendale, in a ranch-style house adjoining a golf course. Lloyd and Kathleen drove there in tense silence, Lloyd thinking of desperation tactics and killers and Kathleen thinking of ways to regain the parity she had lost by appearing loaded.

Dutch greeted them in the doorway, bowing to Kathleen. Lloyd made the introductions.

"Dutch Peltz, Kathleen McCarthy."

Dutch took Kathleen's hand. "Miss McCarthy, a pleasure."

Kathleen returned the bow with a satirical flourish. "Should I call you by your rank, Mr. Peltz?"

"Please call me Arthur or Dutch, all my friends do." Turning to Lloyd, he said, "Circulate for a while, kid. I'll show Kathleen around. We should talk before you leave."

Catching the edge in Dutch's voice, Lloyd said, "We need to talk sooner than that. I'm going to get a drink. Kathleen, if Dutch gets too boring, have him show you his boot trick."

Kathleen looked down at Dutch's feet. Although dressed in a business suit, he was wearing thick-soled black paratrooper boots. Dutch laughed and banged the back of his right heel on the floor. A long, double-bladed stiletto sprang out of the side of his boot. "My trademark," he said. "I was a commando in Korea." He nudged the knife point into the carpet, and the blade retracted.

Kathleen forced a grin. "Macho."

Dutch smiled. "Touché. Come on Kathleen, I'll show you around."

Dutch steered Kathleen toward the dining room buffet, where women were readying dishes of salad and standing over steaming hot trays of corned beef and cabbage, laughing and lauding the food and party preparations.

Lloyd watched them depart, then walked into the living room, whistling when he saw that every inch of floor space was eclipsed by heavyweight high brass: commanders, inspectors, and up. He counted heads—seven commanders, five inspectors, and four deputy chiefs. The lowest ranking officer in the room was Lieutenant Fred Gaffaney, standing by the fireplace with two inspectors wearing cross-and-flag lapel pins. Gaffaney looked over and caught Lloyd's eye, then turned quickly away. The two inspectors followed suit, flinching when Lloyd stared straight at them. Something was *off.*

Lloyd found Dutch in the kitchen, regaling Kathleen and a deputy chief with one of his dialect anecdotes. When the chief walked away shaking his head and laughing, Lloyd said, "Have you been holding out on me, Dutchman? Something's got to be up; I've never seen this many heavy hitters in one place in my whole career."

Dutch swallowed. "I took the commander's exam and passed high. I didn't tell you because I—" He nodded toward Kathleen.

"No," Lloyd said, "she stays. Why didn't you tell me, Dutch?"

"You don't want Kathleen to hear this," Dutch said.

"I don't care. Tell me, goddamnit!"

Dutch spat it out. "I didn't tell you because with me on the commander's list there would be no end to the favors you would have asked. I was going to tell you *if* I passed and *when* I got assigned. *Then* I got the word from Fred Gaffaney—They're going to offer me the command of Internal Affairs when Inspector Eisler retires. Gaffaney is on the captain's list; he's almost certain to be my exec. Then *you* blew up at him, causing *me* to lose a great deal of face. I patched it up; old Dutch always looks out for his temperamental genius. Things are changing, Lloyd. The department has been taking a beating from the media—shootings of blacks, police brutality, those two cops busted for possession of coke. There's a shake-up coming. I.A.D. is filled with born-agains, and the chief *himself* wants a crackdown on officers shacking up, fucking whores, chasing pussy, that kind of bullshit. I'm going to have to go along with it, and I don't want *you* to get hurt! I told Gaffaney that you'd apologize to him, and I *expected* you to show up with your wife, not one of your goddamned girlfriends!"

"Janice left me!" Lloyd screamed. "She took the girls with her, and I wouldn't apologize to that sanctimonious cocksucker to save my life!"

Lloyd looked around. Kathleen stood rigid against the wall, shock-stilled, her hands balled into fists. A group of officers and wives filled the dining room door. When he saw nothing but awe and self-righteous judgment in their eyes, Lloyd whispered, "I need five men, Dutch. For thirty-one suspect interviews. Just for a few days. It's the last favor I'll ever ask you for. I don't think I can get him by myself."

Dutch shook his head. "No, Lloyd."

Lloyd's whisper became a sob. "Please."

"No. Not now. Sit on it for a while. Take a rest. You've been working too hard."

The crowd in the doorway had spilled over into the kitchen. Moving his eyes over the entire assembly, Lloyd said: "Two days, Dutch. Then I'm taking my act on TV. Watch for me on the six o'clock news."

Lloyd turned to walk away, then hesitated. He about-faced and swung his open right hand at Dutch's face. The crack of flesh on flesh died into a huge collective gasp. "Judas," Lloyd hissed.

Kathleen snuggled close to Lloyd in the car, abandoning herself to wanting his reckless courage. She was afraid of saying the wrong thing, so she stayed silent and tried not to speculate on what he was thinking.

"What do you hate?" Lloyd asked. "Be specific."

Kathleen thought for a moment. "I hate the Klondike Bar," she said. "That's a leather bar on Virgil and Santa Monica. A sadist hangout. The men who park their motorcycles in front frighten me. I know you wanted me to say something about killers, but I just don't feel that way."

"Don't apologize. It's a good answer."

Lloyd pulled a U-turn, throwing Kathleen off to the other side of the seat. Within minutes they were parked in front of the Klondike Bar, watching a group of short-haired, leather-jacketed men snort amyl nitrate, then throw rough arms around each other and walk inside.

"One other question," Lloyd said. "Do you want to spend the rest of your life as a cut-rate Emily Dickinson or do you want to go for some pure white light?"

Kathleen swallowed. "Pure white light," she said.

Lloyd pointed to the neon sign above the swinging bar doors. A muscular Yukon adventurer, wearing nothing but a Mountie hat and jock strap, glared down at them. Lloyd reached into the glove compartment and handed Kathleen his off-duty .38. "Shoot it," he said.

Kathleen shut her eyes and fired blindly out the window until the gun was empty. The Yukon adventurer exploded with the last three shots, and suddenly Kathleen was breathing cordite and pure white light. Lloyd gunned the car and peeled rubber for two solid blocks, driving with one hand on the wheel and the other on the squealing Kathleen's tartan lap.

When they pulled up in front of her bookstore, he said, "Welcome to the heart of my Irish Protestant ethos."

Kathleen wiped tears of laughter from her eyes and said, "But I'm an Irish Catholic."

"No matter. You've got heart and love, and that's what matters."

"Will you stay?"

"No. I have to be alone and figure out what I have to do."

"But you'll come by soon?"

"Yes. In a couple of days."

"And you'll make love to me?"

"Yes."

Kathleen closed her eyes and Lloyd leaned over and kissed her alternately soft and hard, until her tears ran between their lips and she broke the embrace and ran from the car.

At home, Lloyd tried to think. Nothing happened. When plans, theories, and contingency strategies wouldn't coalesce in his mind he had a brief moment of panic. Then the classic simplicity hit him. His entire life had been the prelude to this breathless pause before flight. There was no turning back. His divine instinct for darkness would take him to the killer. The rabbit had gone down the hole and would never return to daylight.

Part Four
Moon Descending

12

His intended was named Peggy Morton, and she was chosen for the challenge her consummation presented as much as for her persona.

Since Julia Niemeyer and her manuscript and his curbside assignation he had been feeling slippage on all fronts. His lean, strong body looked the same, but *felt* sluggish and flaccid; his normally clear blue eyes were evasive, clouded with fear when he stared at himself in the mirror. To combat these little crumblings the poet had resurrected several of his pre-Jane Wilhem disciplines. Hours were spent practicing judo and karate and firing his handguns at the N.R.A. range, doing push-ups and chin-ups and sit-ups until he was one mindless ache. They worked only as a picayune holding action, and nightmares still gnawed at him. Fetching young men on the street seemed to be pantomiming obscene overtures; cloud formations twisted into bizarre patterns that spelled his name for all of Los Angeles to read.

Then his tape recorder was stolen and he gained a faceless nemesis: Sergeant Lloyd the homicide fisherman. In the eleven hours since first hearing the man's voice on the tape he had exploded four times, progressively more graphic Boy's Town fantasies driving him into a near stuporous state that would evaporate within minutes, leaving him ready to explode again, but afraid of the price. Looking at the memorabilia on his walls didn't help; only the voice excited him. Then he thought of Peggy Morton, who lived only a few blocks from a street filled with young men for hire, young men to match the shame-including voice on the tape, young men who shared the hideous lifestyle of Officer Pig and his lackey. He drove to West Hollywood and consummation.

Peggy Morton lived in a "security" building on Flores Avenue, two blocks south of the Sunset Strip. He had followed her home one morning from the all-night market on Santa Monica and Sweetzer, staying along the tree-shrouded sidewalk, listening as she conjugated verbs in French. There was something very simple and wholesome about her; and in the traumatic aftermath of Julia he had seized on that simplicity as the basis for his ardor.

It had taken him a scant week to establish the pretty young redhaired woman as an extreme creature of habit: She left her cashier's job at Tower Records at precisely midnight, and her lover Phil, the night manager of the store, would walk her down to the market, where she would buy groceries, then walk her home. Phil would sleep over only on Tuesdays and Fridays.

"It's our deal, sweetie," he heard Peggy say a half dozen times. "I have to study my French. You promised you wouldn't press me."

The good-natured, doltish Phil would protest briefly, then grab Peggy and her shopping bag in an exasperated embrace and walk away shaking his head. Peggy would then shake *her* head as if to say, "Men," and dig a bunch of keys out of her purse and unlock the first of the many doors that would take her up to her fourth-floor apartment.

The apartment building fascinated and challenged him. Seven stories of glass and steel and concrete, advertised by signs in its entrance foyer as "a 24-hour total electronic security environment." He shook his head at the sadness of people needing such protection and rose to the challenge. He knew that there were four keys on Peggy's key ring, and that they were all necessary to gain access to her apartment—he had heard Phil joke about it. He knew also that wall-mounted electronic movie cameras patrolled the foyer constantly. The first step had to be to obtain keys . . .

It was easily accomplished, but gained him only partial access. After three days of studying Peggy's routine, he knew that when she arrived at work at four o'clock she went first to the employees' "breakroom" at the back of the store. She would then leave her purse on a table next to the Coke machine and walk to the adjoining storeroom to check out the incoming supply of albums. He observed this through a sliding glass door for three days running. On the fourth day he made his move—and botched it when Peggy's returning footsteps forced him to run back into the store proper with only one key in his hand.

But it was the key to the front entrance foyer, and that night, dressed as a woman and carrying a bag of groceries as camouflage, he brazenly unlocked the door and walked straight to a bank of mailboxes that designated Peggy's apartment as 423. From there he circled the foyer and learned that a separate key was required for the elevator door. Undaunted, he noticed a door off to his left. It was unlocked. He opened it and walked down a dingy hallway to a laundry room filled with coin-operated washers and dryers. He scanned the room and noticed a wide ventilator shaft in the ceiling. Noise from the apartments above him caught his ears, and his wheels started to turn . . .

Again dressed as a woman, but this time wearing a tight cotton jumpsuit underneath the feminine garb, he parked across the street to wait for Peggy to return home. His tremors of expectation were so great that no thoughts of the homicide fisherman's voice crossed his mind.

Peggy showed at 12:35. She shifted her grocery bag and fumbled her new key into the lock and let herself in. He waited for half an hour, then walked over demurely and followed suit, partially shielding his face with his own shopping bag. He walked through the foyer to the laundry room and placed a hand-lettered "Out of Order" sign on the door, then bolted it shut from the inside. Breathing shallowly, he stripped off his loose fitting gingham dress and emptied his work tools from the bag: screwdriver, chisel, ball peen hammer, hacksaw, and silencer-fitted .32 automatic. He stuck them into the compartments of an army surplus cartridge belt, then wrapped the belt around his waist and donned surgical gloves.

Bringing to mind his few fond memories of Peggy, he stood up on top of the washer directly beneath the ventilator shaft and peered into the darkness, then took a deep breath and placed his hands above his head in a diving position and leaped upward until his arms caught the corrugated metal walls of the shaft's interior. With a huge, lung-straining effort he hoisted himself up into the shaft, flattening out his arms, shoulders, and legs to gain a purchase that propelled him slowly up. Feeling like a worm doing penance in hell, he inched forward, a foot at a time, modulating his breathing in concert with his movement. The shaft was stifling hot and the metal stung his skin through his jumpsuit.

He reached the second-floor connecting shaft, and found it wide enough to climb through. He moved along it, savoring the feeling of again being horizontal. The crawl space terminated at a metal plate covered with tiny holes. Cool air was pouring through them, and he squinted and saw that he was at ceiling level across the hallway from apartments 212 and 214. He rolled onto his back and removed the hammer and chisel from his cartridge belt, then twisted back on his stomach and wedged the chisel head into the edge of the plate and snapped it off with one sharp hammer blow. The plate dropped onto the blue carpeted hallway, and he crawled through the open hole and dropped to the floor in a handstand. He caught his breath and re-placed the metal plate crookedly in the shaft, then walked down the hall, his eyes constantly trawling for hidden security devices. Seeing none, he walked through two connecting doorways and up two flights of concrete service stairs, feeling his heartbeat reach a new crescendo with each step he took.

The fourth floor corridor was deserted. He walked to the door of apartment 423 and placed his ear to it. Silence. He took the .32 automatic from his belt and checked to see that the silencer was screwed tight to the barrel. Concentrating on the timbre of doltish Phil's voice, he rapped on the door and said, "Peg? It's me, babe."

There was a shuffling of feet within the apartment, followed by the fondly muttered words, "You crazy . . ." The door opened a moment later. When Peggy Morton saw the man in the black jumpsuit her hands flew to her mouth in surprise. She looked into his light blue eyes and saw longing. When she saw the gun in his hand she tried to scream, but nothing came out.

"Remember me," he said, and fired into her stomach.

There was a soft plop, and Peggy sank to her knees, her terrified mouth trying to form the word "No." He rested the gun barrel against her chest and squeezed the trigger. She pitched backward into her living room and ex-pelled a soft "No" along with a mouthful of blood. He stepped inside and closed the door behind him. Peggy's eyelids were fluttering and she was gasping for breath. He bent down and opened her robe. She was naked underneath it. He placed the barrel to her heart and fired. Her body lurched and her head snapped upwards. Blood poured from her mouth and nostrils. Her eyelids fluttered a last time, then closed forever.

He walked into the bedroom and found an oversized shift dress that looked like it would fit him, then rummaged in the dresser until he found a brunette wig and a large straw hat. He put the outfit on and checked his getaway image in the mirror, deciding that he was beautiful.

A circuit of the kitchen yielded a large, double-strength shopping bag and a stack of newspapers. He carried them into the living room, then placed them on the floor beside the body of his most recent beloved. He removed Peggy's blood-soaked robe and got his hacksaw. He lowered the saw and closed his eyes and felt sharp sprays of blood cut the air. Within minutes tissue, bone, and viscera had been separated and the pale yellow carpet had turned dark crimson.

He walked to the balcony and looked out at the silent jetstream of cars on the Sunset Strip. He wondered briefly where all the people were going, then walked back to his twenty-third beloved and picked up her severed arms and legs. He carried them to the edge of the balcony and flung them to the world, watching as they disappeared, weighted down with his power.

Now only the head and torso remained. He let the torso lie and wrapped the head in newspaper and placed it in the supermarket bag. Sighing, he walked out the door of the apartment and through the silent security building and into the street. At curbside he slid out Peggy Morton's dress and removed her wig and straw hat and dumped them in the gutter, knowing that he had met the equivalent of all of mankind's wars and had emerged the victor.

He took his trophy out of the shopping bag and walked along the sidewalk. At the corner he saw a beautiful, pristine white Cadillac. He placed Peggy Morton's head on the hood. It was a declaration of war. Warrior slogans passed through his mind. "To the victor belong the spoils" caught and stuck. He got his car and went looking for spartan revelry.

Benevolent voices propelled him down Santa Monica Boulevard. He drove slowly in the right lane, the tight rubber gloves numbing his hands on the wheel. There was little traffic, so the absence of street noise left him free to *listen*; to *hear* the thoughts of the young men lounging against stop signs and bus benches. Keeping eye contact was hard, and it would be even harder to make up his mind based on looks alone, so he stared straight ahead, throwing his encounter open to the voice of fate.

Near Plummer Park, crude hustler catcalls and importunings assailed him. He kept going; better *nothing* than someone nasty.

He crossed Fairfax, moving out of Boy's Town, frightened and relieved that his gauntlet was ending. Then he hit the red light at Crescent Heights and voices came down on him like shrapnel: "Good weed, Birdy. You carry dime bags for your johns and you'll clean up."

"I already cleaned up, what do you think I am, a fucking janitor?"

"It might not be a bad idea, beauty. Janitors get social security, jockers get the clap."

All three voices dissolved into laughter. He looked over. Two young blondes and the lackey. He gripped the wheel so hard that his numb hands came to life and twisted in spastic tremors, hitting the horn by accident. The voices stopped at the noise. He could feel their gazes zeroing in. The light turned green, the color reminding him of tape slithering through bloody apertures. He stood his ground; to run now would be cowardice. Cancer cells started to crawl over his windshield, and then a soft voice was at his passenger window.

"You looking for company?"

It was the lackey. Staring at the green light, he ran through a mental litany of his twenty-three beloveds. Their images calmed him; they *wanted* him to do it.

"I *said*, 'You want some company?'"

He nodded in return. The cancer cells vanished at the act of courage. He forced himself to look over and open the door and smile. The lackey smiled back, no recognition in his eyes. "The silent type, huh? Go ahead, stare. I know I'm gorgeous. I've got a pad down near La Cienega. Five minutes and Larry the Bird flies you straight to heaven."

The five minutes stretched into twenty-three eternities; twenty-three female voices saying "Yes." He nodded each time and felt himself go warm all over.

They pulled into the motel parking lot, Larry leading the way up to his room and closing the door behind them, whispering, "It's fifty. In advance." The poet reached into his jumpsuit and extracted two twenties and a ten. He handed them to Larry, who put them in a cigar box on the nightstand and said, "What'll it be?"

"Greek," the man said.

Larry laughed. "You'll love it, doll. You ain't been fucked till you been fucked by Larry the Bird."

The man shook his head. "No. You've got it mixed up. I want to fuck you."

Larry breathed out angrily. "Buddy, *you* got it all wrong. I don't take it up the ass, I give it up the ass. I been rippin' off butthole since high school. I'm Larry Bir—"

The first shot caught Larry in the groin. He crashed into the dresser, then slid to the floor. The man stood over him and sang, "On, o' noble Marshall, roll right down that field; with your banner flying o'er us, we will never yield." Larry's eyes came alive. He opened his mouth, and the man stuck the silencer-fitted barrel into it and squeezed off six shots. The back of Larry's head and the dresser behind it exploded. He removed the spent clip and reloaded, then rolled the dead hustler onto his back and pulled off his pants and jockey shorts. He spread Larry's legs and wedged the gun barrel into his rectum and pulled the trigger seven times. The last two shots ricocheted off the spinal cord and tore through the jugular as they exited, sending criss-crossed geysers of blood into the cordite-reeking air.

The poet got to his feet, surprised to find that he could hold himself steady. He held both of his hands in front of his face and noticed that they were steady, too. He pulled off his rubber gloves and felt symbolic life return to his hands. He had now killed twenty-three times for love, and once for revenge. He was capable of bringing death to man and woman, lover and rapist. He knelt beside the corpse and reached his hands into a pile of dead viscera and immersed them in blood, then turned on all the lights in the room and wrote on the wall in bloody finger strokes: "I am not Kathy's Klown."

Now that he knew it himself, he pondered the proper means of spreading the news to the world. He found the telephone and dialed "Operator," requesting the number of the Homicide Division, Los Angeles Police Department. The operator gave it to him and he dialed, drumming bloody fingers on the nightstand as he listened to the dial tone. Finally, a gruff voice answered, "Robbery/Homicide, Officer Huttner speaking. May I help you?"

"Yes," the man said, going on to explain that a very kind Detective Sergeant had rescued his dog. His daughter wanted to send the nice policeman a Valentine. She forgot his name, but remembered his badge number—1114. Would Officer Huttner get the word to the nice policeman?

Officer Huttner said "Shit" to himself and "Yes sir, what's the message?" into the mouthpiece.

The man said, "Let the war begin," then yanked the cord out of the wall and hurled the phone across the bloody motel room.

13

Lloyd drove to Parker Center at dawn, the possible ramifications of his outburst at the party banging in his head like cymbals gone mad. Whatever the upshot, from formal assault charges to departmental censure, he was going to be the object of an I.A.D. investigation that would result in his being immediately placed on a full-time specific assignment that would preclude investigating the killings. It was time to take his investigation underground, stay unavailable to the department in general and the I.A.D. witch-hunters in particular, make his amends to Dutch later and get the killer, whatever the price to his career.

Lloyd ran the six flights of stairs up to his office. There was a note on his desk from the night officer downstairs: "Badge 1114. Let the war begin? Probably a crank—Huttner." I.A.D. psychological warfare, Lloyd decided; religious fanatics were never subtle.

Lloyd walked down the hall to the junior officers' lounge, hoping that there would be no night-watch dicks lingering there. He was going to be out on the street for a long stretch, and coffee alone wouldn't do it.

The lounge was deserted. Lloyd checked the undersides of the lunch tables, the classic "Long-term surveillance" cops' hiding place. On his fourth try he was rewarded: a plastic baggie filled with Benzedrine tablets. He grabbed the whole bag. Thirty-one names on his stereo supply list *and* a one man stake-out of Whitey Haines's apartment. Better too much speed than too little.

The Parker Center corridors were coming alive with early arriving officers. Lloyd saw several unfamiliar men with crew cuts and stern looks give him the eye, and immediately made them for I.A.D. detectives. Back in his office, he saw that the papers on his desk had been gone over. He was raising his fist to slam the desk when his phone rang.

"Lloyd Hopkins," he said into the mouthpiece. "Who's this?"

A distressed male voice answered. "Sergeant, this is Captain Magruder, West Hollywood Sheriff's. We've got two homicides out here, separate locations. We've got a set of prints, and I'm certain they match the ones in your teletype on the Niemeyer killing. Can you . . ."

Lloyd went cold. "I'll meet you at the station in twenty minutes," he said.

It took him twenty-five, running red lights and siren all the way. He found Magruder at the Information Desk, in uniform, poring over a stack of folders. Noting his name tag, Lloyd said, "Captain, I'm Lloyd Hopkins."

Magruder jumped back as if stung by a swarm of bees. "Thank God," he said, sticking out a trembling hand. "Let's go into my office."

They walked down a hallway crowded with uniformed officers talking in animated whispers. Magruder opened his office door and pointed Lloyd to a chair, then sat down behind his desk and said, "Two homicides. Both last night. One woman, one man. Murder scenes a mile apart. Both victims blown to hell with a .32 automatic. Identical spent casings at both scenes. The woman was dismembered, probably with a saw. Her arms and legs were found in the swimming pool of the adjoining apartment building. Her head was wrapped up in a newspaper and placed on the hood of a car directly outside her apartment house. A nice girl, twenty-eight years old. The second victim was a fruit hustler. Worked out of a motel a few blocks from here. The killer stuck the .32 in his mouth and up his ass and blew him to shit. The night manager, who lives directly below, didn't hear a thing. She called us when blood started dripping down through her ceiling."

Lloyd, stunned beyond thought at the news of the male victim, watched Magruder reach into his desk drawer and pull out a fifth of bourbon. He poured a large shot into a coffee cup and downed it in one gulp. "Jesus, Hopkins," he said. "Holy Jesus Christ."

Lloyd declined the bottle. "Where were the prints found?" he asked.

"The fruit hustler's motel room," Magruder said. "On the telephone and the nightstand and next to some writing in blood on the walls."

"No sexual assault?"

"No way to tell. The guy's rectum was obliterated. The M.E. told me he'd never seen—"

Lloyd raised a hand in interruption. "Do the papers know about it yet?"

"I think so . . . but we haven't released any information. What have you got on the Niemeyer killing? Any leads you can give my men?"

"I've got nothing!" Lloyd screamed. Lowering his voice, he said, "Tell me about the fruit hustler."

"His name was Lawrence Craigie, a.k.a. Larry "The Bird," a.k.a. "Birdman." Middle thirties, blonde, muscles. I think he used to hustle off the street down near Plummer Park."

Lloyd's mind exploded, then coalesced around an incredible series of connections: Craigie, the witness at the 6/10/80 suicide; the "Bird" in Whitey Haines's bugged apartment. It *all* connected.

"You *think?*" Lloyd shouted. "What about his rap sheet?"

Magruder stammered, "We . . . We've run a make on him. All we got was unpaid traffic warrants. We—"

"And this guy was a known male prostitute? With no record at *all?*"

"Well . . . maybe he paid a lawyer to get his misdemeanors wiped."

Lloyd shook his head. "What about your vice files? What do your vice officers say about him?"

Magruder poured himself another drink and knocked it back. "The Vice

Squad doesn't come on duty until nightwatch," he said, "but I've already checked their files. There's nothing on Craigie."

Lloyd felt widening connections breathing down his neck. "The Tropicana Motel?" he asked.

"Yes." Magruder said. "How did you know?"

"Body removed? Premises sealed?"

"Yes."

"I'm going over. You've got officers stationed there?"

"Yes."

"Good. Call the motel and tell them I'm coming."

Lloyd stilled his mental tremors and ran out of Magruder's office. He drove the three blocks to the Tropicana Motel, expecting rare glimpses of hell and his own destiny.

He found an upholstered slaughterhouse, reeking of blood and shattered flesh. The young deputy who guarded the door contributed gory details. "You think this is bad, Sergeant? You shoulda been here earlier. The guy's brains were all over that dresser over there. The coroner had to scoop them into a plastic bag. They couldn't even mark the outline of the stiff with chalk, they had to use tape. Jesus."

Lloyd walked over to the dresser. The light blue carpet next to it was still sopping wet with blood. In the middle of the dark red expanse was the metallic tape outline of a spread-eagled dead man. He ran his eyes over the rest of the room: a large bed with purple velour coverlet, muscle boy statuettes, a cardboard box filled with chains, whips, and dildos.

Surveying the room again, Lloyd noticed that a large part of the wall above the bed had been covered with brown wrapping paper. He called to the deputy, "What's with this paper on the wall?"

The deputy said, "Oh, I forgot to tell you. There's some writing underneath. In blood. The dicks covered it up so the TV and newspaper guys wouldn't see it. They think maybe it's a clue."

Lloyd grabbed a corner of the wrapping paper and pulled it free. "I Am Not Kathy's Klown" stared down at him in bold, blood-formed letters. For one brief second, his computer jammed, whirled, and screeched. Then all the fuses blew out and the words blurred and metamorphosed into noise, followed by perfect silence.

Kathleen McCarthy and her court—"We had a following of equally bookish, lonely boys. Kathy's Klowns they were called." Dead women who resembled wholesome early sixties high school girls. A dead fruit hustler and his perverse, corrupt cop buddy and . . . and . . .

Lloyd felt the young deputy tugging at his sleeve. His silence became pure Satanic noise. He grabbed the deputy by the shoulders and pushed him into the wall. "Tell me about Haines," he whispered.

The young officer quaked and stammered out, "Wh-what?"

"Deputy Haines," Lloyd repeated slowly. "Tell me about him."

"Whitey Haines? He's a loner. He sticks to himself. I've heard talk that he takes dope. Th-that's all I know."

Lloyd released the deputy's shoulders. "Don't look so scared, son," he said.

The deputy swallowed and straightened his tie. "I'm not scared," he said.

"Good. You keep quiet about our conversation."

"Yes . . . Sir."

The telephone rang. The deputy picked it up, then handed it to Lloyd. "Sergeant, this is Officer Nagler from S.I.D.," a frenzied voice blurted out. "I've been trying to get you for hours. The switchboard at the Center tol—"

Lloyd cut him off. "What *is* it, Nagler?"

"Sergeant, it's a match. The index and pinky on the Niemeyer teletype match perfectly with the index and pinky I got off the tape recorder."

Lloyd dropped the receiver and walked out onto the balcony. He looked down at the parking lot filled with rubber-necking ghouls and sad curiosity seekers, then shifted his gaze to the street scene. Everything he saw was as awesome as a baby's first glimpse of life out of the womb and into the breach.

14

Propelled by a whirlwind of interlocking fates, Lloyd drove to Kathleen McCarthy's house. There was a note on the front door: "Buying books— Will return at noon—U.P.S. leave packages on steps."

Lloyd snapped the lock on the door with a short, flat kick. The door burst open, and he closed it behind him and headed straight for the bedroom. He went through the dresser first; intimate apparel, scented candles, and a bag of marijuana were revealed. He checked the walk-in closet. Boxes of books and record albums covered every inch of rack and floor space. There was a shelf at the back, partially hidden by an ironing board and rolled-up carpet. Lloyd ran a hand across it and hit smoothly finished wood that shifted at his touch. He reached up with both hands and pulled the object out. It was a large box of beautifully varnished oak with a brass hinged top. It was heavy; Lloyd strained as he lowered it first to his shoulders, then to the bedroom floor.

He pulled the box over to the bed and knelt beside it, wedging the ornamental gold lock off with his handcuff holder.

The box contained narrow, gold-bordered picture frames, arranged lengthwise on their edges. Lloyd pulled one out. Encased behind glass were shriveled red rose petals pressed on parchment. There was minute writing beneath the petals. He carried the frame over to a floor lamp and switched on the light and squinted to read it. Under the first petal on the left was written:

"12/13/68: Does he know that I broke up with Fritz? Does he hate me for my short interludes? Was he that tall man browsing through the Farmer's Market? Does he know how much I need him?"

Lloyd followed the floral tributes across the picture frame and across time: "11/24/69: O dearest, can you read my mind? Do you know how I return your homage in my diary? How it is all for you? How I would forever eschew fame to continue the growth our anonymous rapport gives me?" "2/15/71: I write this in the nude, darling, as I know you pick the flowers you send me. Do you feel my telepathic poetry? It comes from my *body*."

Lloyd put the frame down, knowing something was wrong—he should be more moved by Kathleen's words. He stood very still, knowing that if he forced it, it would never come. He closed his eyes to increase the depth of the silence, and then . . .

Even as it hit him, he started to shake his head in denial. It couldn't be, it was too incredible.

Lloyd emptied the oak box onto the bed. One by one, he held the picture frames to the light and read the dates beneath the withered petals. The dates corresponded with the murder dates of the women in his computer printouts, either exact matches or with a variance factor of two days at the most. But there were more than sixteen rose petals—there were twenty-three, going back to the summer of 1964.

Lloyd recalled Kathleen's words at the power plant. "The first time there was a poem, the second time just the flowers. And they kept coming for over eighteen years." He went through the glass cases again. The oldest rose fragments were dated 6/10/64—over eighteen years ago. The next oldest were dated 8/29/67, over three years later. What had the monster been doing during those three years? How many more had he killed, and *Why? Why? Why?*

Lloyd read over Kathleen's words and recalled the dead faces that matched them. Jeanette Willkie, D.O.D. 4/15/73, caustic poisoning; flowers dated 4/16/73, "Darling, have you kept yourself chaste for me? I have now been celibate four months for you." Mary Wardell, D.O.D. 1/6/74, strangled to death; flowers dated 1/8/74, "Thank you for my flowers, dearest. Did you see me last night by my window? I was nude for you." And on and on through Julia Niemeyer, D.O.D. 1/2/83, heroin overdose, butchered after death; flowers dated 1/3/83, "My tears stain this parchment, my love. I need you inside me so much."

Lloyd sat down on the bed, willing his raging mind silent. Innocent, romantic Kathleen, a mass murderer's obsessive love object. *"We had a following of equally lonely, bookish boys."*

Lloyd's mind jerked his body upright. Yearbooks—the *Marshall Baristonian*. He tore through drawers, shelves, closets and bookcases until he found them, wedged behind a disused TV set. 1962, 1963, 1964; pastel Naugahyde bound. He flipped through '62 and '63—no Kathleen, Kathy Kourt, or Kathy Klowns.

He was halfway through 1964 when he hit pay dirt—Delbert "Whitey" Haines, caught for posterity giving the raspberry sign. On the same page was a skinny, acne-faced boy named Lawrence "Birdman" Craigie, wittily denoted as "Bad news for L.B.J.'s Great Society." Lloyd flipped through a dozen more pages of blasted innocence before he found the Kathy Kourt: four plain-pretty girls in tweed skirts and cardigan sweaters looking up in awe at a similarly attired, heartbreakingly young Kathleen McCarthy. When he saw what it all meant, Lloyd started to tremble. The dead women were all variations of the girls in Kathy's Kourt. The same wholesome features, the same fatuous innocence, the same incipient acceptance of defeat.

Lloyd's tremors became full-out body shudders. Whispering "rabbit down the hole," he dug the list of tape recorder purchasers from his pocket and turned to the index of the 1964 *Baristonian*. Seconds later the final connection sprung to life: Verplanck, Theodore J., member of the Marshall

High School Class of 1964; Verplanck, Theodore, 1976 purchaser of a Watanabe A.F.Z. 999 recorder.

Lloyd studied the photograph of the genius killer as a smiling teenager. Intelligence formed the face; a terrible arrogance rendered the smile ice-cold. Theodore Verplanck had looked like a boy who had lived within himself, who had created his own world and armed it to the teeth with highly developed adolescent conceits. Shuddering, Lloyd pictured the coldness in the young eyes magnified by almost twenty years of murder. The thought filled him with awe.

Lloyd found the phone and dialed the California Department of Motor Vehicles Office in Sacramento, requesting a complete make on Theodore J. Verplanck. It took the switchboard operator five minutes to come back with the information: Theodore John Verplanck, D.O.B. 4/21/46, Los Angeles. Brown hair, blue eyes. 6', 155 lbs. No criminal record, no outstanding traffic warrants, no record of traffic violations. Two vehicles: 1978 Dodge Fiesta Van, P-O-E-T, 1980 Datsun 280Z, DLX-191. Address, res. and bus.—Teddy's Silverlake Camera, 1893 North Alvarado, L.A. 90048. (213) 663-2819.

Lloyd slammed down the receiver and finished writing the information in his notepad. His awe moved into a sense of irony: The poet-killer still lived in the old neighborhood. Taking a deep breath, he dialed 663-2819. After three rings, a recorded message came on. "Hi, this is Teddy Verplanck, welcoming your call to Teddy's Silverlake Camera. I'm out right now, but if you'd like to talk about camera supplies, photo-finishing or my super-high-quality portrait photography and candid group shootings, leave a message at the beep. Bye!"

After hanging up, Lloyd sat down on the bed, savoring the killer's voice, then clearing his mind for the final decision: Take Verplanck himself or call Parker Center and request a back-up team. He wavered for long minutes, then dialed his private office number. If he let it ring long enough, someone would pick it up and he could get a fix on what trustworthy officers were available.

The phone was picked up on the first ring. Lloyd grimaced. Something was wrong; he hadn't plugged in his answering machine. An unfamiliar voice came on the line. "This is Lieutenant Whelan, Internal Affairs. Sergeant Hopkins, this message was recorded to inform you that you are suspended from duty pending an I.A.D. investigation. Your regular office line is open. Call in and an I.A.D. officer will arrange for your initial interview.

You may have an attorney present and you will receive full pay until our investigation is settled."

Lloyd dropped the phone to the bed. So it ends, he thought. The final decision: They couldn't and wouldn't believe him, so they had to silence him. The final irony: They didn't love him the way he had loved them. The fulfillment of his Irish Protestant ethos would cost him his badge.

Noticing a small backyard through the bedroom window, Lloyd walked outside. Rows of daisies growing out of loosely packed dirt and a makeshift clothesline greeted him. He knelt down and plucked a daisy, then smelled it and ground it under his heel. Teddy Verplanck would probably not give up without a fight. He would have to kill him, which would mean never knowing *why*. Some sort of explanation from Whitey Haines had to be his first step, and if Verplanck took it into his mind to kill or flee while he was drumming a confession out of Haines he—

The sound of weeping interrupted Lloyd's thoughts. He walked back into the bedroom. Kathleen was standing over her bed, replacing the glass encased flowers in the oakwood box. She brushed tears out of her eyes as she worked, not even noticing his presence. Lloyd stared at her face; it was the most grief-stricken visage he had ever seen.

He walked to her side. Kathleen shrieked when his shadow eclipsed her. Her hands flew to her face and she started to back away; then recognition hit and she threw herself into Lloyd's arms. "There was a burglar," she whimpered. "He wanted to hurt my special things."

Lloyd held Kathleen tightly; it felt like grasping the loose ends of a trance. He rocked her head back and forth until she murmured, "My *Baristonians*," and shook herself free of his embrace and reached for the yearbooks scattered on the floor. Her desperate ruffling of pages angered Lloyd, and he said, "You could have gotten duplicates. It wouldn't have been much trouble. But you're going to have to rid yourself of them. They're killing you. Can't you see that?"

Kathleen came all the way out of her trance. "What are you talking about?" she said, looking up at Lloyd. "Are . . . Are you the one who broke in and hurt my things? My flowers? Are you?" Lloyd reached for her hands, but she yanked them away. "Tell me, goddamnit!"

"Yes," Lloyd said.

Kathleen looked at her yearbooks, then back at Lloyd. "You animal," she hissed. "You want to hurt me through my precious things." She clenched her hands into fists and hurled them at him. Lloyd let the ineffectual blows glance off his chest and shoulders. When she saw that she was inflicting no damage, Kathleen grabbed a brick bookend and flung it at his head.

The edge caught Lloyd's neck. Kathleen gasped and recoiled from the act. Lloyd wiped off a trickle of blood and held it up for her to see. "I'm proud of you," he said. "Do you want to be with me?"

Kathleen looked into his eyes and saw madness and power and harrowing need. Not knowing what to say, she took his hand. He cradled her to him and closed the door and turned off the light.

They undressed in the semidarkness. Kathleen kept her back to Lloyd. She pulled off her dress and stepped out of her pantyhose, afraid that another look at his eyes would prevent her from consummating this rite of passage. When they were nude they fell onto the bed and into each other's arms. They embraced fiercely, joined at odd places, her chin locked in his breastbone, his feet twisted into her ankles, her wrists bearing into his bloody neck. Soon they were coiled into one force and the pressure of their interlocking limbs forced them to separate as they began to go numb and lightheaded. In perfect synchronization they created a space between themselves, offering the most tentative of overtures to close that gap, a stroking of arms and shoulder blades and stomachs; caresses so light that soon they ceased to touch flesh and the space between them became the object of their love.

Lloyd began to see pure white light in the space, growing in and around and out of Kathleen. He drifted into the permutations of that light, and all the forms that came to him spoke of joy and kindness. He was still adrift when he felt Kathleen's hand between his legs, urging him to grow hard and fill the light-hallowed void between their bodies. Brief panic set in, but when she whispered, "Please, I *need* you," he followed her lead and violated the light and entered her and moved inside her until the light dissipated and they coiled and peaked together and he knew that it was blood he expelled; and then awful noise wrenched him from her, and she said very softly as he twisted into the bedcovers, "Hush, darling. Hush. It's just the stereo next door. It's not *here*. I'm *here*."

Lloyd dug into the pillows until he found silence. He felt Kathleen's hands stroking his back and turned around to face her. Her head was surrounded by floating amber halos. He reached up and stroked her hair, and the halos scattered into light. He watched them disappear and said, "I . . . I think I came blood."

Kathleen laughed. "No, it's just my period. Do you mind?"

Unconvinced, Lloyd said, "No," and shifted over to the middle of the bed. He took a quick inventory of his body, touching odd parts of himself, probing for wounds and disconnected tissue. Finding nothing but Kathleen's internal flow, he said, "I guess I'm all right. I think I am."

Kathleen laughed. "You *think* you are? Well, I'm wonderful. Because now I know that after all these years it was you. Eighteen long years, and now I know. Oh, darling!" She bent down and kissed his chest, running her fingers over his ribs, counting them.

When her hands dropped to his groin, Lloyd pushed her away. "I'm not your dream lover," he said, "but I know who he is. He's the murderer, Kathleen. I'm certain that he kills out of some twisted kind of love for you. He's killed twenty-odd women, going back to the middle sixties. Young women who looked like the girls in your court. He sends you flowers after each murder. I know it sounds incredible, but it's true."

Kathleen heard every word, nodding along in cadence. When Lloyd finished she reached over and switched on the lamp next to the bed. She saw that he was perfectly serious and therefore perfectly insane, terrified at violating his anonymity after close to two decades of courtship.

She decided to bring him out very slowly, as a mother would a brilliant but disturbed child. She put her head on his chest and pretended to need comfort while her mind ran in circles, looking for a wedge to break through his fear and give her access to his innermost heart. She thought of opposites: yin-yang, dark-light, truth-illusion. After a moment, she hit it: fantasy-reality. He must think that I believe his story, and so *I* must barter for his *real* story, the story that will let me break through fantasy and make our consummation real. He hates and fears music. If I am going to be his music, *I must find out why.*

Lloyd reached an arm over and drew Kathleen closer.

"Are you sad?" he asked. "Are you sad that it had to end this way? Are you frightened?"

Kathleen nuzzled into his chest. "No, I feel safe."

"Because of me?"

"Yes."

"That's because you have a real lover now."

He stroked her hair absently. "We have to talk about this," he said. "We have to get Marshall High circa '64 out of the way before we can be together. I need to get a handle on the killer before I take him. I need to learn all I can about him, to get this thing straight in my mind before I act. Do you understand?"

Kathleen nodded, shielding her eyes. "I understand," she said. "You want me to dig into my past for you. That way you can solve your puzzle and we can be lovers. Right?"

Lloyd smiled. "Right."

"But my past hurts, darling. It hurts to rehash it. Especially when you're such a puzzle yourself."

"I'll be less of a puzzle as we go on."

Angered at the condescension, Kathleen raised her head. "No, that's not true. I need to *know* you, don't you understand? No one knows you. But I *have* to."

"Look, sweetheart . . ."

Kathleen batted away his placating hand. "I need to know what happened to you," she said. "I need to know why you're afraid of music."

Lloyd began to tremble, and Kathleen saw his pale gray eyes turn inward and fill with terror. She took his hand. "Tell me," she said.

Lloyd's mind moved backward in time, collating moments of joy to counterbalance the horror story that only he and his mother and brother knew. He gained strength with each recollection, and when his mental time machine came to a halt in the spring of 1950 he knew that he had the courage to tell his story. Taking a deep breath, he began.

"In 1950, around my eighth birthday, my maternal grandfather came to Los Angeles to die. He was Irish; a Presbyterian minister. He was a widower with no family except my mother, and he wanted to be with her while the cancer ate him up. He moved in with us in April, and he brought everything he owned with him. Most of the stuff was junk; rock collections, religious knickknacks, stuffed animal heads, that kind of thing; but he also brought a fabulous collection of antique furniture—desks, dressers, wardrobes—all made of rosewood so well varnished that you could see your reflection just as in a mirror. Grandfather was a bitter, hateful man; a rabid anti-Catholic. He was also a brilliant storyteller. He used to take my brother Tom and me upstairs and tell us stories of the Irish Revolution and how the noble Black and Tans wiped out the Catholic rabble. I liked the stories, but I was smart enough to know that Grandfather was twisted with hate and that I shouldn't take what he said completely to heart. But it was different with Tom. He was six years older than me and already twisted with hate himself. He took Grandfather seriously, and the stories gave his hatred a form; he started aping Grandfather's broadsides against Catholics and Jews.

"Tom was fourteen then, and he didn't have a friend in the world. He used to make me play with him. He was bigger than me, so I had to go along with it or he'd beat me up. Dad was an electrician. He was obsessed with television. It was new, and he thought it was God's greatest gift to mankind. He had a workshop in our backyard. It was crammed to the rafters with TV sets and radios. He spent hours and hours out there, mixing and matching tubes and running electrical relays. He never watched TV for enjoyment; he was obsessed with it as an electrician. Tom loved TV, though. He believed everything he saw on it, and everything he heard on the old radio serials. But he hated being alone while he watched and listened. He didn't have any friends, so he used to make me sit with him out in the workshop, watching *Hopalong Cassidy*, and *Martin Kane, Private Detective* and all the rest. I hated it; I wanted to be outside playing with my dog or reading. Sometimes I tried to escape, and Tom would tie me up and make me watch. He . . . He . . ."

Lloyd faltered, and Kathleen watched his eyes shift in and out of focus, as if uncertain of what time period they were viewing. She put a gentle hand on his knee and said, "Go on, *please*."

Lloyd drew in another breath of fond memories.

"Grandfather's condition got worse. He started coughing up blood. I couldn't stand seeing it, so I took to running away, ditching school and hiding out for days at a time. I was befriended by an old derelict who lived in a tent on a vacant lot near the Silverlake Power Plant. His name was Dave. He was shell-shocked from the First World War, and the neighborhood merchants sort of looked after him, giving him stale bread and dented cans of beans and soup that they couldn't sell. Everyone thought Dave was retarded, but he wasn't; he slipped in and out of lucidity. I liked him; he was quiet, and he let me read in his tent when I ran away."

Lloyd hesitated, then plunged ahead, his voice taking on a resonance unlike anything Kathleen had ever heard.

"My parents decided to take Grandfather to Lake Arrowhead for Christmas. A last family outing before he died. On the day we were to leave I had a fight with Tom. He wanted me to watch television with him. I resisted, and he beat me up and tied me to a chair in Dad's workshop. He even taped my mouth shut. When it came time to leave for the lake, Tom left me there. I could hear him in the backyard telling Mother and Dad that I had run away. They believed him and left, leaving me alone in the shack. There was no way I could move a muscle or make a sound. I was there for a day or so, cramped up in awful pain, when I heard someone trying to break into the shack. I was scared at first, but then the door opened, and it was Dave. But he didn't rescue me. He turned on every TV set and radio in the shack and put a knife to my throat and made me touch him and eat him. He burned me with tube testers and hooked up live wires and stuck them up my ass. Then he raped me and hit me and burned me again and again, with the TVs and radios going full blast the whole time. After two days of hurting me, he left. He never turned off the noise. It grew and grew and grew and grew . . . Finally my family came home. Mother came running into the shack. She took the tape off my mouth and untied me and held me and asked me what happened. But I couldn't talk. I had screamed silently for so long that my vocal cords had shredded. Mother made me write down what had happened. After I did, she said, 'Tell no one of this. I will take care of everything.'

"Mother called a doctor. He came over and cleansed my wounds and sedated me. I woke up in my bed much later. I heard Tom screaming from his bedroom. I snuck over. Mother was lashing him with a brass studded belt. I heard Dad demanding to know what was happening and Mother telling him to shut up. I snuck downstairs. About an hour later, Mother left the house on foot. I followed her from a safe distance. She walked all the way up to the Silverlake Power Plant. She went straight up to Dave's tent. He was sitting on the ground reading a comic book. Mother took a gun from her purse and shot him six times in the head, then walked away. When I saw what she had done, I ran to her, and she held me and walked me back home. She took me to bed with her that night and gave me her breasts, and she taught me how to speak again when my voice returned and she nurtured me with many stories. After Grandfather died she would take me up to the attic and we would talk, surrounded by antiquity."

Rigid with pity and terror, tears streaming down her face, Kathleen breathed out: "And?"

"And," Lloyd said, "my mother gave me the Irish Protestant ethos and made me promise to protect innocence and seek courage. She told me stories and made me strong again. She's mute now, she had a stroke years ago and can't speak; so I talk to *her*. She can't respond, but I know she understands. And I seek courage and protect innocence. I killed a man in the Watts Riot. He was evil. I hunted him down and killed him. No one ever suspected Mother of killing Dave, no one ever suspected me of killing Richard Beller and if I have to kill him, no one will suspect me of ridding the world of Teddy Verplanck."

Kathleen went shock-still at the words "Teddy Verplanck." Caught in a benign web of her own memories, she said, "Teddy Verplanck? I knew him in high school. He was a weak, ineffectual boy. A very kind boy. He—"

Lloyd waved her quiet. "He's your dream lover. He was one of the Kathy Klowns back in high school; you just never knew it. Two of your other classmates are involved in the killings. A man named Delbert Haines and a man who was killed last night—Lawrence Craigie. I discovered a bugging device—a tape recorder, at Haines's apartment—that's what put me on to Verplanck. Now listen to me . . . Teddy has killed over twenty women. What I need from you is information on him. I need your insights, your . . ."

Kathleen leaped from the bed. "*You* are insane," she said softly. "After all these years you have to construct this policeman's fantasy to protect yourself? After all these years, you—"

"I'm not your dream lover, Kathleen. I'm a police officer. I have a duty to perform."

Kathleen shook her head frantically. "I'll *make* you prove it. I still have the poem from 1964. I'll make you copy it, then we'll compare handwritings."

She ran nude into the front room. Lloyd heard her murmuring to herself, and suddenly knew that she could never accept reality. He got up and pulled on his clothes, noting that in the aftermath of confession his sweat-drenched body was both relaxed and incandescently alive. Kathleen returned a moment later, holding a faded business card. She handed it to Lloyd. He read:

"6/10/64

My love for you
   now etched in blood;
My tears caked in
   resolute passion;
Hatred spent on me
   will
   metamorphose into
    love

> Clandestinely you
>   will be mine."

Lloyd handed the card back. "Teddy, you poor, twisted bastard." He bent and kissed Kathleen's cheek. "I have to go," he said, "but I'll be back when this is settled."

Kathleen watched him walk out the door, closing it on her entire past and all her recent hopes for the future. She picked up the phone and dialed Information, securing two telephone numbers. She dialed the first one breathlessly, and when a male voice came on the line, said, "Captain Peltz?"

"Yes."

"Captain, this is Kathleen McCarthy. Remember me? I met you at your party last night?"

"Sure, Lloyd's friend. How are you, Miss McCarthy?"

"I . . . I . . . I think Lloyd is crazy, Captain. He told me he killed a man in the Watts Riot, and that his mother killed a man and that—"

Dutch cut in, "Miss McCarthy, please be calm. Lloyd is in a bit of a crisis within the department, and I'm sure he's behaving erratically."

"But you don't understand! He's talking about killing people!"

Peltz laughed. "Policemen talk about such things. Please have him call me. Tell him it's important. And don't worry."

When she heard the receiver click, Kathleen steeled herself for the next call, then dialed. After six rings a soft tenor voice said: "Teddy's Silverlake Camera, may I help you?"

"Y . . . Yes . . . Is this Teddy Verplanck?"

"Yes, it is."

"Thank God! Look, you probably don't remember me, but my name is Kathleen McCarthy, and I . . ."

The soft voice went softer. "I remember you well."

"Good . . . Look, you may not believe this, but there's a crazy policeman out to get you. I—"

The soft voice interrupted. "Who is he?"

"His name is Lloyd Hopkins. He's about forty, and very big and tall. He drives a tan unmarked police car. He wants to hurt you."

The soft voice said, "I know that. But I won't let him. No one can hurt me. Thank you, Kathleen. I remember you very fondly. Goodbye."

"G . . . Goodbye."

Kathleen put down the phone and sat on the bed, surprised to find that she was still nude. She walked into the bathroom and stared at her body in the full-length mirror. It looked the same, but she knew that somehow it had changed and would never be completely hers again.

15

Running red lights and using his siren, Lloyd drove downtown. He left the car in an alley and ran the four blocks to Parker Center, taking a service elevator to the third floor S.I.D. offices, sending up silent prayers that Artie Cranfield would be the only data analyst on duty. Opening a door marked "Data Identification," he saw his prayers rewarded—Cranfield was alone in his office, hunched over a microscope.

The technician looked up when Lloyd closed the door behind him. "You're in trouble, Lloyd," he said. "Two I.A.D. bulls were here this morning. They said you were talking about becoming a TV star. They wanted to know if you had processed any evidence lately."

"What did you tell them?" Lloyd asked.

Artie laughed. "That you still owe me ten scoots on last year's World Series pool. It's true, you know."

Lloyd forced himself to laugh back. "I can do better than that. How'd you like your very own Watanabe A.F.Z. 999?"

"What?"

"You heard me. Nagler from Fingerprints has it. He's at his father's house in San Berdoo. Call the San Berdoo P.D., they'll give you the phone number."

"What do you *want*, Lloyd?"

"I want you to outfit me with a body wire, and I want six .38 caliber blank slugs."

Artie's face darkened. "When, Lloyd?" he asked.

"Right now," Lloyd said.

The outfitting took half an hour. When he was satisfied with the concealment and feedback check, Artie said, "You look scared, Lloyd."

This time Lloyd's laughter was genuine. "I am scared," he said.

*   *   *

Lloyd drove to West Hollywood. The body recorder constricted his chest, and each of his raging heartbeats felt like it was bringing him closer to a short-circuit suffocation.

There were no lights on in Whitey Haines's apartment. Lloyd checked his watch as he picked the lock with a credit card. 5:10. Daywatch ended at 5:00, and if Haines came home directly after getting off duty, he should arrive within half an hour.

The apartment was unchanged since his previous entry. Lloyd chased three Benzedrine tablets with sink water and stationed himself beside the door, accustoming himself to the darkness. After a few minutes the speed kicked in and went straight for his head, obliterating the smothering feeling in his chest. If it didn't take him too high, he would have enough juice for days of manhunting.

Lloyd's calm deepened, then shattered when he heard a key inserted into the lock. The door swung open a split second later, and blinding light caused him to reach up to shield his eyes. Before he could move, a flat handed karate chop glanced off his neck, long fingernails gouging his collarbone. Lloyd dropped to his knees as Whitey Haines shrieked and swung his billy club at his head. The club smashed into the wall and stuck, and as Haines tried to jerk it free Lloyd rolled onto his back and kicked out with both feet at Haines's groin, catching him full force and knocking him to the floor.

Haines retched for breath and went for his holstered revolver, wrenching it free just as Lloyd managed to get to his feet. He pointed the gun upward as Lloyd sidestepped, yanked the billy club out of the wall, and slammed it into his chest. Haines screamed and dropped the gun. Lloyd kicked it out of the way and drew his own .38 from his waistband. He leveled it at Haines's nose and gasped, "On your feet. Up against the wall and walk it back. Do it real slow."

Haines drew himself slowly upright, massaging his chest, then spread-eagling against the wall, his hands above his head. Lloyd nudged the .38 on the floor over to where he could pick it up without relinquishing his bead on him. When the gun was safely in his waistband he ran his free hand over Haines's uniformed body. He found what he was looking for in the lining of his Eisenhower jacket—a plain manila folder stuffed with paper, Craigie, Lawrence D., a.k.a. Bird, Birdy, Birdman, 1/29/46, typed on the front.

Haines started to blubber as he sensed Lloyd's eyes boring into the folder.

"I . . . I . . . I didn't kill him. It . . . It . . . was probably some crazy faggot. You gotta listen to me. You got—"

Lloyd kicked Haines's legs out from under him. Haines crashed to the floor and stifled a scream. Lloyd squatted beside him and said, "Don't fuck with me, Haines. I'll eat you up. I want you to sit on your couch while I do some reading. Then we're going to talk about the good old days in Silverlake. I'm a Silverlake homeboy myself, and I know you're going to love walking down memory lane with me. On your feet."

Haines stumbled over to his Naugahyde sofa and sat down, clenching and unclenching his fists and staring at the gleaming toes of his boots. Lloyd took a chair across from him, the manila folder in one hand, his .38 in the other. With one eye on Haines, he read through the pages of the Vice files.

The notations went back ten years. In the early '70s, Lawrence Craigie had been arrested regularly for soliciting homosexual acts and had been frequently questioned when found loitering in the vicinity of public restrooms. Those early reports carried the signatures of the entire eight-man Vice Squad. After 1976, all entries pertaining to Lawrence Craigie were filed by Deputy Delbert W. Haines, #408. The reports were ridiculously repetitive, and dubious question marks covered the later ones. When he saw the report dated 6/29/78, Lloyd laughed aloud. "Today I employed Lawrence Craigie as my vice finger man. I have told the men on the squad not to bust him. He is a good snitch. Respectfully—Delbert W. Haines, #408."

Lloyd laughed; booming stage laughter to cover the sound of his pushing the activator button on his body recorder. When he felt mild electric tendrils encircle his chest, he said, "An L.A. County Deputy Sheriff running dope and male prostitutes, getting kickbacks from fruit hustlers all over Boy's Town. What are you going to do with the Birdman dead? You'll have to find yourself a new sewer, and when the Sheriff's dicks link you to Craigie you'll have to find a new career."

Whitey Haines stared at his feet. "I'm clean all the way down the line," he said. "I don't know what the fuck you're talking about. I don't know nothing about Craigie's murder or any of that other shit. This is some kind of outlaw shit you're pulling on me or you would have brought another cop with you. You're a punk cop who likes to hassle other cops. I had your number the other day when you asked me about them suicides I reported. You wanna bust me for ripping off that vice folder, then bust on, homeboy, 'cause that's all you got on me."

Lloyd leaned forward. "Look at me, Haines. Look at me real close."

Haines took his eyes from the floor. Lloyd looked into them and said, "Tonight you pay your dues. One way or the other you are going to answer my questions."

"Go fuck yourself," Whitey Haines said.

Lloyd smiled, then held up his .38 snub nose and opened the chamber. He emptied five of the six rounds into his hand, then snapped the chamber shut and spun it. He cocked the hammer and placed the barrel on Haines's nose. "Teddy Verplanck," he said.

Whitey Haines's florid face went pale. His clenched hands mashed together so hard that Lloyd could hear tendons cracking. A network of veins pulsated in his neck, jerking his head away from the gun barrel. A thick layer of dry spittle coated his lips as he stammered, "J—just—a g—guy from high school."

Lloyd shook his head. "Not good enough, Whitey. Verplanck is a mass murderer. He killed Craigie and God knows how many women. He sends your old classmate Kathy McCarthy flowers each time he kills. He had your apartment bugged; that's how I connected you to Craigie. Teddy Verplanck was obsessed with you, and you're going to tell me why."

Haines fingered the badge pinned above his heart. "I—I don't know nothing."

Lloyd spun the chamber again. "You've got five chances. Whitey."

"You haven't got the guts," Haines whispered hoarsely.

Lloyd aimed between Haines's eyes and squeezed the trigger. The hammer clicked on an empty chamber. Haines started to dry-sob. His twitching hands grabbed at the sofa and ripped out hunks of Naugahyde and foam.

"Four chances," Lloyd said. "I'll give you a little help. Verplanck was in love with Kathy McCarthy. He was a Kathy Klown. Remember the Kathy Kourt and the Kathy Klowns? Does the date June 10th, 1964, mean anything to you? That was the day that Verplanck first contacted Kathy McCarthy. He sent her a poem about blood and tears and hatred being spent on him. You and Verplanck and the Birdman were all at Marshall High then. Did you and Craigie hurt Verplanck, Haines? Did you hate him and bleed him and—"

"No! No! No!" Haines screamed, wrapping his arms around himself and banging his head on the couch. "No! No!"

Lloyd stood up. He looked at Haines and felt the last piece of the puzzle slip into place, fusing Christmas of 1950 and a score of June 10ths into a door that unlocked the inner sanctum of hell. He put his gun to Haines's head and pulled the trigger two times. At the first hammer click Haines shrieked; at the second he clasped his hands and began murmuring prayers. Lloyd knelt beside him. "It's over, Whitey. For you, for Teddy, maybe even for me. Tell me why you and Craigie raped him."

Lloyd listened to Haines's prayers wind down, catching the tail end of the rosary in Latin. When he finished, Haines smoothed his sweat drenched khaki shirt and adjusted his badge. His voice was perfectly calm as he said, "I always figured that someone knew, that God would tell someone to hurt me for it. I've been seeing priests in my dreams for years. I always figured God would tell a priest to get me. I never figured he'd send a cop."

Lloyd sat down facing Haines, watching his features soften in his prelude to confession.

"Teddy Verplanck was weird," Whitey Haines said. "He didn't fit in and he didn't care. He wasn't a sosh and he wasn't an athlete and he wasn't a badass. He wasn't a loner, he was just different. He didn't have to prove himself by doing crazy shit, he just walked around school in his fruity ivy league clothes, and every time he looked at you you knew he thought you were scum. He printed up this poetry newspaper and stuffed it into every locker on the fucking campus. He made fun of me and Birdy and the Surfers and Vatos and nobody would fuck with him because he had this weird kind of juice, like he could read your mind, and if you fucked with him he'd put it in his newspaper and everyone would know.

"There were these love poems that he used to put in his paper. My sister was real smart; she figured out all the big words and the symbolic shit and told me that the poems were ripoffs of the great poets and dedicated to that snooty bitch Kathleen McCarthy. Sis sat next to her in Home Ec, she told me that the McCarthy cunt lived in this fantasy world where she thought that half the guys at Marshall had the hots for her and the other stuck-up bitches she hung out with. 'Cathy's Clown' was a big hit song then, and the McCarthy bitch told Sis that she had a hundred personal 'Cathy Clowns.' But Verplanck was the only clown, and he was afraid to hit up on McCarthy and she didn't even know he had the hots for her.

"Then Verplanck printed these poems attacking the Bird and me. People started giving us the fisheye in the quad. I was cracking jokes when Kennedy got knocked off, and Verplanck stared me down. It was like he was ripping off my juice for himself. I waited for a long time, until just before graduation of '64. Then I figured it out. I had my sister write this fake note from Kathy McCarthy to Verplanck, telling him to meet her in the bell tower room after school. Birdy and I were there. We were only going to hurt him. We kicked his ass good, but even when he was all beat up he still had more juice than we did. That's why I did it. Birdy just followed me like he always did."

Haines hesitated. Lloyd watched him grope for words to conclude his story. When nothing came, he said, "Do you feel shame, Haines? Pity? Do you feel anything?"

Whitey Haines pulled his features into a rock hard mask that brooked no mercy. "I'm glad I told you," he said, "but I don't think I feel nothing. I feel bad about the Birdman, but he was born to die freaky. I've been revenging myself all my life. I was born to live hard. Verplanck was just in the wrong place at the wrong time. He got what he paid for. I say tough shit. I say I've paid my dues all the way down the line. I say fuck 'em all and save six for the pallbearers." It was the most eloquent moment of his life. Haines looked at Lloyd and said, "Well, Sergeant. What now?"

"You have no right to be a policeman," Lloyd said, opening his shirt and showing Haines the tape recorder hook-up. "You deserve to die, but I'm not equipped for cold-blooded killing. This tape will be on Captain Magruder's desk in the morning. You'll be through as a Deputy Sheriff."

Haines breathed out slowly as his sentence was passed. "What are you going to do with Verplanck?" he asked.

Lloyd smiled. "Save him or kill him. Whatever it takes."

Haines smiled back. "Right on, homeboy. Right on."

Lloyd took out a handkerchief and wiped the door knob, the arms of the chair and the grips of Haines's service revolver. "It'll only take a second, Whitey," he said.

Haines nodded. "I know."

"You won't feel much."

"I know."

Lloyd walked to the door. Haines said, "Those were blanks in your gun, right?" Lloyd raised a hand in farewell. It felt like a giving of absolution. "Yeah. Take care, homeboy."

When the door closed, Whitey Haines walked into the bedroom and unlocked his gunrack. He reached up and took out his favorite possession—a sawed-off .10 gauge double barrelled shotgun, the weapon he was saving for the close quarters apocalypse that he knew would one day come his way. After slipping shells into the chambers, Whitey let his mind drift back to

Marshall High and the good old days. When the memories started to hurt he jammed the barrels into his mouth and tripped both triggers.

Lloyd was unlocking his car when he heard the explosion. He sent up a plea for mercy and drove to Silverlake.

16

Teddy Verplanck was parked across the street from his camera store sanctuary, waiting for the arrival of a tan unmarked police car. Within minutes of the incredible phone call he had thrown his entire set of consummation tools into a canvas duffle bag and had run for his safeguard unregistered car and the one-on-one combat that would decide his fate. Somehow, through chance or divine intervention, he had been given the opportunity to fight for the very soul of his beloved Kathy. He had been passed the torch by Kathy herself, and an eighteen-year-old covenant was about to be fulfilled. He thought of the armaments now resting in his trunk: silencer-fitted .32, .30 caliber M-1 carbine, two-edged fire axe, custom-made six-shot Derringer, spiked, lead-filled baseball bat. He had the technology and the love to make it work.

Two hours after the call, the car pulled up. Teddy watched a very tall man get out and survey the front of the shop, walking the length of its facade, peering into the windows. The big man seemed to be savoring the moment, collating instinctive information for use against him. Teddy was beginning to enjoy his first glimpse of his foe when the big man bolted for his car, hung a U-turn and headed south on Alvarado.

Teddy took deep breaths and decided to pursue. He waited ten seconds and followed, catching the tan car at Alvarado and Temple and keeping a discreet distance behind as it led him to the Hollywood Freeway westbound. When it hit the on-ramp, the Matador accelerated full force into the middle lane. Teddy followed suit, certain that the policeman was so lost in thought that he would never notice the headlights behind him.

Ten minutes later the Matador exited at the Cahuenga Pass. Teddy let two cars get between them, keeping one eye on the road and the other on his foe's long radio antenna. They drove into the hills surrounding the Hollywood Bowl. Teddy saw the tan car come to an abrupt halt in front of a small thatch-covered house. He pulled to the curb several doors down and quietly squeezed out the passenger side, watching his policeman-adversary walk up the steps and knock on the door.

Moments later a woman opened the door and exclaimed, "Sarge! What brings you here?!"

The voice that answered her was hoarse and tight. "You won't believe what's been happening. I don't know if I believe it myself."

"Tell me about it," the woman said, closing the door behind them.

Teddy walked back to his car and settled in to wait, weighing the dark practicalities of his situation. He knew that it had to be a vendetta waged by one man—Detective Sergeant Lloyd Hopkins—or he would have been deluged with policemen before this. It *had to be* that Hopkins wanted Kathy for himself and was willing to forgo due process to get her.

Comforted by the knowledge that the force arrayed against him consisted of only one man, Teddy formulated a plan for elimination, then thought of the path that had brought him to this point.

He had spent the days after June 10, 1964, regrouping in his art and observing the mutiny of Kathy's Kourt.

His initial outrage against his violators had become tragic validation of his art; he had paid for his art in blood, and now it was time to take his blood knowledge and reach for the stars. But the pages he filled up were turgid and hollow, timid and obsessed with form. And they were completely subservient to the drama that was taking place in the rotunda court: a betrayal so brutal that he knew it rivaled his own recent devastation.

One by one, hurling maiming prose, the girls of Kathy's Kourt attacked their leader in the very spot where she had given them every sustaining ounce of her love. They called her frigid and a no-talent shanty mick. They told her that her no-dating policy was a cheap ploy to save them for scuzzy lesbian encounters that she was too cowardly to initiate. They called her a prissy, derivative poet. They left her with nothing but tears, and he knew that they had to pay.

But the price eluded him, and he was too fragmented in his own life to pursue the payoff. He spent a year writing an epic poem on the themes of rape and betrayal. When the poem was completed he knew that it was trash and burned it. He grieved for the loss of his art and turned to the sad efficacy of a craft—photography. He knew the rudiments, he knew the business end, and above all he knew that it would supply him with the means to live well and seek beauty in an ugly world.

He became a proficient, unimaginative commercial photographer, earning a decent living by selling his photographs to newspapers and magazines. But Kathy was always with him, and thoughts of her brought back the terror of June 1964 full force. He knew that he had to combat that terror, that he would not be worthy of Kathy's memory until he had conquered the fear that always came with it. So for the first time in his life, he sought the purely physical.

Hundreds of hours of weightlifting and calisthenics transformed the puny body he had always secretly despised into a rock-hard machine; a like amount of time earned him a black belt in karate. He learned about weaponry, becoming an expert rifle and pistol shot. With the gathering of these worldly skills came a concurrent lessening of terror. As he grew stronger his fear became rage and he began to contemplate the murder of the Kathy Kourt betrayers. Death schemes dominated his thoughts, yet last vestiges of fear prevented him from taking action.

Self-disgust was returning in force when he hit on the solution. He needed a rite of blood passage with which to test himself before beginning his revenge. He spent weeks speculating on the means, without results, until one night a phrase from Eliot jumped into his mind and stuck there: "Below, the boardhound and the boar, pursue their pattern as before, yet reconciled among the stars."

He knew immediately where that pattern was taking him—the inland regions of Catalina Island, where wild boars roamed in herds. He sailed over the following week, bringing with him a six-shot Derringer and a weighted baseball bat with sharpened ten-penny nails driven into the head. Carrying only those weapons and a canteen of water, he hiked by nightfall into the middle of the Catalina outback, prepared to kill or die.

It was dawn when he spotted three boars grazing next to a stream. He raised his baseball bat and charged them. One boar retreated, but the other two stood their ground, their tusks pointing straight at him. He was within killing range when they charged. He feinted, and they rushed past him. He waited two seconds, then feinted in the opposite direction, and when the boars snorted in frustration and turned to ram him, he sidestepped again and swung his bat downward at the closest one, catching it in the head, the impact of the blow wrenching the bat from his hands.

The wounded boar writhed on the ground, squealing and flailing at the embedded bat with its hooves. The other boar turned around, then stood on its hind legs and leaped at him. This time he didn't feint or sidestep. He stood perfectly still, and when the boar's tusks were almost in his face he raised the Derringer and blew its brains out.

On his exultant return hike he let the dozens of boars that he saw live in peace. At last "reconciled among the stars," he took the tourist steamship back to L.A. proper and began plotting the deaths of Midge Curtis, Charlotte Reilly, Laurel Jensen, and Mary Kunz, first determining their whereabouts through phone calls to the Marshall High Records Office. When he learned that all four girls were scholarship students at Eastern colleges he felt his hatred for them grow in quantum leaps. Now their motive for betraying Kathy was clearly delineated. Academically validated, and thrilled with the prospect of leaving Los Angeles, they had spurned their mentor's plans to remain in L.A. and be their teacher, attributing it to the basest of desires. He felt his rage branch out into deepening areas of contempt. Kathy would be avenged, and soon.

He compiled his college itinerary and left for points east on Christmas day, 1966. Two carefully staged accidental deaths, one forced drug overdose and one killing that matched the Boston Strangler M.O. comprised his mission.

He landed in snowbound Philadelphia and rented a hotel room for three weeks, then set out by rented car on his circuit of Brandeis, Temple, Columbia, and Wheaton Universities. He was armed with caustic agents, strangling cord, narcotics, and formidable reserves of bloodstained love. He was invulnerable at all levels but one, for when he saw Laurel Jensen sitting alone in the Student Union at Brandeis he knew she was *of* Kathy, and that he could never harm anyone who was once so close to his beloved. Glimpses of Charlotte Reilly browsing the Columbia bookstore confirmed the symbiotic thrust of their union. He didn't bother to search out the other two girls; he knew that to see them would render him as vulnerable as a child at its mother's breast.

He flew home to Los Angeles, wondering how he could have paid such a severe price and not even have his art or his mission as a reward. He wondered what he was going to do with his life. He fought fear by strict adherence to the most stringent martial arts disciplines and by the penance of prolonged fasting followed by ascetic desert sojourns where he clubbed coyotes to death and roasted their carcasses over fires he built and nurtured with desert tools and his own breath. Nothing worked. The fear still drove him. He was certain that he was going insane, that his mind was a tuning fork that attracted hungry animals who would one day eat him up. He couldn't think of Kathy—the animals might pick up his thoughts and descend on her.

Then suddenly things changed. He heard the meditation tape for the first time. And then he met Jane Wilhelm.

Emboldened by his sojourn in the past, Teddy walked over to the thatch-covered house and stationed himself behind the towering hibiscus plants adjoining the front porch. After a few minutes he heard voices coming from inside, and seconds later the door opened and the policeman was standing there, shivering against the chill night air.

The woman joined him, huddling into his arms, saying softly, "You promise that you'll be real careful and call me after you catch the son of a bitch?"

The big man said, "Yes," then bent and kissed her on the lips. "No protracted farewells," the woman said as she closed the door behind her.

Teddy got to his feet as he watched the tan police car drive off. He pulled a pushbutton stiletto from his pocket. Lloyd Hopkins was going to die soon, and he was going to die regretful of this last visit to his mistress.

He walked to the front door and drummed light knuckles across it. Joyous laughter answered the intimacy of the knock. He heard footsteps approaching the door and flattened himself off to the side of it, the knife held against his leg. The door burst open and the woman's voice called out, "Sarge? I knew you were too smart to turn down my offer. I knew—"

He jumped from his hiding place to find the woman framed in the doorway in an attitude of longing. It took seconds for her hopeful face to turn terrified, and when he saw recognition flash in her eyes he raised his knife and held it before her, then flicked it lightly across her cheek. Her hands jumped to her face as blood spurted into her eyes, and he raised a hand to her throat to silence her potential screams. His hand was at the neck of her sweater when he slid on the doormat and crashed to his knees. Joanie's sweater ripped free in his hands, and as he tried to get to his feet she swung the door onto his arm and kicked at his face. A pointed toe caught his mouth and ripped it open. He spit out blood and stabbed blindly through the crack in the doorway. Joanie screamed and kicked again at his face. He ducked at the last second and grabbed her ankle as it descended, yanking it upward, bringing her down in a flailing tangle of limbs. She scuttled backward as he got to his feet and walked inside, weaving the stiletto in front of him in a slow figure-eight pattern. He turned to close the door, and she kicked out and sent a floor lamp crashing into his back. Stunned, he jumped backward, his body weight slamming the door shut.

Joanie got to her feet and stumbled back into her dining room. She wiped blood from her eyes and banged her arms sideways, looking for weapons, her eyes never straying from the jumpsuited figure advancing slowly toward her. Her right arm caught the back of a deck chair, and she hurled it at him. He kicked it out of his way and inched forward teasingly, in a parody of stealth, his knife movements becoming more and more intricate. Joanie crashed into her dining room table and grabbed blindly at a stack of dishes, scattering them, getting her hands on only one dish, then finding herself without the strength to throw it.

She dropped the dish and stepped backward. When she touched the wall she realized that there was no place left to run and opened her mouth to scream. When a gurgling sound came out, Teddy raised his stiletto and threw it at her heart. The knife caught and Joanie felt her life burst, then seep out in a network of fissures. As bright light became darkness she slid to the floor and murmured, "Do-wah, wah-wah-do . . . ," then surrendered herself to the dark.

Teddy found the bathroom and cleansed his split lips with mouthwash, wincing against the pain but going on to douse the wounds with the whole bottle as penance for allowing himself to be bloodied. The pain enraged him. Hatred of Lloyd Hopkins and contempt for the puny bureaucracy he represented burst out of his every pore.

Let them all know, he decided; let the world know that he was willing to play the game. He found the telephone and dialed O. "I'm in Hollywood and I want to report a murder," he said.

The stunned operator put him directly through to the switchboard at the Hollywood station. "Los Angeles Police Department," the switchboard officer said.

Teddy spoke succinctly into the mouthpiece: "Come to 8911 Bowlcrest Drive. The door will be open. There's a dead woman on the floor. Tell Sergeant Lloyd Hopkins that it's open season on police groupies."

"And what is your name, sir?" the switchboard officer asked.

Teddy said, "My name is about to become a household word," and hung up.

The bewildering phone call was relayed from the switchboard officer to the desk officer, who flashed on the name "Lloyd Hopkins" and remem-

bered that Hopkins was a good friend of Captain Peltz, the daywatch commander. Having heard rumors that Hopkins was in trouble with I.A.D., the
desk officer called Peltz at home with the information. "The operator got
the message slightly garbled, Captain," he said. "She thought it was a crank,
but she did mention a dead woman and your buddy Sergeant Hopkins, so I
thought I'd call you."

Dutch Peltz went cold from head to foot. "What *exactly* was the message?" he asked.

"I don't know. Just something about a dead woman and your bu . . ."

Dutch's voice, filled with worry, interrupted. "Did the caller leave an address?"

"Yes, sir. 8911 Bowlcrest."

Dutch wrote it down and said, "Have two officers meet me there in
twenty minutes and tell no one about this call. Do you understand?"

Dutch didn't wait for an answer, or bother to hang up the phone. He
threw on slacks and sweater over his pajamas and ran for his car.

17

Frock-coated figures wielding razor-edged crucifixes chased him across an
open field. In the distance a large stone house shimmered in the glow of a
white hot spotlight. The house was encircled by iron fencing linked together by musical clefs, and he knew that if he could hit the fence and sur-
round himself with benevolent sound he would survive the onslaught of the
cross killers.

The fence exploded as he made contact, hurtling him through barriers of
wood, glass, and metal. Hieroglyphics flashed before his eyes; computer
printouts that twisted into the shapes of contorted limbs and bombarded
him past a last barrier of pulsating red light and into a sedately furnished
living room fronted with triangular bay windows. The walls were covered
with faded photographs and gnarled flower branches. As he moved closer
he saw that the pictures and branches formed a door that he could will
open. He was willing himself into a pitch-black trance when a succession of

crosses slammed into him and pinned him to the wall. The photographs and branches descended on him.

Lloyd jerked awake, slamming his knees into the dashboard. It was dawn. He looked through the windshield and saw a half-familiar Silverlake side street, then looked at his haggard face in the rearview mirror and felt it all come back: Haines, Verplanck and his planned stakeout around the corner from Silverlake Camera. The speed had boomeranged and had combined with his nervous tension to knock him out. The killer was a block away, asleep. It was time.

Lloyd walked over to Alvarado. The street was perfectly still, and no lights issued from the red brick building that housed the camera store. Remembering that Verplanck's motor vehicle registration listed an identical business and home address, he stared up at the second-story windows, then checked the parking lot next door. Verplanck's Dodge van and Datsun sedan were parked side by side.

Lloyd walked around to the alley in back of the building. There was a fire escape that reached up to the second floor and a metal fire door. The door looked impregnable, but there was an unshaded window with a deep brick ledge about four feet off to its right. It was the only possible access.

Lloyd leaped for the bottom rung of the fire escape. His hands caught iron and he hauled himself up the steps. At the second-story landing he gave the metal door a gentle push. No give; it was locked from the inside. Lloyd eyed the window, then stood up on the railing and flattened himself into the wall. He took a bead on the ledge and pushed off, landing on it squarely, grasping the window runner to hold himself steady. When his heartbeat subsided to the point where he could think, he looked down and saw that the window led into a small, darkened room filled with cardboard boxes. If he could get in he could reach the apartment proper without rousing Verplanck.

Squatting on the ledge, Lloyd got a grip on the bottom of the window runner and pushed in and up. The window squeaked open and he lowered himself into a closet-sized storage space reeking of chemicals and mildew. There was a door at the front of the room. Lloyd drew his .38 and nudged it open, entering into a carpeted hallway. Using his gun as a directional finder, he crept down it until he came to an open door.

He braced himself head first into the wall and peered in. An empty bedroom with a neatly made bed. Picasso prints on the walls. A connecting door into a bathroom. Complete silence.

Lloyd tiptoed into the bathroom. Immaculate white porcelain; polished brass fixtures. There was a half-open door next to the sink. He looked through the crack and saw steps leading downstairs. He inched down them with painstaking slowness, his gun arm extended to its maximum length, his finger on the trigger.

The steps ended at the back of a large room filled with cardboard photographic displays. Lloyd felt his tension ridden body breathe out of its own accord. Verplanck was gone, he could *feel* it.

Lloyd surveyed the front of the store. It looked like camera stores everywhere: wood counter, neatly arrayed cameras in glass cases, cheerful children and cuddly animals beaming down from the walls.

Treading silently, he walked back upstairs, wondering where Verplanck had spent the night and why he hadn't taken one of his cars.

The second floor was still eerily silent. Lloyd walked through the bathroom and bedroom and down the hall to an ornate oak door. He pushed it open with his gun barrel and screamed. Triangular bay windows made up the front wall. Huge photographs of Whitey Haines and Birdman Craigie covered the side walls, interspersed with taped-on rose branches, the whole collage united by crisscrossed smearings of dried blood.

Lloyd walked along the walls, looking for details to prove his dream a fake, a coincidence, anything but what he couldn't let it mean. He saw dried semen on the photos, crusted over the genital areas of both Haines and Craigie, the word "Kathy" finger-painted in blood. Beneath the photographs there were small holes in the wall stuffed with excrement. The holes were at waist level; higher up the white wallpaper surrounding the photographs bore fingernail tracks and bite marks.

Lloyd screamed again. He ran back through the hallway and bathroom and downstairs. When he reached the first floor he crashed over a pile of cartons and stumbled out the front door. If his dream was for real, then music would save him. Dodging traffic, he ran across Alvarado and around the corner to his car. He hit the ignition and fumbled the radio on, catching the end of a commercial jingle. His mental colors and textures were returning to normal when an alarmed electronic voice leaped out at him:

"The 'Hollywood Slaughterer' has claimed his third victim in twenty-four hours, and police are gearing up for the greatest manhunt in Los Angeles history! Last night the body of forty-two-year-old actress-singer Joan Pratt was discovered in her Hollywood Hills home, making her the third person to die violently in the Hollywood area in the past two days. Lieutenant Walter Perkins of the L.A.P.D.'s Hollywood Division and Captain Bruce Magruder of the West Hollywood Sheriff's are holding a joint news conference this morning at Parker Center to discuss the massive manhunt and to advise the Hollywood area populace on security measures to thwart the killer or killers. Captain Magruder told reporters this morning that 'The Sheriff's department and L.A.P.D. have deployed our largest force of street officers ever in our effort to catch this killer. We firmly believe that this person's insanity is peaking and that he will try to kill again soon. There will be helicopter patrols throughout the Hollywood–West Hollywood areas, as well as a concentrated deployment of officers on foot. Our efforts will not cease until the killer is caught. Our entire detective force is tracking down every available lead. In the meantime, remember: This killer has killed both men *and* women. I urge all Hollywood residents not, repeat, *not* to stay alone tonight. Buddy up, for your own safety. We bel . . .'"

Lloyd began to whimper. He kicked the radio housing, then ripped the metal box free of the dashboard and hurled it out the window. Joanie was dead. His genius had become the door to a telepathic charnel house. He could read Teddy's thoughts and Teddy could read his. The dream and Joanie's death; a logic-defying fraternal bonding that would spawn more and more and more horror; a horror that would only end with the killing of his evil symbiotic twin. He looked in the rearview mirror and saw Teddy Verplanck's yearbook picture. The transmogrification was complete. Lloyd drove to the old neighborhood to tell his family that the Irish Protestant ethos was a one-way ticket to hell.

Dutch Peltz sat in his office at the Hollywood Station, armed for betrayal with the Polaroid snapshot of a nude man and woman.

Since he had refused to press assault charges, the Internal Affairs officers investigating Lloyd had been swarming over him in an attempt to find other perfidies that they could bring to light to offset Lloyd's threatened media barrage. They had no idea that the L.A.P.D.'s most brilliant detective had been intimately familiar with Joan Pratt, the third victim of the Hollywood Slaughterer. The photograph was enough evidence to end Lloyd's career at best and have him shot on sight at worst.

Dutch walked to the window and looked out, thinking that he may have already signed away his own best years. His refusal to file charges would cost him his command of I.A.D., and if anyone found out that he had withheld the photograph and of his knowledge of the anonymous phone call that had mentioned Lloyd's name, he would be brought to departmental trial and suffer the ignominy of possible criminal prosecution. Dutch swallowed and asked himself the only question that made any sense. Was Lloyd a murderer? Was his protégé/mentor/son a killer brilliantly concealed by the cloak of genius? Was he a textbook schizophrenic, an academically identifiable split-personality monster? *It couldn't be.*

Yet there was a logical narrative line that said "maybe." Lloyd's erratic behavior throughout the years, his recent obsession with murdered women, his outburst at the party. *That* he had seen himself. When coupled with the traumatic aftermath of his wife and daughters' desertion and Kathleen McCarthy's phone call and the anonymous phone call and Joan Pratt's body and the nude snapshot and—

Dutch couldn't finish the thought. He looked at his telephone. He could call I.A.D. and save himself, dooming Lloyd, but maybe saving innocent lives. He could do nothing or he could track down Lloyd himself. His sleepless night, filled with images of Joan Pratt's body, had given him a good command of his options. Then Dutch asked himself the only other question that made sense. Who mattered the most*!* When "Lloyd" resounded through him, he tore up the photograph. He would clear the case himself.

When he got to the old wood-framed house on Griffith Park and St. Elmo, Lloyd went straight to the attic and a thirty-two-year-old treasure trove of antiquity. He traced patterns on dust-covered rosewood surfaces and marveled at his mother's foresight. She had never sold the furniture because she knew that one day her son would need to commune in the very spot that had formed his character. Lloyd felt another hand resting on his, guiding him in his artwork. The hand forced him to draw death's heads and lightning bolts. He took a last look at his past and future, then went downstairs to wake up his brother.

While Lloyd stood over him, Tom Hopkins ripped out the squares of synthetic grass that covered the ground adjoining their father's electronics shack. When he got to bare dirt he whimpered, and Lloyd handed him a shovel and said, "Dig." He obeyed, and within minutes Lloyd was hauling out wooden boxes filled with shotguns and a steamer trunk containing handguns and automatic rifles. Astonished to find the weaponry well oiled and ready to use, he looked at his brother and shook his head. "I've underestimated you," he said.

Tom said, "Bad times are coming down, Lloydy. I gotta get my shit to-gether."

Lloyd reached down into the hole and pulled out a reinforced plastic bag filled with individually wrapped .44 magnums. He hefted one, then stuck it in his waistband. "What else have you got?" he asked.

"I got a dozen A.K. 47s, five or six sawed-offs and a shitload of ammo," Tom said.

Lloyd slammed his hands onto Tom's shoulders, forcing him to his knees. "Just two things, Tommy," he said, "and then our slate will be clean. One, when you get your shit together you've got nothing but a big pile of shit; two, stay scared of me and you'll survive."

Lloyd grabbed a Remington 30.06 and a handful of shells. Tom pulled a pint of bourbon from his pocket and took a long drink. When he offered him the bottle Lloyd shook his head and looked up at his mother's bedroom window. After a second the mute old woman appeared. Lloyd knew that she knew and had come to offer a silent goodbye. He blew her a soft kiss and walked to his car.

All that remained was to set a time and place.

Lloyd drove to a pay phone and dialed Silverlake Camera. The call was answered on the first ring, as he knew it would be.

"Teddy's Silverlake Camera, may I help you?"

"This is Lloyd Hopkins. Are you about ready to die, Teddy?"

"No, I have too much to live for."

"No more innocent ones, Teddy. You've been waiting for me all these years. I'm ready, but don't hurt anyone else."

"Yes. It's just you and me. *Mano a mano?*"

"Yes. You want to pick the time and place, homeboy?"

"Do you know where the Silverlake Power Plant is?"

"Yes, it's an old friend of mine."

"I'll meet you there at midnight."

"I'll be there." Lloyd hung up, his mind bursting with lightning bolts and death.

Kathleen woke up late and put on coffee. She looked out her bedroom window to appraise the growth of her daisies and saw that they had been trampled. She thought of the neighborhood kids, then saw a huge footprint in the dirt and felt her stratagems for putting the crazy policeman out of her mind coalesce around a unifying thread. Instead of her planned day of opening the store and taking care of paperwork she would write her dream lover-betrayer into oblivion, consigning him to villainhood on the wings of a scathing broadside against weak, violence-obsessed men. She would meet Detective Sergeant Lloyd Hopkins head-on and defeat him.

After coffee, Kathleen sat down at her desk. Words fluttered through her mind, but refused to connect. She considered smoking a joint to get things going, then rejected the notion; it was too early for a reward. Feeling both her resistance and determination deepen, she walked into the front room and stared at the table by the cash register. Her own books, all six of them, arranged in a circle around a pasteboard blow-up of a four-star review in Ms.

Kathleen leafed through her own words at random, looking for old ways to say new things. She found passages decrying male hierarchies, but saw that the underlying symbolism centered on glass. She found acid portraits of men seeking shelter, but saw that the central theme was her own need to nurture. When she saw that her most righteously hateful prose featured crimson-flowered redemption, she felt her narcissistic nostalgia die. Her six volumes of poetry had earned her seven thousand four hundred dollars in advances and nothing in royalties. The advances for *Knife-edged Chaste* and *Notes from a Non-Kingdom* had paid off her long-standing Visa card bill, which she promptly ran up again, paying off the following year with the advance for *Hollywood Stillness*. *Staring down the Abyss*, *Womanworld*, and *Skirting the Void* had secured her her bookstore, which was now skirting the edge of bankruptcy. Her remaining volumes had bought her an abortion and a trip to New York, where her editor had gotten drunk and had stuck his hand up her dress at the Russian Tea Room.

Kathleen ran into her bedroom and hauled out her glass encased rose petals. She carried them back to her bookstore—living room and one by one hurled them at the walls, the sound of breaking glass and falling book-shelves drowning out her own screamed obscenities. When the detritus of the past eighteen years of her life had devastated the room, she wiped tears from her eyes and savored the destruction: books lying dead on the floor, glass shards reflecting off the carpet, plaster dust settling like fallout. The overall symbolism was perfection.

Then Kathleen noticed that something was off. A long black rubber cord was dangling from a torn-out section of her ceiling. She walked over and yanked on it, pulling loose spackle-covered wiring that extended all the way around the room. When she got to the wire's terminus a tiny micro-phone was revealed. She took up the cord and yanked a second time. The opposite end led to her front door. She opened the door and saw that the wire continued up to the roof, shielded by the branches of the eucalyptus tree that shaded the front porch.

Kathleen got a ladder. She stood it up on the ground beside the tree and followed the wire up to her roof. She could see that on the rooftop it had been concealed by a thin coat of tar. Squatting down, she ripped the wiring out and let it lead her to a mound of tar paper covered with shellac. She pulled the cord a last time. The tar paper ripped open and she looked down at a tape recorder wrapped in clear plastic.

At Parker Center, Dutch went through Lloyd's desk, hoping that the I.A.D. officers hadn't picked it clean. If he could find any of the homicide files that Lloyd was working with, maybe he could form a hypothesis and go from there.

Dutch rifled the drawers, prying the locks open with the buck knife he carried strapped to the inside of his gunbelt, coming away with nothing but pencils, paper clips and wanted posters. Slamming the drawers shut, he pried open the filing cabinets. Nothing; the Internal Affairs vultures had gotten there first.

Dutch emptied the wastebasket, sifting through illegible memos and sandwich wrappers. He was about to give up when he noticed a crumpled piece of Xerox paper. He held it up to the light. There was a list of thirty-one names and addresses in one column, and a list of electronic stores in the other. His heart gave a little leap; this had to be Lloyd's "suspect" list— the men that he had wanted him to detach officers to interview. It was slim—but something.

Dutch drove back to the Hollywood Station. He handed the list to the desk officer. "I want you to call all the men on this list," he said. "Lay out a *heavy* spiel about 'routine questioning.' Let me know who sounds panicky. I'm going out, but I'll be calling in."

From his office, Dutch called Lloyd's house. As he expected, there was no answer. He had called in vain every half hour throughout the night, and now it had become obvious that Lloyd had run to ground. But to where? He was either hiding out from I.A.D. and/or stalking his real or imaginary killer. He might also be—

Unable to complete the thought, Dutch recalled that Kathleen Mc-Carthy had mentioned at the party that her bookstore was on Yucca and Highland. She had fearfully denounced Lloyd on the phone last night, but *might* know of his whereabouts; Lloyd always sought out women when he was under stress.

Dutch drove to Yucca and Highland, pulling up in front of the *Feminist Bibliophile*, noticing immediately that the front door was half open and the porch was littered with broken glass.

Drawing his gun, Dutch walked inside. Mounds of broken glass, plaster, and books covered the floor. He walked back through the kitchen and into the bedroom. No more evidence of destruction, only the eeriness of a leather purse lying on the bed.

Dutch dug through the purse. Money and credit cards were intact, throwing the scene way out of kilter. When he found more money and Kathleen McCarthy's driver's license and car registration inside a calfskin wallet, he grabbed the telephone and dialed the desk at the station.

"This is Peltz," he said. "I want an all points bulletin issued. Kathleen Margaret McCarthy, white female, 5'9", 135, brown and brown, D.O.B. 11/21/46. Beige 1977 Volvo 1200, license LQM 957. Have the officers detain for questioning only. No force—this woman is not a suspect. I want her brought to my office."

"Isn't this a little irregular, Captain?" the switchboard officer asked.

"Shut up and issue it," Dutch said.

After checking the blocks around the bookstore unsuccessfully for Kathleen and her car, Dutch began to feel like a pent-up Judas having second thoughts. He knew that movement was the only antidote. Any destination was better than no destination.

Dutch drove to Silverlake. He knocked on the door of the old house that Lloyd had driven him by so many times, only halfheartedly expecting someone to answer; he knew that Lloyd's parents were old and lived in silent solitudes. When no one came to the door, he walked around the side of the house to the backyard.

Peering over the fence, Dutch saw a man swigging from a pint of whiskey and waving a large handgun in front of him. He stood perfectly still, recalling Lloyd's stories about his crazy older brother Tom. He watched the sad spectacle until Tom dropped the handgun to the ground and reached into a packing crate next to it, pulling out a machine gun.

Dutch gasped as he watched Tom weave drunkenly, muttering, "Fuckin' Lloyd don't know shit, fuckin' fuzz don't know how to deal with the fuckin' niggers, but I know for fuckin' sure. Fuckin' Lloyd thinks he can fuck with me, he's got another fuckin' think comin'."

Tom dropped the machine gun and fell to the dirt along with it. Dutch drew his .38 and squeezed through a gap in the fence. He crept along the side of the house, then sprinted over to Tom, his gun aimed straight at his head. "Freeze," he said as Tom looked up, bewildered.

"Lloydy took my goodies," he said. "He never wanted to play with me. He took my *best* stuff and still wouldn't play with me."

Dutch noticed a large hole in the ground next to him. He looked into it. The muzzles of a half-dozen sawed-off shotguns stared up at him. Leaving Tom weeping in the dirt, he ran back to his car. He gripped the steering wheel and wept himself, praying for God to give him the means to indict Lloyd with pity or release him with love.

18

Kathleen zigzagged through Hollywood side streets, destinationless, numbing the discovery of the tape recorder with silent chantings of her very best prose, the big policeman and his murder theory battling her words point-counterpoint until she ran a red light on Melrose and fishtailed across the intersection, narrowly missing a crossing guard and a flock of children.

She pulled to the curb, shaking, her literary holding action drowned out by the honking of angered motorists. She was past words now. Lloyd Hopkins and his conspiracies demanded to be disproved on the basis of fact. The tape recorder was evidence that would require the negation of superior evidence. It was time to visit an old classmate and let *his* words speak.

Dutch watched from the back of the room as Lieutenant Perkins, the commanding officer of the Hollywood Division detective squad, briefed his men on the Hollywood Slaughterer case:

"Our black-and-white units and helicopter patrols are going to keep the bastard from killing again, but you guys are going to find out who he is. The Sheriff's dicks are handling the Morton and Craigie cases, and may have an angle—some deputy who used to work West Hollywood Vice blew his brains out last night at his pad, and some of his old Vice partners say he was in tight with Craigie. Robbery/Homicide downtown is handling the Pratt case, which leaves you guys the job of rousting every pervert, burglar, dope addict, and all-purpose scumbag known to use violence in the Hollywood area. Utilize your snitches, your parolee files, your brains, and the feedback of the guys from patrol. Use whatever force you deem necessary."

The men got up and headed for the door. Noticing Dutch, Perkins called out, "Hey skipper, where the fuck is Lloyd Hopkins now that we really need him?"

Kathleen pulled up in front of the red brick building on Alvarado. She noticed a "Closed Due to Illness" sign on the front door and peered through the plate-glass window. Seeing nothing but shadow-covered countertops and stacks of boxes, she walked to the parking lot, immediately spotting a long yellow van with a license plate reading "P-O-E-T." She had her hand on the rear-door latch when darkness reached out and smothered her.

Lloyd waited for darkness in the park-playground a half mile below the Silverlake Power Plant. His car was hidden from street view behind the maintenance shed, the 30.06 and .44 magnum in the trunk, loaded and waiting. Sitting on a child's swing that shuddered under his weight, he compiled a list of the people he loved. His mother and Janice and Dutch headed the list, followed by his daughters and the many women who had brought him joy and laughter. Casting out hooks of memory to sustain the loving moments, he reeled in fellow cops and engaging criminals and even passersby he had glimpsed on the street. The more obscure the people became, the deeper the feeling of love touched him, and when twilight came and went Lloyd knew that if he died at midnight he would somehow live on in the vestiges of innocence that he saved from Teddy Verplanck.

Kathleen came out of the darkness with her eyes open, chemical stench and a glaze of tears her prelude to vision. She tried to blink to adjust her focus, but her eyelids wouldn't move. When squinting with all her might brought nothing but a flood of burning teardrops, she opened her mouth to scream. Some unseen closure rendered her mute, and she twisted her arms and kicked out with her legs, gouging the air for sound. Her arms remained fixed while her feet scraped an invisible surface, and as she flailed and heaved with every inch of her sense-blunted body she heard "sssh, sssh," and then there was a soft blackness daubing at her eyes, followed by bright light. *I am not blind and deaf, but I am dead,* she thought.

Kathleen's vision centered in on a low wooden table. When squinting brought her greater clarity she saw that it was only a few feet in front of her. As if in answer, the table, with a scraping sound, moved up to where she could touch it. She twisted her arms again, pain cutting through her numbness. *I am dead, but I am not cut in pieces.*

Willing all her senses into her eyes, Kathleen stared at the table. Gradually a room came into view behind it, and then the soft blackness was on and off her like the clicking of a camera shutter, and when the light returned the table was in her face, covered with naked plastic dolls with pins stuck into their crotches and huge heads made out of black-and-white photographs. *I am in hell and these are my fellow exiles.*

Sensing familiarity in the photograph heads, Kathleen forced her mind to function. *I am dead, but I can think.* She knew that the heads were somehow *of* her, somehow close to her, somehow—

Kathleen's senses snapped. Her arms contracted and her legs jerked upward, sending her chair to the floor. *I am alive and those are the girls from my court and the policeman was right and Teddy from high school is going to kill me.*

Invisible hands picked up the chair and turned it around. Kathleen squirmed and dug her heels into a soft white carpet. *My eyelids are forced open and my mouth is taped shut, but I am alive.*

Kathleen rolled her eyes to the far edges of the periphery, memorizing the wall in front of her in hopes of combining sight and thought into something more. When she assimilated all that she saw she began to sob, and tears once again turned her blind. Blood, rose branches, desecrated photographs and excrement. The stench assaulted her. *I am going to die.*

There was a whirring sound. Kathleen followed it with her mind and what remained of her vision. She saw a tape recorder on a nightstand. She tried to scream, and felt the tape across her mouth begin to give. *If I can scream, I—*

A soft sighing came over the tape machine. Kathleen breathed in through her nose and blew out with all her strength. The tape strained against her mouth and came loose along her lower lip. The soft sighing became a soft singsong voice:

"I am only worthy to love you in verse,
To spread my love on the wings of a curse;

They betrayed you and ripped you,
Buried in dread;
I avenged your heartache by killing them dead;
Then *you* betrayed me with
   Badge one-one-one-four-
You let him hurt me and make you his whore;
I cannot blame you—but tonight you must choose;
With your eyes sewn open you will watch
   him lose;
I will always love—love . . . love . . ."

The soft voice receded back into a sigh. Kathleen contorted her eyebrows and felt the stitches at the corners of her eyelids loosen. *I am going to kill him before he kills me.*

The tape recorder clicked off. Kathleen's chair was hoisted into the air and spun around in a perfect circle. She screamed and heard the faintest vibration of her own voice, then looked up at Teddy Verplanck in a skin-tight black jumpsuit. She formed words to keep from screaming and ripping the tape from her mouth prematurely. *He has become so handsome. Why are cruel-looking men always the most handsome?*

Teddy put a piece of paper in front of Kathleen's eyes. Biting down on her tongue, she read the block printed script: "I cannot speak to you yet. I am going to take out a knife and mark myself. I will not hurt you with the knife."

Kathleen nodded up and down, probing the tape with the tip of her tongue. Feeling was returning to her feet, and she could tell that she was wearing her blunt-toed wingtip flats. *Good kicking shoes.*

Teddy smiled at her nodding acquiescence and turned the paper over. The reverse side was covered with faded newspaper clippings. Kathleen's gaze zeroed in on them. When she saw that the clippings detailed accounts of women's murders she stifled a dry sob by biting her cheeks and methodically reading every word on the page. Her terror turned to rage and she bit down hard, until blood and spittle filled her mouth. She breathed deeply through her nose and thought: *I am going to maim him.*

Teddy threw the paper to the floor and unzipped the top of his jumpsuit, letting it fall to his waist. Kathleen looked at the most perfect male torso she had ever seen, transfixed by the rock-hard perfection until Teddy reached behind his back and drew out a penknife. He held the blade in front of his chest and twirled it like a baton, then pointed the blade at the area above his heart. When the tip drew blood, Kathleen twisted her hands on the arms of her chair, pushing out with her elbows, feeling her right hand bonds give way completely. *Now. Now. Now. Please God let me do it now. Now. Now.*

Teddy wiped his torso and squatted in front of Kathleen, holding his chest at her eye level. He whispered, "It's 10:30. We have to go soon. You were so beautiful with your eyes rolled back." He wiped his chest a second time. Kathleen saw that he had carved "K Mc" beside his left nipple. She gagged, but held on. *Now.*

Teddy squatted lower and smiled. Kathleen spat in his face and kicked out with both her legs, catching him in the groin, jerking her right hand free and pushing forward, toppling her chair just as Teddy crashed to the floor. She screamed and kicked again, her legs glancing off Teddy's stomach. Teddy dropped his knife and shrieked, wiping bloody spittle from his eyes. Kathleen lunged with her whole body and got her free hand on the knife, hooking her right leg around Teddy to draw her within stabbing range. Teddy twisted and flailed blindly with his arms. Kathleen brought the knife down in a swooping roundhouse at his abdomen. Teddy jerked backward and the blade cut air. Kathleen stabbed again, the knife snagging into the carpet. Teddy got to his knees and wrapped his fists into a hammer and swung down. Kathleen bared her teeth to bite as the blow arced toward her. She screamed and tasted blood when the hammer made contact. Then there was a throbbing red darkness.

Dutch watched the muster-room clock strike eleven. He shifted his gaze out the door to the front desk. The desk officer looked up from his telephone and called out, "Nothing yet, skipper. I've made contact with twenty-three out of the thirty-one. The rest are no answers or recorded messages. Nothing even remotely suspicious."

Nodding curtly in answer, Dutch said, "Keep trying" and walked out to the parking lot. He looked up at the black sky and saw the crisscrossed beacons of the helicopter patrols light up low cloud formations and the tops of Hollywood skyscrapers. Save for a skeletal station contingent, every Hollywood Division officer was on the street, on foot, in the air or in a black-and-white, armed to the teeth and pumped up for glory. Rolling imaginary dice, Dutch calculated the odds on accidental shootings by overeager cops at ten to one, rookies and promotion happy hot dogs the most likely blood spillers.

With Lloyd still missing and no clues to his whereabouts, he found that he didn't care. Blood was in the air, and nihilist rectitude was the night's prevailing logic. He had gone through cartons of Lloyd's arrest records from his Hollywood Division days, finding no indicators pointing to trauma that might have festered to the point of combustion; he had telephoned every one of Lloyd's girlfriends whose name he could recall. Nothing. Lloyd was guilty or Lloyd was innocent and Lloyd was nowhere. And if Lloyd was nowhere, then he, Captain Arthur F. Peltz, was a spiritual seeker who had gone to Mecca and had come away with unimpeachable evidence that life was shit.

Dutch walked back inside the station. He was halfway up the stairs to his office when the desk officer ran up to him. "I got a response to your A.P.B., Captain. Vehicle only. I wrote down the address." Dutch grabbed at the paper the officer was holding, then ran downstairs to the front desk and ran frenzied eyes over Lloyd's interview list. When 1893 N. Alvarado screamed out from both pieces of paper, he yelled, "Call the officers who called in the bulletin and tell them to resume patrol; this is mine!"

The desk officer nodded. Dutch ran up to his office and got his Ithaca pump. Lloyd was innocent and there was a monster to slay.

19

A winding two-lane access road led up to the Power Plant. It terminated at the base of a scrub-bush dotted hillside that rose steeply to the tall barbed-wire fence that enclosed the generator facility. There was a dirt parking lot off the left of the road, next to a tool shack sandwiched between two stanchions hung with high powered spotlights. Another spotlight housing was stationed directly across the blacktop, with feeder wires connecting to the Silverlake Reservoir a quarter of a mile north.

At 11:30, Lloyd walked up from the playground, staking out the territory as he trudged uphill, the 30.06 resting on his shoulder, the .44 magnum pressed to his leg. He knew only that since assuming his position on the street side of the playground at eight-thirty, six cars had driven northbound on the access road. Two were official Water and Power Department vehicles, presumably headed for the plant's administration offices. The four remaining cars had returned within an hour, meaning that the occupants had gotten stoned or laid on the hillside and had retreated back to L.A. proper. Which meant that Teddy Verplanck had arrived on foot or was in the process of driving up.

Lloyd walked north on the dirt shoulder, hugging the embankment that branched into Power Plant Hill. When he reached the last turn in the road he saw that he was correct. Two cars were parked next to the fence beside the tool shack; both were Water and Power vehicles.

The embankment ended, and Lloyd had to walk a stretch of pavement before he could scale the hill and establish a killing ground. He treaded lightly, his eyes constantly scanning his blind side. If Verplanck was nearby, he was probably hiding in the clump of trees adjoining the parked cars. He checked his watch: eleven forty-four. At precisely midnight he would blow that clump of trees to kingdom come.

The pavement ended, and Lloyd began to climb uphill, pushing forward slowly, dirt mounds breaking at his feet. He saw a tall scattering of scrub bushes looming in front of him and smiled as he realized that it was the perfect vantage point. He stopped and unslung his 30.06, checking the clip and flipping off the safeties. Everything was operative and set to go at a split second's notice.

Lloyd was within a yard of his objective when a shot rang out. He hesitated for a brief instant, then hurled himself head first into the dirt just as a second shot grazed his shoulder. He screamed and burrowed into the ground, waiting for a third shot to give him a direction to fire in. The only sound was the pounding of his own chest.

An electrically amplified voice cut the air: "Hopkins, I have Kathy. She has to choose."

Lloyd rolled into a sitting position and aimed his 30.06 at the sound of the voice. He knew that Verplanck was a conjuror who could assume shapes and voices and that Kathleen was safe somewhere in her web of fantasies. Clenching his bloodied shoulder into a huge ache to allow for the recoil, he fired off a full clip. When the shattering echoes died out, a laughing voice answered them. "You don't believe me, so I'll make you believe me."

A series of hellish shrieks followed, noises that no conjuror could artifice. Lloyd muttered "No, no, no," until the electronic voice called out, "Throw down your weapons and come out to meet me or she dies."

Lloyd hurled his rifle at the road. When it clattered onto the pavement he stood up and jammed his .44 magnum into the back of his waistband. He stumbled downhill, knowing that he and his evil counterpart were going to die together with no one but the strident woman poet to write their epitaph. He was murmuring "rabbit down the hole, rabbit down the hole," when white light blinded him and a white-hot hammer slammed him just above the heart. He flew back into the dirt and rolled like a dervish as the light bored into the ground by his side. Wiping dirt and tears from his eyes, he crawled for the pavement, watching the spotlight's reflections gradually illuminate Teddy holding Kathleen McCarthy in front of the toolshed. He tore through his blood-drenched shirt and felt his chest, then twisted his right arm and pawed at his back. A small frontal and a crisp exit wound. He would have the juice to kill Teddy before he bled to death.

Lloyd pulled out his .44 and spread himself prone, his eyes on the two spotlights next to the toolshed. Only the top light was on. Teddy and Kathleen were right below the housings, forty feet of blacktop and dirt away from the muzzle of his handcannon. One shot at the spotlight; one shot to take off Teddy's head.

Lloyd squeezed the trigger. The light exploded and died at the precise second that he saw Kathleen break free of Teddy's grasp and fall to the ground. He got to his feet and stumbled across the pavement, his gun arm extended, his left hand holding his trembling wrist steady. "Kathleen, hit the other light!" he screamed.

Lloyd moved forward into his last gauntlet of darkness, a red-black curtain that masked all his senses and enveloped him like a custom-made shroud. When the spotlight went on Teddy Verplanck was ten feet in front of him, coming to meet his destiny with a .32 automatic and a nail-studded baseball bat.

Both men fired at the same instant. Teddy clutched his chest and pitched backward just as Lloyd felt the bullet tear into his groin. His finger jerked the trigger and recoil sent the gun flying from his hand. He fell to the pavement and watched Teddy crawl toward him, the spikes on the baseball bat gleaming in the white-hot light.

Lloyd pulled out his .38 snub nose and held it upright, waiting for the moment when he could see Teddy's eyes. When Teddy was on top of him and the bat was descending and he could see that his blood brother's eyes were blue he pulled the trigger six times. There was nothing but the soft click of metal on metal as Lloyd screamed and blood burst from Teddy's mouth. Lloyd wondered how that could be and if he was dead, and then just before losing consciousness he saw Dutch Peltz wipe the blade that stuck out of his steel-toed paratrooper's boot.

20

The long transit of horror ended, and the three survivors began the longer process of healing.

Dutch had carried Lloyd and Teddy to his car, and with Kathleen weeping beside him had driven to the home of a doctor under indictment for dealing morphine. With Dutch's gun at his head the doctor had examined Lloyd, pronouncing him in need of an immediate transfusion of three pints of blood. Dutch checked Lloyd's driver's license and the I.D. cards he had taken from the body of Teddy Verplanck. Both men were type O+. The doctor performed the transfusion with a makeshift centrifuge to stimulate Teddy's heartbeat while Dutch whispered over and over that he would kill all the charges against him, regardless of the cost. Lloyd responded favorably to the transfer of blood, regaining consciousness as the doctor sedated Kathleen and removed the catgut stitches that anchored her eyelids to her brows. Dutch didn't tell Lloyd where the blood had come from. He didn't want him to know.

Leaving Lloyd and Kathleen at the doctor's house, Dutch drove the remains of Teddy Verplanck to their final resting place, a stretch of condemned beach known to be rife with industrial toxins. Hauling the body over a series of barbed wire fences, he had watched as the poisonous tide swept it away on the wings of a nightmare.

Dutch spent the next week with Kathleen and Lloyd, convincing the doctor to oversee their medical recovery. The house became a hospital with two patients, and when Kathleen came out of her sedation she told Dutch of how Teddy Verplanck had gagged her and slung her over his back, carrying her through the Silverlake hills on his way to ambush Lloyd.

He told her of how verse notations on Teddy Verplanck's calendar had led him to the reservoir and how if Lloyd was to survive as a policeman and a human being she would have to be very gentle and never talk to him about Teddy. Weeping, Kathleen agreed.

Dutch went on to say that he would destroy every official trace of Teddy Verplanck, but it would be her job to blunt Lloyd's terror-driven memory with love. "With all my heart," was her answer.

Lloyd was delirious for over a week. As his physical wounds healed, his nightmares took over, and gradually, between the gentlest of caresses, Kathleen succeeded in convincing him that the monster was dead and that mercy had somehow prevailed. Holding a mirror to his eyes, she told him tender stories and made him believe that Teddy Verplanck was not his brother but a separate entity who was sent to close out the books on all the anguish in his first forty years. Kathleen was a good storyteller, and tenuously, Lloyd started to believe her.

But as Kathleen pieced together the story of Teddy and Lloyd her own terror began. Her phone call to Silverlake Camera had caused the death of Joanie Pratt. Her reluctance to believe Lloyd and smash her own pitiful illusions had resulted in the destruction of a living, breathing woman. She felt it with *her* every breath, and when she touched Lloyd's devastated body it felt like a death sentence. Writing about it compounded the grief. It was a life sentence with no parole and no means of atonement.

A month to the day after the Silverlake *walpurgisnacht*, Lloyd discovered that he could walk. Dutch and Kathleen had discontinued their daily visits and the indictment-free doctor had taken him off his pain medication. He would have to retrieve his family and face his I.A.D. inquisitors soon, and before he did that there was a place that he had to visit.

The cab dropped him in front of a red brick building on North Alvarado. Lloyd picked the lock on the door and walked upstairs, not knowing if he wanted the worst of his nightmares confirmed or denied. Whatever he saw would determine the course of the rest of his life, but he still didn't know.

The nightmare room was empty. Lloyd felt his hopes soar and shatter. No blood, no photographs, no body waste, no rose branches. The walls had been painted a guileless light blue. The bay windows were boarded shut. He would never know.

"I knew you'd come."

Lloyd turned around at the voice. It was Dutch. "I've been staking the place out for days," he said. "I knew you'd come here before you got in touch with your family or reported back to duty."

Running light fingertips over the wall, Lloyd said, "What did you find here, Dutch? I have to know."

Dutch shook his head. "No. Not ever. Don't ever ask again. I doubted you and I almost betrayed you, but I've made my amends and I won't tell you that. Everything that I could find pertaining to Teddy Verplanck is destroyed. He never existed. If you and Kathleen and I believe that then maybe we can live like normal people."

Lloyd slammed the wall with his fist. "But I have to know! I've got to pay for Joanie Pratt, and I'm not a cop anymore, so I've got to figure out what it means so I can know what to do! I had this dream that Jesus God I just can't ex—"

Dutch walked over and put his hands on Lloyd's shoulders. "You're still a cop. I went to the Chief myself. I lied and I threatened and I groveled and it cost me my promotion and my I.A.D. command. Your trouble with I.A.D. never happened, just like Teddy never happened. But you owe me, and you're going to pay."

Lloyd wiped tears from his eyes. "What's the price?"

Dutch said, "Bury the past and get on with your life."

Lloyd got Janice's new address and flew up to San Francisco the following night. Janice was gone for the weekend, but the girls were there with her friend George, and when he walked through the door they pounced on him until he was certain that they would bruise every inch of his battered body. He had a brief moment of panic when they demanded a story, but the tale of the gentle lady poet and the cop satisfied them until it burst apart in a torrent of tears. Penny was the one to supply the conclusion. Holding Lloyd tightly, she said: "Happy stories are a new mode for you, Daddy. You'll get the hang of it. Picasso switched his style late in life, so can you."

Lloyd got a hotel room near Janice's apartment and spent the weekend with his daughters, taking them to Fisherman's Wharf and the zoo and the Museum of Natural History. When he dropped them off Sunday night George told him that Janice had a lover, an attorney specializing in tax shelters. He was the one Janice was spending the weekend with. Brief thoughts of wreaking havoc on the affair crossed his mind and he reflexively balled his hands into fists. Then images of Joanie Pratt rendered his blood thoughts stillborn. Lloyd kissed and hugged the girls goodbye and walked back to his hotel. Janice had a lover and he had Kathleen and he didn't know what he felt, let alone what it all meant.

On Monday morning Lloyd flew back to Los Angeles and took a cab to Parker Center. He walked up to the sixth floor, feeling the sore muscles around his groin wound stretch and tighten. It would still be weeks before he could make love, but when old doc dope pusher gave him the word he would sweep Kathleen off for a whole shitload of weekends.

The sixth-floor corridors were empty. Lloyd checked his watch. 10:35. Morning coffee break. The junior officers' lounge was probably packed. Dutch had undoubtedly covered his prolonged absence with some sort of story, so why not get the reunion amenities out of the way in one fell swoop?

Lloyd pushed the lounge door open. His face lit up at the sight of a huge roomful of shirt-sleeved men hunched over coffee and donuts, laughing and joking and making good-natured obscene gestures. He stood in the doorway savoring the picture until he felt the noise recede to a hush. Every man in the room was looking at him, and when they all rose to their feet and began to applaud he looked back into their faces and saw nothing but awe and love. The room swayed behind his tears, and shouted "bravos" coupled with the applause to drive him back out into the corridor, dashing more tears from his eyes, wondering what on earth it all *meant*.

Lloyd ran toward his office. He was fumbling in his pocket for his keys when Officer Artie Cranfield came up beside him and said, "Welcome back, Lloyd."

Lloyd pointed down the hallway and wiped his face. "What the fuck was that all about, Artie? What the fuck did all that *mean?*"

Artie looked puzzled, then wary. "Don't shit a shitter, Lloyd. There's a rumor all over the department that you cleared the Hollywood Slaughterer case. I don't know where it started, but everyone in Robbery/Homicide believes it, and so does half the L.A.P.D. The word is that Dutch Peltz told the chief himself and that the chief pulled the Internal Affairs bulls off your ass because keeping you *on* the Department was the best way to keep your mouth *shut*. You want to tell me about it?"

Lloyd's tears of bewilderment became tears of laughter. He opened his door and wiped his face with his sleeve. "The case was cleared by a woman, Artie. A left-wing cop-hater poet. Dig the irony and enjoy your tape recorder."

Lloyd closed the door on Artie Cranfield's baffled face. When he heard him walk away muttering to himself he switched on the light and looked at his cubicle. Everything was the same as when he had last seen it, except for a single red rose sticking out of a coffee cup on his desk. There was a piece of paper next to the cup. Lloyd picked it up and read:

Dearest L.—Protracted goodbyes are terrible, so I'll be brief. I have to go away. I have to go away because you have given me back my life, and now I have to see what I can do with it. I love you and I need your shelter and you need mine, but the mortar that binds us is blood, and if we stay together it will own us and we will never have the chance to be sane. I have given up the bookstore and my apartment. (It belongs to my creditors and the bank, anyway.) I have my car and a few hundred dollars in cash, and am taking off sans excess baggage for parts unknown. (Men have been doing it for years.) I have much on my mind, much writing to do. Does "Penance for Joanie Pratt" sound like a good title? She owns me, and if I give her my best then maybe I'll be forgiven. I hurt for our past, L.—But I hurt for your future most of all. You have chosen to stalk ugliness and try to replace it with your numbing kind of love, and that is a painful road to follow. Goodbye. Thank you. Thank you. Thank you.

K.

P.S. The rose is for Teddy. If we remember him, then he'll never be able to hurt us.

Lloyd put the paper down and picked up the flower. He held it to his cheek and juxtaposed the image with the spartan accoutrements of his trade. Floral-scented terror merged with metal filing cabinets, wanted posters, and a map of the city, producing pure white light. When Kathleen's words turned the light into music he drew the moment into the strongest fiber of his heart and carried it away.

BECAUSE THE NIGHT

To Edith Eisler

I must take charge of the liquid fire,
and storm the cities of human desire

—W. H. Auden

1

The liquor store stood at the tail end of a long stretch of neon, where the Hollywood Freeway cut across Sunset, the dividing line between bright lights and residential darkness.

The man in the yellow Toyota pulled into the bushes beside the on-ramp, twisting the wheel outward and snapping on the emergency brake in a single deft motion. He took a big-bore revolver from the glove compartment and stuck it inside a folded-up newspaper with the grip and trigger guard extended, then turned the ignition key to *accessory* and opened the car door. Breathing shallowly, he whispered, "Beyond the beyond," and walked up to the blinking fluorescent sign that spelled L-I-Q-U-O-R, the dividing line between his old life of fear and his new life of power.

When he walked through the open door, the man behind the counter noticed his expensive sports clothes and folded *Wall Street Journal* and decided he was a class Scotch buyer—Chivas or Walker Black at the least. He was about to offer assistance when the customer leaned over the counter, jabbed the newspaper at his chest and said, "Forty-one-caliber special load. Don't make me prove it. Give me the money."

The proprietor complied, keeping his eyes on the cash register to avoid memorizing the robber's features and giving him a reason to kill. He felt the man's finger on the trigger and caught the shadow of his head circling the store as he fumbled the cash into a paper bag. He was about to look up when he heard a sob behind him near the refrigerator case, followed by the sound of the robber cocking his gun. When he did look up, the *Wall Street Journal* was gone and a huge black barrel was descending, and then there was a cracking behind his ear and blood in his eyes.

The gunman leaped behind the counter and dragged the man, kicking and flailing, to the rear of the store, then crept to the cardboard beer display that stood next to the refrigerator case. He kicked the display over and saw a young woman in a navy pea coat huddled behind an old man in coveralls.

The robber weaved on his feet; nothing he had been taught had prepared him for three. His eyes shifted back and forth between the two whimpering in front of him and the counterman off to his left, searching for a neutral ground to tell him what to do. His vision crisscrossed the store, picking up geometric stacks of bottles, shelves piled with junk food, cut-outs of girls in bikinis drinking Rum Punch and Spañada. Nothing.

A scream was building in his throat when he saw the beige curtain that separated the store from the living quarters behind it. When a gust of wind ruffled the curtain he *did* scream—watching as the cotton folds assumed the shape of bars and hangman's nooses.

Now he knew.

He jerked the girl and the old man to their feet and shoved them to the curtain. When they were trembling in front of it, he dragged the counterman over and stationed him beside them. Muttering, "Green door, green door," he paced out five yards, wheeled and squeezed off three perfect head shots. The horrible beige curtain exploded into crimson.

2

Detective Sergeant Lloyd Hopkins stared across the desk at his best friend and mentor Captain Arthur Peltz, wondering when the Dutchman would end his preliminaries and get down to the reason why he had called him here. Everything from the L.A.P.D.'s touch football league to recent robbery bulletins had been discussed. Lloyd knew that since Janice and the girls had left him Dutch had to fish for conversational openers—he could never be direct when he wanted something. The rearing of families had always been their ice-breaker, but now that Lloyd was familyless, Dutch had to establish parities by roundabout means. Growing impatient and feeling ashamed of it, Lloyd looked out the window at the nightwatch revving up their black-and-whites and said, "You're troubled, Dutch. Tell me what it is and I'll help."

Dutch put down the quartz bookend he was fingering. "Jungle Jack Herzog. Ring a bell?"

Lloyd shook his head. "No."

Handing him a manila folder, Dutch said, "Officer Jacob Herzog, age thirty-four. Thirteen years on the job. An exemplary cop, balls like you wouldn't believe. Looked like a wimp, bench pressed two-fifty. Worked Metro, worked Intelligence Division plants, worked solo on vice loan-outs to every squad room in the city. Three citations for bravery. Known as the 'Alchemist,' because he could fake *anything*. He could be an old crippled man, a drunk marine, a fag, a low rider. You name it."

Lloyd's eyes bored in. "And?"

"And he's been missing for three weeks. You remember Marty Bergen? 'Old Yellowstreak'?"

"I know two jigs blew his partner in half with a ten-gauge and Bergen dropped his gun and ran like hell. I know he faced a trial board for cowardice under fire and got shitcanned from the Department. I know he published some short stories when he was working Hollenbeck Patrol and that he's been churning out anticop bullshit for the *Big Orange Insider* since he was fired. How does he figure in this?"

Dutch pointed to the folder. "Bergen was Herzog's best friend. Herzog spoke up for him at the trial board, made a big stink, dared the Department to fire him. The chief himself had him yanked off the streets, assigned to a desk job downtown—clerking at Personnel Records. But Jungle Jack was too good to be put to pasture. He's been working undercover, on requests from half the vice commanders on this side of the hill. He'd been here at Hollywood for the past couple of months. Walt Perkins requested him, paid him cash out of the snitch fund to glom liquor violators. Jack was knocking them dead where Walt's guys couldn't get in the door without being recognized."

Lloyd picked up the folder and put it in his jacket pocket. "Missing Person's Report? Family? Friends?"

"All negative, Lloyd. Herzog was a stone loner. No family except an elderly father. His landlord hasn't seen him in over a month, he hasn't shown up here *or* at his personnel job downtown."

"Booze? Dope? A pussy hound?"

Dutch sighed. "I would say that he was what you'd call an ascetic intellectual. And the Department doesn't seem to care—Walt and I are the first ones to even note his absence. He's been a sullen hardass since Bergen was canned."

Lloyd sighed back. "You've been using the past tense to describe Herzog, Dutchman. You think he's dead?"

"Yeah. Don't you?"

Lloyd's answer was interrupted by shouting from the downstairs muster room. There was the sound of footsteps in the hall, and seconds later a uniformed cop stuck his head in the doorway. "Liquor store on Sunset and Wilton, Skipper. Three people shot to death."

Lloyd began to tingle, his body going alternately hot and cold. "I'm going," he said.

3

The man in the yellow Toyota turned off Topanga Canyon Road and drove north on the Pacific Coast Highway, dawdling at stoplights so that his arrival at the Doctor's beach house would coincide exactly with dusk. As always, the dimming of daylight brought relief, brought the feeling of another gauntlet run and conquered. With darkness came his reward for being the Doctor's unexpendable right arm, the one person aside from the Night Tripper who knew just how far his "lonelies" could be tapped, dredged, milked, and exploited.

Spring was a sweet enemy, he thought. There were torturously long bouts of sunshine to contend with, transits that made nightfall that much more satisfying. This morning he had been up at dawn, running an eight-hour string of telephone credit checks on the names gleaned from the john books of the Doctor's hooker patients. A full day, with, hopefully, a fuller evening in store: his first grouping since taking three people for the mortal coil shuffle and maybe later a run to the South Bay singles bars to trawl for more rich lonelies.

The man's timing was perfect; he pulled off P.C.H. and down the access road just as the Doctor's introductory music wafted across the parking area.

Six cars—six lonelies; a full house. He would have to run for the speaker room before the Night Tripper got impatient.

Inside the house, the man ignored the baroque quartet issuing over the central speakers and made for a small rectangular room lined with acoustical padding. The walls held a master recording console with six speakers— one for each upstairs bedroom, with microphone jacks for each outlet and six pairs of headphones and an enormous twelve-spooled tape deck capable of recording the activity in *all* the bedrooms with the flick of a single switch.

He went to work, first turning on the power amp, then hitting the volume on all six speakers at once. A cacophony of chanting struck his ears and he turned the sound down. The lonelies were still shouting their mantras, working themselves into the trancelike state that was a necessary precondition to the Doctor's counseling. Getting out his notebook and pen, the man settled into a leather chair facing the console, waiting for the red lights on the amplifier to flash—his signal to listen in, record, and assess from his standpoint as Dr. John Havilland's executive officer.

He had held that position for two years; two years spent prowling Los Angeles for human prey. The Doctor had taught him to control his compulsions, and in payment for that service he had become the instrument that brought about realization of Havilland's own obsession.

As the Doctor explained it, a "consciousness implosion" had replaced the "consciousness explosion" of the 1960s, resulting in large numbers of people abandoning the old American gospels of home, hearth, and country, *and* the counterculture revelations of the sixties. Three exploitable facts remained, one indigenous to the naive pre-sixties psyche, two to the jaded post: God, sex, and drugs. Given the right people, the variations on those three themes would be infinite.

His assignment was to find the right people. Havilland described his prototypical chess piece as: "White, of either gender, the offspring of big money who never fit in and never grew up; weak, scared, bored to death and without purpose, but given to a mystical bent. They should be orphaned and living on trust funds or investment capital or severely estranged from their families and living on remittances. They should accede to the concept of the 'spiritual master' without the slightest awareness that what they really want is someone to tell them what to do. They should love drugs and possess marked sexuality. They should consider themselves rebels, but their rebelliousness should always have been actualized as timid participation in mass movements. Find these people for me. It will be easier than you might think; because as you search for them, they will be searching for me."

The search took him to singles bars, consciousness workshops, the ashrams of a half dozen gurus, and lectures on everything from New Left social mobilization to macrobiotic midwifery, and resulted in six people who met Havilland's criteria straight down the line and who fell for his charisma hook, line, and sinker. Along the way he served the Doctor in other capacities, burglarizing the homes of his legitimate patients; reconnoitering for information that would lead to the recruitment of more lonelies; screening sex ads in the underground tabloids for rich older people to pimp the lonelies to; planning his training sessions and keeping his elaborately cross-referenced files.

He had moved forward with the Doctor, indispensable as his procuror of human clay. Soon Havilland would embark on his most ambitious project, with him at his side. Last night he had proved his mettle superbly.

But the headaches . . .

The light above speaker number one flashed on, causing the man to drop his pen and reach for the headphones. He had managed to adjust them and plug in the jack when he heard the Doctor cough—his signal that it was time to pay careful attention and make notes about anything that seemed special or particularly useful.

First came a profusion of amenities, followed by the two lonelies praising the bedroom's decor. The man could hear the Doctor pooh-poohing the rococo tapestries, assuring his charges that such surroundings were their birthright.

"Get to it, Doc," the man muttered.

As if in answer, the Doctor said, "So much for light conversation. We're here to break through the prosaic, not dawdle in it. How did your ménage in Santa Barbara work out? Did you learn anything about yourselves? Exorcise any demons?"

A soft male voice answered. The man recognized the voice immediately and recalled his recruitment: the gay bar in West Hollywood; the plump executive type whose wary mien was a virtual neon sign announcing "frightened first-timer seeking sexual identity." The seduction had been easy and the seducee had met all the Doctor's criteria.

"We used the coke to get things started," the soft voice said. "Our client was old and afraid of displaying his body, but the coke got his juices running. I—"

A woman's voice interrupted: "*I* got the old geezer's juices going. He wasn't even down to his skivvies when I grabbed his crotch. He wanted the *woman* to take the lead; I sensed that as soon as we walked in the door and I saw all that science fiction art on the walls—amazons with chains and whips, all that shit. He—"

The soft male voice rose to a wail. "I was savoring the lead-in! Doctor said to take it slow, the guy wasn't pre-screened. We got him from the sex ads, and Doctor said that—"

"Bullshit!" the woman barked. "You wanted to get coked yourself, and you wanted the old guy to like you because you were the one with the dope, and if we played it your way the whole assignment would have been a cocaine tea party."

The man put down his pen as the executive type started to blubber. After a short interval of silence, the Doctor whispered, "Hush, Billy. Hush. Go out and sit in the hallway. I want to talk to Jane alone."

There were the sounds of footsteps over a hardwood floor and of a door slammed in rage. The man smiled in anticipation of some vintage Havilland. When the Doctor's voice came over the speaker, he took up his pen with a glee akin to love.

"You're letting your anger run you, Jane."

"I know, Doctor," the woman said.

"Your power lies in exercising it judiciously."

"I know."

"Was the assignment fulfilling?"

"Yes. I chose the sex and made them like it."

"But it felt hollow afterwards?"

"Yes and no. It was satisfying, but Billy and the old man were so *weak*!"

"Hush, Janey. You deserve to traffic with stronger egos. I'll keep my eye on the high-line personals. We'll find you some feisty intellectuals to butt heads with."

"And a partner with balls?"

"Nooo, you'll go solo next time."

The man heard Jane weep in gratitude. Shaking his head in loathing, he listened to the Doctor deliver his coup de grâce: "He paid you the full five thousand?"

"Yes, Doctor."

"Did you do something nice for yourself with your gratuity?"

"I bought myself a sweater."

"You could have done better than that."

"I—I wanted you to have the money, Doctor. I took the sweater just as a symbol of the assignment."

"Thank you, Jane. Everything else all right? Reciting your fear mantras? Following the program?"

"Yes, Doctor."

"Good. Then leave the money with me. I'll call you at the pay phone later this week."

"Yes, Doctor."

The sounds of departure forced the man to catch up with his note-taking. As if on cue, the Doctor clapped his hands and said, "Jesus, what an ugly creature. Speaker three, Goff. Efficacy training."

Goff plugged a jack into speaker number three and hit the *record* switch. When the tape spool began to spin, he tiptoed upstairs to watch. This would be his first visual auditing since blasting his "beyond" to hell, and he had to see how far the Night Tripper was taking his recruits. Only one of them was capable of approaching his own degree of extremity, and all his instincts told him that Havilland was just about to push him to it.

Goff was wrong. Peering through a crack in the door, he saw the Professor and the Bookworm kneeling on gym mats facing the mirror that covered the entire west wall. Their hands were clasped as if in prayer and Havilland was standing over them, murmuring words of encouragement. With Billy Boy and the Bull Dagger already counseled, it meant that the Doctor was saving the foxy redhead and the real psycho for last.

Goff pressed himself into the wall and stared into the bedroom just as the two men on the mats pulled off their undershirts and began shouting their fear mantras. "*Patria infinitum patria infinitum patria infinitum patria infinitum patria infinitum.*" With each repetition of the phrase they smashed their hands into their chests, each time harder, shouting louder and louder as the blows hit home. Throughout, they retained eye-to-eye contact with their own mirror images, never flinching, even as blood-dotted welts rose on their torsos.

Goff checked the second hand of his watch. One minute. Two. Three. Just when he thought the chanters would have to collapse, he heard the word "*Stop!*"

Havilland knelt on the mat, facing the men. Goff watched them move their eyes from the mirror to the eyes of the Doctor, then extend their right arms and squeeze their hands into fists. Havilland reached into the pocket of his lab coat and withdrew a disposable syringe and a handful of cotton balls. First he injected the Bookworm; then he wiped the needle and injected the Professor. Both lonelies swayed on their knees but remained upright.

The Doctor got to his feet, smiled, and said, "Think pure efficacy. Robert, you have been placed in a very wealthy home on assignment. A couple, an older man and woman, are drooling for your favors. The phone rings. They both go to answer it. Where do *you* go?"

Robert stammered, "T-to the b-bathroom? To check for drugs?"

Havilland shook his head. "No. You have drugs on the brain; it's a weak point of yours. Monte, what would *you* do?"

Monte wiped sweat from his chest and twisted to stare at himself in the mirror. "*I* would wonder why the call was so important that they both had to run for the phone, especially when I was there looking so groovy. So what I would do would be to run for an extension and pick it up the very second that the old fucker did, then listen in and see if there was any salient info I could get from the call."

Havilland smiled and said, "Bravo," then slapped Monte across the face and whispered, "Bravo, but always look at *me* when you answer. If you look at yourself you get the notion that you thought independently. Do you see the fallacy in that kind of thinking?"

Monte lowered his eyes, then brought them up to meet Havilland's. "Yes, Doctor."

"Good. Robert, a hypothetical question for you. Think pure efficacy and answer candidly. My supply of legally obtained pharmaceutical drugs runs out, because of new laws passed limiting hypnotics and the like to physicians with hospital affiliations. You crave them and come to realize that they are what you like most about being in my tutelage. What do you do?"

The Bookworm pondered the question, shifting his gaze back and forth from the mirror to the Doctor. Goff grinned when he realized that Havilland had given the lonelies a Pentothal jolt.

Finally, Robert whispered, "It would never happen to you. It just couldn't."

Havilland put his hands on Robert's shoulders and gave them a gentle squeeze. "The perfect answer. Monte would have intellectualized it, but your response was pure candor and pure heart. And of course you were right. I want you to both chant your mantras now. Hold eye contact with yourself, but think of *me*."

When Havilland started for the door, Goff padded downstairs and back to the speaker room. He rewound the efficacy training tape and placed the spool in a large manila envelope, then plugged his headphones into the middle speaker just in time to hear male/female sexual grunting move into strangled sighs and girlish giggles. The giggle became a high-pitched smoker's cough, and Goff himself laughed. It *was* the tight little redhead he had picked up at the Lingerie Club, the one who had devastated him with her Kundalini yoga positions. He had been lucky to get out of her Bunker Hill Towers condo alive.

The Doctor was the first to speak. "Bravo. Bravo." His monotone sent the woman into new gales of laughter. The man she had coupled with was still trying to catch his breath. Goff imagined him lying on the bed on the verge of a coronary.

The Doctor spoke again. "Later, Helen. I want to check the victim's pulse. You may have gone too far this time."

"Beyond the beyond," Helen said. "Isn't that our motto, Doctor?"

"Touché," the Doctor said. "I'll call you Thursday."

When a full five minutes of silence followed the sound of little Helen skipping gaily out the bedroom door, Goff's gut clenched. He knew that the male lover was the real psycho and that the Night Tripper was taking him a major step closer to his brink. Thus the shattering of glass and the obscenities that came in the wake of the stillness were expected, as were the expressions of concern from the Doctor. "It's all right, Richard, it really is. Sometimes 'beyond the beyond' means hating. First you have to accept that reality, then you have to work through it. You can't hate yourself for being what you are. You are basically *good* and *powerful*, or you wouldn't be with me now. You just happen to have an exceptionally high violence threshold to overcome in order to achieve your selfhood."

Thomas Goff shifted into memories of Richard Oldfield's recruitment, beginning with the crippled whore with the three-hundred-dollar-a-day smack habit he had met at Plato's Retreat West. She had told him of the stockbroker/bodybuilder/remittance man who paid five C-notes a pop to work her over because of her resemblance to the governess who had tortured him as a child. The approach at the health club had had the thrust of a nightmare; Oldfield looked enough like Goff to be taken for his fraternal twin, and he was dead-lifting four hundred pounds. But the bodybuilder had capitulated to the Doctor's machinations like a baby going for its mother's tit.

More breaking glass. Oldfield weeping. Havilland alternately whistling a

tune and murmuring, "There, there." Goff knew that the reversal was coming.

It arrived in the form of a slap in the face that filled the speaker with static. "You weakling," Dr. John Havilland hissed. "You picayune poseur. You
sycophantic whoremonger. I give you the best fuck in our program, promise
to take you where your chickenshit conscience would never permit you to
stray, and you respond by smashing windows and bawling."

"Doctor, please," Richard Oldfield whimpered.

"Please *what*, Richard?"

"Ple—you know . . ."

"You have to say it."

"Ple-please take me as far as I can go."

The Doctor sighed. "Soon, Richard. I'm going to be collecting a great
deal of information, and it should yield the name of a woman suitable for
you. Think of that when you go through your fear mantras."

"Thank you, Doctor John."

"Don't thank me, Richard. Your green doors are my green doors. Go
home now. I'm tired, and I'm going to dismiss the grouping early."

Goff heard the Doctor escort Oldfield to the door. The tape machine
recorded a hissing silence. The Night Tripper's executive officer imagined
it as being inhabited by nightmares in repose, manifested in cold manila
folders spilling out data that would transform human beings into chess
pieces. The Alchemist and his six offerings were just the beginning. A series of Havilland's slogans caused Goff to shudder back the headache that
was burning behind a beige curtain in his mind. Last night. Three. What if
the data keepers couldn't be bought? The headache throbbed through the
curtain, like a hungry worm eating at his brain.

Doors slamming above him; periods of stillness, followed by the staggered
departures of the lonelies. Mercedes and Audis pulling out onto P.C.H. and
more silence. Suddenly Goff was terrified.

"Bad thoughts, Thomas?"

Goff swung around in his chair, knocking his shorthand pad to the floor.
He looked up into the light brown eyes of Dr. John Havilland, locking his
own eyes into them exactly as the Doctor had taught him. "Just thoughts,
Doctor."

"Good. The papers are full of you. How does it feel?"

"It feels dark and quiet."

"Good. Does the 'psycho killer' speculation disturb you?"

"No, it amuses me because it's so far from the truth."

"You had to take out three?"

"Yes. I—I remembered your efficacy training. Some-sometime I might have to do it again."

"A cold gun? Untraceable?"

"Cold city. I stole it."

"Good. How are the headaches?"

"Not too bad. I chant if they really start to hurt."

"Good. If your vision starts to blur again, see me immediately, I'll give you an injection. Dreams?"

"Sometimes I dream about the Alchemist. He was good, wasn't he?"

"He was superb, Thomas. But he's gone. I scared him off the face of the earth."

Havilland handed Goff a slip of paper. "She's a legitimate patient—she phoned the office for an appointment. I checked her out with some girls in the life. She's a thousand dollars a night. Check out her john book—anyone who can afford her can afford us."

Goff looked at the slip: Linda Wilhite, 9819 Wilshire Blvd, 91W. He smiled. "It's an easy building. I've hit it before."

Havilland smiled back. "Good, Thomas. Go home now and enjoy your dreams."

"How do you know I'll enjoy them?"

"I *know* your dreams. I made them."

Goff watched the Doctor about-face and walk to the latticework patio that overlooked the beach. He let the Doctor's exit line linger in his mind, then turned off the tape console and walked outside to his car. He was about to hit the ignition when he noticed a mound of wadded up plastic on top of the dashboard. He grabbed at it and screamed, because he knew that it was *beige* plastic, and that meant that *he* knew.

Goff ripped the plastic trashbag to shreds, then slammed his fists into the dashboard until the pain numbed the screaming in his mind. Turning on the headlights, he saw something white under his windshield wiper. He got out of the car and examined it. The embossed business card of John R. Havilland, M.D., Practice in Psychiatry, stared at him. He turned the card over. Neatly printed on the back were the words *I know your nightmares*.

4

After thirty-six nonstop hours on the liquor store case, Lloyd Hopkins fell asleep in his cubicle at Parker Center and dreamed of annihilation. Sound waves bombarded him, predator birds attacked the willfully shut-off part of his brain where the man he had killed in the Watts Riot and the man he had tried to kill last year resided. The birds tore open jagged sections of sky, letting in crystals the color of blood. When he awakened he bludgeoned the images with quiet still-lifes of Janice and the girls in San Francisco, waiting for time to heal the wounds or reinforce the division. The liquor store/charnel house memory took over from there, pushing family love back into the safety compartment with his nightmares. Lloyd was relieved.

The death scene expanded in his mind, chalked like a forensic technician's marking grid. Off to his left were an open cash register, a counter scattered with tens and twenties, broken liquor bottles all along the lower shelves. Heel marks where the proprietor had been dragged to his execution. The right hand grid revealed an overturned cardboard beer display and heel marks where the two other victims had probably crouched to hide from the killer. Bisecting the grids was the crimson wind tunnel into the store's rear room, three bodies crumpled across a once beige curtain that was torn free from the doorway by the muzzle velocity of three hollow point .41 slugs smashing through three cranial vaults. There were no discernible trajectory or spatter marks; exploded brain and bone debris had rendered the tiny stockroom a slaughterhouse.

Lloyd shook himself further awake, thinking: *psychopath.* He walks into the store, pulls out a monster handcannon and demands the money, then sees or hears something that flips his switch. Enraged, he hops over the counter and drags the proprietor by the hair over to the doorway. The girl and the old man betray their presence. He knocks over the display cutout and makes them walk to the curtain. Then he takes them out with three bull's-eyes from a top-heavy, unvented revolver with monster recoil, leaving the money on the counter. A volcano with ice-water fuel injection.

Lloyd stood up and stretched. Feeling the last residue of sleep dissipate, he walked down the hall to the men's room and stood before the sink, alternately staring at himself in the mirror and running cold water over his face. He ignored the sound of early arriving officers laughing and primping quietly around him, aware for a split second that they were keeping their voices at a low register out of deference to his reputation and well-known hatred of loud noise. Feeling his rage start to peak, he defined his killer with self-righteous cop invective: *psychopathic scumbag. Take him out before his switch flips again.*

The first thirty-six hours of his investigation had been spent thinking and chasing computer type. After noticing a "No Parking" zone outside the liquor store and extending all the way down the block, Lloyd theorized that the killer had either walked to the location or had parked in the bushes beside the freeway on-ramp. His latter thesis had been rewarded—under fluorescent arc lights the forensic technicians had found fresh tire tracks in the soft dirt and minute yellow paint scrapings stuck to the tips of sharp branches. Four hours later the L.A.P.D.'s Scientific Investigation Division completed its tests on the paint and announced the results of the technician's plaster of paris moldings of the tire tracks: The car was a Japanese import, late model; the paint the standard brand in every Japanese automotive plant; the tires standard equipment radials—used solely by Japanese manufacturers. R&I and a computer cross-check of recent armed robbery and homicide bulletins revealed that there were no yellow Japanese imports registered to convicted and paroled armed robbers or murderers and that none had been mentioned as figuring in any robberies or homicides dating back over a year. The California Department of Motor Vehicles supplied the most frustrating information: There were 311,819 yellow Japanese automobiles, 1977 to 1984 models, registered in Los Angeles County, making a concerted check for criminal records a clerical impossibility. Even the L.A. County "Hot Sheet" yielded zilch—a total of eight yellow Toyotas, Subarus, and Hondas had been reported stolen over the past six weeks, and all eight had been recovered. The car was a dead end.

Which left the gun.

Lloyd considered the still awaited latent print workup a foregone conclusion: smudges, streaks, partials, and at best a few completes belonging to local juiceheads who patronized the store. Let the three officers he had assigned to run background checks on the victims have carte blanche there—fingerprint mania or the "kill three to get one" angle his superiors at Robbery/Homicide had told him to stress were as dead as the car. Every ounce of Lloyd's instinct told him that, just as every ounce had told him that the trinity of this case was the killer's psychosis, his cool, his *gun*.

The Ballistics Report and the Autopsy Protocol were rife with flat-out wonderment. Henry McGuire, Wallace Chamales, and Susan Wischer were killed by a .41 revolver fired from a distance of twelve to fifteen feet, all three slugs hitting them square between the eyes. The killer was a marksman, the gun an anomaly. Forty-one revolvers predated the Wild West days, going out of manufacture before the Civil War. They were too unwieldy, too heavy, and had a marked tendency toward misfiring. Forty-one ammunition was even worse: hardball or hollow point, its unpredictable reports were capable of jerking the shooter's arm seemingly out of its socket or of going off like a soggy popcorn kernel. Whoever had shot the three people at Freeway Liquor had mastered a difficult antique handgun with antique ammo and had exercised his mastery under a state of extreme duress.

Lloyd stared deeper at his own mirror image, wondering what to do now that he had already sent stolen gun queries to every police agency in California and had personally questioned every antique gun dealer in the Central Yellow Pages. Negative answers all the way down the line—no .41s in stock, let alone purchased, and it would probably be another twenty-four hours before the responses to his queries began trickling in. All the paperwork was digested; all the facts were lodged. There was nothing he could do but wait.

And waiting was antithetical to his nature. Lloyd walked back to his cubicle and stared at the walls. Snapshots of his daughters formed a spray around the fed's ten most wanted; a pincushion map of L.A. County showed that homicides were up in Hollywood, South Central, and the East Valley. On the Freeway Liquor case the obvious next step was a call to Hollywood dicks to see what their snitches had come up with. Looking for something to perk his mental juices, he picked up the file that Dutch Peltz had given him just before the start of the frantic thirty-six hours. *Herzog, Jacob Michael, 5/3/49*, was typed on the front of the manila folder and inside were Xerox copies of statistical records forms, fitness reports, commendation certificates and odd memoranda from superior officers. Thinking of Herzog as a dead man and of the folder as his epitaph, Lloyd pulled up a chair and read every word in it five times.

A singular man emerged. Jungle Jack Herzog had a 137 I.Q., barely met the L.A.P.D.'s height and weight requirements and was born in Beirut, Lebanon. He was fluent in three Middle Eastern languages and had protested the Vietnam war in college, before joining the Air National Guard. He had graduated twelfth in his academy class and received scrolls in scholarship, marksmanship, and physical training. His first four years on the job had been spent working Wilshire Patrol and Wilshire Vice, receiving Class A fitness reports, earning praise from all superior officers save one vice squad lieutenant, who shunted him back into uniform for refusing to serve in a public restroom deployment to catch persons engaged in homosexual acts. That same lieutenant had then recanted his criticism—later requesting that Herzog train his men in operating bookmaking and prostitution surveillances, heavily emphasizing the use of disguise. Herzog's "seminars" had been so successful that he gained consultant status, training plainclothes officers citywide, staying in demand while doing four and three year tours of duty at West L.A. and Venice Divisions.

Jungle Jack became known as the "Alchemist," a reference to his ability to transform himself and render himself virtually invisible on the street. He was also spectacularly brave—twice resolving hostage situations, the first time by offering himself to the gunman who had taken over a bar he was staking out for liquor violations.

The gunman had grabbed a young prostitute and was holding a knife to her throat while his accomplice tapped the cash register and grabbed the purses and billfolds of the bar's patrons. Herzog, in the guise of a crippled drunk, taunted the knife wielder to release the girl and take him in her stead, screaming obscenities at him, inching closer as the blade drew a trickle of blood at the girl's throat. When he was two feet away, the gunman shoved the prostitute aside and grabbed Herzog, screaming when Jungle Jack's elbow crashed into his windpipe. Herzog disabled the man with a flat-handed karate chop and took off after his accomplice, catching him after a five-block foot pursuit.

The second hostage situation was resolved even more boldly. A man known to local officers as a heavy angel dust user had snatched a little girl and was holding her at gunpoint while a crowd gathered around him. Jack Herzog, in uniform, walked through the crowd and up to the man, who dropped the little girl and fired at him three times. The shots missed, and Herzog blew the man's brains out at point-blank range.

Herzog's reputation grew within the Department; requests from vice squad and plainclothes commanders multiplied. Then Sergeant Martin Bergen, Herzog's best friend, committed an act of cowardice as noteworthy as Herzog's acts of bravery. A trial board followed, and Herzog went to the wall for his friend, calling in favors in hope of saving Bergen's career, testifying as a character witness at his trial, decrying the L.A.P.D.'s hero mentality from his standpoint as one of its greatest heroes. Martin Bergen was banished from the Department in disgrace and Jungle Jack Herzog was banished to a file clerk job—a defeat as ignominious as Bergen's. Even a hero shouldn't fuck with the bosses.

Lloyd put the folder down when he realized that a shadow had fallen across the pages. He looked up to find Officer Artie Cranfield from S.I.D. staring at him.

"Hello, Lloyd. How's tricks?"

"Tricky."

"You need a shave."

"I know."

"Any leads on the liquor store job?"

"No. I'm waiting on queries. Ever hear of a cop named Jungle Jack Herzog?"

"Yeah, who hasn't? A real gunslinger."

"Ever hear of an ex-cop named Marty Bergen?"

"What is this, a guessing game? Everyone knows Old Yellowstreak and that toilet paper tabloid he writes for. Why?"

"Herzog and Bergen were best buddies. Mr. Guts and Mr. Chickenshit. You like it?"

"Not particularly. You look sardonic, Lloyd."

"Waiting makes me feel sardonic. Not sleeping makes me look sardonic."

"Are you going home to sleep?"

"No, I'm going to look for Mr. Guts."

Artie shook his head. "Before you go, say something macho about the liquor store asshole."

Lloyd smiled. "How about 'his ass is grass and I'm the fucking lawn-mower'?"

"I like it! I like it!"

"I thought you would."

*   *   *

Lloyd drove to Jack Herzog's last known address, a twenty-unit apartment house on the valley side of the Hollywood Hills. The pink stucco building was sandwiched between two shopping malls and featured a video game arcade in the front lobby. The directory listed Herzog as living in apartment 423. Lloyd walked up four flights of stairs and checked the hallway in both directions, then jimmied the lock with a credit card and closed the door behind him, almost stumbling over the pile of unopened mail that was spread out on the floor.

He flipped a light switch and let his eyes fall on the first thing that greeted them, a trophy case filled with award scrolls and loving cups. The ink on Herzog's death certificate was the scouring powder wipe marks that covered the wood and glass surfaces. A quick check of the rest of the apartment revealed that wipe marks streaked with abrasive powder were spread over every surface capable of sustaining latent prints. It was the job of a conscientious professional.

Lloyd leafed through the envelopes on the floor. No personal letters or postcards—every piece was either a utility bill or junk mail. Letting his eyes stray over the living room walls, he saw an impersonal habitat come into focus—no artwork of any kind; no masculine disarray; furniture that had probably come with the lease. The award scrolls and loving cups had the look of hand-me-downs, and when he squinted to read the names and dates embossed on them, Lloyd saw that they were track and field awards won by Herzog's father in Lebanon during the late '40s.

The kitchen was even more spare—dishes and silverware stacked neatly by the drainboard, no food of any kind in the refrigerator or on the shelves. Only the bedroom bore signs of personality: a closet stuffed with L.A.P.D. uniforms and a huge supply of civilian clothes, outfits ranging from ragpicker overcoats to skinny-lapel pimp suits to outlaw motorcycle leathers. Beside the bed were tall shelves crammed with books. Lloyd scanned the spines. All the titles were biographies, the lives of generals, conquerors and religious iconoclasts predominating. One whole shelf was devoted to works on Richard the Lion Hearted and Martin Luther; another to books on Peter the Great. Romantic plunderers, despots, and mad visionaries. Lloyd felt a wave of love for Jungle Jack Herzog.

After checking out the bathroom, Lloyd found the phone and called Dutch Peltz at the Hollywood station. When Dutch came on the line, he said, "I'm at Herzog's pad. It's been wiped by a pro. You can scratch Herzog for real, but don't let anyone know, okay?"

"All right. Was the pad trashed?"

"No. I get the feeling the killer was just being cautious, covering his ass from all standpoints. Can you do me a few favors?"

"Name them."

"When the Vice Squad comes on, find out from Walt Perkins what bars Herzog was working. Glom any reports he may have filed. I'm going to check out Marty Bergen myself, and I'll come back here and interview Herzog's neighbors tonight. I'll call you at home around seven."

"Sounds good."

"Oh, and Dutch? Have your guys feel out their snitches on antique gun freaks, or any assholes known to use violence who've been taking up guns lately. Even if it's just street bullshit and jive, I want to know about it."

"You're fishing, Lloyd."

"I know. I'll call you at seven."

Lloyd walked through Jungle Jack Herzog's barren dwelling place. Locking the door behind him, he said, "You poor noble son-of-a-bitch, why the fuck did you have to prove yourself so hard?"

It took Lloyd half an hour to drive to the West Hollywood office of the *Big Orange Insider*. Heat, smog, and lack of sleep combined to produce a head pounding that had the pavement wobbling before his eyes. To combat it he rolled up the windows and turned the air conditioning on full, shivering as a fresh adrenaline rush overtook him. Two new cases, three dead and one presumed dead. No sleep for at least another twelve hours.

The *Big Orange Insider* occupied the first floor of a pseudo art-deco chateau on San Vicente a block south of Sunset. Lloyd walked in, bypassing the receptionist, knowing she made him for a cop and would be instantly buzzing the editorial offices to tell them the enemy was coming. He walked into a large room crammed with desks and smiled as suspicious eyes darted up from typewriters to appraise him. When the eyes turned hostile he bowed and blew the assembly a kiss. He was beginning to feel at ease when two women waved back. Then he felt a tugging at his sleeve and turned to see a tall young man pressed into him.

"Who let you back here?" the young man demanded.

"No one," Lloyd said.

"Are you a policeman?"

"I'm a defector. I've quit the cops, and I'm seeking asylum with the counterculture fourth estate. I want to peddle my memoirs. Take me to your wisest ghost writer."

"You have thirty seconds to vacate the premises."

Lloyd took a step toward the young man. The young man took two steps backward. Seeing the fear in his eyes, Lloyd said, "Shit. Detective Sergeant Hopkins, L.A.P.D. I'm here to see Marty Bergen. Tell him it's about Jack Herzog. I'll be waiting by the reception desk."

He walked back to the reception area. The woman at the desk gave him a deadpan stare, so he busied himself by perusing the enlarged and framed editorial cartoons that adorned the four walls. The L.A.P.D. and L.A. County Sheriff's were attacked in vicious caricatures. Fat, porcine-featured policemen cloaked in American flags poked sleeping drunks with tridents; Chief Gates was dangled on a puppet's string by two men in Ku Klux Klan robes. Wolf-faced cops herded black prostitutes into a paddy wagon, while the officer at the wheel guzzled liquor, a speech balloon elaborating his thoughts: "Wow! Police work sure is exciting! I hope these bimbos are holding some cash. My car payment is overdue!"

"I'll admit it's a bit hyperbolic."

Lloyd turned to face the voice, openly sizing up the man who owned it. Martin Bergen was over six feet tall, blonde, with a once strong body going to flab. His florid face was contorted into a look of mirthless mirth and his pale blue eyes were liquid but on target. His breath was equal parts whiskey and mint mouthwash.

"You should know. You had what? Thirteen or fourteen years on the job?"

"I had sixteen, Hopkins. You've got what?"

"Eighteen and a half."

"Pulling the pin at twenty?"

"No."

"I see. What's this about Jack Herzog?"

Lloyd stepped back in order to get a full-body reaction. "Herzog's been missing for over three weeks. His pad has been wiped. He was working Personnel Records downtown and on a loan-out to Hollywood Vice. No one at Parker Center or Hollywood Station has seen him. What does that tell you?"

Marty Bergen began to tremble. His red face turned pale and his hands plucked at his pants legs. He backed into the wall and slid down into a folding metal chair. The woman at the desk brought over a glass of water, then hesitated and hurried off into the ladies' room when she saw Lloyd shake his head.

Lloyd sat down beside Bergen and said, "When did you see Herzog last?"

Bergen's voice was calm. "About a month ago. We still hung out. Jack didn't blame me for what I did. He knew we were different that way. He didn't judge me."

"What was his state of mind?"

"Quiet. No—he was always quiet, but lately he'd been moody, up one minute, down the next."

"What did you talk about?"

"Stuff. Shit. Books, mostly. My novel, the one I've been writing."

"Did you and Herzog discuss his assignments?"

"We never talked police work."

"I've heard Herzog described as a 'stone loner.' Is that accurate?"

"Yes."

"Can you name any of his other friends?"

"No."

"Women?"

"He had a girlfriend he saw occasionally. I don't know her name."

Lloyd leaned closer to Bergen. "What about enemies? What about men within the Department who hated him for the way he stood by you? You know the rank-and-file cop mentality as well as I do. Herzog must have engendered resentment."

"The only resentment that Jack engendered was in me. He was so much better than me at everything that I always loved him the most when I hated him the most. We were so, so different. When we talked last, Jack said that he was going to exonerate me. But I ran. I was guilty."

Bergen started to sob. Lloyd got up and walked to the door, looking back on the hack writer weeping underneath framed excoriations of what he had once been. Bergen was serving a life sentence with no means of atonement. Lloyd shuddered under the weight of the thought.

The return trip to the Valley eased Lloyd's fatigue. Snug in his air-conditioned cocoon, he let his mind run with images of Herzog and Bergen, intellectual cop buddies, two men who his instincts told him were as much alike as Bergen said they were different. The Freeway Liquor case receded temporarily to a back burner, and when he parked in front of Jack Herzog's building he felt his mental second wind go physical. He smiled, knowing he would have the juice for a long stretch of hunting.

Herzog's neighbors began returning home from work shortly after five. Lloyd sized the first several of them up from his car, noting that their common denominator was the weary lower middle class look indigenous to Valley residents of both genders. Prime meat for the insurance payoff ploy. He pulled a stack of phony business cards from the glove compartment and practiced his glad-hander insurance man smile, preparing for a performance that would secure him the knowledge of just how much a loner Jungle Jack Herzog was.

Three hours later, with two dozen impromptu interviews behind him, Lloyd felt Herzog move from loner to cipher. None of the people he had talked to recalled even *seeing* the resident of apartment 423, assuming that the unit was kept vacant for some reason. The obvious candor of their statements was like a kick in the teeth; the fact that several had mentioned that the landlord/manager would be out of town for another week was the finishing blow. It was a solid investigatory angle shot to hell.

Lloyd drove to a pay phone and called Dutch Peltz. Dutch answered on the first ring. "Peltz, who's this?"

"Anyone ever tell you you answer the phone like a cop?"

Dutch laughed. "Yeah, you. Got a pencil?"

"Shoot."

"Herzog was working two singles bars, the First Avenue West and Jackie D.'s, both on Highland north of the Boulevard. He was specifically looking for bartenders taking bribes to serve minors and hookers giving head in the hat-check room; we'd had a dozen complaints. He worked those joints for over six weeks, never blowing his cover, always calling narco or patrol from a pay phone when he saw something coming down. He figured in six coke busts and one for prostitution. As a result, the A.B.C. has both joints up for suspension of their liquor licenses."

Lloyd whistled. "What about the reports he filed?"

"No reports, Lloyd. Walt Perkins's orders. The arresting officers filed. Walt didn't want Jack compromised."

"Shit. That means you can scratch revenge as a motive."

"Yeah, at least as far as his recent arrest record is concerned. What happened with Bergen?"

"Nothing. Bergen hasn't seen Herzog in over a month, says he was

moody, troubled. He took the news hard. He was drunk at two in the afternoon. Poor bastard."

"We're going to have a file a Missing Persons Report, Lloyd."

"I know. Let Internal Affairs handle it, which means you and Walt
Perkins are going to catch shit for not reporting it earlier and probably even
heavier shit for working Herzog off the payroll."

"You might get the case if it goes to Robbery/Homicide."

"They'll never find the stiff, Dutch. This job is pro all the way. I.A.D. will
go at it sub rosa, then stonewall it. Let me give it another forty-eight hours
before you call them, okay?"

"Okay."

"What have you got from your snitches on the liquor store job?"

"Nothing yet. I sent out a memo to all officers on it. It's still too early for
a response. What's next on Herzog?"

"Barhopping, Dutchman. Yours truly as a swinging single."

"Have fun."

Lloyd laughed and said, "Fuck you," then hung up.

Bombarded by disco music, Lloyd competed for floor and bar space at
First Avenue West. Showing his insurance agent's business card and Jack
Herzog's personnel file photo to three bartenders, four cocktail waitresses
and two dozen singles, he got negative responses, distinguished only by hostile looks and shakes of the head from low-rider types who made him for fuzz
and annoyed brush-offs from young women who didn't like his style. Lloyd
walked out the door angrily shaking *his* head as the washout continued.

Jackie D.'s, three doors down, was almost deserted. Lloyd counted heads
as he took a seat at the bar. A couple doing a slow grind on the dance floor
and two overaged swingers feeding coins to the jukebox. The bartender
slipped a napkin in front of him and explained why: "Twofers at First Avenue West. Every Tuesday night I get killed. First Ave. can afford it, I can't.
I keep my prices low to do volume and I still get killed. Is there no mercy
in this life?"

"None," Lloyd said.

"I just wanted a confirmation. What are you drinking?"

Lloyd put a dollar bill on the bar. "Ginger ale."

The bartender snorted, "You see what I mean? No mercy!"

Lloyd took out the snapshot of Jack Herzog. "Have you seen this man?"

The bartender scrutinized the photo, then filled Lloyd's glass and nodded. "Yeah, I seen him around here a lot."

Lloyd's skin prickled. "When?"

"A while back. A month, six weeks, maybe two months ago, right before those A.B.C. cocksuckers filed on me. You a cop?"

"That's right."

"Hollywood Vice?"

"Robbery/Homicide. Tell me about the man in the picture."

"What's to tell? He came in, he drank, he tipped well, he didn't hit on the chicks."

"Ever talk to him?"

"Not really."

"Did he ever come in with or leave with anyone?"

The bartender screwed his face into a memory search, then said, "Yeah. He had a buddy. A sandy-haired guy. Medium height, maybe early thirties."

"Did he meet him here?"

"That I can't tell you."

Lloyd walked over to the pay phone outside the men's room and called Hollywood Station, requesting Lieutenant Perkins. When he came on the line, Lloyd said, "Walt, this is Lloyd Hopkins. I've got a question."

"Hit me."

"Did Herzog work his bar assignments alone?"

There was a long moment of silence. Finally Perkins said, "I'm not really sure, Lloyd. My *guess* is sometimes yes, sometimes no. I've always given Jack carte blanche. Any arrangements he made with individual squad members would be up to him. Shall I ask around tomorrow night at roll call?"

"Yes. What about a sandy-haired man, medium height, early thirties. Herzog might have worked with him."

"That's half our squad, Lloyd."

There was another stretch of silence. Finally Lloyd said, "He's dead. I'll be in touch," and replaced the receiver. The barman looked up as he strode toward the door. "There's no mercy!" he called out.

Battered by sleeplessness and dwindling options, Lloyd drove downtown to Parker Center, hoping to find an easily intimidated nightwatch supervisor on duty at Personnel Records. When he saw the man behind the records counter dozing in his chair with a science fiction novel lying on his chest, he knew he was home.

"Excuse me, Officer!"

The records supervisor jerked awake and stared at Lloyd's badge. "Hopkins, Robbery/Homicide," Lloyd said. "Jack Herzog left some files for me in his desk. Will you show me where it is?"

The supervisor yawned, then pointed to a bank of Plexiglas enclosed cubicles. "Herzog's daywatch, so I don't know exactly where his desk is. But you go help yourself, Sergeant. The names are on the doors."

Lloyd walked into the Plexiglas maze, noting with relief that Herzog's cubicle was well out of the supervisor's sight. Finding the door unlocked, he rummaged through the desk drawers, feeling another impersonal habitat come into focus as pencils, notepads, and a series of blank office forms were revealed. One drawer; two drawers; three drawers. Herzog the cipher.

Lloyd was raising his fist to slam the desktop when he noticed the edges of several slips of paper on the floor, wedged into the juncture where the wall met the carpet. Squatting, he pulled them out, going cold when he saw file requisition slips with the officer's name, rank, date of birth, and badge number on top and the requesting officer's name and division below. Squinting, he read over the five slips. The officers' names were unknown to him, but the requesting officer's name wasn't. Captain Frederick T. Gaffaney, Internal Affairs Division, had requested all five files. Old born-again Christian Fred, who had given him grief as a Robbery/Homicide lieutenant. Squinting harder, Lloyd felt the coldness run up his spine into his brain. He knew Gaffaney's signature. These were blatant forgeries.

Lloyd got out his notebook and wrote down the names of the officers whose files had been requested. Tucker, Duane W., Lieutenant, Wilshire Division; Murray, Daniel X., Captain, Central Division; Rolando, John L., Lieutenant, Devonshire Division; Kaiser, Steven A., Captain, West Valley Division; Christie, Howard J., Lieutenant, Rampart Division.

He stared at the names, then on impulse ran his hand under the carpet again, coming away with a last slip of paper, going dead ice cold when he read the name printed on top: *Hopkins, Lloyd W. #1114, 2/27/42, Sergeant, Robbery/Homicide Division.*

5

Thomas Goff's surveillance photographs had not prepared him for the woman's beauty; nothing in Goff's oral and written reports came close to describing her aura of refinement. A thousand-dollar-a-night whore in a thousand-dollar raw silk dress. Dr. John Havilland leaned back in his chair, pretending to be tongue-tied. Give the woman the temporary upper hand, let her think her charisma had dented his professionalism. When Linda Wilhite didn't fidget under his gaze, he broke the long introductory silence. "Will you tell me something about yourself, Ms. Wilhite? The reasons why you've decided to enter therapy?"

Linda Wilhite's eyes circled the office; her hands smoothed the arms of her chair. Brilliantly varnished oak walls, a framed Edward Hopper original. No couch. The chairs she and the Doctor were sitting in were upholstered in pure cashmere. "You love nice things," she said.

Havilland smiled. "So do you. That's a very beautiful dress."

"Thank you. Why do most people come to see you?"

"Because they want to change their lives."

"Of course. Can you guess what I do for a living?"

"Yes. You're a prostitute."

"How exactly did you know that?"

"You called my service and made an appointment without asking to speak to me personally, and you wouldn't say who referred you. When a woman contacts me in that manner, I assume that she's in the Life. I've counseled a great many prostitutes, and I've published several monographs on my findings, without ever violating the anonymity of my patients. In criminal parlance I'm a 'stand-up guy.' I don't have a receptionist or a secretary, because I don't trust such people. Women in the Life trust *me* for these reasons."

Linda traced patterns on her silk and the Doctor's cashmere. "This dress cost thirteen hundred dollars. My shoes cost six hundred. I love nice things and you love nice things, and we both make a lot of money. But what I do to make money is killing me, and I have to stop."

Havilland leaned forward as the woman's words settled in on him. He brought his voice down to its lowest register and said, "Are you ready to sacrifice picayune shit like thirteen hundred dollar dresses to achieve your true power? Are you ready to dig through your past to find out why you need creature comforts at the expense of your integrity? Are you willing to break yourself down to ground zero in order to help me take you as far as you can go?"

Linda flinched at the battery of questions. "Yes," she said.

Havilland stood up, stretched and decided to go in full bore. Sitting back down, he said, "Linda, my brand of therapy is a two-way street. What you think I need to know and what I need to know may well be two different things. I would like this first session to consist of questions and answers. I'll throw out some educated guesses and assumptions about you, and you tell me how accurate I am. What I want to establish is some kind of instinctive rapport. Do you follow me?"

Her voice quavering, Linda said, "How far is as far as I can go?"

Dr. John Havilland threw back his head and laughed. "My educated guess is that you can hit the ball out of the ballpark and into the next county."

Linda smiled. "Then let's do it," she said.

Havilland got up and walked to the window, glancing down on the jet-stream of cars and people twenty-six stories below him. He coughed and pressed the activator button inlaid on the window ledge, sending current to the tape recorder housed behind a section of wall panel.

Turning to face Linda Wilhite, he said, "You're thirty-one or two, large family, northern Midwest—Michigan or Wisconsin. The best and brightest of your siblings. Adored by your brothers, despised by your sisters. Your parents are new money, uneasy about it, terrified of losing their hard-earned status. You dropped out of college in your senior year and worked at odd jobs before a series of disillusionments led you slowly into the Life. How close am I?"

Linda was already shaking her head. "I'm twenty-nine, from L.A., an only child. My parents died when I was ten. I lived in a series of foster homes until I graduated from high school. I never attended college. My parents were semi-poor. I made a conscious decision to become a prostitute, just as I've made a conscious decision to quit being one. Please don't consider me typical."

Circling the office, his eyes shifting back and forth between Linda Wilhite and the Persian rug that cushioned his footfalls, Havilland said, "Is being typical a crime? No, don't answer, let me continue. You enjoy sex with certain kinds of older men among your customers, and it hurts you if they sleep with anyone else. If you find a customer attractive, then you fantasize about him and hate yourself for it afterwards. You despise hookers who consider themselves 'therapists' and the like. Your basic dilemma is a conservative nature, one grounded in the work ethic, undercut with the knowledge that what you do is shit, antithetical to every decent moral instinct you possess. You have rationalized this contradiction for years, bolstered yourself with self-help books and spiritual tracts, but now it won't wash anymore and you came to me. Touché, Ms. Wilhite?"

The Doctor's voice had risen higher and higher, little crescendos of truth that Linda knew would grow in scope and intimacy without the man's resonance ever cracking. Her hands fluttered over her lap, looking for something of and by herself to touch. When they descended on green paisley silk, she jerked them back and said, "Yes. Yes. Yes. How did you know those things?"

Dr. John Havilland sat back down and stretched his legs until his feet dangled a few inches from Linda's alligator shoes. "Linda, I'm the best there is. To be blunt, I am a work of fucking art."

Linda laughed until she felt a blush creep up from her bodice. "I've got a john who says the same thing to me. He collects Colombian art, so I know it's an informed opinion. And you know the funny thing? He calls me 'a work of fucking art,' and he never fucks me—he just takes pictures of me. Isn't that a hoot?"

Havilland laughed along, first uproariously, then sedately. When his laughter wound down, he said, "What does this man do with the photographs of you?"

"He has them blown up, then he frames them and hangs them in his bedroom," Linda said.

"How do you feel about that? Worshiped? Adored?"

"I . . . I feel worthy of my beauty."

"Did your parents recognize your beauty early on? Did they fawn over you because of it?"

"My father did."

"Did your parents take photographs of you?"

Linda flinched at the word *photographs*. She stammered, "N-no."

Havilland leaned forward and put his hand on her knee. "You've gone pale, Linda. Why?"

Flinching again, Linda said, "This is happening so fast. I wasn't going to tell you today because most of the time it seems so remote. My father was a violent man. He was a longshoreman, and he used to fight bare knuckles for money on the docks at San Pedro. He'd win or he'd lose and he'd always bet heavily on himself, so if he won he showered mother and me with gifts and if he lost he brooded and smashed things. Most of the time it was fifty-fifty, win, lose, win, lose—so that I never knew what to expect.

"Then, when I was ten, Daddy hit a losing streak. He brooded worse than ever and punched out all the windows in our house. It was winter and we were broke and the heat was shut off and cold air blew in through the broken windows. I'll never forget the day it happened. I came home from school and there were police cars in front of the house. A detective took me aside and told me what happened. Daddy had put a pillow over Mother's head and shot her in the face. Then he stuck the gun in his mouth and shot himself. I was sent to Juvenile Hall, and a couple of days later a matron told me I had to identify the bodies. She showed me photographs from the autopsy—Daddy and Mother with half their faces blown away. I cried and I cried, but I couldn't stop looking at the pictures."

"And, Linda?" Havilland whispered.

Linda said, "And I went to live with an elderly couple who treated me like a princess. I swiped the pictures the matron showed me and forced myself to laugh and gloat over them. Those pictures gave me freedom from the shitty life I had, and laughing at them was like getting revenge on my parents. I—"

Havilland raised a hand in interruption. "Let me finish. Your foster parents caught you laughing over the photographs and punished you? It was never the same with them after that?"

"Yes," Linda said.

The Doctor circled his office again, running light fingertips over the oak walls. "A few more questions, then we'll end the session. Is the type of man—of customer—that you're attracted to large and physical, possessed of intelligence and breeding but also possessed of a certain aura of violence?"

Linda's whisper was astonished. "Yes."

Havilland smiled. "World-class progress in one session. Does the day after tomorrow—Friday—suit you for our next one? Say ten-thirty?"

Linda Wilhite stood up, surprised to find her legs steady. She smoothed the front of her dress and said, "Yes. I'll be here. Thank you."

Havilland took her arm and walked her to his outer office door. "It was my pleasure."

After Linda Wilhite was gone, the Doctor, armed with her image and facts from Goff's reconnaissance, turned off the lights and played the time-travel game.

When Linda was two and living in a San Pedro dive with her white-trash parents, he was twelve and gaining clandestine access to wealthy homes in Bronxville and Scarsdale, New York, exorcising his nocturnal heart by delivering himself to the quiet muse of other peoples' dwellings, sometimes stealing, sometimes not . . .

When Linda was fourteen and sexually experimenting with surfer morons in Huntington Beach, he was twenty-four and graduating from Harvard Medical School at the top of his class, the legendary Doctor John the Night Tripper, the genius dope chemist/abortionist who held instructors rapt with his digressions on the theories of Kinsey, Pomeroy, and Havelock Ellis . . .

When Linda was growing into her exquisite beauty in a series of foster homes, filled with wonder at her parents' deaths and the apostasy that their bloodletting had spawned, he—

The Time Machine screeched, shuddered, and ground to a halt. A green door opened to reveal a man in a gray uniform standing beside a salmon-pink '56 Ford Victoria ragtop. Little girls in party dresses thronged the car, and just before it exploded into flames they turned to point and laugh at him.

The Night Tripper walked to the wall and turned on the light, seeking confirmation. He found it in glass-encased tributes; framed diplomas from New York University and Harvard Med and St. Vincent and Castleford Hospitals—parchment that spelled out plainly that he was the best. The dates on them told him why the Time Machine had malfunctioned. Linda was powerful. Linda had sustained a catastrophe as he had and required that he juxtapose his story against hers from the beginning . . .

1956. *Scarsdale, New York.* Johnny Havilland, age eleven, known as "Spaz," "Wimpdick," and "Shitstick." Sherry-guzzling mother with the inbred look indigenous to high-line Wasps who have never had to work for a living; big bucks father, a hunter whose shotgun volleys have decimated the varmint population of six New York counties. Johnny hates school; Johnny hates to play ball; Johnny loves to dream and listen to music on his portable radio.

Johnny's father considers him a wimp and decrees a rite to prompt his manhood: Shoot the family's senile golden retriever. Johnny refuses and is sent by his father to a "training school" run by an extremist sect of nuns. The nuns lock Johnny in a basement full of rats, with no food or water and only a shovel for protection. Two days go by. Johnny huddles in a corner and screams himself hoarse as the rats nip at his legs. On the third day he falls asleep on the floor and wakes up to find a large rat scampering off with a chunk of his lip. Johnny screams, picks up the shovel and beats every rat in the basement to death.

Johnny's father takes him home the following day, tousling his hair and calling him "Dad's little ratter." Johnny goes straight for his father's gun rack, grabs a twelve-gauge pump and strides outside to the kennel, where five Labradors and short-haired Pointers frolic behind barbed wire. Johnny blows the dogs to kingdom come and turns to face his father, who turns white and faints. Weeks go by. His father shuns him. Johnny knows that his father has given him a precious gift that is far more valuable than standard manhood. Johnny loves his father and wants to please him with his new-found strength.

1957. "Green Door" by Jim Lowe climbs the hit parade and fills Johnny with portents of dark secrets.

> "Midnight, one more night without sleeping.
> Watching, 'till the morning comes creeping.
> Green door, what's that secret you're keeping?"

Johnny wants to know the secret so he can tell his father and make him love him.

The quest for the secret begins with a shinny up a drainpipe into a neighbor's darkened attic. Johnny finds coyotes mounted on roller-skate wheels and department store mannequins. The mannequins have been gouged in the facial and genital regions and red paint has been daubed in the holes and left to trickle off in simulation of wounds. Johnny steals a coyote's glass eye and leaves it on his father's desk. His father never mentions the gift. As other gifts from other dark houses follow, Johnny perceives that his father is terrified of him.

Johnny's housebreaking career continues; the spacious homes of Westchester County become his teacher and friend. Thoughts of earning his father's love grow mute beside the haphazard tides of passion that he assimilates in shadow-shrouded bedrooms and hallways. Green door after green door after green door bursts open. And then there was the next to the last door and the man in the uniform, and the last door opening on a pitch-black void . . .

The darkness deepened as the Time Machine suffered its final malfunction, its chronograph needle stuck permanently on June 2, 1957. The void stretched into months. The callow Johnny Havilland who entered was only a shell compared to the self-sufficient John who emerged . . .

Always this memory gap, the Night Tripper thought. Father was there when he entered and gone when his recollections again assumed a linear sequence. He took Goff's photographs of Linda Wilhite from his desk and fanned them like a deck of cards. Linda came briefly to life, the slash of her mouth speaking bewilderment. She wanted to know *why* he was as great as he was.

Havilland ruffled the photos again, making Linda beg for the answer. He smiled. He would tell her, and he would not need the Time Machine to help him.

1958. Father had been gone for months; Mother, in a perpetual sherry haze, didn't seem to care. Checks came in bimonthly, drawn from the tax-exempt trust funds that Father's father had started almost half a century before. It was as if a giant puppetmaster had snatched the man into eternity, leaving his material wealth as wonder bait to ensure that Johnny could have *anything* he wanted.

Johnny wanted knowledge. He wanted knowledge because he knew it would give him sovereignty over the psychic pain that all the human race save himself was subject to. His grief over his father's disappearance had transmogrified into armor sheathed in one-way transparent glass. *He* could look out and see *all*; no one could look in and see *him*. Thus invulnerable, Johnny Havilland sought knowledge.

He found it.

In 1962 John Havilland graduated from Scarsdale High School, number one in his class, hailed by the school's principal as a "human encyclopedia." N.Y.U. and more scholastic honors followed, culminating in a Phi Beta

Kappa key, Summa Cum Laude graduation and a full scholarship to Harvard Medical School.

It was at Harvard Med that John Havilland was able to combine his knowledge-lust and dominion over human feelings into dominion over other people. Like his early burglary career, it began with a shinny up a drainpipe and a vault into an open window. But where before he had come away with knickknacks to please his father, this time he came away with questions and answers that he knew would make *him* the spiritual patriarch to scores of pliant souls.

The window yielded tape recordings of confidential interviews conducted by Alfred Kinsey in 1946 and 1947. The interviewees were described in terse sentences and were then asked to describe themselves. The variance factor was astonishing—the people almost always defined themselves by some physical abnormality. The Q. and A. sessions that followed proceeded along uniform patterns, revealing mundane matters—lust, guilt, and adultery—things which John Havilland's immune system had surmounted in early adolescence.

After over two hundred hours of listening to the tapes, John knew two things: One, that Kinsey was an astute interviewer, a scholar who considered factual admissions illuminating in themselves; and, two, that that knowledge was *not* enough and that Kinsey had failed because he could *not* get his interviewees to talk openly about fantasies beyond variations of fucking and sucking. He could elicit no admissions of dark grandeur, because he felt none himself. His interviewees were hicks who didn't know shit from Shinola. Kinsey operated from the Freudian/humanist ethic: Provide knowledge of behavior patterns to enable the subject a viewpoint of objectivity in which to relegate his neuroses to a scrap heap of things that don't work. Show him that his fears and most extreme fantasies are irrational and convince him to be a loving, boring, happy human being.

After over six hundred hours of listening, John knew two more things: That the most profound truth lay in the labyrinths that coiled behind a green door in the interviewee's mind the very second that Alfred Kinsey said, "Tell me about your fantasies"; and, two, that with the proper information and the correct stimuli he could get carefully chosen people to break through those doors and act out their fantasies, past moral strictures and the boundaries of conscience, taking *him* past his already absolute knowledge of mankind's unutterable stupidity into a new night realm that he as yet was incapable of imagining. Because the night was there to be plundered; and only someone above its laws could exact its bounty and survive.

Now armed with a mission, there remained only to discover and actuate the means toward its fulfillment. It was 1967. Drugs and hard rock flooded Harvard yard, spawned by a backwash of students, townies, and traveling hippies willing to protest anything, try anything, and ingest anything in order to gain themselves, lose themselves, or achieve a "transcendental experience." Social change was in the wind, producing a "consciousness explosion" that John Havilland considered fatuous and propagated by failures, many of whom would not live to see the period dwindle out of its own emptiness, replaced by a new reactionary fervor. Giving the youth culture a life expectancy of two years at the most, he decided to become one of its icons. People would follow him; they would have no choice.

Two abortions performed gratis in his antiseptically clean Beacon Hill apartment gained him a hushed reputation among Harvard undergrads; a record heard at a pot party provided him with a powerful sobriquet. "Doctor John the Night Tripper" was a Creole who shrieked odes to dope and sex, backed up by two saxes, drums, and an electric organ. At the party, a heavily stoned anthropology professor shoved an album cover in John Havilland's face and yelled, "That's you, man! Your name is John and you're in med school! Dig it!"

The nickname stuck, fueled by the young doctor's forays into manufacturing LSD and liquid methamphetamine. Drug concocting med students were commonplace, but a dope doc who gave the stuff away with no strings was the subject of much speculation. People started to come around to his apartment, seeking his knowledge. He told them what they wanted to hear, a hodgepodge of counterculture thought combed from all their heroes. They never knew they were being bullshitted, not even when the Night Tripper revealed that there were indeed strings.

The experiments began. Do you *really* want to find out who you are? Dr. John would ask his would-be subject. Do you *really* want to find out the depth of your potential? Do you understand that my exploring your most secret fantasies will gain for you in one weekend what psychoanalysis will never discover?

The subjects were all "pre-screened" drop-ins at the Beacon Hill apartment. They were, male and female, all of a type: Aesthetes devoid of original thought; rich-kid spiritual seekers whose rebellious streaks cloaked long histories of overdependence on their parents. A weekend to help out Dr. John with his med school thesis? Sure.

The weekends would begin with high quality marijuana and jokingly phrased sex questionnaires. More weed and oral questions followed, the Doctor regaling the subjects with made-up sexual anecdotes of his own. When the subjects were plied almost to sleep with weed and music, Dr. John would give them a skin pop of sodium Pentothal and tell them horror stories and gauge their responses. If they responded with glee, he would go straight for the fantasy jugular, interweaving his horror stories with the subject's own, creating tapestries ranging from family slaughter to wholesale sexual conquest. When the subject fell asleep, the Night Tripper would fall asleep at his side, savoring the feel of clothed bodies almost touching in the fellowship of nightmares.

Increasingly smaller doses of sodium Pentothal accompanied by visual aids took up the rest of the weekend, bringing the subject to the fantasy/reality juncture point where they had some cognizance of what they had revealed. Anti-war activists guffawed over photographs of napalm-barbecued babies, felt momentary remorse, then laughed it off in the joy of newfound freedom. The Doctor described beloved parents in postures of debasement with barn-yard creatures; the subjects supplied gory and humorous embellishments. Psyches broke through green doors, retreated into normalcy and left their weekend revelations to simmer benignly, waiting for the right time or the right catalyst, or waiting for nothing.

After four months of weekends, Dr. John discontinued his experiments. They had become boringly repetitive, and he had reached the point where he could unfailingly predict the responses of his subjects. He had quantum leaps to take in his mission, but he knew those leaps were years away.

Upon graduation from medical school in 1969, Havilland was assigned to the Intern Program at St. Vincent's Hospital in the Bronx, New York, where he spent twelve-hour shifts tending to the needs of welfare families. It was boring medicine, and he grew more restive by the day, sending out resumés to every hospital in the metropolitan New York area known to have a lackluster psychiatric staff. A three-year residency was required of all physicians training in psychiatry, and he wanted to be sure that he would be able to dominate his instructors—even at entry level.

Sixteen applications sent out; sixteen acceptances. Three months of detective work. Conclusion: Castleford Hospital, one hour north of New York City. Low pay, alcoholics in key administrative posts, a psychiatric staff of four aged doctors and a pillhead R.N. Heavy Medicaid contracts with the New York State Parole Board, which meant plenty of court-referred criminal types. He would play the game with all the finesse he was capable of and they would give him carte blanche. On March 4, 1971, Dr. John Havilland moved into his new quarters outside the main administration building at Castleford Hospital in Nyack, New York, knowing that something was about to happen. He was right. After six months of counseling dreary low-lifes, he met Thomas Goff.

At their first counseling session Goff had been hyperkinetic and witty, even under the stress of a migraine headache. "My goal in life used to be to do *nothing* exceedingly well; my downfall was the fact that I liked to do it in stolen cars. . . . I'll do anything to keep from going back to prison, from skin-diving for Roto-rooter to servicing Jewish spinsters in Miami Beach. What do you recommend, Doc? Grow gills or get circumcised? Jesus fucking Christ, these daylight headaches are killing me!"

Havilland had felt instincts clicking into place, telling him to act now. Obeying those instincts, he gave Goff a large intravenous shot of Demerol. While Goff was off on a painless dope cloud he asked him questions and found out that Goff liked to hurt people and that he never talked about it because they put you in jail for that. He had hurt lots of people, but the Trashbag Man had been his cellie at Attica and the headaches had started about then, and wasn't that wild psychedelic ceiling *beige? Give me back my headaches!*

Havilland had put him completely out, reading his file while he was unconscious. Thomas Lewis Goff, D.O.B. 6/19/49; light brown and blue, 5' 10", 155. High school dropout, 161 I.Q., car thief, burglar, pimp. Suspect in three aggravated assault cases, cases dismissed when the women victims refused to testify. Convicted of first degree auto theft with two priors, sentenced to five years in state prison, sent to Attica on 11/4/69, considered a model prisoner. Paroled after the recent riots, when psychiatrists at the prison judged that he would go psychotic if he remained incarcerated. Psychosomatic headaches and terror of daylight chief symptoms, dating from the time of the riot, when he was shut in a secluded cell block with one Paul Mandarano, a convicted murderer known as the "Trashbag" killer. Mandarano had committed suicide by hanging himself from the cell bars, and Goff had remained in the cell with his body until the riot was quelled. No presence of neurological damage; judged an excellent parole risk.

Fate embraced Dr. John Havilland. When Thomas Goff regained consciousness, he said, "It's going to be all right, Thomas. Please trust me."

The Night Tripper stalked Goff's nightmares, then blunted them with drugs and fantasies until Goff wasn't sure that Attica and the Trashbag Man had really happened. Under sodium Pentothal and age regression hypnosis, the Doctor took him back to the trauma flux point, learning that Paul Mandarano had hanged himself with a beige plastic trashbag and that a blower fan stationed outside the cell block had blown the loose ends of the bag continually over the bars, acting in concert with safety arc lights, turning the cell where Goff had huddled with a rotting body into an alternately brightly lit and pitch-black horror show. Classic symbolism: Light magnified the terror; darkness diminished it. After seven months of therapy sessions in a cool, dim room, Thomas Goff's fear of daylight abated to the point where it became tolerable. "I'll always hate oysters, Doc; but sometimes I'll have to watch other people eat them. Daylight is pretty unavoidable, but as Nietzsche said, 'What does not destroy me makes me stronger.' Right, Doc?"

The Night Tripper felt tremors of love at Goff's words. It was right for Goff to love him, but the reverse was not tolerable. "Yes, Thomas, Nietzsche was right. You'll find that out even more as we continue our journey together."

That journey was interrupted for over ten years.

Thomas Goff disappeared, gone into mists that would always be at best a witches' brew of fantasy and reality. The Doctor grieved for the loss of his would-be right hand and concentrated on practicing the craft of psychiatry, specializing in counseling criminals and prostitutes at Castleford and then in private practice in Los Angeles, seeking and storing knowledge, writing and publishing monographs and establishing a reputation of maverick brilliance that grew and grew as his designs for conquest seethed within him. And then one day Thomas Goff was at his door, whimpering that the headaches were back and would the Doctor please help him?

Fate snapped its fingers. "Yes," Dr. John Havilland said.

Neuro scans, electro-encephalograms, blood tests, and extensive therapy followed, each physical and mental probe another step toward the starting gate of the Night Tripper's mission. Thomas Goff's last ten years had been extraordinary. Havilland described them in his journal:

Since my previous analysis of the subject, he has gone on to assume classic criminal behavior patterns, exemplifying the paranoic/sociopathic textbook personality, but with one notable exception: His criminal behavior is pathologically derived, but not pathologically executed. Goff shows great adaptability in subjugating his violent urges to circumspection in the choosing of his victims, and he always stops short of inflicting great bodily harm or murder. He has committed nighttime burglaries all over the East Coast for a decade and has never been caught; he has performed an estimated two hundred assaults on women, experiencing simultaneous sexual release *without reverting to the mayhem that characterized his assault career prior to our 1971 counselings.* Since Goff is in the truest sense a psychopath, this restraint (and his pride in it, that he attributes to my earlier counseling!) is beyond extraordinary—it is almost unbelievable. It is evident that he credits me with saving his life (i.e., alleviating his terror of daylight and blunting his memory of the suicide he witnessed at Attica); and that, implicitly, he credits me with "teaching" him the restraint that has armed him with a virtual criminal carte blanche. In fact, Goff (a 161 I.Q.!) says that *I have taught him to think.* It is evident that this brilliant criminal is seeking a father-son bonding with me, and that his "headaches" are a psychosomatic device to bring the two of us together to achieve the purposes he senses I have planned. His attraction to me is *not* either overtly or covertly homosexual; Goff simply equates me, on the sensory/stimuli level, with peace, tranquility and the fulfillment of dreams.

Three weeks into the new counseling, with Goff's recurring headaches quelled with hallucinogen-laced codeine, the Night Tripper went in full tilt and gained complete capitulation.

"Do you know that I love you, Thomas?"

"Yes."

"Do you know that I am here to take you as far as you can go?"

"Yes."

"Will you help me to help other people? To bring them out the way I've brought you out?"

"You know I will."

"Will you help me gain knowledge?"

"Name it, point the finger, I'll do it."

"Would you kill for me?"

"Yes."

That night the Doctor outlined Goff's role in his mission. Recruit lonely men and women, journeymen spiritual seekers, spineless "new agers" with no family and plenty of money. The counterculture consciousness circuit and singles nightspots should be rife with them. Goff was to judge their susceptibility, draw them out, and bring them to him, utilizing the greatest discretion and caution, employing no physical violence. He was also to perform burglary-reconnaissance forays, entering the homes of the Doctor's hooker patients, checking their john books for the names of wealthy customers—the objective being men with weak wills and monogamous relationships with their whores. "Be slow and cautious, Thomas," Havilland said. "This is a lifetime process."

That process yielded three lonelies in the first year. Havilland was satisfied with the progress he was making with their psyches, but frustrated by the lack of pure knowledge he was reaping. Eight more months passed; another three lonelies were recruited. The Doctor refined his techniques and filled up hundreds of pages on what he had learned. Yet still he hungered for pure data; molding clay that he could hold in his hands, savor and then mix into the human tapestry he was creating. The frustration had him slamming his desk in rage, beseeching time warps in his past for the answer to unanswerable questions. Then two events coincided and provided an answer.

Despite medication, Thomas Goff's headaches grew worse. Havilland ran a new series of tests and found his psychosomatic diagnosis rebuked. Goff had leptomeningitis, a chronic brain inflammation. It was the cause of his headaches and had probably been a contributing factor to his violent behavior throughout the years. For the first time in his professional life, the Doctor found himself in a crisis. Leptomeningitis could be cured by surgery and a wide assortment of drugs. His executive officer could be restored to health, and it would be business as usual. Leptomeningitis was also known to induce homicidal rages in normally peaceful men and women, yet, somehow, Thomas Goff, a violent sociopathic criminal, had sustained the disease for over a decade without letting it push him across the line into mindless slaughter. Without treatment, Goff would soon go insane and die of a massive cerebral hemorrhage. *But if, through a careful application of antibiotics and painkillers, Goff's disease could be de-escalated and escalated to suit his whims, he would possess his very own terminal man, and it would provide him*

with the opportunity to observe an absolutely emotionless human machine run
gauntlets of stress unparalleled in psychiatric history. And if need be, Goff could
be put to use as the ultimate killing machine.

The Night Tripper decided to sacrifice his executive officer/protégé/son
to the god of knowledge.

Then the Alchemist appeared.

Goff's leptomeningitis was three weeks into a "remission" when he told
the Doctor of the vice cop he had met, the disguise-artist reader of hero biographies who he could tell was just dying to bend to someone. Havilland
had at first been wary—the man was, after all, a police officer—but then
after seven counseling sessions devoted to bringing the Alchemist through
his obvious green door, the cop supplied the last piece of the Night Tripper's
long-sought puzzle: cruel, merciless data. Levers of manipulation that would
allow him to bend hundreds of people like twigs. The six folders that he offered in acquiescence to the Doctor's charisma were the first key. Four data
keepers and two police legends. The Alchemist had tried very hard to
please him, and in his gratitude the Doctor had brought him through his
green door much too fast, and he had run from the self-discoveries that were
unfolding before him.

Now the Alchemist was gone. Only his legacy of potential knowledge
remained.

Back in the present, the Night Tripper let his mind play over the files in
his wall safe. Cops. Men used to violence as a way of life. Goff would have
to be his go-between, but he was approaching his terminus—the lepto
would become uncontrollable within a few months. His training mission
was unsettling, a violation of his efficacy counseling. He should have
searched the liquor store for possible witnesses, then retreated until the proprietor was alone. One killing was perfection; three was dangerous.

Havilland walked to his window and looked out, watching the microcos-
mic progression of the people below him, scuttling like laboratory animals
in an observation maze. He wondered if they would ever know that at odd
moments he loved them.

6

Seventy-two hours into the liquor store case; over two thousand man hours spent probing every possible scientific angle. Yield: Zero. Extensive background checks on the three victims: Zero multiplied by the silence of the random factor—decent people at the wrong place at the wrong time, loved ones importuning God for the reason why, the unearthing of dull facts leading nowhere. The fingerprint report was a pastiche of swirls, streaks, and smudges; the heel marks and fabric elements found at the death scene were all attributed to the victims. The snitch reports that filtered back to Hollywood Division officers had the air of hyperbole and were inimical to Lloyd's concept of the killer as being very smart and very cool and not at all interested in reaping renown for his handiwork. If the queries on stolen .41 revolvers came back negative, the only remaining option would be to initiate nationwide gun queries and have a team of computer jockeys and astute paperwork detectives run through the over three hundred thousand automobile registration records for yellow Japanese imports, cross-checking them with criminal records and records of known criminal affiliates, looking for combustion points. If no two facts struck sparks and if the gun queries washed out, the case would be shunted into the bureaucratic backlog.

Lloyd recoiled at the knowledge that time was running out. Seated at Dutch Peltz's desk, savoring the feel of a silent Hollywood Station drifting toward dusk, he read over Xeroxes of the Field Interrogation Reports he had requisitioned citywide. On the night of April 23, eleven yellow Japanese cars had been stopped for traffic violations and/or "suspicious behavior." Four of the people cited and detained had been women, five had been ghetto black men, two with no criminal record, three with misdemeanor records for possession of drugs and nonpayment of child support. The two remaining white men were a lawyer stopped and ultimately arrested for drunk driving and a teenager popped for driving under the influence of a narcotic substance, which the arresting officer surmised to be airplane glue. No sparks.

Lloyd yelled, "Shit!" and stormed through his makeshift command post looking for a pen and paper. Finding a yellow legal pad and a stack of pencils atop Dutch's bookcase, he wrote:

Dutchman—time running out. There's a shitload of hotel stick-ups downtown, so I'll probably get yanked to a robbery assignment soon. The 4/23 F.I.s and the snitch feedback are goose-egg. Will you do the following for me?

1. Have another team of uniformed officers house-to-house (6–8 block radius) the area surrounding Freeway Liquor. Have them ask about:

A. Yellow Jap cars recently seen in area. (Lic. #)

B. Recent loiterers.

C. Recent conversations with the three deceased. All 3 victs. were locals. Did *they* mention anything suspicious?

D. *Have officers check previous canvass report filed by patrolmen who house-to-housed the night of the killings. Have them check residences of people who were not home that night.*

E. Tell the men that Robbery/Homicide has allocated unlimited overtime on this case—they'll get the $ in their next check.

2. Glom all H.W. Div. F.I.'s for past 6 mos. mentioning yellow Jap. autos. Set aside all incoming F.I.s featuring same, and collate all incoming rob. & homicide bulletins mentioning same.

3. Re: Herzog. I've got a weird feeling about this—even beyond the fact J.H. stole my file. I want some kind of handle on it before we call I.A.D. Have you run your grapevines on the 6 officers? Are the files still missing? I'm going to sleep at J.H.'s pad for the next several nights—(886-3317) see what happens—also, if the Rob./Hom. brass can't find me, they can't reassign me—L.H.

There was a knock at the door, followed by the sound of coughing. Lloyd put his memo under Dutch's quartz bookend and called out, "Enter!"

Lieutenant Walt Perkins walked in and shut the door behind him. When he shuffled his feet nervously, Lloyd said, "Looking for me or the Dutchman, Walt?"

"You," Perkins said.

Lloyd pointed to a chair. Perkins ignored it. "I checked with the squad," he said. "Herzog always worked alone. A lot of the men wanted to work with him because of his rep, but Jack always nixed it. He used to joke that ninety-five percent of all vice cops were alcoholics. He . . ." Perkins faltered as Lloyd came alive with tension. The sandy-haired man was not a cop.

Perkins shuffled his feet again, drawing figure eights on the floor. "Lloyd, I don't want I.A.D. nosing around the squad."

"Why?" Lloyd asked. "The worst you'll get is a reprimand. Vice commanders have been working Herzog off the payroll for years. It's common knowledge."

"It's not that."

"Then what is it?"

Perkins ceased his figure eights and forced himself to stare at Lloyd. "It's you. I know the whole story of what happened with you last year. I got it straight from a deputy chief. I admire you for what you did, that's not it. It's just that I know the promotion board has a standing order not to ever promote you or Dutch, and I—"

Lloyd's peripheral vision throbbed with black. Swallowing to keep his voice down, he said, "And you want me to sit on this? A brother officer murdered?"

Shaking his head and lowering his eyes, Perkins whispered, "No. I paid off a clerk at Personnel Records. He's going to carry Herzog present for another week or so, then report him missing. There'll be an investigation."

Lloyd kicked out at a metal wastebasket, sending a mound of wadded paper onto Perkins's pants legs. The lieutenant flinched back into the door and brought his eyes up. "The born-agains in I.A.D. have a hard-on for you, Hopkins. Gaffaney especially. You're a great cop, but you don't give a fuck about other cops and the people close to you get hurt. Look at what you've done to Dutch Peltz. Can you blame me for wanting to cover my ass?"

Lloyd released the hands he had coiled into fists. "It's all a trade-off. You're an administrator, I'm a hunter. You're a well liked superior officer, which means that the guys you command are shaking down hookers for head jobs and ripping off dope dealers for their shit and slopping up free booze all over Hollywood. I'm not so well liked, and I get strange, scary ideas sometimes. But I'm willing to pay the price and you aren't. So don't judge me. And get out of the way if you don't want to get hurt, because I'm seeing this thing through."

Lloyd pretended to fiddle with the papers on Dutch's desk. The second he averted his eyes, Perkins slipped out the door.

An hour later, when the last remnants of twilight dissolved into night, Lloyd drove to Jackie D.'s bar. The barman he had talked to two nights before was on duty and the place was still empty. The barman had the same weary look and automatically put down a napkin as Lloyd took a seat at the bar, shaking his head and saying, "No mercy. The ginger ale drinkers always return. There is no mercy."

"What's the complaint this time?" Lloyd asked.

"Wet T-shirt contest next door. First I gotta compete with free booze, now I gotta compete with free tits. I heard the guy who owns that puspocket is gonna throw in female mud wrestling, maybe female bush shaving, maybe female dick measuring, make a bundle and go into something stable like pushing heroin. No mercy!"

"Isn't his liquor license up for suspension, too?"

"Yeah, but he's young and he's got the chutzpah to think big and diversify. You know, a forty-story swingers' condo shaped like a dick, with an underground garage shaped like a snatch. You drive in and an electric beam shoots you an orgasm. No mercy!"

"There is mercy. I'm here to prove it."

The barman poured Lloyd a ginger ale. "Cops do not give mercy, they give grief."

Lloyd drew a paper bag from his jacket pocket. "You remember the man I was asking you about the other night? You said you saw him here with another man, sandy haired, early thirties?"

"Yeah, I remember."

"Good. We're going to create a little picture of that guy. You're going to be the artist. Come over on this side of the bar."

Lloyd spread out his wares on the bartop. "This is called an Identikit. Little composite facial features that we put together from a witness's description. We start with the forehead and work down. We've got over thirty nose types and so forth. See how the slots fit together?"

The barman fingered cardboard eyebrows, chins, and mouths and said, "Yeah. I just put these pieces together until it looks like the guy, right?"

"Right. Then I put the finishing touches in with a pencil. You got it?"

"Do I look dumb?"

"You look like Rembrandt."

"Who's he?"

"A bartender who drew pictures on the side."

It took the barman half an hour of sifting, comparing, rejecting, and appraising to come up with a composite. Lloyd looked at the portrait and said, "Not bad. A good-looking guy with a mean streak. You agree with that?"

"Yeah," the barman said. "Now that you mention it, he did look kinda mean."

"Okay. Now show me what these composite pieces have missed."

Lloyd took out a pencil and poised it over the Identikit picture. The barman studied his portrait from several different angles, then grabbed the pencil and went to work himself, shading the cheeks, broadening the nose, adding a thin line of malevolence to the lips. Finishing with a flourish, he said, "There! That is the cocksucker in the flesh!"

Holding the cardboard up to the light, Lloyd saw a vividly lean countenance come into focus, the thin mouth rendering the handsomeness ice cold. He smiled and felt the barman tugging at his sleeve. "Where's this fucking mercy you were telling me about?"

Lloyd stuck the portrait in his pocket. "Call the A.B.C. tomorrow at ten o'clock. They'll tell you the complaints against you have been removed and that you're no longer facing a license suspension."

"You've got that kinda clout?"

"Yeah."

"Mercy! Mercy prevails!"

Driving over the Cahuenga Pass to Jack Herzog's apartment, Lloyd thought: Only the hunt prevails. Trace all evidential links backward and forward in time and you will find that you are in the exact place that you were in four or eight or sixteen years ago, chasing ghouls too twisted to be called human and too sad to be called anything else, finding or not finding them, holding surveillance on patterns of hatred and fear, imparting morally ambiguous justice, running headlong into epiphanies that were as ever-changing as your need to know them was immutable. That the hunt was always conducted on the same landscape was the safest mark of permanence. Los Angeles County was thousands of miles of blacktop, neon, and scrub-brush-dotted hillside, arteries twisting in and around and back on themselves, creating human migrations that would unfailingly erupt in blood, stain the topography and leave it both changed and the same.

Lloyd looked out the window, knowing by off-ramp signs exactly where he was. He strained his eyes to see Ray Becker's Tropics, a bar he had worked as a vice officer fifteen years before. It wasn't there. The whole block had been razed. The Tropics was now a coin laundry, and the Texaco Station on the corner was a Korean church. A thought crossed his mind. If the city became unrecognizable, and the blood eruptions became the only sign of permanence, would he go insane?

The entrance foyer of Herzog's building was crowded with teenagers playing Pac-Man. Lloyd walked past them to the elevator and took it up to the fourth floor. The corridor was again deserted, with a wide assortment of music and TV noise blasting behind closed doors. He walked to the door of 423 and listened. Hearing nothing, he picked the lock and moved inside.

Flipping the wall switch, he saw the same sterile apartment illuminated, the only addition since his previous entry a fresh stack of junk mail and final notices from Bell Telephone and L.A. County Water and Power. Knowing the bedroom and the kitchen would be the same, Lloyd sat down on the couch to be still and think.

His mind was doing tic-tac-toe, .41 revolvers and Herzog's file requisition slips as x's and o's, when the phone rang. Lloyd picked up the receiver and slurred into the mouthpiece, "Hello?"

"Dutch, Lloyd."

"Shit."

"Expecting someone else?"

"Not really. I'd forgotten I left the number."

"Anything new on Herzog?"

"A good composite I.D. on a man Herzog was seen with. That's it."

"I've got some feedback on those file slips. Got a pencil?"

Lloyd dug a pen and spiral notebook out of his pocket. "Shoot."

"Okay," Dutch said. "First off, all the files are still missing. Second, they were *not* requisitioned from anywhere within the Department. Third, all the six officers are in good standing in the Depart—"

Lloyd cut in. "What about common denominators? I'm the only one of the six below lieutenant. Have you—"

"I was getting to that. Okay, six files. One, there's you, regarded as the best homicide dick in the L.A.P.D. Two, there's Johnny Rolando. You've heard of him—he's been a technical advisor on half a dozen TV shows. Both of you fall into what you might call the legendary-cop category. Now the other four—Tucker, Murray, Christie, and Kaiser—are just hardworking uniformed brass with over twenty years on the job. What—"

Lloyd interrupted: "That's *all* you've got?"

Dutch sighed. "Just listen, okay? The other four have one thing in common: Moonlight gigs as head of security for industrial firms. You know the kind of deal—plants that hire lots of cheap labor, lots of dopers and ex-cons on the payroll, lots of pilfering, lots of chemicals lying around that can be used to manufacture dope, so you have to keep the lid on—let the employees only rip you off so much, that kind of thing."

Lloyd's mental wheels turned. "How did you grapevine this info, Dutch?"

"Through a friend on the feds. He said the four firms—Avonoco Fiberglass, Junior Miss Cosmetics, Jahelka Auto King, and Surferdawn Plastics are what you'd call semi-sleazy. Shitkicker security guards who couldn't make the cops, files with lots of juicy dirt on their employees, to use as levers in case they go batshit from sniffing too much paint thinner. *Heavy* files on the workers at Avonoco—they've got a class-two security rating. They make fasteners for the space program at Andrews Air Force Base and they pay the minimum wage to everyone below management level. You like it?"

"I don't know. What's the theory behind it? Hire legit cops as figureheads, keep the shitkickers in line, have them act as go-betweens if a wayward employee gets busted?"

Dutch yawned. "Basically, yeah, I'd say that's it."

"Any *hard* dirt on the officers themselves?"

"Not really. Johnny Rolando screws TV stars; Christie, the Avonoco Fiberglass security man, has a history of compulsive gambling and psychiatric care; you like to give superior officers shit and never go home to sleep. Just a random sampling of L.A.'s finest."

Lloyd didn't know whether to laugh or take offense at the remark. Suddenly regret coiled around him and forced the words out. "I'll apologize to Perkins."

Dutch said, "Good. You owe him. I'll move on your liquor store memo and I'll give you another forty-eight on Herzog. After that *I'm* reporting him missing. Herzog's father is old, Lloyd. We owe it to him to give him the word."

"Yeah. What's Perkins afraid of, Dutch?"

"None of the stuff you hit him with. He runs one of the cleanest Vice Squads in the city."

"What, then?"

"You. A forty-two-year-old hardcharger cop with nothing to lose is a scary fucking thing. Sometimes you even scare me."

Lloyd's regret settled like a stone at the center of his heart. "Good night, Dutch."

"Good night, kid."

Lloyd replaced the receiver, immediately thinking of new angles on the case. His mental x's and o's were settling around blackmail, but his eyes kept straying back to the phone. Call Janice and the girls in San Francisco? Tell them that the house was sealed off almost exactly the way they had left it, that he only used the den and the kitchen, preserving the rest of the rooms as a testament to what they had once had and could have again? His phone conversations with Janice had at last progressed beyond civility. Was this the time to push for the fullest possible restoration of the family's past?

The job provided the answer. No. The officers who took over the formal investigation of Herzog's disappearance would check his phone bill and discover the long distance call. Janice's snotty off-and-on live-in lover would probably not accept a collect call. Fucked again by the verities of being a cop.

Stretching out on the couch, Lloyd dug in for a long stint of mental machinations. He was at it for half an hour, playing variations on blackmail themes, when there was a rapping on the door, followed by a woman's softly spoken words, "Jack? Jack, are you there?"

Lloyd walked to the door and opened it. A tall blonde woman was framed by the hall light. Her eyes were blurry and her blouse and designer jeans were rumpled. She looked up at him and asked, "Are you Marty Bergen? Is Jack here?"

Lloyd pointed the woman inside, scrutinizing her openly. Early thirties, a soft/strong face informed with intelligence. A lean body clenched against stress and bringing it off with grace. *Play her soft.*

When she was standing by the couch, he said, "My name is Hopkins. I'm a police officer. Jack Herzog has been missing from both his work assignments for close to a month. I'm looking for him."

The woman took a reflexive step backward, bumping the couch with her heels and then sitting down. Her hands flew to her face, then grasped her thighs. Lloyd watched her fingers turn white. Sitting down beside her, he asked, "What's your name?"

The woman released her hands, then rubbed her eyes and stared at him. "Meg Barnes."

Taking her steady voice as a signal to press the interrogation, Lloyd said, "I've got a lot of personal questions."

"Then ask them," Meg Barnes answered.

Lloyd smiled. "When did you see Herzog last?"

"About a month ago."

"What was the basis of your relationship?"

"Friends, occasionally lovers. The sexual part came and went. Neither of us pushed it. The last time I saw Jack he told me he wanted to be alone for a while. I told him I'd come by in a month or so."

"Which you did tonight?"

"Yes."

"Did Herzog contact you at any time during the month?"

"No."

"Was the sexual part of your relationship on immediately before you saw Herzog last?"

Meg flinched and said, "No, it wasn't. But what does this have to do with Jack's disappearing?"

"Herzog is an exceptional man, Miss Barnes. Everything I've discovered about him has pointed that out. I'm just trying to get a handle on his state of mind around the time he disappeared."

"I can tell you about that," she said. "Jack was either exhilarated or depressed, like he was on a roller-coaster ride. Most of his conversation had to do with vindicating Marty Bergen. He said he was going to fuck the L.A.P.D. high brass for what they did to him."

"Why did you think I was Bergen?" Lloyd asked.

"Because Bergen and I are the only friends Jack has in the world, and you're big, the way Jack described Bergen."

Lloyd spent a silent minute mustering his thoughts. Finally he asked, "Did Herzog say specifically how he was going to vindicate Bergen or fuck the high brass?"

"No, never."

"Can you give me some specific instances of his exhilarated or depressed behavior?"

Meg Barnes pondered the question, then said, "Jack was either very quiet or he'd laugh at absolutely everything, whether it was funny or not. He used to laugh hysterically about someone or something called Doctor John the Night Tripper. The last time I saw him he said he was really scared and that it felt good."

Lloyd took out his Identikit portrait. "Have you ever seen this man?"
She shook her head. "No."

"Do the names Howard Christie, John Rolando, Duane Tucker, Daniel Murray, or Steven Kaiser mean anything to you?"

"No."

"Avonoco Fiberglass, Jahelka Auto King, Surferdawn Plastics, Junior Miss Cosmetics?"

"No. What are they?"

"Never mind. What about my name—Lloyd Hopkins?"

"No! Why are you asking me these things?"

Lloyd didn't answer. He got up from the couch and tossed the upholstered pillow he was leaning against on the floor, then carried the coffee table over to the wall. When he turned around, Meg Barnes was staring at him. "Jack's dead," she said.

"Yes."

"Murdered?"

"Yes."

"Are you going to get the person who did it?"

Lloyd shuddered back a chill. "Yes."

Meg pointed to the floor. "Are you sleeping here?" Acceptance had taken the controlled edge off her voice. Lloyd's voice sounded numb to his own ears. "Yes."

"Your wife kick you out?"

"Something like that."

"You could come home with me."

"I can't."

"I don't make that offer all the time."

"I know."

She got up and walked to the door. Lloyd saw her strides as a race between her legs and her tears. When she touched the door handle, he asked, "What kind of man was Herzog?"

Meg Barnes's words and tears finished in a dead heat. "A kind man afraid of being vulnerable. A tender man afraid of his tenderness, disguising it with a badge and a gun. A gentle man."

The door slammed shut as tears rendered words unnecessary. Lloyd turned off the lights and stared out the window at the neon-bracketed darkness.

7

"Tell me about your dreams."

Linda Wilhite measured the Doctor's words, wondering whether he meant waking or sleeping. Deciding the latter, she plucked at the hem of her faded Levi skirt and said, "I rarely dream."

Havilland inched his chair closer to Linda and formed his fingers into a steeple. "People who rarely dream usually have active fantasy lives. Is that true in your case?" When Linda's eyelids twitched at the question, he thrust the steeple up to within a foot of her face. "Please answer, Linda."

Linda slapped at the steeple, only to find the Doctor's hands in his lap. "Don't push so hard," she said.

"Be specific," Havilland said. "Think exactly what you want to say."

Linda breathed the words out slowly. "We're barely into the session and you start taking command. I had some things I wanted to discuss, things that I've had on my mind lately, and you barge right in with questions. I don't like aggressive behavior."

The Doctor collapsed the steeple and clasped his hands. "Yet you're attracted to aggressive men."

"Yes, but what does that have to do with it?"

Havilland slumped forward in his chair. "Touché, Linda. But let me state my case before I apologize. You're paying me a hundred and fifteen dollars an hour, which you can afford because you earn a great deal of money doing something you despise. I see this therapy as an exercise in pure pragmatism: Find out why you're a hooker, then terminate the therapy. Once you stop hooking you won't need me or be able to afford me, and we'll go our separate ways. I feel for your dilemma, Linda, so please forgive my haste."

Linda felt a little piece of her heart melt at the brilliant man's apology. "I'm sorry I barked," she said. "I know you're on my side and I know your methods work. So . . . in answer to your question, yes, I do have an active fantasy life."

"Will you elaborate?" Havilland asked.

"About six years ago I posed for a series of clothed and semi-nude photographs that ultimately became this arty-farty coffee table book. There was this awful team of gay photographers and technicians, and they posed me in front of air conditioners to blow my hair and give me goose bumps and beside a heater to make me sweat buckets, and they turned me and threw me around like a rag doll, and it was worse than fucking a three hundred pound drunk."

"And?" Havilland whispered.

"And I used to fantasize murdering those fags and having someone film it, then renting a big movie theater and filling it with girls in the Life. They'd applaud the movie and applaud me like I was Fellini."

The Doctor laughed. "That wasn't so hard, was it?"

"No."

"Is that a recurring fantasy?"

"Well . . . no . . ."

"But variations of it recur?"

Linda smiled and said, "You should have been a cop, Doctor. People would tell you whatever you wanted to know. Okay, there's this sort of upbeat version of the movie fantasy. You don't have to be a genius to see that it derives from my parents' deaths. I'm behind a camera. A man beats a woman to death, then shoots himself. I film it, and it's real and it isn't real. What I mean is, *of course* what happens is real, only the people aren't *permanently* dead. That's how I justify the fantasy. What I think I—"

The Doctor cut in: "Interpret the fantasy."

"Let me finish!" Linda blurted out. Lowering her voice, she said, "I was going to say that somehow it all leads to love. These real or imaginary or whatever people die so that I can figure out what my fucked-up childhood meant. Then I meet this big, rough-hewn man. A lonely, no-bullshit type of man. He's had the same kind of life as me and I show him the film and we fall in love. End of fantasy. Isn't it syrupy and awful?"

Looking straight at the Doctor, Linda saw that his features had softened and that his eyes were an almost translucent light brown. When he didn't answer, she got up and walked over to the framed diplomas on the wall. On impulse, she asked, "Where's your family, Doctor?"

"I don't really have a family," Havilland said. "My father disappeared when I was an adolescent and my mother is in a sanitarium in New York."

Turning to face him, Linda said, "I'm sorry."

"Don't be sorry, just tell me what you're feeling right now."

Linda laughed. "I feel like I want a cigarette. I quit eight months ago, one of my little control trips, and now I'm dying for one."

Havilland laughed in return. "Tell me more about the man you fall in love with."

Linda walked around the office, running her fingertips along the oak walls. "Basically, all I know is that he wears a size forty-four sweater. I know that because I had a john once who had the perfect body and he wore that size—for some reason I looked at the label while he was getting dressed. When I first started having these fantasies I used to picture the john's face—then I made myself forget his face, because it interfered with my fantasy. Once I even drove downtown to Brooks Brothers and spent two hundred dollars on a size forty-four navy blue cashmere sweater."

Linda sat down and drummed the arms of her chair. "Do you think that's a sad story, Doctor?"

Havilland's voice was very soft. "I think I'm going to enjoy taking you beyond your beyond."

"What's that?"

"Just a catch phrase of mine dealing with patients' potentialities. We'll talk more about that later. Before we conclude, please give me a quick response to a hypothetical situation. Among my patients is a young man who wants to kill. Wouldn't it be terrible if he met a young woman who wanted to die and if someone were there with a camera to record it?"

Linda slammed the arms of her chair. The floor reverberated with her words: "Yes! But why does that idea titillate me so?"

Havilland got up and pointed to the clock. "No souls saved after fifty minutes. Monday at the same time?"

Linda took his hand on the way to the door. "I'll be here," she said, her voice receding to a whisper.

Havilland drove home to his condominium/sanctuary in Beverly Hills and went straight to his inner sanctum, the only one of the six rooms not walled from floor to ceiling with metal shelves spilling psychology texts.

The Night Tripper thought of his three dwellings as a wheel of knowledge exploration, with himself as the hub. His Century City office was the induction spoke; his condo the fount of study and contemplation; the Malibu beach house the spoke of dispatch, where he sent his lonelies beyond their beyonds.

But the central point of his work was here behind a door he had personally stripped of varnish and painted an incongruous bright green. It was the control room of the Time Machine.

A swivel chair and a desk holding a telephone were centered in the room, affording a swivel view of four information-covered walls.

One wall held a huge map of Los Angeles County. Red pins signified the addresses of his lonelies, blue pins denoted the pay phones where he contacted them—a safety buffer he had devised. Green pins indicated homes where the lonelies had been placed on assignment, and plastic stick figures marked Thomas Goff, ever mobile in his quest to find more red pins.

Two walls comprised a depth gauge, to probe the Night Tripper's childhood void. Serving as markings on the gauge were WCBS top-forty surveys from Spring 1959, attached to the walls with red and blue pins, and a shelf containing roller-skate wheels that were once the feet of dead animals, lockets of soft brown hair stolen from inside a family Bible, and a swatch of carpet stained with blood.

Clues.

The remaining wall was covered with typed quotations from inhabitants of the void, taped on in approximate chronological order:

December 1957: Mother—"Your father was a monster, and I'm glad he's gone. The administrators of the trust fund have been instructed to tell us nothing, and I'm glad. I don't want to know." (Current disposition: Residing in a Yonkers, N.Y., sanitarium with severe alcoholic senility.)

March 1958: Frank Baxter (father's lawyer)—"Just think the best, Johnny. Think that your dad loves you very much, which is why he's sending you and your mother all that nice money." (Disposition: Committed suicide, August 1960)

Spring 1958: (Imagined? Recalled from previous summer?) Police detectives questioning mother as to father's whereabouts—obsequious; deferential to wealth. (Disposition: Complete disregard of all my in-

quiries to Scarsdale P.D. and Westchester County P.D. 1961–1968)
Dreamt?

June 1958: Nurse & doctor at Scarsdale Jr. High (overheard)—"I
think the boy has a touch of motor aphasia"; "Bah! Doctor, that boy
has got a tremendous mind! He just wants to learn what he wants to
learn"; "I'll believe the X ray before I believe your analysis, Miss
Watkins." (Disposition: doctor dead, nurse moved away, address unknown. Note: X rays and other tests taken at Harvard indicate no
aphasiac lesions.)

Walls of clues. Hubs within the hub of himself and all the spokes of his
wheels.

Havilland swiveled in his chair, pushing off with his feet, spinning himself faster and faster, until the room was a blur and the four walls and their
clues metamorphosed into rapid-fire images of Linda Wilhite and her home
movie fantasies. He shut his eyes and Richard Oldfield was standing nude
in front of a movie camera, with other lonelies laboring over arc lights and
sound equipment. The chair was close to toppling off its casters when the
phone rang and froze the moment. Deep breathing to bail out of his reverie,
the Night Tripper let the chair come to a halt. When he was certain his
voice would be calm, he picked up the phone and said, "Is this good news,
Thomas?"

Goff's voice was both self-satisfied and hoarse with tension. "Bingo. Junior
Miss Cosmetics. I never even had to contact the cop. I played one of his
stooges like an accordion. Murray won't know anything about it."

"Have you got them?"

"Tonight," Goff said. "It's only costing us a grand and some pharmaceutical coke."

"Where? I want to know the exact time and place."

"Why? You told me this was my baby."

"Tell me, Thomas." Hearing the hoarseness in his own voice, Havilland
coated his words with sugar. "You've done brilliantly, and it *is* your baby. I
just want to be able to picture your triumph."

Goff went silent. The Doctor pictured a proud child afraid to express his
gratitude at being wooed with cheap praise. Finally the child bowed to the
father. "At ten-thirty tonight. The end of Nichols Canyon road, in the little park with the picnic benches."

Havilland smiled. Throw the child a crumb. "Beyond brilliant. Perfection. I'll meet you at your apartment at eleven. We'll celebrate the occasion by planning our next grouping. I need your feedback."

"Yes, Doctor." Goff's voice was one step above groveling. Havilland hung up the phone and replayed the conversation, realizing that Linda Wilhite had remained a half step back in his mind the whole time, waiting.

At nine-thirty Havilland drove to Nichols Canyon and parked behind a stand of sycamore trees adjacent to the picnic area. He was shielded from view by mounds of scrub-covered rock which still allowed him visual access to Goff's meeting spot. The lights that were kept on all night to thwart off gay assignations would frame the picture, and unless Goff and the security stooge spoke in a whisper their voices would carry up to his hiding place. It *was* perfection.

At ten past ten, Goff's yellow Toyota pulled up. Havilland watched his executive officer get out and stretch his legs, then withdraw a large revolver from his waistband and go into a gunfighter's pirouette, swiveling in all directions, blowing away imaginary adversaries. The overhead lights illuminated a throbbing network of veins in his forehead, the storm warning of a lepto attack. Havilland could almost feel Goff's speeded-up heartbeat and respiration. When the sound of another car approaching hit his ears and Goff stuck his gun back and covered the butt with his windbreaker, Havilland felt his body go cold with sweat.

A battered primer-gray Chevy appeared, doing a little fishtail as the driver applied the brakes. A fat black man in a skin-tight uniform of pale blue shirt, khaki pants, and Sam Browne belt got out, making a big show of slamming the door and chugging from a pint of whiskey. Havilland shuddered as he recalled one of Goff's favorite death fantasies: "Drawing down on niggers."

The black man sauntered up to Goff and offered him the bottle. Goff declined with a shake of the head and said, "You brought them?" Havilland squinted and saw that Goff's fingers were trembling and involuntarily plucking at his waistband.

The black man knocked back a long drink and giggled. "If you got the money, I've got the honey. If you got the dope, I got the . . . shit, I can't rhyme that one. You look nervous, homeboy. You been tootin' a little too much of your own product?"

Goff took a step backward. His whole left side was alive with tremors.

Havilland could see his left leg buckle as though straining to kick out at a right angle. The black man raised his hands in a supplicating gesture, fear in his eyes as he saw Goff's face contort spastically. "Man, you reelin' with the feelin'. I get you the stuff and you pay me off, and we do this all real slow, all right?"

Goff found his voice. Willing it even made his tremors subside. "Rock steady, Leroy. You want it slow, you got it slow."

"My name ain't Leroy," the black man said. "You dig?"

"I dig you, Amos. Now cut the shit and bring me the stuff. *You* dig?" Goff's thumbs were hooked in his belt loops. His hands twitched in the direction of the gun. Havilland saw the black man bristle, then smile. "For a K note and two grams of righteous blow you can call me anything short of Sambo." He walked to his car and reached into the backseat, coming away with two large cardboard suitcases. Returning to Goff and putting them down at his feet, he said, "Fresh off the Xerox machine. Nobody but me knows about it. Come up green, homeboy."

Goff stuck a shaking hand into his windbreaker and pulled out a plastic baggie, then tossed it in the dirt beside the black man's car. "Ride, Leroy. Buy yourself a Cadillac and get your hair processed on me."

The black man picked up the baggie and balled it in his fist, then killed the pint and threw it at Goff's Toyota. When it hit the trunk and shattered, Goff grabbed at his waistband, then stifled a shriek and jerked his gun hand to his mouth and bit it. Havilland stifled his own outcry and watched the black man raise his hands and back up slowly toward his car, murmuring, "I'll be rockin' steady, rockin' steady real slow. *Reeeal* slow." His back touched the driver's side door and he squirmed in behind the wheel, rolled up the window and gunned the car in reverse. When the dust from his exit cleared, Havilland could see Thomas Goff weeping, aiming his handcannon at the moon.

An hour after Goff's sobbing departure, the Doctor drove to his underling's apartment in the Los Feliz district, the moon catching the edge of his vision, constantly drawing his eyes from the road. Parking outside Goff's building, he checked the contents of his black leather "Truth Kit": sodium Pentothal ampules, ten c.c. bottles of liquid morphine and an assortment of disposable syringes. He would quash Goff's pain and gauge the degree of his slippage.

Goff opened the door on the first knock. He was stripped to the waist, his torso oozing sweat. Havilland stepped inside and felt the chill of an air-conditioner on full blast. He looked at Goff. His extremities were tensed as if to contain earthquakes and his eyes were a feverish yellow. Doing a quick hypothetical run-through based on observation and carefully studied case histories, he gave his pawn a month to live.

When the door closed on his diagnosis, the Doctor took Goff by the arm and led him to the couch. The two cardboard suitcases rested by the coffee table, unopened. Goff smiled through his tremors and pointed to them. "We're on our way, Doctor John."

Havilland smiled in return and opened his leather bag. He withdrew a fresh syringe and a morphine bottle, poking the needle through the porous rubber top, extracting just enough dope for an enticing mainline. Goff wet his lips and said, "It's the worst it's ever been. I've been doing some more reading on migraines. They get worse in a person's thirties. I think I'm really scared."

The Doctor took a bead on a large pulsating vein behind Goff's left ear. He formed a tourniquet with the flat of his hand, placing it just above Goff's collarbone. Whispering, "Easy, Thomas, easy," he inserted the needle square into the vein and depressed the stopper. A sharp jet of blood squirted out as the morphine entered. Goff's features unclenched in relief and Havilland smiled and amended his death sentence: A small dose still brought comfort. Sixty days.

Goff's limbs went languorous and the veins in his forehead receded to their normal dimensions. Havilland studied his patient and devised a spur of the moment contingency plan: If the pain began again within the next half hour, give Goff thirty days of maintenance doses, risk him on one more security-file run, then take him out of L.A. to terminate, and go solo on the remaining runs. If the pain remains abated, give him sixty days of tether for two more runs. Play the truth game with him to explain the tension with the jigaboo. The problem was *covered*.

Goff closed his eyes and drifted off into a dope/exhaustion cloudbank. Havilland got up and walked around the living room, purposely averting his eyes from the suitcases. The low ceiling was painted black and the walls were painted a military brown. Goff's therapy-controlled brightness phobia had driven him to turn a cheery dwelling place into a neuroses decompression chamber. Every time he visited the apartment, the Doctor looked for splotches of color, indicators that he had at long last instigated a total failure of memory, thereby giving Goff some peace of mind to go with his total ac-

quiescence. But everything that could be purchased or rendered dark remained that way, room carpeting to cabinet hardware.

The Doctor surveyed the decompression chamber from a possible farewell
standpoint. Various shades of darkness hit his senses, producing a pleasant vertigo that resurrected a childhood memory of a ferris wheel at a Bronx amusement park. The wheel was about to grab him when a burst of non-sequitur pink
threw a wrench into its gears.

Snapping back to the present, Havilland saw that it was a pink slip of
paper on the end table near the bedroom door, partially covered by a black
ceramic ashtray. He picked it up and felt the room reel. It was an L.A.P.D.
release slip, issued to Thomas Goff upon the presentation of sixty-five dollars bail money. The charge was 673.1—Failure to appear in traffic court.
The Doctor read the heavily abbreviated type at the bottom and crumpled
the paper in his hand. His executive officer had been arrested for nonpayment of jaywalking citations.

The ferris wheel stopped at the top of its circuit, then plummeted to
earth, dropping him into a land of treason. He looked over at Goff, who
stirred in his stupor, kneading his shoulders into the couch.

The Doctor felt a wave of rage and loathing hit him like a one-two punch
in the solar plexus. To combat it he breathed in-out, in-out until the coun-
terproductive emotions leveled off into professional calm. When he was certain he could maintain his decorum he arrayed the tools of his truth kit on
the coffee table, filling one syringe with morphine and another with sodium
Pentothal. As Goff's stirrings became more violent, he reached over and
pinched his nostrils shut and counted slowly to ten. At nine Goff jerked fully
awake and screamed. Havilland took his hand from his nostrils and clamped
it over his mouth, pinning his head to the wall. Whispering, "Easy, Thomas,
easy," he took the morphine syringe and skin-popped Goff in his left arm and
left pectoral muscle. Seeing that Goff's relief was instantaneous, he released
his hand and said, "You didn't tell me that you were arrested last month."

Goff shook his head until his body shook with it all the way down to his
toes. "I haven't been in the slam since Attica, you know that, Doc."

It was the hoarse rasp of a terrified man speaking the perfect truth. Havilland smiled and whispered, "Your left forearm, Thomas." When Goff
obeyed, he jammed a 30 c.c. jolt of sodium Pentothal into the largest vein
at the crook of his elbow. Goff gasped and began to giggle. Havilland withdrew the needle and leaned back on the couch. "Tell me about the Junior
Miss file transaction," he said.

Goff giggled and fixed his glazed eyes on the far wall. "I scoped out the security bimbos from the bar across from the parking lot," he slurred. "All white trash and niggers. The niggers looked too shifty, so I settled on this Okie type. I asked some of the regulars about him, casual like. They said he was a coke fiend, but controlled, and a closed-mouthed type. He sounded like prime meat, so I brought him out slowly and closed the deal yesterday. I met him a couple of hours ago. Those two suitcases are the files."

Havilland felt his mind buzz, like someone had stuck a live wire into his brain. Goff was so far gone that he was now immune even to massive doses of hypnotic drugs. Time was running out for his executive officer—he had two weeks to live. At best.

Thomas Goff continued to squeal with laughter, his hands dancing over his body. Havilland examined the pink release slip. No vehicle license plate mentioned. Goff had obviously been stopped for questioning while on foot, a routine warrant check turning up his old jaywalking tickets. He waved the slip in front of Goff's eyes. Goff ignored the flash of brightness and laughed even harder.

Havilland got to his feet and swung a roundhouse open hand at Goff's face. Goff screeched, "No please," as the blow made contact, then wrapped his head in his hands and curled into a fetal ball on the couch. The Doctor squatted beside him and put a hand on his shoulder. "You need a rest, Thomas," he said. "The migraines are sapping your strength. We're going to take a little vacation together. I'm going to confer with some specialists about your headaches, then treat you myself. I want you to stay home and rest, then call me in forty-eight hours. All right?"

Goff twisted to look at the Doctor. He wiped a trickle of blood from his nose and whimpered, "Yes, but what about the next grouping? We were going to plan it, remember?"

"We'll have to postpone it. The important thing now is to deal with your migraines."

Thomas Goff's eyes clouded with tears. The Doctor extracted a bottle of tetracycline-morphine mixture from his bag and prepped a syringe. "Antibiotics," he said. "In case your migraines have gone viral." Goff nodded as Havilland found a vein in his wrist and inserted the needle. His tears spilled over at the act of mercy, and by the time the doctor withdrew the syringe he was asleep.

Dr. John Havilland picked up the two suitcases, surprised to find that he wasn't thinking of the merciless information inside. As he turned off the light and shut the door behind him, he was thinking of a black vinyl Vietnam body bag he had won as a joke prize at a med school beer bust and of dogs exploding into red behind a barbed wire fence.

8

Lloyd awoke in his den, already calculating hours before he was fully conscious. Thirty-six since Dutch's ultimatum and no new leads—report Herzog missing. Well over a hundred hours since the liquor store slaughter—all leads dead-ended. Start cross-checking the three hundred thousand yellow Jap cars and begin hauling in known armed robbers, leaning on them hard, squeezing all known and suspected pressure points in hope of securing information. Shit work all the way down the line.

Lloyd stretched and rolled off the convertible bed in one motion, then walked into the kitchen and opened the refrigerator, letting the cold air bring him to full consciousness. When goose bumps formed beneath his T-shirt and boxer shorts he shivered and dug out a half consumed container of cottage cheese, eating with the spoon that was still stuck inside. Almost gagging on the sticky blandness, he looked around the three small rooms he had allotted himself in his family's absence: den to sleep, think, and study in; kitchen for the preparing of such gourmet fare as cottage cheese and cold chili from the can; the downstairs bathroom for hygiene. When he started doing calculations as to the number of hours since Janice and the girls had left, his mental calculator quit in midtransaction. If you start running tabs you'll go crazy and do something crazy to get them back. Let it be. If you stalk them, they'll know you haven't changed. It's a penance waiting game.

Finishing his breakfast, Lloyd showered hot and cold, then dressed in a day old button-down shirt and his only clean suit, an unseasonable summer pinstripe. Murmuring "Now or never," he sat down at his desk, dug out a spiral notebook and wrote:

4/28/84
To: Chief of Detectives

From: Det. Sergeant Lloyd Hopkins, Rob/Hom. Div.

Sir:

Four days ago I was contacted by my friend, Captain Arthur Peltz, the commander of Hollywood Division. He told me that Officer Jacob Herzog, a Personnel Records clerk at Parker Center who was working on a sub-rosa loan-out to Hollywood Vice, had been missing for nearly a month. Captain Peltz asked me to investigate, and in doing so I discovered that Herzog's (intact) apartment had been professionally wiped of fingerprints. I questioned Herzog's best friend, former L.A.P.D. Sergeant Martin Bergen, who told me that *he* hadn't seen Herzog in over a month and that Herzog had been "moody" at the time of their last meeting. An interview with Herzog's girlfriend confirms his month long absence and "moody" behavior. My opinion is that Herzog is the victim of a well-planned homicide and that his disappearance should be immediately and fully investigated. I realize that I should have reported this earlier, but my sole purpose in *not* reporting was to first establish evidence (however circumstantial) of wrongdoing. Captain Peltz ordered me to report to you immediately, but I violated that order.

Respectfully, Lloyd Hopkins, #1114

Lloyd read over his words, strangely satisfied at having taken the bulk of the risk in incurring high brass wrath. He ripped the page out of the notebook and put it in his inside jacket pocket, then clipped on his .38 and handcuffs and made for the front door. He had his hand on the doorknob when the phone rang.

He let it ring ten times before answering—only Penny pursued a phone call that persistently.

"Speak, it's your dime."

Penny's giggle came over the wire. "No, it's *not*, Daddy! It's my dollar-forty."

Lloyd laughed. "Excuse me. I forgot inflation. What's the scoop, Penguin?"

"The same old same old. What about you? Are you getting any?"

Lloyd feigned shock. "Penny Hopkins, I'm surprised at you!"

"No, you're not. You told me I was jaded in my crib. You didn't answer my question, Daddy."

"Very well, in answer to your question, I am *not* getting any."

Penny's giggle went up an octave. "Good. Mom read me that first letter of yours, you know. We were talking about it the other night. She said it was excessive, that *you* were excessive, and even when you were admitting to being a sleazy womanizer your admissions were excessive. But I could tell she was impressed."

"I'm glad. Is Roger still staying with you?"

"Yes. Mom sleeps with Roger, but she talks about you. One of these nights I'm going to get her stoned and get her to admit you're her main love. I'll report her words to you verbatim."

Lloyd felt a little piece of his heart work itself loose and drift up to San Francisco. "I want all of you back, Penguin."

"I know. I want to come back, and so does Anne. That's two votes for you. Mom and Caroline want to stay in Frisco. Dead heat."

"Annie and Caroline are okay?"

"Anne is big into vegetarianism and Eastern thought and Caroline is in love with this punk rock fool next door. He's a high school dropout. Gross."

Lloyd laughed. "Par for the teenage course. Let me hit you with something. Doctor John the Night Tripper. Ring any bells?"

"Ancient ones, Daddy. The sixties. He was this wild rock and roller. Caroline has one of his records—*Bad Boogaloo.*"

"That's it?"

"Yeah. Why?"

"A case I'm on. Dutch is on it, too. It's probably nothing."

Penny's voice went low and shrewd. "Daddy, when are you going to tell me about what happened right after the breakup? I'm no dummy, I know you were shot. Uncle Dutch practically admitted it to Mom."

Lloyd sighed as their conversation came to its usual conclusion. "Give it another couple of years, babe. When you're a world-weary fifteen I'll spill my guts. Right now all it means is that I owe a lot of people."

"Owe what, Daddy?"

"I don't know, babe. That's the tricky part."

"Will you tell me when you figure it out?"

"You'll be the first to know. I love you, Penny."

"I love you, too."

"I've got to go."

"So do I. Love love love."

"Likewise."

"Bye."
"Bye."

With "Owe what, Daddy?" trailing in his mind, Lloyd drove downtown to Parker Center. His memo to the chief of detectives rested like a hot coal in his jacket pocket. Deciding to check his incoming basket before dropping it with the chief's secretary, he took the elevator to the sixth floor and strode down the hall to his cubicle, seeing the note affixed to his door immediately: "Hopkins—call Det. Dentinger, B.H.P.D., re: gun query."

Lloyd grabbed his phone and dialed the seven familiar digits of the Beverly Hills Police Department, saying, "Detective Dentinger," when the switchboard operator came on the line. There was the sound of the call being transferred, then a man's perfunctory voice: "Dentinger. Talk."

Lloyd was brusque. "Detective Sergeant Hopkins, L.A.P.D. What have you got on my gun query?"

Dentinger muttered "shit" to himself, then said into the mouthpiece, "We got a burglary from two weeks ago. Unsolved, no prints. A forty-one-caliber revolver was listed on the report of missing items. The reason you didn't get a quicker response on this is because the burglary dicks who originally investigated think that the report was padded, you know, for insurance purposes. A bunch of shit was reported stolen, but the burglar's access was this little basement window. He couldn't have hauled all the shit out—it wouldn't have fit. I've been assigned to investigate the deal, see if we should file on this joker for submitting a false crime report. I'll give you the sp—"

Lloyd cut in. "Do you think there *was* a burglary?"

Dentinger sighed. "I'll give you my scenario. Yes, there was a burglary. Small items were stolen, like the jewelry on the report, the gun, and probably some shit the victim didn't report, like cocaine—I've got him figured for a stone snowbird, really whacked out. You know the clincher? The guy owns two of these antique guns, mounted in presentation cases, with original ammo from the Civil War, but he only reports *one* stolen. I don't doubt that the fucker *was* stolen, but any intelligent insurance padder would stash the other gun and report it stolen too, am I right?"

Lloyd said, "Right. Give me the information on the victim."

"Okay," Dentinger said. "Morris Epstein, age forty-four, eight-one-six-seven Elevado. He calls himself a literary agent, but he's got that Hollywood big bucks fly-by-night look. You know, live high on credit and bullshit, never know where your next buck is coming from. Personally, I think these—"

Lloyd didn't wait for Dentinger to finish his spiel. He hung up the phone and ran for the elevator.

8167 Elevado was a salmon pink Spanish-style house in the Beverly Hills residential district. Lloyd sat in his car at the curb and saw Dentinger's "big bucks fly-by-night" label confirmed: The lawn needed mowing, the hedges needed trimming, and the chocolate brown Mercedes in the driveway needed a bath.

He walked up and knocked on the door. Moments later a small middle-aged man with finely sculpted salt-and-pepper hair threw the door open. When he saw Lloyd, he reached for the zipper at the front of his jumpsuit and zipped up his chest. "You're not from Roll Your Own Productions, are you?" he asked.

Lloyd flashed his badge and I.D. card. "I'm from the L.A.P.D. Are you Morris Epstein?"

The man shuffled back into his entrance foyer. Lloyd followed him. "Isn't this out of your jurisdiction?" the man said.

Lloyd closed the door behind them. "I'll make it easy on you, Epstein. I have reason to believe that the forty-one revolver you reported stolen might have been used in a triple homicide. I want to borrow your other forty-one for comparison tests. Cooperate, and I'll tell the Beverly Hills cops that your insurance report was exaggerated, not padded. You dig?"

Morris Epstein went livid. Spittle formed at the corners of his mouth. He flung an angry arm in the direction of the door and hissed, "Leave this house before I have you sued for police harassment. I have friends in the A.C.L.U. They'll fix your wagon for real, flatfoot."

Lloyd pushed past Epstein's arm into an art-deco living room festooned with framed movie posters and outsized gilt-edged mirrors. A glass coffee table held a single-edged razor blade and traces of white powder. There was a large cabinet against the wall by the fireplace. Lloyd opened and shut drawers until he found the glassine bag filled with powder. He turned to see Epstein standing beside him with the telephone in his hand. When he held the bag in front of Epstein's eyes, the little man said, "You can't bluff me. This is illegal search and seizure. I'm personal friends with Jerry Brown. I've got clout. One phone call and you are adios, motherfucker."

Lloyd grabbed the telephone from Epstein's hand, jerked the cord out of the wall and tossed it on the coffee table. The table shattered, sending glass shards exploding up to the ceiling. Epstein backed into the wall and whispered, "Now look, pal, we can bargain this out. We can—"

Lloyd said, "We're past the bargaining stage. Bring me the gun. Do it now."

Epstein unzipped the top of his jumpsuit and kneaded his chest. "I still say this is illegal search and seizure."

"This is a legal search and seizure coincident to the course of a felony investigation. Bring me the gun—in its case. Don't touch the gun itself."

Morris Epstein capitulated with an angry upward tug of his zipper. When he left the room, Lloyd gave it a quick toss, searching the remaining drawers, wondering whether or not he should go to the Beverly Hills Station and check out the burglary report. Dentinger had said that no prints were found, but maybe there were F.I.'s on yellow Jap imports or other indicators to jog his brain.

He went through the last drawer, then turned his attention to the mantel above the fireplace. He could hear Epstein's returning footsteps as his eyes caught a cut-glass bowl filled with matchbooks. He grabbed a handful. They were all from First Avenue West—one of the two bars that Jungle Jack Herzog was working.

"Here's your gun, shamus."

Lloyd turned around and saw Epstein holding a highly varnished rosewood box. He walked to him and took the box from his hands. Opening the lid, he saw a large blue steel revolver with mother-of-pearl grips mounted on red velvet. Arranged in a circle around it were copper-jacketed soft-nosed bullets. Taking a pen from his pocket, he inserted it into the barrel and raised the gun upward. Clearly etched on the barrel's underside were the numbers 9471.

"Satisfied?" Epstein said.

Lloyd lowered the barrel and closed the lid of the box. "I'm satisfied. Where did you get the guns?"

"I bought them cheap from the producer of this Civil War mini-series I packaged last year."

"Do you know the serial number of the other gun?"

"No, but I know the two guns had consecutive numbers. Listen, do the Beverly Hills fuzz really think I padded that burglary report?"

"Yes, but I'll slip them the word about how you cooperated. I saw some matches here from First Avenue West. Do you go there a lot?"

"Yeah. Why?"

Lloyd took a photograph of Jack Herzog from his billfold. "Ever see this man?"

Epstein shook his head. "No."

Withdrawing a photocopy of his Identikit portrait of the man seen with Herzog, Lloyd said, "What about him?"

Epstein looked at the picture, then flinched. "Man, this is fucking weird. I did some blow with this guy outside Bruno's Serendipity one night. This is a great fucking likeness."

Lloyd felt two divergent evidential lines intersect in an incredible revelation. "Did this man tell you his name?" he asked.

"No, we just did the blow and split company. But it was funny. He was a weird, persistent kind of guy. He kept asking me these questions about my family and if I was into meeting this really incredibly smart dude he knew. What's the matter, shamus? You look pale."

Lloyd gripped the gun box so hard that he could hear his finger tendons cracking. "Did you tell him your name?"

"No, but I gave him my card."

"Did you tell him about your guns?"

Epstein swallowed. "Yeah."

"When did you talk to the man?"

"Maybe two, three months ago."

"Have you seen him since?"

"No, I haven't been back to Bruno's. It sucks."

"Did you see the man get into a car?"

"Yeah, a little yellow job."

"Make and model?"

"It was foreign. That's all I know. Listen, what's this all about? You come in here and hassle me, break my coffee table—" Epstein stopped when he saw Lloyd run for the door. He called out, "Hey, shamus, come back and shmooze sometime! I could package a badass fuzz like you into a series!"

Running roof lights and siren, Lloyd made it back to Parker Center in a record twenty-five minutes. Cradling the gun box in the crook of his arm, he ran the three flights of stairs up to the offices of the Scientific Indentification Division, then pushed through a series of doors until he was face to face with Officer Artie Cranfield, who put down his copy of *Penthouse* and said, "Man, do you look jazzed."

Lloyd caught his breath and said "I *am* jazzed, *and* I need some favors. This box contains a gun. Can you dust it for latents real quick? After you do that, we need a ballistics comparison."

"This is a suspected murder weapon?"

"No, but it's a consecutive serial number to the gun I think is the liquor store murder weapon. Since the ammo in this box and the murder ammo is antique, probably from the same casting, I'm hoping that the rifling marks will be so similar that we can assume th—"

"We can't make those kinds of assumptions," Artie interjected. "That kind of theorizing won't hold up in court."

Lloyd handed Artie the gun box. "Artie, I'll lay you twenty to one that this one gets settled on the street. Now will you please dust this baby for me?"

Artie took a pencil from his desk and propped open the lid of the box, then stuck another pencil in the barrel of the revolver, the end affixed to the upper hinge of the box, forming a wedge that held the gun steady. When the box and gun were secure, he took out a small brush and a vial of fingerprint powder and spread it over every blue steel, mother-of-pearl, and rosewood surface. Finishing, he shook his head and said, "Smooth glove prints on the grip, streak prints on the barrel. I dusted the box for kicks. Smudged latents that are probably you, glove prints that indicate that the box was carefully opened. You're dealing with a pro, Lloyd."

Lloyd shook his head. "I really didn't think we'd find anything good. He stole the companion gun, but I figured he might have touched this one, too."

"He did, with surgical rubber gloves." Artie started to laugh.

Lloyd said, "Fuck you. Let's take this monster down to the tank and see how it kicks."

Artie led Lloyd through the Crime Lab to a small room where water and tufted-cotton-layered ballistics tanks were sunk into the floor. Lloyd slipped three slugs into the .41's chamber and fired into the top layer of water. There was the sound of muffled ricocheting, then Artie squatted and opened up a vent on the tank's side. Withdrawing the "catcher" layer of cotton, he pulled out the three expended rounds and said, "Perfect. I've got a comparison microscope in my office. We'll sign for the liquor store shells and run them."

Lloyd signed a crime lab chit for the three rounds taken from the bodies of the liquor store victims and brought them, in a vinyl evidence bag, to

Artie's office. Artie placed them on the left plate of a large, double-eyepieced microscope, then placed the three ballistics tank rounds on the right plate and studied both sets, individually and collectively, for over half an hour. Finally he got up, rubbed his eyes and voiced his findings: "Discounting the fact that the set of rounds fired at the liquor store were flattened by their contact with human skulls, while the tank rounds were intact, and the fact that the impact of the liquor store rounds altered the rifling marks, I would say that the basic land and groove patterns are as identical as slugs fired from two different guns can be. Nail the bastard, Lloyd. Give him the big one where it hurts the most."

Bruno's Serendipity was a singles bar/backgammon club on Rodeo Drive, in the heart of Beverly Hills's boutique strip. The club's interior was dark and plush, with a long sequin-studded black leather bar dominating one half of the floor space, and lounge chairs and lighted backgammon boards the other. A sequined velvet curtain divided the two areas, with a raised platform just inside the doorway that was visible from both sides of the room. Lloyd smiled as he approached the bar. It was a perfect logistical setup.

The bartender was a skinny youth with a punk haircut. Lloyd sat down at the bar and took out his billfold, removing a ten dollar bill and his Identikit portrait and letting the bartender see his badge all in one motion. When the youth said, "Yes, sir, what can I get you?" Lloyd tucked the ten into his vest pocket and handed him the photocopy.

"L.A.P.D. Have you seen this man here before? Take it over to the light and look at it carefully."

The bartender complied, switching on a lamp by the cash register. He studied the picture, then shook his head and said, "Sure. Lots of times. Kind of an intense dude. I think he swings both ways, I mean I've seen him in these really intense conversations with both men and women. What did he do?"

Lloyd gave the youth a stern look. "He molests little boys. When was the last time you saw him?"

"Jesus. Last week sometime. This guy's a chicken hawk?"

"That's right. What time does he usually show up?"

The bartender pointed in the direction of the backgammon tables. "You see how dead it is? Nobody shows up here much before eight. We only open up this early because we usually get some businessmen boozehounds in the late afternoon."

Lloyd said, "I noticed that you don't have a parking lot. Have you got any kind of valet parking setup?"

The youth shook his head. "We don't need one. Plenty of street parking after the boutiques close." He pointed to the platform inside the doorway. "You'll be able to see him real good, though. After dark, every time the door opens disco music goes on and colored lights flash down from the ceiling, white, then blue and red, you know, to let people know who's arriving. You'll be able to see him real good."

Lloyd put a dollar bill on the counter, then walked to a stool at the far end of the bar. "Ginger ale with lime. And bring me some peanuts or something. I forgot to eat lunch."

For six hours Lloyd drank ginger ale and plumbed logic for something to explain his two cases converging into a single narrative line. Nothing but a sense of his own fitness for the unraveling emerged from his ruminations, which were accompanied by a disco light show at the club's front door. From six o'clock on, every person who entered was centered in a flashing light show that was stereo-synced to upbeat arrangements of tunes from *Saturday Night Fever*. Most of the people were young and stylishly dressed and did a brief dance step before heading for the bar or backgammon tables. Lloyd scrutinized every male face as the first white light hit it; no one even vaguely resembled his suspect. Gradually the male and female faces merged into an androgynous swirl that made his eyes ache, combining with the noise of subtle and blatant mating overtures to tilt all his senses out of focus.

At eleven o'clock, Lloyd went to the men's room and soaked his head in a sink filled with cold water. Revived, he dried himself with paper towels and walked back into the club proper. He was about to take his seat at the bar when the Identikit portrait walked past him in the flesh.

Lloyd's skin prickled and he had to ball his gun hand to kill a reflex reach for his .38. The men's eyes locked for a split second, Lloyd averting his first, thinking *Take him outside at his car*. Then he heard a hoarse gasp behind him, followed by a clicking of metal on metal.

Both men turned at the same instant. Lloyd saw the Identikit man raise his monster handgun and sight it straight at him. He ducked to his knees as the muzzle burst with red and the report of the shot slammed his ears. Bottles exploded behind the bar as the shot went wide; screams filled the room. Lloyd rolled on the floor toward the sequined divider curtain, drawing his .38 and attempting to aim from a backward roll as odd parts of frantic bodies blocked a shot at his target. Two more thunderous explosions; the bar mirror shattering; the screaming reaching toward a crescendo. Lloyd rolled free of the curtain, crashing into a backgammon table. He got to his feet as another shot hit the curtain housing and sent the curtain crashing to the floor. People were huddling under tables, pressing together in a tangle of arms and legs. Muzzle smoke covered the bar area, but through it Lloyd could see his adversary arcing his pistol, looking for *his* target.

Lloyd extended his gun arm, his left hand holding his wrist steady. He fired twice, too high, and saw the Identikit man turn and run back in the direction of the restrooms. Stumbling over an obstacle course of trembling bodies, Lloyd pursued, flattening himself to the wall outside the men's room, nudging the door inward with his foot. He heard strained breathing inside and pushed the door open, firing blindly at chest level, jerking himself backward just as a return shot blew the door in half.

Lloyd slid to the floor, counting expended rounds: five for psycho, three for himself. Charge him and kill him. He fumbled three shells from his belt into the chamber of his snub nose, then fired into the bathroom in hope of getting a return shot in panic. When none came, he pushed through the half-destroyed door, catching a blurry glimpse of a pair of legs pulling themselves up and out of a narrow window above the toilet.

Stripping off his jacket, Lloyd leaped up and tried to squeeze out the window. His shoulders jammed and splintered the woodwork, but even by squirming and contracting every inch of his body he wouldn't fit. Jumping down, he ran back through the club proper, now a wasteland of shattered glass, upended furniture, and shelter-seeking mounds of people. He was only a few feet from the entrance promenade when the door burst open and three patrolmen with pump shotguns came up in front of him and aimed their weapons at his head. Seeing the fear in their eyes and sensing their fingers worrying the triggers, Lloyd let his .38 drop to the floor. "L.A.P.D.," he said softly. "My badge and I.D. are in my jacket pocket."

The middle cop poked Lloyd in the chest with the muzzle of his shotgun. "You ain't got a jacket, asshole. Turn around and put your hands on the wall above your head, then spread your legs. Do it real slow."

Lloyd obeyed in the slowest of slow motion. He felt rough hands give him a thorough frisking. In the distance he could hear the wail of sirens drawing nearer. When his hands were pinned behind his back and cuffed, he said, "My jacket is in the bathroom. I was here on a homicide stakeout.

You've got to issue an A.P.B. and a vehicle detain order. It's a yellow Japan—"

A heavy object crashed into the small of his back. Lloyd twisted around and saw the middle cop holding his shotgun, butt extended. The other two cops hung a few feet back, looking bewildered. One of them whispered, "He's got a cross draw holster. I'll check the bathroom."

The middle cop silenced him. "Shitcan it. We'll take him in. You check these people, look for anyone wounded, take statements. The meat wagon will be here in a second, so you help the paramedics. Jensen and I will take asshole in."

Lloyd squinted and read the leader cop's nameplate—Burnside. Straining to keep his voice steady, he said, "Burnside, you are letting a mass murderer and probable cop killer walk. Just go into the bathroom and get my jacket."

Burnside spun Lloyd around and shoved him out the door and into a patrol car at curbside. Lloyd looked out the window and saw other Beverly Hills black-and-whites and paramedic vans pull up directly on the sidewalk. As the patrol car accelerated, he looked in vain for a yellow Japanese import and felt his whole body smolder like dry ice.

The ride to the Beverly Hills Station took two minutes. Burnside and Jensen hustled Lloyd up the back stairs and led him down a dingy hallway to a wire mesh holding tank. Shoving him inside, still cuffed, Burnside said to his partner, "This bust feels like fat city. Any legit L.A.P.D. dick would have taken one of our guys with him on a stakeout. Let's go get the skipper."

When the two cops locked the cage door and ran off down the hallway, Lloyd leaned back against the wire wall and listened to the laughing and shouting coming from the drunk tank at the far end of the corridor. Letting his mind go blank, he gradually assimilated a mental replay of the events at Bruno's Serendipity. One thought dominated: Somehow the Identikit man had instantly seized upon him as his enemy. True, his size and outdated business suit would alert any streetwise fool; but the I.K. man had glimpsed him for only a brief moment in a crowded, artificially lighted environment. Lloyd held the thought, testing it for leaks, finding none. *Something was way off the usual criminal ken.*

"You fucked up, Sergeant."

Lloyd shifted his gaze to see who had spoken. It was a Beverly Hills captain, in uniform. He was holding his suit coat and .38 and shaking his head slowly.

"Let me out and give me my jacket and gun," Lloyd said.

The captain shook his head a last time, then slid a key into the cage door and swung it open. He took a handcuff key from his pocket and unlocked Lloyd's cuffs. Lloyd rubbed his wrists and took his coat and gun out of the captain's hands, realizing that the man was at least a half dozen years his junior. "Yeah, I fucked up," he said.

"Nice to hear the legendary Lloyd Hopkins admit to fallibility," the captain said. "Why didn't you notify the head of our detective squad of your stakeout? He would have given you a backup officer."

"It happened too fast. I was going to wait for the suspect outside by his car. I would have called for one of your units to assist me, but he made me for a cop and freaked out."

"What are you, six-four? Two-twenty-five? It doesn't take a genius to figure out what you do for a living."

"Yeah? Your own officers couldn't figure it out too well."

The captain flushed. "Officer Burnside will apologize to you."

Lloyd said, "Goody. In the meantime a stone psychopathic killer drives out of Beverly Hills a free man. An A.P.B. and a vehicle detain order might have gotten him."

"Don't try my patience, Hopkins. Just be grateful that no one at Bruno's was hurt. If you had been responsible for the injury or death of a constituent of mine, I would have crucified you. As it stands, I'll let your own Department deal with you."

Lloyd's vision pulsed with red. He shut his eyes to keep the throbbing localized and said, "Do you want to hear the whole story?"

"No. I want a complete report, in triplicate. Go upstairs and find a desk and write it now. I've informed your superiors at Robbery/Homicide. You are to report to the Chief of Detectives tomorrow morning at ten. Good night, Sergeant."

Fuming, Lloyd watched the captain walk away. He gave himself ten minutes to cool down, then took an elevator to the third-floor vehicle registration office. A night clerk gave him a yellow legal pad and a pen, and over the next two hours he block printed three reports detailing the events at Bruno's and summarizing his investigations into the liquor store homicides and the disappearance of Officer Jack Herzog, copying over his unsubmitted memo to the chief of detectives verbatim in hopes that it would be construed as an effort at "team play." When he finished, he left the pages with the night desk officer and headed for the parking lot. He was almost out the door when an intercom voice jerked him back in. "Urgent call for Sergeant Hopkins. Paging Sergeant Hopkins."

Lloyd walked to the night desk and picked up the phone. "Yes?"

"It's Dutch, Lloyd. What happened?"

"Lots of shit. Who told you?"

"Thad Braverton. You're supposed to see him tomorrow."

"I know. Is he pissed?"

"Depends on what you have to say. What *happened?*"

Lloyd laughed through his anger and fatigue. "You won't *believe* what happened. The same guy did the liquor store job and killed Jack Herzog. I'm sure of it. He fired on me with his liquor store piece. We did our best to destroy a Beverly Hills singles bar. It was wild."

Dutch shouted, *"What!"*

"Tomorrow, partner. I'll call you after I talk to Braverton."

Dutch's voice was soft. "Jesus fucking Christ."

Lloyd's was softer. "Yeah, on a popsicle stick. You got any good news for me? I could use some."

Dutch said, "Two items. One, I checked around on that weird name you asked about. Doctor John the Night Tripper. He was a rock bimbo from years ago, and it's also the nickname of a psychiatrist who does lots of counseling of hookers and court-referred criminal types. He's very well respected. His real name is John Havilland and his office is in Century City. Two, you're in good shape with I.A.D. I called Fred Gaffaney this morning and reported Herzog missing. I took the grief, which consisted of Gaffaney screaming 'fuck' a few times."

Lloyd memorized the first item and laughed at the second. "Good work, partner. I'll talk to you tomorrow."

Dutch laughed back. "Stay alive, kid."

Lloyd hung up and walked out into the parking lot, threading his way through a maze of erratically parked black-and-whites and unmarked cruisers. When he got to the sidewalk he saw Officer Burnside striding toward him. Burnside snickered as he passed, and Lloyd halted and tapped him on the shoulder. "You got something to say to me?"

Burnside turned and said, "Yeah. Ain't you a little old to be hotdogging outside your jurisdiction?"

Lloyd smiled and drove a short right hand into Burnside's midsection. Burnside gasped and doubled over. Lloyd propped up his chin with his left hand, then swung a full force right at the bridge of his nose, feeling it crack beneath his fist. Burnside flew back onto the pavement, moaning and draw-ing himself into a ball to escape more blows. Lloyd walked to his car feeling old and numb and tired of his profession.

9

The Night Tripper was on his fourth reading of the Junior Miss Cosmet-ics files when the phone in his private study rang, twenty-four hours before Goff's next scheduled call. Picturing his terminal man straining against a bacterial fever, he picked up the receiver and whispered, "You're early, Thomas. What is it?"

Goff's reply came out in series of gasps. "Cop! Big man from the cop files! I tried to wax him like the liquor store scum, but he—" The gasps became a horrified wailing.

Havilland envisioned Goff hyperventilating and frothing and burning up the phone booth with his fever and bewildered rage. Passing sentence in his mind, he said aloud, "Go home, Thomas. Can you understand that? Go home and wait for me. Draw in three breaths and tell me you'll go home. Will you do that for me?"

The three breaths drew out the semblance of a human voice. "Yes . . . yes . . . please hurry."

The Doctor replaced the receiver and held his hands in front of his eyes. They were perfectly steady. He walked into the bathroom and stared at himself in the mirror. His light brown eyes were unwavering in their knowl-edge that although Goff had fallen, he was invulnerable. He reached below the sink and picked up the death kit he had prepared the previous night, then went back to his study and stuffed it inside the old leather briefcase he had saved since med school. Squatting down, he pulled up a section of loose carpeting and opened his floor safe, extracting a single manila folder, think-ing for a split second that the man in the photo attached to the first page looked exactly like his father.

Thus armed for mercy, he left his apartment and walked out to the street to look for a cab. One cruised by a few minutes later. "Michael's Restaurant on Los Feliz and Hillhurst," Havilland told the driver. "And please hurry." The driver sped through the late evening traffic, never looking back at his passenger. Pulling up in front of the restaurant, he said, "Fast enough for you?"

The Doctor smiled and handed him a twenty. "Keep the change," he said.

When the cab drove away, Havilland walked the four blocks to Goff's apartment, noting with relief that all the lights in the adjoining units were off. He rapped softly on the door, hearing otherworldly moans respond to his knock. The inside chain was withdrawn, and Goff was framed in the doorway, beseeching him with terrified eyes and hands pressed together in prayer. The doctor stared at the hands as they trembled a few inches in front of him. The fingers were bloody stubs, as if Goff's animal panic had driven him to try to dig a way out of his life. Looking at the inside of the door, he saw gouge marks and trickles of blood.

Havilland put gentle hands on Goff's shoulders and pushed him back into the living room, seeing his cordite-stinking handgun on the coffee table. Shutting and bolting the door, he pointed Goff to the couch, then rummaged in his briefcase for his instruments of accusation and mercy. Laying the manila folder face down on the floor and filling a syringe from a lab vial of strychnine, he whispered, "Two questions before I sedate you, Thomas. One, did the police see your car?"

Goff shook his head and tried to form 'no' with his lips. The Doctor looked into his eyes. *Probable truth.*

Whispering, "Good, good," he clasped his left hand over Goff's mouth and pressed his head to the wall with all his strength. Goff's eyes bulged but remained locked into the eyes of his master. Havilland took the manila folder from the floor and slipped off the front page photograph. Holding it up for Goff to see, he said, "Is this the policeman?"

Goff's eyes widened, the pupils dilated. A scream rose in his throat and he twisted his head and bit at the Doctor's hand. Havilland pushed forward with all his weight, flailing with his free arm for the syringe, finding it just as Goff's teeth grazed his palm. Throwing himself across Goff's squirming torso, he stabbed the needle into his neck, missing his target vein, pulling it free as the point struck muscle tissue. Aiming again, he saw his father and the cop in the photo fuse into one persona just as the ferris wheel at the Bronx amusement park began its descent. The spike struck home; his thumb worked the plunger; the poison entered. Goff's back arched as his feet twisted and pushed off the wall in a huge full-body seizure. Both master and minion were thrown to the floor. Goff writhed, foam at his mouth. Havilland got to his knees, seeing his father and the cop separate into individual entities, replaced by a little girl in a fifties-style party dress laughing at him. He shook his head to destroy the vision, then heard Goff's vertebrae popping as he attempted to turn himself inside-out. Getting to his feet, he saw a door opening on blackness and headstones behind a barbed wire fence. Then he held his hands in front of his face and saw that they were steady. He looked down on the floor and saw Thomas Goff, dead, frozen in a final configuration of anguish.

"Father," the Night Tripper whispered. "Father. Father."

Now only the disposal remained.

The Doctor dug through his briefcase, removing the black vinyl body bag and laying it out lengthwise on the floor, zipped open. He tossed Goff's handgun into the bottom, then stuffed in Goff himself and zipped the bag up.

Goff's car keys were on the coffee table. Havilland pocketed them, then squatted down and hoisted the pain-free Goff onto his right shoulder. Picking up his briefcase and flicking off the ceiling light, he shut the door and walked outside to the street.

Goff's Toyota was parked four buildings down. Havilland unlocked the trunk and wedged the dead man inside, securing the body bag by placing a spare tire and bumper jack across Goff's midsection. Satisfied with the concealment, the Doctor slammed the trunk shut and drove him to his final resting place.

Thomas Goff's grave was the basement maintenance area of a storage garage in the East Los Angeles industrial district. It was owned by one of the Doctor's former criminal counselees, currently doing ten to life for a third armed robbery conviction. Havilland paid the taxes and sent the man's wife a quarterly check; the gloomy old red-brick fortress would be his for at least another eight years.

It took the Night Tripper ten minutes to secure the gravesite, rummaging through the ring of keys his counselee had given him, opening up a series of double padlocked doors, driving through an obstacle course of mildewed cartons and rotting lumber until he was in the pitch black bowels of the building. Wiping the car free of his fingerprints and retracing his steps in the dark, he felt a sense of satisfaction and completion hit him harder with each padlock he snapped shut: Thomas Goff had spent his adult life seeking the absence of light and the Doctor had promised to help; now he would have layer upon layer of darkness to cradle his eternity.

When the street door lock was fastened behind him, the Night Tripper walked toward downtown L.A. and shifted his thoughts to the future. With Goff dead, he was flying solo; all the file runs were his. It was time to put off his current lonelies with talk of forthcoming "ultimate" assignments and concentrate on the acquisition of data and his possible combat with the policeman who so resembled his father. Crossing the Third Street bridge, the lights of the downtown business monoliths hovering in front of him, Havilland thought of chess moves: Richard Oldfield, clinically insane yet superbly cautious, who resembled the late Thomas Goff like a twin brother. *Pawn to queen*. Linda Wilhite, the hooker who fantasized snuff films and who desired a life of blissful domesticity with a big, rough-hewn man. *Queen to king*.

And finally the highly tarnished "king" himself: Detective Sergeant Lloyd Hopkins, the outsized L.A. cop with the off-the-charts I.Q., the man of whom the Alchemist had said: "I glommed his file because he is simply the best there is. If he weren't such an up-front womanizer and so outlaw in his methods, he'd be chief of detectives. He's got close to complete autonomy within the Department, because the high brass knows he's the best and because they think he's slightly off his nut. He was the one who closed the 'Hollywood Slaughterer' case last year. No one really knows what happened, but the rumor is that Hopkins simply went out and killed the bastard."

Havilland replayed the words in his mind, juxtaposing them with the superlative arrest record and erratic home life detailed in the folder. *Checkmate*. Staring deeper into the lights before him, he thought of unlocking the door to his childhood void with symbolic patricide.

10

"Before we start, I want you to read this morning's *Big Orange Insider*."

Lloyd shifted in his chair and lowered his eyes, wondering if Thad

Braverton bought his look of phony contrition. Their handshake had been a good start, but Braverton's eyes were pinpoints of barely controlled rage, belying the authoritative calm of his voice.

"Martin Bergen's byline?" Lloyd asked.

The chief of detectives shook his head. "No. Surprisingly, it was written by some other cop-hating hack. Just read it, Hopkins. The comments of one Officer Burnside are particularly interesting."

Lloyd stood up and took the folded tabloid from the chief, handing him his neatly typed report on the liquor store–Herzog case in return. Sitting back down, he read the *Insider*'s hyperbolized account of the shoot-out at Bruno's Serendipity. The three-column piece was written as an indictment of "Gunslinger Justice" and heavily emphasized the "Innocent young singles whose lives were placed in jeopardy by a trigger-happy L.A.P.D. detective." The concluding paragraph featured the observations of Beverly Hills Officer Carl D. Burnside, twenty-four, "whose nose was in a splint from a recent jogging accident."

"Sergeant Hopkins attempted to arrest his suspect in a room filled with innocent people, even though he knew the guy was armed and dangerous. He should have had a Beverly Hills officer go with him. His callous disregard for the safety of Beverly Hills citizens is disgusting. Hotdog cops like Hopkins give sensitive, safety-conscious policemen like me a bad name."

Lloyd stifled a burst of laughter by wadding up the tabloid and watching the chief of detectives read his report. He had labored over it at home for five hours, detailing his two cases from their beginnings, charting their convergence step by step, underlining his certainty of Martin Bergen's innocence in Jack Herzog's presumed death, Herzog's theft of the six L.A.P.D. Personnel files and how the Identikit man *had to have seen those files*—it was the only way he could have identified him as a policeman in a crowded, smoky room.

The last page was the clincher, the evidence documentation that Lloyd hoped would bowl Thad Braverton over and save him the ignominy of departmental censure. At dawn he had driven back to Bruno's Serendipity and had bribed the two workmen cleaning up the previous night's damage into letting him make a check for expended .41 rounds. By charting approximate trajectories and scanning the walls with a flashlight he had been able to recover two flattened slugs. Artie Cranfield and his comparison microscope had done the rest of the work, delivering the irrefutable ballistics confirmation: *The three liquor store rounds and the two rounds extracted from the walls at Bruno's Serendipity had been fired by the same gun.*

Thad Braverton finished reading the report and fixed Lloyd with a deadpan stare. "Muted bravos, Hopkins. I was going to suspend you, but in the light of this I'll let you slide with a reprimand: Do not ever go into another department's jurisdiction without greasing the skids with their watch commander. Do you understand me?"

Lloyd screwed his face into a semblance of sheepishness. "Yes, Chief."

Braverton laughed. "Don't try to act contrite, you look like a high school kid who just got laid. You're the official Robbery/ Homicide supervisor on the liquor store job, right?"

"Right."

"Good. Stay on that full time. I'm turning over the Herzog case to I.A.D. They'll go at it covertly, which is essential; if Herzog was engaged in any criminal activity I don't want it getting back to the media. They're also better equipped to check out the file angle discreetly—those security firms are big bucks, and I don't want you stepping on their toes. *Comprende?*"

Lloyd flushed. "Yes."

"Good. I'll set up some sort of liaison so that you and I.A.D. can compare notes. What's your next move?"

"I want a full-scale effort to identify this asshole. The Identikit portrait is an exceptional likeness, and I want every cop in the county to have a look at it. Here's what I'm thinking: A closed briefing here at the Center this afternoon. Representatives of every L.A.P.D. and Sheriff's division to attend. No media shitheads. I'll get up about ten thousand copies of the I.K. portrait and tell the men to distribute them at their roll calls. I'll brief the men on my experience with the suspect and offer my observations on his psych makeup and M.O. Every cop in L.A. County will be looking for him. Once we get a positive I.D., we can issue an A.P.B. and take it from there."

Thad Braverton slammed his desk with both palms and said, "You've got it. I'll have my secretary start phoning the various divisions immediately. How's two-thirty sound? That will allow time for the men to go back to their stations and put out the copies before nightwatch. You can take care of getting them in the meantime."

Lloyd got to his feet and said, "Thanks. You could have given me a lot of grief, but you didn't." He started to walk for the door, then turned around and added, "Why?"

Braverton said, "You really want to know?"

"Yes."

The chief of detectives sighed. "Then I'll tell you. Only four men know *exactly* what happened with you last year. You and Dutch Peltz, obviously, and the big chief and myself. I'm sure you know that rumors have circulated and that some cops admire you for what you did while other cops think you should be in Camarillo for it. I love you for what you did. I'm a hard ass with most people, but I'll take a lot of shit from the people I love."

Lloyd ducked out the door at the chief's last words. He didn't want him to see that he was a half step away from tears.

Four hours later, Lloyd stood behind the lectern at the front of Parker Center's main briefing room, staring out at what he estimated to be two hundred uniformed and plainclothes police personnel. Every man and woman present had been issued a manila folder upon entering the room. Each folder contained fifty copies of the Identikit portrait of the man designated and M.O.-typed as:

Multiple homicide suspect, W.M., 30–35, lt. brn., eye color unknown, 5'9"–5'11", 150–160. Drives late model yellow Japanese import; armed with .41 antique handgun. Known to frequent singles bars and use cocaine. *This man is the perpetrator of the April 23 Hollywood liquor store killings. Consider him armed and extremely dangerous."*

When the last late-arriving officers took their seats, Lloyd held up a copy of the *Los Angeles Times* and spoke into the microphone. "Good afternoon. Please give me your complete attention. On page two of today's *Times* there is an accurate report of my encounter last night with the man whose portrait you are now holding. The only reason I am alive today is because this man uses a single-action revolver. I heard him cock the hammer before he fired at me and was able to avoid his first shot. Had he been using a more practical double-action weapon, I would be dead."

Lloyd let his eyes circuit the audience. Feeling them securely in his hand, he continued, "After exchanging fire with me, the man escaped. All the *hard* facts regarding him are on your Identikit pictures. The portrait, by the way, is a superb likeness—it was put together by an intelligent witness and was immediately confirmed by two others. *That is our man*. What I would like to add are my observations of this killer."

He paused and watched the assembled officers study their folders and take out pens and notepads. When there was a gradual shifting of eyes to the lectern, he said, "Last week this man killed three people with clean head shots worthy of a practiced marksman. Last night he fired at me from a distance of ten feet and missed. His four subsequent rounds were wild, fired in panic. I believe that this man is psychotic and will kill until he himself is killed or captured. There must be a concerted effort to identify him. I want these portraits distributed to *every* officer in L.A. County and every trustworthy snitch. He uses coke and frequents singles bars, so every vice and narco officer should utilize *their* snitches and question *their* bar sources. Witnesses have said that he has mentioned 'an incredibly smart dude' he knows, so our suspect may have a partner. I want men *strongly* resembling this suspect to be *carefully* detained for questioning, at *gunpoint*. All suspects detained should be brought to the Central Division jail. I'll be there from five o'clock on, with a legal officer and a stack of false arrest waivers. Some innocent men are going to be rousted, but that's unavoidable. Direct all queries from police and non-police sources to me, Sergeant Lloyd Hopkins, at Central Division, extension five-one-nine."

Lloyd let the officers catch up on their note taking, knowing that up to now their rapt attention had been on a purely professional level. Clearing his throat and tapping the microphone, he went straight for their purely personal jugulars. "I've given you ample reasons why the apprehension of this suspect is the number one police priority in Southern California, but I'll go a notch better: This man is the prime suspect in the disappearance and probable murder of a Los Angeles police officer. Let's nail the mother-fucker. Good day."

It took Lloyd two hours to establish a command post at the Central Division jail's booking facility. Anticipating a deluge of phone calls, he had first appropriated three unused telephones from the Robbery/Homicide clerical supply office, plugging them into empty phone jacks adjacent to the jail's attorney room, securing an immediate hookup to the existing extension number by intimidating a series of Bell Telephone supervisors. Central Division switchboard operators were instructed to screen incoming calls and give all police *and* civilian calls regarding the Identitkit picture first priority in the event of tied-up lines. Any *live* suspects brought in were to be placed in a soundproof interrogation room walled with one-way glass. Once Lloyd's negative identification certified their innocence, they were to be gently coerced into signing false arrest waivers by Central Division's ad hoc "legal officer," a patrolman who had graduated law school, but had failed the California Bar exam four times. The detainee would then be driven back to his point of "arrest" and released.

Lloyd settled in for a long tour of duty, setting out notepads and sharpened pencils for jotting information and a large thermos of coffee for fuel when his brain wound down. Every angle had been covered. The two officers working under him on the liquor store case had been yanked from their current duties and told to compile a list of all singles bars in the L.A.P.D.'s jurisdiction. Once this was accomplished, they were to phone vice squad commanders citywide and have them deploy surveillance teams. Watch commanders had been instructed to highlight the Identikit man at evening roll call and to order all units to approach all suspects with their pump riot guns. If the I.K. man was on the street, there was a good chance of taking him.

But not alive, Lloyd thought. Ruffling through the false arrest forms on his desk, he knew that his killer would not give up without a fight and that on this night the odds of innocent blood being spilled were at their optimum. A panicky, overeager cop might fire on a half-drunk and belligerent businessman who resembled the I.K. suspect; an overly cautious officer might approach a yellow Jap import with a placating smile and get that smile blown off his face by a .41 hollow point. The detain/identify/release approach was desperation—any experienced Homicide dick would know it implicitly.

At six o'clock the first call came in. Lloyd guessed the source immediately: Nightwatch units had been on the street for an hour, and scores of patrolmen had been putting out the word to their snitches. He was right. A self-described "righteous dope dealer" was the caller. The man told Lloyd how he was certain the liquor store killer was a "nigger with a dye job" who "wasted" the three people as part of a "black power conspiracy." He then went on to offer *his* definition of black power: "Four coons pushing a Cadillac into a gas station for fifty cents worth of gas." Lloyd told the man that his definition would have been amusing in 1968 and hung up.

More calls followed.

Lloyd juggled the three phone lines, sifting through the ramblings of drunks, dopers, and jilted lovers, writing down every piece of information that issued from a reasonably coherent voice. The offerings were of the third- and fourth-hand variety—someone who knew someone who said that someone saw or knew or *felt* this or that. It was in all probability a labyrinth of *mis*information, but it had to be written down.

At ten, after four hours on the phones, Lloyd had filled up one entire legal pad, all with non-police input. He was beginning to despair of ever again dealing with a fellow professional when a pair of callow-looking Newton Street Division patrolmen brought in the night's first "hard" suspect, a rail-thin, six-foot-six blonde youth in his early twenties. The officers acted as though they had death by the tail, each of them clasping a white-knuckled hand around the suspect's biceps.

Lloyd took one look at the terrified trio, said, "Take off the cuffs," and handed the youth a false arrest waiver. He signed it as Lloyd told the officers to take their "killer" wherever he wanted and to buy him a bottle of booze on the way. The three young men departed. "Try to stay alive!" Lloyd called after them.

Within the next two hours, three reasonable suspect facsimiles were brought in, two by Hollywood Division patrol teams, one by Sheriff's detectives working out of the San Dimas Substation. Each time Lloyd shook his head, said, "Cut him loose" and force-fed the suspect a hard look, a waiver and a pen. Each time they signed willingly. Lloyd imagined them envisioning every "innocent man falsely imprisoned" movie ever made as they hurriedly scrawled their names.

Midnight came and went. The calls dwindled. Lloyd switched from coffee to chewing gum when his stomach started to rumble. Thinking that the twelve o'clock change of watch would allow him a hiatus from the phones, he settled back in his chair and let the normal jail noises cut through his caffeine fatigue and lull him into a half sleep. Full sleep was approaching when a voice jerked him awake. "Sergeant Hopkins?"

Lloyd swiveled his chair. An L.A.P.D. motorcycle officer was standing in front of him, holding an R&I computer printout. "I'm Confrey, Rampart Motor," the officer said. "I just came on duty and saw your I.D. kit want. I popped a guy who looks exactly like it last month. Jaywalking warrants. I remembered him because he had this weirdness about him. I got his R&I sheet and his D.M.V. record. There's a mug shot from my warrant bust."

Lloyd took the sheet and slipped off the mug-shot strip. The Identikit man jumped out at him, every plane and angle of his face coming into focus, like a paint-by-numbers portrait finally completed.

"Is it him?" Confrey whispered.

Lloyd said, "Yes," and stared at the full-face and profile shots of the man who had almost killed him, trembling as he read the cold facts that described a monster:

Thomas Lewis Goff, W.M., D.O.B. 6/19/49, brn., blu., 5'10", 155. Pres. Add.—3193 Melbourne #6, L.A. Crim. Rec. (N.Y. State): 3 agg. asslt. arrst.—(Diss.); 1 conv.—1st Deg. Auto Theft—11/4/69—sent. 3–5 yrs. Paroled 10/71. (Calif. State): Failure to app.—3/19/84—Bail $65—paid. Calif. dr. lic. # 01734; Vehic.—1980 Toyota Sed. (yellow) lic. # JLE 035; no mov. viol.

Lloyd put the printout down and said, "Who's the morning watch boss at Rampart?"

Confrey stammered, "Lu-Lieutenant Praeger."

"Good. Call him up and tell him we've got the big one on Melbourne and Hillhurst. Hold him for me; I'll be right back."

While Confrey made the call, Lloyd ran down the hall to the Central Division armory and grabbed an Ithaca pump and box of shells from the duty officer. When he returned to the jail area, Confrey handed him the phone and whispered, "Talk slow, the loot is an edgy type."

Lloyd took a deep breath and spoke into the mouthpiece. "Lieutenant, this is Hopkins, Robbery/Homicide. Can you set something up for me?"

"Yes," a taut voice answered. "Tell me what you need."

"I need a half dozen unmarked units to check the area around Melbourne and Hillhurst for a yellow nineteen-eighty Toyota, license JLE oh-three-five. No approach—sit on it. I need the thirty-one hundred block of Melbourne sealed at both ends in exactly forty minutes. I want five experienced squad room dicks to meet me at Melbourne and Hillhurst in exactly forty minutes. Tell them to wear vests and to bring shotguns. Have them bring a vest for me. I want *no* black-and-whites inside the area. Can you implement this now?"

Lloyd didn't wait for an answer. He handed the phone back to Confrey and ran for his car.

By zigzagging through traffic and running red lights, Lloyd made it to Melbourne and Hillhurst in twenty minutes. No other unmarked cruisers were yet on the scene, but he could feel the too perfect silence that preceded impending explosions all around him. He knew that the silence would soon be broken by approaching headlights, two-way radio crackle and the hum of powerful engines held at idle. Last name introductions and his orders would follow, leaving nothing but the explosion itself.

Parking under a streetlamp at the edge of the intersection, Lloyd turned on his emergency flashers as a signal to the other officers and jacked shells into his shotgun, pumping one into the chamber and setting the choke on full. Grabbing his flashlight, he walked down Melbourne, staying close to the trees that bordered the sidewalk, grateful that there were no late night strollers or dog walkers out. The street was a solid mass of two-story apartment buildings, identical in their sideways exposures and second-story landings. Three-one-nine-three was in the middle of the block, a dark gray stucco with wrought-iron railings and recessed door without screens. Lloyd flashed his light on the bank of mailboxes at the front of the building. T. Goff—Apt. 6, true to the R&I printout. He counted mail slots, then stepped back and counted the doorways themselves, playing his beam over them to illuminate the numerals embossed at eye level. Ten units; five up, five down. Apartment six was the first unit on the second story. Lloyd shivered when he saw muted light glowing behind drawn curtains.

He walked back to Hillhurst, scanning parked cars en route. No yellow Toyotas were stationed at curbside. When he got to the intersection, he found it blocked off by sawhorse detour signs affixed with blinking red lights. Radio static broke the silence, followed by hoarse whispers. Lloyd squinted and saw three unmarked Matadors parked crossways behind the barricade. He blinked his flashlight at the closest one, getting a double blink in return. Then there was the opening of car doors and five men wearing bullet-proof vests and holding shotguns were standing in front of him.

"Hopkins," Lloyd said, getting "Henderson," "Martinez," "Penzler," "Monroe," and "Olander" in return. A vest was handed to him. He slipped into it and said, "Vehicle?"

Five negative head shakes answered him at once. One of the officers added, "No yellow Toyotas in an eight block radius."

Lloyd shrugged. "No matter. The target building is halfway down the block. Second story, light on. Henderson and I are going in the door. Martinez and Penzler, you stand point downstairs, Monroe and Olander, you hold a bead on the back window." Feeling a huge grin take over his face, he bowed and whispered, "Now, gentlemen."

The men formed a wedge and ran down Melbourne to 3193. When they

were on the sidewalk in front of the building, Lloyd pointed to the first upstairs back window, the only one on the second story burning a light. Monroe and Olander nodded and hung back as Martinez and Penzler
automatically took up their positions at the bottom of the stairs. Lloyd
nudged Henderson with his gun butt and gestured upwards, whispering,
"Opposite sides of the door. One kick."

With Lloyd at the lead, they tiptoed up the stairs and fanned out to cover
both sides of the door to apartment 6. Henderson put his ear to the doorjamb and formed "nothing" with his lips and tongue. Lloyd nodded and
stepped back and raised his shotgun. Henderson took up an identical position beside him. Both men raised their right feet simultaneously and kicked
out at the same instant. The door burst inward, ripped loose at both sides,
dangling from one remaining hinge. Lloyd and Henderson pressed into the
wall at the sound of the implosion, listening for reflex movement within
the apartment. Hearing nothing but the creaking of the door, they stepped
inside.

Lloyd would never forget what he saw. While Henderson ran ahead to
check the other rooms, he stood in the doorway, unable to take his eyes
from the nightmare hieroglyphics that surrounded him on all sides.

The living room walls were painted dark brown; the ceiling was painted
black. Taped across the walls were photographs of nude men, obviously
clipped from gay porno books. The bodies were composites formed of mis-
matching torsos, heads, and genital areas, the figures linked by magazine
photos of antique handguns. Each collage had a slogan above it, block
printed in contrasting yellow paint: "Chaos Redux," "Death's Kingdom,"
"Charnel Kong," and "Blitzkrieg." Lloyd studied the printing. Two of the
slogans were in an unmistakable left-hander's slant; the other two in a
straight up right-handed motion. Squinting at the wall area around the
cutouts, he saw that they were bracketed by abrasive powder wipe marks.
He ran his fingers over the walls in random circles. A film of white powder
stuck to them. Like Jack Herzog's apartment, this place had been professionally secured against latent print identification.

Henderson came up behind Lloyd, startling him. "Jesus, Sarge, you ever
see anything like it?"

Lloyd said, "Yes," very softly.

"Where?"

Lloyd shook his head. "No. Don't ask me again. What are the other
rooms like?"

"Like a normal pad, except for the colors of the wall and ceiling paint. All the surfaces have been wiped, though. Ajax or some shit like that. This motherfucker is whacked out, but smart."

Lloyd walked to the door and looked out. Martinez and Penzler were still stationed downstairs and there was as yet no general awakening of the other tenants. He turned and said to Henderson, "Go round up the other men, then wake up the citizens." He handed him the mug-shot strip of Thomas Goff and added, "Show this to every person and ask them when they saw the bastard last. Bring anyone who's seen him in the past twenty-four hours to me."

Henderson nodded and went downstairs. Lloyd counted to ten to clear his mind of any preconceived notions of what he should look for and let his eyes take a quick inventory of the living room, thinking: darkness beyond the aesthetic limits of the most avant garde interior decorator. Black Naugahyde sofa; charcoal gray deep-pile rug; black plasticene high-tech coffee table. The curtains were a thick olive drab velour, capable of shutting out the brightest sunlight, and the one floor lamp was sheathed in black plastic. The overall effect was one of containment. Although the living room was spacious for a small apartment, the absence of color gave it a stiflingly claustrophobic weight. Lloyd felt like he was enclosed in the palm of an angry fist. In reflex against the feeling he slipped off his bullet-proof vest, surprised to find that he was drenched in sweat.

The kitchen and bathroom were extensions of the darkness motif; every wall, appliance and fixture had been brushstroked with a thick coat of black enamel paint. Lloyd scrutinized potential print-sustaining surfaces. Every square inch had been wiped.

He walked into the bedroom. It was the disarrayed heart of the angry fist; a small black rectangle almost completely eclipsed at floor level by a large box spring and mattress covered by a purple velour bedspread. Lloyd stripped the bedspread off. The dark blue patterned sheets were crumpled and rank with sweat. Male clothing, varied in color, was strewn across them. Squatting to examine it, he saw that the pants and shirts were stylish and expensive and conformed in size to Thomas Goff's dimensions. An overturned cardboard box lay next to the front of the bed. Upending it, Lloyd sifted through a top layer of male toiletries and a second layer of paperback science fiction novels, coming to a tightly wedged stack of battered record albums on the bottom.

He thumbed through them, reading the titles on the jackets. Dozens of albums by the Beatles, Rolling Stones, and Jefferson Airplane, all bearing the block printed warning: "Beware! Property of Tom Goff! Hands off! Beware!" Lloyd held two albums up and examined the printing. It was right-hand formed and identical to the printing on the living room walls. Smiling at the confirmation, he read through the remaining records, knowing that the common denominator of Goff's musical taste was the 1960s, going cold when he saw a garish album entitled *Doctor John the Night Tripper—Bayou Dreams*.

Lloyd studied the jacket. A frizzy-haired white man wearing red satin bell bottoms was honking a saxophone at a snarling alligator. The song titles listed on the back were the typical sixties dope, sex, and rebellion pap, almost nostalgic in their naïveté. Putting the album down, he wondered if it were a Herzog-Goff link beyond general aesthetic strangeness—a link that could be plumbed for evidence.

There was a rapping on the wall behind him. Lloyd stood up and turned around, seeing Henderson and a small man in a terrycloth bathrobe. The man was casting unbelieving eyes over the black walls, mashing shaky hands together inside the pockets of his robe. "This guy's the manager, Sarge. Said he saw our buddy this afternoon."

Lloyd smiled at the man. "My name's Hopkins. What's yours?"

"Fred Pellegrino. Who's going to pay for my busted door and this crazy paint job?"

"Your insurance company," Lloyd said. "When did you see Thomas Goff last?"

Fred Pellegrino pulled rosary beads from his pocket and fondled them. "Around five o'clock. He was carrying a suitcase. He smiled at me and hot-footed it out to the street. 'See you soon,' he said."

"You didn't ask him where he was going?"

"Fuck no. He's paid up three months in advance."

"Was he alone?"

"Yeah."

"How long has he lived here?"

"About a year and a half or so."

"Good tenant?"

"The best. No noise, no complaints, always paid his rent on time."

"Did he pay by check?"

"No, always cash."

"Job?"

"He said he was self-employed."

"What about his friends?"

"*What* friends? I never seen him with *nobody*. What if my insurance company don't pay for this batshit paint job?"

Lloyd ignored Pellegrino and motioned Henderson over to the far side of the room. "What did the other tenants have to say?" he asked.

"The same spiel as Pops," Henderson said. "Nice, quiet, solitary fellow who never said much besides 'good morning' or 'good night.' "

"And no one else has seen him today?"

"No one else has seen the scumbag in the past week. This is depressing. I wanted to eighty-six the cop-killer motherfucker. Didn't you?"

Lloyd gave a noncommittal shrug and took Goff's R&I printout from his pocket. He handed it to Henderson and said, "Go back to Rampart and give this to Praeger. A.P.B., All Police Network. Tell him to add 'armed and extremely dangerous' and 'has left-handed male partner,' and to call the New York State Police and have them wire me all their existing info on Goff. Tell Pellegrino that I'm spending the night here as a safety precaution and shoo him back to his pad."

"You're gonna crash here?" Henderson was slack-jawed with disbelief.

Lloyd stared at him. "That's right, so move it."

Henderson walked away shaking his head, taking a pliant Fred Pellegrino by the arm and leading him out of the apartment. When they were gone, Lloyd walked to the landing and looked down on the knot of people milling in the driveway. Bullet-proof vested cops with shotguns were assuring pajama-clad civilians that everything was going to be all right. After a few minutes the scene dispersed, the citizens walking back to their dwellings, the cops to their unmarked Matadors. When Henderson pointed a finger at his head and twirled it, then pointed upstairs, Lloyd dragged the sofa over to the devastated front door and barricaded himself in to think.

Two divergent cases had merged into one and had now yielded one *known* perpetrator and one accomplice, an *unknown* quantity whose only *known* crime thus far was defacing rented property. With an A.P.B. in effect and I.A.D. covering the personnel file angle, his job was to deduce Thomas Goff's behavior and go where less intelligent cops wouldn't think to look.

Lloyd let his eyes circuit the living room, knowing that it would merge with another horror chamber the very second he closed them, knowing that it was essential to juxtapose the imagery and see what emerged.

He did it, shuddering against the memory of Teddy Verplanck's bay-windowed apartment, deciding that *it* was worse because he had known the extent of the Hollywood Slaughterer's carnage and that he was driving to be destroyed. Thomas Goff's home bespoke a more subtle drive—the drive of a seasoned street criminal who had very probably not been arrested for anything since 1969, a man with a partner who might well be a restraining influence; a man who spread his insanity all over his walls and walked away saying 'see you soon' a few hours ahead of a massive police dragnet.

Lloyd walked through the apartment again, letting little observations snap into place and work in concert with his instincts: the photos of nude men and guns spoke "homosexual," but somehow that seemed wrong. There was no telephone, which confirmed Goff as a basic loner. The lack of dishes, cooking utensils, and food were typical of ex-convicts, men who were used to being served and who often developed a craving for cafeteria food. The incredible darkness of the rooms was sheer insanity. All indicators pointing to the enormous question of *motive*.

Lloyd had almost completed his run-through of the apartment when he noticed a built-in wall cupboard in the hall between the living room and bedroom. It had been painted over like the rest of the wall, but cracks in the paint by the wooden opener knob indicated that it had been put to use. He swung the cupboard door open and recoiled when he saw what was affixed to the back.

There was a magazine cutout of a blue uniformed policeman with his hands upraised as if to placate an attacker. Surrounding the cop were outsized porno book penises studded with large metal staples. A circle of handgun cutouts framed the scene, and square in the middle of the cop's chest was a glued-on white paper facsimile of an L.A.P.D. badge, complete with a drawing of City Hall, the words, "Police Officer" and the number 917.

Lloyd slammed the cupboard with his fist. Jack Herzog's badge number burned in front of his eyes. He tore the door off by the hinges and hurled it into the living room. Just then Penny's "Owe what, Daddy?" hit him like a pile driver, and he knew that getting Thomas Goff would be the close-out on all his debts of grief.

11

The Night Tripper stared at the stunning female beauty that now adorned the walls of his outer office. Thomas Goff's surveillance photographs of Linda Wilhite were blown up and framed behind glass, woman bait that would lure his policeman/adversary into a trap that would be sprung by his own sexual impulses. The Doctor walked into his private office and thought of how he had planned over a decade in advance, creating a series of buffers that would prevent anyone from knowing that he and Thomas Goff had ever met. He had destroyed Goff's file at Castleford Hospital; he had even stolen his prison file while visiting Attica on a psychiatric seminar, returning it three weeks later, altered to show a straight, no-parole release. He had never been seen with Goff, and they had always communicated via pay phones. The only possible connection was several times removed—through his lonelies, all of whom Goff had recruited. If the manhunt for his former executive officer received pervasive media play, one of them might snap to a newspaper or TV photograph accompanied by scare rhetoric.

Yet even that avenue of discovery was probably closed, Havilland thought, picking up the morning editions of the *L.A. Times* and *L.A. Examiner*. There was no further mention of the shoot-out at Bruno's Serendipity and no mention of the late night raid on Goff's apartment. If Hopkins had initiated some sort of media stonewall to keep a lid of secrecy on his investigation, then his complicity in his own destruction would reach epic proportions.

The Night Tripper trembled as he recalled the past thirty-six hours, and his acts of courage. After disposing of Goff's body, he had walked through downtown L.A., thinking of the probable course of events that had led Hopkins to at least identify Goff at the level of physical description. One thing emerged as a reasonable certainty: It was the Alchemist's disappearance and presumed death, *not* the liquor store killings, that had led the policeman to Goff. Goff and Herzog had spent a good deal of time together at bars, and some perceptive witness had probably provided Hopkins with the description that took him to Bruno's Serendipity. Thus, hours later, after he had smeared Goff's walls with homosexual bait, he had left the albums that Goff had stashed at Castleford in 'seventy-one and added the touch that would arouse Hopkins' cop rectitude. Pique his rage with the faggot image of the Alchemist; pique his brain with the wipe marks, diverse script styles, and Goff's old copy of *Bayou Dreams*.

The most thrilling act of courage had been in implementing Richard Oldfield, dressing him in a bulky sweater that downplayed his musculature and a tweed cap that was very much in Thomas Goff's style, yet shielded his upper face and non-Goff haircut. He had pumped him up for hours, promising him his very own handpicked victim as his "ultimate assignment," then had watched from a parked rental car across the street as Oldfield went through his impersonation perfectly, fooling Goff's landlord dead to rights, with Hopkins and his dragnet only hours away.

Havilland unlocked his desk drawer and dug out the Junior Miss Cosmetics file he had been studying, hoping that fresh work and thoughts of the future would quiet the sense of excitement that made him want to *live* in the hours just past.

It didn't help. He kept recalling the flashlights approaching and how he knew that he was now *inside* the police cordon; how he had hunkered down in the car seat and had heard the officers repeat Goff's license number over and over, one of them whispering that "Crazy Lloyd" was "leading the raid," his partner replying with something about "Crazy Lloyd going after that Hollywood psycho with a thirty-ought-six and a forty-four mag." When the raid itself transpired a half hour later, he could see Hopkins across the street, holding a shotgun, much taller than any of the men he led, looking exactly like his father. It had taken monumental self-control to drive away from the scene without confronting the policeman face to face.

With an effort, the Night Tripper returned to the cosmetics file, reading notations on the life and sleazy times of the woman who he was certain would become his next pawn.

Sherry Shroeder was a thirty-one-year-old former assembly line worker at Junior Miss Cosmetics, recently fired for stealing chemicals used in the manufacture of angel dust. It had been her fourth and final pilfering "arrest" within the company, resulting in her dismissal under threats of criminal prosecution. Daniel Murray, the L.A.P.D. captain who moonlighted as the Junior Miss security chief, had made her sign a confession and had told her that it would not be submitted to the police if she signed a waiver stating that she would not apply for unemployment benefits or workmen's compensation. Her three previous "arrests" had been resolved through Daniel Murray's coercion. Sherry Shroeder was a frequent co-star of low budget pornographic films. Murray had obtained a print of one of her features and had threatened to show it to her parents should she fail to return the chemicals she had stolen. Sherry agreed, eager to retain her four-dollar-an-hour job and spare her parents the grief of viewing her performance. There was no photograph attached to the folder, but her vital statistics of five-seven, 120, blonde hair, and blue eyes were enticing enough. There was a final notation in the file, stating that since her dismissal Sherry Shroeder had been seen almost daily in the bars across the street from Junior Miss, drinking with her former fellow employees and "turning tricks" in the back of her van on paydays.

Havilland wrote down Sherry Shroeder's address and phone number and put it in his pocket. Relieved that his next move was ready to be implemented, he let his thoughts return to Lloyd Hopkins, making a spur of the moment decision that felt uncommonly sound: If the policeman didn't come his way within forty-eight hours, he would initiate the confrontation himself.

12

After a twenty-four hour stint of Robbery/Homicide conferences and paper chasing at Parker Center, Lloyd drove to Century City to grasp at the wildest of straws, getting honest with himself en route: His investigation was stymied. Every cop in Southern California was shaking the trees for Thomas Goff, and he, the supervising officer and legendary "big brain," did not yet have a psychological mock-up to work from. If he could use the legendary criminal shrink's nickname as his entree, he could probably interest him in the Goff case and get him to offer his observations. It was slim, but at least it was movement.

The twenty-four hours at the Center had yielded nothing but negative feedback. The New York State Police had reacted promptly to his inquiry on Thomas Goff, issuing the L.A.P.D. a teletype that ran to six pages. Lloyd learned that Goff was a sadist who picked women up in bars, seduced and then beat them; that he liked to steal late model convertibles, that he had "no known associates" and was given a no-parole release from Attica, most likely a bureaucratic stratagem to encourage his departure from New York State.

The day's major frustration had been at a late afternoon conference in Thad Braverton's office, where the chief of detectives had read a strongly worded memo from the *big* chief stating that there was to be a total media blackout on the Goff case, for reasons of "public safety." Lloyd had laughed aloud, then had sat fuming as Braverton and his old nemesis Captain Fred Gaffaney of I.A.D. gave him the fish-eye. He knew that "public safety" translated to "public relations," and that the media kibosh was undertaken out of apprehension regarding Jack Herzog's possible criminal activities and his relationship with the disgraced cop Marty Bergen. The icing on that cake was the industrial firms and the brass hats who were moonlighting for them. It would not do to step on their toes. A media blitz might flush Goff out, but the Department was covering its ass.

Lloyd parked in a subterranean facility on Olympic and Century Park East, then took an elevator up to ground level and found the shrink's building, a glass and steel skyscraper fronted by an astroturf courtyard. The directory in the foyer placed "John Havilland, M.D.," in suite 2604. Lloyd took a glass-encased elevator to the twenty-sixth floor and walked down a long hallway to an oak door embossed with the psychiatrist's name. He pushed the door open, expecting to be confronted by the saccharine smile of a medical receptionist. Instead, he was transfixed by photographic images of the most beautiful woman he had ever seen.

She was obviously tall and slender, with classic facial lines offset by little flaws that made her that much more striking, that much less the trite physical ideal. Her nose was a shade too pointed; her chin bore a middle cleft that gave her whole face an air of resoluteness. Dark hair cascaded at the edge of soft cheekbones and formed a complement with large eyes whose focus was intense, but somehow indecipherable. Walking up to the wall to examine the photographs at close range, Lloyd saw that they were candid shots, and that much more stunning for the fact. Closing his eyes, he tried to picture the woman nude. When new images wouldn't coalesce, he knew why: her beauty rendered all attempts at fantasy stillborn. This woman demanded to be seen naked in reality or not at all.

"She's exquisite, isn't she?"

The words didn't dent Lloyd's reverie. He opened his eyes and saw and heard and felt nothing but the feminine power captured in front of him. When he felt a tap on his shoulder, he turned around and saw a slight man in a navy blazer and gray flannel slacks staring up at him, hand outstretched, light brown eyes amused by his reaction to the photographs. "I'm John Havilland," the man said. "What can I do for you?"

Lloyd snapped back into a professional posture, taking the man's hand and grasping it firmly. "Detective Sergeant Hopkins, Los Angeles Police Department. Could I have a few minutes of your time?"

Dr. John Havilland smiled and said, "Sure. We'll go into my office." He pointed toward an oak door and added, "I've got over half an hour until my next session. You're blushing, Sergeant, but I don't blame you."

Lloyd said, "Who is she?"

"A counselee of mine," Havilland said. "Sometimes I think she's the most beautiful woman I've ever seen."

"I was thinking the same thing. What does she think about being your pinup girl?"

Havilland's cheeks reddened; Lloyd saw that the man was smitten beyond the bounds of professionalism. "Forget I asked, Doctor. I'll keep it to business from here on in."

The Doctor lowered his eyes and led Lloyd into an oak paneled inner office, pointing him to a chair, taking an identical seat a few feet away. Raising his eyes, he said, "Is this personal or an official police inquiry?"

Lloyd stared openly at the psychiatrist. When Havilland didn't flinch, he realized that he was in the company of an equal. "It's both, Doctor. The starting point is your nickname. I—"

Havilland was already shaking his head. "It's a secondhand nickname," he said. "Doctor John the Night Tripper was a sixties rock and roller. I was given the monicker in med school, because my name was John and I did a certain amount of night tripping. I've also counseled a great many criminals, court referred and otherwise. These people have perpetuated the nickname. Frankly, I like it."

Lloyd smiled and said, "It does have a certain ring." He dug two snapshots out of his jacket pocket and handed them to Havilland. "Have you ever counseled either of these men?"

The Doctor looked at the photos and handed them back. "No, I haven't. Who are they?"

Lloyd ignored the question and said, "If you had treated them, would you have told me?"

Havilland formed his fingers into a steeple and placed the point on his chin. "I would have given you a 'yes' or 'no' answer, then asked, 'Why do you want to know?' "

"Good direct answer," Lloyd said. "I'll reciprocate. The light-haired man recently walked into a liquor store and blew three people to shit. The dark-haired man is an L.A. policeman, missing and presumed dead. Before he disappeared he was hysterical and obsessed with your nickname. I'm certain that the light-haired man killed him. Old light-hair is a world-class psycho. Two days ago we shot it out in a Beverly Hills singles bar. You probably read about it in the papers. He escaped. I want to cancel his ticket. Atascadero or the morgue, preferably the latter."

Lloyd leaned back and loosened his necktie, chagrined that he had raised his voice and probably blown his professional parity with the psychiatrist. He felt a headache coming on and shut his eyes to forestall it. When he opened his eyes, Dr. John Havilland was beaming from ear to ear and shaking his head in delight. "I love macho, Sergeant. It's one of my weak points as a headshrinker. Since we've established a certain base of candor, can I ask a few candid questions?"

Lloyd grinned. "Shoot, Doc."

"All right. One, did you honestly think that I knew these two men?"

Lloyd shook his head. "No."

"Then is it safe to assume that you came to exploit my renowned knowledge of criminal behavior?"

Lloyd's grin widened. "Yes."

The Doctor grinned back. "Good. I'll be glad to offer my observations, but will you phrase your case or questions or whatever nonhypothetically? Give me the literal information as succinctly as possible, then let me ask questions?"

Lloyd said, "You've got it," then walked to the window and looked down on the street twenty-six stories below him. With his back to the doctor, he spoke for ten uninterrupted minutes, recounting a streamlined version of the Herzog/Goff investigation, excluding mention of the security files and

Herzog's relationship with Marty Bergen, but describing the Melbourne Avenue horror show in detail.

When he concluded, the Doctor whispered, "God, what a story. Why hasn't there been mention of this man Goff on TV? Wouldn't that help flush him out?"

Turning to face Havilland, Lloyd said, "The high brass have ordered a total media blackout. Public safety, public relations, take your pick—I don't want to go into it. Also, my options are dwindling. I haven't got the slightest handle on Goff's partner. The A.P.B. is hit or miss. I'll be staking out some bars myself, but that's needle in a haystack stuff. If I don't get any leads soon, I'll have to fly to New York and interview people who knew Goff there, which, frankly, seems futile. Run with the ball, Doc. What I'm interested in are your assumptions on Goff's relationship with his partner and the condition of his apartment. What do you think?"

Havilland got up and paced the room. Lloyd sat down and watched him circuit the office. Finally the Doctor stopped and said, "I buy your appraisal of Goff's basic psychoses and the left-handed man as a restraining influence, but only to a degree. Also, I don't think that the men are homosexual lovers, despite the symbolism of the wall cutouts. I think you're dealing with subliminally exposed false clues; the nude men and the slogans especially. The slogans are reminiscent of the sixties—maybe Goff and his friend were inspired by the sloganeering of the Manson family. I think that the left-behind record albums point to the subliminality of the subterfuge, because every single record was some kind of sixties musical archetype. The apartment was cleaned out thoroughly, yet these albums were left behind. That strikes me as odd. Now one thing is obvious—Goff's cover was blown after his gunplay with you; he knew he had to run, that he would be positively identified very soon. *So his friend wiped the walls to eliminate his own fingerprints*, probably after Goff had vacated—but he didn't remove the cutouts because they pointed only to *Goff's* psychoses. He didn't *see* the cupboard cutout that bore the missing officer's badge number, because it was an inside surface that he himself had never touched, and because he didn't know that Goff had created it. The other wall clues could be construed as ambiguous, but not the cupboard cutout. It pointed to the murder of a Los Angeles policeman. Had Goff's friend known of it, he would have destroyed it. What do *you* think, Sergeant?"

Riveted by the brilliantly informed hypothesis, Lloyd said, "It floats on all levels. I was thinking along similar lines, but you took it two steps further. Can you wrap the whole package up for me?"

The Doctor sat down facing Lloyd, drawing his chair up so that their knees were almost touching. He said, "I think that the basic motivational clues, subliminal and overt, are the nude men, which represent not homosexual tendencies, but a desire to destroy male power. I think that Goff's friend is highly disturbed while Goff himself is psychotic. I think both men are highly intelligent, highly motivated pathological cop haters."

Lloyd let the words sink in, retaining eye contact with the Doctor. The thesis was sound, but what was the next investigative step?

Finally Havilland lowered his eyes and spoke. "I'd like to help you, Sergeant. I have lots of informed criminal sources. My own mini-grapevine, so to speak."

"I'd appreciate it," Lloyd said, taking a business card from his jacket pocket. "This has my office and home numbers on it. You can call me regardless of the time." He handed Havilland the card. Havilland pocketed it and said, "Could I have that picture of Goff? I'd like to show it to some of my counselees."

Lloyd nodded. "Don't mention that Goff is a homicide suspect," he said as he placed the snapshot in the Doctor's hand. "Try to sound casual. If your patients think this is a big deal, they might try to exploit the situation for money or favors."

"Of course," Havilland said. "It's the only professional way to do it. By the same token, let me state this flat out: I cannot and will not jeopardize the anonymity of my sources, under any circumstances."

"I wouldn't expect you to."

"Good. What will you do next?"

"Hit the bricks, chew on your thesis, go over the existing paperwork forty or fifty times until something bites me."

Havilland laughed. "I hope the bite won't be fatal. You know, it's funny. All of a sudden you look very grave, and just like my father. Bad thoughts?"

Lloyd laughed until his sides ached and tears ran down his cheeks. Havilland chuckled along, forming a series of steeples with his fingers. Regaining his breath, Lloyd said, "God, that feels good. I was laughing at how ironic your question was. For a solid week I've had nothing but homicide on my brain, but when you said 'bad thoughts' I was thinking of that incredible woman on your walls."

Laughing wildly himself, the Doctor blurted out, "Linda Wilhite has that effect on a man. She can tur—" He caught himself in mid-sentence, stopped and said, "She can move men to the point of wanting to speak her name out loud. Forget what I said, Hopkins. My counselees' anonymity is sacred. It was unprofessional of me."

Lloyd got to his feet, thinking that the poor bastard was in love, beyond rhyme or reason, with a woman who probably caused traffic jams when she walked down the street to buy a newspaper. He smiled and stuck out his hand. When Havilland took it, he said, "I do unprofessional things all the time, Doc. Guys with our kind of juice should fuck up once in a while out of *noblesse oblige*. Thanks for your help."

Dr. John Havilland smiled. Lloyd walked out of his office, willing his eyes rigid, away from the photographs of Linda Wilhite.

13

The Night Tripper began to hyperventilate the very second that Lloyd Hopkins walked out his door. The suppressed tension that had fueled his performance, *his brilliant performance*, started to seep out through his pores, causing him to shiver uncontrollably and grab at his desk to fight his vertigo. He held the desktop until his knuckles turned white and cramps ran up his arms to his shoulders. Concentrating on his own physiology to bring his control back to normal, he calculated his heartbeat at one twenty-five and his blood pressure as stratospheric. This professional detachment in the face of extreme fear/elation calmed and soothed him. Within seconds he could feel his vital signs recede to something approaching normalcy. "Father. Father. Father," Dr. John Havilland whispered.

When his physical and mental calm united, the Doctor replayed his performance and assessed the policeman, astonished to find that he was not the right-wing plunderer he had expected, but rather a likable fellow with a sense of humor that was offset by the violence he held in check just below the surface of his intellect. Lloyd Hopkins was a bad man to fuck with. So was he. He had taken their first round easily, running on instinct. Round two would have to be meticulously planned.

Checking his desk calendar, the Doctor saw that he had no patients for the rest of the day and that Linda Wilhite's next session was still two days off. Thoughts of Linda spawned a long series of mental chess moves. Hopkins would be leaving for New York, unless he discovered evidence to keep him in Los Angeles. It would not do to have "Crazy Lloyd" talk to the administrators at Attica. Round two would have to be initiated today, but how?

Just then it hit him. At their first session Linda had spoken of a "client" who collected Colombian art and who took nude photos of her and hung them in his bedroom. *Another pawn.*

Havilland opened the wall safe hidden behind his Edward Hopper original and took out Thomas Goff's verbatim transcription of Linda's john book/journal. He sifted through pages of sexual facts, figures, and ruminations before he found mention of the man.

8/28/83; Stanley Rudolph, 11741 Montana (at Bundy) 829-6907. Referred by P.N.

A truly ambivalent man. He lives in a condo full of Colombian art (aesthetic!) that he claims he buys dirt cheap from doper rip-off bimbos (macho obnoxiousness!). The statues were atavistic, *virile*, wonderful. Stanley talks them up so much prior to business that I know he wants something other than straight fucking—especially when he starts calling me a work of fucking art. Lead in to (of course!) a photography session! (Reading between the lines—Stan baby is impotent, digs nudie shots juxtaposed against his phallic statues.) Stan takes his shots (no beavers—actually tasteful)—(Stan the Aesthete)—then tells me stories about all the women who beg for his donkey dick (Stan the macho buffoon.) I lounge around nude trying to keep from cracking up. $500.00.

9/10/83—Ambivalent Stan has become a regular at $500.00 per. I am now framed on his walls in naked splendor. Weird. I wish my breasts were bigger.

Havilland replaced the transcript in his safe and thought of another faceless pawn living a sleazy life in the Valley industrial district, then locked up his office and went looking for her.

*   *   *

Junior Miss Cosmetics was situated at the northeast edge of the San Fernando Valley, a squat green stucco building enclosed by rusted cyclone fencing. Outside the wire perimeter was a huge dirt lot filled with carelessly parked cars, and across the street stood an entire city block of cocktail lounges, all of them flashing neon signs at three o'clock in the afternoon. Parking underneath a sign advertising "Nude Workingman's Lunch," Dr. John Havilland felt like he had just entered hell.

The Doctor locked his car and counted neon blinking doorways all the way up the block, ending with a total of nine. He walked into the first door, wincing against a blast of country western music, squinting until he could make out a bandstand and an overweight redhead doing a listless nude boogie. There was a horseshoe-shaped bar off to his left. Steeling himself for his role, Havilland took a twenty dollar bill from his money clip and walked over.

The bartender looked up as he approached. "You drinking or you want the lunch?" he asked.

Havilland placed the twenty flat on the bar and willed his voice to suit the environment. "I'm looking for Sherry Shroeder. A buddy of mine says she hangs out here."

"Sherry's eighty-six," the bartender said. "She gets coked or juiced and gets rowdy. You looking to pour some pork?"

The Doctor gawked, then said, "What?"

The bartender spoke slowly, as if to an idiot child. "You know, push the bush? Slake the snake? Drain the train? Siphon the python?"

Havilland swallowed and took another twenty from his pocket. "Yes. All those things. Where can I find her? Please tell me."

Snatching up the two bills, the bartender leaned over and spoke into the Doctor's ear. "Go down the street to the Loafer Gopher. Sherry should show up there sooner or later. Sit at the bar, and sooner or later she'll come up and try to sit on your face. And, buddy? Keep your roll to yourself. They got some righteous shitkickers down there."

The Loafer Gopher was dark and featured punk rock. Havilland sat at the bar and sipped scotch and soda while Cindy and the Sinners sang their repertoire of "Prison of Your Love," "Nine Inches of Your Love," and "Gimme Your Love" over and over. He arrayed a stack of one dollar bills in front of him and tried to avoid eye contact with the topless barmaid, who considered eye-to-eye meetings a signal to refresh drinks. Playing Mozart in his mind to kill the hideous music and conversation surrounding him, the Doctor waited.

The waiting extended into hours. Havilland sat at the bar, buying a drink every twenty minutes, nursing the top, then, unseen, dumping the rest on the floor. When mental Mozart began to pall, he fantasized Sherry Shroeder as everything from a Nordic ice maiden to a platinum-coiffed slattern, using her security file statistics as his physical spark point. He was nearing the limits of both his patience and imagination when coy fingers caressed his neck and a coy female voice asked, "Care to buy a lady a drink?"

Havilland swiveled his stool to face the come-on. The woman who had delivered it looked like a burned-out beach bunny. Her face was seamed from too much sun and chemical ingestion, with deep furrows around the mouth and eyes that bespoke many desperate attempts to be fetching and an equal number of rejections. Her blonde hair was set in a lopsided frizzy style that added to her look of anxiousness. But her features were pretty, and her designer jean and tanktop-clad body was lean and womanly. If this was his actress, Richard Oldfield would love her.

"I'm Sherry," the woman said.

Havilland signaled the barmaid and smiled at his pawn. "I'm Lloyd."

She giggled as the barmaid placed a tall drink in front of her and grabbed two of the Doctor's one dollar bills as payment. She took a long sip and said, "That's a good name. It goes with your blazer. You don't really dress for the Gopher, but that's okay, 'cause there's so many bars on this strip that you can't go home and change every time you hop one, can you? I mean, is that the truth?"

"That's the truth," Havilland said. "I dress conservatively because the bigwigs at the studio demand it. I'm just like you. I can't go home and change every time I go out on a talent search."

Sherry's eyes widened. She gulped the rest of her drink and stammered, "Ar-ar-are you an agent?"

"I'm an independent movie producer," Havilland said, snapping his fingers at the barmaid and pointing to Sherry's empty glass. "I sell art movies to a combine of millionaires, who screen the films in their special screening rooms. As a matter of fact, I'm here looking for actresses."

Sherry downed her fresh drink in three fast swallows. Havilland watched her eyes expand and bodice flush. "I'm an actress," she said in a rush of breath. "I've done extra work and I've done loops and other stuff. Do you think you—"

Havilland silenced her with a finger to her lips, then looked around the bar. No one seemed interested in their business. "Let's go outside and talk," he said. "This place is too loud."

Sherry led him across the street to the Junior Miss parking lot and her battered VW van. "I used to work there," she said as she unlocked the passenger door. "They fired me because I was overqualified. They found out I had a bigger I.Q. than the president of the company, so they let me go."

Havilland sat down in the passenger seat and made a mental note not to touch anything inside the vehicle. Sherry walked around the front of the van and squeezed in behind the wheel. When she looked at him importuningly, the Doctor said, "Sherry, I'll be frank. I produce high-budget adult films. Normally I would not advise a serious young actress like yourself to appear in such a movie, but in this case I would—because only a private audience of Hollywood bigshots will be viewing it. Now let me ask you, have you had experience in adult films?"

Sherry's answer came out in a gin-fueled torrent of words. "Yeah, and this is perfect because before I did loops and the camera guy said my mom and dad would never know. We shot in the boys' gym at Pacoima Junior High, 'cause the camera guy knew the janitor and he had the key, and we had to shoot late at night 'cause then nobody would be around. Ritchie Valens went to Pacoima Junior High, but he got killed with Buddy Holly on February 3, 1959. I was just a little girl then, but I remember."

The final memory numbed the Doctor. He took out his billfold and said, "We'll be shooting in two days or so, at a big house in the Hollywood Hills. Two performers—you and a very handsome young man. Your pay is a thousand dollars. Would you like an advance now?"

Sherry Shroeder threw her arms around Havilland and buried her head in his neck. When he felt her tongue in his ear, he grabbed her shoulders and pushed her away. "Please, Sherry, I'm married."

Sherry gave a mock pout. "Married men are the best. Can I have a C-note now?"

Havilland took three hundreds from his billfold. He handed them to Sherry and whispered, "Please keep quiet about this. If word gets out, other actresses will be bothering me for parts, and I think I want to stick with you exclusively. All right?"

"All right."

Havilland smiled. "I need your phone number."

Sherry reached in the glove compartment, then flicked on the dashboard light and handed the Doctor a red metallic flaked business card bearing the words, "Sherry—Let's Party! Incall and outcall, 632-0140." Havilland put the card in his pocket and nudged the passenger door open with his shoulder. He smiled and said, "I'll be in touch."

Sherry said, "Party hearty, Lloyd baby," and gunned her engine. The Doctor watched the VW van peel rubber into the night.

The Night Tripper drove to a pay phone and called Richard Oldfield at his home, speaking a single sentence and hanging up before Oldfield could reply. Satisfied with the force of his words, he drove to the Hollywood Hills and his third stellar performance of the day.

Oldfield had left the front door unlocked. The Night Tripper walked through it to find his pawn kneeling on the living room floor in his efficacy training posture, head thrust out and eyes closed, hands clasped behind his back. He was stripped to the waist, and his pectoral muscles were twitching from a recent workout.

Havilland walked up and flung a whiplike backhand at Oldfield's face, gashing his cheek with his Harvard signet ring. Oldfield leaned into the blow and remained mute. Havilland reared back and swung again, catching his pawn on the bridge of the nose, ripping flesh and severing a vein below his left eye. When Oldfield betrayed no pain, the Doctor unleashed a whirlwind of open palms and backhands, until his pawn's face contorted and a single tear escaped from each eye and merged with the blood from his lashings.

"Are you ready to hurt and twist and loathe and gouge the woman who ruined you as a child?" the Night Tripper hissed. "Are you ready to go as far as you can go? Are you ready to enter a realm of pure power and relegate the rest of the world to the shit heap that it really is?"

"Yes," Richard Oldfield sobbed.

The Doctor took a silk handkerchief from his blazer pocket and swabbed his counselee's face. "Then you shall have all of it. Now listen and don't ask questions. The time is two days from now, the place is here. Don't go out of the house until I tell you, because a policeman is looking for someone who looks exactly like you. Do you understand all these things?"

"Yes," Oldfield said.

Havilland walked to the phone and dialed seven digits he had memorized early that afternoon. When a weary voice answered, "Yes?" he said,

"Sergeant, this is John Havilland. Listen, I've got a line on your suspect. It's rather vague, but I think I credit the information."

"Jesus fucking Christ," Lloyd Hopkins said. "Where did you get it?"

"No," Havilland said, "I can't tell you that. I can tell you this—the man is right-handed, and in my professional opinion he knows nothing about any homicides, or about Goff's whereabouts."

Lloyd said, "I've got my notebook, Doc. Talk slowly."

"All right. This man says he met Goff last year at a singles bar. They pulled a burglary together, he forgets the location, and stole some art objects. Goff had a customer for the stuff. My man says his name was either Rudolph Stanley or Stanley Rudolph. He had a condo in Brentwood, somewhere near Bundy and Montana."

"That's it?"

"Yes. My counselee is a basically decent, very disturbed young man, Sergeant. Please don't press me for his identity. I won't yield on that."

"Don't sweat it, Doc. But if I get Goff on your info, be prepared for the best dinner of your life."

"I look forward to it." Havilland waited for a reply, but the policeman had already hung up.

Putting down the phone, he saw that Richard Oldfield had not budged from his supplicant position. He looked at the blood on his hands. Twist the cop. Gouge him. Maim him. Make him pay for the childhood darkness and infuse the void with light.

14

At dawn, Lloyd was stationed in his car at the southeast corner of Bundy and Montana, armed with skin-tight rubber gloves and a selection of burglar's picks. After receiving Havilland's phone call, he had made a battery of his own calls, to the L.A.P.D.'s R&I, the All Police Computer Network, the feds, and the California Department of Motor Vehicles Night Information line. The results were only halfway satisfying: A man named Stanley Rudolph lived at 11741 Montana, # 1015, but he possessed no criminal record and had never been cited for anything more serious than running a red light. A solid citizen type who in all probability would scream for his attorney when confronted with the fact that he was a receiver of stolen goods. There was only the tried-and-true and highly illegal daylight recon run. Rudolph's D.M.V. application had yielded the facts that he was unmarried, worked as a broker at the downtown stock exchange, and was the owner of a light blue 1982 Cadillac Seville bearing the personalized license plate "Big Stan," which was now parked directly across the street. Lloyd fidgeted and looked at his watch. 6:08. The exchange would be opening at seven. "Big Stan" would have to leave soon or be late for work.

Sipping coffee directly from the thermos, he thought of his other, nonprofessional telephone inquiries. Against his better judgment, he had called R&I and the D.M.V. to learn what he could about Linda Wilhite. The information gleaned was lackluster: Date of birth, physical stats, address, and phone number and the facts that she was "self-employed," drove a Mercedes and had no criminal record. But the act of pursuit was thrilling, fueled by fantasies of what it would be like to need and be needed by a woman that beautiful. Thoughts of Linda Wilhite had competed with thoughts of his investigation for control of his mind, and it was only Havilland's astonishing phone call that bludgeoned them to second place.

At 6:35, a portly man wearing a three-piece business suit trotted up to the Cadillac, holding a sweet roll in one hand and a briefcase in the other. He got in the car and gunned it southbound on Bundy. Lloyd waited for three minutes, then walked over to 11741 Montana and took the elevator up to the tenth floor.

1015 was at the end of a long carpeted corridor. Lloyd looked in both directions, then rang the bell. When thirty seconds went by without an answer, he studied the twin locks on the door and jammed his breaker pick into the top mechanism, feeling a very slight click as a bolt loosened. He leaned his shoulder into the door, accentuating the give of the top lock. With his free hand he stuck a needle-thin skeleton pick into the bottom keyhole and twisted it side to side. Seconds later the bottom lock slid open and the door snapped inward.

Lloyd stepped inside and closed the door behind him. When his eyes became adjusted to the darkness, he found himself in a treasure trove of primitive art. There were shelves filled with Colombian fertility statues and African wood carvings covering the tops of empty bookcases. Windowsills and ottomans held Mayan pottery, and the walls were festooned with framed oil paintings of Peruvian Indians and shrines in the Andes. The living room carpeting and furniture were bargain basement quality, but the artwork looked to be worth a small fortune.

Lloyd slipped on his rubber gloves and reconnoitered the rest of the condo, coming to one nonincriminating conclusion: Except for the artwork and the late model Cadillac, "Big Stan" lived on the cheap. His clothing was off the rack and his refrigerator was stuffed with TV dinners. He shined his own shoes and owned nothing electronic or mechanical except the built-in appliances that came with the pad and an inexpensive 35mm camera. Stanley Rudolph was a man obsessed.

Lloyd took a generic brand cola from the refrigerator and sat down on a threadbare sofa to consider his options, realizing that it would be impossible to secure latent prints from any art objects that Goff or Havilland's anonymous source might have touched. Stanley Rudolph had probably fondled the statues and pottery repeatedly, and the shrink had said that his source was both right-handed and innocent of knowledge of Goff's whereabouts and homicides in general. Havilland was a pro; his assessments could be trusted.

This left three approaches: Lean hard on "Big Stan" himself; toss the pad for levers of intimidation, and find his address book and run the names through R&I. Since "Big Stan" was unavailable, only the last two approaches were practical. Lloyd killed his soft drink and went to work.

It took him three hours to comb every inch of the condo and confirm his conclusion that Stanley Rudolph was a lonely man who lived solely to collect art. His clothes were poorly laundered, his bathroom was a mess, and the bedroom walls were blanketed with dust, except for rectangular patches where paintings had obviously recently hung. The sadness/obsessiveness combo made Lloyd want to send up a mercy plea for the entire fucked-up human race.

This left the address book, resting beside the telephone on the living room floor. Lloyd leafed through it, noting that it contained only names and phone numbers. Turning to the G's, he saw that there was no mention of Thomas Goff and that Stanley Rudolph's scrawl was unmistakably right-handed. Sighing, he thumbed back to the A's and got out his notepad and pen and began copying down every name and phone number in the book.

When he got to "Laurel Benson," Lloyd felt a little tremor drift up his spine. Laurel Benson was a high-priced call girl he had rousted while working West L.A. Vice over ten years before. Thinking that it was merely a coincidence and that it was nice to know that "Big Stan" got laid occasionally, he continued his transcribing until he hit "Polly Marks" and put down his pen and laughed out loud. Thus far, the only two women listed in the book were hookers. No wonder Rudolph had to shine his own shoes and drink generic soda pop—he had *two* expensive habits.

The N through V section contained the names of over fifty men and only four women, two of them hookers that Lloyd had heard about from vice squad buddies. Writers cramp was coming on when he turned to the final page and saw "Linda Wilhite—275-7815." This time the little tremor became a 9.6 earthquake. Lloyd replaced the address book and left the obsessive little condo before he had time to think of his next destination and what it all meant.

Parked outside Linda Wilhite's plush high-rise on Wilshire and Beverly Glen, Lloyd ran through literal and instinctive chronologies in an attempt to logically explain the remarkable coincidence that had just fallen into his lap. Dr. John Havilland was in love with Linda Wilhite, who was probably a very expensive prostitute, one who had tricked with Stanley Rudolph, who had bought stolen goods from Thomas Goff and the Doctor's anonymous source. Havilland did not know Goff or Rudolph, but did know Wilhite and the source. The coincidence factor was strong, but did *not* reek of malfeasance. Unanswered questions: Did Linda Wilhite know Goff or the source; or, the wild card—was the shrink, who had the air of a man in love, protecting Linda Wilhite, *the real source*, by giving him correct information from a bogus "informant," this way protecting both his professional ethics and the woman he loved? Was the Doctor playing a roundabout game, *wanting* to aid in a homicide investigation, yet not wanting to relinquish confidential information? Lloyd felt anger overtake his initial sex flush. If Linda Wilhite knew *anything* about Thomas Goff or his left-handed friend, he would shake it out of her.

He ran into the high-rise and bolted three flights of service stairs. When he raised his hand to knock on the door of Linda Wilhite's apartment, he saw that *he* was shaking.

A security peephole slid open. "Yes?" a woman's voice said.

Lloyd put his badge up in front of the hole. "L.A.P.D.," he said. "Could I speak to you for a moment, Miss Wilhite?"

"What's this about?"

Lloyd felt his shaking go internal. "It's about Stanley Rudolph. Will you open up, please?"

There was the sound of locks being unlatched, and then *she* was there, wearing an ankle-length paisley caftan. Lloyd tried to stare past her into the apartment, but Linda Wilhite held the center of his vision and rendered the background dull black.

"What *about* Stanley Rudolph?" she asked.

Lloyd walked into the apartment uninvited, taking a quick inventory of the entrance hall and living room. It was still hazy background stuff, but he knew that everything was tasteful and expensive.

"Don't be shy, make yourself right at home," Linda Wilhite said, coming up behind Lloyd and pointing him toward a floral-patterned easy chair. "I'll have the butler bring you a mint julep."

Lloyd laughed. "Nice pad, Linda. Out of the low-rent district."

Linda feigned a return laugh. "Don't be formal, call me suspect."

Lloyd stuck his hand in his jacket pocket and pulled out snapshots of Thomas Goff and Jungle Jack Herzog. He handed them to Linda and said, "Okay, suspect, have you seen either of these men before?"

Linda looked the photos over and returned them to Lloyd. There was not the slightest flicker of recognition in her eyes or her hands-on-hips pose. "No. What's this about Stan Rudolph? Are you with Vice?"

Lloyd sat down in the easy chair and stretched his legs. "That's right. What's the basis of your relationship with Rudolph?"

Linda's eyes went cold. Her voice followed. "I think you know. Will you state your purpose, ask your questions, and get out?"

Lloyd shook his head. "What do *you* know?"

"That you're no fucking Vice cop!" Linda shouted. "You got a snappy comeback for that one?"

Lloyd's voice was his softest; the voice he saved for his daughters. "Yeah. You're no hooker."

Linda sat down across from him. "Everything in this apartment calls you a liar."

"I've been called worse than that," Lloyd said.

"Such as?"

"Some of the choicer shots have included 'urban barracuda,' 'male chauvinist porker,' 'fascist cocksucker,' 'wasp running dog,' and 'pussy hound scumbag.' I appreciate articulate invective. 'Motherfucker' and 'pig' get to be boring."

Linda Wilhite laughed and poked a finger at Lloyd's wedding ring. "You're married. What does your wife call you?"

"Long distance."

"What?"

"We're separated."

"Serious splitsville?"

"I'm not sure. It's been a year and she's got a lover, but I intend to outlast the bastard."

Linda stretched out her legs, matching Lloyd's pose, but in the opposite direction. "Do you always discuss intimate family matters with total strangers?"

Lloyd laughed and stilled an urge to reach over and touch her knee. "Sometimes. It's good therapy."

"I'm in therapy," Linda said.

"Why?" Lloyd asked.

"That's your first dumb question," Linda said. "Everyone has problems, and people who have money and want to get rid of them go to shrinks. *Comprende?*"

Lloyd shook his head. "Most troubled people are swamped by petty neuroses, stuff that they haven't got the slightest handle on. Offhand, I'd say that you're not that kind of person. Offhand, I'd say that some sort of catalyst led you to the couch."

"My shrink doesn't have a couch. He's too hip."

"That's a strange thing to call a psychiatrist."

"All right. Hip translates to brilliant, concerned, dedicated, and brutally honest."

"Are you in love with him?"

"No. He's not my type. Look, this conversation is getting a little weird and a bit far afield. You *are* a cop, aren't you? That wasn't a dime-store badge you showed me, or anything like that, was it?"

Lloyd saw a large stack of newspapers lying on top of a coffee table an arm's length away. He pointed to them and said, "If you've got Tuesday's *Times,* look at the second page. 'Shootout at Beverly Hills Nightclub.' "

Linda went to the table and leafed through the papers, then read the article standing up. When she turned around to face Lloyd, he had his badge and I.D. card extended. Linda took the leatherette holder and examined it, then smiled from ear to ear. "So you're Sergeant Lloyd Hopkins and one of those pictures is the unidentified homicide suspect you shot it out with. Very impressive. But what do Stan Rudolph and I have to do with it?"

Lloyd mulled the question over as Linda sat back down without relinquishing the I.D. holder. Deciding on an abridged version of the truth, he said, "An informant told me that Thomas Goff, my previously 'unidentified homicide suspect,' sold Stanley Rudolph some art objects, aided by a still unidentified partner. I came across Rudolph's address book and noticed the names of several call girls I'd busted years ago. I also noticed your name, and concluded that since the only other women in the book were in the Life, you had to be also. I needed an outside lever to pry some information out of Rudolph, and since the other women probably still hate me for busting them, I decided on you."

Linda handed the I.D. holder back. "Are you that fucking brash?"

Lloyd smiled. "Yes," he said.

"Why don't you just question Stan baby yourself?"

"Because he'd probably want an attorney present. Because any admission of knowing Goff is an implicit admission of receiving stolen goods, accessory to first degree burglary and criminal conspiracy. What kind of man is Rudolph?"

"A pathetic little nerd who gets his rocks off taking nude pictures. A loud-mouthed buffoon. What specifically did this guy Goff do?"

"He's murdered at least three people."

Linda went pale. "Jesus. And you want me to pry information about him out of Stan baby?"

"Yes. And about his partner, who I'm certain is left-handed. Does Rudolph ever talk about his art collection and how he acquired it?"

Linda tapped Lloyd's arm and said, "Yes. His art collection is his favorite topic of conversation. It's all tied in to his sex M.O. He's told me a dozen times that he buys his stuff from rip-off guys. That's as specific as he gets. He used to have nude photographs of me on his bedroom walls, but he took them down because he was expecting some more Colombian statues. I haven't tricked with him in six weeks or so, so maybe he and Goff got together recently."

Lloyd thought of the rectangular patches on Rudolph's bedroom wall, imagining the nude Linda he could have seen had he pulled his B&E a few months before. "Linda, do you think you—"

Linda Wilhite silenced him with a breathtaking coconspirator's smile.

"Yes. I'll call Stan baby and set up a date, hopefully for tonight. Call me around one A.M., and don't worry, I'll be very cool."

Lloyd's conspiratorial smile felt like a blush. "Thank you."

"My pleasure. You were right, you know. I did enter therapy for a reason."

"What was it?"

"I want to quit the Life."

"Then I was right on two counts."

"What do you mean?"

"I told you you were no hooker."

Lloyd got up and walked out of the apartment, letting his exit line linger.

With the Stanley Rudolph angle covered, Lloyd remembered an investigatory approach so rudimentary that he knew its very simplicity was the reason he had forgotten to explore it. Cursing himself for his oversight, he drove to a pay phone and called Dutch Peltz at the Hollywood Station, asking him to go across the street to the Hollywood Municipal Court and secure a subpoena for Jack Herzog's bank records. Dutch agreed to the errand, on the proviso that Lloyd fill him in at length on the case when he came by the station to pick up the paperwork. Lloyd agreed in return and drove to Herzog's apartment house in the Valley, thinking of Linda Wilhite all the way.

At Herzog's building, Lloyd went straight to the manager's apartment, flashed his badge, and asked him what bank the missing officer's rent checks were drawn on. Without hesitation, the frail old man said, "Security-Pacific, Encino branch," then launched into a spiel on how other officers had been by the previous day and had sealed the nice Mr. Herzog's nice apartment.

After thanking the manager, Lloyd drove back over the Cahuenga Pass to the Hollywood Station. He found Dutch Peltz in his office, muttering, "Yes, yes," into the telephone. Dutch looked up, drew a finger across his throat and whispered, "I.A.D." Lloyd took a chair across from him and put his feet up on the desk. Dutch muttered, "Yes, Fred, I'll tell him," and hung up. He turned to Lloyd and said, "Good news and bad news. Which would you prefer first?"

"Take your pick," Lloyd said.

Dutch smiled and poked Lloyd's crossed ankles with a pencil. "The good news is that Judge Bitowf issued your subpoena with no questions asked. Wasn't that nice of him?"

Lloyd took in Dutch's grin and raised his feet as if to kick his precious quartz bookend off the desk. "Tell me what Fred Gaffaney had to say. Omit nothing."

"More good news and bad news," Dutch said. "The good news is that *I* am your official liaison to I.A.D. on all matters pertaining to the Goff-Herzog case. The bad news is that Gaffaney just reiterated in the strongest possible language that you are to go nowhere near the officers working the moonlight gigs or go near the firms themselves. Gaffaney is preparing an approach strategy, and he and his top men will be conducting interviews within a few days. *I* will be given Xeroxes of their reports, *you* can get copies from me. Gaffaney also stated that if you violate these orders, you will be suspended immediately and given a trial board. You like it?"

Lloyd reached over and patted the bookend. "No, I don't like it. But you do."

Dutch flashed a shark grin. "I like anything that keeps you reasonably restrained and thereby a continued member of the Los Angeles Police Department. I would hate to see you get shitcanned and go on welfare. You'd be drinking T-bird and sleeping in the weeds within six months."

Lloyd stood up and grabbed the subpoena off Dutch's desk. He laid the notebook containing the names from Stanley Rudolph's address book in its place and said, "I know why you're acting so sardonic, Dutchman. You had a martini with your lunch. You have one drink a year, and your low tolerance gets you plowed. I'm a detective. You can't fool me."

Dutch laughed. "Fuck you. What's with this notebook and where do you think you're going? You were going to fill me in on the case, remember?"

Lloyd took a playful jab at the bookend. "Fuck you twice. I don't confide in alcoholics. Have one of your minions run those names through R&I, will you?"

"I'll think about it. Hey Lloydy, how come you took my bad news so easy? I expected you to throw something."

Lloyd tried to imitate Dutch's shark grin, but knew immediately that it came out a blush. "I think I'm in love," he said.

Lloyd drove back to the Valley, highballing it northbound on the Ventura Freeway in order to hit the Encino branch of the Security-Pacific Bank before closing time, making it with two minutes to spare. He showed his I.D. and the subpoena to the manager, a middle-aged Japanese man who led him to the privacy of a safe deposit box examination room, returning five minutes later with a computer printout and a thick transaction file. Bowing, the manager closed the door, leaving Lloyd in impeccable silence.

That silence soon became inhabited by dates and figures that detailed an atypical cop life. Jack Herzog's savings and checking accounts went back five years. Lloyd started at the beginning of the transaction file and waded through paychecks deposited twice monthly, rent checks drawn monthly and savings stipends deposited every third L.A. City pay period. Jack Herzog was a frugal man. There were no large withdrawals indicating spending sprees; no checks for amounts exceeding his monthly rent payment of $350.00, and out of every third paycheck he deposited $300.00 in a 7½% growth savings account. When Herzog opened his dual accounts in 1979, his total balance was less than six hundred dollars. At the transaction file's last entry date four months before, he was worth $17,913.49.

Noting that the last entry was on 1/4/84, Lloyd turned to the computer sheet, hoping it contained facts updating Herzog's two accounts to the present.

It did. The same deposit/check withdrawal motif continued, this time detailed in hard to read computer type. Lloyd was about to shake his head at the sadness of close to nineteen grand belonging to a dead man when the final transaction came into focus, grabbing him by the throat.

On March 20, around the time of his disappearance, Jack Herzog closed out both his accounts and purchased an interbranch bank draft for his total balance of $18,641.07. There was a photocopy of the draft clipped to the computer sheet. It stated that the above amount was to be transferred to the West Hollywood branch of Security-Pacific, to the savings account of Martin D. Bergen. Lloyd let the facts sink in, then walked slowly out of the examination room and through the bank proper, bowing to the bank manager and running as soon as he hit the sidewalk.

By speeding through the Hollywood Hills, Lloyd was able to reach the *Big Orange Insider* office in just under half an hour. The same receptionist gave him the same startled look as he pushed through the connecting door to the editorial department, and seconds later the young man he had tangled with on his previous visit attempted to block his progress by standing in his path with his legs dug in like a linebacker. "I told you before you can't come back here," he said.

Lloyd took a bead on his head, then caught himself. "Marty Bergen," he said. "Official police business. Go get him."

The young man wrapped his arms around his chest. "Marty is on vacation. Leave now."

Lloyd took the bank subpoena from his pocket and rolled it up, then tickled the underside of the young man's chin with the end. When he jerked backward, Lloyd said, "This is a court order to search Bergen's desk. If you don't comply with it, I'll get an order to search the entire premises. Do you dig me, Daddy-o?"

Turning beet red, then pale, the youth flung an arm toward the back of the room. "The last desk against the wall. And let me see that court order."

Lloyd handed the subpoena over and weaved through a crammed maze of desks, ignoring the stares of the people sitting at them. Bergen's desk was covered with a pile of papers. Lloyd leafed through them, pushing the stack aside when he saw that every page contained notes scrawled in an indecipherable shorthand. He was about to go through the drawers when a woman's voice interrupted him. "Officer, is Marty all right?"

Lloyd turned around. A tall black woman wearing an ink-stained printer's smock was standing beside the desk, holding a long roll of tabloid galley paper. "Is Marty *all right?*" she repeated.

"No," Lloyd said. "I don't think so. Why do you ask? You sound concerned."

The woman fretted the roll in her hands. "He's been gone since the last time you were here," she said. "He hasn't been at his apartment and nobody from the *Orange* has seen him. And right before he took off he grabbed all his columns for the following week, except one. I'm the head typesetter, and I needed to set those issues. Marty really screwed the *Orange*, and that's not like him."

"Has he taken off like this before?"

The woman shook her head. "No! I mean sometimes he rents a motel room and goes on a toot, but he always leaves copies of his column for the time he expects to be gone. This time was *weird* because he took *back* his columns, and *they* were really *weird* to begin with."

Lloyd motioned the woman to sit down. "Tell me about those columns," he said. "Try to remember everything you can."

"They were *just weird,*" the woman said slowly. "One was called 'Moonlight Malfeasance.' It was about these bigshot L.A. cops who had these figurehead jobs bossing around all these low-life rent-a-cops. *Weird.* The other columns were offshoots on that one, about the L.A.P.D. manipulating the media, because they got all the inside dirt from the moonlight cops. *Weird.*

I mean the *Orange's* meat is its anti-fuzz policy, but this stuff was *weird*, even for Marty Bergen, who was a lovable dude, but *weird* himself."

Lloyd felt fragments of his case burst into a strange new light: *Marty Bergen had seen the missing L.A.P.D. Personnel files.* Swallowing to hold his voice steady, he said, "You told me that Bergen let you keep one of the columns. Have you still got it?"

The woman nodded and rolled out her galley sheet on the desk. "Marty gave real specific instructions on how to set it," she said. "He said it had to have a heavy black border and that it had to run on May the third, because that was the birthday of this buddy of his. *Weird*." She located the section and jabbed it with her finger. "There. Read it for yourself."

The black-bordered piece was entitled "Night Train to the Big Nowhere." Lloyd read it over three times, feeling his case move from its strange new light into a stranger darkness.

When a cop jumps on the Night Train to the big nowhere, he doesn't care about its exact destination, because any terminus is preferable to living inside his own head, with its awful knowledge of how the solar age will never penetrate the Big Iceberg.

When my friend jumped on the Night Train to the Big Nowhere, he probably foresaw only relief from his locked-in knowledge of the big nightmare, and the vise grip of the new nightmare that spelled out his role to play in the shroud dance that owns us all.

That you didn't purchase your ticket with your gun spoke volumes. Like me, you were a blue-suit sham. You did not use that tool of your trade in your nihilist last hurrah, reaffirming your masquerade. Instead you strangled on a pink cloud of chemical silence, giving yourself time to think of all the puzzles you had solved, and of the cruelty of your final jigsaw revelations. At the end you confronted, and *knew*. It was your most conscious act of courage in a life vulgarized by fearful displays of bravery. I love you for it, and offer you this twenty-one gun verse valedictory:

Resurrect the dead on this day,
open the doors where
they dare not to stray;
Cancel all tickets to the horror shroud dance,
Burn down the night in the rage of a trance.

Lloyd handed the sheet back to the bewildered typesetter. "Print it," he said. "Redeem your piece of shit newspaper."

The woman said, "It ain't the *New York Times*, but it's a regular gig."

Lloyd nodded, but didn't reply. When he walked out of the office the strident young man was scrutinizing the bank subpoena with a magnifying glass.

Knowing that he couldn't bear to recon Marty Bergen's apartment, Lloyd drove home and called the West Hollywood Sheriff's, briefly explaining the case and relegating the job to them, omitting his knowledge of the bank draft, telling them to make a check of local motels and to detain Bergen if they found him.

New questions burned in the morass that the Herzog-Goff case had become. Was Jungle Jack Herzog a suicide? If so, where was his body, who had disposed of it, and who had wiped his apartment free of fingerprints? Marty Bergen's "weird" columns indicated that he had seen the files Herzog had stolen. Where were the files, what was the literal gist of the suicide column, where was Bergen, and what was the extent of his involvement in the case?

When nothing came together for him, Lloyd knew that he was over-amped, undernourished, and coming unconnected, and that the only antidote was an evening of rest. After a dinner of cold sliced ham and a pint of cottage cheese, he sat down on his porch to watch the twilight dwindle into darkness, warming to the idea of not thinking.

But he thought.

He thought of the terraced hills of the old neighborhood, and of sleepless fifties nights spent listening to the howling of dogs imprisoned in the animal shelter two blocks away. The shelter had given his section of Silverlake the nickname of "Dogtown," and for the years of 'fifty-five and 'fifty-six, when he had been a peewee member of the Dogtown Flats gang, it had supplied *him* with the sobriquets of "Dogman" and "Savior." The constant howling, plaintive as it was, had been mysterious and romantic dream fuel. But sometimes the dogs chewed and clawed their way to freedom, only to get obliterated by late-night hot-rodders playing chicken on the blind curve blacktop outside his bedroom window. Even though the corpses were removed by the time he left for school in the morning, with the pavement hosed down by old Mr. Hernandez next door, Lloyd could feel and smell and almost taste the blood. And after a while, his nights were spent not listening, but cringing in anticipation of coming impacts.

Lack of sleep drew Lloyd gaunt that fall of 'fifty-six, and he knew that he had to act to reclaim the wonder he had always felt after dark. Because the night was there to provide comfort and the nourishing of brave dreams, and only someone willing to fight for its sanctity deserved to claim it as his citadel.

Lloyd began his assault against death, first blocking off "Dead Dog Curve" at both ends with homemade sawhorse detour signs to prevent access to chicken players. The stratagem worked for two nights, until a glue-sniffing member of the First Street Flats crashed his 'fifty-one Chevy through the barricade, sideswiping a series of parked cars as he lost control, finally coming to a halt by rear-ending an L.A.P.D. black-and-white. Out on bail the next day, the driver went looking for the *puto* who had put up the sawhorse, smiling when Dogtown buddies told him it was a crazy fourteen-year-old kid called Dogman and Savior, a loco who was planning to flop in a sleeping bag by Dead Dog Curve to make sure that nobody played chicken on his turf.

That night fourteen-year-old Lloyd Hopkins, six foot one and a hundred and eighty pounds, began the series of *mano a mano* choose-off's that rendered the nicknames Dogman and Savior passé and earned him a new title: "Conquistador." The fights continued for ten nights straight, costing him a twice broken nose and a total of a hundred stitches, but ending chicken on Griffith Park and St. Elmo forever. When his nose was set for the second time and his swollen hands returned to their normal size, Lloyd quit the Dogtown Flats. He knew he was going to become a policeman, and it would not do to have a gang affiliation on his record.

The ringing of a telephone jerked him back to the present. He walked into the kitchen and picked it up. "Yes?"

"Hopkins, this is Linda."

"What?"

"Are you spaced out or something? Linda Wilhite."

Lloyd laughed. "Yeah, I am spaced out. How's tricks?"

"Not funny, Hopkins, but I'll let you slide because you're spaced. Listen, I *did* just trick with Stanley, and I very subtly pried some not too encouraging info out of him."

"Such as?"

"Such as you were misinformed somehow. Stan baby has never heard of Goff. I described the picture you showed me to him, and he doesn't know anyone resembling it. Ditto any left-handed man. Stan said he buys his stuff from a black guy who works solo. He *did* buy some stuff from a white guy, once, last year, but the guy charged too much. Sorry I couldn't be of more help."

"You were a lot of help. How did you get my phone number?"

Linda laughed. "You *are* spaced. From the phone book. Listen, will you let me know how this turns out?"

"Yes. And thanks, Linda."

"My pleasure. And by the way, if you feel like calling, you don't have to have a reason, though I'm sure you'll think one up."

"Are you telling me I'm devious?"

"No, just lonely and a bit guilt-ridden."

"And you?"

"Lonely and a bit curious. Bye, Hopkins."

"Goodbye, Linda."

15

After a handshake and brief salutations, Linda Wilhite took her seat across from the Doctor and began to talk. When Havilland heard vague self-analysis fill the air, he clicked off his conscious listening power and shifted into an automatic overdrive that allowed him to juxtapose Linda's beauty against the single most important aspect of his life: *thinking one step ahead of Lloyd Hopkins.*

Since they were both geniuses, this kept the Night Tripper's mental engine pushed to its maximum horsepower, searching for loopholes and overlooked flaws in the logical progression of his game. With his physical concentration zeroed in on Linda, he thought of the game's one possible trouble spot: Jungle Jack Herzog.

Their relationship had been based on mutual respect—Herzog's genuine, the Doctor's feigned. The Alchemist was a classic psychiatric prototype—the seeker after truth who retreats into a cocoon of rationalization when confronted with harrowing *self*-truths. Thus the Doctor had played into his pathetic fantasy of using the stolen files to create an "L.A.P.D.

credibility gap" that would by implication exonerate his friend Marty Bergen, while at the same time plumbing the basis of his attraction to a man whose cowardly actions he despised. The truth had finally become too strong, and Herzog had run to some unknown terminus of macho-driven shame. Goff had wiped his apartment shortly after he disappeared, and the odds against his leaving records or contacting Bergen or L.A.P.D. colleagues were astronomical—his shameful new self-knowledge would preclude it. Yet Hopkins had tied in Herzog to the late Thomas Goff, although he had *not* mentioned the missing files. *That* was potentially damaging, although Herzog had had no knowledge of his *hard* criminal activity. The most important part of the game was now to convince Hopkins that he was shielding someone close to Goff; that he was strangling on the horns of an ethical dilemma. He would play the role of every wimpy liberal man of conscience that policemen hated, and "Crazy Lloyd" would buy it—hook, line, and sinker.

The Night Tripper mentally decelerated, catching bits of psychobabble sloganeering as Linda's monologue wound down. Knowing that she would expect him to respond, he made brief mental notes to contact and placate his lonelies with excuses for his absence, then smiled and said, "I let you go on like that without interjecting questions because such thinking is living in the problem, not the solution. You've got to be able to exposit *facts*, gauge them for their basic truths and nuances, solicit my feedback, accept it or reject it, then move on the next *fact*. You've obviously read every lunatic and well-intentioned self-help book ever written, and it's mired you down with a great deal of *useless* food for thought. *Give me facts*."

Linda flushed, clenched her jaw and slammed the arms of her chair. "Facts," she said. "You want facts, then I'll give you facts. Fact: I'm lonely. Fact: I'm horny. Fact: I just met a very interesting man. Fact: I can tell that he's turned on to me. Fact: He's mooning for his estranged wife and will probably not hit on yours truly, as much as he'd like to. Fact: I'm pissed off about it."

Havilland smiled. The litany sounded like his fish swallowing a huge chunk of bait. "Tell me about the man. Facts, physical and otherwise, then your conclusions."

Linda smoothed the hem of her skirt and smiled back. "All right. He's about forty and very large, with intense gray eyes and dark brown hair, sort of unkempt. Ruddy complexion. His clothes are out of style. He's funny and arrogant and sarcastic. He's very smart, but there's nothing contrived or academic about it. He just *has* it. He's a *natural*."

At Linda's last words the Doctor felt his fish gobble the bait, then inexplicably start to chew through the line. When he spoke, his voice sounded disembodied, as if it had been filtered through an echo chamber. "He *has* it? He's a *natural*? Those aren't facts, Linda. Be more specific."

"Don't get angry," Linda said. "You wanted conclusions."

Havilland leaned back in his chair, feeling his own line snap with the realization that he had displayed anger. "I'm sorry I raised my voice," he said. "Sometimes nonspecific information makes me angry."

"Don't apologize, Doctor. You know human emotions better than I do."

"Yes. More facts then, please."

Linda stared at her clenched hands, then counted facts on her fingers. "He's a cop, he's proud to a fault, he's lonely. He—oh shit, he just has *it*."

Havilland felt barbed-wire hooks gouge his jugular, Linda's beauty the hook wielder. Her voice supplied a verbal gouging that honed the hooks to razor sharpness. "I just don't feel factual about this man, Doctor. It's weird meeting him so soon after entering therapy, and nothing will probably come of it, but my only facts are my *intuitions*. Doctor, are you all right?"

Havilland stared through Linda to a mental chessboard he had constructed to resurrect his professional cool. Kings, queens, and knights toppled; and in the wake of their fall he was able to dredge up a smile and a calm voice. "I'm sorry, Linda. One of my little bouts of vertigo. I'm also sorry for impugning your intuitions. One thing struck me when you were describing this fellow, and that's that he sounds very much like your size forty-four sweater fantasy man. Has that occurred to you?"

Linda covered her mouth and laughed. "Maybe the Rolling Stones were wrong."

"What do you mean?"

"You're obviously not a rock fan," Linda said. "I was referring to an old Stones tune called 'You Can't Always Get What You Want.' Although they could be *right*, because if Lloyd-poo doesn't want to be had, then I'm sure that he will *not* be had. That's part of his charm."

Havilland made a steeple and brought it up to his face, framing Linda inside the triangle. "How has he affected your fantasy life?"

Linda gave the Doctor a rueful smile. "You don't miss much. Yes, this man is the basic forty-four sweater prototype; yes, he possesses that certain aura of violence I mentioned earlier; yes, I have cast him as the man who watches my gory home movies with me. I also like the fact that he's a cop. And you know why? Because he doesn't judge me for being a prostitute. Cops and hookers work the same street, so to speak."

Collapsing the steeple into his lap, the Doctor said, "For the record, Linda, you've made a great deal of progress in only three sessions. So much so that I'm considering a rather avant-garde visual aid session a week or so down the line. Would you be up for that?"

"Sure. You're the doctor."

"Yes," Havilland said, "I am. And doctors have certain results that they must achieve. Mine involve confronting my counselees' most hideous secrets and fears, taking them through their green doors and beyond their beyonds. You know that your confrontations are going to be particularly painful, don't you, Linda?"

Linda stood up and adjusted the pleats in her skirt, then slung her handbag over her shoulder. "No pain, no gain. I'm tough, Doctor. I can handle all the truth you can hit me with. Friday at ten-thirty?"

Havilland got to his feet and took Linda's hand. "Yes. One thing before you go. What were your parents wearing at the time of their deaths?"

Linda held the doctor's hand while she pondered the question. Finally she said, "My father was wearing khaki pants, a plaid lumberjack shirt and a Dodger baseball cap. I remember the pictures the policemen showed me. The detectives were amazed that he could blow his brains out and still keep the cap on his head. My mother was doing part-time practical nursing then, and she was wearing a white nurse's uniform. Why?"

Havilland lowered her hand. "Symbolic therapy. Thank you for digging up such an unpleasant memory."

"No pain, no gain," Linda said as she waved goodbye.

Alone in his office with the scent of Linda's perfume, the Night Tripper wondered why validation of his most audacious move should cause such a bizarre reaction. He played back the session in his mind and got nothing but a static hiss that sounded like an air-raid siren about to screech its doom warning. Reflexively, he grabbed his desk phone and dialed one of his pawn's numbers, getting a recorded message: "Hi, lover, this is Sherry! I'm out right now, but if you want to party or just rap, talk to the machine. Bye!"

He put down the receiver, knowing immediately that he had made a mistake. Sherry Shroeder lived in the Valley. He had made a toll call that would appear on his phone bill. Havilland took a deep breath and closed his eyes, searching for a train of thought to provide a counteraction to the blunder. It arrived in the form of *facts*: the remaining Junior Miss Cosmetics files were boring. They were boring because they detailed unimaginative sleaze. Thus a higher class line of confidential dirt should be procured. The Avonoco Fiberglass Company had a class two security rating. The Alchemist had said, "If you cut a fart they've got a file on you. They hire lots of parolees and work furlough inmates as part of an L.A. County kickback scam." The L.A.P.D. file on their security chief had described him as a compulsive gambler with a history of psychiatric counseling. Choice meat for Thomas Goff. *Choicer* meat for a trained psychiatrist.

The Night Tripper locked up his office and took the elevator down to the bank of pay phones in the lobby. He was leafing through the Yellow Pages when the reason for his erratic behavior stunned him with its implications of cheap emotion: *he was jealous of Linda Wilhite's attraction to Lloyd Hopkins*.

16

Lloyd spent the morning at the West Hollywood Sheriff's Substation, reading over the report filed by the team of detectives who had searched Marty Bergen's apartment.

The report ran a total of eight pages, and contained both the officers' observations regarding the apartment's condition and a six-page inventory of items found on the premises. There was no mention of the personnel files or any other official police document, and nothing that pointed to Jack Herzog or his murder/suicide/disappearance. What emerged was a clipped word portrait of an alcoholic ex-cop reaching the end of his tether.

On the ambiguous pretext of a "routine check," the detectives had learned from Bergen's landlady that she had not seen her tenant in over a week, and that in her opinion he was "holed up swacko in some motel on the Strip." The state of Bergen's apartment confirmed this appraisal. Empty scotch bottles were strewn across the floor, and there were no clothes or toilet articles to be found. All four rooms reeked of booze and waste, and a portable typewriter lay smashed to pieces on the kitchen floor.

The officers had followed the landlady's advice and had checked every motel and cocktail bar on the length of the Sunset Strip, showing Bergen's *Big Orange Insider* byline photo to every desk clerk and bartender they encountered. Many recognized Bergen as a frequent heavy binger, but none had seen him in over two weeks. Deciding to sit on the information before assigning L.A.P.D. detectives to search for the ex-cop/writer, Lloyd drove to West L.A. and his last remaining uncharted link to the whole twisted mess, wondering if his motives were entirely professional.

Linda Wilhite opened her door on the second knock, catching Lloyd in the act of straightening his necktie. Pointing him inside, she looked at her watch and said, "Noon. Fourteen hours after my call, and you're here in person. Got a good reason?"

Lloyd sat down on a floral-patterned sofa. "I came to cop a plea," he said. "I haven't been entirely honest with you, and I—"

Linda silenced him by leaning over and adjusting the knot in his tie. "And you want something. Right?"

"Right."

"So tell me," Linda said, sitting down beside him.

Lloyd gave her an unrepentant stare. "Dr. John Havilland put me on to you, unconsciously. I saw those pictures of you in his outer office. Then he—"

Linda grabbed his arm. "What!"

"The framed photographs of you. Don't you know about that?"

Linda shook her head angrily, then sadly. "That poor, wonderful man. I told him about this arty-farty picture book I posed for, and he went out and bought it. How sad. I figured he was some sort of ascetic asexual, then this morning I told him about a man I'm attracted to, and he freaked out. I've never seen anyone so jealous."

"He blurted your name when I commented on the pictures," Lloyd said. "And he obviously takes them down before he sees you. Havilland counsels lots of criminal types. In the course of my investigation I blundered onto his name and decided to exploit his expertise in matters of the criminal psyche. As I suspected, he had his own underworld grapevine. He queried his source and came up with a man who, along with Thomas Goff, sold Stanley Rudolph some art objects. I snuck into Rudolph's pad and found your name in his phone book. Even though Rudolph himself doesn't know Goff, this anonymous man *does*. The whole Rudolph connection was a weird bunch of information and *mis*information, which doesn't alter the fact that Havilland's source *knows* Goff."

Lloyd paused when he saw that Linda's face had become a mask of rage. Lowering his voice, he continued. "Havilland is legally protected by a shitload of statutes regarding professional privilege. He does not have to reveal the name of his source, and all my instincts tell me that no amount of coercion would move him to divulge the name of Goff's cohort."

Lloyd put his hand on Linda's shoulder. She cringed at his touch, then batted his hand away and hissed, "There are people who can't be coerced, Hopkins, and the Doctor is one of them. He can't be coerced because unlike you, he has principles. There are also people who can't be manipulated, and even though I'm a whore, I'm one of them. Do you honestly think that I'd manipulate information out of a man who wants to help me and give it to a man who at best wants to fuck me? You want an addition to your epithet list, Sergeant? How about 'uncaring manipulative sleazebag'?"

Seeing red, Lloyd walked out of the apartment and down to the street and his unmarked cruiser. Ten minutes later he was sitting in Dr. John Havilland's outer office, staring at the photographs of Linda Wilhite and asking his seldom sought God not to let him do anything stupid.

The Doctor appeared just as the red throbbing behind Lloyd's eyes began to subside. He was ushering an elderly woman wearing a "Save the Whales" T-shirt out of his private office, cooing into her ear as she checked the contents of her purse. When he saw Lloyd, he said, "One moment, Sergeant," issued a final goodbye to his patient, then turned and laughed. "That very rich woman thinks that she can communicate telepathically with whales. What can I do for you? Have you made any progress in your investigation?"

Lloyd shook his head and spoke with a deliberate slowness. "No. Your source was somewhat inaccurate in his information. I questioned Stanley Rudolph. He has no knowledge, guilty or otherwise, of Thomas Goff. His primary source of stolen goods is a black man who works by himself. Rudolph bought goods from a *solo* white man only once, sometime last year. You said that your source met Goff at a singles bar. Did he tell you the name of it?"

Havilland sighed and sat down in an armchair across from Lloyd. "No, he didn't. To be frank, Sergeant, the young man has a drug problem, an addiction that sometimes involves blackouts. His memory isn't always completely trustworthy."

"Yet you believe that he knows Goff?"

"Yes."

"And you credit his statement that he has no knowledge of Goff's where-abouts and no knowledge regarding the liquor store homicides?"

Havilland hesitated, then said, "Yes."

Keeping his voice deliberately slow, Lloyd said, "No, you don't. You're shielding someone who knows something hot about Goff, and you're scared. You want to tell me what you know, but you don't want to compromise your ethics and jeopardize your patient's well-being. I understand these things. But understand *me*, Doctor. You're my only shot. We're dealing with mass murder here, not petty neuroses. You have to tell me his name, and I think you know it."

"No," Havilland said. "That's absolute."

"Will you reconsider over a period of twenty-four hours? I'll have an at-torney present when I question the man, and he won't know that you in-formed on him. I'll concoct a story that would satisfy a genius."

Havilland lowered his eyes. "God damn it, I said no!"

Lloyd felt his slow-motion strategy burst. He jammed his hands into his front pockets, closing them around open handcuff ratchets and a metal studded sap. Staring straight at the doctor, he squeezed the concealed weaponry so hard that the pain forced his words out in a wince. "You fuck with me and I'll hit you with an I.R.S. audit and more writs, petitions, sub-poenas, and court orders than you thought existed. I'll initiate motions re-questing the case files of every court-referred patient who ever crossed your door. I'll hire shyster lawyers out of my own pocket and keep them on re-tainer just to dream up ways to hassle you. I'll have badass nigger vice cops keep your office under surveillance and scare the shit out of the rich neu-rotics you feed from. Twenty-four hours. You've got my number."

A red tide propelled Lloyd out of the office. When he took his hands from his pockets, he saw that they were bleeding.

Hook, line, and sinker.

Havilland walked into his private office and removed an array of bait from his wall safe. Ten thousand dollars in a brown paper bag and a newly typed psychiatric report accompanied by a snapshot. He placed the report in his top desk drawer, then looked at his watch. One-thirty. He had six hours until his next move. Leaning back in his chair, the Night Tripper closed his eyes and tried to will a dreamless sleep.

He succeeded and failed.

Sleep came, interspersed with semi-conscious moments that he knew to be his memory. As each image passed through him he felt like a surgical bonesaw was slicing his body in two, leaving him the choice of going with his symbolic past or of drifting into the cloud cover of anesthesia. Off to his left was sleep; off to his right was a blood-spattered corkboard equipped with arm and legholes, a rigor-mortised ankle encircled by a steel manacle, and the Bronx ferris wheel spinning off its axis. Full consciousness was a pinpoint of light between his eyes, an escape hatch that could trigger *full sleep* if concentrated upon in tandem with recitation of his mantra, *patria sanctorum*. Three roads inward: to wakefulness, to oblivion, to his child-hood void. Feeling fearless, the Night Tripper succumbed to memory and let his right side disengage.

A huge magnifying glass descended on the void, serving up details: "McEvoy-D Block," etched on the manacle; gouged and cauterized arteries marking the ankle; father whispering in his ear as the ferris wheel reached its apex, suspending them above blocks of Puerto Rican tenements. Strain-ing to read the lips of the people traversing below him, he caught long snatches of conversation and shock waves of laughter. Then his two sides fused.

Havilland awoke, refreshed, at six-forty-five. His yawn became a smile when the new void embellishments passed the credibility test by returning to his conscious mind. His smile widened when he realized that his one-on-one with Lloyd Hopkins was the catalyst that had supplied the fresh details. Thus fortified by sleep and memory, he picked up his bag of money, locked the office, and drove to Malibu and the acquisition of data.

The rendezvous point was a long stretch of parking blacktop overlooking the beach. Havilland left his car in the service area of a closed gas station on the land side of the Pacific Coast Highway and took the tunnel under-pass across to the bank of lighted pay phones adjoining the spot where he was to meet the Avonoco Fiberglass security chief. He checked his watch and walked to the railing: 8:12 P.M., the last remnants of an amber sun turn-ing the ocean pink. Savoring the moment, he watched the ball of fire meld into a pervasive light blue. When the blue died into a dark rush of waves, he walked to the phone booth nearest the railing and dialed the number of his actress pawn.

"Hello?"

Havilland grimaced; Sherry's salutation was slurred into three stoned syl-lables.

"Hello? Who's this? Is that you, Otto, you horny hound?"

Havilland's grimace relaxed. Though loaded, his pawn was lucid. "This is Lloyd, Sherry. How are you?"

"Hi, Lloyd!"

"Hi. Do you remember our deal?"

"Of course, baby. I got ripped off to the max on *Steep Throat* and *Nuclear Nookie*. I'm not letting this one get away."

Havilland turned around and stretched, catching a glimpse of a man hunched over the phone in the last booth at the end. Even though the caller was a good ten yards away, he turned back and lowered his voice to a whisper. "Good. We're shooting tomorrow night. Your co-star will pick you up. That's a little idea of mine. You know, let the stars get acquainted so that they can perform more realistically. He'll bring an outfit for you to wear. Is that your current address on your business card?"

"Yeah, that's my crib. And I'll get the rest of my money then?"

"Yes. Your co-star's name is Richard. He'll pick you up at nine. I'll see you on the set."

Sherry laughed. "Nine P.M. Tell Richard to be there or be square. Bye, Lloyd."

"Goodbye, Sherry."

Havilland hung up and stared through the Plexiglas booth enclosures, noting with relief that the caller was gone. He checked his watch again, then walked to the railing and over to the approximate middle of the parking strip. 8:24. Hopefully, Lieutenant Howard Christie would be punctual.

At precisely eight-thirty, slow footsteps echoed on the blacktop. The Doctor squinted and saw a man materialize out of the shadows and walk straight toward him. When he was ten feet away, a sudden burst of moonlight illuminated his features. It was the man in the phone booth. Shunting that knowledge aside, the Doctor walked forward with his hand extended, watching an archetypal cop come into focus.

He was a big crew-cutted man going to fat. He had a blunt face and cold eyes that measured the Doctor up, down, and sideways without revealing a hint of his appraisal. When they were face to face, he took the extended hand and said, "Doctor Havilland, I presume?"

The words rendered the Doctor mute and faint. He tried to jerk his hand free. It was futile; the force that grasped it was crushing it into numbness.

The force spoke: "Did you think you were dealing with amateurs? I've been a cop for twenty-two years, fourteen of them on the take. I know the ropes. I saw you park your car half an hour ago, and ran you through the D.M.V. The White Pages told me the rest. A psychiatrist. Very fucking unimpressive. Do you know how many shrinks I've gamed to get out of trouble in the Department? Did you think I'd let you pull this clandestine rendezvous horseshit anonymously? Did you think I believed that snow job you gave me on the phone? A book about secret information abuse? Really, Doctor, you insult my intelligence."

With a final squeeze, Howard Christie released the Doctor's hand, then put an arm around his shoulders and led him to the railing. Havilland concentrated on his mantra. He sat on the railing and forced an appropriately frightened laugh. When Christie laughed in return, he felt his newfound courage click in.

Christie took a deep breath of ocean air. "Don't look so scared, Doc. One thing my first shrink taught me: In all relationships, power bondings are established in the first five minutes. I had to establish the fact that *I* am the power broker, because *I* have what *you* want, and since we are dealing with class two security clearance stuff, this scam is felonious. *Capice?*"

"Yes," Havilland said. "I understand. But where are the files?" He ran his right foot nervously over the blacktop in wider and wider circles. A big rock caught his toe. He nudged it toward him and added, "Does anyone else know my name or that I contacted you?"

Christie shook his head. "I told you I knew the ropes. No one at Avonoco knows, and I just found out your name from a D.M.V. clerk who's already forgotten it. But listen: Where did you get *my* name?"

Lowering his head, Havilland saw a holstered revolver clipped to Christie's belt, half covered by his open sports jacket. "I—I—met an L.A.P.D. officer at a bar. He—he told me you had a gambling problem."

Christie slammed the railing with both palms. "Loudmouthed motherfuckers. For your info, Doc, cops are just like crooks, you can't trust any of them. What was his name?"

"I—I—don't remember. Honestly."

"No problem. People who go to bars forget things fast, which is why they go to bars. I'm glad I'm not a drunk. Two addictions would be too fucking much. Let's cut the shit and get down to business. First off, don't tell me why you want the files—I don't want to know. Second, we're talking about a long process of photocopying them and moving them out a few at a time. If you want quick gratification, tough shit—discuss it with *your* shrink.

Third, your offer of ten thou doesn't cut it. I owe a lot of money to some *very* bad dudes to owe money to. I want thirty K, no less. *Capice?*"

Havilland faked a coughing attack, leaning over with his head between his knees. When he felt Christie slap his back, he pretended to retch and braced his hands on the pavement, palming the rock, then shoving it into his right jacket pocket as he resumed a sitting position. Wiping his eyes, he inched closer to his adversary, seeing the gun butt fully exposed, Christie's badge attached to his belt next to it.

Christie slapped his back a last time. "Breathe deep, Doc. That good sea air will put hair on your chest. What do you think of my terms?"

Havilland took a deep breath and stuck his hand in his pocket, closing it around the rock. He calculated potential arcs and slid over to where his left shoulder and Christie's right shoulder were brushing. "Yes, it's a deal. You're holding all the aces."

Christie laughed. "No gambling metaphors, I'm trying to quit." He reached his arms up as if to embrace the sky, then brought them down in a huge yawn. "I'm tired," he said. "Let's wrap this up for tonight. Here's what I'm thinking: Six payments of five K apiece, the files to be very cautiously siphoned out at my discretion. You'll have to trust me on that. I'm the dominant ego in this relationship, but I'll be benevolent about it. Look at it as a father-son type of gig. *Capice?*"

Dr. John Havilland gasped at the worst insult ever hurled at him. He recalled a quote from Christie's L.A.P.D. file: *Long history of overdependence upon supportive figures.* Thinking, *So be it,* the Doctor said, "What do you think *I* am, an amateur? Don't you think I know that compulsive gamblers have a need to counterbalance their self-destruction by asserting themselves in business relationships, an unconscious ploy to overrule their awful dependency on their closest loved ones, the ones who rule them and own them and give them the tit they suck on?"

Christie stood up and stammered, "W-w-why you little fuck," just as Havilland smashed the rock into his face. The cop teetered on the railing, grabbing it with one hand, wiping blood from his eyes with the other. Havilland reached for his waistband and pulled the gun free, then closed his eyes and aimed at where he thought Christie's face should be. He pulled the trigger twice, screaming along with the explosions, then opened his eyes and saw that Christie's face was not a face, but a charred blood basin oozing brain and skull fragments. He fired four more times, eyes open and not screaming, ripping Christie's badge from his belt just as his last shot sheared off his head and sent him pitching over the railing to the rocks thirty feet below. Drenched in blood and inundated by horror and memory, the Night Tripper ran.

17

At ten o'clock, after nine straight hours of prowling singles bars and simple drinking bars for Thomas Goff and Marty Bergen, Lloyd gave up, surrendering himself to the idea of a trip to New York to prowl Goff's old haunts. The Department would pay for his ticket and per diem, and before he left he would consult an attorney on legal loopholes to exert against Dr. John Havilland. Defeat loomed like a stark black banner. Lloyd succumbed to the knowledge that there was no place to go but backward in time.

The old neighborhood greeted him with banners that mocked his cop exigencies. Parking at Sunset and Vendome, he sprinted up the cracked concrete steps to the highest point in Silverlake, hoping to find a reprise of old themes that would affirm the forty-two-year-old warrior persona he had paid so dearly to assume.

But the timeless L.A. haze blanketed, then shut down his would-be reverie. He could not see his parents' house a scant half mile away; whole vistas of landmarks were covered by a witch's brew of evaporating low clouds, industrial fumes and neon. Lloyd's affirmation became a rhapsody of high prices paid for dubious conquests.

In the 1965 Watts riot he had killed a fellow National Guardsman who had fired into a storefront church filled with innocent blacks partaking of coffee and prayer. No one had ever made him for the killing, and two months later he entered the Los Angeles Police Academy.

His career as a policeman was sustained brilliance, his concurrent role as husband and father a series of blundering attempts to instill his family with benign equivalents of his knowledge. When the force of his will elicited anger and hurt, he ran back to the job, and when the job swirled him into vortexes of boredom and terror and loathing, he found women who wanted to touch briefly what he was, offer their innocence as barter, and then get out before his hard line fervor destroyed their hard-earned and fatuous sense of life's amenities.

And then, last year, Teddy Verplanck merged into his path, turning his universe into chaos. When that symbiosis was completed, death and rebirth occurred simultaneously, and as his wounds healed, Lloyd became a hybrid warrior formed of his past and its validity and of accredited blood testimony as to where it would ultimately take him.

And his hard line fervor cracked and solidified, leaving him to tread air in the middle of a fissure.

Before he could consciously recall his vow of abstinence, Lloyd drove to Wilshire and Beverly Glen and the only destination that gave the softer part of his fissure credibility. Finding the door open, he walked into the entrance hall and cleared his throat to announce his presence. His answer was the shuffle of feet and an unexpected giggle.

"You're early," Linda called out.

Trying to track the voice, Lloyd said, "It's Hopkins, Linda."

Linda stepped out of a closet next to the dining room, dressed in a silk robe. "I know it is."

Lloyd walked forward to meet her. "Am I that predictable?"

Nodding her head both "yes" and "no," Linda said, "I don't know. Just don't apologize for this afternoon. I was as out of line as you. No pretexts this time?"

"No."

"Want to talk before or after?"

"After."

Linda smiled and tilted her head toward the bedroom, then let Lloyd step ahead of her and walk in. When his back was turned, she slipped off her robe and let it fall to the floor. Lloyd swiveled to face the soft sound, seeing Linda nude, framed in the doorway, backlighted by the glow of a hall lamp. Keeping the frame at arm's length, he undressed, wincing when his gunbelt hit the carpet. Linda giggled at the impact, then laughed outright when he leaned over and fumbled off his shoes and socks and snagged his zipper and nearly fell out of his pants. Whispering something that sounded like "beyond the beyond," she slid past him and lay down on the bed. Lloyd saw her take up a beckoning position, a single shaft of light fluttering across her abdomen. Using the light as a beacon, he came to her.

She talked while he held her and felt her and tasted her; little sighs about love and green doors. When his kisses became more persistent and then trailed down to her breasts, those sighs became the gasped word "Yes." Lost in the word's repetition, he let his lips move lower, until "yes" crescendoed into "Now, please, now!"

Lloyd obeyed, joining their two halves in a single abrupt motion, then pulling back to a sustaining movement as Linda coiled herself around him and pushed upward. He moved slowly; she with the unrestrained fervor of a graceful animal exploding with gracelessness, forming a point-counterpoint give and take that battered awareness of technique to death. Then he began to move with her fury, and the cop/whore entity pushed itself into a wordless, gasping trance.

Linda succumbed to reality first, twisting her head from the crook of Lloyd's collarbone. She traced his back with her palms and kissed his neck softly, until he pulled his head from the pillow and looked down on her, revealing a blank, tear-mottled face. All she could think of to say was, "Hopkins."

Lloyd rolled over and took her hand. When he remained silent, Linda said, "It's after. We were going to talk, remember?"

Twisting sideways to face her, Lloyd said, "What do you want to talk about?"

"Anything except what just happened. It was perfect; let's not mess with it."

Lloyd positioned himself so that his eyes and Linda's were only inches apart. "No earth-shaking postcoital revelations?"

Nodding her head so that their noses rubbed, Linda said, "Yes. I'm quitting the Life. I've got seventy grand tucked away, which should set me up in some kind of business enterprise. I'm quitting the shrink, too. If I quit hooking on my own I won't need him, and therapy is too expensive for a fledgling businesswoman."

"He'll be very sorry to see you go."

"I know. He's a very brilliant shrink, but I shouldn't associate with men who are obsessed with me. Having pictures of me on the wall is just too sad. Even though he takes them down for my visits, I still feel manipulated. Do you remember the pictures? Exactly how was I posed?"

"You weren't posed. They were candid type shots."

Linda's face clouded. "Really? That's strange. *All* the pictures in the book were posed."

Lloyd shrugged, then felt an overlooked connection hit him. "*Never* underestimate your power, even over hardnoses like Havilland. Listen, did you ever mention Stanley Rudolph to him?"

Linda said, "Yes, but not by name. All I mentioned was that he liked to take nude pictures of me. Why? I don't want to talk about *your* case or *my* clients."

"Neither do I. What do you want to talk about?"

"Tell me why you broke up with your wife."

"It's not a pretty story."

"It never is."

Lloyd turned over on his back, wanting to distance himself from Linda. He tried to find the appropriate words to begin his story, then realized that unless he looked her straight in the eye, his prelude would be self-serving lies. Twisting back around and locking into eye contact, he said, "It happened last year. I had been neglecting my family and cheating on my wife with various women for years before that, but last year was when it all exploded.

"I was working Robbery/Homicide, pretty much on the cases I pleased, when I got an anonymous phone call that led me to a murder victim. A young woman. I headed the investigation and dug up information that pointed to a mass murderer who was so fucking smart that no police agency in L.A. County connected any of his killings. At the time I went to my superiors with my information, he had killed at least sixteen women."

Linda raised a hand to her face and bit the knuckles. Lloyd said, "My superiors wouldn't authorize an investigation; it was too potentially embarassing to too many police departments. So I went after him myself. Janice left me about that time, taking the girls with her. There was just me and the killer. I found out who he was—a man named Teddy Verplanck. He made the media very big as the Hollywood Slaughterer. You probably heard about him. I went out to get him, but a woman I was seeing got in the way. He killed her. I went out to kill Verplanck. We shot each other up, and another officer, my best friend, killed him. That part of it never hit the media. Janice and the girls don't know exactly what happened, but they do know that I was shot, and that the whole episode almost cost me my career. Now I've got some nightmares to live with and a lot of innocent blood to atone for."

Linda astonished Lloyd by smiling. "I was expecting some tawdry little tale of other men and other women, not a gothic epic."

Baffled by the reaction, Lloyd said, "You almost sound titillated by it."

Linda kissed his lips softly. "My father shot my mother and then blew his brains out. I was ten. I'm no neophyte. Sometimes my thoughts are very dark. Let's go to sleep on a happy note, though. I want us to be together."

Lloyd got up and closed the bedroom door, shutting out all traces of light. "So do I," he said.

The morning began with a muffled cadence counting issuing from the living room. Lloyd put it off as Linda gyrating to a TV exercise program and went back to sleep, only to be awakened again minutes later by a firm bite on his neck. He opened his eyes and saw Linda squatting beside the bed in a black leotard. She was sweating and holding one hand behind her back. He leaned forward to kiss her, only to have her dart out of the way of his lips. "What size sweater do you wear?" she asked.

Lloyd sat up and rubbed his eyes. "No kiss? No offer of breakfast? No 'when will I see you again?' "

"Later. Answer my question."

"Size forty-six. Why?"

Linda muttered "shit," and handed Lloyd a Brooks Brothers box tied with a pink ribbon. He opened it and saw a carefully folded navy blue pullover sweater. Stroking its downy front, he whistled and said, "Cashmere. Did you buy this for me?"

Linda shook her head. "I'll tell you the story some day. It's a size too small, but please wear it."

Standing up, Lloyd grabbed Linda and consummated their morning kiss. "Thank you. I'll lose weight so it'll fit better."

"I wouldn't put it past you. What's the matter, Hopkins? You're scowling."

Lloyd broke the embrace. "Delayed reaction to joy. My already complicated life has just gotten much more complicated. I'm glad."

"It's mutual. What happens next?"

"I'm going to New York in a day or so. Thomas Goff comes from there. I'm going to cruise his old haunts and talk to people who knew him. It's my only remaining out. When I get back I'll call you."

"You'd better. Why don't you shower while I make some coffee and toast? I've got my yoga class in an hour, but at least we can have breakfast together."

Lloyd showered, alternating hot and cold jets of water over his body, lost in the sound of the spray and the hum of music coming from the kitchen.

After drying off and dressing, he walked into the kitchen and found Linda fiddling with the radio dial. "I hate to be a downer," she said, "but I just heard some bad news. An L.A. policeman was murdered in Malibu. I didn't get all the details, but—"

Lloyd grabbed the radio and flipped the tuner to an all-news station, catching static and the conclusion of a weather report. He sat down and looked at Linda, then put a finger to her lips and said, "They'll repeat the story. Cop killings are hot news."

The weatherman said, "Back to you, Bob," and a stern-voiced announcer took over: "More details on that Malibu killing. L.A. County Sheriff's detectives have just announced that the dead man found on the beach near Pacific Coast Highway and Temescal Canyon Road is a twenty-two-year L.A.P.D. veteran named Howard Christie, a lieutenant assigned to the Rampart Division. Christie's decapitated body was found early this morning by local surfers, who called the Malibu Sheriff's Substation to inform them of the grisly find. Captain Michael Seidman of the Malibu Station told reporters: 'This is a homicide, but as yet we do not know the cause of death and have no suspects. We have, however, determined that Lieutenant Christie was killed in the parking lot immediately above the spot on the beach where his body was found. We are now appealing to anyone who was in the vicinity of Pacific Coast Highway and Temescal Canyon Road last night or early this morning, people who might have seen or heard something suspicious. Please come forward. We need your assistance.' Further details on this story as it breaks. And now—"

Linda turned off the radio and stared at Lloyd. "Tell me, Hopkins."

"It's Goff," Lloyd said, with a death's-head grin. "I'm not going to New York. If you don't hear from me in forty-eight hours, send up a flare." He grabbed his sweater and ran out the door. Linda shuddered, imagining her new lover's departure as a race into hell.

Pacific Coast Highway and Temescal Canyon Road was a pandemonium of police vehicles with cherry lights flashing, TV minicam crews, mobs of reporters, and a large crowd of rubbernecks that spilled over from the parking blacktop, forcing southbound P.C.H. traffic into the middle lane.

Lloyd pulled up to the dirt shoulder on the land side of the highway and killed his siren, then pinned his badge to his jacket front and dodged cars over to a diagonal stretch of pavement sealed with a length of rope hung with "Official Crime Scene" warnings. The area behind the cordon was filled with plainclothes officers and technicians with evidence kits, and a long bank of pay phones was crowded with uniformed sheriff's deputies calling in information. At the rear of the scene a half dozen plainclothesmen squatted beside the wooden railing overlooking the cliffs and the ocean, spreading fingerprint powder on a cracked piece of timber.

"I'm surprised it took you this long."

Recognizing the voice, Lloyd pivoted and saw Captain Fred Gaffaney push his way through a knot of patrol deputies and plant himself in his path. The two men stared at each other until Gaffaney fingered his cross-and-flag tie bar and said, "This is one sensitive piece of work, and I forbid you to interfere. It's in the sheriff's jurisdiction, with I.A.D. handling any connections to collateral cases."

Lloyd snorted, "Collateral cases? Captain, this is Thomas Goff all the way down the line!"

Gaffaney grabbed Lloyd's arm. Lloyd buckled, but let himself be led over to the shadow of an empty pay phone.

"Internal Affairs is moving on the other officers whose files were stolen," the captain said. "They're going to be interrogated and perhaps taken into protective custody, along with their families. Except for you. Let's put the past aside, Sergeant. Tell me what you've got so far, and if possible, I'll help you move on it."

Lloyd drummed his fingers on the side of the phone booth. "Marty Bergen has at the very least *seen* the stolen files. He's missing, but some columns that he left for advance publication indicate conclusively that Herzog passed the files to him. I think we should issue an A.P.B. on Bergen, and get a court order to seize everything at the *Big Orange Insider*."

Gaffaney whistled. "The media will crucify us for it."

"Fuck the media. I've also got a hearsay line on Goff, through a hotshot psychiatrist who has a patient who knows him. But the cocksucker is hiding behind professional privilege and won't kick loose with the name of his source."

"Have you considered talking to Nathan Steiner?"

Lloyd nodded. "Yeah. I'm going to run by his office today. What have *you* got? The radio report said Christie was decapitated, which sounds like possible forty-one stuff."

Gaffaney's hands played over his tie bar. "I've got an excellent reconstruction from a team of very savvy sheriff's dicks. The M.E.'s verdict won't be in for hours, but this is the way they see it:

"One—yes, it's a gunshot homicide. Christie was shot over by that broken piece of railing, and was blown down to the beach by the impact. I saw the body. It landed on some rocks up from the tide, so it stayed dry. I saw powder burns on his shirtfront, so the shots were obviously fired point-blank. Two—Christie *was* decapitated, but the biggest piece of his head the technicians have been able to find so far is a skull fragment about the size of a half dollar. You know why? He was almost certainly killed with his own gun. It wasn't found on his body or anywhere around here. His badge was stolen, too. I talked to one of the top dogs at Rampart, and he told me that Christie packed a three-fifty-seven Python on and off duty, and that he kept it loaded with Teflon-tipped dum-dum's." Gaffaney reached into his pants pocket and handed Lloyd a copper-jacketed slug. "Feel the weight of that monster, Hopkins. I took it off of Christie's gunbelt while the medics weren't looking. The expended rounds and Christie's head are probably halfway to Catalina by now."

Lloyd gouged the slug's teflon head with his fingernail. "Shit. Those Sheriff's dicks are probably right, this is a much heavier load than a forty-one. What else? Anything from Avonoco? Christie's vehicle? Other vehicles? Witnesses? Blood tracks on the pavement?"

The Captain put a restraining hand on Lloyd's chest. "Slow down, you're making me nervous. There's nothing on any of that yet, except a trail of blood leading from the railing across the parking lot and through the underpass to the other side of P.C.H. The trail got fainter as it went along, which indicates that the killer himself wasn't wounded, he was just soaked with Christie's blood. The techs are doing their comparison tests now; we'll know for sure soon. What's *your* next move?"

"Pump Nate Steiner for some legal advice. Hassle the shrink. You?"

Captain Fred Gaffaney grinned. "Interrogate the other security chiefs, go over their records, rattle skeletons. The feds are at Avonoco now. Christie's security rating makes him a quasi federal employee, so this is a collateral F.B.I. beef. Stay in touch, Hopkins. If you want transcripts of the I.A.D. interrogations, call Dutch Peltz."

Lloyd walked back to his car, oblivious to the ghouls lining P.C.H., drinking beer and standing on their tiptoes to get a glimpse of the drama. He had his hand on the door when the young man from the *Big Orange Insider* drove by and flipped him the finger.

Nathan Steiner was a Beverly Hills attorney who specialized in defending drug dealers. His forte was "obstructionist" tactics—filing writs and court orders, suits and countersuits, and motions requesting information on prospective jurors, potential witnesses, and courtroom functionaries; all strategies aimed at securing dismissals on the grounds of prejudiced testimony or "courtroom bias." These strategies often worked, but more often "Nate the Great" won his cases by outlasting judges and prosecutors and by harassing them into foolish blunders with his paperwork onslaughts. It was well known that many judges granted his minor petitioning requests automatically, in the hope that it would keep his clients *out* of their courtrooms and thus save them the pain of a protracted Steiner performance; it was *not* well known that "Nate the Great" felt deep guilt over the scores of dope vultures cut loose from jail as the result of his machinations and that despite his loud advocacy of civil liberties, he atoned for that guilt by advising L.A.P.D. officers on ways to circumvent laws regarding probable cause and search and seizure.

Thus, when Lloyd barged through his office door unannounced, he was ready to listen. Taking a seat uninvited, Lloyd outlined a hypothetical case involving a doctor's legal right not to divulge professionally secured information, stressing that *all* of the doctor's records would have to be seized, because at this point the name of the patient was unknown.

Concluding his case, Lloyd sat back and waited for an answer. When Steiner grunted and said, "Give me three or four days to look at some statutes and think about it," Lloyd got to his feet and smiled. Steiner asked him what the smile meant.

"It means that I'm an obstructionist, too," Lloyd said.

After stopping at a taco stand and wolfing a burrito plate, Lloyd drove home and changed clothes, outfitting himself in soiled khaki pants and shirt, work boots, and a baseball cap advertising Miller High Life. Satisfied with his workingman's garb and one-day stubble, he rummaged through his garage and came up with a set of burglar's tools he had scavenged from a Central Division evidence locker ten years before: battery-powered hand drill with cadmium steel bits; assorted hook-edged chisels, and a skinny-head crowbar and mallet. Packing them inside a tool kit, he drove to Century City and the commission of a Class B felony.

The reconnoitering took three hours.

Parking on a residential side street a half mile from Century City proper,

Lloyd walked to Olympic and Century Park East and found a uniformed custodian sweeping the astroturf lawn in front of his target building. He explained to the man that he was here to help with a private wiring job for a firm situated on the skyscraper's twenty-sixth floor. Only one thing worried him. He needed an electrical hook-up with wall sockets big enough to accommodate his industrial-sized tools. Also, it would be nice to have a sink in which to scrape off rusted parts. The location didn't matter; he had plenty of cord. Was there a custodian's storeroom or something like that on the twenty-sixth floor?

The man had nodded with a befuddled look in his eyes, making Lloyd grateful for the fact that he seemed stupid. Finally he gave a last nod and said that yes, every floor had a custodial room, in the identical spot—the northeast edge of the building. Would the custodian on that floor let him use it for his job? Lloyd asked.

The man's eyes clouded again. He was silent for several moments, then replied that the best thing to do was wait until the custodians went home at four, then ask the guard in the lobby for the key to the storeroom. That way, everything would be cool. Lloyd thanked the man and walked into the building.

He checked the northeast corners of the third, fifth, and eighth floors, finding identical doors marked "Maintenance." The doors themselves looked solid, but there was lots of wedge space at the lock. If no witnesses were around, it would be easy.

With two hours to kill before the custodial crew left work, Lloyd took service stairs down to ground level, then walked to a medical supply store on Pico and Beverly Drive and purchased a pair of surgical rubber gloves. Walking back slowly to Century City, all thoughts of the Goff/Herzog/Bergen/Christie labyrinth left his mind, replaced by an awareness of one of his earliest insights: crime was a thrill.

Stationed in the shade of a plastic tree on the astroturf lawn in front of his target, Lloyd saw a dozen men wearing maintenance uniforms exit the building at exactly 4:02. He waited for ten minutes, and when no others appeared, grabbed his toolbox and walked in, straight past the guard and over to the service stairs next to the elevators, donning his gloves the second he hit the privacy of the empty stairwell. Breathing deeply, he treaded slowly up twenty-six stories and pushed through a connecting doorway, finding himself directly across from Suite 2614.

The hallway was empty and silent. Lloyd got his bearings and assumed a

casual gait as he walked past Dr. John Havilland's door. When he got to the
maintenance room, he scanned the hallway one time, then took the crowbar from his tool kit and wedged it into the juncture of door and jamb. He
leaned forward with all his weight, and the door snapped open.

The storeroom was six feet deep and packed with brooms, mops and industrial chemicals. Lloyd stepped inside and flicked on the light switch,
then closed the door and loaded his hand drill with a two-inch bit. Squatting, he pressed the start switch and jammed the bit into the door two feet
above floor level. Pushing the drill forward and rotating it clockwise simultaneously, he bored a hole that was inconspicuously small yet provided a
solid amount of air. Hitting the kill switch, he sat down and tried to get
comfortable. Seven o'clock was the earliest safe break-in time; until then,
all he could do was wait.

Swallowed up by darkness, Lloyd listened to the sounds of departing office workers, checking their departures against the luminous dial of his
wristwatch. There was a deluge at five, others at five-thirty and six. After
that it was uninterrupted silence.

At seven, Lloyd got up and stretched, then opened the storeroom door
halfway, reaccustoming his eyes to light. When all his senses readjusted, he
picked up his tool kit and walked down the hall to Suite 2604.

The lock was a single unit steel wraparound, with the key slot inset in the
doorknob. Lloyd tried his burglar's picks first, starting with the shortest and
working up, getting inside the keyhole but jamming short of the activator
button. This left the options of drilling or jimmying. Lloyd gauged the odds
of individual suites in a security building having individual alarms and decided that the odds were in his favor. He got out his skinny-head crowbar
and pried the door open.

Darkness and silence greeted him.

Lloyd shut the door quietly, brushing slivers of cracked wood off the doorjamb and onto the outer office carpet. He fumbled for the wall switch,
found it, and lit up the waiting room. Linda Wilhite beamed down from the
walls. Lloyd blew her a kiss, then tried the door to Havilland's private office. It was unlocked. He flicked off the waiting room light and took a penlight from his pocket, letting its tiny beam serve as his directional finder.
Whispering, "Let's go real slow, let's be real cool," he walked inside.

Playing his light over the walls, Lloyd caught flashes of highly varnished
oak, framed diplomas, and the Edward Hopper painting he had seen on his
initial visit. Arcing his light at waist level, he circuited the entire room,

picking up bookcases filled with leather-bound medical texts, straight-backed chairs facing each other, and Havilland's ornate oak desk. *No filing cabinets.*

Thinking, *safe*, Lloyd felt along the walls, stopping to read the diplomas before reaching behind them. Harvard Medical School; St. Vincent's and Castleford Hospitals. East Coast money all the way, but nothing except wood paneling in back of them.

Lloyd slid back the Hopper painting and hit pay dirt, then slammed the wall when he saw that the safe was an Armbruster "Ultimate," triple lead-lined and impregnable. It was the shrink's desk or nothing.

Lloyd moved to the desk, holding the penlight with his teeth and getting out his burglar's picks. He grabbed the top drawer to hold it steady for the insertion, then nearly fell backward when it slid open in his hand.

The drawer was stuffed with pens, blank paper, and paper clips and a bottom layer of manila folders. Lloyd pulled them out and scanned the index tabs stuck to their upper right hand corners. Typed last names, first names, and middle initials. *Patients.*

There were five folders, all of them filled with loose pages. Seeing that the first three bore women's names, Lloyd put them aside and read through the fourth, learning that William A. Waterston III had difficulty relating to women because of his relationship with his domineering grandmother, and that he and Havilland had been exploring the problem twice a week for six years, at the rate of one hundred and ten dollars per hour. Lloyd scrutinized the photograph that accompanied the psychiatric rundown. Waterston did not sound or look like the type of man who would know Thomas Goff; he looked like an aristocratic nerd who needed to get laid.

Lloyd checked the index tab on the last file, seeing that a string of aliases forced the typist to move from the tab onto the front of the folder: Oldfield, Richard; a.k.a. Richard Brown; a.k.a. Richard Green; a.k.a. Richard Goff.

The last alias went through Lloyd like a convulsion. He opened the folder. A color snapshot was attached to the first page; a head and shoulders shot of a man who resembled Thomas Goff to a degree that fell just short of twinhood. Lloyd read through the entire fourteen pages of the file, shuddering when the facts of the resemblance were made clear.

Richard Oldfield was Thomas Goff's illegitimate half-brother, the result of a union between Goff's mother and a wealthy upstate New York textile manufacturer. He had entered therapy with Dr. John Havilland four years before, his love/hate relationship with his half-brother his "salient neurosis." Thomas Goff was a brilliant criminal; Richard Oldfield a stockbroker-remittance man living largely on stipends shamed and coerced out of his father by Goff's alcoholic mother, who had raised the two boys together. After wading through long paragraphs of psychiatric ruminations, Lloyd felt the blood theme emerge: Richard Oldfield's desire to emulate Thomas Goff had driven him to undertake a sporadic criminal career, burglarizing homes known to contain art objects, acting on information from stock exchange acquaintances. *Hence the Stanley Rudolph connection,* obscured by Havilland's cowardly manipulations: he wanted to surrender *the Goff connection* to police scrutiny, without divulging the name of his patient. Richard Oldfield's occasional usage of his half brother's name was what Havilland termed "cross-purpose identification—the desire to assume a person's identity and act out both loved and hated aspects of their personalities, thereby restoring order to their own psyches, resolving the love-hatred ambivalence into an acceptable norm."

Reading the file a second time, paying close attention to the most recently dated additions, Lloyd learned that Oldfield's surrender to the Goff psyche was becoming more pronounced, assuming "pathological dimensions." Goff hated women and prowled bars looking for ones to abuse; Oldfield paid prostitutes to let him beat them. Goff hated policemen and spoke often of his desire to kill them; Oldfield now aped his half brother's broadsides. The last file entry was dated 2/27/84, slightly over two months earlier, and stated that "Richard Oldfield was assuming the proportions of the classic paranoid/schizophrenic criminal type."

Lloyd put the folder down, wondering if Oldfield had discontinued therapy in February or if Havilland had more data on him elsewhere. He rummaged through the other drawers until he found a metal Rolodex file. Oldfield's address and phone number were right there under the O's—4109 Windemere, Hollywood, 90036; 464-7892.

Lloyd sat still for a full minute, fuming at the fact that his illegal entry would destroy the possibility of ever hanging an accessory rap on Havilland. Then he thought of Richard Oldfield and went calm beneath his rage. Putting the files back in their proper place, and sorting the ramifications of the B&E, he picked up the tool kit and made for the door, thinking: Don't let Havilland know that his secrets have been plundered; don't give him reason to warn Oldfield, who might warn Goff. *Cover your tracks.*

Lloyd looked at the splintered doorjamb and calculated more odds, then got out his crowbar and padded over to the door of the adjoining suite. Thinking, *just do it,* he pried the door open.

Only the sound of cracking wood assailed him. He hit the next door and the door after that, then heard the blare of an alarm cut through the echoes of his destruction.

The noise grew, then leveled off to a piercing drone. Lloyd grabbed his tool kit and ran toward the maintenance storeroom, checking the elevator bank as he passed it. The flashing numbers on top said that armed help was on the sixth floor and ascending rapidly.

Lloyd opened the storeroom door, then let it close halfway. He paced off three yards to the service stairs across the hallway and closed the door behind him, leaving himself just enough of a crack to peer through. Seconds later he heard the elevator door open, followed by the sounds of running footsteps and strained breathing drawing nearer. When he saw a single uniformed guard draw his gun and step cautiously inside the storeroom, he nudged his door open and hurled himself across the hallway, pushing the storeroom door shut. There was a panicked "What the fuck!" from the guard trapped inside, and then six shots tore through the door and ricocheted down the hallway.

Lloyd stepped inside the service stairs, picked up his toolbox and hurtled down twenty-six stories to ground level. Chest heaving and soaked with sweat, he pushed the connecting door into the lobby open. No one. He walked out the door and across the astroturf lawn to Century Park East, restraining himself by assuming a nothing-to-hide gait. He was safely inside his unmarked cruiser when he heard the wail of sirens converge on the scene of his crime. With shaking hands, he drove to the Hollywood Hills.

Windemere Drive was a residential side street in the shadow of the Hollywood Bowl. One-story Tudor cottages dominated the 4100 block, and the sidewalk was free of tree and shrub overhang. It was a good surveillance spot.

Lloyd parked at the corner and circled the block on foot. No yellow Toyota. Coming back around, he flashed his penlight at the numbers stenciled on the curb. 4109 was two doors down from where he had left his car, on the opposite side of the street. He checked his watch. At 8:42 the stucco and wood Tudor house was pitch dark.

He walked back to his unmarked Matador and grabbed the Ithaca pump stashed under the driver's seat. After jacking a shell into the chamber, he walked over to 4109 and rang the doorbell.

No answer and no light coming from inside. Lloyd pressed his face to the front picture window. Heavy curtains blocked his vision. Hugging close to the walls, he padded across the porch and around the driveway to the back-yard. No car; thick drapes covering all the windows. The opposite side of the house was shielded from foot access by an overgrown hedge connected to the house next door. Lloyd craned his neck to get a quick look, glimps-ing more darkened windows. Sounds from brightly lit neighboring dwellings underlined 4109's lack of habitation. He walked back to his car to wait.

Slouching low in the driver's seat, Lloyd waited, keeping a sustained eye-ball fix on 4109. It was almost an hour later that a white Mercedes pulled to the curb in front of the house. A man too tall to be Thomas Goff and a woman in a white nurse's uniform got out and moved into a side-by-side lovers' drape. The woman squealed as the man nuzzled her neck. Together they walked up the steps and into the house. A light glowed behind the heavy curtains as the door was shut.

Lloyd stared at the curtains and thought of the woman. If she was a pros-titute, Oldfield would probably pay her to stand his abuse. But that didn't click; her uniform and affectionate manner spelled girlfriend or pick-up. Keeping his impatience at bay by concentrating on the need not to risk the woman's safety, Lloyd settled in to wait out the night.

18

Laughing voices and a burst of light cut across the Night Tripper's field of vision, casting a rainbow haze over his infrared image of Lloyd Hopkins slouching in the front seat of his car. He put down the magnification lens he was holding to his eye and smiled. "Hello, Sherry. Hello, Richard," he said.

Sherry giggled. "Hi, Lloyd." Her uniform was a size too small and looked like it would split down the middle should she attempt anything more strenuous than walking in a straight line. She sniffed back a wad of mucous and giggled again. Havilland smiled. Coked to the gills.

He sized up his leading man.

Oldfield stood with his back up against the bolted door, in a posture that reminded the Doctor of a staunch medieval warrior trying to keep demons at bay, never guessing that they resided inside him. Last night Havilland had called him to his Malibu grouping retreat and had primed him for his performance by whispering death poems in his ear while he scrubbed Howard Christie's blood from the seats of his Volvo. The recitation had had a calming effect on them both; and now Richard Oldfield was a quiet nuclear warhead.

Sherry laughed and undid the top button of her uniform blouse. Oldfield walked to the middle of the living room and said, "Ready when you are, C.B."

Sherry giggled at the remark; Havilland could hear traces of stage fright. He walked to Oldfield and threw an arm around his shoulder. "Hold on just a minute, will you, Sherry? I want to talk to your co-star alone."

Sherry nodded and kicked off her shoes. The Doctor led Oldfield back to the bedroom and swept an arm toward its new furnishings. "Isn't it wonderful, Richard? One of your co-counselees helped me set it up while you were asleep out at the retreat."

Oldfield darted his eyes over white velvet curtains shuttering the windows; his mattress removed from the bedstead and centered on the middle of the floor, covered with light blue silk sheets; a movie camera on a tripod with its gaze zeroing downward. He dry swallowed and whispered, "Please take me as far as I can go."

Havilland embraced him, letting his lips touch his ear. "Yes. You helped *me* last night, Richard. I was afraid. You took me through that fear, just as I have taken you through your fears. Just one reminder. When she abuses you, think of all the abuse that governess made you take as a child. Keep your fuel intake at optimum, right up until the moment. Now wait here."

The Doctor walked back into the living room. Sherry Shroeder was sitting on the couch, her uniform top completely unbuttoned. "I didn't know whether or not to strip," she said.

Sitting down beside her, Havilland said, "Not yet. Button up your outfit while I give you directions." He put a hand on her knee as she fumbled at her top. "What we are filming is a variation on the corny old nurse routine. You know, nurses are supposed to be very experienced, because they know so much about bodies."

Sherry laughed. Havilland noticed that her nervousness had subsided. Squeezing her knee gently, he said, "This variation is the nurse spanking the boy, who of course is Richard—really a man—and then getting so aroused that she has to seduce him. What I want you to do is pull down Richard's pants and spank him *hard*, very *hard*, then do the most seductive striptease you are capable of. After that I'll give both of you more specific instructions. Do you understand?"

Sherry waggled her eyebrows. "I used to play tennis when I was a little girl. I've got a great backhand." She laughed and covered her mouth. "Richard's got a really sharp bod. Where's the camera guy?"

"Well . . ." Havilland said, "to be frank, I can't afford one, so I'm filling in. You and Richard came too high, so to cut costs, I'm standing in behind the camera myself. I—"

Sherry poked a teasing finger in the Doctor's ribs. "Come on, Lloyd. As Gary Gilmore said, 'Let's do it.' "

They walked into the bedroom. Oldfield was sprawled on his back across the mattress, fully clothed. Havilland got behind the camera, adjusting the tripod and swiveling the lens until the mattress was captured in a wide-angle shot. Clearing his throat, he said, "Since this is a silent movie, please feel free to talk—but *quietly*. I don't want to upset the neighbors." He turned the camera on and listened to the whir of film. "Sherry, you know what to do. Richard, follow Sherry's lead, but position your face on the *near* side of the mattress, so I can get some close shots. Okay, action!"

Sherry sat down on the edge of the mattress, facing the camera. She extended her legs in front of her, resting her heels on the floor. Patting her lap, she said, "Come on, you bad boy."

Oldfield obeyed, getting to his feet and loosening his belt, then lying down across Sherry's legs, positioning his buttocks just above her knees. "Bad, bad boy," she said as she pulled down his pants and undershorts. "Bad, bad boy."

Havilland zoomed in for a close-up reaction shot just as Sherry's first slap hit naked flesh. Oldfield grimaced. "Harder, Sherry," the Doctor said.

Sherry redoubled her efforts, grunting "Bad, bad boy," each time her palm made contact. Oldfield's lens-framed eyes contracted with the blows. Havilland hissed, "Harder, Sherry, harder. Remember your tennis stroke."

"Bad bad bad bad boy!" Sherry brought her hand down full force. Oldfield's eyes glazed over and dry spittle formed at the corners of his mouth. Havilland took his eye from the camera and saw that raised red dots were forming on his buttocks. "Bad bad bad bad bad boy!"

"Cut!"

The Doctor's own shout startled him. "Cut," he repeated softly. "That's a print. Richard, go wait in the hall. Sherry, step off the mattress and do your striptease."

The actors obeyed, Oldfield drawing himself to his feet and cinching his pants without meeting Sherry's eyes; Sherry kneading her flushed right hand. When Richard was outside the bedroom, Havilland said, "Be your sexiest," and swung the camera up. "Now," he said.

Sherry Shroeder began to undress, plucking at the buttons on her uniform. She took off her blouse and dropped it on the floor, then snagged the zipper at the back of her skirt. Jerking it loose, she muttered, "Shit," then caught herself and pouted at the camera, stepping out of the skirt and twirling it on a finger above her head. Letting it drop, she unhooked her bra and pulled down her stockings and panties. Nude, she did a pelvis grinding dance step that caused her breasts to shake in opposite directions. Covered with goosebumps, she silently mouthed song lyrics and tried to pout at the same time. Zooming in for a close-up, the Doctor thought that he could detect the words to "Green Door."

"Cut!"

Again the Doctor's own voice jolted him. "Lie down, Sherry," he said. "Richard, you can come in now."

Oldfield re-entered the bedroom, naked, holding his hands over his genitals. Havilland pointed to the bed, then shut off the camera and checked the expended film cylinder. Film to burn. He framed a long shot of the mattress and the two performers on it, then locked in the tripod and said, "I'm a little shy, so I'll let you pros do what comes naturally. I'll come back and check on you in a few minutes."

Sherry laughed and Oldfield flinched. Havilland flipped the automatic forward switch and walked out to the dining room. Poking his infrared lens through a crack in the curtains, he saw his *best* actor perform.

Lloyd Hopkins, stuffed fat with bait, was still sitting inside his car, still staring daggers at the house. The allusions to illegal searches in his personnel file had been accurate—he was not above committing crime to solve crimes. He was a hypocritical snake, *and* a cowardly one—undoubtedly afraid of approaching his suspect for fear of jeopardizing the fair damsel in the bedroom. Havilland watched him yawn, scratch, and stretch without ever taking his eyes from the Tudor cottage. Each tiny move was like a laser beam piercing the childhood void.

Checking his watch, the Doctor saw that ten minutes had passed. He walked to the bedroom. Sherry and Richard were lying on opposite sides of the mattress. He turned the camera off and stared at his performers. Sherry was positioned on one elbow, an arm across her breasts. Richard lay rock still, eyes closed, twitching.

"We did it soft," Sherry said. "I think we faked it pretty good. Richard couldn't, you know, but I think it still looked okay. If you want we can try again and shoot some hard shots."

Havilland walked to the bedroom closet and ran his hand over a ledge at the back, coming away with a thick roll of adhesive bandage. "No, that does it, except for some clothed shots I want to get. You can get dressed now."

"*Really?*"

"Really. I'll give you the rest of your money in a minute."

Richard's eyes twitched open at the phrase. He got to his feet and stretched, then pulled on his pants and shirt and took the tape from the Doctor's hand. "Thank you for helping me go beyond my beyond," he said.

Havilland looked into his eyes and saw frozen rage. He focused the camera at Sherry and hit the on switch. Sherry finished buttoning her blouse and said, "Lloyd, can we make this quick? There's a party in the Valley at eleven-thirty, and since this was quicker than I thought, I'd like to make it."

Havilland nodded assent and telescoped the lens so that Sherry's face was held in an extreme close-up. "Now, Richard," he said.

The viewfinder went black as Richard Oldfield hurled himself beyond his beyond. A high-pitched shriek died into a struggle for breath; crashing bodies caused a blank wall to sway before the camera's eye. The Night Tripper tried to refocus, then gave up. Richard pinned Sherry to the floor with his knees, one hand holding her head, the other swirling tape up from her mouth to her nose. When both passages were shut air tight, he stood up and watched her face turn red, then blue and her arms and legs flail. Soon her entire body became a collective gasp; her torso pushing off the floor in an adrenaline-fueled death throe.

Oldfield fell to his knees and pummeled the flailing body, throwing right-left combinations at the groin and ribcage until all resistance ended in a last shudder of asphyxiation. Now weeping, he stood up on wobbly legs and saw the Doctor with the camera strapped to his shoulder, bending down, pulling the bandage off of Sherry Shroeder's face.

"Now, Richard. Now, Richard. Now, Richard."

The Night Tripper was holding out a silencer-fitted revolver. Richard took it in his hand, then looked down, seeing the dead woman's face covered with a transparent plastic pillow.

"Now, Richard. Now, Richard. Now, Richard."

The camera zoomed in and whirred; Oldfield pressed the barrel to the pillow and pulled the trigger. There was a dull plop, then the hiss of escaping air, then a spread of crimson as the deflated plastic filled with blood.

"Yes, Richard. Yes, Richard. Yes, Richard."

The Night Tripper steadied the camera, pushing the eyepiece out of his way. He took the gun from Richard's hand and flipped the cylinder open, letting the spent round fall to the floor. The Bronx ferris wheel became a whirling corkboard. He took two fresh rounds from his pocket and placed them in adjoining chambers, then flicked the cylinder shut and spun it.

Richard Oldfield stood slack-jawed, swaying to self-contained music. The Night Tripper took a Dodger baseball cap and Howard Christie's badge from his jacket, placing the cap on Richard's head, pinning the badge to his left breast pocket. He placed the camera back on the tripod, then filmed close-ups of the badge, the cap and Richard's face. Thinking of Linda Wilhite and toppling chess pieces, he picked the gun up off the floor and placed it in Richard's right hand. Getting back behind the camera, he said, "Do you feel complete now, Richard?"

"Yes," Richard said.

"Articulate how you feel."

"I feel as if I've conquered my past, that I've broken through all my green doors with the promise of peace as my reward."

"Will you go one step further for me? It will help a beautiful woman to resolve her nightmares."

"Yes. Name it."

"Stick the gun in your mouth and pull the trigger twice."

Richard obeyed without question. The hammer clicked on empty chambers. The Night Tripper captured his finest moment on film, then ran to the dining room curtains and looked out with his blood-colored lens. Lloyd Hopkins was asleep, his head cradled into the half-open car window.

19

Lloyd awoke at dawn, startled out of a dreamless sleep by a sharp cramp in his leg. Rubbing his calf, he looked out of the car window and saw the Tudor cottage and the white Mercedes parked in the same spot as the night before. Oldfield's shackup was still in progress. He had time to go home and call for reinforcements to aid him in a continued surveillance and possible approach.

Lloyd swung his Matador around and pulled up behind the Mercedes. He wrote down the license number, then called R&I on his two-way radio and read it off, requesting a complete readout on both vehicle and owner. After three minutes of static crackle, the operator came back on the air with her information. FHM 363—No wants; no warrants. Registered to Richard Brian Oldfield, 4109 Windemere, L.A. 90036. No wants; no warrants; no criminal record. Discouraged and exhausted despite his hours of sleep, Lloyd drove home, thinking of a shave, shower, and lots of coffee.

A three-day accumulation of newspapers greeted him on his front porch. The previous day's *L.A. Times* bore a banner headline: "Policeman Murdered in Malibu." A sidebar added, "Execution Style Death for L.A.P.D. Lieutenant." Lloyd kicked the papers aside and unlocked the door, seeing the stapled together notebook pages on the floor immediately. Picking them up, he read:

Memo to: Lloyd
From: Dutch
Read now.
L.—Where have you been? Shacking? I thought you turned over a new leaf. I'm your liaison, and we were supposed to be in daily contact,

remember? This info is straight from Gaffaney. I'll save the good stuff for last.

*A.P.B. issued on Marty Bergen—no response as yet.

*Seizure order for *Big Orange Insider* granted, yield—zilch. Punk kid editor had contents of M.B.'s desk destroyed after your last visit. Is threatening "police brutality" suit.

*Intensive questioning of P.C.H./Temescal Cyn. area residents—zilch.

*Phone-in info. on Christie—so far crank bullshit. (No eyewitnesses have come forth.)

*Blood on pavement—conclusively Christie's.

*Additional skull fragment and flattened slug found on beach (.357 Teflon tipped). This, + coroner's report—"Death caused by massive neurological destruction inflicted by gunshots fired at point-blank range," indicate that Christie was killed with his own gun.

*Sacramento D.M.V. night info. operator (she saw account of Christie's death in papers) called in, said that Christie called at 8:30 or so on the night of the murder, requesting D.M.V. make on car license. She gave info., but cannot remember the name of the person she gave him, or the lic. #, or the make of the car. Interesting, because the M.E. fixed the time of H.C.'s death at around the time of the call.

*On afternoon of his death, Christie was seen around classified file section at Avonoco. He told secretary he was meeting a "heavy hitter" at the beach that night. When secretary asked why, he clammed up. She said he seemed agitated and elated.

*Re: I.A.D. interviews—Rolando, clean. Kaiser, Tucker, Murray, in protective custody, appear to be clean.

****! Important—while I.A.D. officers were checking out offices of Junior Miss Cosmetics, security guard freaked out and tried to run. He was apprehended and taken into custody. (Pos. of marijuana.) Gaffaney is convinced he has guilty knowledge. This man (Hubert Douglas, M.N., age 39) yelped for you (said you were "cool" when you busted him for G.T.A. years ago). *Will talk only to you.* Come to P.C. *immediately* (Gaffaney's orders) before Douglas makes bail or wangles a writ.

***Call me—D.P.

Lloyd didn't bother to shave or shower or change clothes. Still wearing his B&E outfit, he drove straight to a liquor store. As he recalled, Hubert

Douglas was a bonded sourmash fiend. A pint of Jack Daniel's seemed like the ticket to soothe his soul and loosen his tongue. After purchasing the bottle, he raced downtown to Parker Center.

Hubert Douglas was being held in an interrogation cubicle adjoining Fred Gaffaney's office. Lloyd looked through the one-way glass and saw him sitting across a table from the captain, dressed in security guard's uniform replete with gold epaulets and a Sam Browne belt. A loudspeaker about the window crackled with his story of Come-San-Chin, the Chinese cocksucker. Gaffaney listened with his head bowed, fingering his cross-and-flag tie bar.

Lloyd walked in the door just as Douglas delivered his punch line and doubled over with laughter, slapping the table and exclaiming, "Dig it! Dig it!" Seeing Lloyd, he said, "Hopkins, my man!" and got up and extended his hand. Lloyd took it and said, "Hello, Hubert. My colleagues treating you okay?"

Douglas nodded toward Gaffaney, who looked up and glared at Lloyd. "This joker keeps asking me questions. I keep tellin' him I'll talk to you, and he keeps tellin' me you out of touch, the heavy implication bein' that you out pourin' the pork somewhere. I know my rights. I been in custody almost twenty-four hours. You gots to arraign me within twenty-four hours or cut me loose."

Lloyd looked at Gaffaney, then back at Douglas. "Wrong, Hubert. This is Saturday. We can legally hold you until Monday morning. Have a seat. I'll be back to talk to you after I have a few words with the captain."

Gaffaney got up and followed Lloyd outside. Measuring him with disdainful eyes, he said, "You need a shave and your clothes are filthy. Where have you been?"

"Out pulling burglaries," Lloyd said. "What's with Hubert?"

Gaffaney pushed the cubicle door shut. "I was at Junior Miss Cosmetics, along with an aide. We were talking to Dan Murray in his office. We had just gotten word that Christie was checking out the classified file section at Avonoco several hours before he was shot. Since my instincts regarding Murray's behavior told me he was clean, I mentioned it. Douglas was washing windows in the next room. My aide thought he looked hinky and copwise, so he kept an eye on him. He bolted when the conversation turned to files. My aide caught him with a big bag of weed in his pocket. He *knows* something, Hopkins. Get it out of him."

Lloyd let his mental wheels spin. "Captain, have you thrown the name Thomas Goff at that D.M.V. operator who called in about Christie?"

"Yes. I talked to her myself. She said that Goff was *not* the name she dug up for Christie. I also gave her the license number and a description of Goff's vehicle. Negative on that too. What do you—"

Lloyd hushed the captain with a hand on his shoulder. "Has Douglas seen the mug shots of Goff?"

"No."

"Then get me a copy of them now, and run me a complete all-police computer check on this name—Richard Brian Oldfield, white male, about thirty. Four-one-oh-nine Windemere, Hollywood. White Mercedes, FHM-three-six-three. He's clean on wants and warrants, but I need all the details I can get."

Gaffaney nodded, then said, "What are you fishing for?"

"I'll tell you after I've spoken to Douglas. Will you get me those mug shots now?"

The captain walked into his office, flushing from his neck all the way up to his crew cut. Returning to Lloyd and handing him the mug-shot strip, he hissed, "Don't make Douglas any promises of leniency."

Lloyd gave his superior officer a guileless smile. "No, sir." When Gaffaney walked back to his office, he entered the cubicle and flipped off the loud-speaker. "Let's make a deal," he said to Hubert Douglas, placing the pint of Jack Daniel's on the table between them. "Tell me what I want to know, and you walk. Fuck me around, and I hotfoot it up to Narco Division and glom a pound of reefer to add to the bag the I.A.D. bulls took off you, making it a felony possession bust. What'll it be?"

Douglas grabbed the bottle and downed half of it in one gulp. "Do I look stupid, Hopkins?"

"No, you look intelligent and handsome and full of savoir faire. Let's accomplish this with a minimum of bullshit and jive. The I.A.D. bulls think that you have some guilty knowledge regarding the classified files at Junior Miss. Let's take it from there."

Douglas coughed and breathed bourbon in Lloyd's face. "But what if that there guilty knowledge involves coppin' to some illegal shit I pulled?"

"You still walk."

"No shit, Dick Tracy?"

"If I'm lyin', I'm flyin'. Talk, Hubert."

Douglas knocked back a drink and wiped his lips. " 'Bout three weeks ago

I was drinkin' in a juke joint down the street from Junior Miss. This paddy dude starts a conversation with me, asks me if I like workin' security at Junior Miss, what my duties was, how tight I was in with the security boss, that kind of rebop. He buys me drinks up the ying-yang, gets me righteously lubed, then splits. I ain't no dummy, I knows this dude and I ain't seen the last of each other."

Douglas paused and grabbed the bottle. Lloyd snatched it out of his hand before he could bring it to his lips. Placing the mug-shot strip on the table, he said, "Is this the man?"

Douglas stared at the photos and grinned from ear to ear. "Righteous. That's the dude. What kind of shit did he pull?"

"Never mind. Finish your story."

Casting sad eyes at the pint, Douglas said, "I was right. The dude shows up the very next day, and offers to get me coked. We toot some righteous pharmaceutical blow in the john, then he starts talkin' about this righteous smart fuckin' buddy of his, how the guy was fuckin' obsessed with fuckin' *data*, you know, obsessed with knowin' the fuckin' skinny on other people's lives. You dig?"

"I dig," Lloyd said. "Did he tell you the man's name? Did he describe him? Did he say that the man was his half-brother?"

Douglas shook his head. "The fucker didn't even tell me his own fuckin' name, let alone the name of his fuckin' buddy. But dig, that day he makes his pitch: one K and two grams of pharmacy blow for Xerox copies of all the classified files. I tell him it's gonna take time, I gotta make them copies a couple at a time, on the sly. So I does it, without Murray or anyone else at Junior Miss knowin' about it. The dude calls me at the bar to set the tr—"

Lloyd interrupted: "Did he give you an address or a phone number where he could be reached?"

"Fuck, no! He kept callin' himself a 'justified paranoid' and said that he covered his tracks when he took a fuckin' piss, just to stay in fuckin' practice. He wouldn't even call me at my fuckin' crib; it had to be the fuckin' bar. Anyways, we sets up the trade-off, last week sometime, Tuesday or Wednesday night, and man, it was righteously fuckin' strange. Kick loose with that jug, will you, homeboy? I'm thirsty."

Lloyd slid the bottle across the table. "Tell me about the trade-off. Take it slow and be very specific."

Douglas guzzled half of the remaining whiskey. "Righteous. Anyway, I been observin' the dude, and to my mind he seems like he ain't wound together too tight. You know, this seems to be a dude that you might wanta call seriously nervous and itchy. We sets up the meet for Nichols Canyon Park, at night. The dude shows up in his little yellow car, lookin' sweaty, shaky and bug-eyed, lookin' like a righteous fuckin' rabid dog lookin' to die, but lookin' to get in a few righteous fuckin' bites before he goes. He kept grabbin' at himself like he was packin' a roscoe and he kept baitin' me with all this racist shit. Hopkins, this fucker looked like righteous fuckin' *death*. I gave him the files and he gave me the K and the blow and I got the fuck out fast. I don't know what the fucker done, but I wouldn't worry too much about catchin' him, because no fuckin' human bein' can look like that and fuckin' survive. I been to 'Nam, Hopkins. Righteous fuckin' Khe Sahn. I seen lots of death. This fucker looked worse than the terminal yellow jaundice battle fatigue walkin' dead over there. He was righteous fuckin' death on a popsicle stick."

Lloyd let the barrage of words settle in on him, knowing that they confirmed Thomas Goff's Melbourne Avenue horror show, and *possibly* the killing of Howard Christie; but that they somehow contradicted the revelation of Richard Oldfield and his sibling rivalry with Goff. He said, "Kill the jug, Hubert, you've earned it," and walked out into the hallway. A secretary passed him and said, "Captain Gaffaney went to lunch, Sergeant. He left your query reply with the duty officer."

Lloyd thanked the woman and nonchalantly walked into Gaffaney's office. A plastic bag of marijuana tagged with an official evidence sticker was lying on his desk. He pulled off the sticker and put it in his pocket, then opened the window and hurled the bag out into the middle of Los Angeles Street, where it came to rest in the bed of a passing Dodge pickup.

"Support your local police," Lloyd called out. When only traffic noise answered him, he walked by the interrogation cubicle and gave Hubert Douglas the thumbs up sign. Douglas grinned through the open doorway and raised his empty pint in farewell.

Lloyd took the elevator down to the first floor and walked to the front information desk. The duty officer did a double take on his outfit and handed him a slip of paper. He leaned against the desk and read: Subject D.O.B. 6/30/53, L.A. Calif. driv. lic. # 1679143, issued 7/69, no moving violations; no wants, warrants or record in Cont. U.S. *squeaky clean*—F.G.

Lloyd felt nameless little clicks assail him. He put his mind through a twenty-four-hour instant replay until he hit the source of his confusion: Thomas Goff was born and raised and sent to prison in New York State.

Havilland's psychiatric report on his half-brother Richard Oldfield stated that their mother raised the two boys together, presumably in New York. Yet this computer run-through fixed Oldfield's place of birth as Los Angeles. Also, Oldfield was issued a California driver's license in 1969, shortly after his sixteenth birthday, which at least *hinted* at long-term California residency.

Lloyd grabbed the desk phone and dialed Dutch's office number at the Hollywood Station.

"Captain Peltz speaking."

"It's me, Dutch. You busy?"

"Where the hell have you been? Did you get my memo?"

"Yeah, I got it. Listen, I need your help. Two-man stakeout on a pad near the Hollywood Bowl. It's got to be very cool, no unmarked units, nothing that smacks of heat. I don't want to approach this guy just yet; I only want him pinned."

"*This guy?* Who the hell is *this guy?*"

"I'll tell you about him when I see you. Can you meet me at my place in an hour? I want to change clothes and grab my civilian wheels."

Dutch sighed. "I've got a meeting in half an hour. Make it two hours."

Lloyd sighed back. "Deal."

Driving home, his little clicks worked themselves into the tapestry of the case, assuming the shape of a man who might or might not be Richard Oldfield; a man adept at manipulating *violent men* in order to achieve his purpose, which now emerged as the accruing of potential blackmail knowledge. Fact: Jack Herzog had stolen six L.A.P.D. Personnel files for his *personal* aim of "vindicating" Marty Bergen, and had told his girlfriend that he was "really scared" in the days before his disappearance/murder/suicide. Bergen considered his best friend's attempt at vindication ridiculous and had destroyed the columns the files had inspired. Yet, Thomas Goff and/or his still unknown "hotshot," "really smart" accomplice/partner, had used the L.A.P.D. information to cunningly circumvent Captain Dan Murray, wresting confidential file copies from his stooge Hubert Douglas, *killing* Lieutenant Howard Christie, probably for his refusal to deliver the files or on the basis of his demands for exorbitant amounts of money. This evidential and theoretical narrative line was cohesive and arrow straight.

But it contradicted most of his instincts regarding Thomas Goff. Goff was obsessed with his .41 revolver. He had used it on the three liquor store victims, a crime *still lacking a motive*; he had fired it at Lloyd himself, its single-action clumsiness giving him away. *Yet* . . . Howard Christie was killed with his own gun. Goff, assuming he was the killer, had eschewed a violent pattern in a time of stress, grabbing a weapon from a seasoned police officer, then shooting him with it. *It didn't wash.* The Christie job had the earmarks of a killing perpetrated by a novice, someone who had lulled the cop/security chief into considering him harmless—not the fever- or dope-driven Goff.

This left four potential suspects—Herzog, Havilland, Bergen, and Oldfield. The first three were ridiculous prospects: Herzog was a ninety-nine percent sure dead man; Havilland a love- and conscience-struck coincidental link with no motives; Bergen a pathetic, guilt-ridden drunk. Only Oldfield remained, and even he was shot full of logical holes.

His blood relationship with Goff was, of course, the key tie-in. Still, hearsay evidence indicated that Goff was dominated by his unknown partner, while Havilland's psychological workup portrayed Oldfield as being subservient to Goff. And the fact that he strongly resembled Goff and still walked around the streets pointed to his innocence. If he were Goff's accomplice, he would know that every cop in Southern California was looking for his mirror image. He would not go out and cruise for comely nurses to bring back to his pad.

Lloyd hit the Harbor Freeway southbound, feeling his clicks work into truth. He was dealing with two killers, two men whose drives had spawned an apocalypse.

20

The chess game progressed. The lonelies had been tapped for data purchasing capital, and tonight, with his cop/adversary dead, he would inject himself with sodium Pentothal and images of his past hours and make the void explode. The homecoming was in sight.

The Night Tripper stood on his balcony and stared at the ocean, then closed his eyes and let the sound of waves crashing accompany a rush of fresh images: Hopkins departing Windemere Drive at dawn; the industrial-sized trashbag containing Sherry Shroeder thumping against Richard Old-field's shoulder as he carried it to his car; the sated look on Richard's face as they lowered her to her grave in the shadow of the Hollywood sign. Satis-fying moments, but not as fulfilling as watching his lonely Billy develop and then edit his movie into a co-mingling of Linda Wilhite's childhood trauma and adult fantasy. Billy had at first warmed to the challenge of a rush job, then had become frightened when Sherry Shroeder died in his developing room. It had taken a brilliantly ad-libbed therapy session to see him through completion of the assignment.

Opening his eyes, Havilland recalled the day's *minor* testimonials to his will: The manager of his office building had called his condo with the news that he had been burglarized and that workmen were now repairing the damage to his front office door; his answering service had an urgent "call me" message from Linda Wilhite. Those telephone tidings had been such obvious capitulations to his power that he had succumbed to their symbol-ism and had used the beach phone to call the lonelies with an "assessment" request—ten thousand dollars per person. They had all answered "Yes" with doglike servility.

Let the capitulations continue.

The Night Tripper walked over to the kitchen wall phone and punched Linda Wilhite's number. When he heard her "Hello?" he said, "John Hav-illand, Linda. My service said that you needed to speak to me."

Linda's voice took on force. "Doctor, I realize that this is short notice, but I want to let you know that I'm quitting therapy. You've opened me up to lots of things, but I want to fly solo from here on in."

Havilland breathed the words in. When he breathed his own words out, they sounded appropriately choked with sentiment. "I'm very sad to hear that, Linda. We were making such progress. Are you sure you want to do this?"

"I'm positive, Doctor."

"I see. Would you agree to one more session? A special session with vi-sual aids? It's my standard procedure for final sessions, and it's essential to my form of therapy."

"Doctor, my days are very tied up. There's lots of—"

"Would tonight be all right? My office at seven? It's imperative we con-clude this therapy on the right foot, and the session will be free."

Sighing, Linda said, "All right, but I'll pay."

Havilland said, "Goodbye," and hung up, then punched another seven digits and began hyperventilating.

"Yes?" Hopkins's voice was expectant.

"Sergeant, this is John Havilland. Strange things have been happening. My office was broken into, and besides that, my source just contacted me. I—I—I—"

"Calm down, Doctor. Just take it slow."

"I—I was going to say that I still can't give you his name, but Goff contacted *him*, because he heard that he was in need of a gun and some money Goff owed him. The money and the gun are in a locker box at the Greyhound Bus Depot downtown. Fr-frankly, Sergeant, my source is afraid of a setup. He's considering returning to therapy, so I was able to get this information out of him. He-he has a strange relationship with Goff. . . . It's fr-fraternal almost."

"Did he give you the number of the box?"

"Yes. Four-one-six. The key is supposed to be with the man at the candy counter directly across from the row of lockers. Goff gave it to him yesterday, my man told me."

"You did the right thing, Doctor. I'll take care of it."

Dr. John Havilland replaced the receiver, thinking of Richard Oldfield stationed in the bar across from Box 416, armed with Lloyd Hopkins's personnel file photo and an Uzi submachine gun.

21

Lloyd was lead-footing it northbound on the Harbor Freeway when he realized that he had forgotten to leave Dutch a note explaining his absence. He slammed the dashboard with his palm and began shouting obscenities, then heard his cursing drowned out by the wail of sirens. Looking in his rearview mirror he saw three black-and-whites roar past with cherry lights flashing, heading for the downtown exits. Wondering why, he flipped on his two-way radio. When a squelch filtered voice barked "All units, all units, code three to the bus depot, Sixth and Los Angeles, shot fired," he shuddered back a wave of nausea and joined the fray.

Sixth and Los Angeles Streets were a solid wall of double-parked patrol cars. Lloyd parked on the sidewalk outside the bus terminal's south entrance and ran in past a bewildered-looking group of patrolmen carrying shotguns. They were jabbering among themselves, and one tall young officer kept repeating "Psycho. Fucking psycho," as he fondled the slide of his Ithaca pump. Pushing through a knot of unkempt civilians milling around in front of the ticket counters, Lloyd saw a uniformed sergeant writing in a spiral notebook. He tapped him on the shoulder and said, "Hopkins, Robbery/Homicide. What have we got?"

The sergeant grinned. "We got a machine-gun nut case. A wino was checking the doors of the lockers across the walkway from the gin mill by the Sixth Street entrance when this psycho runs out of the bar and starts shooting. The wino wasn't hit, but the lockers were torn up and an old bag lady got grazed by a ricochet. The meat wagon took her to Central Receiving. The juicehounds inside the bar said it sounded like a tommy gun—rat-tat-tat-tat-tat-tat-tat-tat. My partner is at the gin mill now, taking statements from the wino and potential witnesses. Rat-tat-tat-tat-tat-tat-tat-tat."

Lloyd felt little clicks resound to the beat of the sergeant's sound effects. "Is there a candy counter directly across from the shooting scene?"

"Yessir."

"What about the suspect?"

"Probably long gone. The wino said he tucked the burpgun under his coat and ran out to Sixth. Easy to get lost out there."

Lloyd nodded and ran to the hallway by the Sixth Street entrance. Gray metal lockers with coin slots and tiny key holes covered one entire wall, the opposite all inset with narrow cubicles where vendors dispensed souvenirs, candy and porno magazines. Checking the lockers close up, he saw that numbers 408 through 430 were riddled with bullet dents, and as he had suspected, the bar the gunman had run out of was directly across from 416.

Crossing to the bar, Lloyd eyeballed the man at the candy counter, catching a cop-wise look on his face. Doing a quick pivot, he walked over and stuck out his hand. "Police officer. I believe someone left a key for me."

The candy man went pale and stammered, "I—I—didn't think there'd be no gunplay, Officer. The guy just asked me if I wanted to make twenty scoots for holding on to the key, then whipping it on the guy who asked for it. I didn't want no part of no shooting."

The fury of his mental clicking made Lloyd whisper. "Are you telling me that the man who gave you the key is the man who fired off the machine gun?"

"Th-that's right. This don't make me no kind of accessory after the fact, does it?"

Lloyd took out a well-thumbed mug shot of Thomas Goff. "Is this the man?"

The candy man shook his head affirmatively and then negatively. "Yes and no. This guy looks enough like him to be his brother, but the gun guy had a skinnier face and a longer nose. It's a real close resemblance, but I gotta say no."

Taking the key from the vendor's shaking hands, Lloyd said with a shaking voice, "Describe the wino the gunman fired at."

"That's easy, officer. He was a big husky guy, ruddy complexion, dark hair. He looked kinda like you."

The final click went off like a flashing neon sign that spelled, "Fool. Patsy. Dupe. Sucker bait." *It was Havilland.* The setup was for *him*, not Oldfield; it was perpetrated by *Oldfield*, not Goff. Whatever the unrevealed intricacies of the case, Havilland had set him up from the beginning, acting on knowledge of his methods gathered from his L.A.P.D. file. The shrink had set up the psychiatric report on Oldfield as a calculated move based on old Hollywood Division fitness reports that had mentioned his penchant for "search methods of dubious legality." He had been strung out from before their first meeting; the Night Tripper albums and the Linda Wilhite office photos ploys, with Linda and Stanley Rudolph and Goff and Oldfield and Herzog and how many others dangling on their own puppet strings as the Doctor's willing or unwitting accomplices? The simple brilliance of it was overpowering. He had pinioned himself to a steel wall with self-constructed steel spikes.

Before the spikes could draw more blood, Lloyd walked to Box 416 and inserted the key. The door jammed briefly, then came open. Inside was a .357 Colt Python and a roll of twenty dollar bills held together with a rubber band. He picked the gun up. The cylinder was empty, but the barrel exuded a faint odor of paraffin and the underside of the vent housing bore a plastic sticker reading Christie—L.A.P.D.

The spikes dug in again, wielded from within and without. Lloyd slammed the locker door shut and drove to Parker Center.

He found the sixth-floor I.A.D. offices packed with detectives and civilian personnel. A uniformed officer passed him in the hallway and threw words of explanation: "My partner and I just brought in Marty Bergen, grabbed him in MacArthur Park, feeding the ducks. He waived his rights. Some Internal Affairs bulls are getting ready to pump him."

Lloyd ran to the attorney room at the end of the hall. A knot of plainclothes officers were staring through the one-way glass. Squeezing in beside them, he saw Marty Bergen, Fred Gaffaney, a stenographer, and an unidentified woman who had the air of a deputy public defender sitting around a table covered with pencils and yellow legal pads. The woman was whispering in Bergen's ear, while the stenographer poised fingers over his machine. Gaffaney worried his tie bar and drummed the tabletop.

Noticing wires running along the ceiling wainscoting, Lloyd nudged the officer nearest him and said, "Is there a backup transcription going down?"

The officer nodded. "Tape hookup to the skipper's office. He's got another steno at his desk."

"Headphones?"

"Speaker."

Lloyd took out his notepad and wrote, John Havilland, M.D., office 1710 Century Park East—*All phone #'s from business & residence calls for past 12 mos.*, then walked down the hall and rapped on the glass door of Fred Gaffaney's outer office. When his secretary opened it and gave him a harried look, he handed her the notepad. "The captain wants me to listen in on the interview. Could you do me a favor and call Ma Bell and get this information?"

The woman frowned. "The captain told me not to leave the office. Some marijuana that constituted evidence was stolen earlier. He had to release a suspect, and he was very angry about it."

Lloyd smiled. "That's a rough break, but this request is direct from Thad Braverton. I'll hold down the fort."

The woman's frown deepened. "All right. But please keep all unauthorized people out." She closed her hand around the notepad and walked off in the direction of the elevator bank. Lloyd locked the door from the inside and moved to the captain's private office. A grandmotherly stenographer was sitting at the desk, pecking at her machine while Gaffaney's sternly enunciated words issued from a wall speaker above her head.

". . . and legal counsel is present. Before we begin this interview, Mr. Bergen, do you have anything you wish to say?"

Lloyd pulled up a chair and smiled at the stenographer, who put a finger to her lips and pointed to the speaker just as a burst of electronically amplified laughter hit the room, followed by Marty Bergen's voice. "Yeah. I wish to go on the record as saying that your tie clasp sucks. If the L.A.P.D. were a just bureaucracy, you would be indicted on five counts of aesthetic bankruptcy, possession of fascist regalia, and general low class. Proceed with your interview, Captain."

Gaffaney cleared his throat. "Thank you for that unsolicited comment, Mr. Bergen. Proceeding, I will state some specific facts. You may formally object if you consider my facts erroneous. One, you are Martin D. Bergen, age forty-four. You were dismissed from the Los Angeles Police Department after sixteen years of service. While on the Department, you became friends with Officer Jacob M. Herzog, currently missing. Are these facts correct?"

"Yes," Bergen said.

"Good. Again proceeding, six days ago you were questioned by an L.A.P.D. detective as to the current whereabouts of Officer Herzog. You told the officer that you had not seen Herzog in approximately a month, and that on the occasions of your last meetings Herzog had been 'moody.' Is that correct?"

"Yes."

"Again proceeding, do you wish to alter your statement to that officer in any way?"

Bergen's voice was a cold whisper. "Yes, I do. Jack Herzog is dead. He killed himself with an overdose of barbiturates. I discovered his body at his apartment along with a suicide note. I buried him in a rock quarry up near San Berdoo."

Lloyd heard Bergen's attorney gasp and begin jabbering words of caution at her client. Bergen shouted, "No, goddamn it, I want to tell it!" There was a crescendo of voices, with Gaffaney's finally predominating: "Do you remember where you buried the body?"

"Yes," Bergen said. "I'll take you there, if you like."

The speaker went silent, then slowly came to life with the sound of animated whispers. Finally Gaffaney said, "Not wanting to put words in your mouth, Mr. Bergen, would you say that the previous statement you made to the police regarding Officer Herzog was misleading or incorrect?"

"What I told Hopkins was pure bullshit," Bergen said. "When I talked to him Jack was already three weeks in his grave. You see, I thought I could walk from all this. Then it started eating at me. I went on a drunk to sort it out. If those cops hadn't found me I would have come forward before too long. This has got to be heavy shit that Jack was involved in, or you wouldn't have put out an A.P.B. on me. I figure that you've got me for two misdemeanors—some jive charge for disposing of Jack's body and receiving stolen documents. So just ask your questions or let me make my statement, so I can get charged and make bail. Okay, Fred baby?"

There was another long silence, this one broken by Fred Gaffaney. "Talk, Bergen. I'll interject questions if I find them necessary."

Breath noise filled the speaker. Lloyd's body clenched in anticipation. Just when he thought he would snap from tension, Bergen said, "Jack was always stretched very thin, because he didn't have the outlets that other cops have. He didn't booze or carouse or chase pussy; he just read and brooded and competed with himself, wanting to be like these warrior mystics he worshipped. He got on mental kicks and ran wild with them. For about six months prior to his death he was obsessed with this notion of exonerating me by creating this L.A.P.D. credibility gap—showing the Department in a bad light so that the shame of my dismissal would be diminished by comparison. He talked it up and talked it up and talked it up, because he was a hero, and since he loved me he had to turn me from a coward into a hero to make our friendship real.

"About this time he met some guy in a bar. The guy introduced him to another guy, a guy that Jack called a 'file-happy genius.' This guy was some kind of guru who charged big bucks to all these sad guru-worshipper types, helping them with their problems and so forth. He convinced Jack to steal some personnel files that would suit their individual purposes—Jack's 'credibility gap' and the guru's loony hunger for confidential information. Jack showed me the files. Four of them were brass working outside security gigs where more personnel files were involved, one was Johnny Rolando, the TV guy, and the other was, you know, Lloyd Hopkins. Jack figured that the information in these files would comprise a sleazy picture of the L.A.P.D. *and* satisfy the guru's needs."

"Do you still have the files?" Gaffaney asked.

"No," Bergen said. "I read them and gave them back to Jack. I tried to put the information to use in a series of columns, as a memorial tribute to him, but finally I decided that it was just a tribute to his disturbance and gave up on the idea."

"Tell me more about this so-called guru and his friend."

"All right. First off, I don't know either of their names, but I do know that the guru was counseling Jack, helping to bring him through some things that were disturbing him. The guru used ambiguous phrases like 'beyond the beyond' and 'behind the green door,' which is an old song title. Both those phrases were included in Jack's suicide note."

Lloyd grabbed the telephone and dialed a number that he knew was a ninety-nine percent sure bet to confirm Havilland's complicity all the way down the line.

"Hello?"

Turning his back on the stenographer, he whispered, "It's me, Linda."

"Hopkins baby!"

"Listen, I can't talk, but the other night you whispered 'beyond the beyond' and something about green doors. Where did you get those phrases?"

"From Dr. Havilland. Why? You sound really spaced, Hopkins. What's all this about?"

"I'll tell you later."

"When?"

"I'll come by in a couple of hours. Stay home and wait for me. Okay?"

Linda's voice went grave. "Yes. It's him, isn't it?"

Lloyd said "Yes," and hung up, catching Bergen in midsentence. ". . . so from the froth around Jack's mouth I knew he'd O.D.'d on barbiturates. He used to say that if he ever took the Night Train, he'd never do it with his gun."

Gaffaney sighed. "Sergeant Hopkins searched Herzog's apartment and said that the surface had been wiped free of prints by scouring powder. When you discovered the body, did you notice any wipe marks?"

"No. None."

"Do you recall the exact words of Herzog's suicide note, in addition to those phrases you mentioned? Did Herzog elaborate on his reasons for killing himself?"

"This is where we part company, Fred baby," Bergen said. "I'll tell you anything you want to know, except that. And you haven't got the juice to get it out of me."

The sound of palms slamming a table top rattled the speaker. "On that note we'll break for a few hours. We've prepared a detention cage for you, Mr. Bergen. Your attorney can keep you company if she wishes to. We'll pick up where we left off later. Sergeant, show Mr. Bergen to his interim housing."

The speaker went dead. Lloyd got up and walked to the outer office window, catching a glimpse of a plainclothes officer hustling Marty Bergen and his attorney to the stairs leading to the fifth floor detention cages. Bergen's post-confession posture signified pure exhaustion: stooped shoulders; glazed eyes; shuffling walk. Lloyd saluted his back as he rounded the corner out of sight, then turned to see Gaffaney's secretary tapping on the door, holding up a sheaf of papers for him.

"I got your information, Sergeant."

Lloyd opened the door and took the woman's pages. "Let me explain this readout," she said. "The supervisor got me the business and residence calls up to two days ago; that's as far up-to-date as their computer is fed. When you go through it you'll notice that only a few of the numbers have names or addresses after them. That's because virtually all of this person's calls were made to pay phones. Isn't that strange? The locations of the pay phones are listed next to the number. Is this what you needed?"

Lloyd felt another soft click. "This is excellent. Will you do me one other favor? Call the *top* managing supervisor at Bell and have her try to get me the numbers called from both phones in the past two days. Have her call me at Robbery/Homicide with the information. Tell her it's crucial to an important murder investigation. Will you do that for me?"

"Yes, Sergeant. Are you going to talk with the captain? I know that he's interested in what you're doing."

Lloyd shook his head. "No. If he needs me, I'll be in my office. I'm not going to bother him with this phone business until I have something conclusive. He has enough to worry about."

Gaffaney's secretary lowered her eyes. "Yes. He works much too hard."

Lloyd jogged up to his office, wondering if the born-again witch-hunter cheated on his wife. Closing the door, he read over the list of phone numbers dialed from Havilland's office and Beverly Hills apartment, feeling his clicks collide with Hubert Douglas's snatch of Thomas Goff dialogue: "He kept callin' himself a 'justified paranoid' and said that he covered his tracks when he took a fuckin' piss, just to stay in fuckin' practice."

The pay phone calling translated to *Havilland's* "justified paranoia." The majority of the calls were made to phone booths situated within a quarter mile radius of the homes of Jack Herzog, Thomas Goff, and Richard Old-field. The calls to Herzog began last November, which coincided with Marty Bergen's statement that Herzog met "the guru" six months ago; they ended in late March, around the time of Herzog's suicide. The Goff calls ran from the beginning of the readout until the day after the liquor store slaughter; the Oldfield communications all the way through until the readout terminated forty-eight hours before.

Turning his attention to the other pay phone locations, Lloyd got out his Thomas Brothers L.A. County street map binder, hoping that his theory meshed with Bergen's statement about the "guru" charging "big bucks" to "these sad guru-worshipper types." Phone readout to map index to map; five locations, five confirmations. Click. Click. Click. Click. Click. All five pay phones were located in shopping centers in expensive residential neighborhoods—Laurel Canyon, Sherman Oaks, Palos Verdes Estates, San Marino, and the Bunker Hill Towers complex. Conclusion: Not counting other potential "worshipper types" living *inside* his non-toll-call area of Century City and Beverly Hills, Dr. John Havilland had at least five people, perhaps innocent, perhaps violently disturbed, that he was "counseling." Unanswered question: Citing Havilland's "justified paranoia" structure, it was obvious that he wanted to be heavily buffered against *any* kind of scrutiny. *Then where did he meet with his patients?*

Lloyd recalled the diplomas on Havilland's office wall: Harvard Medical School; two hospitals from the metropolitan New York area. Click. Click. Click. Thomas Goff was New York born and bred. Could his association with the Doctor date back to his days as a psychiatric resident? All the clues lay in the past, cloaked in medical secrecy. Lloyd imagined himself as a guru-worshipper type about to write a book, armed with nothing but good intentions and a telephone. Five minutes later that telephone became a time machine hurtling toward Dr. John Havilland's past.

The book ploy worked. Years before he became dedicated to secrecy, John Havilland had possessed an autobiographical bent, one that was captured for posterity in the form of a Harvard Medical School entrance essay that his faculty advisor called "the very model of both excellence in English skills and the exposition of sound motives for becoming a psychiatrist."

From the gushing advisor's recollections of Havilland and his essay, Lloyd learned that the guru shrink was born in Scarsdale, New York, in 1945, and that when he was twelve his father disappeared, never to be seen again, leaving young John and his mother lavishly well provided for. After weeks of speculating on his father's absence, John sustained a head injury that left him with fragmented memories and fantasies of the man who had sired him, a patchwork quilt of truth and illusion that his alcoholic mother could not illuminate in any way. Recurring memory symbols of good and evil—loving rides on a Bronx ferris wheel and the persistent questioning of police detectives—tore at John and filled him with the desire to know *himself* by unselfishly helping others to know *themselves*. In 1957, at age twelve, John Havilland set out to become the greatest psychiatrist who ever lived.

Lloyd let the advisor gush on, learning that while at Harvard Med Havilland studied symbolic dream therapy and wrote award-winning papers on psychological manipulation and brainwashing techniques; that during his Castleford Hospital residency he counseled court-referred criminals with astounding results—few of the criminals ever repeated their crimes. After concluding with the words, "and the rest of Dr. Havilland's work was performed in Los Angeles; good luck with your book," the advisor waited for a reply. Lloyd muttered, "Thank you," and hung up.

Calls to Castleford and St. Vincent's Hospitals proved fruitless; they would not divulge information on Havilland and would not state whether Thomas Goff had ever been treated there. The only remaining telephone destination was a twelve-year-old boy's "memory symbol" of evil.

Lloyd called the Scarsdale, New York, Police Department and talked to a series of desk officers and clerk typists, learning that the department's records predating 1961 had been destroyed in a fire. He was about to give up when a retired officer visiting the station came on the line.

The man told Lloyd that some time back in the fifties a filthy rich Scarsdale man named Havilland had been the prime suspect in the murder of a Sing Sing Prison guard named Duane McEvoy, who was himself a suspect in the sex murders of several young Westchester County women. Havilland was also suspected of torching a whole block of deserted houses in an impoverished section of Ossining, including a ramshackle mansion that the then Scarsdale police chief had described as a "torture factory." Havilland had disappeared around the time that McEvoy's knife-hacked body was found floating in the Hudson River. So far as the retired officer knew, he was never brought to justice or seen again.

After hanging up, Lloyd felt his clicking form a tight web of certainty. John Havilland had seized upon him as an adversary, casually remarking on his resemblance to his father at their initial meeting. An obsession with paternal power had led him to acquire a coterie of weak-willed "offspring"—

Goff and Oldfield among them—that he was molding into carriers of his own plague and dispatching on missions of horror. Thomas Goff had probably collided with the Doctor at Castleford Hospital, some time shortly after his parole from Attica. Havilland's "counseling" had steered him away from the criminal tendencies that had ruled his life to that time, accounting for his post-Attica one hundred percent clean record. He had probably been Havilland's recruiter of "guru-worshipper types"—his bar prowling M.O. and the testimony of Morris Epstein and Hubert Douglas pointed to it.

Lloyd's clickings departed the realm of certainty and jumped into the realm of pure supposition with a wild leap that nonetheless felt *right*: Thomas Goff was dead, murdered by Havilland after he freaked out at the liquor store with his .41. Havilland had done the interior decorating at Goff's apartment, leaving the "Doctor John the Night Tripper" album as bait. The man that Goff's landlord had seen the afternoon before the police raid was *Oldfield—impersonating Goff*. Havilland himself had killed Howard Christie.

Fool. Dupe. Patsy. Chump. Sucker bait. The reprisals jarred Lloyd's mind. He got up and started down the hall to Thad Braverton's office, then stopped when the door embossed with "Chief of Detectives" loomed in his path as a barrier rather than a beacon. *All of his evidence was circumstantial, suppositional, and theoretical.* He had no evidential basis on which to arrest Dr. John Havilland.

Shifting physical and mental gears, Lloyd walked down to the fifth-floor detention area, finding Marty Bergen alone in the first cage, staring out through the wire mesh.

"Hello, Marty."

"Hello, Hopkins. Come to gloat?"

"No. Just to say thanks for your statement. It was a help to me."

"Great. I'm sure you'll make a smashing collar and carve another notch on your legend."

Lloyd peered in at Bergen. The crisscrossed wire cast shadows across his face. "Have you got any idea how big this thing is?"

"Yeah. I just heard most of the story. Too bad I can't report it."

"Who told you?"

"A source. I'd be a shitty reporter if I didn't have sources. Got any leads on the guru guy?"

Lloyd nodded. "Yes. I think it's almost over. Why didn't you tell me what you knew when I talked to you before?"

Bergen laughed. "Because I didn't like your style. I did what I had to do by coming forward, Hopkins, so I'm clean. Don't ask me to kiss your ass."

Lloyd gripped the wire a few inches from Bergen's face. "Then kiss this, motherfucker: if you'd talked to me before, Howard Christie would be alive today. Add that one to your guilt list."

Bergen flinched. Lloyd walked away, letting his words hang like poisonous fallout.

Driving west toward Hollywood, Lloyd asked himself his remaining unanswered questions, supplying instinctive answers that felt as sound as the rest of his hypothesis. Did John Havilland know that Jungle Jack Herzog was dead? No. Most likely he assumed that the shame of Herzog's "beyond" would prevent him from clueing in the world at large or the police in specific to the man who had "brought him through" it. The wipe marks in Herzog's apartment? Probably Havilland; probably the day after the liquor store murders, when he realized that Goff was irrevocably flipped out. Goff had recruited Herzog, so it was likely that he might have visited Jungle Jack's pad and left prints. Havilland would want that potential link to him destroyed. Yet the Doctor had left himself vulnerable at the level of Herzog.

Lloyd forced himself to say the word out loud. Homosexual. It was there in Herzog's hero worship; in his awful need to court danger as a policeman; in his lack of sexual interest in his girlfriend immediately before his death. Bergen would not elaborate on the suicide note because that piece of paper said it explicitly, illuminating Havilland's tragic flaw by implication: he wanted Jack Herzog to roam the world as a testimonial to the power of a man who brought a macho cop out of the closet.

Hatred gripped Lloyd in a vice that squeezed him so hard he could feel his brains threaten to shoot out the top of his head. His foot jammed the gas pedal to the floor in reflex rage, and Highland Avenue blurred before his eyes. Then a line from Marty Bergen's memorial column forced him to hit the brake and decelerate. "Resurrect the dead on this day." He smiled. Jungle Jack Herzog was going to return from "beyond the beyond" and frame the man who sent him to his death.

Lloyd passed the Hollywood Bowl and turned onto Windemere Drive, cursing when he saw that Oldfield's Mercedes was not in front of his house and that a profusion of front lawn barbecues would prevent him from a quick B&E. After parking, he walked over and peered in the front window, finding it still covered with heavy curtains. Swearing again, he gave the front lawn a cursory eyeballing, stopping when he saw a patch of white on the otherwise green expanse.

He walked over. The patch was a piece of adhesive bandage, with a streak of what looked like congealed blood on the sticky side. Another soft click, this one followed with a soft question mark. Lloyd picked the bandage up and headed south toward the purchasing of material for his frame.

Parked outside the Brass Rail gun shop on La Brea, he took Howard Christie's .357 Magnum from the glove compartment and checked the grips. They were checkered walnut with screw fasteners at the top and bottom; interchangeable, but too ridged to sustain fingerprints. Cursing a blue streak, Lloyd took the gun into the shop and flashed his badge at the proprietor, telling him that he wanted a large handgun with interchangeable smooth wooden grips that would also fit his magnum. The proprietor got out a small screwdriver and arrayed a selection of revolvers on the counter. Ten minutes later Lloyd was three hundred and five dollars poorer and the owner of a Ruger .44 magnum with big fat cherrywood grips, the proprietor having waived the three-day waiting period on the basis of a certified police affiliation. Thus armed, Lloyd crossed his fingers and drove to a pay phone, hoping that his luck was still holding.

It was. The Robbery/Homicide switchboard operator had an urgent message for him—call Katherine Daniel—Bell Telephone, 623-1102, extension 129. Lloyd dialed the number and seconds later was listening to a husky-voiced woman digress on how her respect for her late policeman father had fueled her to "kick ass" and get him the information he needed.

". . . and so I went down to the computer room and checked the current feed-in on your two numbers. No calls were made either yesterday or today from either the business or residence phones. That got my dander up, so I decided to do some checking on this guy Havilland. I started by checking the computer files on his phone bills, going back a year and a half. He paid by check on both bills—with the exception of last December, when a man named William Nagler paid both bills. I then checked this Nagler guy out. He paid his *own* bill every month, plus the bill for a number in Malibu. He *lives* in Laurel Canyon, because his checks have his address on them, and *his* number has a Laurel Canyon prefix. But—"

Lloyd interrupted: "Take it slow from here on in, I'm writing this down."

Katherine Daniel drew in a breath and said, "All right. I was saying this guy Nagler paid the bill for this number in Malibu—four-five-two, six-one-five-one. The address is unlisted—as long as Nagler pays the bill on the phone there, Ma Bell doesn't care if it's in Timbuctu. Anyway, I ran a random sampling of the six-one-five-one toll calls over the past year, and got a lot of the same pay phone numbers the other supervisor gave you on your earlier query. I also ran the computer feed-in from yesterday and today and got some toll calls, all in this area code. Do you want them?"

"Yes," Lloyd said. "Slow and easy. Have you got names and addresses on them?"

"Do you think I'd do a half-assed job, Officer?"

Lloyd's forced laugh sounded hysterical to his ears. "No. Go ahead."

"Okay. Six-two-three, eight-nine-one-one, Helen Heilbrunner, Bunker Hill Towers, unit eight-forty-three; three-one-seven, four-zero-four-zero, Robert Rice, one-zero-six-seven-seven Via Esperanza, Palos Verdes Estates; five-zero-two, two-two-one-one, Monte Morton, one-twelve LaGrange Place, Sherman Oaks; four-eight-one, one-two-zero-two, Jane O'Mara, nine-nine-zero-nine Leveque Circle, San Marino; two-seven-five, seven-eight-one-five, Linda Wilhite, nine-eight-one-nine Wilshire, West L.A.; four-seven-zero, eight-nine-five-three, Lloyd W. Hopkins, three-two-nine-zero Kelton, L.A. Hey, is that last guy related to you?"

Lloyd had his laugh perfected. "No. Hopkins is a common name. Have you got Nagler's phone number and address?"

"Sure. Four-nine-eight-zero Woodbridge Hollow, Laurel Canyon. Four-six-three, zero-six-seven-zero. Is that it?"

"Yes. Farewell, sweet Katherine!"

Husky chuckles came over the line.

Sweating, his legs weak from tension, Lloyd called Dutch's private line at the Hollywood Station, connecting with a desk sergeant who said that Captain Peltz was out for the afternoon, but would be calling in hourly for his messages. Speaking very slowly, Lloyd explained what he wanted: Dutch was to dispatch trustworthy squadroom dicks to the following addresses and have them lay intimidating "routine questioning" spiels on the people who answered the door, using "beyond the beyond" and "behind the green door" as buzzwords. Holding back William Nagler's name and address, he read off the others, having the officer repeat the message. Satisfied, Lloyd said that *he* would be calling back hourly to clarify the urgency of the matter with Dutch and hung up.

Now the risky part. Now the conscious decision to jeopardize an innocent woman's life for the sake of a murder indictment, an action that was an indictment of his own willingness to deny everything that had happened with Teddy Verplanck. Driving to Linda's apartment, Lloyd prayed that she would do or say something to prove the jeopardy move right or wrong, saving them both indictments on charges of cowardice or heedless will.

Linda opened the door with a drink in one hand. Lloyd looked at her posture and the light in her eyes, seeing indignation moving into anger, a prostitute who got fucked once too often. When he moved to embrace her, she stepped out of his way. "No. Tell me first. Then don't touch me, or I'll lose what I'm feeling."

Lloyd walked into the living room and sat down on the sofa, outright scared that Linda's rectitude said all systems go. He pulled out the .44 magnum and laid it on the coffee table. Linda took a chair and stared at the gun without flinching. "*Tell me,* Hopkins."

With his eyes tuned in to every nuance of Linda's reaction, Lloyd told the entire story of the Havilland case, ending with his theory of how the Doctor had played off the two of them, counting on at least a one-way attraction developing. Linda's face had remained impassive during the recounting, and it was only when he finished that Lloyd could tell that her gut feeling was awe.

"Jesus," she said. "We're dealing with the Moby Dick of psychopaths. Do you really think he has the hots for me, or is that just part of his scam?"

"Good question," Lloyd said. "I think initially it was part of the scam, because he wanted to portray himself as a fellow lover of women. Afterwards, though, I think he was genuinely jealous of your attraction to me, if only because he has me slotted in the role of adversary. Make sense? You know the bastard better than I do."

Linda considered the question, then said, "Yes. My first impression of Havilland was that he was essentially asexual. What next, Hopkins? And why is that gun on my table?"

Lloyd flinched inwardly. Linda was allaying his doubts with perfect responses and the right questions. A light went on in his mind, easing the constricted feeling in his chest. Only if she made the perfect statement voluntarily would he sanction the jeopardy gambit. "I have no hard evidence. I can't arrest Havilland and make it stick. He called you today, right?"

"Yes. How did you know that?"

"That telephone read-out I mentioned. What did he want?"

"I called to tell him I was quitting therapy. His service forwarded the call to him. He almost begged me to come for one more session. I agreed."

"When?"

"Tonight at seven."

Lloyd checked his watch. 6:05. "One question before we get to the gun. The other night you told me about your parents' deaths and said that sometimes you have very dark thoughts. Does Havilland know about that? Has he emphasized your parents' deaths in the course of his counseling?"

Linda said, "Yes. He's obsessed with it, along with some violent fantasies I have. Why?"

Lloyd choked back a wave of fear. "I need Havilland's fingerprints on the grips of that gun. Once I have them, I'll switch the grips to Howard Christie's gun, get Havilland's prints from the D.M.V. and arrest him for Murder One and make it stick while I dig up corroborative evidence. I want you to take the gun to your session tonight. Keep it in your purse and don't touch the grips. Tell Havilland that your fantasies are becoming more violent and that you bought a gun. Hand it to him nervously, holding it by the cylinder housing and barrel. If my reading of him is correct, he'll grab it by the grips, showing you the proper handling procedure, then give it back. Hold it nervously by the barrel and trigger guard and put it back in your purse. After the session, go home and wait for my call. Havilland has no idea that I'm on to him, so you'll be in no danger."

Linda's smile reminded Lloyd of Penny and how she was her most beautiful in moments of rebellion. "You don't believe that, Hopkins. You're shaking. I'll do it on one condition. I want the gun loaded. If Havilland freaks out, I want to be able to defend myself."

A green light flashed in response to Linda's perfect voluntary statement. Lloyd took six .44 shells from his jacket pocket and put them on the coffee table. The moment froze, and he felt himself treading air. Linda put a hand on his arm. "I think I've been waiting a long time for this," she said.

22

The Time Machine sped backward, fueled by a high octane sodium Pentothal mainline. Calendar pages ruffled in the wind. Bombardments of imagery from recent gauntlets pushed the pages closer and closer, until the black-on-white type smothered him, then turned him outside in.

Saturday, June 2, 1957. Johnny Havilland has heard from the J.D.'s at school that an auto graveyard on the edge of Ossining niggertown is a chrome treasure trove. The old jig who looks after the place sells nifty hood ornaments for the price of a pint of jungle juice, and if you hop the fence you can swipe something sharp and get away before he catches you. Jimmy Vandervort got a bulldog from a Mack truck for thirty-nine cents; Fritz Buckley got a gunsight hood hanger off a 'forty-eight Buick for free, flashing a moon on the spook when he demanded the scratch for some T-bird. Johnny imagines all manner of chrome gadgetry that he could kipe and give to his father to jazz up his 'fifty-six Ford Vicky ragtop. He takes a series of buses up to Ossining, and within an hour he is walking the streets of a Negro shanty town in the shadow of Sing Sing Prison.

The streets remind him of photographs he has seen of Hiroshima after Uncle Sam slipped the Japs the A-bomb: Rubble heaps on the front lawns of abandoned houses; gutters filled with empty wine bottles and sewage overflow; emaciated dogs looking for someone or something to bite. Even the Negroes reinforce the A-bomb motif: they look gaunt and suspicious, like mutant creatures fried by atomic fallout. Johnny shivers as he recalls the spate of horror movies he has seen against his mother's wishes. Somehow this is scarier, and because it is scarier he will become that much more of a man by stealing here.

Johnny is about to ask one of the Negroes for directions to the auto graveyard when he spots a familiar flash of color down the block. He walks over and sees his father's Vicky parked outside an old wood-framed house patched over with tarpaper. Painted obscenities and swastikas cover all sides of the house. Johnny climbs in through a broken window, as if drawn by a magnetic force.

Once inside, standing in darkness on rotting wood planks, Johnny's magnet takes on the form of his father's laughter, issuing from the top of a staircase off to his left. He walks over, hearing his father's baritone glee meld with the high-pitched squealing of another man. The whir and click of gears joins with the voices as Johnny treads up the stairs, holding tightly to the banister.

When he reaches the second-story landing, Johnny sees a door and squints in the darkness to see if it is green. The laughter and the gear noise grow louder, then the door blows open a crack. Johnny tiptoes over and peers inside.

A stench assails him as his eyes hone in on the backs of his father and a man in a gray uniform standing in front of a whirling circular object. The smell is of blood and body waste and sweat. A green blanket marked off like a crap table lies on the floor, covered with coins and folding money. The walls and ceiling are dotted with bright red, and rivulets of pale red drip toward the floor. Johnny squints and sees that his father is holding a chisel. He moves the chisel toward the whirling object, and a spritz of red liquid cuts the air. The man in the gray uniform laughs and exclaims, "Shit, that's a ten pointer!" He steps back and sticks his hand in his pocket, then drops a wad of cash on the blanket. The whirling circular object comes to a halt and into view.

A nude woman is attached to a plywood reinforced corkboard mounted on a foundation of bricks. A gear train composed of motorcycle chains and lawnmower belts stands behind it. The woman is manacled at the ankles and pinioned at the top with spikes through her wrists. Slash wounds oozing blood cover her chest and extremities, and a black rubber handball is stuck in her mouth, held there by crisscrossed strips of friction tape.

Johnny bites his hand to keep from screaming, feeling his fingers crack beneath his teeth. He squints at the first naked woman he has ever seen and notes her swollen belly and knows that she is pregnant.

His father grabs a handle at the top of the corkboard and leans his whole body into a downward pull. The woman spins end over end, and the man in the uniform squeals, "How about ten bucks on a roulette abortion?"

Johnny watches the chisel descend, clamping his eyes open with self-mauled fingers, knowing he has to see, knowing what *must* be happening, but seeing instead his daddy sitting beside him in the whirling ferris wheel at Playland in the Bronx, whispering that everything would always be all right and he could go on *all* the rides and eat all the cotton candy he wanted and that Mommy would quit drinking and they would be a real family. Then the uniform man was saying "It's a boy!" and he hears the sound of his own scream, and the uniform man was on top of him with his chisel, and then father was stabbing the uniform man with a knife and stabbing *him* with a needle, whispering, "Easy, Johnny, easy, beauty, easy, babe."

The Time Machine pushed through days of sedative haze filled with the sound of mother weeping and Baxter the lawyer telling her that the money would always be there, and stern-looking men in cheap summer suits asking her where father was, and did he know a man named Duane McEvoy? Mother's scream: "No, you cannot talk to the boy—he knows nothing!" Then Baxter the lawyer takes him to a horror triple feature in White Plains and tells him father is gone forever, but he will be his pal. Midway through *The Curse of Frankenstein* images of the whirling circular object hit him. It all starts to come back, and thoughts of the ferris wheel die, slaughtered by a Cinemascope and Technicolor replay of the Caesarean birth.

"It's a boy!"

Johnny runs out of the theater and hitchhikes to Ossining niggertown. The same A-bomb Negroes and hungry dogs maneuver on the periphery of the area, but the block itself has burned to the ground.

But it happened here.

No, it was a nightmare.

But it *did* happen here.

I don't know.

Weeks pass. The newspapers attribute the Ossining fire to "heedless Negro children playing with matches" and express gratitude that no one was hurt. Johnny grieves for his lost father and listens in on mother's phone calls to Baxter. She repeatedly tells the lawyer to buy the cops off once and for all, regardless of the price. Baxter finally calls back and tells mother that it is all set, but to be sure she should destroy everything belonging to father, including everything in his safe-deposit boxes. Johnny knows that there is nothing interesting in father's study—only his guns and ammo and his books; but the safe deposit boxes are something he has forgotten to scope out. He steals the keys to the boxes from father's desk and forges a note to the manager of the First Union Bank in Scarsdale Village. The old fart buys it hook, line, and sinker, chuckling over the twelve-year-old boy doing banking errands for his dad. Johnny walks away from the bank with a brown paper bag full of blue chip stocks and a black leather-bound diary that looks like a bible.

Johnny walks to the train station, intending to go to the movies in the city. A very un-Scarsdale-like bum tries to panhandle train fare from him. Johnny gives him the stock certificates. Once on the train heading toward Manhattan, Johnny opens up the diary and reads his father's words. The words prove conclusively that what he saw on June 2, 1957, in Ossining niggertown was for real.

Since 1948, alone and with the aid of a Sing Sing Prison guard named Duane McEvoy, father had tortured and murdered eighteen women, some in Westchester County, some in upstate cities adjoining his favorite duck hunting preserves. The mutilations, sexual abuse, and ultimate dismemberments are described in vivid detail. Johnny forces himself to read every word. Tears are streaming down his face and the ferris wheel memory battles the words for primacy. The benevolent whirling object is winning as the train pulls into Grand Central Station. Then Johnny gets to the passages that prove how much his father loves him and everything goes crazy.

The boy is so much smarter than me that it's scary.

Brains are everything. I've been able to keep Duane as my lackey for so long because the dumbfuck knows that I'm the one who keeps him from getting caught. When Johnny killed the rats and shot the dogs I saw him go cold almost overnight, and when I saw him go smart and wary and cautious too, I knew I was scared. I wanted to go to him and love him, but staying away makes him stronger and more fit for life.

Johnny boy is like an iceberg—cold and 7/10's below the surface.

He's probably afraid to kill human prey; too manipulative, too asexual. It's going to be interesting watching him hit adolescence. How will he attempt to prove himself?

Johnny walks through Grand Central, openly weeping. Coming out onto 42nd Street, he throws the death bible into a storm drain and hurls a silent vow to his father: he will show him that he is afraid of nothing.

Fall 1957. Johnny considers potential victims at Scarsdale Junior High. To fulfill his father's legacy, he knows that they must be female. Beyond that first essential qualification, he sets his own criteria: All his prey must be snooty, giggly, and stay late after school participating in kiss-ass extracurricular activities, then walk home via the Garth Road underpass, where he would be waiting with a razor-sharp Arkansas toad stabber like the one Vic Morrow wielded in *Blackboard Jungle*.

Johnny's selection process narrows as he stakes out the underpass. Finally he settles on Donna Horowitz, Beth Shields, and Sally Burdett, grinds who remain until after dark each day in the Chem Lab, washing test tubes and brown-nosing Mr. Salcido for a good grade. Stab. Stab. Stab. Johnny sharpens his switchblade every night and wonders if father ever bagged three at once. He sets the execution date: November 1, 1957. The three grinds will walk through the underpass at their usual time of 5:35 to 5:40, giving him twelve minutes to bump them off, then hotfoot it over to the station and catch the 5:52 to the city. Stab. Stab. Stab.

November 1, 1957. At 5:30 Johnny is stationed on the left-hand side of the Garth Road underpass, wearing blue jeans and a hunting vest that he has scavenged from his father's left-behinds. The vest has loops to hold shotgun shells and hangs down to his knees. The toad stabber is affixed to his belt in a plastic scabbard.

The three victims approach the underpass right on time. Donna Horowitz notices Johnny and starts to giggle. Sally Burdett hoots, "Is that Johnny Havilland or Chucko the Clown? Dig that crazy vest!" Johnny draws his knife as Beth Shields sidles past him, taunting, "Wimpdick, Wimpdick." He lunges and snags the stiletto on his vest pocket. The blade pokes his ribcage and he screams and falls to his knees. The girls gather around him and shriek with laughter. Johnny sees a kaleidoscope of the Caesarean birth, the ferris wheel and his father joining in the laughter. He screams again to drown it all out. When that doesn't work, he bangs his head on the pavement until everything goes silent and black.

The banging continues. When a woman's voice calls out, "Dr. Havilland, are you there?" the Night Tripper is catapulted back to the present. His office, the projector and a portable movie screen come into focus. The voice must belong to Linda Wilhite, banging on his outer office door. His first conscious thought of his now destroyed childhood void is appreciation for his very own God, who did not give him the courage to break down the void until he had given him the courage to kill, and earn his father's love. His destiny had been dealt with split-second accuracy.

"Dr. Havilland, are you there? It's Linda Wilhite."

The Doctor got to his feet and took a deep breath, then rubbed his eyes.

His steps were rubbery from the sodium Pentothal jolt, but that was to be expected—he was, technically speaking, a newborn creature. Trying his new voice, he called, "Hold on, Linda. I'm coming." Hearing his familiar baritone, he walked to the outer office door and opened it.

Linda Wilhite stood there, looking uncharacteristically nervous. "Hello, Linda," Havilland said. "Are you all right? You seem slightly on edge."

Linda walked past the Doctor into his private office and took her usual seat. When Havilland followed her in, she said, "I've been having some very strange, violent fantasies. I've even bought a gun." Pointing to the movie screen and projector, she added, "Are those the visual aids you mentioned?"

Havilland sat down facing Linda. "Yes. Tell me about your new fantasies. You look full of stress. Are you sure you want to quit therapy under such conditions?"

Linda twisted in her chair, clutching her purse in her lap. As the last fuzziness from his Pentothal trip died, Havilland saw that underneath her nervousness she was very angry. "Yes, I still want to quit therapy. *You* look full of stress. Woozy, too. Everyone is full of stress. These are stressful times, don't you know that, goddamn it?"

Havilland raised placating hands. "Easy, Linda. I'm on your side."

Linda sighed. "I'm sorry I barked."

"That's all right. Tell me about the new fantasies."

Linda said, "They're weird, and variations on my sweater man fantasies. Basically I'm just menaced by the same type of man I used to have the hots for. I fantasize being chased by men like that. The fantasies always end with me shooting them." She reached into her purse and pulled out a large blue steel revolver, grasping it by the barrel and cylinder. "See, Doctor? Do you think I'm crazy?"

Havilland reached over and took the revolver from Linda, holding it firmly by the smooth wood grips, sighting it at the movie screen. "I'm proud of you," he said as he handed it back, butt first.

Linda returned the gun to her purse. "Why?"

"Because, as you said, these are stressful times. You're a strong person, and in stressful times strong people go beyond their beyonds. Move your chair over here. I want to run a little home movie for you."

Linda pulled her chair over to where it was facing the screen. Havilland got up and threaded a length of film through the projector's feeder device, then hit the on switch and turned off the wall light. A series of blank frames flashed across the screen, followed by a jerky panning shot of a bedroom, followed by more blank frames.

Then a blonde woman in a nurse's uniform began to undress. Close-up shots caught everything fallible about her body: a small abdominal scar, networks of varicose veins, patches of cellulite. When she was naked, she did an awkward vamp dance, then lay down on a mattress covered by a single blue sheet.

A nude man joined her, averting his face from the camera. The couple moved into an embrace, broke it, and moved to opposite sides of the mattress. The woman looked bewildered and the man mashed his face into the sheet. After holding these poses for long moments, the woman rolled underneath the man and they faked intercourse.

Linda clutched her purse and said, "What is this, amateur porno film night? I thought this was going to be a therapy session."

"Shhh," Havilland whispered. "You'll catch the drift in just a few seconds."

The screen went blank, then filled up with a long shot of the blonde woman, now dressed in her nurse's uniform, leaning against the bedroom wall. Suddenly a man, also clothed, threw himself on top of her. The screen again went blank, then segued into an extreme close-up of a transparent plastic pillow. The muzzle of a gun was pressed to the pillow. A finger pulled the trigger and the screen was awash in red. The camera caught a close-up of the man's face. When Linda saw the face she screamed "Hopkins!" and fumbled in her purse for the gun. Her finger was inside the trigger guard when the lights went on and the man from the movie jumped out of the closet and smothered her with his body.

23

Lloyd slammed down the phone in response to Dutch's news: the two women and one man that Hollywood Division detectives had leaned on with "behind the green door" and "beyond the beyond" had immediately clammed up, first threatening the officers with lawsuits, then going into repeated recitations of the phrase *"patria infinitum."* No breakdowns, no re-cantings of past sins, just indignation at police scare tactics and the rapid expulsion of seasoned cops. Dutch would be deploying a new team of de-tectives for runs at the guru worshippers, but they would probably be in mantra comas by then. There was only himself, Linda and her magnum, and the unknown quantity of William Nagler.

Lloyd checked the clock on the kitchen wall. 7:45. Linda would still be at her "therapy" session. He could wait and call and ease his mind, or he could move. The ticking of the clock became deafening. He locked up the house and walked to his car.

Headlights flashed across the driveway as he slipped behind the wheel, and a panel truck pulled in front of his unmarked cruiser. Lloyd got out and saw Marty Bergen step in front of the headlights and jam his hands into his pockets. A gun butt extended from his waistband.

"My lawyer glommed me a writ," he said. "Fred Gaffaney almost shit shotgun shells."

Lloyd said, "Amateurs shouldn't pack hardware. Beat it. I've got no sto-ries for you."

Bergen laughed. "When I was on the job I was in love with my piece. Off duty, I always made sure that people could see it. I was in love with it until I had to use it. Then I dropped it and ran. Jack's dead, Hopkins."

"Tell me something I don't know."

"It's on me. It's all on me."

"Wrong, Bergen. It's the Department's and it's mine."

Bergen kicked the grill of the Matador, then stumbled backward into the hood of his truck. "I *owe*, goddamn you! Can't you see that? All I ever had was what Jack gave me, and even that was all twisted. Some piece of shit took him where he shouldn't have fucking gone and made him feel things that he shouldn't have fucking felt, and it was *me* that he felt them about, and I owe! Don't make me say the words, Hopkins. Please don't make me say the fucking words."

Lloyd sent up a prayer for all guilt-driven innocents seeking jeopardy. "What do you want, Bergen?"

Former L.A.P.D. Sergeant Martin D. Bergen wiped tears from his eyes. "I just want to pay off Jack."

"Then get in the car," Lloyd said. "We're going to Laurel Canyon to good guy–bad guy a suspect."

*　　　*　　　*

William Nagler was not at home.

Lloyd parked across the street from his two-story redwood A-frame and walked over and knocked on both the front and back doors. No answer, no lights burning and no sounds of habitation. After checking the mailbox and finding two catalogs and a Mastercard bill, he returned to the car and his improbable partner.

"Are you going to open up this thing?" Bergen asked as Lloyd squeezed in behind the wheel.

Lloyd shook his head. "No. I don't trust the fourth estate. Just play the interrogation by ear. You ever work plainclothes?"

"Yeah. Venice Vice. I'm going to be the good guy, right?"

"No. You've got booze breath and you need a shave. You're big, but I'm bigger, so I can play savior. I'll ask the questions, you just be abusive. Just imagine yourself as a typical fascist pig out of the pages of the *Big Orange Insider* and you'll be cool."

Bergen laughed. "You're the kind of joker who hands out compliments one minute, then rags people who hand out compliments the next, which means one of two things—you either love to give people shit, or you don't know where your own head is at. Which one is it?"

With his eyes on Nagler's front door, Lloyd said, "Don't jerk my chain. If I didn't want you here, you wouldn't be here. If I didn't understand what you have to do, I would have busted you for carrying a concealed weapon and kicked your ass back to the slam."

Bergen scratched his razor stubble and poked Lloyd in the arm. "I apologize for saying I didn't like your style. What I should have said was that you *have* style, but you don't know what to do with it."

Lloyd turned on the dashboard light and stared at Bergen. "Don't tell me about style. I read some of your early stuff. It was damn good. You could have been something big, you could have said things worth saying. But *you* didn't know what to do with it, because being really good is really scary. I know fear, Bergen. Two niggers blew away your partner and you ran. I can understand that and not judge you for it. But you had the chance to be great and you settled for being a hack, and that I can't understand."

Bergen toyed with the knobs of the two-way radio. "You Catholic, Hopkins?"

"No."

"Tough shit, you're going to hear my confession anyway. Jack Herzog taught me to write. He ghosted my first published stories, then edited the ones I actually did write. *He* formed my style; *he* was the one who had the chance to be great. It's weird, Hopkins. You're supposed to be the pragmatist, but I think you're really a romantic innocent with an incredible nose for shit. It's funny. Jack gave me everything I have. He made me a derivative fiction stylist and a competent journalist. He'd been writing a novel, and I was serving as *his* editor, helping him hold it together as he got crazier and crazier. I've never had the chance to be great. But if I had *your* brains and drive and guts, I'd be more than a gloryhound flatfoot."

Lloyd turned on the radio and listened to code ones and twos. "It's a stalemate, Marty, and a life sentence for both of us. But we're lucky we can play the game."

Bergen took the pistol from his waistband and rolled down the window and took a bead on the moon. "I believe that," he said.

Two hours passed in silence. Bergen dozed off and Lloyd stared out the window at William Nagler's driveway, wondering if he should make a run to a phone and call Linda; wondering also if Havilland's worshippers were in contact with each other and if the already hassled followers had alerted Nagler to the approaching heat. No, he decided finally. Havilland was too well buffered. The worshippers probably had no way of contacting Havilland or each other besides Havilland's pay phone communiqués, which logic told him were rigidly pre-scheduled. *His* investigatory parries were buffered against discovery. Then the truth hit. He was pumping himself up with logic because Linda was part of the game and part of him, and if she fell the game was over forever.

Shortly after ten o'clock, a silver Porsche convertible pulled up in front of the A-frame. Lloyd nudged Bergen awake and said, "Our buddy is here. Follow my lead and when I touch my necktie interrupt me and buzz him with 'behind the green door' and 'beyond the beyond.' This guy had nothing to do with Jack Herzog, so don't even mention his name. You got it?"

Bergen nodded and squared his shoulders in preparation for his performance. Lloyd grabbed a flashlight and opened the car door just as a man got out of the Porsche and crossed the sidewalk in front of the A-frame. Bergen slammed his door, causing the man to turn around at the foot of the steps. "Police officers," Lloyd called out.

The man froze at the words, then walked forward in the direction of his car. Lloyd flashed the light square in his face, forcing him to throw up his hands to shield his eyes. "It—it's—ma-my car," he stammered. "I've got the pink in the glove compartment."

Lloyd studied the face. Blonde, bland, and cultured were his first impressions. He pointed his five cell at the ground and said, "I'm sure it is. Are you William Nagler?"

The man stepped off the curb and stroked the hood of the Porsche. Touching its sleekness gave an edge of propriety to his voice. "Yes, I am. What is this in regard to?"

Lloyd walked up to within inches of Nagler, forcing him back on the sidewalk. He held up his badge and played his light on it, then said, "L.A.P.D. My name is Hopkins, that's Sergeant Bergen. Could we talk to you inside?"

Nagler shuffled his feet. Lloyd held his light on the little dance of fear and saw that the worshipper was pigeon-toed to the point of deformity. "Why? Have you got a warrant? Hey! What are you doing!"

Lloyd turned around and saw Marty Bergen leaning into the Porsche, feeling under the seats. Nagler wrapped his arms around himself and shouted, "Don't! That's my car!"

"Cool it, Partner," Lloyd said. "The man is cooperating, so just maintain your coolness." Lowering his voice, he said to Nagler, "My partner's a black glove cop, but I keep him on a short chain. Can we go inside? It's cold out here."

Nagler brushed a lock of lank blonde hair up from his forehead. Lloyd eyed him openly and added competent and smart and very scared to his initial assessment.

"What's a black glove cop?"

As if on cue, Bergen walked over and stood beside Lloyd. "We should toss the vehicle," he said. "This bimbo's a doper, I can tell. What are you flying on, citizen? Ludes? Smack? Dust? Give me thirty seconds inside that glove compartment and I'll get us a righteous dope bust."

Lloyd gave Bergen a disgusted look. "This is a routine questioning of burglary victims, not a narc raid, so be cool. Mr. Nagler, can we go inside?"

Nagler's feet did another fear dance. "I'm not a burglary victim. I've never been burglarized and I don't know anything about any burglaries."

Lloyd put an arm around Nagler's shoulders and moved him out of Bergen's earshot. "All the houses on this block have been crawled," he said. "Sometimes the guy steals, sometimes not. A snitch of mine heard a tip that he's a panty freak, that he checks out all the pads he crawls for lingerie. What I want to do is check for fingerprints on your bedroom drawers. It will only take five minutes."

Nagler jerked himself free. "No. I can't allow it. Not without a warrant."

Pointing at Bergen, Lloyd whispered, "He's the senior officer, I'm just a forensic technician. If I can't print your drawers, he'll go cuckoo and frame you on a drug charge. His daughter O.D.'d on heroin and it flipped him out. He's about one step ahead of the net, so it wouldn't do to rile him. Please cooperate, Mr. Nagler, for both our sakes."

Nagler looked over his shoulder at Marty Bergen, who was now squatting and examining the front wheel covers of his Porsche. "All right, Officer. Just keep that man *away* from me."

Lloyd whistled, drawing Bergen away from his hubcap scrutiny. "Mr. Nagler is going to cooperate, Sergeant. Let's make it quick. He's a busy man."

"Dopers always are," Bergen said, walking over. He gave the Porsche a last glance and added, "I'll bet it's hot. We should check the hot sheet. We could get us a righteous G.T.A. bust." Leaning into Lloyd in a psuedo drunk's weave, he whispered, "What's my job inside?"

Seeing that Nagler was walking ahead to open the door, Lloyd faked a coughing attack, then said sotto voce, "Toss the pad for official papers, especially anything pertaining to property in Malibu. See if you can find something illegal to squeeze him with. Be menacing."

Nagler unlocked the door and turned on a light in the entrance foyer. He pointed inside and shivered, then wrapped his arms around himself and moved his inwardly bent feet together so that the toes were touching. Lloyd thought of a frightened animal trying to protect itself by curling into a ball and blending in with the scenery. The fear in the man's eyes made him want to strangle John Havilland for his complicity in that fear and strangle himself for what he might have to do. He caught Bergen's eyes and saw that his bogus partner was thinking along parallel lines and hoped that his rage would hold for the duration of his performance. When he felt his own rage subside in a wave of pity, he resurrected it by thinking of the guru-shrink slipping through loopholes in the legal process and said, "Let's sit down and talk for a minute first, Mr. Nagler. There's a few questions I have."

Nagler nodded assent. Lloyd walked through the foyer into a living room furnished with plastic high-tech chairs and a long sofa constructed of bean-bags and industrial tubing. Bergen sauntered in behind him, going straight for a portable bar on casters. Sitting down in a lavender armchair that creaked under his weight, Lloyd saw Western movie posters beam down at him from all four walls. Nagler perched himself on the edge of the sofa and said, "Will you *please* make this fast?"

Lloyd smiled and said, "Of course. This is a charming living room, by the way." He pointed to the posters. "Are you a movie buff?"

"I'm a free-lance art director and an amateur filmmaker," Nagler said, leveling worried eyes at Marty Bergen. "Now please get to your questions."

Bergen chuckled and poured himself a large shot of Scotch. "I think this pad sucks, and I think this bimbo is just holding down this art director gig as a front for his dope racket." He downed the drink and poured another. "What are you dealing, citizen? Weed? Speed? *Dust?* That's it, Hoppy! This is a *dust bust!*"

Nagler fretted his hands and pleaded to Lloyd with his eyes. Bergen guzzled Scotch, then blurted out, "Jesus, I'm gonna be sick. Where's the can?"

Lloyd waved an arm toward the back of the house as Nagler drew his feet together and slammed the edge of the sofa with outwardly cocked wrists. Bergen took off running, making gagging sounds and holding his hands over his mouth. Lloyd shook his head and said, "I apologize for my colleague, Mr. Nagler."

"He's a terrible man," Nagler whispered. "He has a low karma consciousness. Unless he changes his life radically, he'll never go beyond his low efficacy image."

Lloyd noted that the recitation of the mini-spiel had had a calming effect on Nagler. He honed his own spiel to razor sharpness and said, "Yes, I do pity him. He has so many doors to go beyond before he finds out who he really is."

The razor drew blood. Nagler's whole body relaxed. Lloyd threw out a smile calculated to flash "kindred soul." Thinking, *hook him now*, he said, "He needs spiritual guidance. A spiritual master is just the ticket for him. Don't you agree?"

Nagler's face lit up, then clouded over with what looked to Lloyd like an aftertaste of doubt and fear. Finally he breathed out, "Yes. Please get on with your business and leave me in peace. *Please.*"

Lloyd was silent, charting interrogation courses while he got out a pen and notepad. Nagler fidgeted on the edge of the sofa, then turned around when footsteps echoed behind him.

"*Achtung*, citizen!"

Lloyd looked up from his notepad to see Marty Bergen hovering next to the sofa, holding a glass freebase pipe out at arm's length. "Thought you were cool, didn't you, citizen? No dope on the premises. However, you overlooked the new possession of drug paraphernalia law recently passed by the state legislature. This pipe and the ether on your bathroom shelf constitute a misdemeanor."

Bergen dropped the pipe into Nagler's lap. Nagler jerked to his feet and threw his hands up to his face; the pipe fell to the floor and shattered. Bergen, florid faced and grinning from ear to ear, looked at Lloyd and said, "This is fucking ironic. I wrote an editorial condemning that law as fascist, which of course it is. Now I'm here enforcing it. Ain't life a bitch?" He reached into his back pocket and pulled out a wad of paper. "Check this out," he said.

Lloyd stood up, grabbed the papers and walked over to the shivering worshipper. Steeling himself against revulsion, he said, "You have the right to remain silent. You have the right to have legal counsel present during questioning. If you cannot afford counsel, an attorney will be provided. Do you have a statement to make regarding that paraphernalia, Mr. Nagler?"

The answer was a series of body shudders. Nagler pressed himself into the wall, trembling. Lloyd put a gentle hand on his shoulder and felt a jolt of almost electric tension. Looking down at the worshipper's feet, he saw that they were twisting across each other, as if trying to gouge the ankles. The brutality of the posture made Lloyd turn away and seek out Marty Bergen for a semblance of sanity.

The image backfired.

Bergen was standing by the bar, guzzling Scotch straight from the bottle. When he saw Lloyd staring at him, he said, "Learning things you don't like about yourself, Hot Dog?"

Lloyd walked to Bergen and grabbed the bottle from his hands. "Guard him. Don't touch him and don't talk to him; just let him be."

This time the answer Lloyd got was Bergen's grin of self-loathing; a smile that looked like a close-up of his own soul. Taking the bottle with him, he walked to a small den off the living room hallway and found the phone. He dialed Linda's number and let it ring ten times. No answer. Checking his watch, he saw that it was 10:40. Linda had probably gotten tired of waiting for his call and had left.

Lloyd put down the phone, knowing that he had wanted the comfort of Linda's voice more than her confirmation of Havilland's prints on the magnum. Remembering Bergen's wad of paper, he reached into his pocket and extracted it, smoothing it out on the desk beside the phone.

It was a real estate brochure listing properties in Malibu and the Malibu Colony. Attached to the top of the front page were "complimentary" Pacific

Coast Highway parking stickers for the period 6/1/84 to 6/1/85. A soft "bingo" sounded in Lloyd's mind. Beach area realtors gave away the hundred-dollar-a-year resident stickers to their preferred customers. It was a solid indication that Nagler had property in Malibu—property that he let John Havilland use, but held the deed to for tax purposes and secrecy. Havilland would undoubtedly *not* let his worshippers confer with him at his office or Beverly Hills condo—but a beach house owned by an *especially* trusted worshipper would be the ideal place for individual or group meetings.

He read the name of the realtor on the front of the brochure—Ginjer Buchanan Properties. The phone number was listed below it. Lloyd dialed it on the off-chance that an eager beaver salesperson might still be at the office. When all he got was a recorded message, he called information and got a residential listing for a Ginjer Buchanan in Pacific Palisades. He dialed that number and got another machine, this one featuring reggae music and the realtor's importunings to "leave a message at the tone and I'll call you from the Twilight Zone."

Thinking of the Los Angeles Police Department as both the keepers and inmates of the Twilight Zone, Lloyd rifled the desk drawers looking for official paper pertaining to Malibu property. Finding nothing but stationery and invoices for movie equipment, he walked down the hall looking for other likely rooms to toss. The bathroom and kitchen would probably yield zilch, but at the end of the hallway stood a half-opened door.

Lloyd walked to it and fumbled at the inside wall for a light switch. An overhead light went on, framing a small room filled with haphazardly discarded movie cameras, rolls of film, and developing trays. The floor was a mass of broken equipment, with plaster chips torn loose from the walls. Noticing a Movieola that remained intact atop a metal desk, Lloyd peered in the viewfinder and saw a celluloid strip showing a pair of inert legs clad in white stockings.

He was about to examine the equipment more closely when singing and chanting blasted from the living room. Walking back to investigate, Lloyd saw and heard a hellish two-part harmony.

Marty Bergen was standing over a kneeling William Nagler, strumming an imaginary guitar and singing, "They had an old piano and they played it hot behind the green door! don't know what they're doin', but they laugh a lot behind the green door! Won't someone let me in so I can find out what's behind the green door!"

When Bergen fell silent, fumbling for more verses, Nagler's chanting took precedence. *"Patria infinitum patria infinitum patria infinitum."* Muttered in a droning monotone punctuated by the worshipper's banging of his prayer-clasped hands against his chest, the words seemed to rise from a volition far older and darker than John Havilland or his murderer-father. *"Patria infinitum patria infinitum patria infinitum patria infinitum patria infinitum."*

Bergen snapped to Lloyd's presence and shouted above the chanting, "Hi, Hoppy! Think I'll make the top forty with this? Green Door Green Door Green Door!"

Lloyd grabbed Bergen and shoved him to the wall and held him there, hissing, "Shut the fuck up now, and don't drink another drop. Go toss the rest of the pad for Nagler's I.R.S. forms and income tax returns. Don't say another fucking word, just do it."

Bergen tried to smile. It came out a death grin. "Okay, Sarge," he said.

Lloyd released Bergen and watched him ooze off the wall. When he shambled away, the chanting became the dominating aspect of the room. *"Patria infinitum patria infinitum patria infinitum patria infinitum patria infinitum."*

Lloyd knelt in front of the worshipper, watching his trance grow deeper with each blow to the heart, memorizing every detail of the flagellation in order to justify his next move. When Nagler's glazed eyes and heaving lungs were permanently imprinted in his mind, he swung a full power open hand at his head and saw the trance crumble as the worshipper was knocked off his knees screaming, "Doctor!"

Lloyd, knocked loose of his own equilibrium, pinned Nagler's shoulders to the floor and shouted, "Havilland's dead, William. Before he died he said that you were a chump and a fool and a dupe."

Nagler's glazed eyes zeroed in on Lloyd. "No. No. No. *Patria infinitum. Patria infin—*"

Lloyd dug his fingers into the worshipper's collarbone. "No, William, you can't. You can't go back."

"Doctor!"

"Shhh. Shhh. You can't, Bill. You can't go back."

"Doctor!"

Lloyd dug his fingers deeper, until Nagler started to sob. Withdrawing his hands altogether, he said, "He talked about how he used you, Bill. How he got you to pay his phone bills, how he made you his slave, how he laughed at you, how your movies were shit, how you had all that expensive equipment, but you did—"

Lloyd stopped when Nagler's sobs trailed off into a terrified stutter. "Hor-hor-hor-moo-hor-moo."

"Shhh, shhh," Lloyd whispered. "Take it slow and think the words out."

Nagler stared up at Lloyd. The look on his face wavered between grief and bliss. Finally the bliss prevailed long enough for him to say, "Horror movie. Doctor John made a horror movie. That's how I know you're lying about what he said about me. He appreciates my talent. I edited the movie and Doctor said—he said . . ."

Lloyd stood up, then helped Nagler to his feet and pointed him toward the sofa. When Nagler was seated, he studied his face. He looked like a man about to enter the gas chamber who didn't know whether or not he wanted to die. Knowing that the bliss/death part of the worshipper had the edge and possessed the potential to produce lucid answers, Lloyd quashed his impulse to bludgeon Nagler into grief/life. Sighing, he sat down beside the ravished young man and stabbed in the dark. "Havilland isn't really dead, Bill."

"I know that," Nagler said. "He was here this morning with—" He stopped and flashed a robot smile. "He was here this morning."

Lloyd said, "Finish the thought, Bill."

"I did. Doctor John was here this morning. End of thought."

"No. Beginning of thought. But let's change the subject. You don't really think I'm a policeman, do you?"

Nagler shook his head. "No. Doctor John told me that there was a three percent leak factor in our program. I know exactly what the leak was—it came to me while I was chanting. You're an Internal Revenue agent. I paid Doctor John's phone bills while he went skiing in Idaho last December. You checked the records out, because you're with big brother. You also cross-checked my bank records and the Doctor's, and saw that I sent him a big check last year. He probably forgot to report it on his tax return. You want a bribe to keep silent. Very well, name your amount and I'll write a check." Nagler laughed. "How silly of me. That would leave a record. No, name your amount and I'll pay you off in cash."

Lloyd gasped at Nagler's recuperative powers. Five minutes earlier, he had been a groveling mass. Now he held the condescending authority of a plantation owner. A "horror movie" and the wrecked equipment in the back room were the dividing points. Thinking, *Break him,* he said, "Didn't it surprise you that my partner knew enough to sing you that song?"

"No. A song is a song."

"And a movie is a movie," Lloyd said, reaching into his pocket. "Bill, it's time I came clean. Doctor John sent me to test your loyalty." He held out the mug-shot strip of Thomas Goff. "I'm the replacement for the old recruiter. You remember this fellow, don't you? There's a guy on Doctor John's program who looks just like him. I know all about the meetings at the house in Malibu and how you bought the house for the Doctor and how you pay the phone bill. I know about the pay phone contacts and how you don't fraternize outside the meetings. I know because I'm one of you, Bill."

First grief, then bliss, now bewilderment. Lloyd had kept his eyes averted from Nagler, letting him feast on Thomas Goff's image instead of his own. When he finally reestablished eye contact he saw that the man had fingered the mug-shot strip to pieces and that his spiel had turned him into clay. Feeling like a bullfighter going in for the kill, Lloyd said, "I also lied when I said that Doctor John said that your movies were shit. He really loves your movie work. In fact, just today he told me that he wants you to both star in *and* direct the script he's working on. He tol—"

Lloyd stopped when Nagler's grief took him over. "*Patria infinitum patria infinitum patria infinitum patria infinitum.*"

Lloyd thought of Linda and got up and walked toward the den and the telephone. He had his hand on the receiver when a tap on his shoulder forced him to jump back, turn around, and ball his fists.

It was Bergen, looking eerily sober. "I couldn't find any I.R.S. papers," he said, "but I did find our pal's diary under his bed. Renaissance weird, Hopkins. Fucking gothic."

Lloyd took the morocco bound book from Bergen's hands and sat down on the desk. Opening it, he saw that the first entry was dated 11/13/83, and that it and all the subsequent entries were written in an exquisitely flourished longhand. While Bergen stood over him, he read through accounts of Havilland's "programming," picking up a cryptically designated cast along the way. There was the "Lieutenant," who had to be Thomas Goff; the "Fox," the "Bull dagger," the "Bookworm," the "Professor," the "Muscleman," and "Billy Boy," who had to be Nagler himself.

The entries themselves detailed how Havilland ordered his charges to fast for thirty-six hours, then stand nude in front of full-length mirrors and chant their "fear mantras" into tape recorders, until "subliminal dream consciousness" took over and led them to babble "transcendental fantasies" that he would later sift through for "key details" to translate into "reality fodder." How he paired them off sexually at the "Beach Womb," interrupting the couplings to take vital signs and "stress readings"; how he forced them to kill dogs and cats as "insurance against moral flaccidity"; how the "Lieutenant" interrupted their REM sleep with late night phone calls and brutal interrogations into their dreams.

Alternately using the first person "I" and the third person "Billy Boy," Nagler described how he and Doctor John's other counselees were pimped out to wealthy people who advertised for "fantasy therapists" in privately published and circulated sex tabloids, the weekend "lovemaking seminars" often netting Havilland several thousand dollars, and how the "beach womb groupings" were taped and transcribed by the "Lieutenant," who sometimes served as the "Chef"—concocting mixtures of pharmaceutical cocaine and other prescription drugs that the Doctor would administer to his counselees under "test-flight conditions."

Lloyd leafed full-speed through the diary, looking for incriminating facts: names, addresses and dates. With Marty Bergen hovering beside him and Nagler's muffled chanting coming in from the living room, he felt like the sole outpost of sanity in a lunatic landscape, the feeling underlined by the fact that the diary contained *no* facts—only narrated disclosures peopled with coded characters.

Until an entry dated the day before jumped out at him:

Helped set up movie equipment at the Muscleman's house in the Hollywood Hills. Doctor John supervised. I showed him how to operate the camera. I hope Muscleman won't break anything. He scares me—and he looks more and more like the Lieutenant these days.

The entry was followed by a blank page, followed by the diary's concluding entry, dated that morning. Lloyd felt an icepick at his spine as he read,

It's not real. They faked it. You can fake anything with new camera technology. It's a fake. It's not real.

Lloyd shoved Bergen aside and walked back to the movie room and searched among the upended equipment for film scraps, finding three strips of celluloid wedged underneath the editing machine. Running them through the machine's feeder-viewfinder, he saw four close-ups of a woman's white nyloned legs, a long shot of a mattress on a carpeted floor and a blurred extreme close-up of a broad-chested man with what looked like an L.A.P.D. badge pinned to his shirt.

The icepick jabbed his heart. Lloyd thought of the white-stockinged nurse that Richard Oldfield had brought to his house twenty-four hours before. The knife twisted, dug and tore, accompanied by a deafening burst of *patria infinitums* from the living room.

Lloyd walked toward the sound, finding Nagler still in his mantra pose and Bergen standing beside the fireplace, pouring bottles of liquor over the acrylic "firewood" on the grate. "Long-term interrogation, Sarge," he said. "It won't do to get tempted. What's next?" His ghoul grin had become a feisty smirk, and for one split-second Lloyd found a beacon of sanity.

"I'm leaving, you're staying here," he said. "I have to check on someone. Then, if she got my evidence, I have to take our friend's guru out. You stay here and watchdog him. Hang by the phone. If I need you, I'll ring once, then call back immediately."

"I want in on the bust," Bergen said.

Lloyd shook his head. "No. Just having you *here* could cause me lots of grief, and I'm not risking my job or *you* any further." He watched Bergen's smirk go hangdog. "What are you going to do when all this is over?"

Bergen laughed as he poured out a bottle of Courvoisier V.S.O.P. "I don't know. Jack left me close to twenty grand, maybe I'll just see where that takes me." When Lloyd didn't react to his mention of the money, he said, "You *knew* about the bank draft, right?"

Lloyd said, "Yeah. I didn't report it because I knew I.A.D. would try to seize your account as evidence."

"You're a good shit, Hopkins. You know that?"

"Sometimes."

"What are *you* going to do when this is over?"

Lloyd thought of Linda and Janice and his daughters, then looked over at the devastated William Nagler, still chanting at demons. "I don't know," he said.

24

The Night Tripper sat at the recording console in the Beach Womb, listening to Richard Oldfield and Linda Wilhite make frightened small talk upstairs in bedroom number three. The split-second accuracy of his fate had taken on ironic overtones. Linda's screaming of "Hopkins" combined with the gun in her purse was a tacit admission that the genius cop had figured it out on the same day that he had broken through his childhood void. Richard had blown his chance to kill Hopkins, and his contingency plan to drive Linda over the edge with the snuff film and have *her* commit the murder had backfired. After twenty-seven years devoted to venting his terror through others, it had all come down to himself. He had claimed his father's heritage, gaining autonomy along with the knowledge that the game was over. God was a malevolent jokester armed with a blunt instrument called irony.

Havilland leaned back in the chair that Thomas Goff used to occupy, feeling a conscious version of his dream disengagement split him in two. His left side imagined whirling corkboards, while his right side heard words issuing from the bedroom where Richard guarded the object of his corkboard fantasies. Soon exhaustion crept up. The spinning of the corkboard dominated, while the words played on, like dim music at the edge of sound.

". . . why are you staring at me?"

"Doctor said to watch you."

"Do you do everything he tells you to do?"

"Yes. Why are you making nasty faces at me? I've been gentle with you."

"Because Doctor said to be gentle? No, don't answer, it'll only make me hate you more. For your information, drugging and kidnapping is not a gentle activity. Are you aware of that?"

"Yes. No. You're very beautiful."

"Jesus. Was that movie for real? I mean, there was the awful part, and then this close-up of you. Listen, are you Thomas Goff?"

"I told you my name was Richard."

"All right, but what about the movie. *Was* it real? My mother was killed like that, with a pillow and a gun. Is the movie part of your crazy guru's plans for me?"

"What movie?"

"Jesus. Are you high? I mean, on something besides insanity? You know, on drugs?"

"Doctor gives me tranquilizers and antidepressants. Prescription stuff. He's a doctor, so it's legal and not bad."

"*Not bad?* Havilland's a Doctor Feelgood to boot? No, don't answer, I know he's capable of anything. I'm not going to let you hurt me, you know. Never. Not ever."

"I don't want to hurt you."

"Jesus, you sound like Peter Lorre. Does it turn you on that I'm not scared?"

"Yes. No. No!"

"First responses are always the most honest, Richard. If you or that psychopath downstairs tried to hurt me, I'd kick and bite and scratch and rub lye in your eyes. I—"

"I don't want to hurt you! I've done my hurting! It wasn't good!"

"Y-you—you mean you hurt other women?"

"Yes! No! I mean they hurt *me*. Me! Me! Me! Me. Me."

"Who hurt you? What are you talking about?"

"No. Doctor said I should talk to you, but not about bad things."

"Bad things, hmm? Okay, we'll change the subject. Let me ask you a question. Do you honestly think that those overdeveloped muscles of yours are a turn-on to women?"

"No. Yes. Yes!"

"First responses, Richard, and you're right. A woman sees a man like you and thinks, 'This guy is so insecure that he spends three hours a day at the gym with all the fags and narcissists, building himself up outside so I won't know how scared he is inside.' I've got a lover who's bigger than you and probably almost as strong, but he's got a trace of flab on his stomach and hips. And I dig it. You know why? Because he lives in reality and does a good job of it, and he hasn't got time to pump iron. So don't think that your muscles impress me."

"The . . . they're for protection."

"From the people who hurt you? From the *woman* who hurt you?"

"Yes."

"Aha, the truth outs. Let me set you straight on something. Muscles don't rule the world, brains do. Which is how a wimp like Havilland can make a slave out of someone big and strong like you. People protect each other with their love, not their muscles. Someone, probably some woman, hurt you really badly. She didn't do it with her muscles, because she didn't have any. You can't get revenge by hitting back at people the way they hit at you, because then the people who hurt you win—by making you like them. Aren't you hip to that?"

"No. It's different with Doctor John. He took me beyond my beyond."

"What's your beyond?"

"No!"

"Hurting women? You can't hurt me, because I'm smarter than you and stronger than you, and because that wimp downstairs told you not to. Some fucking beyond. Brown-noser to a freaked-out headshrinker who's going to end up in the locked ward at Camarillo for life. Who's going to protect you when he's wearing a straitjacket and sucking baby food out of a straw?"

"No! No! No no no no no. No."

"Yes, Richard. Yes. Besides, how many beyonds have you got? One? Two? Three? You don't seem too fulfilled to me. It's old wimpy's beyonds we're talking about, Richard. I almost wish you'd try to get violent with me, so I'd know you had the guts to disobey your slavemaster."

"What makes you think you're so smart and so tough?"

"I don't know. Do you know that I'm not scared of you?"

"Yes."

"Then that's your answer."

"What would you do if I tried to hurt you?"

"Fight back. Watch you get turned on and watch you lose."

"Doctor said you're a whore. Whores are wrong. Whores are bad."

"You almost got me there, but you missed by a few days. I quit. I walked. *I walked.* You can, too. You can walk out the door and wave goodbye to the Doctor, and he'll be terrified, because without you he's just another L.A. fruitcake with no place to hang his hat. Think on that. I'm going to try to sleep, but you think on that."

The Night Tripper awakened, instantly aware that his corkboard dreams had destroyed the music voices in bedroom number three. He checked the console and saw that he had forgotten to hit the "record" switch, then heard a soft male sobbing come over the speakers and pictured Richard distraught over his dictate not to hurt the whore.

Richard was a day too late. Linda was his. In the morning he would sacrifice her to his father's memory. He would end the game on his own terms.

25

Dawn.

Lloyd sped north on Pacific Coast Highway, running on adrenaline, rage, and terror. His jeopardy gambit had become a sacrificial offering, and if the fires had already been fed, he would have to take out the Beach Womb and everyone in it and throw himself into the flames. He looked at the pump shotgun resting on the seat beside him. Five rounds. Enough for Havilland, Oldfield, two miscellaneous worshippers, and himself.

The thought of self-immolation jerked his mind off of the immediate future and back to the immediate past. After leaving Bergen and Nagler, he had driven to Linda's apartment. She was not there, and her Mercedes was not in the garage. Now frightened, he had run dome light and siren to Havilland's Century City office. The night watchman in the lobby told him that he had admitted a very beautiful young woman at about seven o'clock, and that an hour later the nice Dr. Havilland and another man had brought her downstairs, looking high as a kite. "Emergency tooth extraction," the Doctor had said. "I'm not a dentist, but I gave it a go anyway." The two men had then hustled the near-comatose woman off in the direction of the parking lot.

After frantically driving by Havilland's Beverly Hills condo and finding no one there, Lloyd had run code three to the Pacific Palisades residential address of Ginjer Buchanan of Ginjer Buchanan Properties. The woman was not at home, but her live-in housekeeper succeeded in rousing her by phone at her boyfriend's apartment in Topanga Canyon. After Lloyd explained the urgency of the matter, the realtor agreed to meet him at her office with the information he needed. An hour later, at five A.M., he was staring at a floor plan of the Beach Womb.

Then the terror that he had held at bay by movement took over. If he called the Malibu sheriffs for assistance, they would storm the beachfront house S.W.A.T. style, with all the accoutrements of military/police overkill: Gas, machine guns, bullhorns, and the substation's lackluster hostage negotiation team. Loudspeaker amplified pleas, counterpleas and simplistic psychological manipulation that Havilland would laugh at; itchy-fingered deputies weaned on TV cop shows; automatic weaponry fired in panic. Linda in the crossfire. No. The jeopardy gambit came down to himself.

Again Lloyd looked at his Ithaca pump. When the taste of cordite and charred flesh rose in his throat, he pulled over to the side of the highway and a long row of pay phones. Jungle Jack Herzog redux—with a blackmail demand.

He had the receiver to his ear and a handkerchief over the mouthpiece when a strangely familiar vehicle ground to a halt behind his cruiser. Squinting through the Plexiglas, he saw Marty Bergen get out on the driver's side door and walk over to the booths, holding a quart bottle of beer out at arm's length, as though he were afraid of being contaminated. Lloyd slammed down the receiver, wondering how someone so sad could look so scary.

Bergen smiled. "Maintenance jug. I haven't touched it yet. Emergencies only. You looked scared, Hopkins. Really scared."

Lloyd grabbed the bottle and smashed it to pieces on the pavement. Only when the smell of beer hit his nostrils did he realize what he had done. "I told you to stay with Nagler."

"I couldn't. I had to move, so I tied him up and split. Is that a misdemeanor or a felony? When I was on the job I never did learn the penal code."

"How did you find me?"

"That one I do know: 413.5—Impersonating a Police Officer. I called the number on the real estate brochure. The woman told me you'd just walked out the door. She gave me the guru guy's address. I was headed up there when I saw your car."

Lloyd started to see red. "And?"

Bergen squared his shoulders. "And this is vigilante shit all the way. Where's the backup units? Where's the sheriff's black-and-whites? It's all about to come down, and you're here by your lonesome looking scared.

Why? Personally, I think we should go in full bore, fire team, copters, tear gas, snipers, I—"

Lloyd swung an overhand right at Bergen's jaw. Bergen caught the blow flush and went down on his back, then got up on one knee and began flailing with both arms, his eyes squeezed shut. Lloyd started to bring up an uppercut, then hesitated and moved backward into the phone booth. He fed dimes to the coin slot until he realized he had deposited four times the required amount. Cracking the door for air, he deep breathed and dialed.

"Hello?"

The voice was Havilland's. Lloyd cleared his throat and brought his voice up to tenor register. "Doctor, this is Jack Herzog. I've been away for a while. I need to see you."

The Doctor's response was a startling burst of laughter. "Hello, Sergeant. Congratulations on a job well done."

Lloyd said, "I know all about you and your father. Herzog left a pile of notes. Let Linda go, Havilland. It's over."

"Yes, it is over, but Herzog's green door would prevent him from keeping notes, and if you had any evidence, storm troopers would already have assaulted me. And Linda is here of her own free will."

"Let me talk to her."

"No. Later perhaps."

"Hav—"

Lloyd doubled over as a blunt force crashed into his kidneys; he dropped the receiver and slid down the wall as Bergen uncoiled his fists and elbowed his way into the booth. Lloyd tried to get up, but stomach cramps forced him to remain bent over, retching for breath.

Bergen picked up the dangling receiver and spoke into it. "Hey guru man, this is Martin Bergen. I'm a reporter for the *Big Orange Insider*. Maybe Jack Herzog told you about me. Listen, Hopkins and I just broke Billy Boy Nagler. He told us all about your scam. The *Orange* is going to do an exposé on you, talk about how you cheated your way through medical school, how you studied pimp techniques with Western Avenue spades, how chronic impotence led you to become a spiritual master. You like it, guru? You feel like consenting to an interview?"

Lloyd got to his feet and shoved his ear in the direction of the receiver, shouldering Bergen partially aside, so that both men were able to hear the tail end of Havilland's scream, the long silence that came in its wake and the calm words that finally emerged. "Yes. An interview. You obviously know where I am. Come over. We'll barter for the truth."

The line went dead. Lloyd shoved Bergen out of the booth and limped over to his car, his abdominal pain abating with each step he took. Grabbing Ginjer Buchanan's floor plan from the glove compartment, he said, "Have you still got your thirty-eight?"

"Yes," Bergen whispered.

Lloyd spread the floor plan out on the hood of the cruiser. "Good. You knock on the front door, I'll go in upstairs on the beach side. There's a woman in the house. She's innocent. Don't go near her. Keep the Doctor talking for at least two minutes. If he tries to pull anything weird, kill him."

26

The Night Tripper switched on the living room amplifier and the bedroom number three speaker, then walked into the kitchen and found the 1984 equivalent of his 1957 Arkansas toad stabber, a short-bladed, serrated-edged steak knife. He stuck the weapon in his back pants pocket and called upstairs, "Richard, come here a second."

Oldfield appeared at the head of the stairs. "Yes, Doctor?"

"We're having a visitor," Havilland said. "Maybe more than one. Stay upstairs in number three and stick close to Linda. Listen for strange noises. When you hear 'now' come over the speaker, bring Linda down to me."

Nodding mutely, Oldfield about-faced and walked back down the hall. Havilland stared at the front door and counted seconds, savoring each little increment of time. He was up to six hundred and forty-three when the doorbell rang.

The Doctor opened the door, extending his second count to six hundred and fifty, standing perfectly still as he eyed the burned-out figure who had maneuvered at the center of the Alchemist's life and the unseen periphery of his own. "Please come in," he said.

Bergen entered, hunching forward with his hands jammed in his windbreaker pockets. "Nice décor," he said. "Too bad I didn't bring my note-book. I can never remember details unless I write them down."

Havilland pointed to a pair of armchairs facing the latticework patio and the beach. Bergen walked over and sat down, stretching his legs and cram-ming his hands deeper into his pockets. Sitting down beside him, the Doc-tor said, "Where's Hopkins?"

Bergen licked his lips. "Parked over on P.C.H., scared shitless. He's crazy about this girl you're holding, and he's afraid to move because he thinks you'll kill her. He suspects you of all kinds of felony shit, but his superiors won't let him move—no hard proof. We glommed Billy Boy's diary, but all we could get out of it were possible pandering beefs. You're clean, Doc."

Havilland breathed out slowly, wondering if the burnout's right hand was holding a gun. "Then you really have no intentions of writing an article on me? You came here to offer me a deal?"

"Right. Hopkins and I both want something personal. I want all your records pertaining to Jack Herzog destroyed. I don't want anyone to know that you counseled him. Hopkins wants the girl released safely. If you com-ply, Hopkins drops his investigation and lets the L.A.P.D. high brass deal with you, and I never write a word about you and your scam. What do you think?"

Havilland let the deal settle in on him. The selfishness of the men's mo-tives rang true, but they obviously didn't know that he knew the game was *over*. "And if I don't comply?"

Bergen pulled out his left hand and looked at his watch. "Then I attack you in print with a yellow journalistic fervor you wouldn't believe, and Crazy Lloyd goes after you with everything *he's* got. A word to the wise, Doc. They don't call him Crazy Lloyd for nothing."

Lloyd skirted the ocean side of the house, looking for the foundation stanchions mentioned on the floor plan. Holding the Ithaca pump in the crook of his arm, he hugged the edge of the sand, shielded from view from within the house by a wooden screen of crisscrossed trelliswork.

The rear stanchion was an ornately carved wooden pole leading up to a second-story balcony that was open at the front and enclosed by a trellis-work arbor immediately before the upstairs windows. Lloyd grabbed the pole with his right arm and inched himself up the narrow footholds pro-vided by the carving indentations, holding the shotgun out at arm's length. When he was just underneath the edge of the balcony, he slid the Ithaca pump up and over, wincing at the clatter and scrape of metal. Leaning his weight into the pole, he released his right arm and grabbed the edge with both hands, then hoisted himself onto the tar papered surface.

Hearing nothing but silence, Lloyd picked up the shotgun and tiptoed over to the enclosure, looking for an entry point. There were no built-in doors, but dead in the middle a section of wood had cracked and separated, providing a crawl space. Seeing no other way, Lloyd wedged himself through, splintering a large network of boards in the process. The sound exploded in his ears, and he closed his eyes to blot out the overwhelming sense that the whole world could hear it. When he opened them, he again heard nothing but silence, and realized that his finger had the Ithaca's trigger at half-squeeze.

Early morning light played through the gaps in the trelliswork and reflected off the second-floor windows. Lloyd threaded his way past piles of lounge chairs and over to the windows, hoping to find at least one unlatched. He was about to begin trying the hasps when he saw that the middle window was wide open.

Holding the shotgun out in front of him, he walked over and pulled back the curtains that blocked his view. Seeing nothing but an empty bedroom, he stepped inside and padded to the door. Opening it inward with trembling hands, he saw a long carpeted hallway and heard Marty Bergen's voice *surrounding* him: "We're reasonable men, aren't we? Compromise in the basis of reason, isn't it? We—"

Lloyd pulled the door shut, wondering how Bergen's voice would be carrying from two places at once. Then it hit him: William Nagler's diary had stated that Thomas Goff taped the Beach Womb groupings. The house was obviously equipped with speakers, amplifiers and bugging apparatus. Bergen and Havilland were downstairs talking, while an upstairs speaker was blasting their conversation.

Lloyd pushed the door open and peered out, cocking his ears in order to get a fix on the speaker. The sound of amplified coughing delivered it: The room across the hallway two doors down. Linda was flashing across his mind until Havilland's voice destroyed the image. "But you want innocence for Jack, and you can't have it. Hopkins wants the woman and he can't have her. *Now!*"

And then Linda was there in reality, propelled out of the speaker bedroom by an unseen force. Lloyd jumped out into the hallway when he saw her, catching a blurred glimpse of a moving object that she seemed to be

shielding. When Linda saw him, she screamed, "No!" and tried to duck
back into the room, revealing Richard Oldfield behind her.

"Hopkins, no!"

Linda stumbled and fell to the floor as Oldfield froze in the doorway.
Lloyd fired twice at eye level, blowing away Oldfield's retreating shadow
and half the doorframe. Muzzle smoke and exploding wood filled the hallway. Lloyd ran through it to find Linda on her feet, blocking his entrance
into the bedroom. She pummelled him with tightly balled fists until he
shoved her aside and saw an empty room and a half-open picture window
reflecting a descending object on its opposite side. Screaming "Oldfield!"
Lloyd pumped a shell into the chamber and blew the reflection and the
window to bits, staring into the rain of glass for geysers of red that would
mark first blood. All he saw was glass fallout; all he heard and felt was Linda
pushing herself into him, shrieking, "No!"

Until a shot reverberated stereophonically from downstairs and the bedroom speaker, tearing him away from Linda and down the hall to the head
of the stairs, from which he saw Bergen and Havilland wrestling on the
floor for Bergen's .38, kicking, flailing and gouging at each other, twisted
into one entity that made a clean shot at the Doctor impossible.

Lloyd fired blindly at the far downstairs well. Startled by the explosion,
Bergen and Havilland jerked apart from each other, letting the .38 fall between them. Lloyd hurtled down the stairs, pumping in another round and
taking a running bead on the Doctor's head. He was within a safe firing
perimeter when Havilland got his left hand on the revolver and aimed it at
Bergen's midsection. Bergen twisted away and brought his knees up to de-
flect Havilland's arm, again voiding Lloyd's target.

The Doctor's finger jerked the trigger twice. The first shot ricocheted off
the hardwood floor, the second shot tore through Bergen's jugular. Lloyd
saw *innocent* first blood cut the air and screamed, hearing his own terrified
wail dissolve into the sound of his Ithaca kicking off a wild reflex round and
the .38 blasting three times in its echo. When his tear-wasted vision
cleared, he saw Havilland stabbing Bergen in the stomach with a short-
bladed knife.

Lloyd felt everything move into a thunderous slow motion. Slowly he
worked the slide of his weapon; slowly he walked to the death scene and
aimed point-blank at Havilland's head. Slowly the Doctor looked up from
his second generation fate, dropped the knife and smiled.

Lloyd rested the muzzle on his forehead and pulled the trigger. The empty chamber click resounded like hollow thunder, snapping the slow motion sequence, sending everything topsy-turvy and breakneck fast. Suddenly Lloyd had the shotgun reversed and was slamming the butt into Havilland's face over and over again, until a jagged section of his cheek was sheared off and blood started to seep from his ears. Then the speed diminished into a vertiginous absence of light, and from deep nowhere a beautiful voice called out, "Walk, Richard. *Walk*."

27

The legal machinery took over, and for nine straight days, temporarily suspended from duty and held incommunicado at Parker Center, Lloyd watched the state of California and the City and County of Los Angeles bury Dr. John Havilland in an avalanche of felony indictments, a barrage of due process based on his ninety-four page arresting officer's report and Havilland's own written and taped memoirs.

The first indictment was for the murder of Martin Bergen. The Malibu District Attorney expected it to be an open and shut case, because a highly respected veteran police officer had witnessed the killing, and because the defendant appeared to have no known relatives or friends likely to press embarrassing lawsuits against either Sergeant Lloyd Hopkins or the Los Angeles Police Department for their jurisdictional foul-up on the "arrest."

Back-up charges were quick in coming, as federal agents investigating the Howard Christie murder moved in and seized *everything* at Havilland's Century City office, Beverly Hills condominium, and Malibu house. His handwritten notes alone led to three indictments for first degree murder, handwriting experts having examined verified specimens of the Doctor's script along with his diary notations stating that he had ordered Thomas Goff to "kill the proprietor of the liquor store on Sunset and the Hollywood Freeway as proof of your desire to move beyond your beyond." Identical match ups, three murder one indictments and an indictment for criminal conspiracy resulting.

The agents also found the deed to a storage garage in East Los Angeles, and upon checking it out discovered a yellow Toyota sedan and the de-composed body of Thomas Goff. A right index print belonging to John Havilland was found on the car's dashboard. The District Attorney of the City of Los Angeles ordered yet another murder indictment. The federal of-ficers could find no concrete evidence linking Havilland to the murder of Howard Christie, and gave up.

Four days into his forced sequestering, Captain Fred Gaffaney visited Lloyd at his typewriter storage room/domicile and told him that *any* report that he submitted explaining Martin Bergen's presence at the Malibu house would be accepted if he agreed to edit out all mention of former officer Jacob Herzog and all mention of the stolen L.A.P.D. files and the security firms and their files. The various prosecutors thus far involved in the case had read his ninety-four page epic and considered it "overly candid" and "potentially embarrassing to the prosecution." Lloyd agreed. Gaffaney smiled and told him it was a wise move—he would have been summarily shitcanned from the Department had he refused. Before he left, Gaffaney added that he would be appearing before the grand jury in two days. Was there any information he had held back? Lloyd lied and said, "No."

The worshippers of John Havilland were taken into custody, questioned and released after signing depositions elaborating their relationships with "Doctor John." A free-lance "deprogrammer" of religious cult captives was there to aid the district attorneys and D.A.'s investigators in their interro-gations. The combined coercion worked four out of five times, resulting in detailed accounts of brainwashing, dope experimentation, and sexual de-basement. Only William Nagler could not be convinced to talk. He screamed his mantra and ranted about "horror movies" and was ultimately released to the care of his parents, who admitted him to an expensive pri-vate sanitarium. The D.A.s were pleased overall with their questionings; the depositions would be juicy fodder for the grand jury, and they would spare the sad brainwashees the grief of a courtroom appearance.

Lloyd was not spared that grief. He spoke for four straight hours, almost verbatim from his new arrest report, omitting all mention of Herzog, the se-curity files and Martin Bergen's outsized role in his investigation. He ex-plained Bergen's presence at the death house as a simple case of a bulldog reporter hot on a story. When Lloyd concluded his own story, he did not mention Richard Oldfield or Linda Wilhite and their presences at the house, or how he happened to be unconscious when the first wave of sher-iff's deputies arrived on the scene. When he walked back to the witness table, Fred Gaffaney was there with a wink and glad tidings: his violations of L.A.P.D. canon were only going to cost him a thirty-day suspension without pay, a slap on the wrist for his vigilante hooliganism.

The final witness to appear before the grand jury was a Los Angeles County deputy medical examiner, who stated that in his opinion the flurry of indictments leveled at Havilland was overkill, because the Doctor's fall down a steep flight of stairs immediately before his arrest had resulted in severe and irrevocable brain damage. Havilland was destined to live out his years insensate, not knowing who, what, or where he was. The impact sustained by his fall had opened up lesions from a previous head injury, quadrupling the neurological destruction. The M.E. ended with the statement, "I tried to get the man to understand that I was a doctor, that I was there to examine him. It was like trying to explain relativity to a turnip. He kept looking at me so pathetically. He had no idea that it was over."

But Lloyd knew that it wasn't. There was the unfinished business of the horror movie and the big "why" of Linda's behavior at the Beach Womb. And when that was settled, there was the matter of homage to Marty Bergen.

Nine days after the incident the press had dubbed the "Malibu Massacre," Lloyd was released from his "voluntary incarceration" at Parker Center. His thirty-day suspension had twenty-one days left to go, and he was told to remain in Los Angeles for the next two weeks, in order to be available to the myriad D.A.s working on the Havilland case. He was also ordered not to speak to representatives of the media and to refrain from police work on any level.

Returning to Los Angeles at large, Lloyd found that John Havilland had become a cause for ghoulish celebration. The psychiatrist was still front-page news, and a number of nightclub comedians had made him the focal point of their shticks. The Big Orange Insider had dubbed him the "Witch Doctor," and the 1958 novelty song "Witch Doctor" by David Seville and the Chipmunks was re-released and climbing the top forty. Charles Manson was interviewed in his cell at Vacaville Prison and proclaimed Dr. John Havilland "a cool dude."

Medical authorities at the jail ward of the L.A. County Hospital proclaimed the Doctor a vegetable, and Lloyd resisted his own ghoulish impulse to visit his adversary in his padded cell and throw the phrase "snuff film" at what remained of his brain. Instead, before going home or partaking of any post-sequestering amenities, he drove to 4109 Windemere Drive.

No L.A.P.D. or Federal crime scene stickers on the doors or windows; layers of undisturbed dust on the junctures of doors and doorjambs. An ordinary looking Tudor cottage in the Hollywood Hills. Lloyd sighed as he circuited the house on foot. Stonewall. He hadn't mentioned Oldfield in any of his official reports or earlier communiqués, and the feds who had seized Havilland's property either hadn't come across Oldfield's name or had decided to ignore it. In their fearful haste to deny Jack Herzog, the L.A.P.D. and the F.B.I. were letting the sleeping dogs that were John Havilland's minions lie.

Lloyd broke into the house through a back window and went straight for the bedroom. A mattress lay on the carpeted floor, an identical visual match to the film scrap he had seen at Billy Nagler's workshop. Reddish-brown matter stained a swatch of carpet near the window. Recalling the adhesive bandage he had found on the front lawn the day before the Malibu apocalypse, Lloyd bent down and examined it. Blood.

Checking the rest of the house, Lloyd found it cleaned of personal belongings. No male clothing, no toilet articles, no legal or personal documents. Food, appliances and furniture remained. Oldfield had fled. And judging from the dust on the doorjambs, he had a good head start.

Driving back to Parker Center, he put all thoughts regarding Linda Wilhite out of his mind, coming to one solid conclusion. Havilland or Oldfield had destroyed the movie. Had the Department or the feds discovered it, he would have heard. Again he was dealing with theory and circumstantial evidence.

It took Officer Artie Cranfield a scant ten minutes to identify the reddish brown matter on the carpet swatch as type O+ blood. Thus armed with facts, Lloyd called the L.A.P.D. Missing Persons Bureau and requested the stats on all female caucasians age twenty-five to forty with type O+ blood reported missing over the past ten days. Only one woman fit the description—Sherry Lynn Shroeder, age thirty-one, reported missing by her parents six days before. Lloyd wept when the clerk ticked off her last known place of employment—Junior Miss Cosmetics.

He had watched her walk in the door.

Tears streaming down his face, Lloyd ran through the halls and out the door of Parker Center, knowing that he was exonerated and that it wasn't enough; knowing that the woman he wanted to love was innocent of the overall tapestry of evil; she had been psychically violated by a madman. In the parking lot, he slammed the hood of his car and kicked the grill and broke off the radio aerial and molded it into a missile of hate. Hurling it at the twelve-story monolith that defined everything he was, he sent up a vow to Sherry Lynn Shroeder and set out to plumb the depths of his whore/lover's violation.

A call to Telecredit revealed that Linda Wilhite had bank balances totaling $71,843.00 and had made no recent major purchases with any of her credit cards. Richard Oldfield had liquidated his three savings and checking accounts and had sold a large quantity of IBM stock for $91,350.00.

A trip to L.A. International Airport armed with D.M.V. snapshots of the two supplied the information that Oldfield had boarded a flight for New York City four days after the Malibu killing, paying cash for his ticket and using an assumed name. Linda had accompanied him to the gate. An alert baggage handler told Lloyd that the two didn't seem like lovers, they seemed more like "with-it" sister and "out-of-it" brother.

Lloyd drove back to L.A. proper feeling jealous and tired and somehow afraid to go home, afraid that there was something he had forgotten to do. He would have to confront Linda soon, but before he did that he needed to pay tribute to a fallen comrade.

Marty Bergen's landlady opened the door of her former tenant's apartment and told Lloyd that the people from the *Big Orange* had come by and taken his beat-up furniture and typewriter, claiming that he promised them to the tabloid in his common law will. She had let them take the stuff because it was worthless, but she kept the box that had the book he was working on, because he owed two months rent and maybe she could sell it to the real newspapers and make up her loss. Was that a crime?

Lloyd shook his head, then took out his billfold and handed her all the cash it contained. She grabbed it gratefully and ran down the hall to her own apartment, returning with a large cardboard box overflowing with typed pages. Lloyd took it from her hands and pointed to the door. The woman genuflected out of the apartment, leaving him alone to read.

The manuscript ran over five hundred pages, the typing bracketed with red-inked editorial comments that made it seem like a complete co-authorship. It was the story of two medieval warriors, one prodigal, one chaste, who loved the same woman, a princess who could only be claimed by traversing concentrically arrayed walls of fire, each ring filled with progressively more hideous and bloodthirsty monsters. The two warriors started out as rivals, but became friends as they drew closer and closer to the princess, battling demons who entered them as they entered each gauntlet of flame, growing telepathic as the guardians of each other's spirit. When the final wall of fire stood immediately before them, they revolted against the symbiosis and prepared to do battle to the death.

At that point the manuscript ended, replaced by contrapuntal arguments in two different handwritings. The quality of the prose had deteriorated in the last chapters. Lloyd pictured Jack Herzog pushed to the edge of his tether by the Witch Doctor, trying to forge poetry out of the horror of his flickering-out life. When he finally put the book down, Lloyd didn't know if it was good, bad, or indifferent—only that it had to see print as a hymn for the L.A. dead.

The hymn became a dirge as he drove to Linda Wilhite's apartment, hoping that she wouldn't be there, so he could go home and rest and prolong the sense of what might have been.

But she was.

Lloyd walked in the half-opened door. Linda was sitting on the living room sofa, perusing the classified section of the *Times*. When she looked up and smiled, he shuddered. No might-have-beens. She was going to tell him the truth.

"Hello, Hopkins. You're late."

Lloyd nodded at the classifieds. "Looking for a job?"

Linda laughed and pointed to a chair. "No, business opportunities. Fifty grand down and a note from the bank gets me a Burger King franchise. What do you think?"

Lloyd sat down. "It's not your style. Seen any good movies lately?"

Linda shook her head slowly. "I saw a preview of one, and got a vivid synopsis from one of the stars. The one print was destroyed, by me. I'd forgotten how good you were, Hopkins. I didn't think you knew that part of it."

"I'm the best. I even know the victim's name. You want to hear it?"

"No."

Lloyd mashed his hands together and brought them toward his chest, then stopped when he realized he was unconsciously aping Billy Nagler's worship pose. "Why, Linda? What the fuck happened with you and Oldfield?"

Linda formed her hands into a steeple, then saw what she was doing and jammed them into her pockets. "The movie was a crazy reenactment of my parents' deaths. Havilland pushed Richard into it. He ran part of the film for me at his office. I freaked out and screamed. Richard grabbed me, and they doped me and took me out to Malibu. Richard and I talked. I hit the one germ of sanity and decency that he had. I convinced him that he could

walk out the door like the movie and Havilland never existed. We were getting ready to walk when Havilland called out 'Now!' Marty Bergen could
have walked out with us. But then you showed up with your shotgun."

When Lloyd remained silent, Linda said, "Babe, it was the right thing to
do, and I love you for it. Richard and I took off running, and you could have
put the cops on to us, but you didn't, because of what you felt for me.
There's no rights and wrongs in this one. Don't you know that?"

Lloyd brought his eyes back from deep nowhere. "No, I don't know that.
Oldfield killed an innocent woman. He has to pay. And then there's *us*.
What about *that*?"

"Richard has paid," Linda said in a whisper. "God, has he paid. For the
record, he's long gone. I don't know where he is, and I don't want to know,
and if I *did* know, I wouldn't tell you."

"Do you have any idea what you did? *Do you*, goddamn it!"

Linda's whisper was barely audible. "Yes. I figured out that I could walk, and
I convinced someone else that he could, too. He deserves the chance. Don't
lay your guilt on me, Hopkins. If Richard hadn't gotten hooked up with Havilland he never would have killed a fly. What are the odds of his meeting
someone else like the Witch Doctor? It's over, Hopkins. Just let it be."

Lloyd balled his fists and stared up at the ceiling to hold back a flood of
tears. "It's not over. And what about us?"

Linda put a tentative hand on his shoulder. "I never saw Richard hurt
anybody, but I saw what you did to Havilland. If I hadn't seen it, maybe we
could have given it a shot. But now that's over, too."

Lloyd stood up. When Linda's hand dropped from his shoulder, he said,
"I'm going after Oldfield. I'll try to keep your name out of it, but if I can't,
I won't. One way or the other, I'm going to get him."

Linda got to her feet and took Lloyd's hands. "I don't doubt it for a
minute. This is getting funny and sad and weird, Hopkins. Will you hold me
for a minute and then split?"

Lloyd shut his eyes and held the most beautiful woman he had ever seen,
closing out the L.A. end of the Havilland case. When he felt Linda start to
retreat from the embrace, he turned around and walked, thinking that it
was over and it would never be over and wondering how he could get the
Herzog/Bergen book published.

Outside, the night shone in jetstreams of traffic light and in flames from
a distant brush fire. Lloyd drove home and fell asleep on the couch with his
clothes on.

SUICIDE HILL

To Meg Ruley

You're alone and you know a few things.
The stars are pinholes; slits in the hangman's mask

Them, rats, snakes;
the chased and chasers—

Thomas Lux

Psychiatric Evaluation Memorandum

From: Alan D. Kurland, M.D., Psychiatrist, Personnel Division
To: Deputy Chief T. R. Braverton, Commander, Detective Division;
    Captain John A. McManus, Robbery/Homicide Division
Subject: Hopkins, Lloyd W., Sergeant, Robbery/Homicide Division

Gentlemen:

As requested, I evaluated Sergeant Hopkins at my private office, in a series of five one-hour counseling sessions, conducted from 6 November to 10 November 1984. I found him to be a physically healthy and mentally alert man of genius-level intelligence. He was a willing, almost eager, participant in these sessions, belying your initial fears about his cooperation. His response to intimate questions and "attack" queries was unwaveringly honest and candid.

Evaluation: Sergeant Hopkins is a violence-prone obsessive-compulsive personality, this personality disorder chiefly manifesting itself in acts of excessive physical force throughout his nineteen-year career as a policeman. Following secondarily but directly in this overall behavior pattern is a strong sexual drive, which he rationalizes as a "counterbalancing effort" aimed at allaying his violent impulses. Intellectually, both of these drives have been justified by the exigencies of "the Job" and by his desire to uphold his reputation as a uniquely brilliant and celebrated homicide detective; in reality both derive from a strident pragmatism of the type seen in emotionally arrested sociopathic personalities—quite simply, a preadolescent selfishness.

Symptomatically, Sergeant Hopkins, a self-described "hot-dog cop" and admitted sybarite, has followed both his violent impulses and his sexual desires with the heedless fervor of a true sociopath. However, throughout the years he has felt deep guilt over his outbursts of violence and extramarital womanizing. This awareness has been gradual, resulting in both the resistance to eschew old behavior patterns and the desire to abandon them and thus gain peace of mind. This emotional dilemma is the salient fact of his neuroses, yet it is unlikely that it alone, by its long-term nature, could have produced Sergeant Hopkins's current state of near nervous collapse.

Hopkins himself attributes his present state of extreme anxiety, despondency, episodes of weeping and highly uncharacteristic doubts about his abilities as a policeman to his participation in two disturbing homicide investigations.

In January of 1983, Sergeant Hopkins was involved in the "Hollywood Slaughterer" case, a case that remains officially unsolved, although Hopkins claims that he and another officer killed the perpetrator, a psychopath believed to have murdered three people in the Hollywood area. Sergeant Hopkins (who estimated the Hollywood Slaughterer's victims to include an additional sixteen young women) was intimately involved with the psychopath's third victim, a woman named Joan Pratt. Feeling responsible for Miss Pratt's death, and the death of another woman named Sherry Lynn Schroeder, who was connected to the Havilland/Goff series of killings (May 1984), Hopkins has transferred that sense of guilt to twin obsessions of "protecting" innocent women and "getting back" his estranged wife and three daughters, currently residing in San Francisco. These obsessions, which represent delusional thinking of the type common to emotionally disturbed superior intellects, were at the core of the professional blunders which led to Sergeant Hopkins's present suspension from duty.

On October 17 of this year, Sergeant Hopkins had succeeded in locating a third Havilland/Goff suspect, Richard Oldfield, in New Orleans. Believing Oldfield to be armed and dangerous, he requested officers from the New Orleans P.D. to aid him in the arrest. Told to remain at a safe distance while the team of N.O.P.D. plainclothesmen apprehended the suspect, Hopkins disobeyed that order and kicked down Oldfield's door, hesitating when he saw that Oldfield was with a partially clothed woman. After screaming at the woman to get dressed and get out, Hopkins fired at Oldfield, missing him and allowing him to escape out the back way while he attempted to comfort the woman. The New Orleans officers apprehended Oldfield some minutes later. Two plainclothesmen were injured, one seriously, while making the arrest. Sergeant Hopkins said that his episodes of weeping began shortly after this incident.

At Oldfield's arraignment, Sergeant Hopkins was caught prevaricating on the witness stand by Oldfield's attorney. During our second session, he admitted that he faked evidence to obtain an extradition warrant for Oldfield, and that the reason for his courtroom lies was a desire to protect a woman involved in the Havilland/Goff/Oldfield case—a woman he was intimately involved with during the investigation. Sergeant Hopkins became verbally abusive at this point, bragging that he would never relinquish the woman's name to the district attorney or any police agency.

Conclusions: Sergeant Hopkins, forty-two, is experiencing cumulative stress reaction, severe type; is suffering severe nervous exhaustion, exacerbated by an intransigent determination to solve his problems himself—a resolve that implicitly reinforces his personality disorder and makes continued counseling untenable. As of this date I deem it impossible for Sergeant Hopkins to conduct homicide investigations without exploiting them in some social or sexual context. It is highly improbable that he can effectively supervise other officers; it is equally improbable that, given his grandiose self-image, he would ever submit to the performing of nonfield duties. His emotional stability is seriously impaired; his stress instincts disturbed to the point where his armed presence makes him at best ineffective, at worst highly dangerous as a Robbery/ Homicide detective. It is my opinion that Sergeant Hopkins should be given early retirement and a full pension, the result of a service-connected disability, and that the administrative processes involving his separation from the L.A.P.D. should be expedited with all due speed.

Sincerely,
Alan D. Kurland, M.D.
Psychiatrist

1

The sheriff's transport bus pulled out of the gate of Malibu Fire Camp #7, its cargo sixteen inmates awaiting release, work furlough and sentence modification, its destination the L.A. County Main Jail. Fifteen of the men shouted joyous obscenities, pounded the windows and rattled their leg manacles. The sixteenth, left unencumbered by iron as a nod to his status as a "Class A" firefighter, sat up front with the driver/deputy and stared at a photo cube containing a snapshot of a woman in punk-rock attire.

The deputy shifted into second and nudged the man. "You got a hard-on for Cyndi Lauper?"

Duane Rice said, "No, Officer. Do you?"

The deputy smiled. "No, but then I don't carry her picture around with me."

Thinking, fall back—he's just a dumb cop making conversation—Rice said, "My girlfriend. She's a singer. She was singing backup for a lounge act in Vegas when I took this picture."

"What's her name?"

"Vandy."

"Vandy? She got one name, like 'Cher'?"

Rice looked at the driver, then around at the denim-clad inmates, most of whom would be back in the slam in a month or two tops. He remembered a ditty from the jive-rhyming poet who'd bunked below him: "L.A.—come on vacation, go home on probation." Knowing he could outthink, outgame and outmaneuver any cop, judge or P.O. he got hit with and that his destiny was the dead opposite of every man in the bus, he said, "No, Anne Atwater Vanderlinden. I made her shorten it. Her full name was too long. No marquee value."

"She do everything you tell her to?"

Rice then gave the deputy a mirror-perfected "That's right."

"Just asking," the deputy said. "Chicks like that are hard to come by these days."

With banter effectively shitcanned, Rice leaned back and stared out the window, taking cursory notice of Pacific Coast Highway and winter deserted beaches, but *feeling* the hum of the bus's engine and the distance it was racking up between his six months of digging firebreaks and breathing flames and watching mentally impoverished lowlifes get fucked up on raisinjack, and his coming two weeks of time at the New County, where his sentence reduction for bravery as an inmate fireman would get him a job as a blue trusty, with unlimited contact visits. He looked at the plastic band on his right wrist: name, eight-digit booking number, the California Penal Code abbreviation for grand theft auto and his release date—11/30/84. The last three numbers made him think of Vandy. In reflex, he fondled the photo cube.

The bus hit East L.A. and the Main County Jail an hour later. Rice walked toward the receiving area beside the driver/deputy, who unholstered his service revolver and used it as a pointer to steer the inmates to the electric doors. Once they were inside, with the doors shut behind them, the driver handed his gun to the deputy inside the Plexiglas control booth and said, "Homeboy here is going to trusty classification. He's Cyndi Lauper's boyfriend, so no skin search; Cyndi wouldn't want us looking up his boodie. The other guys are roll-up's for work furlough and weekend release. Full processing, available modules."

The control booth officer pointed at Rice and spoke into a desk-mounted microphone. "Walk, Blue. Number four, fourth tank on your right."

Rice complied. Placing the photo cube in his flapped breast pocket, he walked down the corridor, working his gait into a modified jailhouse strut that allowed him to keep his dignity *and* look like he fit in. With the correct walk accomplished, he made his eyes burn into his brain a scene that he would never again relinquish himself to:

Prisoners packed like sardines into holding tanks fronted by floor-to-ceiling cadmium-steel bars; shouted and muffled conversations bursting from within their confines, the word "fuck" predominating. Trusties wearing slit-bottomed khakis listlessly pushing brooms down the corridor, a group of them standing outside the fruit tank, cooing at the drag queens inside. The screech and clang of barred doors jerking open and shut. Business as usual for institutionalized bulls and cons who didn't know they'd be shit out of luck without each other. Death.

The door to #4 slid open. Rice did a quick pivot and walked in, his eyes settling on the only other inmate in the tank, a burly biker type sitting on the commode reading a paperback Western. When the door slammed shut, the man looked up and said, "Yo, fish. You going to classification?"

Rice decided to be civil.

"I guess so. I was hoping for a blue trusty gig, but the bulls have obviously got other ideas."

The biker laid his book on the floor and scratched his razor stubble. "Obviously, huh? Just be glad you ain't big like me. I'm going to Trash and Freight sure as shit. I'll be hauling laundry bags with niggers while you're pushing a broom somewhere. What you in for?"

Rice leaned against the bars. "G.T.A. I got sentenced to a bullet, did six months at fire camp and got a modification."

The biker looked at Rice with eyes both wary and eager for information. Deciding to dig for his own information, Rice said, "You know a guy named Stan Klein? White guy about forty? He would have hit here about six and a half, seven months ago. Popped for possession and sale of cocaine, lowered to some kind of misdemeanor. He's probably out by now."

The biker stood up, stretched, and scratched his stomach. Rice saw that he was at least six-three, and felt a warning light flash in his head. "He a friend of yours?"

Rice caught a belated recognition of the intelligence in his eyes. Too smart to bullshit. "Not really."

"Not really?" The big man boomed the words. "Not really? *Obviously* you think I'm stupid. *Obviously* you think I don't know how to put two and two together or count. *Obviously* you think I don't know that this guy Klein ratted on you, made a deal with the fuzz and walked around the same time you got busted. *Obviously* you do not know that you are in the presence of a superior jailhouse intellect that does not enjoy being gamed."

Rice swallowed dry, holding eye contact with the big man, waiting for his right shoulder to drop. When the biker took a step backward and laughed, Rice stepped back and forced a smile. "I'm used to dealing with dumbfucks," he said. "After a while you start gearing your thinking to their level."

The biker chuckled. "This guy Klein fuck your woman?"

Rice saw everything go red. He forgot his teacher's warnings about never initiating an attack and he forgot the ritual shouts as he swung up and out with his right leg and felt the biker's jaw crack under his foot. Blood sprayed the air as the big man crashed into the bars; shouts rose from the adjoining tanks. Rice kicked again as the biker hit the floor; through his red curtain he heard a rib cage snap. The shouts grew louder as the electric door slammed open. Rice swiveled to see a half dozen billy clubs arcing toward him. Brief thoughts of Vandy kept him from attacking. Then everything went dark red and black.

Module 2700 of the Los Angeles Main County Jail is known as the Ding Tank. Comprised of three tiers of one-man security cells linked together by narrow catwalks and stairways, it is the facility for nonviolent prisoners too mentally disturbed to exist in the general inmate population: droolers, babblers, public masturbators, Jesus shriekers and mind-blown acidhead mystics awaiting lunacy hearings and eventual shipment to Camarillo and county-sponsored board-and-care homes. Although the "ding" inmates are kept nominally placid through the forced ingestion of high-powered tranquilizers, at night, when their dosages wear down, they spring verbally to life and create a din heard throughout the entire jail. When he returned to consciousness in a cell smack in the middle of Tier #2, Module 2700, Duane Rice thought he was dead and in hell.

It took him long moments to discover that he wasn't; that the tortured shouts and weeping noises were not blows causing the aches and throbs all over his torso. As full consciousness dawned, the pain started for real and it *all* came back, drowning out a nearby voice screaming, "Ronald Reagan sucks cock!" Reflexively, Rice ran his hands over his face and neck. No blood; no lumps; no bruises. Only a swelling around his carotid artery. Choked out and thrown in with the dings, but spared the ass-kicking the jailers usually gave brawlers. Why?

Rice took a quick inventory of his person, satisfying himself that his genitals were unharmed and that no ribs were broken. Taking off his shirt, he probed the welts and bruises on his torso. Painful, but probably no internal damage.

It was then that he remembered the photo cube and felt his first burst of panic, grabbing the shirt off the floor, slamming the wall when plastic shards fell from the wad of denim. His fists were honing in on the cell bars when the intact photo of Anne Atwater Vanderlinden dropped out of the right pocket and landed faceup on his mattress. Vandy. Safe. Rice spoke the words out loud, and the Ding Tank cacophony receded to a hush.

Her hush.

Rice sat down on the edge of the mattress and moved his eyes back and forth between the photograph and the scratched-on graffiti that covered the cell walls. Obscenities and Black Power slogans took up most of the print space, but near the wadded-up rags that served as a pillow laboriously carved declarations of love took over: Tyrone and Lucy; Big Phil & Lil Nancy; Raul y Inez por vida. Running his fingers over the words, Rice held the aches in his body to a low ebb by concentrating on the story of Duane and Vandy.

He was working as pit boss at a Midas Muffler franchise in the Valley, pilfering parts from the warehouse and selling them to Louie Calderon at half pop, twenty-six and on Y.A. parole for vehicular manslaughter, going nowhere and waiting for something to happen. Louie threw a party at his pad in Silverlake, promising three-to-one women, and invited him. Vandy was there. He and Louie stood by the door and critiqued the arriving females, concluding that for pure sex the skinny girl in the threadbare preppy clothes was near the bottom of the list, but that she had *something*. When Louie fumbled for words to explain it, Rice said, "Charisma." Louie snapped his fingers and agreed, then pointed out her shabby threads and runny nose and said, "Snowbird. I never seen her before. She just sees the open door and walks in, maybe she thinks she can glom some blow. Maybe she got charisma, but she got no fucking control."

Louie's last word held. Rice walked over to the girl, who smiled at him, her face alive with little tics. Her instant vulnerability ate him up. It was over as soon as it started.

They talked for twelve hours straight. He told her about growing up in the projects in Hawaiian Gardens, his boozehound parents and how they drove to the liquor store one night and never returned, his ability with cars and how his parents' weakness had given him a resolve never to touch booze or dope. She scoffed at this, saying that she and her brother were dopers because their parents were so uptight and controlled. Their rapport wavered until he told her the *full* truth about his manslaughter bust, wrapping up both their defiances with a bright red ribbon.

When he was twenty-two, he had a job tuning sports cars at a Maserati dealership in Beverly Hills. The other mechanics were loadies who were always ragging him about his disdain for dope. One night they fashioned a speedball out of pharmacy meth and Percodan and slipped it into his coffee, right before he went out to test the idle on a customer's Ferrari. The speedball kicked in as he was driving down Doheny. He immediately realized what was happening and pulled to the curb, determined to wait the high out and do some serious ass-kicking.

Then it got really bad. He started hallucinating and thought he saw the dope-slippers walking across the street a half block down. He gunned the engine, speed-shifted into second and plowed into them at seventy. The front bumper was torn off, the grille caved in, and a severed arm flew across the windshield. He downshifted, turned the corner onto Wilshire, got out and ran like hell, an incredible adrenaline jolt obliterating the dope rush. By the time he had run out of Beverly Hills, he felt in control. He knew that he had gotten his revenge, and now he had to play the game with the law and get off cheap.

A two-hour steam bath at the Hollywood Y sweated the rest of the speedball out of his system. He took a cab to the Beverly Hills police station, gouged his arm with a penknife to induce crocodile tears and turned himself in. He was charged with two counts of third-degree manslaughter and hit and run. Bail was set at $20,000, and arraignment was set for the following morning.

At arraignment, he learned that the two people he had killed were not the dope-slipping mechanics, but a solid-citizen husband and wife. He pleaded guilty anyway, expecting a deuce maximum, back on the street in eighteen months tops.

The judge, a kindly-looking old geezer, gave him a ten-minute lecture, five years state time suspended and his sentence: one thousand hours of picking up paper refuse from the gutters of Doheny Avenue between Beverly Boulevard on the north and Pico Boulevard on the south. After courtroom spectators applauded the decree, the judge asked him if he had anything to say. He said, "Yes," then went on to tell the judge that his mother sucked giant donkey dicks in a Tijuana whorehouse and that his wife turned tricks with the gorillas in the Griffith Park Zoo. The judge recanted his sentence suspension and hit him with five years in the California Youth Authority Facility at Soledad—the "Baby Joint" and "Gladiator School."

When Rice finished his story, Anne Vanderlinden doubled over with laughter and launched *her* rap, chain-smoking two full packs, until all the guests had either split or were coupled off in Louie's upstairs bedrooms. She told him about growing up rich in Grosse Pointe, Michigan, and her hard-ass tax lawyer father, Valium-addict mother and religious crackpot brother, who got bombed on acid and stared at the sun seeking mystical synergy until he went totally blind. She told him how she dropped out of college because it was boring and how she blew her $50,000 trust fund on coke and friends, and how she liked blow, but wasn't strung out. Rice found her use of street argot naive, but pretty well done. Knowing she was on the skids and probably sleeping around for a place to stay, he steered her talk away from the present and into the future. *What did she really want to do?*

Anne Vanderlinden's little facial tics exploded as she tripped over words to explain her love of music and her plans to spotlight her singing and dancing talents in a series of rock videos: one for punk, one for ballads, one for disco. Rice watched her features contort as she spoke, wanting to grab her head and smooth her face until she was perfectly soft and pretty. Finally he clutched her lank blonde hair and drew it back into a bun that tightened the skin around her eyes and cheeks, whispering, "Babe, you won't have shit until you quit sticking that garbage up your nose, and you find someone to look after you."

She fell sobbing into his arms. Later, after they made love, she told him it was the first time she'd cried since her brother went blind.

It was over the next few weeks, after Anne Atwater Vanderlinden had moved in with him and become Vandy, that he figured it out: you don't wait for things to happen—you make them happen. If your woman wants to become a rock star, you regulate her coke use and buy her a sexy wardrobe and cultivate music business connections who can do her some good. Vandy could sing and dance as well as a half dozen female rock stars he knew of, and she was too good to go the tried-and-untrue route of demo tapes, backup gigs and lackluster club dates. She had an ace in the hole. She had him.

And *he* had a chump change job at Midas Muffler, a parole officer who looked at him like he was something that crawled out from under a rock, and an overpriced apartment with world-class cockroaches. With his debits cataloged, Rice figured out his credits: he was a great mechanic, he knew how to deactivate automobile alarm systems and bore steering columns for a forty-second start, any car, anywhere, anytime; he knew enough industrial chemistry to compound corrosive solutions that would eat the serial numbers off engine blocks. He had solid Soledad connections who would fix him up with good fences. He would *make* it happen: become a world-class car thief, set up Vandy's career and get out clean.

For a year and a half, it worked.

With three strategically located storage garages rented, and armed with a battery-powered ignition drill, he stole late model Japanese imports and sold them at two-thirds their resale value to a buddy he'd known in the joint, supervising the engine block dips that rendered the cars untraceable, rotating his rip-off territory throughout L.A. and Ventura counties to avoid the scrutiny of individual auto theft details. In two months he had the down payment for a classy West L.A. condo. In three months he had Vandy primed for stardom with a health food diet, daily aerobics, coke as an occasional reward and three walk-in closets stuffed with designer threads. In four months he had the feedback of two high-priced voice teachers: Vandy was a weak, near tone-deaf soprano with virtually no range. She had a decent vibrato growl that could be jazzed up with a good amplifier, and gave great microphone head. She had the haunted sex look of a punk-rock star—and very limited talent.

Rice accepted the appraisals—they made him love Vandy more. He altered his game plan for crashing the L.A. rock music scene and took Vandy to Vegas, where he dug up three out-of-work musicians and paid them two bills a week to serve as her backup group. Next he bribed the owner of a slot machine arcade/bar/convenience store into featuring Vandy and the Vandals as his lounge act.

Four shows a night, seven days a week, Vandy's vibrato growled the punk lyrics of the group's drummer. She drew wolf whistles when she sang and wild applause when she humped the air and sucked the microphone. After a month of watching his woman perform, Rice knew she was *ready*.

Back in L.A., armed with professional photographs, bribed press raves and a doctored demo tape, he tried to find Vandy an agent. One brick wall after another greeted him. When he got past secretaries, he got straight brush-offs and "I'll call yous"; and when he got past them and whipped out Vandy's photos, he got comments like "interesting," "nice bod" and "foxy chick." Finally, in the Sunset Strip office of an agent named Jeffrey Jason Rifkin, his frustration came to a head. When Rifkin handed back the photos and said, "Cute, but I have enough clients right now," Rice balled his fists and took a bead on the man's head. Then inspiration struck, and he said, "Jew boy, how'd you like a brand-new silver gray Mercedes 450 SL absolutely *free?*"

A week later, after he picked up his car, Rifkin told Rice that he could introduce him to a lot of people who might help Vandy's career, and that her idea of showcasing her talent via a series of rock videos was an excellent "high-exposure breakthrough strategy," albeit expensive: $150–200 K minimum. *He* would do what he could with *his* contacts, but in the meantime he also knew a lot of people who would pay hard cash for discount Benzes and other status cars—people in the "Industry."

Rice smiled. Use and be used—an arrangement he could trust. He and Vandy went Hollywood.

Rifkin was partially good to his word. He never procured any recording or club gigs, but he did introduce them to a large crowd of semisuccessful TV actors, directors, coke dealers and lower-echelon movie executives, many of whom were interested in high-line cars with Mexican license plates at tremendous discounts. Over the next year, paperwork aided by an Ensenada D.M.V.-employed cousin of his old Soledad buddy Chula Medina, Rice stole 206 high-liners, banking close to a hundred fifty thou toward the production of Vandy's rock videos. And then just as he was about to drill the column of a chocolate-brown Benz ragtop, four L.A.P.D. auto theft dicks drew down on him with shotguns, and one of them whispered, "Freeze or die, motherfucker."

Out on $16,000 bail, his show biz attorney gave him the word: for the right amount of cash, his bank account would not be seized, and he would get a year county time. If the money were *not* paid, it would be a parole violation and probable indictments on at least another fifteen counts of grand theft auto. The L.A.P.D. had an informant by the balls, and they were squeezing him hard. He could only buy the judge if he acted now. If he were quickly sentenced, the L.A.P.D. would most likely drop its investigation.

Rice agreed. The decision cost him an even $100,000. His attorney's fees cost him an additional forty. Ten K for Vandy and bribe money his lawyer slipped to an L.A.P.D. records clerk to learn the identity of the informant had eaten up the rest of his bank account, and had not yielded the name of the snitch. Rice suspected the reason for this was that the shyster pocketed the bread because he knew that the snitch was Stan Klein, a coke dealer/entrepreneur in the Hollywood crowd they ran with. When he learned Klein had been popped for conspiracy to sell dangerous drugs and that it was later dropped to a misdemeanor, he became the number one suspect. But he had to be sure, and the decision to be sure had cost him his last dime and gotten him zilch.

And two weeks away from the release date he'd eaten smoke, fire and bullshit to earn, he'd fucked it up and probably earned himself a first-degree assault charge and *at least* another ninety days of county time.

And Vandy hadn't written to him or visited him in a month.

"On your feet, Blue. Wristband count."

Rice jerked his head in the direction of the words. "I won't let you medicate me," he said. "I'll fight you and the whole L.A. County Sheriff's Department before I let you zone me out on that Prolixin shit."

"Nobody wants to medicate you, Blue," the voice said. "A few of L.A. County's finest might wanta shake your hand, but that's about it. Besides, I can *sell* that goose juice on the street, make a few bucks *and* serve law and order by keeping the Negro element sedated. Let's try this again: wristband count. Walk over to the bars, stick your right wrist out to me, tell me your name and booking number."

Rice got up, walked to the front of the cell and stuck his right arm through the bars. The owner of the voice came into focus on the catwalk, a pudgy deputy with thin gray hair blown out in a razor cut. His name tag read: G. Meyers.

"Rice, Duane Richard, 19842040. When do I get arraigned on the new charge?"

Deputy G. Meyers laughed. "What new charge? That scumbag you wasted was in for assault on a police officer with a half dozen priors, and you carried three L.A. County firemen to safety during the Agoura fire. Are you fucking serious? The watch commander read your record, then scumbag's, and made scumbag a deal: he presses charges on you, then the county presses charges on him for grabbing your shlong. Not wanting a fruit jacket, he agreed. He gets to spend the rest of his sentence in the hospital ward, and you get to serve as blue trusty here in the Rubber Ramada, where hopefully you will not get the urge to whip any more ass. Where did you learn that kung fu shit?"

Rice kicked the news around in his head, sizing up the man who'd delivered it. Friendly and harmless, he decided; probably close to retirement, with no good guys/bad guys left in him. "Soledad," he said. "There was a Jap corrections officer who taught classes. He gave us a lot of spiritual stuff along with it, but nobody listened. The warden finally got wise to the fact that he was teaching violent junior criminals to be better violent junior criminals, and stopped it. What's a ding trusty do?"

Meyers took a key from his Sam Browne belt and unlocked the cell. "Come on, we'll go down to my office. I've got a bottle. We'll belt a few and I'll tell you about the job."

"I don't drink."

"Yeah? What the fuck kind of criminal are you?"

"The smart kind. You booze on duty?"

Meyers laughed and tapped his badge. "Turned my papers in yesterday. Twenty years and nine days on the job, iron-clad civil service pension. I'm only sticking around until they rotate in a new man to fill my spot. Ten days from now I am adios, motherfucker, so till then I'm playing catch-up."

As Gordon Meyers explained it, the job was simple. Sleep all day while the dings were dinged out on their "medication," eat leftovers from the officers' dining room, have free run of his collection of *Playboy* and *Penthouse*, be cool with the daywatch jailer. At night, his duties began: feed the dings their one meal per day, move them out of their cells one at a time and mop the floors, get them to the showers once a week.

The most important thing was to keep them reasonably quiet at night, Meyers emphasized. He would be using his on-duty time to read the classified ads and write out job applications, and he did not want the dings dinging his concentration. Talk softly to them if they started to scream, and if that failed, scream back and make them scared of you. If worse came to worse, give them a spritz of the fire hose. And any ding who smeared shit on his cell walls got five whacks in the ass with the lead-filled "dingdonger" Meyers carried. Rice promised to do a good job, and decided to wait five days before manipulating the fat-mouthed cop for favors.

The job *was* simple.

Rice slept six hours a day, ate the high-quality institutional fare the jailers ate, and did a minimum of one thousand pushups daily. At night, he would bring the dings their chow, G.I. their cells and stroll the catwalk exchanging words with them through the bars. He found that if he kept up a continuous line of cell-to-cell communication, the dings screamed less and he thought of Vandy less. After a few days he got to know some of the guys and tailored his spiels to fit their individual boogeymen.

A-14 was a black guy popped for getting dogs out of the Lincoln Heights Shelter and cooking them up for Rastafarian feasts. The bulls had shaved off his dreadlocks before they threw him in the tank, and he was afraid that demons could enter his brain through his bald head. Rice told him that dreadlocks were "out," and brought him a copy of *Ebony* that featured ads for various Afro wigs. He pointed out that the Reverend Jesse Jackson was sporting a modified Afro and getting a lot of pussy. The man nodded along, grabbed the magazine and from then on would yell "Afro wig!" when Rice strolled by his cell.

C-11 was an old man who wanted to get off the streets and back to Camarillo. Rice falsely reported him as a shit-smearer for three nights running, and gave him three fake beatings, thumping the ding-donger into the mattress and screaming himself. On the third night, Meyers got tired of the noise and turned the old man over to the head jailer of the hospital ward, who said the geezer was Camarillo quail for sure.

The tattooed man in C-3 was the hardest to deal with, because the white trash Rice grew up with in Hawaiian Gardens all had tattoos, and he early on figured tattooing as the mark of the world's ultimate losers. C-3, a youth awaiting a conservatorship hearing, had his entire torso adorned with snarling jungle cats, and was trying to tattoo his arms with a piece of mattress spring and the ink off newspapers soaked in toilet water. He had managed to gouge the first two letters of "Mom" when Rice caught him and took his spring away. He started bawling then, and Rice screamed at him to quit marking himself like a low-life sleazebag. Finally the young man quieted down. Every time he walked by the cell, Rice would roust him for tattooing tools. After a few times, the youth snapped into a frisking position when he heard him coming.

Around midnight, when the dings began falling asleep, Rice joined Gordon Meyers in his office and listened to *his* dinged-out ramblings. Biting his cheeks to keep from laughing, Rice nodded along as Meyers told him of the crime scams he'd dreamed up in his sixteen years working the tank.

A couple were almost smart, like a plan to capitalize on his locksmith expertise—getting a job as a bank guard and pilfering safe-deposit box valuables to local beat cops who frequented the bank, staying above suspicion by not leaving the bank and letting the beat cops do the fencing; but most were Twilight Zone material: prostitution rings of women prisoners bused around to construction sites, where they would dispense blowjobs to horny workers in exchange for sentence reductions; marijuana farms staffed by inmate "harvesters," who would cultivate tons of weed and load it into the sheriff's helicopters that would drop it off into the backyards of high-ranking police "pushers"; porno films featuring male and female inmates, directed by Meyers himself, to be screened on the exclusive "all-cop" cable network he planned to set up.

Meyers rambled on for three nights. Rice moved his plan up a day and started telling him about Vandy, about how she hadn't written to him or visited him in weeks. Meyers sympathized, and mentioned that he was the one who made sure his photo of her wasn't destroyed when the bulls choked him out. After thanking him for that, Rice made his pitch: Could he use the phone to make calls to get a line on her? Meyers said no and told him to write her name, date of birth, physical description and last known address on a piece of paper. Rice did it, then sat there gouging his fingernails into his palms to keep from hitting the dinged-out deputy.

"I'll handle it," Gordon Meyers said. "I've got clout."

Over the next forty-eight hours Rice concentrated on *not* clouting the dings or the inanimate objects in the tank. He upped his push-up count to two thousand a day; he laid a barrage of brownnosing on the daywatch jailer, hoping for at least a phone call to Louie Calderon, who could probably be persuaded to check around for Vandy. He stayed away from Gordon Meyers, busying himself with long stints of pacing the catwalks. And then, just after midnight when the ding noise subsided, Meyers's voice came over the tank's P.A. system: "Duane Rice, roll it to the office. Your attorney is here."

Rice walked into the office, figuring Meyers was fried and wanted to bullshit. And there *she* was, dressed in pink cords and a kelly green sweater, an outfit he'd told her never to wear. "Told you I had clout," Meyers said as he closed the door on them.

Rice watched Vandy put her hands on her hips and pivot to face him, a seduction pose he'd devised for her lounge act. He was starting toward her when he caught his first glimpse of her face. His world crashed when he saw the hollows in her cheeks and the blue-black circles under her eyes. Strung out. He grabbed her and held her until she said, "Stop, Duane, that hurts." Then he put his hands on her shoulders, pushed her out to arm's length and whispered, "Why, babe? We had a good deal going."

Vandy twisted free of his grasp. "These cops came by the condo and told me you were really sick, so I came. Then your friend tells me you're *not* really sick, you just wanted to see me. That's not fair, Duane. I was going to taper off and be totally clean by the time you got out. It's not fair, so don't be mad at me."

Rice stared at the wall clock to avoid Vandy's coke-stressed face. "Where have you been? Why haven't you been to see me?"

Vandy took her purse off Meyers's desk and dug through it for cigarettes and a lighter. Rice watched her hands tremble as she lit up. Exhaling a lungful of smoke, she said, "I didn't come to see you at camp because it was too depressing, and you know I hate to write."

Rice caught *his* hands shaking and jammed them into his pants pockets. "Yeah, but what have you been *doing,* besides sticking shit up your nose?"

Vandy cocked one hip in his direction, another move he'd taught her. "Making friends. Cultivating the right people, like you told me I should do. Hanging out."

"Friends? You mean *men?*"

Vandy flushed, then said, "Just friends. People. What about *your* friends? That guy Gordon is looney tunes. When he brought me up from the parking lot, he told me he was going to organize this hit squad of Doberman pinschers. What kind of friends have *you* been making?"

Rice felt his anger ease; the fire in Vandy's eyes was hope. "Gordon's not a bad guy, he's just been hanging around wackos too long. Listen, are you okay on bread? Have you got any of the money I gave you left?"

"I'm okay."

Vandy lowered her eyes; Rice saw the fire die. "You holding out on me, babe? Ten K wouldn't have lasted you this long if you were on a coke run. You feel like telling me about these fr—"

Vandy threw her purse at the wall and shrieked, "Don't be so jealous of me! You told me I should get in with people in the Industry, and that's what I've been doing! I hate you when you're this way!"

Rice reached out for her wrist, but she batted his hand and moved backward until she bumped the wall and there was no place to go except forward into his arms. With her elbows pressed into herself, she let him embrace her and stroke her hair. "Easy, babe," he cooed, "easy. I'll be out in a few days, and I'll get working on your videos again. I'll make it happen. *We'll* make it happen."

Wanting to see Vandy's face, Rice dropped his arms and stepped back. When she brought her eyes up to him, he saw that she looked like the old Anne Atwater Vanderlinden, not the woman he molded and loved. "How, Duane?" she said. "You can't steal cars anymore. Another job at Midas Muffler?"

Rice let the ugly words hang there between them. Vandy walked past him and picked her purse up off the floor, then turned around and said, "This whole thing wasn't fair. I've been making friends who can help me, and I deserve to do a little blow if I want to. Your control trip is really uptight. Uptight people don't make it in the Industry."

There was a rapping at the door, and Meyers poked his head in and said, "I hate to break this up, but the watch commander is walking, and I don't think he'll buy Vandy here as an attorney."

Rice nodded, then walked to Vandy and tilted her chin up so that their eyes locked. "Go back to the pad, babe. Try to stay clean, and I'll see you on the thirtieth." He bent over and kissed the part in her hair. Vandy stood still and mute with her eyes closed. "And don't ever underestimate me," Rice said.

Meyers was waiting for him on the catwalk, tapping a billy club against his leg. "Listen. A-8 is acting up. He shit on his mattress and smeared food on the walls. You go give him a few whacks with the ding-donger while I escort your girl downstairs. When you get him pacified, come back to the office and we'll bat the breeze."

Rice grabbed the billy club and strode down the catwalk, pushing images of Vandy's decay out of his mind by concentrating on the jumble of ding noises, wishing the babbles and shouts would engulf him to the point where all his senses were numbed. Slapping the ding-donger harder and harder into his palm, he turned into the open front of A-8, wondering why the light was off. He was about to call out for Meyers to hit the electricity when the door slid shut behind him.

The darkness deepened, and the ding noise grew still, then fired up again. Rice yelled, "Unlock A-8, Gordon, goddammit!" then squinted around the cell. As his eyes became accustomed to the dark, he saw that it was empty. He smashed the billy club into the bars full force; once, twice, three times, hoping to scare the dings into temporary quiet. The crash of metal on metal assailed him, and the force of the blows sent shock waves through his entire body. A hush came over the tank, followed by Meyers's mocking laugh and the words "Told you I had clout."

When the meaning clicked fully in, Rice began smashing the club into the wall, four shots at a time, hearing hellish whispers in the wake of the noise: "It's real pharmaceutical blow, baby"; "Duane wouldn't want me to"; "Come on sweetie, party hearty." When the voices degenerated into giggles, he slammed the ding-donger harder and harder, until the wood casing cracked and the dings screamed along in cadence with his blows. Then sections of plaster exploded in his eyes and into his mouth, and his head started to reel. He surrendered himself to the asphyxiation and fell backward into total silence.

A severed arm spraying blood across a windshield; the steam room at the Hollywood Y. Rice came to with a ringing in his ears and a hazy red curtain in front of his eyes, snapping immediately to the bandage at the crook of his elbow and the wall-to-wall padding that surrounded him. Goose-juiced because he had destroyed A-8, because Gordon had—

Rice held his breath until he passed out, his last half-conscious thought to kill the dope with sleep and get even.

He slept; wakened; slept. Stumbling trips to the toilet, untouched trays of food and a thickening razor stubble marked his drifting in and out of consciousness. Dimly, he knew his kick-out date was coming and the bulls were leaving him alone because they were afraid of him. But Vandy . . .

No. Again and again he plunged into self-asphyxiation.

Finally hunger jerked him fully awake. He counted twelve trays of stale sandwiches, and figured his Prolixin jolt had lasted four days, leaving him three days from the streets. Ravenous, he ate until he threw up. That night a Mexican deputy came by his cell to bring him a fresh tray, and told him he was in Hospital Isolation, between the Ding and the High-Power tanks, and that his release date was two days away. The jailer was wearing a paper party hat. Rice asked him why. "The nightwatch ding jailer just retired," he said. "The watch commander threw him a party."

Rice nodded. *It couldn't have happened.* Vandy would never let a wimp like Gordon Meyers touch her. But when the jailer walked away, the doubts came back. He tried to force sleep, but it wouldn't come. The edge of his vision started to go red.

Hours of push-ups and leg lifts produced an exhaustion that felt pure and nonchemical. Rice drifted off again, then awakened to muffled voices coming from somewhere outside his cell.

He followed the sound to a grated ventilator shaft next to the toilet. Peering through the grates, he saw two pairs of denim-clad legs facing each other. The white stripes along the pants seams were a dead giveaway—he was looking into a High-Power Tank cell.

Laughter; then a deep voice taking over, his words echoing clearly through the shaft.

"I heard a dream score the other day, from this black guy on the Folsom chain. He and his partner were gonna do it, then he got violated on a liquor store heist. He was one smart nigger. He had it documented, the whole shot."

A different, softer voice: "Smart nigger is a contradiction in terms."

"Bullshit. Dig this: three-man stick-up gang, a bonaroo kidnap angle, an ace fucking safeguard.

"Here's the play: two guys hold the *girlfriend* of a *married* bank manager, at her pad, while the outside man calls the manager at *his* crib and has him call his chick, who of course is scared fucking shitless. The outside man calls back and gives him the drill: 'Meet me a half block from the bank an hour before opening, or your bitch gets killed and everyone knows you've been cheating on your wife.'

"Now, dig: the phone booth the outside man's been calling from is down the street from the manager's pad, so he can make sure the fuzz ain't been called. He trails the manager to the bank—still no fuzz—walks in with him, hits only the cashboxes, because the vault has gotta be time-locked, walks out, takes the manager out to his car, slugs him and ties him up, calls the inside men at the chick's pad, they tie *her* up, split, then meet later and divvy up the bread. Is that not fucking brilliant?"

The soft-voiced man snorted: "Yeah, but how the fuck are you supposed to find happily married bank managers with girlfriends on the side? You gonna put an ad in the paper: 'Armed robber seeks cooperative pussy-hound bank managers to aid him in career advancement? Send résumé to blah, blah, blah?' Typical nigger bullshit and jive."

"Wrong, bro," the deep-voiced man said. "I don't know how he got the info, but the black guy had two jobs cased—righteous rogue bank managers, girlfriends, the whole shot."

"And I suppose he gave you the skinny?"

"Yeah, he did, and I believe him. He got ten to life as a habitual offender, why not share the wealth, he's looking at a dime minimum. One chick lives in Encino, on the corner of Kling and Valley View, in a pink apartment house; the other, Christine something, lives in Studio City, a house on the corner of Hildebrand and Gage. I told you: one smart fucking nigger."

"I still don't believe it."

"If Bo Derek offered you a headjob, you'd think she was a drag queen. You're just a terminal fucking skeptic."

Rice listened as the conversation deteriorated into the usual jailhouse shtick of sports and sex. When the talk died altogether, he lay down with his head next to the ventilator shaft and once more fell asleep.

Vandy took over his dreams, short-take images of her laughing, moving around in bed. Then she was there with the Vandals, vibrato growling their closing number: "Gotta get down in the prison of your love. Get down, get down, gonna drown, gonna come so good, so hard, burn my body in your prison yard, prison of your love!"

Rice awakened for the final time in L.A. County Jail stint just as Vandy and the Vandals brought "Prison of Your Love" to its off-key crescendo. Coward, he said to himself. Coward. Using sleep the way a junkie uses smack. Maybe she fucked him and maybe she didn't; when you look into her eyes, you'll know. *So stay awake and fight.*

He stood up and looked around the cell, his eyes catching a wad of newspaper beside the toilet and a book of matches on top of the sink. Thinking, *let them know,* he struck a match on the ventilator grate, then lit the newspaper and watched it fireball. When it started to burn his hand, he dropped it into the toilet and listened to the sizzle and hiss of newsprint. Satisfied with the way the ink was running, he turned his attention to the floor-to-wall-to-ceiling padding.

Gouging was the only way.

Rice dug his fingernails into a seam of wall padding and pulled outward. Naugahyde, foam and a layer of webbed cotton were revealed. He poked a finger into the hole and felt metal in back of the webbing. Spring reinforcement. He gouged his way to it, then twisted the nearest piece of metal back and forth until it broke off in his hand.

It took him hours to hone his tool on the ventilator shaft grates. When the spring was razor sharp, he pressed it into a sodden ball of newspaper and darkened the tip. Flexing his left biceps into a hard surface, he thought of Hawaiian Gardens and Vandy. Then he marked himself with his past and future, so the whole world would know. The words were *Death Before Dishonor.*

2

Bobby "Boogaloo" Garcia watched his kid brother Joe loosen his clerical collar and do air guitar riffs in front of the bedroom mirror. He felt his own priest outfit constrict his body and said, "I can't take none of your rock and roll rap today, *pendejo.* I quit fighting 'cause niggers kept knocking me out in the third round, and you'll never make it as a musician 'cause you got no drive and no talent. But we both got a job to do, and we're behind for the month. So let's *do* it."

Joe cut off the music in his head; his lyrics put to an old Fats Domino tune, "Suicide Hill" substituted for "Blueberry Hill." Leave it to Bobby to puncture both their balloons with one shot, so he wouldn't have a good comeback. "Tomorrow's December first. The Christmas rush and the rainy season. We'll double up on Bibles and prayer kits, *and* siding jobs." Bobby's jaw clenched at the last words, and Joe added, "And we'll give some money to Saint Sebastian's. A tithe. We'll find some suckers with bucks, and rip them off and give the *dinero* to earthquake re—"

Bobby stopped him with a slow finger across the throat. "Not earthquake relief, *puto!* It's a scam! You don't do penance for one scam by giving bucks to another one!"

"But Henderson gave two grand to that priest from the archdiocese for earthquake relief. He—"

Bobby shook his head. "A scam within a scam within a scam, *pendejo.* He gave the priest a check for two K and got a receipt for three. That priest has got a brother in the D.A.'s office. The Fraud Division. Need I say fucking more?"

Joe tightened his collar, feeling his nice guy/musician self slip back into Father Hernandez, the phone scam padre. He grabbed a stack of Naugahyde-bound Bibles off the floor and carried them out to the car, wondering for the ten millionth time how Bobby could love hating his brother and his job and his *life* as much as he did.

Bobby and Joe worked for Henderson Enterprises, Inc., purveyors of aluminum siding and Bibles in Spanish. The scam originated in a phone room, where salesmen pitched rustproof patios and eternal salvation through Jesus to unsophisticated and semi-impoverished Angelenos, offering them free gas coupons as a come-on to get the "field representative" out to their homes, where he signed them up for "lifetime protection guarantees," which in reality meant a new siding job or Bible on a "regular installation basis"—meaning debilitating permanent monthly payments to whoever was gullible enough to sign on the dotted line.

Which was where Bobby and Joe, as Father Gonzalez and Father Hernandez, L.A.-based "free-lance" priests, came in. They were the "heavy closers"—psychological intimidation specialists who sized up weaknesses on the follow-up calls and *made* the sucker sign, setting in motion a string of kickbacks originating in the main office of U.S. Aluminum, Inc., and its subsidiary company, the Truth and Light Publishing House.

With the trunk of their '77 Camaro stuffed with Bibles, siding samples and wall hangings of Jesus, the Garcias drove to a "close" in El Monte on the Pomona Freeway. Joe was at the wheel, humming Springsteen under his breath so his brother wouldn't hear; Bobby threw short punches toward the windshield and stared out at the dark clouds that were forming, hoping for thundershowers to spook their closees into buying. When raindrops spattered the glass in front of him, he closed his eyes and thought of how everything important in his life happened when it was raining.

Like the time he sparred with Little Red Lopez and knocked him through the ropes with a perfect right cross. Red said his timing was off because bad weather made his old knife scars ache.

Like the time Joe and his garage band won the "Battle of the Bands" at El Monte Legion Stadium. He played adoring older brother and glommed a groupie who gave him head in his car while he smoked weed and kept the wipers going so he could eyeball prowling fuzz.

Like the righteous burglaries he and Joe pulled in West L.A. during the

'77–'78 floods, when the L.A.P.D. and C.H.P. were all evacuating hillsides and mopping blood off the freeways.

Like the time he felt guilty about treating Joe like dirt, and agreed to rip off the guitars and amplifiers from the J. Geils bass player's pad in Benedict Canyon. Halfway down to Sunset with the loot, the car fishtails and side-swipes a sheriff's nark ark. Joe freaks at the badge and cocked magnum in his face and starts blabbing how a hitchhiker left the stuff in the trunk. No way, Jose, the cop said. Bingo: nine months in the laundry at Wayside.

Like the times when they were kids, and Joe got terrified of thunder and woke him up and made him promise always to protect him.

Bobby switched to left jabs aimed at the wiper blades, pulling his fist back a split second before it hit the glass, watching Joe flinch out of the corner of his eye. "I always carried you, ain't I? Like I promised to when we were kids?"

Joe kept his eyes on the road, but clenched his elbows to his side, like he always did when Bobby started talking scary. "Sure, Bobby, that's true."

"And you've always watchdogged me when I got off too deep into my weird shit. Ain't that true?"

Joe saw what was coming and swallowed so his voice would be steady. "That's true."

"You've got to say it."

Tightening his hands on the wheel, Joe fought an image of their last B&E, of the woman with her skirt up over her head, Bobby with his knife at her throat as he raped her. "Y-you'd be . . . you'd hurt people."

"What kind of people?"

Joe stared straight ahead. The sky was getting darker and taillights began flashing on. Concentrating on their reflections off the wet pavement gave him a moment to think up a new answer that would satisfy Bobby's weird-ness and let him keep a piece of his pride. He was about to speak when a station wagon swerved in front of them.

Joe flinched backward and Bobby grabbed the wheel out of his hands and yanked it hard right. The car lurched forward, missing the station wagon's rear bumper by inches. Bobby jammed his foot onto the accelerator, looked over his shoulder, saw a tight passing space and jerked the car across four lanes and down a darkened off-ramp. He slowly applied the brake, and when they came to a stop at the flooded intersection, Joe was brushing tears from his eyes.

"Say it," Bobby said.

Joe screamed the words, his voice breaking: "You're a rape-o! You're a mind fuck! You're on a wacko guilt trip, and I'm not kicking out any more of *my* money for *your* penance!" He swung the car out into the stream of traffic, punching the gas, doing a deft brody that set off a chain of honks from cut-off motorists. Bobby cracked the passenger window for air, then said softly, "I just want you to know how things are. How they're always gonna be. I owe you for getting us out of burglary. Too many women out there; too many chances to pull weird shit. But you owe me your guts, 'cause without me you ain't got any. We gotta remember that stuff."

Knowing Bobby was trying to get at something, Joe pressed the edge that his tears always gave him. "You sent that woman five K, right? The money orders were cashed, so you know she got them. You sent her a note, so even though the signatures on the checks were false, she knew it was *you*. You haven't done it again, so why are you rehashing all this old stuff? We've got a good deal with Hendy, but you keep talking it down like it's nothing."

Bobby popped short left-right combos until his arms ached and his tunic was soaked with sweat. "I'm just getting itchy, little brother," he said at last. "Like something has gotta happen real soon. Take surface streets, I gotta cool out before the close."

They cruised east on Valley Boulevard, Joe driving slowly in the middle lane, so he could scope out the scene on both sides of the street. The rain died to a drizzle, and Bobby took a hand squeeze from the glove compartment and started a long set of grip builders, dangling his right arm out the window to get a good extension. When Joe saw that the streets were nothing but used-car lots, liquor stores, burrito stands and boredom, he tried to think up some more lyrics to "Suicide Hill." When words wouldn't come, he slumped down in his seat and let the story take over.

Suicide Hill was a long cement embankment that led down to a deep sewage sluice in back of the Sepulveda V.A. Hospital. The hill and the scrubland that surrounded it were encircled by high barbed-wire fencing that was cut through in dozens of places by the gang members who used it as a meeting place and fuck turf.

The hill itself was used to test courage. Steep, and slick from spilled oil, it served as the ultimate motorcycle gauntlet. Riders would start at the top and try to coast down, slowly picking up speed, then popping the bike into first and hurdling the sewage sluice, which was thirteen feet across and rife with garbage, industrial chemicals and a thirty-year accumulation of sharp objects thrown in to inflict pain. Gang rivalries were settled by two riders starting off on top of the hill at the same time, each armed with a bicycle chain, the object to knock the opponent into the muck while hurdling it himself. Scores of bodies were rumored to be decomposing in the sluice. Suicide Hill was considered a bad motherfucker and a destroyer of good men.

So was the man it was named after.

Fritz "Suicide" Hill and the V.A. Hospital dated back to the days immediately following World War II, when scores of returning G.I.s necessitated the creation of veterans' domiciles. Rumor had it that Fritz was housed at the brand-new institution for shell shock, and after his recovery was assigned to a domicile ward to ease his emotional readjustment. Fritz had other ideas. He pitched a tent in the scrubland by the embankment and started an L.A. chapter of the Hell's Angels, then embarked on a career as a motorcycle highwayman, shaking down motorists all over Southern California, always returning to his encampment by the Sepulveda Wash. That part of the legend Joe accepted as fact.

The rest was a mixture of bullshit and tall tales, and the part that Joe wanted to put into his song. Suicide Hill sliced the guy who sliced the Black Dahlia; he masterminded a plot to break Caryl Chessman out of death row; he tommy-gunned niggers from a freeway overpass during the Watts Riot. He turned Leary on to acid and kicked Charlie Manson's ass. The cops wouldn't fuck with him because he knew where the bodies were buried. Even legendary hot dogs like John St. John, Colin Forbes and Crazy Lloyd Hopkins shit shotgun shells when Suicide Hill made the scene.

The most popular ending of the legend had Fritz Hill dying of cancer from all the chemicals he'd sucked in during his many dunks in the Sepulveda Wash. When he saw the end coming, he hauled his 1800 C.C. Vincent Black Shadow up to the roof of the hospital and popped a wheelie over the edge in second gear, flying some five hundred yards before he crashed into the scrubland, igniting a funeral pyre that could be seen all over L.A. Joe knew that the whole story, rebop, truth and all, was the story of everything he and Bobby had ever done, but all he had so far was "and death was a thrill on Suicide Hill"—and those ten bars were enough for a plagiarism beef.

Bobby nudged him out of his reverie. "Hang a right. The pad should be on the next block."

Joe complied, pulling onto a street of identical tract houses, all of them painted pink, peach or electric blue. Bobby scanned addresses, then pointed to the curb and shook his head. "Jesus Christ, Father Hernandez. Another *stone* wacko."

"*Qué*, Father Gonzalez?"

Joe set the brake and got out of the car, then looked over at the front lawn of the closee's pad and answered his own question. "Wacko's not the word, Padre."

The walkway of the peach-colored house was lined with Day-Glo plaster statues of Jesus and his disciples. On one side of the lawn a plastic Saint Francis stood guard over a flock of Walt Disney squeeze toys. On the other side, stuffed teddy bears and pandas were arranged around a papier-mâché nativity scene. Joe walked over and checked out the manger. A Donald Duck doll was wrapped in swaddling clothes. Minnie Mouse and Snoopy leaned against the crib, sheepherder staffs pinned to their sides. The whole collage was sopping wet from the rain. "Holy fuck," he whispered.

Bobby cuffed him on the back of the head. "This is too fucking sad. Anybody this fucking crazy has gotta be a rollover. Let's just get a signature and split." He shoved a turquoise Bible and matching siding sample at Joe, then stared at the opposite side of the lawn. His eyes caught a toppled Jesus statue and a Kermit the Frog puppet going sixty-nine. He grabbed Joe's arm and pushed him up the walkway. "Five minutes in and out. No rosaries, no bullshit."

Before Joe could respond, a fat white woman in a rumpled housedress opened the door and stood on the porch in front of them. Grateful that she wasn't Mexican, Bobby said, "I'm Father Gonzalez, and this is Father Hernandez. We're the field priests from the Henderson Company. We brought you your siding sample and Bible. The workmen will be out to put up your patio next week." He reached into his breast pocket for a blank contract. "All we need is your signature. If you sign today, you get our November bonus, the Henderson Prayer Service: millions of Catholics worldwide will pray for you every day for the rest of your life."

The woman reached into the pockets of her dress and pulled out rosary beads and a wad of one-dollar bills. She bit at her lip and said, "The phone man said I got to give to earthquake relief to get prayed for. He said to give you the money to give to him, and you'd pray for my husband, too. He's got the cancer powerful bad." Joe was reaching for the money when he saw Bobby smile; the slow smile he used to flash just before a fight he knew he was going to lose. He dropped his hand and stood off to one side as the veins in his brother's forehead started to twitch and spit bubbles popped from his mouth. The woman stammered, "He-he's sick powerful bad," and Bobby ran back to the car and began hurling Bibles and siding samples out into the street, covering the pavement with pastel Naugahyde and aluminum. When there were no more phone scam products left to throw, he tore off his priest jacket and his cassock and dropped them into the gutter, followed by the money in his pants pockets. Joe stood on the porch beside the shock-stilled woman, watching the last five years of his life go up in smoke, knowing that what made it so bad was that Bobby believed in God worse than any of the people he hurt.

3

Three weeks into his suspension from duty, Lloyd Hopkins flew to San Francisco and kept his family under a rolling stakeout. He rented a room at a Holiday Inn on the edge of Chinatown and a late-model Ford, and watched from a distance as his wife made her rounds of the city as an antique broker and met her lover for drinks, dinner and overnight visits at her Pacific Heights apartment; from a further distance he followed his daughters to school, on errands and out on dates. After a week of loose surveillance, he knew that he had gleaned no information and gained no special insights that would make his job easier. All he could do was let them find him, and see where it went from there.

He decided to let the girls make the discovery, and drove to their school and parked across the street. At 12:30, classes adjourned for an hour, and Anne and Caroline always ate with friends under the big oak tree in the school's backyard, while Penny skipped lunch and brooded by herself on the steps. If he stood by the car, big and familiar in his favorite herringbone jacket, then sooner or later they would notice him, and he would be able to read their faces and know what to do.

At precisely 12:30, the school's back door opened, and the first wave of students exited and jockeyed for positions under the oak tree. Lloyd got out and leaned against the hood of his car. Anne and Caroline appeared moments later, chattering and making faces as they examined the contents of their lunch sacks. They found spaces on the grass and began eating, Caroline making her usual liverwurst face as she unwrapped her first sandwich.

Penny walked out then, peering around before disappearing into a swarm of children. Lloyd felt tears in his eyes, but kept them on his daughters anyway, waiting for the moment of recognition.

"Loitering in the vicinity of school yards, huh? Let's see your I.D., pervert!"

Lloyd did a slow turn, savoring the sound of Penny's voice and the anticipation of their identical gray eyes meeting. Penny foiled his plan by jumping into his arms and burying her head in his chest. Lloyd held his youngest daughter and dried his eyes on her Dodgers cap. When she started growling and nudging his shoulders like a cat, he growled back and said, "Who's the pervert? And what's with this feline stuff? The last I heard you were a penguin."

Penny stepped back. Lloyd saw that the color in her eyes had deepened, gaining a hint of Janice's hazel. "Penguins are passé. You've lost weight, Daddy. What are you doing in Frisco? This skulking-around scene wasn't too subtle, you know."

Lloyd laughed. "Do the others know I'm here?"

Penny shook her head. "No, they're not too subtle either. I figured it out two days ago. This friend of mine said there was this big man in a tweed jacket checking out the school yard. He said the guy looked like a nark or a perv. I said, 'That sounds like my dad.' I kept peeking outside during classes until I saw you." She stood on her tiptoes and poked Lloyd's necktie. "Speaking of which, my dummy sisters just figured it out."

Looking over his shoulder, Lloyd saw Caroline and Anne staring at him. Even from a distance he could see shock and anger on their faces. He waved, and Anne dropped her lunch sack and grabbed her sister's arm. Together they ran toward the school's back door.

Lloyd looked at Penny. "They're pissed. Why? The last time I came up we got along great."

Penny leaned against the car. "It's cumulative, Daddy. We're the geniuses, they're the plodders. They resent me because I'm the youngest, the smartest, and have the biggest breasts. They—"

"No, goddammit! What really?"

"Don't yell. I'm serious, Annie and Liney have gone très Frisco. They want Mom to divorce you and marry Roger. Mom and Roger are on the rocks, so they're scared. Daddy, are you in trouble in the Department?"

Realizing that his two older daughters weren't going to join him, Lloyd put an arm around his youngest and drew her close. "Yeah. I blew an extradition bust and fucked up at the guy's arraignment. I've been suspended from duty until the first of the year. I'm not sure what's going to happen, but I'm sure I'm finished in Robbery/Homicide. I might get transferred to a uniformed division until my twenty years come up, I might get my choice of flake assignments. I just don't fucking know."

Penny burrowed deeper into her father. "And you're scared?"

"Yeah, I'm scared."

"And you still want all of us back?"

"More than ever."

"Want some advice?"

"Yeah."

"Exploit this rocky period Mom and Roger are going through. Work fast, because they're going away this weekend, and they have this tendency to patch things up during long motel idylls."

Lloyd laughed. "I've been observing you lately. Don't you ever eat lunch?"

Penny laughed back. "The school serves nothing but health food, and Mom's sandwiches suck. I hit a burger joint on the way home."

"Come on, we'll get a pizza and conspire against your mother."

After a long lunch, Lloyd dropped Penny back at school and drove to Janice's apartment. There was a note on the door: "Roger—running late, make yourself at home. Should ret. around 3:30." He checked his watch—3:10—and picked the lock with a credit card and let himself in. When he saw the state of the living room, he realized Janice's success, not her lover, was his chief competition.

Every piece of furniture was a frail-looking antique, the type he had told her never to buy for the house because he was afraid it wouldn't support his 225 pounds; every framed painting was the German Expressionist stuff he despised. The rugs were light blue Persian, the kind Janice had always wanted, but was certain he'd ruin with coffee stains. Everything was tasteful, expensive, and a testament to her freedom as a single woman.

Lloyd sat down carefully in a cherrywood armchair and stretched his legs so that his feet rested on polished hardwood, not pale carpeting. He tried to kill time imagining what Janice would be wearing, but kept picturing her nude. When that led to thoughts of Roger, he let his eyes scan the room for something of or by himself. Seeing nothing, he fought an impulse to check out Janice's bedroom. Then he heard a key in the lock and felt himself start to shiver.

Janice saw him immediately and didn't register an ounce of surprise.

"Hello, Lloyd," she said. "Liney called me at the office and told me you were in town. I expected you to come by, but I didn't expect you to break in."

Lloyd stood up. A red wool suit and a new shorter hairdo. He hadn't been close. "Cops have criminal tendencies. You look wonderful, Jan."

Janice sighed and let her purse drop to the floor. "No, I don't. I'm forty-two, and I'm putting on weight."

"I'm forty-two and losing weight."

"So I can see. So much for the amen—"

Lloyd took two steps forward; Janice one. They embraced hands to shoulders, keeping a space between them. Lloyd broke it off first, so the contact wouldn't make him want more. He took a step backward and said, "You know why I'm here."

Janice pointed to a Louis XIV sofa. "Yes, of course." When Lloyd sat down, she took a chair across from him and said, "I know what you want, and I'm glad that you want it, but I don't know what *I* want. And I may never know. That's as honest an answer as I can give you."

Lloyd felt threads of their past unraveling. Not knowing whether to press or retreat, he said, "You've made a good life for yourself here. This pad, your business, the life you've set up for the girls."

"I also have a lover, Lloyd."

"Yeah, Roger the on-and-off lodger. How's that going?"

Janice laughed. "You're such a riot when you try to act civilized. I read about you in the L.A. papers a couple of weeks ago. Some man you captured in New Orleans."

"Some man whose capture I fucked up in New Orleans, some man whose arraignment I almost blew in L.A."

Janice smoothed the hem of her skirt and leaned forward. "I've never heard you admit to making mistakes before. As a cop, I mean."

Lloyd leaned back. The sofa creaked against his weight and combined with Janice's words to form an accusation. "I never made them before!"

"Don't shout, I wasn't accusing you of anything. What did the man do?"

The creaking grew; for a split second Lloyd thought he could feel the floor start to tremble. "The *man*? He beat a woman to death during a snuff film. Roger ever take out any scumbags like that?"

Janice started to flush at the cheeks; Lloyd grabbed the arms of the sofa to keep from going to her. "Roger doesn't take out scumbags," she said. "He doesn't break into my apartment or carry a gun or beat up on people. Lloyd, I'm a middle-aged woman. I was in love with your intensity for a long, long time, but I can't handle it anymore. Maybe it isn't a nice thing to say, but Roger is a comfortable, no-fireworks lover for a middle-aged antique broker who put in nineteen years as wife to a hot-dog cop. Lloyd, do you know what I'm saying?"

The perfect softness of the indictment rang in Lloyd's ears. "I've made amends as best I could," he said, consciously holding his voice at a whisper. "I've tried to admit the things I did wrong with you and the girls."

Janice's whisper was softer. "And your admissions were excessive and hurt me. You told me things that you shouldn't ever, *ever* tell any woman that you claim to love."

"I *do* love you, goddammit!"

"I know. And I love you, and even if I stay with Roger and divorce you and marry him, I'll always love you, and Roger will never own me the way you have. But I'm too tired for the kind of love you have to give."

Lloyd stood up and walked to the door, averting his eyes from Janice and groping for threads of hope. "The girls? Would you consider how they feel about me?"

"If they were younger, yes. But now they're practically grown up, and I can't let them influence me."

Lloyd turned around and looked at his wife. "You're not yielding on this an inch, are you?"

"I yielded too long and too much."

"And you still don't know what you want?"

Janice stared at the light blue Persian carpet she had coveted since the day of her wedding. "Yes . . . I . . . still don't know."

"Then I guess I'll just have to outyield you," Lloyd said.

4

She was gone, and she'd taken everything that could be converted into quick cash with her.

Duane Rice walked through the condo he'd shared with Vandy, keeping a running tab on the missing items and the risks he'd taken to earn them.

TV console, state-of-the-art stereo system and four rooms' worth of expensive high-tech furniture—gone. Four walk-in closets full of clothes, three for her, one for him—gone. Paintings that Vandy insisted gave the pad class—gone. The down payment and maintenance costs on a flop that he now couldn't live in—adios, motherfucker. Add on the empty carport in back of the building and total it up: two hundred Class A felonies committed in the jurisdictions of the most trigger-happy police departments in the country. Sold down the river by a worthless—

When he couldn't finish the thought, Rice knew that the game wasn't over. He pissed on the living room carpet and kicked the front door off its hinges. Then he went looking for felony number 201 and the means to get back his woman.

The Pico bus dropped him on Lincoln Avenue, a stone's throw from Venice Ghosttown and the likelihood of a shitload of customized taco wagons without alarm systems. On Lincoln and Ocean Park he spotted a hardware store and went in and boosted a large chisel, rattail file and pair of pliers. Exiting the store, he smiled and looked at his watch: two hours and ten minutes out of the rock and back on the roll.

Rice waited for dusk at a burrito stand on the edge of Ghosttown, drinking coffee and eyeballing the East Venice spectacle of overage hippies, overage hookers, overage lowriders and underage cops trying to look cool. He watched horny businessmen in company cars prowl for poontang, tried to guess which hooker they'd hit on and wondered why he had to love a woman before he could fuck her; he watched an aged love child with an amplifier strapped to his back strum a guitar for chump change and suck on a short dog of T-bird. The scene filled him with disgust, and when twilight hit, he felt his disgust turn to high-octane fuel and walked into Ghosttown.

Stucco walk-back apartment buildings, white wood-frame houses spray-painted with gang graffiti, vacant lots covered with garbage. Emaciated dogs looking for someone to bite. The cars either abandoned jig rigs or welfare wagons in mint condition, but nothing exceptional. Rice walked west toward the beach, grateful that the cold weather had the locals indoors, seeing nothing that Louie Calderon would pay more than five bills for out of friendship. He kept walking, and was almost out of Ghosttown when automotive perfection hit him right between the eyes.

It was a '54 Chevy convertible, candy-apple sapphire blue with a canary yellow top, smoked windshield and full continental kit. If the interior was cherry and the engine was in good shape, he was home.

Rice walked up to the driver's-side door and pretended to admire the car while he got out his chisel and pliers. He counted slowly to ten, and when he could feel no suspicion coming down on him, jammed the chisel into the space between the door-lock and chassis and yanked outward. The door snapped open, no alarm went off. Rice saw that the dash was a restored '54 original and felt underneath it for the ignition wires. Pay dirt! He took his pliers and twisted the two wires together. The engine came to life, and he drove the car away.

Two hours later, with the Chevy safely stashed, Rice walked in the door of Louie Calderon's auto body shop and tapped Louie on the shoulder. Louie looked up from the tool kit he was digging through and said, "Duane the Brain! When'd you get out?" Rice ignored the oil-covered hand he offered and placed an arm over Louie's shoulders. "Today." He looked around and saw two mechanics staring at them. "Let's go up to your office."

"Business?"

"Business."

They walked through the shop and up to the office that adjoined the second story of Louie's house. When they were seated across the paper-cluttered desk from each other, Rice said, "Now resting in your hot roller garage out by Suicide Hill is a mint '54 Chevy ragtop. Continental kit, 326 supercharged, full leather tuck and roll, hand-rubbed sapphire blue metal flake paint job. Intact, I'd say it's worth twelve K. Parts, close to ten. The *upholstery* is worth at least two."

Louie opened the refrigerator next to his desk and pulled out a can of Coors. He popped the top and said, "You're crazy. With your record, you have got to be the primo auto theft suspect in L.A. County. You bought your way out of what? A hundred counts? That kind of shit only happens once. Next time, they fuck you for the ones they got you on *and* the ones you got away with. How'd you get in my garage?"

Rice cracked his knuckles. "I cut a hole in the door with a chisel and unlocked it from the inside. Nobody saw me, and I covered up the hole with some wood I found. And I'm not planning on making a career of it. I just did it for a quick stake."

"Nice sled, huh?"

"Primo. If you weren't a Mexican, I'd call it a bonaroo taco wagon."

Louie laughed. "All Chicanos with ambition are honorary Anglos. How much you want?"

"Two grand and a couple of favors."

"What kind of favors?"

"When I was at fire camp, I heard you had a message service. You know, twenty-four-hour, bootleg number, tap proof. That true?"

"*Es la verdad.* Two hundred scoots a month, but be cool who you give the number to, I don't want no shitbirds giving me grief at four in the morning. What else you want? Let me guess . . . Let's see . . . A car!"

"How'd you guess? I don't care what it looks like, all I want is something with legit registration that runs. Deal?"

Louie walked to the back wall and lifted up a framed *Playboy* centerfold, then twirled the dial of the safe and opened it. He pulled out two bank packets and tossed them to Rice. "Deal. The car is ugly, but it runs. Remember this number: 628-1192. Got it?"

Rice said, "Got it," and stuck the money in his pocket. "I also heard you were dealing guns."

Louie's eyes became cold brown slits. "You wanta tell me who told you that?"

"Sure. A guy at the County. Big blonde guy on the Quentin chain."

"Randy Simpson, fat-mouthed motherfucker. Yeah, I've been trying to deal guns, but I can't find no shooters who want my product. I bought these big, heavy-ass army .45 automatics from this strung-out quartermaster lieutenant. He threw in these tranquilizer dart guns, too. A bullshit deal. The shooters want the lightweight Italian pieces, and *nobody* wants the dart guns. I gave my son one of the dart jobs, took the firing pin out so he couldn't hurt himself. Why? You going cowboy, Duane-o?"

Rice shook his head. "I don't know. I heard about a deal, but it might not float. I'll have to check it out."

"What *are* you gonna do for a living?"

"I . . . I don't know. Work on making a few scores, then work on Vandy's career. She split, but I—"

Rice stopped when he saw Louie's face cloud over. He shook his head to blot out the sound of Vandy's "But Duane wouldn't want me to," then said, "What is it? Don't hold back on me."

Louie drained his beer in one gulp. "I was going to tell you, I was just waiting for the right time. A friend of mine saw Vandy, sometime last week. She was walking out of this outcall service place on the Strip, you know, by the All-American Burger. He said at first he didn't recognize her with all this makeup on, but then he was sure. I'm sorry, man."

Rice stood up. Louie saw the look in his eyes and said, "Maybe it don't mean that."

"It means I have to find her," Rice said. "Go get me my car."

Duane Rice drove his "new" '69 Pontiac to the east end of the Sunset Strip, hugging the right-hand lane in order to check out the hookers clustered by bus benches, searching for Vandy's aristocratic features wasted by makeup and dope. Every face he saw burned itself into his brain, where it was superimposed against a reflex image of Gordon Meyers and preppy Anne Atwater Vanderlinden. But none of the faces was *her*, and when he saw three solid blocks of massage parlors, fuck pads and outcall services looming in front of him, he gnawed his lips until he tasted blood.

Rice parked in the All-American Burger lot and walked slowly west on the south side of Sunset. All the streetwalkers now were black, so he kept his eyes glued to the shabby storefronts and their flashing neon signs. He passed Wet Teenagers Outcall and Soul Sisters Mud Wrestling; New Yokohama Oriental Massage and the 4-H Club—"Hot, Handsome, Horny and Hung." After a block, the obscenities blurred together so that he couldn't read individual names, and he stared at front doors waiting for *her* to come out.

When he saw that guilty-looking men were the only ones entering and leaving, he started to see red and walked to a curbside bus bench and braced his hands against it in an isometric press. With his eyes closed, he forced himself to think. Finally he remembered the snapshot of Vandy he'd carried through jail. He reached for his wallet and pulled it from its plastic holder, then turned around and again confronted the flashing beacons. Nuclear Nookie Outcall; Wet and Woolly Massage; Satan's House of Sin. This time the words didn't blur. He pulled out a handful of Louie Calderon's twenties and walked through the nearest door. A bored black man behind a desk looked up as he entered and said, "Yeah?"

Rice held the photo of Vandy and a double saw under the man's nose. "Have you seen this woman?"

The man put down his copy of the *Watchtower*, grabbed the twenty and looked at the snapshot. "No, too good-lookin' for this jive place. If you want to pork this kinda chick, I can fix you up with a cut-rate version who gives mean head."

Rice breathed out slowly; the red trapdoor behind his eyes eased shut. "No thanks, I want *her*. Got any ideas?"

The man stuck the twenty in his shirt pocket. "I don't know what places got what quality pussy, but I know this jive place ain't got nothin' but woof-woofs. You just keep walkin' and whippin' out that green, maybe you find her."

Rice took the man's advice and walked east. He showed the snapshot to every doorman and bouncer at every sex joint on the row, handing out over three hundred dollars, getting nothing but negative head shakes and a consensus that Vandy was too foxy to be doing either Strip outcall or street hooking. After four straight hours of breathing nothing but sleaze, he got coffee at the All-American Burger and sat down at an outside table to think.

He came up with facts that he trusted. Louie and his friends were solid; if one of them saw Vandy out here in whore makeup, it was probably true—without him to look after her she was a stone self-destructor. None of the massage and outcall slimebags he'd talked to had I.D.'d her—and it was to their financial advantage to do so. Louie's friend had seen her sometime last week, probably right after she visited him and cleaned out the pad. It all felt right.

Rice looked at his watch: 3:30, the whores thinning out as the traffic on Sunset dwindled. The only hookers still working were black, and unlikely to have info on Vandy—she avoided all jigs like the plague. Draining his coffee, he stood up and started for the car. Then he saw an incredible redhead walk over to the curb and stick out her thumb.

Rice moved fast, running to his car and pulling up in front of the girl, cutting off a slow-trawling Mercedes. The redhead looked in the passenger window distastefully, then back at the status car. Rice yelled, "A C-note for ten minutes," and the girl hesitated, then opened the door and got in. Rice handed her a wad of twenties as the driver of the Mercedes accelerated and flipped them the bird.

The redhead stuffed the money into her purse and poked a finger at the tufts of foam sticking out of the seat. "This car sucks. Can we go to a motel or something?"

Rice turned around the corner, then pulled over to the curb and flicked on the dashboard light. "I don't want to get laid, I just had a feeling you could help me find this woman." He handed her the photo of Vandy and watched as she examined it, then shook her head.

"No, never. Your chick?"

"That's right."

"She a working girl?"

Rice swallowed a wave of anger. "Yeah. I've heard she's been doing outcall around here, but nobody recognizes her, and I believe them."

The redhead scrutinized the snapshot, then said, "She's real cute. Too classy for most of the places around here."

"What do you mean, 'most'?"

"Well, there's this high-line place a couple of blocks from here, off the Strip. They run only really foxy chicks, to these movies and rock big shots. I worked out of there for a week or so, then I quit. Too much of a drug scene. I'm into health food."

Rice felt his skin prickle. "What's the name of the place?"

"Silver Foxes. No 'outcall,' just 'Silver Foxes.'"

"What's the address?"

"Gardner, just off the Strip. Lavender building, you can't miss it. But they only send chicks out on referrals, you know, it's real exclusive."

"Phone number?"

The girl hesitated. Rice dug in his pocket for more money, then handed it to her. "Tell me, goddammit."

She grabbed the door handle. "You won't tell where you got it?"

"No."

"658-4371." The girl darted out of the car. Rice watched her counting her money as she walked back to the Strip.

It took him less than ten minutes to find the lavender apartment building. It stood just south of Sunset in the glow of a streetlamp, a plain Spanish-style four-flat with no lights burning.

Rice parked and walked across the lawn to the cement porch. Four doors were recessed in the entranceway, illuminated only by mailbox lights. He squinted and saw that three of the apartments belonged to individuals, while the last box was embossed with a raised metal insignia of a fox in a mink coat winking seductively. There was a buzzer beneath the words "Silver Foxes." Rice pressed it three times and heard its echo. No lights went on and no sounds of movement answered the buzzing. He reached into the mailbox and found it empty, then stood back on the lawn so he could eyeball the whole building. Still nothing but darkness and silence.

Rice drove to a pay hone and dialed 658-4371. A recorded woman's voice answered: "Hi, this is Silver Foxes, foxes of every persuasion for every occasion. If you're already registered with us, leave your code number and let us know what you want; we'll get back to you soon. If you're a new friend, let us know who you know, and give us their code numbers and your phone number. We'll get in touch soon."

There was an interval of soft disco music, then a beep. Rice slammed down the receiver and drove back to outcall row.

Only the dregs of the hookers were still out, garishly made-up junkies who stepped into the street and lifted their skirts as cars passed by. Rice sat at a table inside the All-American Burger and drank coffee while he scanned women on both sides of Sunset. Every face he glimpsed looked ravaged; every body bloated or emaciated. Toward dawn, the neon lights on the outcall offices and massage parlors started going off. When street-sweeping machines pushed the few remaining hookers back onto the sidewalk, he took it as his cue to leave and check out business.

Rice drove across Laurel Canyon, coming down into the Valley just as full daylight hit. When he reached Ventura Boulevard, he recalled verbatim the facts he'd heard through the ventilator shaft: "Kling and Valley View, pink apartment house"; "Christine something, Studio City, house on the corner of Hildebrand and Gage." Truth, half-truth or bullshit?

At Hildebrand and Gage he got his first validation. The mailbox of the northeast corner house was tagged with the name "Christine Confrey." That fact gave him a feeling of destiny that built up harder and harder as he drove west to Encino. When he got to Kling and Valley View and saw a faded pink apartment house on the corner, with an out-of-place Cadillac parked in front, the feeling exploded. Rice kept it at a low roar by calculating odds: five to one that the info was correct, making the heists possible.

Checking the mailboxes of the six-unit building, he saw that only one single woman lived there—Sally Issler in #2. He found a door designated 2 on the ground-floor street side, with a high hedge fronting the apartment's large picture window. Rice squatted behind the hedge, waiting for the owner of the Caddy to cut the odds down to zero.

He waited an hour and a half before a door opened and two voices, one male, one female, gave him pay dirt:

"My wife gets back tomorrow. No overnighters for a while."

"Matinees? You know, like the song—'Afternoon Delight'?"

The man laughed. "We can hit Hot Tub Fever during your lunch hour."

"Sounds good, but I read in *Cosmo* that those hot tub places all have herpes germs in the water."

"Don't believe everything you read. Call me at the bank?"

"Yeah."

Rice heard sounds of kissing, followed by a door slamming. He counted to ten, then stood up and peered around the hedge. The Cadillac was just taking off. He ran for his car and pursued it.

It led him to a Bank of America branch on Woodman and Ventura. Rice sized up the man who got out. Tall, broad-hipped, sunken-chested. A wimp whose sex appeal was his money.

The man walked up to the front doors. Rice followed from a safe distance, passing him as he stepped inside. When the manager locked the doors behind him, Rice counted to ten, then peered through the plate-glass window and smiled.

The manager was alone inside the bank, and the surveillance cameras were fixed-focused at the floor. The tellers stations were visible from the street only if a passerby was willing to stand on his tiptoes and crane his neck.

Rice watched the manager walk directly to the teller area and take a key from his pocket, then open drawers and transfer cash to his briefcase, leaving pieces of paper in the money's place—probably doctored tally slips. The odds zoomed to perfection. Rice ran to his car, then drove to a pay phone and called Louie Calderon at his message drop number.

"Speak."

"Louie, it's Duane."

"Already? Don't tell me, the car broke down and you're pissed."

"Nothing like that."

"Another favor?"

"Yeah. I want three .45s and one of those dart guns. You've got darts, too?"

"Yeah. Before we go any further, I don't wanna know what you got in mind. You got that?"

"Right. Silencers?"

"I can get them, but they cut down the range to practically zilch."

"They'll never be fired; it's just an extra precaution."

"Mr. Smooth. Seven bills for the whole shot. Deal?"

"Deal. One more thing. I need two men, smart, with balls, who want to make money. No niggers, no dopers, no trashy gangster types, nobody with robbery convictions."

Louie whistled, then laughed. "You want a lot, you know that? Well, today's your lucky day. I know two Chicano dudes, brothers, who're looking for work. Smart—one righteous vato, one tagalong. Pulled hundreds of burglaries, only got popped once. *Righteous burglars, righteous con men.* They just hung up this phone rip-off gig and they're hurtin' for cash."

"You vouch for them?"

"I fenced their stuff for seven or eight years. When they got busted, they didn't snitch me off. What more you want?"

"Any strong-arm experience?"

"No, but one of them is downright mean, and I'll bet he'd dig it. Used to fight welterweight, ten, twelve years ago. All the top locals stomped on him."

"Can you set up a meet?"

"Sure. But I'm tellin' them and I'm tellin' you: I don't want to know nothin' about your plans. *Comprende?*"

"*Comprende.*"

"Good. I'll call Bobby and set it up. When you meet him, tell him how you saw him knock Little Red Lopez through the ropes with a right cross. He'll eat it up."

The phone went dead. Rice walked back to his car. When he stuck the key in the ignition, he was trembling. It felt good.

5

Even as the dream unfolded, he knew that it was *just* a dream, one of the stock nightmares that owned him, and if he didn't panic, it would run its course and he would wake up safe.

Sometime back in '67 or '68, when he was working Hollywood Patrol, he and his partner Flanders got an unknown trouble call directing their unit to an old house in a cul-de-sac off the Cahuenga Pass, a block of ramshackle pads rented out dirt cheap because noise from the freeway overpass made living there intolerable.

When no one answered their knocks and shouted "Police officers, open up!" he and Flanders kicked in the door, only to be driven back outside by the stench of stale cordite and decomposing flesh. While Flanders radioed for backup units, he drew his service revolver and prowled the pad, discovering the five headless bodies, brain-spattered walls, expended shotgun rounds and the note taped to the TV set: "I keep hearing these voices thru the freeway noise telling Peg and the kids about me and Billy. It's a lie, but they won't believe it was just one time when we was drunk, and that don't count. This way nobody's going to know except Billy, and he don't care."

The man who wrote the note was slumped by the TV set. He had jammed the sawed-off .10 gauge into his crotch and blown himself in two. The shotgun lay beside him in a pile of congealed viscera.

Then the dream speeded up, and he wasn't sure if it was happening or not.

Flanders came back inside and yelled, "Backup, detectives and M.E. on their way, Hoppy." He saw him reach for a cigarette to kill the awful stink, and was about to scream about gas escaping from stiffs, but *knew* Flanders would call it college boy bullshit. He ran toward him anyway, just as the match was struck and the little boy's stomach exploded and Flanders ran out the door with his face on fire. Then *he* was screaming, and ambulances were screaming, and he knew it wasn't a dream, it was the telephone.

Lloyd rolled over and reached for it, surprised to find that he had fallen asleep fully clothed. "Yes? Who is it?"

A familiar voice came on the line. "Dutch, Lloyd. You all right?"

"You woke me up."

"Sorry, kid."

"Don't be; you did me a favor."

"What do you mean?"

"Never mind. What is it, Dutch?"

When there was a long silence on the L.A. end of the line, Lloyd tensed and shook off the last remnants of sleep. He heard the bustle of Hollywood Station going on in the background, and pictured his best friend getting up the guts to tell him something very bad.

"Goddammit, Dutch, tell me!"

Dutch Peltz said, "So far it's just a rumor, but it's an informed rumor, and I credit it. That shrink you saw last month recommended you be given early retirement. You know, emotional disability incurred in the line of service, full pension, that kind of thing. I've heard that Braverton and McManus are behind it, and that if you don't accept the plan, you'll be given a trial board for dereliction of duty. Lloyd, they mean it. If the trial board finds you guilty, you'll be kicked off the Department."

A kaleidoscope of memories flashed in front of Lloyd's eyes, and for long moments he didn't know if he was back in a dream or not. "No, Dutch. They wouldn't do that to me."

"Lloyd, it's true. I've also heard that Fred Gaffaney has got a file on you. Nasty stuff, some sex shit you pulled when you worked Venice Vice."

"That was fifteen fucking years ago, and I wasn't the only one!"

Dutch said, "Sssh, sssh. I'm just telling you. I don't know if Gaffaney is in with Braverton and McManus on this, but I know it's all coming down bad for you. Retire, Lloyd. With your master's, you can teach anywhere. You can do consulting work. You can—"

Lloyd screamed. "No!" and picked up the phone, then saw the framed photograph of his family on the nightstand and put it back down. "No. *No. No.* If they want me out, they'll have to fight me for it."

"Think of Janice and the girls, Lloyd. Think of the time you'd have to spend with them."

"You're talking shit, Dutch. Without the Job, there's nothing. Even Janice knows that. So fuck 'em all except six, and save *them* for the pallbearers. See you in L.A., Captain Peltz."

Dutch's voice was soft and hoarse. "Until then, Sergeant Hopkins."

Lloyd hung up and walked into the bathroom, cursing when he saw the daintily wrapped soap bars and his disposable razor crusted with shaving cream. Muttering "Fuck it," he soaked a washcloth in cold sink water and wiped his face, then straightened his necktie, wondering why he always wore one, even when he didn't have to. When he looked in the mirror, the answer came to him, and he prepared to do battle with the institution that had given him all of his nightmares and most of his dreams.

At a stand of pay phones in the lobby, Lloyd found a copy of the San Francisco yellow pages and leafed through the A's until he hit "Attorneys." Dismissing the shysters who had full-page ads mentioning their low rates and drunk-driving experience, he got out a pencil and notepad and started jotting down names and addresses at random, filling up half a page before he noticed *Brewer, Cafferty and Brown* at an address on Montgomery that was probably only a half dozen blocks from where he was standing. Again muttering "Fuck it," he smoothed his necktie and walked there, jamming his hands into his pockets to keep from running.

The waiting room of Brewer, Cafferty and Brown was furnished in the old-line California style of leather armchairs and brass floor lamps; the photographs on the walls blew the sense of tradition apart. Lloyd walked in and knew immediately that chance had directed him to either *the* best or *the* worst law firm ever to be considered by a defendant in an interdepartmental police trial.

Bobby Seale, Huey P. Newton and Eldridge Cleaver glared down at him, giving the clenched-fist salute; a group photo of the United Bay Area Gay Collective beamed down. Hanging over the reception desk was a purple wall tapestry with "Power to the People!" embroidered in the center, and beside it there was a photographic blowup of dozens of Oriental men in karate stances. Lloyd examined the picture, figuring it for an outtake from a martial arts movie. He was wrong; it was the Boat People's Political Action Army. Sitting down to wait for someone to welcome him, he felt like he had been given the D.T.s without benefit of booze.

After a few minutes, a tall black woman in a tweed suit walked in and said, "Yes, may I help you?"

Lloyd stood up, noticing the woman catch sight of the .38 strapped to his belt. "I came to see an attorney," he said. "Your office was close to my hotel, so I came here."

"Then you don't have an appointment?"

The woman was staring openly at his gun. Lloyd took out his I.D. holder and badge and showed it to her. "I'm a Los Angeles police officer," he said. "I'm looking for an attorney to represent me at a police trial board. An out-of-town lawyer is probably a good idea. I've got forty thousand dollars in the bank, and I'll spend every dime to keep my job."

The woman smiled and walked back out of the room. Lloyd held eye contact with Huey Newton until she returned and said, "This way, please, Mr. Hopkins," and led him to an inner office. A pale man was sitting behind a desk reading a newspaper. "Mr. Brewer, Mr. Hopkins," the woman said, then exited and closed the door behind her.

Brewer looked up from his paper. "L.A.P.D., huh? Well, we know they didn't bring you up on charges of excessive force, because they don't recognize that concept." He stood up and extended his hand. Lloyd shook it, measuring the man's words, deciding his abrasiveness was a test. "I like your office," he said as he took a chair next to the desk. "Out of the low-rent district. You do a lot of oil-leasing contracts on the side, take down the pictures of the niggers when the fat cats come to call?"

Brewer filled a pipe with tobacco and tamped it down. "So much for light conversation. I don't have to agree with a client's ideology in order to represent him. Why are you getting a trial board?"

Lloyd forced himself to talk slowly. "The overall charge will probably be dereliction of duty. I'm currently on a six-week suspension, with pay. The specific charge or charges will have to do with a recent perjury I committed at a murder trial arraignment. I—"

Brewer jabbed the air with his pipe stem. "Why did you commit perjury? Is this a common practice of yours?"

"I lied to protect a woman innocently involved in the case," Lloyd said softy, "and I've lied previously only to circumvent probable-cause statutes in regard to hard felonies."

"I see. By any chance were you intimately involved with this woman?"

Lloyd grasped the arms of his chair. "That's none of your business, Counselor. Next question."

"Very well. Let's backtrack. Tell me about your career with the L.A.P.D."

Lloyd said, "Nineteen years on the Job, fourteen as a detective-sergeant, eleven in Robbery/Homicide Division. I've got a master's in criminology from Stanford, I'm considered the best homicide detective in the Department, I've earned more commendations than I can count, I've successfully investigated a number of highly publicized murder cases. My arrest record is legendary."

Brewer lit his pipe, then blew smoke at the ceiling. "Impressive, but what's more impressive is that someone with such an outstanding record should have incurred such departmental disfavor. I should think that one perjury slipup wouldn't have been sufficient to jeopardize your career. I know the L.A.P.D. looks after their own."

"There's other stuff. Minor fuckups over the years. The high brass sent me to a shrink. I shot my mouth off about things I shouldn't have."

"Why?"

"Because I wanted to get rid of it! Because I never thought they'd try to do this to me!"

"Please calm down, Sergeant. There are ways to get around one psychiatrist's report, usually by mitigating it with the report of a different analyst, one with a superior reputation."

Lloyd gripped the sides of the desk until he felt his hands go numb. "Counselor, this isn't a trial in a court of law, this is a kangaroo cop trial, and academic credentials don't mean shit. Saving my job is a long shot from the gate, and making a department employee look bad would only make the odds worse."

Brewer slid back in his chair and stared past Lloyd at the far wall. "Well . . . there are other approaches. You have a family?"

"Wife and three daughters. I'm separated from them."

"But you remain cordial?"

"Yes." Lloyd stared at the attorney, who kept his eyes fixed on a point just above his head and said, "Then we can exploit them as character witnesses, gain sympathy for you that way. You yourself present an interesting picture, one that can be used to advantage. Are you aware that your clothes don't fit? They're at least two sizes too large. We can portray you in court as a victim of your own conscientiousness, a man driven to radical weight loss by overzealous dedication to duty! If you were to lose even more weight, that sympathy factor would be increased. With proper coaching your daughters would elicit the mo—"

"*Look at me,*" Lloyd hissed, holding down a picture of his hands around Brewer's throat, squeezing until the lawyer's averted eyes popped out of his skull. "Look at me, you cocksucker."

Brewer closed his eyes. "Control your language, Sergeant. I want you to get used to wearing a penitent expression, one that wi—"

Lloyd stepped around the desk, grabbed Brewer by the arms and shoved him into a glass bookcase. The glass shattered; law texts spilled to the floor. Lloyd took hold of Brewer's neck with his left hand, and balled his right hand into a fist and aimed it at the lawyer's squeezed-shut eyes. Then he heard a scream, and his peripheral vision caught the receptionist with her hands clasped over her mouth. He pulled the punch at the last second, sending his fist through an unbroken pane of glass. Shoving Brewer aside, Lloyd held his bloody hand in front of him. "I . . . I'm sorry, goddamn you . . . I'm sorry."

6

Duane Rice looked at Bobby "Boogaloo" Garcia and knew two things: that, ex-welterweight or not, he could take him out easy; and that the little taco bender was incorrigibly *mean.* After a jailhouse handshake, Rice looked around his living room, saw quality stuff and pegged him as a non-doper who gangsterized because he was too lazy to work and in love with the game. Thinking, so far so good, he threw out a line to test his smarts: "I think I saw you fight once. You knocked Little Red Lopez through the ropes at the Olympic about ten, twelve years ago."

Bobby grinned and pointed to the couch; Rice sat down, seeing smarts up the wazoo and a big determination to milk the game. "Likable Louie must have told you that," Bobby said. "Told you I'd dig it. Louie's gotta be the dumbest smart guy I know, because only about six people in the world know about that, and I'm the only one cares, just like you're the only one gives a rat's ass about how you ragged that judge. Fucking Louie. How'd he manage to stay alive so long?"

"He can do things we can't do," Rice said, reaching into the back of his waistband and pulling out a silencer-fitted .45 automatic. "Like this." He worked the slide and ejected the clip, catching the chambered round as it popped into the air. "Dum dum. Likeable Louie has stayed alive for so long because guys who can get nice things are likable. Right, Bobby?"

Laughing, Bobby held out his hands. Rice tossed the .45 up to him, and he grabbed it and did a series of quick draws aimed at the Roberto Duran poster above the fireplace. "Pow, Roberto, pow! Pow! *No más! No más!*" Grinning from ear to ear, he handed the gun back butt first and slumped into a chair across from Rice. "Louie ain't likable, Duane. He's lovable. He's so lovable that I'd suck his daddy's dick just to see where he came from. How many of those you got?"

"Three," Rice said. "One for you, one for me, one for your brother. Is he coming?"

"Any minute. Wanta trade pedigrees?"

"Sure. The vehicular manslaughter conviction you already heard about, three years at Soledad because I lost my temper and reverted to my white trash origins; a bust on one count of G.T.A., a bullet in the County, reduced to six months. Y.A. parole and County probation, both of which I'm hanging up, because car thief/mechanic is what my P.O. calls a 'modus operandi—occupational stress combination.' In other words, he expects me to sling burgers at McDonald's for the minimum wage. No way."

Bobby nodded along, then flashed a grin and said, "How many cars you boost before you got busted?"

"Around three hundred. You and your brother did B&Es, right?"

"Right. At least four, five hundred jobs, with one bust, and that was a fluke."

"What did you do with the money? Louie pays a good percentage, and he said you guys aren't into dope."

Bobby cracked the knuckles of his right hand. "I *own* this house, man. Joe and I used to *own* a coin laundromat and a hot-dog stand, and I bankrolled a couple of fighters after I quit myself. What about *you?* Three hundred G.T.A.s and you drive up in an old nigger wagon looks like something the cat dragged in. What'd you do with *your* money?"

"I spent it," Rice said, boring his eyes into Bobby's, testing for real now, wondering if retreating was the smart thing to do. The two-way stare held until Bobby's eyelids started to twitch and he smiled/winced and said, "Shit, man, I like women as much as the next man."

Stalemate: Bobby had backed off, but returned with a good shot, right on target. Rice tasted blood in his mouth, and felt his teeth involuntarily biting his cheeks. The bloody spittle lubed his voice so his next shot sounded strong to his own ears. "You think you can be cool with that gun? You think you can hold on to it and not shoot it?"

Three seconds into a new eyeball duel, the front door opened and Joe Garcia walked in carrying a bag of groceries. Rice broke the stare and stood up and stuck out his hand. Joe shifted the bag and grabbed the hand limply, then said, "Sorry I'm late," and reached into the bag and pulled out a can of beer. He tossed it at Bobby, who shook it up, then popped the top and let the foam shoot out and spray his face. Chugalugging half the can, he cocked a thumb and forefinger at the Roberto Duran poster and giggled, "Pow! Pow! *No más! No más!*" Rice watched Joe Garcia watch his older brother. He seemed wary and disgusted, a smart reaction for a tagalong criminal. Bobby killed his beer and plugged Roberto Duran a half dozen more times. Rice knew the charade was a machismo stunt to hide his fear. To hide his own contempt and relief, he watched Joe walk into the kitchen, then joined Bobby in laughing. When Joe returned looking outright scared and Bobby gazed over at him and wiped his lips, Rice said, "Let's talk business, gentlemen."

It took him half an hour to outline the plan exactly the way he'd heard it through the ventilator shaft, stressing that no one knew he'd heard it and that he'd cased the locations to a T, getting the facts validated straight down the line. He would be the "inside" man who actually hit the banks; they would be the "outside" men who held the two girlfriends captive at their pads and received the phone calls from the rogue bank manager. Gauging their reactions, Rice saw that Bobby wanted it for the money and the pure unadulterated thrill—every time he mentioned the kidnap angle the ex-welter popped his knuckles and licked his lips; he saw that Joe was afraid of the whole thing, but more afraid of putting the kibosh on his brother's glee. For a two-time-only deal, they were solid partners.

Finishing his pitch, Rice said, "A few other things: park your car on the nearest big street to the chicks' pads. That's Ventura for the Issler woman, Lankershim for Confrey. Wear gloves, but don't put on your ski masks until right before you go in the door. Carry briefcases and dress well so you'll blend in with the neighborhood. We meet at my place, Room 112 at the Bowl Motel on Highland up from the Boulevard, *one hour* after I call you at the girlfriends' pads. Tie the chicks up and tape their mouths, but make sure they can breathe. Questions?"

Bobby Garcia said, "Yeah. You said you been casing both gigs for three days. What do you mean by that?"

"We've got two on-the-sly romances going down," Rice said. "Hawley from the B. of A. and his bitch Issler; Eggers from Security-Pacific and his babe Confrey. Both men open their banks early, by themselves, and pilfer from the tellers boxes, probably small amounts. Okay, three days now, I've seen them tap the tills before opening. I've watched the guards and tellers arrive, parked across the street with binoculars. At both banks the money at the tellers stations is left there overnight!"

Joe Garcia raised his hand. "Why are these banks so lax about their security?"

"Good question," Rice said. "I thought about that, then I did some more checking. First off, Hawley is a fuckup, too wimpy to run a tight ship. He's got nothing but party-hearty types working there, you know, everybody smokes dope on their lunch hour, young squares with no ambition, so they've got to get wasted to make it through the day. Also, the Security-Pacific is only half a block from an L.A.P.D. substation—maybe Eggers thinks he's robbery-proof. Who knows? And who cares?"

Bobby held up his hands, then brought them together and began slowly cracking the knuckles on each finger. Finishing, he said, "Let's cut the shit and get to the cut. It's a righteous fucking plan, but how much are we gonna make?"

Rice said, "I'm guessing at least thirty K per bank minimum, sixty-forty split—sixty for me, forty for you guys to split."

Bobby snorted. Joe said, "That sounds fair to me, you did all the wo—"

"Shut up, *pendejo!*" Bobby yelled. Lowering his voice, he said to Rice, "I like you, Duane, but you're giving me the big one where it hurts the most. Fifty-fifty, or you go take a flying fuck at a rolling donut."

Rice faked a sheepish look; his split strategy had worked to perfection. "Deal," he said, sticking out his right hand for the brothers to grasp, wincing when Bobby slammed it with both callused palms, grinning when Joe's tagalong hands followed. "Day after tomorrow for Hawley and Issler. I'll meet you here tomorrow night at nine for a final briefing. If you need me for anything, call me at Louie's bootleg number."

The three men stood up and shook hands all around. Rice turned to walk out, and Bobby tapped him on the shoulder. "Ain't you forgetting something, Duane?"

Rice smiled and did a two-gun pirouette, drawing one .45 from his back waistband and another from his shoulder holster, flipping them up by the silencered barrels and catching them by the grips. "Be cool," he said as he handed the guns to Bobby.

Bobby "Boogaloo" Garcia grinned and emptied both .45s at his back living room wall, blowing Roberto Duran to shreds and the wall itself into a rubble heap of rotted wood, dust and plaster chips. Joe squinted through the gun smoke and saw that the shots had ripped apart the connecting door to his bedroom. Screaming, "You rape-o motherfucker, you wasted my albums!" he ran back to inspect the damage. Bobby bowed to Rice and said, "Never liked Roberto since Hearns kicked his ass. Silencers work good, Duane."

7

Deputy Chief Thad Braverton slammed down the phone and muttered, "Fuck," then buzzed his secretary. When she appeared in the doorway, he said, "Ring Captain McManus at Robbery/Homicide and have him come up immediately, then call Captain Gaffaney at Internal Affairs and have him come up in fifteen minutes, no sooner."

The woman nodded and about-faced into her vestibule. Braverton sent exasperated eyes heavenward and said, "Crazy Lloyd. Jesus fucking Christ."

McManus rapped on the doorjamb only moments later. Braverton took his eyes from the ceiling and said, "Sit down, John. Close the door behind you. Fred Gaffaney is joining us shortly, and I don't want him to hear any of this."

McManus nodded and eased the door shut, then sat down, waiting for the superior officer to speak first. Close to a minute passed before Braverton said, "Hopkins isn't accepting the retirement deal."

McManus shrugged. "I didn't think he would, sir. I also didn't know that you'd spoken to him."

"I haven't," Braverton said. "Someone leaked the word to him in Frisco. Hopkins went out looking for an attorney to represent him at his trial board and blundered into the office of the most prestigious left-wing firm in the city. He ended up shoving around the head shyster and punching out a bookcase."

McManus breathed out slowly. "Jesus fucking Christ."

"My initial reaction, too."

"Charges filed?"

Braverton shook his head. "S.F.P.D. talked the shyster out of it, applied pressure somehow. I just spoke to the station commander who caught the squeal. He said when the beef came in, Hopkins got a standing ovation from the detective squad."

McManus felt chills dance up his spine. "Typical. Have you decided what you're going to do?"

"No."

"Would you like my feedback?"

"Of course. You're his immediate supervisor, and, as cops go, an atypical thinker."

McManus didn't know if the chief's last remark was a compliment or a jibe; Braverton was a poker voice all the way. Trying hard to keep his own voice level, he said, "Sir, I've been Hopkins's supervisor since Gaffaney made captain and went to I.A.D., and I've handled him the way Fred and his previous bosses did. Let him pick his own shots, let him head up investigations that should have gone to field lieutenants, let him work without a partner. The results he's given me have been outstanding; his methods of obtaining them either dubious or outright illegal. For example: he solved Havilland-Goff brilliantly, but in the process shot it out with Goff in a crowded nightclub, then let him get away. Then he pulled at least two burglaries to obtain evidence. You know how I feel about violation of due process, sir. Hopkins is essentially a criminal. What sets him apart from a run-of-the-mill street thug is a one-seventy I.Q. and a badge. And he's slipping. That foul-up at Oldfield's arraignment is just the beginning. He's obsolescent. Cut him loose."

Braverton remained silent for long moments. McManus fidgeted, then said, "Sir, why have you called Gaffaney in? He was Hopkins's previous sup—"

Braverton cut him off. "I'll tell you after he's left. What you said makes perfect sense, John. You're probably the world's only liberal Irish cop. I th—"

The sound of a buzzer interrupted him. Braverton said, "There he is," then pressed a button on his phone console. There was a tapping on the doorjamb. Braverton called out, "Enter!" and Captain Fred Gaffaney walked in and nodded briskly at both men. "Chief, Captain," he said.

Braverton pointed to a chair. McManus stood up and shook the I.A.D. adjutant's hand, feeling like he had stepped backward in time—Gaffaney's crew cut and bargain-basement blue suit always reminded him of his rookie days, when departmental regulations demanded such a visage. His bone-crusher handshake was another anachronism, and McManus sat down wondering what kind of game Braverton was playing.

Gaffaney settled into his chair and fingered his cross and flag lapel pin. Braverton looked straight at him and said, "Lloyd Hopkins is about to be brought up on a trial board. Dereliction of duty, maybe a criminal prosecution for perjury if he doesn't accept the retirement deal the Department is going to offer him. We're looking for backup dirt. What have *you* got on him?"

"Internal Affairs has a substantial file on Hopkins," Captain Fred Gaffaney said. "Notations covering his numerous insubordinations and illegal search and seizures. What are you using for ammo at the trial board?"

Braverton smiled. "The court transcript of his perjury, a psychiatrist's report that states, essentially, that he's a burnout. If need be, we may utilize his I.A.D. file. Your personal testimony might help."

Gaffaney's left hand jerked up to his lapel pin; McManus watched the witch-hunter's eyes narrow as he said, "You mean as to the information in the file?"

"That's right."

"Of course I'll testify, Chief."

Braverton sighed. "Thanks, Fred, I knew I could count on you."

Gaffaney got to his feet, then said, "If there's nothing else, I have an interview in ten minutes." Braverton nodded dismissal, and McManus watched the crew-cut anachronism exit the office looking *strange*.

The chief's silent deadpan stare compounded the feeling of strangeness. Knowing he was being tested, McManus dropped his usual "sir" and said, "What was that all about?"

Braverton responded with an open-armed gesture that took in his whole office. "You may well be sitting in this chair one day. If you make it, you'll be dealing more with ambitious brass like Gaffaney than with street dicks like Crazy Lloyd."

McManus's whole being tingled; the testing was moving toward a veiled offer of patronage. "And, sir?"

"And I have a nominal regard for due process myself. Gaffaney is on the promotion list. He'll be a commander very shortly, and he'll probably take over I.A.D. when Stillwell retires. As far as that goes, he deserves the job; he's a good exec.

"But he's a born-again Christian loony, so far right that he scares *me*. He's been playing savior to some very well placed junior officers—field sergeants in Metro, I.A.D. dicks, uniformed officers in a half dozen divisions. Sergeants and lieutenants, all born-agains and all ambitious. He's offered them his patronage and promised to move *them* up as *he* moves up."

McManus whistled, then said, "What's his ultimate end?"

Braverton repeated his expansive gesture. "Chief of police, then politics? Who knows? The man is forty-nine years old, twenty-three years on the Job and fucked up on religion. My wife suggested male menopause. What do you—"

McManus raised a hand in interruption. "Sir, where did you get this information?"

"I was getting to that. Gaffaney has a son in the Department, Steve Gaffaney, a rookie working West L.A. Patrol. The kid has been pilfering from the station, clerical supplies, ammo, that kind of thing, for months. Finally the daywatch boss got pissed and called Intelligence Division, because if he initiated an investigation through I.A.D., Gaffaney senior would pick up on it. Intelligence checked the kid out and discovered that he had been suspended from high school for pilfering from lockers and that Captain Fred had bribed the principal of the school to erase all notations pertaining to disciplinary problems on the kid's record, and to improve his grades. Junior wouldn't have been admitted to the Academy with his real transcript."

McManus whispered, "And, sir?"

"And Intelligence did some more checking on Jesus Freak Fred and got wind of his little cross-and-flag coterie, which of course is perfectly kosher within departmental regulations."

"What's the upshot?"

"For now I'm going to sit on it. If the kid fucks up big or Captain Fred gets obstreperous, I'll lower the boom."

McManus smiled as the chief of detectives' machinations moved into out-and-out barter. "Sir, you still haven't told me where Hopkins fits in, and you want something."

Smiling back, Braverton said, "The Intelligence dicks said that Jesus Fred has got a shitload of personal dirt files on officers he hates and wants to curry favor with. He hates Hopkins's guts, and I know for a fact that he's privy to a lot of the sleazy stuff Lloyd has pulled over the years. That charade was to confirm that the files exist. His reaction proved that they do."

"And, sir?"

"And, John, what's *your* reaction to all this?"

"Cut Hopkins loose, blackmail Jesus Fred into retiring by threatening to expose the kid, fire the kid and stonewall the whole fucking mess."

Braverton gave his new protégé a round of applause. "Bravo, except your love of due process and lack of paranoia is appalling. First we have to neutralize Gaffaney's files, which may take a while."

"Then?"

"First things first. Today is December sixth. On January first you will leave Robbery/Homicide and take over the Violent Crime Task Force in South Central L.A. I want a broad-minded man down there, someone who can deal rationally with blacks."

McManus's throat went dry; his first reaction was to offer effusive thanks. Then respect for the barter game took over. "What's it going to cost me?"

Braverton's eyes clouded. "I want to ease Hopkins out," he said. "Hopefully without a trial board. I want you to call him back from San Francisco and give him some sort of assignment that does not involve homicide and will not insult his intelligence. I want him around Parker Center where I can talk to him. He's got to be cut loose, but I want it done gently."

McManus winced at the price of his high-visibility promotion. "You could have made it an order."

"Not my style," Braverton said. "Liberals should be adept at trading up, seeing as how they're handicapped from the gate."

The epiphany clicked into McManus's head and made him forget caution. "You love him."

"Yes. And I owe him, and you owe him. He got the Slaughterer and Havilland and Goff within fifteen months. Do you know the story on the Slaughterer?"

"No."

"Then you don't want to know. Will you do this for me?"

McManus felt old notions of duty crumble in the pit of his stomach. "Yes."

"Good. Do you have an appropriate assignment for him?"

"Not right now. But something should come up soon. It always does."

8

Duane Rice stood in a phone booth adjoining a 7-11 store in Encino. He was wearing a three-piece suit bought for ten dollars at a Hollywood thrift shop, and a curly-haired wig and beard/mustache combo purchased at Western Costume. His shoulder holster held a silencer-attached .45; his rear waistband a tranquilizer dart gun loaded with PCP darts. His hands were covered with surgical rubber gloves. He was ready.

At exactly 7:45 the phone rang. Rice picked up the receiver and said, "Yes?"

The gloating voice was unmistakably Bobby Garcia's: "Got her. Broke in the side door. Nobody saw us, nobody's gonna see us. She's scared shitless, but the kid is playing Mr. Nice Guy and sweet-talking her. Have lover boy call."

Rice said, "Right," then hung up and dialed the home number of Robert Hawley. The phone rang twice, then a female voice yawned, "Hello?"

"Robert Hawley, please," Rice said briskly.

The woman said, "One minute," then called out, "Bob! Telephone!" There was the sound of an extension being picked up, then a male voice calling, "I've got it, Doris. Go back to sleep." When he heard the original line go dead, Rice said, "Mr. Hawley?"

"Yes. Who is it?"

"It's a friend of Sally Issler."

"What the he—"

"*Listen to me* and be real, real cool and we won't kill her. *Are* you listening?"

"Yes, oh God . . . What do—"

Rice cut in, "What do you think we want, motherfucker! The same thing you rip off from your own fucking employer!" When he heard Hawley start to blubber, he lowered his voice. "You want to be cool or you want Sally-poo to die?"

"B-be cool," Hawley gasped.

"Then here's the pitch: One, I've got photographs of you pilfering the B. of A. tellers boxes, with the clock in the background, showing that you're on the job when you're not supposed to be, and some juicy infrared shots of you and Sally fucking. If you don't do what I want, my buddies chop Sally to pieces and the pictures go to your wife, the L.A.P.D., the bank and *Hustler* magazine. Dig me, dick breath?"

The gasp was now a whimper. "Yes. Yes. Yes."

"Good. Now, I want you to call Sally and have her introduce you to my colleagues. I'll call you back in exactly three minutes. There's a tap on your phone, so if you call the cops, another colleague will know and call Sally's roommates and tell them to do some chopping. Do you understand?"

"Y-yes."

Rice said, "Three minutes or chop, chop," then hung up. He watched the second hand on his Timex, pleased that his spontaneous bullshit about the photographs and phone tap had been so easy. When the hand made three sweeps, he again dialed Hawley's number.

"Yes?" A *groveling* whimper.

"You ready?"

"Yes."

"Good. I want you to get in your car and take your usual route to the bank. I've been tailing you for days, so I know the route. Park on the west side of Woodman a half block north of Ventura. I'll meet you there. You're being tailed, so don't fuck up. I'll see you there in twelve minutes."

Hawley's reply was a barely audible squeak. Rice hung up and walked very slowly to his Pontiac, forcing himself to count to fifty before he hit the ignition and eased the car into traffic. When he was six blocks from Hawley's house, he resumed counting, figuring that the bank manager would pass him in the opposite direction before he hit twenty-five. He was right; at twenty-two, Hawley's tan Cadillac approached at way over the speed limit, swerving so close to the double line that he pulled to the right to avoid a head-on. There were no cop cars anywhere. Nothing suspicious. Just business going down.

Rice cut over to side streets paralleling Ventura, pushing the car at forty-five, so that he wouldn't get stuck waiting for Hawley to arrive. At Woodman he turned right and parked immediately, a solid hundred and fifty yards from the spot where the bank man was to meet him. Just as he set the brake and grabbed a briefcase from the back seat, Hawley's Caddy hung an erratic turn off Ventura and slowed. Rice checked his fake mustache in the rearview mirror. Mr. Solid Citizen out for a stroll.

The bank man was acting like Mr. Solid Citizen on a trip to Panic City. Rice walked toward the bank parking lot, watching Hawley scrape bumpers as he parallel-parked his Caddy, plowing into the curb twice before squeezing into an easy space. When he finally got out and stood by the car, he was shaking from head to toe.

Rice approached, swinging the briefcase casually. Hawley frantically eyeballed the street. Their eyes locked for an instant, then Hawley turned around and checked out his blind side. Rice grinned at his protective image and came up on the bank manager and tapped him on the shoulder. "Bob, how nice to see you!"

Hawley did a jerky pivot. "Please, not now. I'm meeting someone."

Rice clapped Hawley on the back and spun him in the direction of the bank, keeping an arm around his shoulders as he hissed, "You're meeting *me*, dick breath. We're going straight to the tellers boxes, then straight back to your car." He dug his fingers into the bank man's collarbone and gouged in concert with sound effects: "Chop, chop, chop." Hawley winced with each syllable and let himself be propelled toward the bank.

At the front door, Hawley inserted keys into the three locks while Rice stood aside with one eye cocked in the direction of Ventura Boulevard. No patrol cars; no unmarked cruisers; nothing remotely off. The doors sprung open and they stepped inside. The bank man locked a central mechanism attached to the floor runner and looked up at the robber. "F-fast, please."

Rice pointed toward the teller area, then stepped back and let Hawley lead the way. When the manager's back was turned, he opened his briefcase and took out a pint bottle of bourbon and stuck it into his right front pants pocket. Hawley stepped over a low wooden partition and began unlocking and sliding open drawers. Rice glanced down and saw rows of folding green, then looked closer and saw that it was *off-green*—fancy traveler's checks done up in a Wild West motif. "The cash," he hissed. "Where's the fucking *money?*"

Hawley stammered, "T-t-time-locked. The vault. You said on the phone you wanted—"

Ignoring him, Rice opened the rest of the drawers himself, finding nothing but fat stacks of B. of A. "Greenbacks" in denominations of twenty, fifty and a hundred. Replaying his casing job in his mind, he snapped to what happened. Hawley was pilfering the traveler's checks. The paperwork he saw him doing was some sort of ass-covering. Seeing the banker outlined in red, he said, "*There's no cash in these drawers?*"

"N-nn-no."

"You've been ripping off *traveler's checks?*"

Shooting a panicky glance at the window, Hawley said, "Just for a while. I've got bad gambling debts, and I'm just trying to get even. Please don't kill me!"

Rice held the briefcase open, thinking of Chula Medina and twenty cents on the dollar tops. When Hawley started stuffing the rows of Greenbacks inside, he said, "Talk, dick breath. Give me a good line on your scam, and maybe I'll let you slide."

Hawley fumbled the packets into the briefcase, his eyes averted from Rice, his voice near cracking as he spoke. "The Greenbacks are tallied by the week. I've got duplicate bankbooks for two old lady customers—they're senile—and I transfer cash from their accounts to the bank and take it out in Greenbacks. I can't do it for much longer, it's wrong, and the paperwork juggling has got to come back on me." He opened the last drawer and transferred its contents to the briefcase, then held up supplicating hands and whispered, "Please, fast."

Rice took in the bank man's "scam," feeling it sink in as truth, knowing that Eggers's pilfer scene was probably something similar—he was a fool to think bank pros would leave cash out overnight. Noting wraparound tabs on the Greenbacks, he flashed a psycho killer smirk and held his jacket open to show off his .45. "I know about exploding ink packets, dick breath. You ink me and I'll come back and chop-chop your whole family."

Hawley shook his head and mashed his hands together. "We do ink only on cash, only on payroll days. *Please*."

He looked up doglike for instructions. Rice closed the briefcase and said, "Back to your car. Stay calm. Think about your golf game and you'll be cool."

Hawley moved toward the front doors in spastic steps; Rice was right behind. When they hit the street and the manager locked the door behind them, he threw his left arm over his shoulders and shifted the tranq gun from his waistband to his right jacket pocket.

They approached the Cadillac from the street. Rice pointed to the driver's-side door, and Hawley got in behind the wheel. Terror hit his face as he saw Rice reach into his waistband, and he squeezed his eyes shut and began murmuring the Lord's Prayer.

Rice shot him twice point-blank: once in the neck, once in the chest just below his left collar point. Hawley jerked backward in his seat, then bounced forward into the steering wheel. Rice watched him slump sideways, his eyes fluttering, his limbs going rubber. Within seconds he was sleeping the open-mouthed sleep of the junkie. Rice leaned into the car and poured the pint of whiskey over his chest and pants legs. *"Bon voyage,"* he said.

After driving to a pay phone and giving Bobby Garcia the all-clear and setting up plans for the split, Rice removed his facial disguise and hit the 405 Freeway to Redondo Beach, the briefcase full of bank checks on the seat beside him. He did another replay of the Eggers case job as he drove, remembering that he had only seen him rummage through the tellers boxes—he'd never seen him with money in hand. That heist had to be a cash rip, and that meant the Garcias couldn't know about the Greenback fuckup. Turning off the freeway onto Sepulveda, he beat time on the dashboard. The melody was a Vandy/Vandals tune; the words he murmured were, "Be home and be flush, Chula."

Chula Medina was at home.

After bolting the door behind him, Rice unceremoniously opened the briefcase and dumped the contents on the floor, then said, "Quarter on the dollar, cash. And fast."

Chula Medina smiled in answer, then sat down cross-legged beside the pile of bank checks. Rice watched him lick his lips as he counted. When he finished, he said, "Nice, but consecutive serial numbers and an off-brand check. These are gonna have to be frozen, then sent east. You've got sixty-four K here. My first, last, final and only offer is a dime on the dollar; here, now, cash, you walk out and we never met. Deal?"

Rice fingered his "Death Before Dishonor" tattoo and knew it was a fucking he had to take. "Deal. Put the money in the briefcase."

Chula got up, gave a courtly Latin bow and went into his bedroom. Rice had the briefcase held open when he returned. Chula dumped in a big handful of real U.S. currency, bowed again and pointed to the door. *"Vaya con Dios,* Duane."

Rice took the 405 to the Ventura to the Hollywood, wondering how the Garcias would react to the low numbers, and if Eggers could be intimidated into the vault for the real stuff. At Cahuenga he exited the freeway, and within minutes he was at his new "home," the Bowl Motel, seventy scoots a week for a room with a sink, toilet, shower and hot plate. Too expensive

for dope fiends; too far up from the Boulevard for hookers; too jig-free to interest the local fuzz. A good interim pad for a rising young criminal. He
parked in his space, grabbed the briefcase and walked to his room, threading his way past groups of beer-guzzling pensioners. Inside, he tossed the
briefcase on the bed and flopped down beside it, grabbing the snapshot of
Vandy off the nightstand. "Coming home, babe; coming home."

Ten minutes later the doorbell rang. Rice put the photo in his shirt
pocket, then walked over and squinted through the peephole, seeing Joe
and Bobby Garcia standing there looking hungry; Joe itchy and anxious,
like he couldn't believe what he'd just done, but drooling for the payoff;
Bobby in a gangstered-back thumbs-in-belt stance, drooling for *more*, the
butt of his .45 clearly outlined through his windbreaker.

Rice opened the door and pointed the brothers inside, then bolted it shut
behind them. He grabbed the briefcase and dumped the money onto the
bed and said, "Count it; it's a little less than I figured." Bobby started to giggle while Joe made a beeline for the cash and began separating it into piles.
Rice locked eyes with Bobby and said, "Tell me about it."

Bobby let his giggle die slowly; Rice saw that the ex-welter was closer to
stone loon than he thought—he couldn't play anything straight.

"Went in easy like I told you," Bobby said. "Wham, blam, thank you,
ma'am. Kept our masks and gloves on, tied her up good, taped her mouth
shut. I think maybe she dug it. Her nipples were all pointy." He went back
to giggling, then segued into sex noises while he jabbed his right forefinger
into a hole formed by his left thumb and pinky. When he started making
slurping sounds, Rice said, "Ease off on that, will you?"

Bobby kiboshed the slurping and started fondling the religious medals
that encircled his neck. "Okay, Duane-o. But she was fine as wine, I'll tell
you that. It go good for you?"

Rice watched Joe stack the loot according to denomination, realizing
that he liked the tagalong as much as he despised his brother. Joe hummed
as he counted, a tune that sounded like "Blueberry Hill." Listening to the
humming made it easy to talk to Bobby without wanting to vomit. "Yeah,
it was pie. Day after tomorrow for Confrey/Eggers. I've got a recon job for
you guys in the meantime."

Bobby giggled and said, "Pie like in hairpie?" and Rice saw red. He was
cocking his fists when Joe jumped up from the bed, frowned and said,
"Sixty-four hundred on the nose. That's really sh—"

Bobby shoved his brother aside, moved to the bed and began recounting the money. Finishing, he spat on the pile of bills and turned to look up at Rice. "Slightly less than you figured, huh? Like twenty-five K less. Like Little Bro and me just risked ten to life for *three fucking grand?*" He paused, then whispered, "You holding out on us?"

Knowing that fire full was the only way out, Rice said, "I'll chalk that up to disappointment and a bad temper, but you say it again and I'll kill you."

Joe stood perfectly still; Bobby gripped the mattress with both hands, his jaw trembling, saliva starting to creep out the corners of his mouth. Seeing more fear than anger, Rice threw him back a chunk of his *cojones*. "Listen, man, I'm just as pissed about it as you. And it's my fault. I should have realized that the real money was left in the vault. But we're still on for the next—"

Bobby screamed, "You're fucking crazy! These bank fools are leaving out peanuts to pilfer, and I'm not risking my ass again for another three grand!"

Thinking, macho counterpunch, Rice smiled and said, "I'm going to make Eggers go into the vault for us. The same hostage plan, for twenty times the money. I'm going to intercept him in person as he enters the bank, then force him to call you guys for confirmation that you're holding his bitch. If he agrees to hit the vault, I'll tell him to sit tight at his desk with his hands in view, and I'll go across the street and keep him eyeball pinned. When the guard and tellers arrive and the real money comes out, Eggers grabs what he can carry on his person and goes across the street to meet me. He figures out a cool way to do this, or his bitch gets chopped. Then I walk him to his car and tranq him."

Grinning like a macho ghoul, Bobby said, "Suppose he don't agree?"

Rice moved to Joe and threw a rough arm around his shoulders. "Then I kill him then and there and take the teller box money. But he'll agree. He always wears a baggy suit. Lots of room, and I'll tell him C-notes only. You in, partners?"

Bobby whooped and jumped up and down, dunking imaginary baskets; Rice tightened his grip on Joe's shoulders. Joe twisted free and stared at him, and Rice snapped to the fact that he was the smarter of the two. Joe's eyes pleaded; Rice whispered, "Two more days and it's over." Joe looked at Bobby, who was throwing left-right body punches at his reflection in the wall mirror. Rice stuck two fingers into his mouth and forced out a loud, shrill whistle.

The noise brought the scene to a halt. Bobby leaned against the mirror and said in exaggerated barrioese, "Thirty-two hundred. Come up green, homeboy."

With an exaggerated shit-eating grin, Rice moved to the bed and began a slow-motion recount of the money, dividing it first in half and shoving that part under the pillow, then separating the remaining half into two portions. Finishing, he offered Joe the first handful of bills, Bobby the second. Both brothers jammed the cash into their front and back pants pockets, then stuffed the overflow into their windbreakers. When the last of the money was stashed, Rice gave them a slow eyeball and shook his head. His crime partners looked like two greedy greaseballs with elephantiasis; like a world-class dose of bad news.

Bobby cracked his knuckles; Joe looked at Rice and blurted, "What about the recon job, Duane? You gonna tell us now?"

Rice leaned back on the bed and shut his eyes, blotting out the bad news. "Yeah. I was thinking that maybe Hawley and Eggers know each other. Remember, we don't know who originally scoped out the heists, how he knew, who he knew, that kind of thing. I'll be watching the papers to see if they mention Hawley and Issler, and I want you guys to keep a loose tail on Eggers and Confrey, see if the cops or feds are nosing around. If they are, we have to call the heist off. I'll call you late tomorrow night. If there's no heat, we hit Friday morning."

Bobby popped his knuckles and said, "What kinda recon you gonna be doing?"

Rice opened his eyes, but kept them away from the brothers. "A little added terror angle, in case Eggers gets uppity. I'm going to trash his pad and steal some kitchen knives, then bring the knives with me when I brace him. That way, I can tell him you're gonna chop up his bitch with a knife with his prints on them. That and the fact that his pad's been violated ought to keep him docile."

Bobby whooped and jumped up and touched the cciling; loose bills started to pop out of his pants pockets. Rice said, "What was your record as a fighter?"

"Eleven, sixteen and zero," Bobby said. "Never went the distance, knocked out or got knocked out. My tops was seven rounds with Harry "The Headhunter" Hungerford. Lost on cuts. Why you asking?"

"I was wondering how you survived this long."

Bobby giggled and shoved Joe in the direction of the door. "Clean living, anonymous good deeds and faith in Jesus, Duane-o," he said, kneading his brother's shoulders. "And a good watchdog. Don't you worry. I'll keep a good tail on Eggers and his mama." He unlocked the door and waggled his eyebrows on the way out. Rice could hear him giggle all the way back to the parking lot.

With the money under his pillow, Rice tried to sleep. Every time he was about to pass out, the staccato beat of the Vandals' gibberish number "Microwave Slave" took over, and Vandy jumped into his mind in the frumpy housedress she wore when she performed the tune. Finally, staying awake seemed like the easier thing to do. Opening his eyes, he saw the ugliness of the room merge with the ugliness of the music. The frayed cord on the hot plate; a line of dust under the dresser; grease spots all along the walls. A lingering echo of Bobby Garcia's psycho/buffoon act was the final straw. Rice packed the money and his shaving gear into the briefcase and went looking for a new pad.

He found a Holiday Inn on Sunset and La Brea and paid $480 for a week in advance. No grease spots, no dust, no senile boozehounds clogging up the parking lot. TV, a view, clean sheets and daily maid service.

After stashing the bulk of his loot, Rice drove up to the Boulevard and spent a K on clothes. At Pants West he bought six pairs of Levi cords and an assortment of underwear; at Miller's Outpost he purchased a half dozen plaid shirts. His last stop was the London Shop, where a salesman looked disapprovingly at his tattoo while fitting him for two sport jacket/slacks combos. He thought about buying a set of threads for Vandy, but finally axed the idea: after he got her off the coke, she'd be healthier and heavier and a couple of sizes bigger.

Now the only white-trash link to be severed was the car. After dropping off his clothes at the new pad and changing into a new shirt and a pair of Levi's, Rice drove to a strip of South Western Avenue that he knew to be loaded with repo lots.

Two hours and six lots got him zilch—the cars looked shitty and none of the sales bosses would let him do under-the-hood checks. The seventh lot, a G.M. repo outlet on Twenty-eighth and Western, was where he hit pay dirt, a bored sales manager in a cubicle hung with master ignition keys telling him to grab a set of diagnostic tools and scope out any sled he wanted.

Rice did timing checks, battery checks, transmission checks and complete engine scrutinies on five domestics before he found what he wanted: a black '76 Trans Am with a four-speed and lots of muscle—good under the hood and even better looking—a car that would impress any crowd he and Vandy sought to crash.

The sales manager wanted four thou. Rice countered with twenty-five hundred cash. The sales manager said, "Feed me," and Rice handed it over, knowing the joker made him for a non–Boy Scout. After signing the purchase papers and pocketing the pink slip, Rice walked over to the street and saw an old wino sucking on a jug in the shade of his '69 Pontiac. He tossed him the keys to his former clunker and said, "Ride, daddy, ride," then strolled back to his sleek muscle car. When he got in and gunned the engine, the wino was peeling rubber down Western in the Pontiac, the bottle held to his lips.

Now Vandy.

Rice drove north to the Sunset Strip, savoring the feel of his Trans Am. He avoided putting the car through speed shifts and other hot-rod pyrotechnics; he was now technically a parole and probation absconder, and traffic tickets would mean a warrant check and instant disaster.

Street traffic on the Strip was light, sidewalk traffic lighter—schoolgirl hookers from Fairfax High turning a few extra bucks on their lunch hour, bouncers sweeping up in front of the massage parlors and outcall offices. Rice turned off Sunset at Gardner and parked. The lavender four-flat that housed Silver Foxes looked bland in the daylight, like just another Hollywood Spanish style. He walked over and rang the bell beneath the sexy fox emblem.

A young man in white dungarees and a Michael Jackson '84 Tour tank top opened the door and blocked the entranceway in a hands-on-hips pose. Rice sized up his muscles and figured him for a bodybuilder who couldn't lick a chicken; strictly adornment and a little jazz for the fag trade. "May I help you?" he asked.

Rice said, "Some friends in the Industry said this was the place to go for female companionship. I'm in town for a week or so, and I haven't got a lot of time to hit the party circuit. Normally paying for it isn't my style, but you were *very* highly recommended." He sighed, pleased with his performance—not a trace of Hawaiian Gardens and Soledad in his speech.

The youth flexed his biceps and imitated Rice's sigh. It came out a pout. "Everybody pays for it somehow, this is the herpes generation. Who were these people who recommended us?"

Rice pointed to the office he could glimpse past the youth's broad shoulders. "Jeffrey Jason Rifkin, the agent, and some buddies of his. I can't remember their names. Can we go inside?"

Nodding, the youth stepped aside just enough to let Rice squeeze through the door sideways. Their arms brushed, and Rice felt his stomach turn over when the kid let out a little grunt of pleasure.

The room was all white, furnished in Danish modern/High Tech—white walls and carpeting, metal tubular desk, bentwood chairs with white fabric backing. Scenes from rock videos were hung on the walls: Elvis Costello in fifties garb superimposed against an A-bomb mushroom cloud; Bruce Springsteen hopping a freight train; Diana Ross drenched to the bone at her Central Park concert. Rice sat down without being asked and watched the kid flip through a white Rolodex on the desk, moving his lips as he read. Thinking of him coupled obscenely with Bobby Garcia kept his revulsion down and gave him an edge of frost.

With a sighing pout, the kid looked up and said, "Yes, we've done business with Mr. Rifkin. In fact, we've sent over lots of foxes for his theme parties."

"Theme parties?" It was a reflex blurt, and Rice knew immediately that it was the wrong thing to say.

The youth hooded his eyes. "Yes, theme parties. Many of our foxes are aspiring actresses, and they enjoy theme parties because they get to act out more than they would on a straight assignment. You know, playing slave queens or topless cowgirls, that kind of thing. What do you do in the Industry?"

Rice said, "I'm a talent scout," and knew from the young man's puzzled expression that it was an outdated term. "I've been out of the Industry for a while," he added, "and Jeffrey Jason is helping me get rolling again. It's a tough racket to get back into."

"Yes," the young man said, "it is. What kind of fox were you looking for?"

Rice stretched his legs and smoothed his shirt front, then said, "Listen, I'm very choosy about my women. If I describe exactly what I want, can you check out your files or whatever and take it from there?"

The young man said, "We can do better than that. We've got *au naturel* photographs of all our foxes." He dug into the top desk drawer, and pulled out a white plastic binder and handed it to Rice. "Take your time, sweetie; it's a fox hunter's candy store, and nobody's rushing you."

Rice opened the binder, feeling a crazo sensation of being ripped upward from the crotch. The first page was a spiel about rare breeds of foxes and fulfillment of fantasies, scripted on lavender paper; on the second page the women began. Posed nude in identical reclining postures, they were all outright beautiful or outright gutter sensual, superbly built in the skinny model and curvy wench modes. White, black, Oriental, and Latina, they all fire-breathed *sex*.

Rice turned the pages slowly, noticing blank spots where other photos had once been pasted; he read the hype printed below each girl's first name and physical stats. "Aspiring actress" and "aspiring singer" were the usual subheadings, and next to them were lurid sex fantasies, supposedly written by the "foxes" themselves. The ridiculous accounts of three ways and four ways made him want to retch, and he flipped through to the end of the binder, looking only for the body he knew by heart. Not finding it, he glanced up at the young man and said, "Is this all your women?"

The youth nodded and flexed his biceps. "You're really hard to please. Those foxes are the crème de la crème."

Rice thought about mentioning former "foxes," then got an idea. "Listen, do you know most of the girls who work out of here?"

"Some. I've only been dispatching for a little over a week. Why?"

Rice said, "I was looking for a chick I saw walk out of here the last time I was in L.A. About five-six, one hundred ten, blonde, skinny, classy features. Preppy clothes. Ring a bell?"

The young man shook his head. "No . . . I'm new on the job, and besides, the owners wouldn't let the foxes dress preppy—no sex appeal."

Another idea clicked into Rice's head. "Too bad. Listen, since I didn't see that particular girl, I'd like you to give me a recommendation. Brains turn me on. I want a smart chick—one I can talk to."

The young man smiled, picked up the binder and leafed through it, then handed it to Rice. "There," he said. "Rhonda. She's got a master's degree in economics, and she's really groovy. A real brain fox."

Rice studied the photograph. Rhonda was a tall buxom woman with a dark brown Afro; deeply tanned except for bikini white across her breasts and pelvis. She was described as an "aspiring stockbroker," and her fantasy was listed as "orgies with rich, intelligent, beautiful men on my own private island in the Adriatic." Rice thought she looked shrewd and probably didn't write the retarded fantasy blurb. Snapping the binder shut, he said, "Great. Can you send her over to the Holiday Inn on Sunset and La Brea, in an hour?"

The youth gave his sigh-pout. "I'll call her. Rhonda is three hundred dollars an hour, one hour minimum. All our foxes gratefully accept tips over that amount. Rhonda carries her own Visa, Mastercard and American Express receipts and imprinter for the basic fee, but please tip her with cash. What room number?"

"814."

"We require a friendship fee of one hundred dollars for first-time fox hunters."

"Like a hunting license?"

The youth giggled; Rice thought he sounded just like Bobby "Boogaloo" Garcia. "That's cute. Yes, call it your deed to the happy hunting grounds. Cash, please, and your name."

Rice slipped a C-note from his shirt pocket and stuck it inside the binder. "Harry 'The Fox Hunter' Hungerford." The youth giggled as he wrote down the name, and Rice walked out wondering if the world was nothing but wimps, pimps, psychos and sex fiends.

Back at the Holiday Inn, he killed time by watching TV for word of the robbery. There was no mention of the heist or of a bank manager zoned on dust, let alone the hostage angle—the bank bigshots had probably stonewalled the media to save face. So far, so good—but his money was running out.

Just as the news brief ended, the door chimes rang. Rice grabbed a wad of twenties from the briefcase and stuck them under the mattress, then walked to the door and opened it.

The woman who stood on the other side in a green knit dress and fur coat was her photograph gone subtle. Expecting sleazy attire and makeup, Rice saw class that rivaled Vandy at her healthiest. No makeup on a face of classic beauty; large tortoiseshell glasses that set off that face and made it even *more* beautiful; a Rolex watch on her left wrist, an attaché case in her right hand. Rice's eyes prowled her body until he snapped to what he was doing and brought them back up to her face. Pissed at his lack of control, he said, "Hi, come in."

The woman entered, then did a slow model's turn as the door was shut, setting her attaché case on the floor, tossing her coat onto a chair. Rice sized up her moves. There was something non-whorish about her act.

Her voice was cool, almost mocking: "In olden times, fox hunting was the private sport of the landed gentry. Today, all natural-born aristocrats, busy men with taste and no time to waste, can enjoy that pleasure with Silver Foxes—the ultimate sensual therapy service for today's take-charge man."

Rice said, "Holy shit," and stepped backward, his heels bumping the attaché case and knocking it over. On impulse, he bent down and opened it up. Inside were three metal credit card imprinters, a stack of charge slips and a copy of *Wealth and Poverty* by George Gilder. The woman laughed as he snapped the case shut, then said, "I'm Rhonda. Most clients either love the intro or get embarrassed by it. You were incredulous. It was cute."

Rice flushed. The last time he'd been called "cute" was the sixth grade, when he nicknamed Hawaiian Gardens "Hawaiian Garbage." Carol Douglas shouted, "You're so cute, Duaney," and chased his ass the rest of the semester. "Cute, huh? Come to any conclusions?"

Rhonda took off her glasses and hooked them into her cleavage by a temple piece. "They're plate glass. I only wore them to look brainy. Yes, I've come to one conclusion—you don't want sex."

Rice sat down on the couch and motioned for Rhonda to join him. When she sat down an arm's length away, he said, "You're a smart lady. Is that a bogus Rolex?"

Rhonda flushed. "Yes. How did you know that?"

"I used to hang out in a Hollywood crowd. Everyone had fake Rolexes, and they used to talk about how their Rolex was real, but everyone else's was phony."

"Are you calling me a phony?"

"No, just seeing if you can level."

"Can you level? You don't look like any Hollywood type I've ever seen. What were *you* into?"

Rice laughed. "I was selling stolen cars. Want me to get to it?"

"If you want to. It's your money."

Rice said, "I'm looking for a woman. My girlfriend. A friend of a friend saw her up on the strip near all the outcall joints. I was in jail for six months, and she was having a tough time, and I—"

Rhonda put a hand on his arm. "And you thought if she needed money badly, she'd turn tricks?"

Pulling his arm away, Rice said, "Yeah. She visited me in jail, and I could tell she was strung out on coke." He thought of Vandy and Gordon Meyers—"It's real pharmaceutical blow, baby"—"Duane wouldn't want me to." The words and a backup flash of Vandy's prep clothes hanging loose on her gaunt frame forced his words out in a tumble: "And I know she'd only do it if she was desperate, and not really like it, and she's a singer, and a lot of girls at Silver Foxes are aspiring singers, and maybe she thought she could help herself while I—"

Something strange and soft in Rhonda's eyes stopped him. He moved to the bed and dug under the mattress until his hands were full of money, then walked back and dumped the stash of twenties in her lap. "That's for starters," he said. "Find her and there's lots more."

Rhonda counted the money and folded it into a tight roll. "Six hundred. What's her name? Have you got a picture?"

Rice took the snapshot from his wallet and handed it to her. "Anne Vanderlinden. She also goes by 'Vandy.'"

Rhonda looked at the photo and said, "Foxy. Does she—"

Rice screamed, "Don't say that!" Catching himself, he lowered his voice. "She's not a fucking animal, she's my woman." Catching Rhonda's strange look again, he said, "Don't stare at me like that."

Rhonda said, "Sorry," then patted the couch. Rice sat down beside her. She put a tentative hand on his knee and asked, "What's your name?"

Rice brushed the hand away. "Duane Rice. Are you in?"

"Yes. Put some things together for me about you and Anne. Who she is, what she likes to do, that kind of thing. Was she in the Hollywood crowd with you?"

Rice stared at the wall and straightened out the story in his head, then said, "First off, I know she isn't working outcall on the Strip; I've already checked those places out. Second, she doesn't really have any friends in L.A. except me. The last time I saw her was in jail close to three weeks ago. She cleaned out the pad we had together. She—"

Rhonda squeezed his arm. "Tell me about the Hollywood crowd."

"I was getting to it. Vandy's a singer. Used to be lead singer with a Vegas lounge group, Vandy and the Vandals. I was sort of her manager. I did some favors for an agent named Jeffrey Jason Rifkin, and he fixed us up with that Hollywood crowd. It took me a while, but I finally figured out that those people were all parasites who couldn't do Vandy a bit of good. But I was unloading cars on them and making a lot of money. I had plenty banked toward making Vandy's rock videos—"

"What?"

"Rock videos. That was my plan: get a stake together to produce rock videos featuring Vandy. It was moving, but then I got busted."

Rhonda said softly, "Look, Duane, I've been with Silver Foxes for over a year, and I've never seen Vandy or heard of her. But lots of outcall girls branch out into other scenes, particularly around here, where there's all this movie and music industry money. Especially girls like Vandy, budding singers looking to get ahead, looking to meet people who can help their careers. Do you follow me?"

Rice imitated Rhonda's soft voice. "I follow that you're bracing me for something. Spit it out; I didn't give you that money for bullshit."

Rhonda tucked the cash roll into her cleavage; Rice saw it as her first whorish move. She said coldly, "Some girls quit outcall because they get heavy into coke or they get offers to live with men in the Industry. Most of these men expect their girls to sexually service their friends, men who can do them favors. The girls get room and board and coke, and if they're *very* lucky, bit parts in movies and rock videos. There's an Industry name for them: coke whores."

Coke whores.

Rice forced the name on himself: tasting it, testing it. He looked at Rhonda and thought about hitting her with "stockbroker groupie" and "moneyfucker," but couldn't do it. The big question jumped into his mind and stuck like glue: Did it happen with Meyers?

Rhonda was staring at him, giving out big sad doe eyes like Carol Douglas back in Hawaiian Garbage. Rice kneaded his tattooed biceps and said, "What do I get for that six hundred?"

"Three hundred," Rhonda said. "Silver Foxes gets three. I didn't want to tell you that, Duane."

"Anyone afraid of the truth is a chickenshit. You're into these 'scenes,' right?"

"On the edges of them, but I'm nobody's kept woman."

"I know. You're just working your way through college."

"Don't be ugly, I want to help you. Was this an A, B, C or D crowd you and Vandy hung out in?"

"What?"

Rhonda's voice revealed exasperation. "In the movie and music biz there are four crowds: A, B, C and D. The A's are the heavy, heavy hitters, B's below them, and so forth. D's are the nerds who are lucky to get work. I was just wondering if Vandy could have hooked up with someone she met in your crowd."

Rice shook his head. "No way. I kept her away from the men, and she doesn't trust women. What crowd are you in?"

Rhonda lowered her eyes at the jibe, then said, "Any crowd with money. If Vandy's in L.A. and into any Industry scenes, I'll find her. Can I call you here?"

Rice looked around his new home, wondering if his talk with the stockbroker/whore had skunked the place past crashing in. "No," he said. "I might split." He took a pad and pencil off the phone stand and wrote down Louie Calderon's bootleg number. "You can call me here and leave a message twenty-four hours a day. You locate Vandy, and you'll see lots of money."

Rhonda took the slip of paper, stood up and collected her attaché case and fur coat. Rice watched her walk toward the door. When her hand was on the knob, she turned around and said, "I'll be in touch."

Rice said, "Find her for me."

Rhonda traced a dollar sign in the air and closed the door behind her.

At dusk, Rice felt the skunk stench close in on the new pad. He knew it didn't come from Rhonda, or Psycho Bobby Garcia, or Hawley or anybody else. It came from being wrapped too tight in his own skull for too long, with no one to talk to except people he wanted to use. It was what it was like all the time before he met Vandy and started to make things happen.

He made the black '76 Trans Am happen.

First he fishtailed out of the Holiday Inn parking lot; then he cruised the Boulevard, idling the engine at stoplights, staying in second gear until he hit Western Avenue. On Western northbound he speed-shifted into third, sized up traffic and vowed not to touch the brake until he hit the Griffith Park Observatory.

So he tapped the horn as he clutched, weaved and shifted, and then Hollywood was behind him and the park road opened up. Then the whole world became a narrow strip of asphalt, headlight glow and a broken white line.

Seventy, eighty, eighty-five. At ninety, on the long upgrade approaching the observatory, the Trans Am started to shimmy. Rice pulled to the side of the road and decelerated, catching a view of the L.A. Basin lit with neon. He thought immediately of Vandy and gauged distances, then turned around and drove toward the tiny pinpoints of light that he knew marked their old stomping grounds.

Their old condo was already up for sale, with a sign on the front lawn offering reasonable terms and fresh molding beside the door he'd kicked off. Splitsville, Cold City, *Nada*.

He drove to the 7-11 on Olympic and Bundy, where he used to send Vandy for frozen pizzas and his custom car magazines. A new night man behind the counter scoped him out like he was a shoplifter. The skunk odor came back, so he grabbed a West L.A. local paper and a candy bar and tossed the chump a dollar bill.

In the parking lot, he ate half the candy bar and looked at the front page. Vandalism at schools in the Pico-Robertson area; church bake-offs in Rancho Park; little theater on Westwood Boulevard. Then he turned the page, and everything went haywire.

The article was entitled, "Sheriff's Vet Heading Security at California

Federal Branch," and beside it was a close-up photo of Gordon Meyers. Rice's hands started to shake. He placed the newspaper on the hood of the Trans Am and read: "California Federal Bank's District Personnel Supervisor Dennis J. Lafferty today announced that Gordon M. Meyers, forty-four, recently retired from the Los Angeles County Sheriff's Department, has taken over as head of security for the Pico-Westholme branch, replacing Thomas O. Burke, who died of a heart attack two weeks ago. Meyers, who served most of his duty time as a jailer in the Main County Jail's facility for emotionally disturbed prisoners, said: 'I'm going to make the most of this job. After a week on the job, Cal Federal already feels like home. It's great to be working with sane, noncriminal people.'"

Rice read the article three more times, then took his hands from the car's hood. They were still trembling, and he could see the blood vessels in his arms pulsate. A scream built up in his throat, then the "Death Before Dishonor" carved on his left biceps jumped out and calmed him. With his tremors now at a low idle, he drove to Pico and Westholme.

The bank was small, dark and still, a low-rent job for a low-rent ex-cop with wacko, low-rent criminal fantasies. Rice cruised by, once, twice, three times, each time forcing himself to say, "Duane wouldn't want me to," "Anyone afraid of the truth is a chickenshit," and "It happened." On the fourth circuit all that came out was, "It happened, it happened, *it happened.*"

Now that he knew it himself, he parked the Trans Am and brainstormed. In and out in three minutes. A block from the 405 north and southbound, two minutes from the Santa Monica east/west, five from Wilshire. Fifty/twenty-five/twenty-five with the Garcias; then adios, greaseballs. The master keys at the repo lot for a foolproof getaway. *Make it happen.*

Rice sat back and made pictures of Vandy, of East Coast rock gigs, of New York crowds that didn't have letters in front of them and big houses in Connecticut. Then noises in his head bombarded the pictures: good metal-on-metal noises that he recognized as the clash of gears, high-powered engines igniting, double-aught loads snapping from breech to barrel.

9

Lloyd sat in the outer office of the Los Angeles F.B.I.'s Bank Robbery Unit, kneading his gauze-bandaged right hand and musing on his new lease on professional life. McManus had called him in Frisco with the word: his suspension was over, he was back on duty with a liaison gig with the feds; report tomorrow morning to Special Agent Kapek at the F.B.I. Central Office and don't fuck up. The "lease" was a phaseout, he decided; a stratagem to keep him occupied and docile while the high brass figured out a discreet way to give him the big one where it would do the most damage. On the flight down and cab ride over he had been exultantly happy, then a look at the clerk/receptionist's face when he flashed his badge brought it all to a crash. It had to be a shit assignment, or they would have given it to a field lieutenant. His glory days were dead.

A severe-looking woman poked her head out of the connecting door and said, "Sergeant Hopkins?"

Lloyd pushed himself out of his chair with both hands; his right hand throbbed. "Yes. To see Special Agent Kapek. Is he here yet?"

The woman walked toward him, holding a manila folder and a sheaf of loose pages. "He'll be here soon. He said you should please wait and read these reports."

Lloyd took the papers with his good hand and sat back down, dismissing the woman with a nod of the head. When he was alone again, he opened the folder, smiling when he saw that it contained a series of L.A.P.D. crime reports.

The first report was submitted by a West Valley Division daywatch patrol unit, and detailed events of Wednesday, 12/7/84, less than twenty-four hours before. While on routine patrol of Woodman Avenue, the officers of Unit Four–Charlie–Z came upon a middle-aged white male urinating in the open window of a 1983 Cadillac Seville. When they approached, they de-

termined that the suspect was heavily under the influence of a narcotic substance, and cautiously advised him of his rights before arresting him for in-
decent exposure and public intoxication. The man screamed incoherently
as he was handcuffed, but the officers were able to pick out the words "bank
rob" and "ray gun."

At the West Valley Station booking area, the suspect was searched. His
identification revealed him to be Robert Earle Hawley, forty-seven, the
owner of the Cadillac Seville. Finding the name familiar, the booking officer checked with the daywatch commander and learned that security personnel at the Bank of America on Woodman and Ventura had entered the
bank at opening time to find the cash boxes ransacked and the bank's manager, Robert Hawley, missing.

Hawley's booking was postponed. The F.B.I. Bank Robbery Unit was no-
tified of the bank manager's incarceration, and a team of detectives drove
him to U.S.C. County General Hospital for detoxification. After determining that Hawley was under the influence of "angel dust," a counterdose
of Aretane was administered. When Hawley returned to a sober state, F.B.I.
Special Agent Peter Kapek and a team of L.A.P.D. detectives again advised
him of his right to remain silent and have an attorney present during questioning. Waiving those rights, Hawley gave the officers the following account of his morning's activities:

At 7:45 A.M. he received a phone call from an unknown man, directing
him to call the home of his "girlfriend," Sally Issler. The man told Hawley
(who is married) that Miss Issler would be killed if his demands were not
met, and that he would call back in exactly three minutes. Hawley called
Miss Issler. A man with a Mexican accent answered, then put Miss Issler on
the line. She screamed that she was being held captive by two men with
guns and knives and to do whatever their friend said. Hawley said he would,
then hung up. The man called back as he said he would, and told Hawley to
meet him on Woodman near the bank in ten minutes, warning him that his
phone was tapped, and any attempts to contact the police would result in
Miss Issler's death. Hawley met the man near the bank, and described him
as "white, late twenties, light brown hair, blue eyes, 5'11"–6'1", 160–170
pounds, with neatly trimmed beard and mustache, wearing three-piece tan
suit." The man forced Hawley to open the bank and empty cashboxes containing approximately $60,000 in traveler's checks into a briefcase, then
walked him back to his car, where he shot him twice with what looked like
a "ray gun." Welts on Hawley's neck and collarbone and small metal darts

still stuck to his clothing indicated that he was telling the truth. Officers were dispatched to the home of Miss Issler. They found her bound and gagged, but otherwise unharmed. She told them that her captors wore ski masks that covered their faces, but were obviously Mexicans. They spoke fluent English with Mexican accents. One man, the "softer-spoken" of the two, was tall and slender; the other, who "talked dirty" to her, was short and muscular. She placed both men as being in their early thirties, and said they were both armed with army-issue .45 automatics with attached silencers.

Lloyd skimmed through the remaining reports, learning that Hawley was treated for toxic poisoning and was not charged with a wienie-wagger beef or with anything pertaining to the robbery, and that Sally Issler was treated for shock at a local hospital and then released. The disparate facts started to sink in, pointing to solid criminal brains. He was about to give the initial pages another go-around when he sensed someone watching him read. He looked up to see a tall man of about thirty hovering near the doorway. "Pete Kapek," the man said. "Nice caper, huh? You like it?"

Lloyd stood up. "Bank robbery's not my meat, but I'll take it." He walked over to the doorway. Kapek stuck out his right hand, then noticed the bandage and switched to his left. Lloyd said, "Lloyd Hopkins," and fumbled a handshake. Kapek said, "I've heard you're smart. What do you think, right off the top of your head?"

Lloyd walked into Kapek's office and went straight for the window and its view of downtown L.A. seven stories below. With his eyes on a stream of antlike people scuttling across Figueroa, he said, "Right off the top, why me? I'm a homicide dick. Two, what's with Hawley? Presumably, he was chosen because his affair with the Issler woman made him particularly vulnerable to a blackmail angle. Again presumably, his wife didn't know about Issler. Then why did he spill his guts so quickly?"

Kapek laughed. "It wasn't in the report, but the phone man told Hawley he had infrared fuck shots of him and Sally. He threatened exposure of the affair as well as Sally's murder. I sized up Hawley as a wimp and made him a deal. Talk, and we wouldn't press charges on him for flashing his shlong, and we'd keep the whole mess out of the media's clutches. You like it?"

Lloyd turned around and looked at Kapek, noticing acne scars that undercut his Fed image and made him seem more like a cop. "Yeah, I like it. Also right off the top of my head: one, we're dealing with brains. Stupider guys would have gone straight for Hawley's wife, right there at his pad, and kept *her* hostage, which might have driven Hawley to the cops from jump street. That's impressive. If the wrong guys got ahold of a family hostage idea and got away with it once, they'd keep going until someone was killed. As it stands, this is probably a one-shot deal, which leads us back to Issler. She been polygraphed?"

Kapek sat down and poked a pencil at the papers on his desk. "She's clean. No polygraph yet, but while she was at the hospital, I had a forensic team and latent prints team do a job on her apartment. They found jimmy marks on the side door, and rubber glove prints on all the surfaces the Mexicans would have touched. We got a bunch of viable latents, and the team stayed up half the night doing eliminations against Sally, Hawley, and a list of friends and relatives that Sally gave us, working with D.M.V., armed forces and passport records. You know what we got? The above non-suspects, and one unaccounted-for set that later turned out to be some dip-shit L.A.P.D. rookie who saw all the black-and-whites out front and thought he'd make the scene. The forensic guys got soil and mashed-up flower petals coming through the side door; the beaners trampled a flower garden on their way in. No, Sally baby was *not* in on it."

Lloyd said, "Shit. Competent print men?"

Kapek laughed. "The best. One guy is a real freak. He dusted the bedposts and logicked that Sally likes to get on top. You like it?"

"Only on Tuesdays. Let's get the obvious stuff out of the way. The phone man wore gloves and Hawley can't I.D. him from mug shots?"

"Right."

"No eyeball witnesses at either crime scene?"

"Right."

"The bank checks bug me. What can they yield cash—a quarter on the dollar?"

"If that. But they're *green*—and from a distance, you know, during a casing job, they might appear to be the real thing, which doesn't make our boys look too smart."

Lloyd nodded. "Employees and ex-employees, known associates of Issler and Hawley?"

"Being checked out. If we don't bust this thing in a week or so, I'll plant a man in the bank. Our approaches are narrowing down. You like it?"

Lloyd collected his thoughts by looking out the window at low-hanging clouds brushing the tops of skyscrapers. "No, I don't. One of the reports said Issler made the Mexicans as carrying army-issue .45s. That's a strange perception for a woman."

Kapek chuckled. "Sexist. Issler's father was a career officer. She knows her stuff. Those old heavy .45s are getting scarce, though. Maybe an approach."

Nodding silently, Lloyd watched dark clouds devour the restaurant atop the Occidental Building; for a moment he forgot that this "case" would probably be his last. Turning to look at Kapek, he said, "So we're stuck with figuring out where the robbers glommed onto Hawley and Issler, and if either of them have other bank manager friends in similarly vulnerable positions, which is a bitch of a fucking intelligence job."

Kapek slapped both thighs. "How about an ad in the singles tabloids— 'Bank Managers involved in extramarital romances please come forward to act as decoy!' No, I've already questioned Hawley and Issler on that—zip. This is a one-shot deal, perpetrated by brainboys who can control themselves. Now the crunch question: what are you going to do about this thing?"

Lloyd cut off Kapek's eagerness with a chopped hand gesture. "No. First, how are we working this? I've been a supervisor and I've worked alone, but I've never worked an interagency gig with the feds. I realize it's your investigation, but I want to know what I can ask for, who I can delegate and how much slack I've got on doing it my way."

Kapek muttered, "Your way," under his breath, then said out loud, "The investigation is structured *this way*. L.A.P.D. is handling the Issler assault-kidnap, with the squad lieutenant from West Valley dicks supervising. He knows you're the liaison; he'll give you any information or assistance you need. I've got three men checking out Issler's and Hawley's known associates, *and* the restaurants and motels they frequented, that kind of thing. They'll be compiling data on the people they come into contact with, checking them out with L.A.P.D. R&I, looking for connections. The traveler's checks are a long shot, but the serial numbers have been broadcast nationwide, and the West Valley cops have put out the word to their snitches. I want you as a floater between agencies. *You've* probably got snitches up the ying-yang, and I want you to utilize them. There is absolutely *nothing* in our computer or files on white/Mexican heist teams period, let alone ones given to kidnap-assaults. This caper sounds like street criminals graduating—more your beat than mine. You take it from there."

Lloyd breathed in the declaration of his second-banana status; it felt like a swarm of nasty little bureaucratic bees buzzing at his brain. His voice was tight and hoarse as he said, "Let's fucking *move*, then. You've got Hawley intimidated, so grab his credit card bills so we can see where he and Sally have been screwing. Don't trust his memory on it—subconsciously he'll be screwing *you*. Lean on him, polygraph him, rattle his skeletons. You like it?"

Kapek snickered, "Rubber hose him? Threaten him with an I.R.S. audit? He's got a son in college who's gay. Squeeze him by putting it on the six o'clock news? Ease off, Sergeant. The man is cooperating."

The buzzing grew deafening. Lloyd looked out the window, then jerked his eyes back when the notion of a seven-story jump to oblivion started feeling good. "I want to have a shot at Issler," he said. "I want to question her about her old boyfriends, and I want to put a tap on her home and work phones. I'll go easy on her."

Kapek stood up, put his hands on the desk and leaned forward so that his face was only a few feet from Lloyd's. "Unequivocally no. That order comes directly from your own immediate superior officer. Captain McManus told me personally to keep you away from her, and all other women involved in this investigation beyond the level of field interrogation. He told me that if you violate that order, he'll suspend you from duty immediately. He means it, and if you cross me on this, I'll report it to him in a hot flash."

Suddenly the bees did a kamikaze attack. Lloyd looked down at his bandaged hand and saw that he had gripped the window ledge so hard that blood was starting to seep through the gauze. He stared out the window at a dark mass of rain clouds. Seeing that the Occidental Building was now completely eclipsed, he said, "It's your ball game, G-man. I'll call you every twenty-four unless something urgent comes up. Call me at home or Parker Center if you get anything. You like it?"

"I like it."

"What else did McManus tell you?"

"He implied that you have emotional problems pertaining to the pursuit of pussy. I told him that my wife's a black belt in karate, so I don't have those problems."

Lloyd laughed. "It's your ball game, but it's my last shot. I'm gonna nail these cocksuckers."

Kapek pointed to the door. "Roll, hot dog."

Lloyd rolled, first in a cab to Parker Center, where he formally reported back for duty, then in a '79 Matador to the West Valley Station, staying ahead of the northbound storm clouds that threatened to drench the L.A. basin to the bone.

In the empty West Valley squadroom, he read the reports filed by plainclothes officers who had canvassed the two crime scenes late the previous day. The Woodman and Ventura house-to-house was a total blank—three housewives had noticed Hawley passed out in his Cadillac, but no one had seen him in the company of another man. The canvass of Sally Issler's neighborhood was an even bigger zero—no male Mexicans, alone or traveling as a pair, were seen on the street, and no unknown or suspicious vehicles were parked on or near her apartment building.

Sally Issler's formal statement, made after she came out of her hospital-administered sedation, was more illuminating. Asked about the personalities of her two captors, she had stated that the "tall, slender" man seemed "passive for a criminal; soft-spoken, maybe even educated," and that the "short, muscular" man "came on like a sex freak, like one of those Mexicans who hit on every chick they meet." When asked exactly what the short man said, she refused to answer.

Lloyd called Telecredit and asked for lists of Robert Hawley's and Sally Issler's recent credit card transactions, emphasizing restaurant and bar bills and motel accommodations. The operator promised to phone him at Parker Center with the information.

Running down options in his mind, Lloyd left a note for the lieutenant handling the Issler investigation to call him at the Center, then wrote out a memo to be teletyped to all L.A.P.D. divisions for roll call: "All units be alert for two-man stickup team: male Mexicans, early thirties, one tall, slender and 'soft-spoken,' one short, muscular and a possible sex offender. Both armed with silencered, army-issue .45 autos. Also be alert for B. of A. Greenback traveler's checks, serial number and denominations in West Valley Div. 12/7/84 robbery bulletin. Direct *all* queries and field interrogation reports to Det. Sgt. Hopkins, Robbery/Homicide Div. x 4209."

On his way out, Lloyd left the memo with the watch commander, who assured him it would be transmitted in time for the nightwatch crime sheet. Then he rolled back to Parker Center, this time straight into the storm clouds.

He was skirting the east edge of Hollywood when the rain hit. Hawley, Issler and Mexican bandits rolled out of his mind, and Janice rolled in, freeze-framed as she looked the last time he saw her. After punching out the lawyer's bookcase, he had walked through Chinatown, pressing his bloody hand into his shirttail, numbed and directionless until it started to rain in buckets and he realized he was only a few blocks from Janice's apartment. He knocked on the door and Roger answered in a bathrobe, his yappy dachshund cowering in back of him.

Roger himself backed off as if fearing a blow. Lloyd walked past him into the kitchen, holding his hand tightly to avoid dripping blood on Janice's Persian carpet. The dog alternately yapped, growled and took a bead on his ankles as he wrapped a dish towel around his gashed knuckles.

Janice had walked in then, carrying a pitcher of frozen daiquiris. She jumped back at the sight of Lloyd, and the pitcher fell to the floor, banana and rum fizz flying in all directions. Lloyd held up his hand and said, "Oh shit, Jan," and the dachshund began lapping up the goo. Roger entered the kitchen as the dog began to reel from the booze. He tried to grab him, but slipped on banana residue and hit the floor ass first. The drunken hound lapped his face, and Janice laughed so hard she had to grab Lloyd for support. He held her with his good arm, and she burrowed into him until he could feel them melding into each other the way they used to. Then Roger broke the spell by blubbering about his robe being ruined, and Janice drew away from her husband and back to her lover. But a brush fire had been ignited. Lloyd whispered, "I love you," as he retreated from the kitchen. Janice formed "yes" with her lips and touched her hands to her breasts.

Back at his Parker Center cubicle, Lloyd let the brush fire smolder as he figured out shit work logistics, first making notes for computer cross-checks, then writing an interdepartmental memo alerting Detective Division personnel to the case and its salient facts. The work forged the facts even deeper into his own mind, pushing back a notion to pad the job and thus postpone the inevitable.

The sense of inevitability dug in like spurs and drove him down to the fourth-floor computer room, where he had the programmer feed in queries on white/Mexican stickup teams and their current dispositions, male Mexicans with both armed robbery and sex offense convictions, and known and suspected gangland armorers. The results came back in twenty minutes—a printout of forty names and criminal records. The first two categories were washouts; the twelve white/Mexican heist teams all had at least two members currently in prison, and the nine Mexican armed robber/sex offenders were all men aged forty-eight to sixty-one.

Lloyd took the list of gun dealers up to his cubicle and read through the twenty-one names and criminal records, immediately dismissing the blacks—Latin and black hoodlums hated each other like poison. This eliminated thirteen names, and the printout showed that four of the eight men remaining were in county jail and state prison on various charges. He wrote down the four names that were left: Mark McGuire,

Vincent Gisalfi, Luis Calderon and Leon Mazmanian, then called his most trusted snitch and gave him the names, an outline of the Hawley/Issler case and the promise of a C-note for hard info. The shit work completed, he looked out his window at the rain and wondered what Janice was doing. Then he balled his bad hand into a fist, checking the gauze for seepage. Seeing none, he pulled off the bandage and dressing and tossed it into the wastebasket.

10

Joe Garcia woke up on the morning of his second strong-arm assault and found himself eyeball to eyeball with another flattened .45 slug, this one mounted on mattress stuffing that had popped out of his Sealy Posturepedic while he slept. Rolling onto his back, he saw the lumber the workmen had stacked for the reconstruction of his bedroom wall and added the spent piece of metal to the ones he'd already dug out of his clothes and books and records. Eleven. Bobby had shot off both guns, a total of fourteen rounds. A stack of his sci-fi paperbacks, his Pendletons and all of his old Buddy Holly records got wasted, and three of the little cocksuckers were still hiding, waiting to tell him that even though he had almost two grand in his kick and Bobby was paying for the damage, he was thirty-one and going nowhere. Figure today's score as ten times the money in a ten times more dangerous plan, and he was going nowhere rich. Then Bobby would talk him into some sleazoid quick-bucks scam, and he'd be going nowhere broke. Pushing himself out of bed, Joe felt shivers at his back and nailed the source: two days ago he became a righteous hardball criminal. If he was going nowhere, at least he was doing it in style.

Then his eyes caught the silencered handgun on top of his dresser, and the source nailed him, turning his knees to rubber. He was an hour away from committing felonies that could send him to prison for the rest of his life or have him shot on sight. The one *good* line from his longtime "epic" song supplied the final nail and made his arms shake like Jell-O: ". . . and death was a thrill on Suicide Hill."

Joe fought the shakes by thinking of Bobby, knowing he'd get pissed or depressed or grateful if he kept running riffs on him. While he dressed he remembered growing up in Lincoln Heights and how Bobby held him when the old man came home juiced and looking for things to hit; how he tied him to his bed so he could go out and play without him; how all the neighbors despised their family because only two kids meant they were bad Catholics, and how Bobby beat up the kids who said they were really Jews in disguise.

Bobby saved his ass then, but when Father Chacon talked the old lady into trying for more rug rats against doctor's advice and she died in childbirth, Bobby kicked the shit out of him when he called the dippy old priest a *puto*.

And Bobby carried him through burglary and jail; and Bobby spit on his dreams; and he could split from him, but he had to stay in L.A. for the music biz, and if he stayed in L.A., Bobby would find him and Bobby would need him, because without him Bobby was a one-way ticket to the locked ward at Atascadero.

The rundown calmed Joe to the point where he could shave, and dress in his camouflage outfit of business suit and shiny black shoes. But when he stuck the .45 into his belt, the shakes returned. This time he fought them with pictures of 10K worth of guitars, amps and recording equipment. It worked until Bobby jumped into the doorway, his arms raised like the Wolfman, growling, "Let's go, *pendejo*. I'm hunnnnggry."

The brothers drove to their target.

At Studio and Gage they parked and fed two hours' worth of coins to the meter, then walked the three blocks north to Hildebrand. Street traffic was scarce, pedestrian traffic nonexistent. At 8:17 they came up on Christine Confrey's ranch-style house, her red Toyota parked in the driveway. Bobby said, "Walk like you're the landlord"; Joe whispered, "Be ultra frosty." Bobby grinned. "Now, little brother."

They took the driveway straight to the back door. Joe looked for witnesses while Bobby took a metal ruler from his jacket pocket and slipped it between the door and doorjamb and pushed up. The catch snapped, and they entered into a tiny room filled with folding lawn chairs. Joe reset the latch and felt his sweat go ice-cold at the moment of B&E terror: if they were seen, it was over.

Bobby eyed the door to the house proper and picked a soiled towel up off the floor; Joe slipped a length of nylon cord from his back pocket, then watched his brother's lips do a silent countdown. At "5" they donned their ski masks and gloves; at "1" they *moved*, pushing through the door at a fast walk.

The connecting hallway was still. Joe heard music coming from a door at the far left end and took that side of the hall, knowing part of his watchdog job was to be the one who grabbed the girl. As the music grew louder, he pressed himself to the wall; when the music drowned out the slamming of his heart, he leaped through the open door and jumped on the woman who was standing with one foot on the bathtub ledge, poising a razor over her leg.

The woman screamed as Joe's arms went around her; the razor gouged a section of calf. Bobby elbowed his way into the bathroom and wrapped the towel over her head, stuffing a large wad of it into her mouth, stifling her screams. Joe fumbled her robe into her breasts so they wouldn't stick out, then circled the cord around her, pressing her arms to her sides. When he got it tied, he lifted her off the floor, kicking and flailing, still tightly grasping the razor. He whispered, "Sssh, sssh, sssh. We're not going to hurt you. We just want money. *We just want money.*"

Bobby got out his roll of tape and pulled a long piece loose, then withdrew the towel. The woman let out a short screech before he was able to loop the tape around her head and press it to her mouth. When he saw the terror in her eyes, his whole body started to twitch, and he whispered, "Get her fucking calmed down."

Joe loosened his grip on the woman as Bobby stumbled out of the bathroom. With one hand he took out his .45 and held it in front of her; with the other he smoothed her disheveled hair. "Sssh. Sssh. We're not going to hurt you. This is a robbery. It's got to do with you and your boyfriend Eggers. You have to do two things: you have to *not* be scared, but you have to *act* scared when the phone rings and you talk to your boyfriend. My buddy's a crazy man, but I can control him. *Be cool and you won't get hurt.*"

Christine Confrey's tremors decelerated just a notch; Joe could feel her thinking. When she dropped the razor, he relaxed his grip and steered her into the hallway. Bobby was there, leaning against the wall, giving the thumbs-up sign. "The phone is gonna ring real soon," he giggled.

Joe nodded and moved Christine into the bedroom, motioning Bobby to stay out. He noticed the phone on a nightstand; it had the look of something about to explode. When it rang shrilly, he looked into his captive's eyes. "*Just be cool,*" he whispered, gently pulling the tape from her mouth.

He picked up the phone on the fifth ring and said, "Eggers?" getting a "Y-yes, Chrissy. P-please p-put her on." Nodding at Christine and holding up the .45 for her to see, he handed the receiver over.

She grasped it with shaking hands and tried to form words. Joe fought a desire to smooth her hair. Finally her voice caught: "John, there's these two men here. They've got guns and they say that all they want is money." She watched Joe stroke the barrel of his .45, and her voice accelerated: "Please, John, goddammit. Don't be fucking cheap—do whatever they tell you to do or they'll kill me. They—"

Joe grabbed the phone and put his free hand over Christine's mouth. He said, "Got it, Eggers?" and got "Yes, you animal" in return. Joe said, "Just do what our friend says," then hung up.

Christine Confrey twisted her head free and said, "Now what?" Joe thought of tire-squealing black-and-whites and shotgun-wielding fuzz. "Now we wait," he said. "An hour tops. Then we get another call, and we tape your mouth and you never see us again."

"You're a slimy piece of Mexican shit," Christine Confrey replied. Joe caught himself starting to nod in agreement, but said instead, "Be cool." His face began sweating beneath the ski mask. It felt like a shroud.

They waited in silence, Christine sitting on the bed, Joe standing by the bedroom door, looking at his watch and listening to Bobby giggle as he prowled the house. It felt like he had two senses, both of them working toward something bad. After thirty-two minutes of scoping out the Timex, Bobby's giggles exploded into a big burst of laughter. Then the door pushed open, and the ski-masked loony was there, a magazine in his hands, growling, "Check the skin book, homeboy. Righteous *hairpie*."

Christine pointed to the magazine Bobby was waving, hyperventilating, then getting out: "I-I-I was nineteen! I needed the money and I only kept it because John likes to see what I was like then and I—"

Joe moved to the bed and wrapped the discarded section of tape around Christine's mouth. Bobby was at his back, holding the copy of *Beaverooney* open, jabbing his right forefinger at the pictures inside. "Dig it, bro! Is this bitch fine as wine, or am I woofin'! Dig it!"

To placate Bobby, Joe glanced at the legs-apart nude spread. "Yeah, but just maintain. *Main-fucking-tain*."

Bobby shoved him aside and sat down on the edge of the bed. Christine strained against the cord and tape, kicking her legs in an effort to propel herself away, working her lips trying to scream. A stream of urine stained the front of her robe and trickled down her thighs. Bobby squealed, "Righteous," and grabbed both her ankles with his left hand and held them to the bed, while his right hand hovered over her pelvis in a parody of a shark about to attack. He grunted, "Duhn-duhn-duhn-duhn," and Joe recognized it as the theme from *Jaws*. Bobby's shark hand did slow figure eights; Bobby himself whispered, "We reconned you good, baby, but I didn't pick up on how fine you are. Fine as wine. I'm the Sharkman, baby. Duhn-duhn-duhn-duhn. I give righteous fin and even better snout."

Joe whimpered, "No, no, no," as Bobby stuck his tongue through the hole in his ski mask and lowered his head; when his mouth made contact with Christine's leg, he shrieked, "No, you fucking rape-o, no!"

The phone rang.

Bobby jerked his head up as Joe moved toward the nightstand. He pulled the .45 from his waistband and aimed it straight between his brother's eyes. "Let it ring, puto. The shark wants to give some snout, and no candy ass watchdog is gonna stop him."

Joe backed into the wall; the phone rang another six times, then stopped. Bobby giggled and started making slurping noises. Christine squeezed her eyes shut and tried to bring her hands together in prayer. Joe shut his own eyes, and when he heard Bobby titter, "Shark goin' down," he stumbled out of the bedroom, picturing tear gas and choppers and death.

Then there was a crashing sound from the rear of the house. Joe opened his eyes and saw Duane Rice running down the hallway holding a briefcase and the .45, no ski mask and no beard disguise on. The house went silent, then Bobby's "Sharkman, Sharkman," reverberated like thunder. Rice crashed into the bedroom, and Joe heard a sound he'd never heard before: Bobby squealing in terror.

He ran to the bedroom door and looked in. Rice had Bobby on the floor and was slamming punches at his midsection. Christine Confrey was still on the bed, trying to scream. Her robe was pulled up over her stomach and her panties were curled around her ankles. Joe ran to the bed and pulled down the robe, then grabbed Duane Rice's shoulders and screamed, "Don't! Don't! You'll kill him!"

Rice's head and fists jerked back at the same instant, and he twisted to look up at the voice. Joe said, "*Please*," and Rice weaved to his feet and gasped, "Get the briefcase."

Bobby moaned and curled into a ball; Christine tried to bury her head in the bed sheets. Rice felt the throbbing redness that was devouring him ease down. When Joe came back holding the briefcase, he pinned his shoulders to the wall and hissed, "You listen to this and we'll survive. Get psycho out of here and run herd on him like you never did before. Tie the woman up even better and don't let that piece of shit near her. If I find out he even *touched* her again, I'll kill him. Do you believe me?"

Joe nodded and said, "Yes." Rice released him, opened the briefcase and started extracting handfuls of money, dropping them on the bed. When the briefcase was half empty, he pointed to the pile and said, "Your share. I'll call you tonight. I trust you for some reason, so you take care of him."

Joe looked at the wads of cash covering the crumpled sheets and Christine Confrey's legs, then looked down at Bobby, slowly rising to his knees. He turned around for sight of Duane Rice, but he was already gone.

Rice forced himself to walk slowly to the Trans Am, parked a block from Christine Confrey's house. He swung the briefcase like Mr. Square Citizen and wondered how good a look the woman got at his face, and why for a split second *her* face looked just like Vandy's. Then he remembered how at their first meeting Joe Garcia had called his brother a rape-o and how it didn't register as anything but jive. Eggers was angel dust pie, but it was Bobby Boogaloo who put them inches away from the shithouse.

After stashing the briefcase in the trunk, Rice drove down Gage to Studio, and at the corner saw the Garcias' '77 Camaro parked at the curb. He pulled into a liquor store lot across the street to observe the brothers' getaway and see if the fuzz approached the Confrey pad. If no black-and-whites descended and Joe and the rape-o looked good, they were clear, and Pico and Westholme was still a possible.

He thought of the score, of the sheer audacity of trashing Eggers's sterile Colonial crib and the look on his face when he showed him the knives he'd stolen and said, "Christine Confrey, chop, chop. Your prints. *You know what I want.*" The look got better as the heist progressed, the bank man realizing there was no way out except to obey. Even though the take was probably only 12K tops, it was twice the amount of the first job—a good omen, and a better appetite whetter.

After ten minutes, no patrol cars or unmarked cruisers appeared, and he could see straight up Gage and tell that the house was still undisturbed. His hands throbbed from whomping Bobby Garcia, and he gripped the steering wheel to control the pain. After twenty minutes, the Garcias swung onto Studio Boulevard from a block east of Gage, walking two abreast with shopping bags partially shielding their faces. Bobby was limping, probably from abdominal pain, and Joe was talking him through the whole scene, more like a daddy than a kid brother. Rice smiled as they got in their Camaro and drove off. For a cowardly tagalong criminal, Joe Garcia had balls. If he could control the rape-o's balls for three hours, he'd make Pico and West-holme happen.

When he got "home" to the Holiday Inn, Rice changed from his bank robber suit into a new shirt-Levi combo and counted the proceeds of the Eggers/Confrey job. His half of the haphazardly split take came to $5,115.00. Fondling the money felt obscene, and he remembered what a soft-hearted old bull at Soledad told him: don't fuck whores, because then all women start looking like whores. He remembered Christine Confrey's terrified face and wondered if you loved a woman, then did all women start looking like her? Even though Christine and Vandy were physical oppo-sites, their resemblance was weird.

Rice looked at the phone and flashed on an idea to call the fuzz and tip them to Christine, then double-flashed on it as suicide and dialed Louie Calderon's bootleg number.

Louie picked up on the first ring. "Talk to me."

"It's Duane. Got any messages for me?"

"Duane the Brain. How's it hangin'?"

"A hard yard. Any calls?"

"Yeah. If a nigger and a Mexican jump off the top of the Occidental Building at the same time, who hits the ground first?"

"Jesus, Louie. Who?"

"The nigger, 'cause the Mexican's gotta stop on the way down and spray his name on the wall!" Louie went into a laughing attack, then recovered and said, "I thought it was funny, and I'm a fuckin' Mexican. Got a pencil?"

"I can remember it. Shoot."

"Okay. Call Rhonda—654-8996. Sexed-out voice, Duane, really fine."

Rice said, "Yeah" and hung up, then dialed Rhonda's number. After six rings, the hooking stockbroker's sleepy voice came on the line. "Yes?"

"It's Duane Rice. What have you got for me?"

"Brace yourself, Duane."

"Tell me!"

Rhonda let out a long breath, then said, "I found out that Anne did work Silver Foxes for a while, a few months ago. Now she's taken up with a man—a video entrepreneur. I'm pretty sure it's a coke-whore scene. He's heavy into rock vid, and, well, I . . ."

Rice said, "Real slow now and you're a K richer. Name, address and phone number. Real slow."

"Can you pay me Monday or Tuesday? I'm going to the Springs for the weekend, and my car payment's due."

Rice screamed, "Tell me, goddammit, you fucking whore!"

Rhonda screamed back, "Stan Klein, Mount Olympus Estates, Number 14! You're a bigger whore than I am and I want my money!"

Klein the dope dealer who probably ratted him off on his G.T.A. bust—

Klein the lounge lizard who he always figured had the hots for Vandy and—

The hotel room reeled; adrenaline juiced through Rice like the shot of dope that had cost him three years of his life. The phone dropped to the floor, and through a long red tunnel Rhonda's voice echoed: "I'm sorry, Duane. I'm sorry. I'm really sorry." Everything went crazy, then a jolt of ice water made the room sizzle like a live wire.

You can't kill him.

You can't kill him because he's a known associate.

You can't kill him because Vandy's a known associate, and the cops will sweat her at Sybil Brand and the dykes will eat her up.

You can't kill him because then you and Vandy can't make the rock scene in the Big Apple and you'll never have the place in Connecticut, and—

It was enough ice-water fuel. Rice ran for the Trans Am, leaving the .45 under the pillow as added insurance. Rhonda's pleas were still coming out of the phone: "I'm sorry, goddammit, but I need money! You promised! You promised!"

Mount Olympus was an upscale tract of two-story Mediterranean villas situated off Fairfax in the lower part of the Hollywood Hills. Rice cruised the access road, looking for Stan Klein's red Porsche with the personalized plate "Stan Man." When all he saw were Benzes, Caddys and Audis, mostly color-coordinated to the houses, he pulled into the empty driveway of Number 14 and got out, grabbing a skinny-head screwdriver from the glove compartment.

The windows were too high to reach, but the door looked flimsy. Rice rang the bell, waited twenty seconds, then rang again. Hearing no sounds of movement inside, he inserted the screwdriver into the door runner just above the lock and yanked. The cheap plywood cracked, and the door opened.

He stepped inside and closed the door, making a mental note not to leave prints. The entrance foyer was dark, but off to his left he could see a big, high-ceilinged living room.

Rice walked in and gasped. Every inch of floor and wall space was covered with stereo and video equipment. V.C.R.s and Betamaxes were stacked along one wall floor to ceiling; home computer terminals, TV sets and giant cardboard boxes piled with Sony Walkmans were lined up on the floor. Three Pac-Man machines were propped by the doorway, and the rest of the room was taken up by mounds of small cardboard boxes. Threading his way into the maze, Rice grabbed a box at random. Rhonda the Fox and a naked man were on the cover, beneath the legend, 'Help me, Rhonda'—the Beach Boys. Private collector's item—available only thru Stan Man Enterprises, Box 8316, L.A., Calif. 90036."

It all went red.

Rice tore through every box in the room; read every cover. Shitloads of naked woman and oldies but goodies, but no Vandy. His frost was returning when he saw a phone and phone machine atop a color TV.

He punched the "Play Message" button and got: "Hi, this is Stan Klein on the line for Stan Man Enterprises. Annie and I are on a video shoot, but we'll be back Monday night. Talk to the beep. Bye!"

Rice pushed "Incoming." There was a tape hiss, followed by a beep and a male voice. "Stanley baby, it's Chick. Listen, Annie was great. Unbelievable skull. So listen, if you're free can we talk ad space like Tuesday? Call me." Beep. "Stan, this is Ward Carter. I . . . uh . . . want to thank you for the, uh, you know, Eskimo trade-off. Annie was fabulous. About the porn vid, it's strictly bootleg on the song rights, but I'm sure I can work out a deal with this man I know who's got a chain of X-rated motels. He's mob, and you know how those guys are into blondes, so maybe you could set up a party? Talk to you Mondayish."

The rest of the messages went unheard; a hideous wailing was drowning them out. Rice wondered where the sound was coming from. When his eyes started to burn, he knew he was weeping for the first time since the sixth grade in Hawaiian Garbage.

11

Lloyd was asleep in his Parker Center cubicle when the phone rang. Snapping awake, he pulled his legs off the desk and checked his watch: 2:40. Afternoon doze-offs: another sign of encroaching middle age. He grabbed the receiver and said, "Robbery/Homicide. Hopkins."

"Peter Kapek. We've got another one. I've got the manager; he's agreed to talk with no attorney. West L.A. Federal Building, fourth-floor interview rooms. Forty-five minutes?"

"Thirty and rolling," Lloyd said, and hung up.

He made the trip in thirty-five, lead-footing it Code Three all the way, then running upstairs to the F.B.I.'s Criminal Division offices. The receptionist looked at his badge and pointed him down a long corridor inset with Plexiglas cubicles on one side and listening rooms on the other. At the far end, he looked through the one-way glass and saw Peter Kapek and a middle-aged man in a tweed suit sitting at a metal table. The man appeared composed, Kapek harried as he jotted notes on a legal pad.

Lloyd stepped across the hall to the booth where a headset-wearing stenographer was transcribing the interrogation. He said, "L.A.P.D." and the woman nodded and tore off the long roll of paper flowing out of her machine. "It's complete," she said. "You didn't miss that much."

Lloyd took the paper and pulled it taut, squinting to read the computer type:

14:45 hrs; 12/9/84, W.L.A. Fed. Crim. Div.

Present: SA Peter Kapek, John Brownell Eggers, W.M., D.O.B. 6/28/39, no wants; no warrants; no criminal record.

Re: Robbery at Security Pacific Bank, 7981 Lankershim Blvd., Van Nuys.

Subject waived attorney.

P.K.: Mr. Eggers, I want you to forget what you already told the L.A.P.D. officers at the station on the ride over. I want a chronological reconstruction of today's events. Take your time, and be as detailed as you like.

J.E.: Of course. I went to the bank early this morning—about 8:30—because I had some papers to go over. As I was about to unlock the door—

P.K.: Excuse me, Mr. Eggers. Was there anyone else there at the bank?

J.E.: No, there wasn't. The staff doesn't arrive until 9:15.

P.K.: Thank you. Please continue.

J.E.: A man approached me as I was about to unlock the doors. He was a white man, about thirty, about six feet, one-seventy or so, medium brown hair, neatly trimmed mustache and beard. He was wearing a cheap tan three-piece suit and carrying a briefcase, and I didn't see him get in or out of a car. (*Long pause*)

The man showed me a gun in a shoulder holster and told me that *he* was the one who had broken into my home two nights before. I had already reported that to the police. He made me unlock the door, then he walked me to my desk. He told me that he wanted vault money, as much as I could carry outside on my person once the time lock went off at opening time. Then . . . (*Pause*)

Then the man took out a knife that he had stolen from my kitchen. He told me that two accomplices of his were holding my wife and daughter hostage at our vacation house in Lake Arrowhead, and that if I didn't cooperate, they would be raped, then dismembered with a second knife of mine, one that he knew had my fingerprints on it. I said I would cooperate, and begged the man not to let his partners hurt my family.

P.K.: Go on, Mr. Eggers. Slowly, please.

J.E.: Thinking of my wife and daughter held hostage terrified me. The man told me to sit at my desk, facing the window, with my hands in my lap, and to remain that way until opening time. He said he would be across the street watching and waiting, and at 9:35, I should walk outside with the money, and he would find me. He said that if I called the police or I wasn't outside at the specified time, my wife and daughter would die—because his partners were going to kill them at exactly 9:40 unless he delivered the "all-clear." (*Pause*)

At 9:30, with money distributed to the tellers, I chitted for the contents of one station. I couldn't think straight, I just mumbled something about a cash draft, stuffed the money in my pockets and walked outside. When I was out of sight of the bank, the robber grabbed me and forced me to hand over the money. Then he led me to my car and made me sit down behind the driver's seat, and he shot me with this ray gun, and I blacked out. When I woke up, around one o'clock, I had an awful headache. I ran to a pay phone and called my wife in Arrowhead, and she and Cathy were safe! No one had held them captive! I had been had! The police were at the bank because I had disappeared for hours, and the rest you know.

P.K.: Backtracking, Mr. Eggers, could you describe any distinctive mannerisms that the robber had?

The computer roll ended. Lloyd handed it back to the steno and walked across the hall and stared at the bank manager through the one-way glass, wondering how much of his bullshit Peter Kapek bought. Thinking "Fuck it," he knocked on the door and stood aside so that Eggers couldn't see him.

Kapek walked into the corridor seconds later, saw Lloyd and smiled. "Is this bimbo slick as shit? You like him?"

Lloyd imitated the smile. "You charging him?"

"With what? Perjury? That's your scene. What we've got so far is a pussy hound trying to protect his reputation. Except for the Lake Arrowhead bullshit and no mention of his sweetie pie, he's leveling. I'm going to goose him, then plea-bargain him into cooperating by giving him immunity on the girlfriend angle."

Lloyd shook his head. "Kapek, we can't do that. This makes two in three days, and the M.O. is getting hairier. We need a media alert on this. Have you hit him with Hawley and Issler?"

"He doesn't know them. That I believe absolutely. This whole shtick is beginning to get to me, Hopkins. You get anything from your files? Your informers?"

Lloyd grabbed Kapek's arm and led him down the hall, out of earshot of the steno booths. "Don't play this joker straight," he said. "He's slick, and he's got a lot of hardball in him, and he'll tie us up for days trying to I.D. his girlfriend."

Kapek yanked his arm free. "He'll cooperate. As soon as I say 'Getting any on the side?' he'll fold."

"Bullshit! You want a reconstruction on this? I buy the stolen knives as our guys—Eggers isn't hip enough to come up with something like that. The robbery went down just like he called it. Our boys got stiffed on the traveler's checks, and they're pissed. Only Eggers came off the dust looking to save his ass. He made the call to Arrowhead from a pay phone, probably with a credit card, so there'd be a record, and he got detoxed from the dust before he hit the bank, so he'd be coherent. He should be zorched to the gills, but he's Mr. Lucidity. You mention adultery, and he'll shut up tighter than a crab's asshole."

"No, *he won't.*"

Lloyd muttered, "Shit. That was gospel about his pad getting burglarized?"

"All the way," Kapek said. "I read the crime report an hour ago—no witnesses, no prints—nothing."

"Eyeball witnesses at the bank?"

"Zero."

"Shit! Let's *lean* on Eggers."

"You're a black-glove cop, Hopkins. I'm not. Eggers is a big man, so the dust shot didn't hit him as hard as Hawley. We play it my way." He shook his head and started to walk away.

Lloyd stepped in front of him and made his voice placating. "Listen, trust me on something. Turn the heat up in the interview room, get him to take off his jacket. You'll see a spike mark or a Band-Aid at the crook of one of his elbows. My guess is that he hasn't even gone by the girlfriend's pad to see if she's okay. The cocksucker hit the family doctor for an antitoxin, then started covering his ass. You release him like everything's copacetic, he'll lead us straight to her."

Kapek smiled. "I like it. But if there's no track or Band-Aid, we play it my way." He walked to the front of the corridor and talked to the receptionist, then returned and winked. "You like it?"

Five minutes later, the corridor started heating up; ten minutes later, it was outright hot. Lloyd watched through the one-way glass as John Eggers fidgeted in his chair, then took off his jacket. Kapek aped his actions, then rolled up his sleeves. This time Eggers aped the F.B.I. man, and by squinting, Lloyd could see the small circular Band-Aid on the inside of his left elbow.

Kapek stood up and stretched, then walked past Eggers and stepped into the corridor. Seeing Lloyd, he closed the door and said, "You're good. I'm sending Slick home in a cab in five minutes. Tail him, but if he goes to his skirt, don't approach, call me." He drew a slow finger across his throat. "I mean that. Also, we should have another confab. Van Nuys Station at six?"

Lloyd said, "Be there or be square," then wiped a line of sweat from his forehead and walked downstairs. In the parking lot, he stood by the side-street entrance and waited for the arrival of the taxi. Shortly, a Yellow Cab pulled in and cruised up to the building's back entrance. John Eggers, his suit coat slung over one shoulder, walked outside and got in. When the taxi swung out onto Veteran Avenue, Lloyd counted to twenty-five and pursued.

He caught the cab at the on-ramp to the 405 northbound, and let a car get between them as they headed toward the Valley. At Ventura, the taxi exited and swung east, staying in the middle lane, the driver cruising so maddeningly slow that Lloyd wanted to ram him with his unmarked unit's snout and shove them all the way to Eggers's destination. Just when his frustration felt like it was about to peak, the cab lurched and hung a sharp left turn onto Gage Avenue and went north. Lloyd started to tingle. Too déclassé a neighborhood for a middle-aged bank exec; they were headed for the girlfriend's pad. When the cab drew to the curb at the corner of Hildebrand, he continued on, looking back through his side mirror.

Eggers got out and walked up the steps of a modest ranch-type house and let himself in. Lloyd parked and walked down the street to his target, eyeing the windows for good listening spots. Deciding to prowl the house's perimeter, he walked down the driveway with his ears perked for sounds of weeping and comforting. He was all the way around the back to the other side when he heard the sounds of pure hard female rage:

". . . and it's all on you, you bastard! They were going to leave me alone until the bad one found that sleazy picture book that you're so fucking in love with!" The voice took on a baby talk tone: "Poor Johnny-poo got held up, and he's sooo afraid that the banky-poo and his wifey-poo are going to find out about his affair with Chrissy-poo. Awww. The mean old robber-poo shot Johnny-poo with dusty-poo, and he got his Brooksie-poo suit *allll* wrinkled. Awww." There was a sharp, flesh-on-flesh noise, then the woman's voice came out soft and dripping with contempt: "That man who robbed you is more of a fucking man than you'll ever be. Think about it, John. Next time you start talking about all the sacrifices you've made to be with me, think about that man beating up one of his partners to keep me from getting raped."

Eggers' retort was a beaten-dog grovel. "But you won't tell the police? Chrissy, my job—*our* future depends on keeping this quiet."

"No," the woman said, "I won't. I care about you too much to hurt you that way. But take this with you when you see your wife in Arrowhead tomorrow. He was sexy, and somewhere down the line when we're screwing, I'm going to be thinking of him, of the man who made you look weak and foolish. Now get out of my sight."

Lloyd leaned against the house and listened to the sound of an impotent, foot-stomping departure. When the door slammed, the woman's weeping took over, and he waited until the sobs trailed off before walking around to the front door. When he rang the bell, his hands were shaking. He looked at the name taped above the buzzer—Christine Confrey—and wondered what the woman with the volatile voice would look like.

The door swung open, and he saw. Chrissy Confrey was a small woman with a face of perfectly mismatched parts: high cheekbones, broad nose and pointed chin. Her hair was straight and long, and her tears had already dried. Lloyd winced at her handsomeness, and realized he didn't know how to play the interrogation. Holding out his badge, he said, "L.A.P.D. I know all about it, Miss Confrey. Two Mexicans with ski masks, one soft-spoken, one the guy who tried to molest you, the white guy you were tell—"

Christine Confrey tried to push the door shut. Lloyd jammed his foot into the floor runner and wedged himself into the house, shouldering the door, and Christine behind it, aside, putting his hands up in a "no harm" pose. "I know what you've been through," he said. "And I don't want you to talk about it. All I want you to do is look at some photographs. Will you do that?"

Christine hissed, "Get out"; Lloyd stepped toward her. "You can give your statement to a woman officer, and I'll try to keep your relationship with Eggers out of it. This is the second one of these assaults, and I want you to look at some photos that the other victims probably didn't see. It won't take long."

Her face a hardening mask of hatred, Christine said, "Have John Eggers look at your pictures. This is his mess, not mine."

"I'm going to," Lloyd said, "but I need you, too. Victims tend to block out the looks of their assailants, and quick cross-check I.D.s can be very helpful. I know you got a good look at the man."

Christine's face mask stiffened to the point where Lloyd thought her features would crack. "You're the assailant. Peeping at windows. Get out!"

Lloyd leaned against the door and wondered what to do, watching Christine Confrey hold her ground in front of him, her feet dug like a frightened animal poised to attack. Strategies to cajole, retreat and press were roiling up in his brain, then blanking out as the violated woman held eye contact. Finally she did attack, rearing back her head and spitting. Lloyd wiped the wad of mucus from his shirt front and returned with an ice-voiced salvo: "Your way, huh? Okay, let's try this: unless we get these scumbags, this is going to happen over and over again. Your feelings and Eggers's job and marriage don't count. So you're going to look at mug shots of your sexy savior. I know he's a handsome fellow with his groovy beard and all th—"

Lloyd stopped when Christine's face registered befuddlement. A light flicked on in his head. The beard and mustache that Hawley and Eggers had described was a fake—one reason why Hawley hadn't been able to I.D. any of the mugs he viewed. Assuming it was only a three-man team, the white partner had probably called the Mexicans to inform them of his success with Eggers, and had gotten either a no answer or word of the impending molestation from the "soft-spoken" man. Panicking, the white robber had driven to the hostage pad, and had entered *without his disguise*.

Still staring at Christine, Lloyd said, "Get dressed. I'm taking you into custody as a material witness."

Christine Confrey broke the stare by spitting at Lloyd's feet, then walking toward the back of the house. When she returned to the living room five minutes later, she was wearing light makeup and a fresh skirt and blouse. As she locked the door, she said, "Don't touch me."

They drove in silence to the Van Nuys Station, Christine chain-smoking and staring out the window, Lloyd steering the cruiser in a circuitous route to give himself time to think. One train of thought dominated: since the L.A.P.D. and F.B.I. both kept their mug shots cross-filed according to M.O. and physical stats, Robert Hawley was probably only shown photographs of convicted armed robbers and men matching his "beard and mustache" description. Both Eggers and Confrey would have to view the entire white male age 25–40 file at Parker Center, but he now had less than two hours before he was to meet Kapek, and if Chrissy Confrey was to be tapped for maximum info during that time, he would have to shove mugs at her while the white robber's face was still fresh in her mind and let Kapek and the feds worry about her statement and known associates.

Thrilled with a solid lead all his own, Lloyd pulled into the station lot. Christine got out of the car without being directed, and walked ahead of him through the station's front doors, eyes downcast. Lloyd caught up with her and pointed her into the detectives' squad room; a plainclothes cop approached with a quizzical look. Lloyd said, "Please have a seat, Miss Confrey," then whispered to the plainclothesman, "Hopkins, Robbery/ Homicide. The woman is an eyeball witness. I want to show her some mug books: white males with nonviolent felony convictions. It's a hunch I'm playing. Can you do that for me?"

The cop nodded and walked into the records booth adjoining the squad room. Lloyd saw that Christine had sat down in the assistant squad commander's chair and was helping herself to his cigarettes. He checked his watch, rankling that he had to have her out before Kapek arrived—kowtowing to a punk G-man ten years his junior. When the whole thing started to rankle, he walked over and said, "Are you going to cooperate?"

Christine blew smoke rings at him. "Of course, Officer."

The plainclothes cop came back with a stack of loose-leaf binders and placed them on the desk in front of Christine. Lloyd opened the top one and saw that the books displayed one man per page, with one close-up head shot, one full-body frontal and one full-body side shot. Below the black-and-white photos, the man's name, date of birth, arrest date and charge were typed, along with a five-digit file number.

Lloyd took a pencil from his pocket and poised it over the first sheet of mugs. "Study the pictures carefully," he said. "If you positively identify the man, tell me. I'll be studying you, and marking the ones you react to, so if you don't make an I.D., we can work up a composite from similar-looking men."

Christine put out her cigarette and lit another. "I only saw him for a second, and I only said he was sexy to hurt John."

"I realize that. Just look at the pictures carefully."

"And the papers and TV won't find out about John and me?"

Lloyd smiled and lied through his teeth. "That's right."

For an hour Christine smoked and looked at snapshots of white male felons. Lloyd sat beside her, reading her face for flashes of recognition. Twice she said, "Sort of, but not him"; three more times she held the binder up and gave it an extra close scrutiny, then shook her head. Lloyd marked the pages that drew her strongest reactions, and when Christine was finished with the last mug book, he wrote down the names and file numbers of the felons and went to the records booth to check their files on the off-chance that there might be some sort of connection to perk his mental juices.

He gave the five files cursory read-throughs, looking for the felons' current dispositions, known associates and brothers with criminal records, learning that George James Turney had been stabbed to death in a San Quentin race war six months previous and had two older brothers in their forties; that Thomas Lemuel Tucker was on federal parole in Alaska, and an orphan; that Alexander "Ramo" Ramondelli had a sister and was dying of cancer at Vacaville Prison Hospital; that Duane Richard Rice was an only child and was serving a year in the county jail for grand theft auto; that Paul Prescott Orchard had a mentally retarded younger brother and was a state parole absconder. The "known associates" were complete washouts—no familiar names, no sparks. It was time to write up a report to mollify Kapek, goose the media, chase snitch feedback and let the feds run with the ball.

Lloyd put the file numbers in a note to the squad lieutenant supervising the Issler assault, telling him to have a police artist utilize them with the assistance of a new eyeball witness the feds had. After dropping the memo off with the desk officer, he walked back to Christine and said, "Let's go. I'll drive you home."

They were walking out the door when Lloyd saw Peter Kapek striding up the steps toward them. He checked his watch: 5:30. The junior G-man had outfoxed him with an early arrival.

Kapek looked at Christine suspiciously; suddenly Lloyd felt sad for the bank manager's mistress. When Kapek started to fume silently for an explanation, Lloyd pulled him out of Christine's earshot. "I had to move fast or lose her. Call me at home and I'll tell you about it. If you don't like it, go fuck yourself and get me detached. She's your witness, but be good to her."

Kapek's fuming rendered him beet red. Lloyd nodded to Christine, then walked back into the station. The desk officer handed him a piece of paper. "Just got the call, from the switchboard at Parker Center. They didn't say who it's from. Sounds like a snitch to me."

Lloyd looked at the message. It said: Luis Calderon dealing army .45s. (Reliable info—call me for details.)

12

The restaurant was cool and dark; the Mexican music soft and harmless; the wraparound booth big and cushiony—a good, private place to talk crime plans. Sipping iced tea and waiting for the Garcias, Duane Rice felt his twenty-four hours of nonstop movement lose its frenzied edge. It was all going to happen; what he'd done since splitting Stan Klein's place proved he could do anything.

After trashing the pad for info on the "video shoot" Vandy and Klein were on, and getting zilch, he knew it was either tend to business or go gonzo, so he'd driven by the Pico-Westholme bank and memorized the floor plan, then cruised the side streets surrounding it for getaway vehicles. Around the corner on Graystone, he noticed an '81 Chevy Caprice parked in the driveway of a house whose screen door was spilling over with rubber-band-wrapped newspapers. He'd walked up and checked the name on the mailbox—Latham—then waited for the paper boy and handed him a spiel about being a friend of the Lathams', and by the way, when were they getting back? The kid said next Friday. Bingo. One vehicle down, one to go.

Then it was *think* or go gonzo, and he forced himself to remember small details all the way back to his kick-out from the slam. It took half an hour of brain-frying concentration, but finally he got it.

At the Burger King down the street from the Bowl Motel there was a fat slob security guard who bragged to the customers about his sixteen-hour shifts and all the money he was making, and how he was spending most of it on his '78 Malibu with a 327 and a B&M Hydrostick. It was never in the lot, but it had to be parked nearby. After a final recon of the Pico-Westholme area, he drove up to Hollywood and found the Malibu parked on De Longpre a half block from the Burger King. Two vehicles down—only the keys to go.

He drove to an art supply store and bought a large piece of molding wax, then cruised by the repo lot on South Western. It was closed up at nine o'clock, and there was no nightwatchman. A simple chisel pry, and he was inside the salesman's hut. There was an oversupply of master keys for *all* late-model Chevys, so he forgot about making wax impressions and glommed the keys outright. The two getaway vehicles were as good as his.

Next he called Rhonda, catching her on her way out the door to her weekend at "The Springs." She told him she didn't know where the video shoot that Vandy and Klein were on was, and that she didn't know whether Vandy performed in any of Klein's X-rated videos. She said she would talk to people in "The Springs" and leave a message if she got any hard info. She mentioned money several times, and he promised to call Silver Foxes Monday night to set up a meet.

Then came the tough part—manipulate the Garcia brothers: both of them for the Pico-Westholme heist; Joe for a watchdog. The heaviest gaming would be groveling to Bobby. Even though it was the right thing to do, it felt all wrong, and he was relieved when he called and got no answer.

Which left him at midnight with nothing to do and no one to do it with, and nowhere near sleep. The Holiday Inn was now total skunk city, so he moved back to the same room at the Bowl Motel, where the same grease spots and lines of dust greeted him, but did not ease him into sleep. Since he now had to stay awake to talk to Joe Garcia, it was either *move* or go gonzo.

So he *moved*, driving the Trans Am like a meek old man, going a weird kind of gonzo, where the superior type English he knew from police reports filled his head with thoughts he didn't want to say or even *think* out loud:

Unlike Stan Klein, Gordon Meyers is not a known associate. In the course of his career as Module 2700 night jailer, he incurred only mild resentment from the thousands of inmates he supervised, all of whom were mentally disturbed misdemeanants incapable of perpetrating armed robbery and murder;

Said unknown perpetrators were obviously seasoned bank robbers, most likely San Quentin or Folsom parolees, institutionalized and subconsciously desirous of committing felony acts in hopes of receiving ten-to-life habitual offender sentences.

The parole officer/cop/shrink rap kept eating at him; finally he started thinking of Vandy to hold it down. He thought of known associate Stan Klein, whom he couldn't touch, and got very calm, even cocky. Deciding to check out Stan Man's new scam, he started asking night clerks at "adult" motels if they had any good "fuck music." The first three clerks took his ten spot and said no; the fourth said yes and offered him a special "short timer" rate for private listening. Steeling himself, he accepted the offer.

The six cassettes stacked atop the V.C.R. in front of the sweat-stained bed all bore the "Stan Man" name and P.O. box. He loaded them into the machine and turned off the lights. Tremors and a flash thought hit him along with the "Stan Man" logo; he didn't want it to be Vandy, but if it was Vandy, he wouldn't be so god-awful alone. Cursing himself, he turned up the volume and watched the show.

A disco beat, then a haggard woman was gobbling a donkey-sized dick while Donna Summer belted, "She Works Hard for the Money." Fade-out, logo, then Rhonda the Fox was taking on four guys at once, the Beach Boys wailing for her to help them. Blank frames, blurred logo, "This Land Is Your Land" on the sound track, Mondale and Ferraro doing a handshaking tour on the screen, intercut with a girl in a red, white and blue negligee giving head to a jig in an Uncle Sam costume.

No Vandy.

If you fuck whores, then all women start looking like whores.

If you love a woman, then all women start looking like her.

Rice kicked over the V.C.R. and ran out of the room and across Sunset to a phone booth. He dialed the Garcias' number; Joe answered on the first ring. All he got out was "Hello?" before Duane the Brain took over in force:

"You want to come to New York, get away from your batshit brother and work a real musician gig?

"You and Bobby want two-thirds of a hundred K foolproof, in and out on Monday morning in six minutes?

"You want to be a fucking *pachuco* for the rest of your life, or do you want out?

"You get your brother to come with you to La Talpa tomorrow at noon. Tell him I'll apologize; tell him I need him."

The words stuck in his throat. Joe's final answer would always stick in his brain: "I'm your man, Duane. And don't worry about Bobby. He likes getting hit. In fact, he said you remind him of this priest he used to know."

"Thanks for sparing my face, Duane-o. The old Sharkman owes you for that. I lit a candle for you last night. Figured you was Protestant, but what the fuck."

Rice looked up to see Bobby Garcia sliding into the booth, his right hand held out. He shook it, glad that the restaurant was dark, so the greasy piece of sharkshit couldn't read the contempt on his face. Thinking, *Ice City*, he said, "Sorry, Bobby. I flipped out."

Bobby sat down across from him and dug into the bowl of nachos and salsa on the table. Between wolfish mouthfuls, he said, "No strain, no gain, no pain. Little brother's coming in a minute. You got another score?"

"Yeah. Straight in and out bank job."

Bobby whistled. "Righteous. Little Bro said a hundred big ones. That true?"

"If I'm lyin', I'm flyin'."

Bobby giggled and slithered a shark hand over the bowl of nachos. "Then you gotta have wings somewhere, 'cause your first two righteous big-time scores netted me and Little Bro about a dollar eighty-nine, and I'm startin' to feel like the bottom man in a Mongolian cluster fuck."

Rice took in a deep breath, hoping his voice would come out just right, giving Sharkshit the perfect amount of slack. "That was secondhand information I acted on. I was crazy to trust it. But we've hit twice. We're on a roll, and this one is all mine. I've had it in mind for a long time, I was just waiting for the right partners."

Bobby smirked. "I hope it ain't a roll into the gutter. I been there twice, and I ain't goin' for sloppy thirds."

"You'll like this one—it's *you*."

"Yeah? *Me*? Tall, dark and handsome? Hung like a mule?"

"No. Nasty, simple and out front. Easy to understand, so I know you'll eat it up."

Bobby giggled. "You said the magic word—eat. You know how to pick up chicks without saying a word? Sit at the bar and part your hair with your tongue."

"It's you, Bobby. So simple and low class that it's got class."

A waitress came up to the booth with menus; Rice grabbed them and said, "We'll order in a few minutes." When she walked away, Bobby said, "We shoulda hit a smorgasbord. The furburger buffet: all you can eat for sixty-nine clams." Rice felt a tide of slime wash over him. Then Joe Garcia was there, saying, "Duane, how's it hanging?"

Rice said, "Long and strong," and squinted across the booth to get a handle on how the tagalong was holding up. Not bad, he decided; scared, but probably cash flushed, and more scared of continuing a crime career with Sharkshit Bobby. A born follower about to trade leaders.

The waitress returned. The brothers ordered Carta Blanca; Rice another iced tea. When she brought the drinks, the three partners fell silent. Then

Rice looked straight at the Garcias, knowing they'd go for the plan: bull-shit, truth, the whole enchilada.

"Nifty little Cal Federal on Pico near the West L.A. freeway crisscross. One camera—we shoot it out. One plainclothes security man—a juicehead. Big payroll payouts on the twelfth and twenty-sixth of the month, so we hit the twelfth, this Monday. I've got one car pegged for the approach, another for the getaway—a family car right around the corner from the bank. The people are away on vacation, and I've got a master key for the doors and ignition. We go in wearing suits and beard-mustache disguises, carrying briefcases. Six tellers stations, two to a man. I know an abandoned garage in Hollyweird where we can stash the getaway sled. In, out, on the freeway by the time the fuzz show up. Three-way equal split. I've been casing this score for a long time, but I didn't know how stand-up you guys were. *Are you with me?*"

Bobby chugalugged his beer, reached into the bowl and crumbled the re-mains of the nachos, then placed his hands palms up on the table. Rice placed his right hand on top of them; Joe sealed the partnership agreement with both of his. Rice said, "You know how to dress and what to bring. Meet me at Melrose and Highland Monday morning at ten."

The partners withdrew their hands and stood up. Bobby squeezed out of the booth, walked over to the waitress and began a soft rendition of the *Jaws* theme. Joe looked at Rice, swallowed and said, "Was that for real about New York and the music gig?"

Rice smiled. "We leave on Wednesday. You stick with me after the job. We have to pick up my old lady, then we have to keep you away from Sharkshit over there. *Comprende?*"

"*Sí, comprendo, mano.*" Joe put out his hand jailhouse style; Rice held it down in a square-john shake. "That low-rider shit is dead. You pull that stuff in New York, and they'll laugh you out of town."

13

Lloyd pulled up to the back entrance of the West L.A. Federal Building and honked his horn. Peter Kapek walked over to the car and got in. Expecting a rebuke for the Confrey approach, Lloyd was stunned when the junior G-man said, "Good work on the girlfriend. I got a good statement out of her. No positive I.D. on the white man, but Confrey and Eggers worked up a composite with an L.A.P.D. artist. It'll be distributed all points by tomorrow morning. Where are we going? And by the way, you look like shit."

Lloyd nosed the Matador out onto Wilshire. "Didn't you get the complete message? We're going to brace a suspected gun dealer. Luis Miguel Calderon, a.k.a. "Likable Louie," male Mexican, age thirty-nine, two convictions for receiving stolen goods, former youth gang member mellowed out into small-time businessman. He's got an auto parts shop in Silverlake, my old neighborhood. A snitch I trust says he's dealing army-issue .45s. And I look like shit because I've been doing police work all night."

Kapek laughed. "I like it! Learn anything?"

Lloyd shook his head. "Not really. I canvassed the Security Pacific area and Confrey's neighborhood; Brawley from Van Nuys dicks couldn't spare any men. I got a big zero—no suspicious people or vehicles. I read every report on Hawley's and Issler's associates eight times—nothing bit me. Then I called a couple of media people and gave them the whole ball of wax. It goes to press and on the air Monday night, giving us exactly forty-eight hours to figure out a strategy. What's the matter, G-man? You're not doing your famous slow burn."

Kapek toyed with the knobs of the two-way radio. "Don't call me 'G-man,' it turns me on. I didn't rat you off on Confrey because I heard these homicide guys at Parker Center talking about you with awe, and I actually started to like you a little bit. Also, I got a good statement from Confrey. The rape guy turned out *not* to be a rape-o, more like a psycho muff diver. He did this rebop about being a shark, then went down on Chrissy's bush. I've computer-fed the info nationwide—nothing—and I've put it in a memo for L.A.P.D. roll calls—maybe we'll get a bite."

"A shark bite?"

"Very fucking amusing. We need a hard lead, Hopkins; this thing is *covered* from every paper angle. Our eyeball witnesses have checked every local and federal mug book—zero. The men checking out the victims' associates have got nothing, and I've got an agent going over Hawley's and Eggers's credit card slips with them—you know, all the places they rendezvoused with the girlfriends have got to be checked out. If nothing breaks by Monday, I'm planting people in the offices where Issler and Confrey work."

Lloyd nodded and said, "I've been kicking around an idea that might account for a connection between Hawley and Eggers and explain why the robbers have escalated their M.O. I'm thinking both these guys might be pilfering traveler's checks—at least Hawley. Here's the reconstruction. While they're casing the B. of A., the robbers see Hawley stealing the *green* traveler's checks, which from a distance look like cash. They think that money is left overnight in the tellers boxes—"

Kapek interrupted. "Hawley said the inside man wanted the bank checks—that he asked for them by name."

Lloyd shook his head. "That's Hawley the pilferer covering his ass, obscuring the robbers' reasons for hitting *his* bank. Here's my reasoning. The robbers have either seen Eggers pilfering similarly, or they figured, and this isn't likely, given their intelligence, that all banks leave loose cash out overnight. So, after the low score on the traveler's checks, they figure that Eggers is just another check stealer, say to themselves 'Fuck that' and decide to make Eggers go for the vault. You like it?"

Grinning, Kapek said, "It floats. But what do we do about it?"

"Have your Bank Fraud Division people give you a crash course in check rip-off scams. Maybe they can tell us something we can use to squeeze Hawley and Eggers. I've got a hunch on this. I think that if these guys are pilferers, it's out of desperation—cash flow problems that they can't talk about. And *that* makes me think *vice*—gambling, dope, sex. Sex the least likely, because they've got the outside stuff going. I'm going to initiate inquiries with every vice squad in the Valley—maybe our boys are heavy in hock to bookies, or loan sharks, or they're into kinky shit we don't know about. If we get a bunch of vice dicks to pump their informants, we might get something."

Kapek elbowed Lloyd and said, "I like it! There's nothing on the traveler's checks, by the way, but on the cash flow problems, I'm going to peruse our boys' bank accounts, see what I get."

Lloyd took the words in silently and, as the old neighborhood drew closer, thought of his family. "You didn't rag me on the media goose," he said. "Come Monday night a lot of innocent people are going to be hurting. I figured a sensitive guy like you would be pissed."

Kapek flushed. "It was the right thing. I would have waited a day or so, then done it. I'm doing the family interviews, though, and *discreetly*."

"We're almost there, G-man. Any thoughts on this interview?"

"No, you?"

"Yeah. Let's test Likable Louie's fuse."

Lloyd pulled to the curb, then pointed to the white adobe building that housed Louie's One-Stop Pit Stop.

"No violence?" Kapek said.

"No violence."

"Then I like it."

They walked across the street and through the wide-open front door of the garage, into a small room filled with stacks of retread tires. A Chicano youth popping a pimple at a wall mirror gave them the fisheye, and Lloyd said, "Where's Louie?"

The youth gouged the zit a last time and reached for an intercom set mounted on the connecting door. Lloyd said, "Don't do that," and motioned for Kapek to walk ahead of him. The kid shrugged, and Kapek pushed through the door. Lloyd was right behind him, tingling at the thought of a razzle-dazzle interrogation.

The garage proper was huge, with pneumatic grease racks, sliding drawers full of auto parts, and a large drive-in space leading to a back entrance and work area. Lloyd and Kapek walked slowly, catching cop-wise squints from the mechanics working beneath the racks. A heavyset man glanced at them, and Lloyd recognized him from his R&I snapshot: Luis Calderon.

He walked over and smiled, revealing buck teeth and a fortune in dental gold. "Good afternoon, Officers. Looking for me?"

Lloyd flashed his badge. "Hopkins, L.A.P.D. This is Special Agent Kapek, F.B.I. We'd like to talk to you."

Calderon sighed. "Have I got a choice?"

Lloyd sighed back. "Yeah, you do. Here or Rampart Station."

"I've already seen it," Calderon said. "Let's go out back and get some air."

Catching an edge in his voice, Lloyd said, "No. Your office." Calderon sighed again and started walking toward the garage's street entrance. Lloyd tapped him on the shoulder. "No, Louie. Your *real* office, where you've got your desk and your files and your invoices."

Louie turned around and walked over to and up a flight of wooden stairs next to the tool bin. Lloyd let Kapek get between them, knowing the mechanic/hood's reaction to a fed roust was out of kilter. When Calderon opened the office door, he squeezed in ahead of him and quickly sized up the room. Soot-stained walls, paper-cluttered desk, refrigerator and a *Playboy* Playmate tacked to the wall, probably hiding a safe. Two phones on the desk, one red, one black; a clipboard holding notebook paper leaning against the red one. Nothing incriminating at first glance.

Calderon opened the refrigerator and took out a Coors, then sat down behind his desk. Popping the can, he said, "Topped out my parole, topped out my probation. Pay my taxes and don't associate with no criminal types. My only vice is brew. I'm a righteous sudser. If outfits were legal, I'd geez the shit. I'm a suds-guzzling motherfucker. I pour the shit on my Rice Krispies in the morning, and sometimes I even shave with it. I give my dog a brew chaser with his Alpo. If I was a fag, I'd squirt the shit up my ass. I am a righteous beerhound motherfucker. So how come you're coming on like storm troopers, when all the Rampart cops know Likable Louie likes to cooperate?"

Lloyd breathed the spiel in, savoring the tension that fueled it. He looked over at Kapek, who was chuckling with genuine amusement, and said, "I don't work out of Rampart, and I didn't come here to catch your Richard Pryor shtick. I could roust your workers for green cards and get myself a bonaroo immigration bust, and I'd love to run the numbers on your engine blocks. A third time receiving conviction is a nickel minimum. State time, Louie, and what you get up the ass there ain't Coors."

Louie Calderon sipped beer. Lloyd saw that his first salvo was on target, but not a wounder. Sensing that Kapek was being quiet out of real respect, he bored in: "You snitching for Rampart dicks, Louie?"

Calderon smiled; Lloyd could almost feel the fat man's blood pressure chill out as he said, "It's well known that Likable Louie likes to cooperate."

Lloyd twisted a wooden chair around and sat down in it, facing Calderon. Smiling and hooking a thumb over his back at Kapek, he said, "Louie, that man over there is an F.B.I. Criminal Division agent. Why haven't you asked me about him?"

"Because unless he wants a boss transmission overhaul, I don't care if he stays, lays, prays or strays."

"How come you've got two phones, different colors?"

"The black phone's for business, the red phone's my hot line to the White House. Ronnie calls me up sometimes. We chase pussy together."

"Who's your connection at Rampart dicks?"

"Who's your tailor? Your suit sucks."

The black phone rang. Calderon picked it up and spoke into it in Spanish. Lloyd raised his eyebrows at Kapek; the F.B.I. man said, "Not a word." Shaking his head, Lloyd watched Likable Louie talk a blue streak, then hang up and say, "Okay, let's see if I can scope this out. You need a favor, and someone at Rampart said I could help. You came on strong to test me, to see if I could be trusted. I'm tired of playing games. What do you need?"

Lloyd was reaching for his most disarming smile when the red phone rang. Louie picked up the receiver and said, "Yes," then nodded and wrote on the clipboard. Lloyd squinted and saw that the top sheet of paper was half covered with pencil scrawl.

Calderon said yes a final time and hung up. Lloyd looked at the veins in his neck and saw the signs of a slamming heart. "Who's your connection at Rampart dicks?"

Louie's voice was hoarse; Lloyd could tell that he was getting genuinely befuddled. "Why you keep asking me that, man?"

Lloyd's third volley began with his most evil shitkicker glare. "I grew up in Silverlake. I was in the Dogtown Flats back when you were in the Alpines. My parents still live over on Griffith Park and St. Elmo, so I like things safe around here. Rampart does a pretty good job of keeping the peace, because they've got snitches like you to rat off the bad dudes that everybody hates. You get to hire wetbacks and turn over some stolen parts, and my mom and dad go to sleep safe at night. Right, Louie?"

"R-r-r-right," Louie stammered.

Lloyd stood up and pulled a .45 automatic from his shoulder holster. Holding it in front of Louie Calderon's trembling face, he said, "There's these three guys perving on women and taking out banks, and maybe they got their pieces from you. Here's the pitch: if you turned the pieces, you've got twenty-four hours to give me the names. If you didn't, you've got forty-eight hours to find out who did, and who he sold them to. If I don't hear from you in forty-eight one way or the other, I go to the commander of Rampart dicks and snitch you off to him as the kingpin motherfucking gun dealer of L.A. County." He dropped his Robbery/Homicide business card on the desk and reholstered the gun. "Be cool, homeboy."

Back at the car, Kapek looked at Lloyd and said, "Jesus fucking Christ."

Lloyd unlocked the door and got in. "Meaning Calderon?"

Kapek took the passenger seat. "No, you. How much of that was bluff?"

"Everything but my threat. Calderon had that self-satisfied look, and he had a shitload of wetbacks working for him, and he didn't want us to see his office. My guess is that he's snitching dope dealers to the Rampart narks in exchange for immunity on the illegals. I know the squad commander at Rampart—he'll let minor shit slide for good information, but he's death on violent crime. If he finds out Louie's dealing guns, Louie's ass is fucking grass."

"But is he *our* gun dealer?"

"I don't know. The important thing is that he's scared. He's between Lieutenant Buddy "Bad Ass" Bagdessarian and me on one side, the robbers and getting a rat jacket on the other. We've got to put a twenty-four tail on him—your men—he's too hip to local cops. He's an old homeboy, a criminal with contacts, and he may damn well *not* be our gun dealer, but be able to put the finger on him, or he may snitch off the robbers straight out to save his ass with Buddy. Either way, we're set. How soon can you implement the surveillance?"

"As soon as you drop me off at Central Office. What are you going to do?"

Lloyd hit the ignition and gunned the car out onto Tomahawk Street. "Read all the paperwork again, then write up my ideas for Brawley at Van Nuys dicks. Then I'm going to visit an old pal of mine. He's a superior court judge, and he's senile and a right-wing loony. He gets his rocks off issuing search-and-seizure warrants. I buy him a case of Scotch every Christmas, and he signs whatever I ask him for. Right before Louie's forty-eight are up, I'm going in his front door with a .12 gauge and due process to seize every scrap of paper he's got. You like it?"

Kapek was pale; his voice was shaky. "Jesus fucking Christ."

"You said that before. One other thing. I'm almost positive that the reason Calderon didn't want us in his office is the red phone. He's either taking bets or running a bootleg message service."

"What's that?"

"A two-way answering service. Mostly it's used by parole absconders and their families. He had a clipboard with writing on it next to the phone—messages for sure. Calderon's house is right next to the garage, and he's probably got someone there monitoring an extension all the time. Sometimes those numbers are legit Ma Bell handouts; sometimes illegal hookups that can't be traced. I want a tap on all Calderon's lines. That requires a federal warrant—your side of the street. Can you swing it?"

Kapek's color was returning, but a thin layer of sweat was creeping over his forehead. He wiped it off with his sleeve and said, "Monday at the earliest. Federal judges *all* go incommunicado on the weekends to avoid warrant hassles. You really want these guys, don't you?"

Lloyd smiled. "I'm probably getting stress-pensioned soon, against my will. I intend to go out in true hot-dog fashion." He pulled up in front of the downtown F.B.I. building, and Kapek got out. Highballing it to Parker Center, the junior G-man's pale face stayed fixed in his mind, and he knew he had taken over the investigation.

With twenty-eight sleepless hours behind him, Lloyd pushed *his* investigation for another twenty-four flat out.

At Parker Center he checked the "monicker" file for every nickname variation of "Shark," coming away with a large assortment of data pertaining to black youth gangs. Useless trivia. An R&I check of male Mexican registered sex offenders with a cunnilingus M.O. yielded seven names, but three of the men were currently in prison and the other four were in their fifties—way above Sally Issler's and Christine Confrey's "late twenties, early thirties" appraisal. The only remaining option was to add the "Shark" and oral sex abuse facts to the roll call reports and distribute the word to all L.A.P.D. informants.

Peter Kapek called in the early evening. Louie Calderon was under constant rolling surveillance. The agents would be keeping a detailed log on his movements and would be running vehicle and address checks on all persons he came into contact with. A team of agents was going over his record for possible armed robbery connections. The Likable Louie angle was covered, as were continuing probes into the recent pasts of Robert Hawley, Sally Issler, John Eggers and Christine Confrey. Come Monday, Channel 7 *Eyewitness News* would leak its "cautionary" report on the bank robbery/extortion gang, without mention of the sex assault facts. This would leave the families of the male victims open for interrogation on the investigation's "Big Question": *how did the robbers get the information on the two extramarital affairs?*

At home late that night, Lloyd phoned in the vice squad query he had mentioned to Kapek, then read the existing files and applied his thinking solely to that question. He came up with four logical answers:

Through connection to the victims' families;

Through connections to the victims' friends and acquaintances;

Through connections at the two banks;

Through the random factor: overheard conversations at meeting places such as bars, restaurants and other public gathering spots, and through informational sources that the four suspects have either consciously or unconsciously refused to reveal.

Knowing that the fourth "answer" was the most likely, Lloyd read through the case file two more times, then wrote out a memorandum stating his conclusions.

0330 hrs; 12/11/84
To: S.A. Peter Kapek, Det. Lieut. S. Brawley

Re: Hawley/Issler–Eggers/Confrey Investigation

Gentlemen:

Having participated in every aspect of this investigation, and having read the case file a dozen times, I have come to one conclusion concerning the robbery gang's access to information on the four victims, one supported by sound suppositions based on existing facts. We know that Robert Hawley and John Eggers, both middle-aged bank managers, are as yet not connected to each other in any discernible personal or professional way. Exhaustive record searches have turned up no common denominators other than:

1. Identical professions;

2. Long-term marriages that appear to be flourishing despite the fact that both men are engaged in extramarital affairs;

3. The said extramarital affairs themselves, both involving women in their late twenties.

The same absence of connections exists between the two women involved. All our victims live and work in the San Fernando Valley, yet interrogations and cross-checks of credit card records show that these two sets of clandestine lovers have not even dined in the same restaurants or drunk in the same bars as each other, at any time in the course of their affairs. The odds of a criminal gang divining the existence of two such potentially lucrative and jeopardy-prone liaisons separately is preposterous. I think there is a viable Hawley/Issler–Eggers/Confrey link, one that the four principals are either willfully or subconsciously suppressing. I believe all four principals should be induced to undergo rigorous polygraph tests, and, should that fail to reveal the link, Pentothal and/or hypnosis questioning—radical investigatory measures that I think are justified in this case. Also, since the basic facts of this series of crimes will be aired and published by the media late tomorrow (released by me in the interest of a public safety precaution), I deem it advisable that the four principals be taken into custody and held without media access on Monday morning, in order to avoid repercussions deriving from familial reaction to exposure of the two affairs. I undertook the media release on my own authority, realizing the full implications. Both my newspaper and television contacts told me they would include a plea for information along with their coverage, and pass said information along to us immediately.

> Respectfully,
> Lloyd W. Hopkins,
> #1114,
> Robbery/Homicide
> Division

Finishing, Lloyd looked out his kitchen window and saw that it was dawn. Feeling the family angle gouging at him, he walked through the downstairs of the house that he once shared with four women; the four rooms he had apportioned himself in their absence. Every step made him both more exhausted and more aware of the need to work. Finally he gave in to the need and slumped into the big leather chair where he used to sit with Penny.

No thoughts came, and neither did sleep. Staring at the telephone, hoping it would ring, supplied one minor brainstorm: Louie Calderon's phone number or numbers. Lloyd called the top supervisor at Bell and gave his name and badge number, then feverishly asked his question. The woman came back with a sadly unfeverish answer: Louis Calderon of 2191 Tomahawk St., L.A., had one house and one business phone—with the same number. The red phone was total bootleg.

More numbing sleeplessness followed, temporarily interrupted by a call from Peter Kapek. The first surveillance shift had just reported that Louie Calderon had left his pad only once, at 6:00 A.M. He walked to the corner and bought a case of beer. "Beer-guzzling motherfucker," Kapek said, promising to call with the next shift's report.

Lloyd shaved, showered and forced himself to eat a packet of cold luncheon meat, chased with a pint of milk and a handful of vitamins. Still unable to sleep, he checked the mailbox for the previous day's mail. There were three bills and a postcard from Penny, Fisherman's Wharf on the front, her perfect script on the back: Daddy—Hang in. Roger's dog peed on Mom's beloved carpet. Rog refused to pay for the cleaning. Mom's response: "Your father, despite his many faults, was housebroken and never cheap." Hang in, Daddy. Love Love Love—Penguin.

Now Lloyd's shot at blissful unconsciousness was broken up by an injection of hope. Feeling a second mental wind coming on, he dialed the home number of Judge Wilson D. Penzler, prepared to listen to a long right-wing

rhapsody before making his warrant request. The judge's housekeeper answered, and said that His Honor was in Lake Tahoe and would be returning
home and to the bench on Wednesday. Lloyd hung up, then picked up the
receiver to call Buddy Bagdessarian at Rampart dicks and blow the whistle
on Louie Calderon. His finger was descending on the first digit when caution struck. No, Buddy would blow the plan by going straight for Louie's
throat. Better to give the beer guzzler some slack.

Daylight came and went. Lloyd remained fitfully awake, swinging on a brain
tether of sharks, old neighborhood homeboy-crooks and his family. He was debating whether to turn on the lights or sit in darkness when the phone rang.

All he got out was "Speak" before Kapek came on the line. "Third shift
just radioed. The beerhound, his wife and rug rats just took off. They're following cautiously. I also grabbed Calderon's jail jacket. The K.A.s are being
checked out. What have *you* been doing?"

Lloyd tingled as the idea took hold. "Thinking. Gotta run, Peter. I'll call
you tomorrow." He hung up and grabbed his burglar tools from the kitchen,
then ran for his L.A.P.D. Burglar Mobile.

Likable Louie's One-Stop Pit Stop and the built-on adobe house were
dark and silent as Lloyd parked on the opposite side of Tomahawk Street
and got up his B&E guts. Pulling on surgical rubber gloves, he brought his
previous visit to the garage to mind and thought of access routes. The house
was probably too well secured; the street door too exposed. There was only
the back way in.

Lloyd checked the contents of his burlap "burglar bag" and pulled out a
battery-operated drill and an assortment of bits, a set of lock picks, a jimmy,
a can of Mace for watchdog debilitation and a large five-cell flashlight. He
dug in the backseat and found an old briefcase left by another officer, stuck
his tools inside it, then walked down the alley that cut diagonally across
Tomahawk Street.

A full moon allowed him a good view of the back entrance, and music
blasting from adjoining houses took care of any noise he might make. Lloyd
looked at the barbed-wire fence encircling the work area and resigned himself to getting cut; he looked at the pulley-operated steel door and knew it
was the window next to it or nothing.

Taking a deep breath, he tossed the briefcase over the fence and hoisted
himself up the links. His right hand ached from his Frisco bookcase smashing, and he had to favor it all the way to the top. When he reached the

barbed wire, he rolled into it, letting his jacket take the clawing until the last possible second, then hooking the strands with his index fingers, gouging his legs until he was free of sharp metal and there was nothing left but a twelve-foot drop. Then he pushed himself off with all his weight, landing feet first on a patch of oil slick blacktop.

No dog; no sounds of approach. Lloyd picked up the briefcase and took the flashlight from it, then walked to the window and compared its circumference to his own bulk. Deciding it would be a tight but makable squeeze, he smashed in the glass with the end of the flashlight and tossed in the briefcase. Then he elbowed himself through the hole, his jacket again taking the brunt of the damage, his legs getting another brief tearing. Coming down hands first into the garage, the smell of gas and motor oil assaulted him.

Still no dog; still nothing to indicate he had been spotted. Lloyd got to his feet and picked up the flashlight and briefcase, then took his bearings. As his eyes got used to the darkness, he picked out the stairway leading up to Louie Calderon's private office.

Lloyd tiptoed over and up the stairs, then tried the door. It was unlocked. He deep-breathed and pushed it open, then flicked on the flashlight and shined it in the direction of the desk. The beam illuminated the red phone and clipboard dead-on.

He walked to the desk, memorizing the exact positions of the invoices and beer cans on top of it, then took a pen and notepad from his back pocket and sat down in Louie Calderon's chair. Holding the flashlight in his left hand, he pushed aside a half-finished Coors and put down the pad in its place. Centering the beam right on top of the clipboard, the office around it went totally dark, and he did his transcribing in a tunnel of eye-grating light.

12/11—A.M.—Ramon V.—Call 629-8811 (mom & bro.) *before* you talk to P.O.

12/11—P.M.—Duane—Rhonda talked to friends in P.S., Stan Klein returning Monday night *late*, remember to call Mon. nite—H.(654-8996)—W.(658-4371)—wants $.

12/11—P.M.—Danny C.—Call home.

12/11—P.M.—Julio M.—Call home.

12/11—P.M.—George V.—Call Louise, Call P.O. No violation.

Completing the copy-over, Lloyd put the pad back in his pocket and returned the beer can to its proper place, pleased that it was a bootleg service rather than a bookie drop. He turned his flashlight toward the floor and retraced his steps downstairs, grabbing a box of baby moon hubcaps on his way to the front door, hoping to put the onus on punks out for a quick score. Driving home, he got his usual post-burglary shakes, followed by his usual post-B&E knowledge: *crime was a thrill.*

In his kitchen, Lloyd copied over the transcribed names and phone numbers for checking against Louie Calderon's K.A. file, then called up the three numbers he had gleaned.

The first one was a sad non-connection. Pretending to be a friend of "Ramon," Lloyd asked his mother about his whereabouts, learning that he had been cut loose from Chino on Friday and hadn't as yet contacted his parole officer or family. The woman was terrified that he was back in Silverlake and on smack.

The two numbers for "Rhonda" were even sadder—both recorded messages that boomed "prostitution" loud and clear: "Hi, this is Rhonda. If you've called for my business and your pleasure, or the converse, leave a message. Bye!"

"This is Silver Foxes. Beautiful women of every persuasion for every occasion. Please leave your name, customer number and wishes at the tone."

Lloyd put down the phone, then added the information to his K.A. check-out list. The singsong lilt of the last message stayed with him as he turned out the lights and flopped down on the couch. While he waited for the sleep that he knew had to come, he toyed with the words. An exhaustion gibberish crept over him. He knew what was behind it: the occasions of *his* persuasion were over. The finality of the thought helped, and unconsciousness was just about there when he grabbed at an escape hatch: *an apocalypse could save him.* The thought was too scary to toy with. Lloyd slammed the hatch shut with every ounce of his will and slept dreamlessly.

14

Clockwork.

Rice looked at his watch as he nosed the '78 Malibu into the shade of a stand of trees by the freeway off-ramp. At 9:43 he'd glommed the car; at 9:56 he'd picked up the brothers, who were outfitted for bear and looking greedy.

At 10:03 he stopped at a 7-11 on the edge of Hollywood for a last-minute acquisition—a brainstorm—and now, at 10:22, there was nothing left but to do it. He glanced at Bobby and Joe as he set the brake. Their suits fit, and their off-color facial hair made them look almost non-Mexican. Their briefcases were big and scuffed. It was all running perfect. "Now," he said.

They walked the half block to the corner of Pico and Westholme and waited for the light. When it turned green, Rice took the lead, striding ahead of the brothers. In front of the bank, he peered through the window and framed the scene inside: six tellers stations on the left, roped-off waiting line with no one standing in it, the execs at their desks in the carpeted area on the right. No armed guards; no sign of Gordon Meyers; the surveillance camera sweeping on its tripod above the doors. *Perfection.*

The brothers caught up, and Rice let them go through the doors first. When they were halfway to the teller area, he took a can of 7-11 shaving cream from his jacket pocket, shook it and fired a test spritz at the ground. When it hit the pavement, it hit *him:* when you look into his eyes, you'll know.

Rice pushed the doors open, wheeled and extended his right arm at the camera, missing his first spray, catching the lens on-center with the second. Coming off his toes, he saw that no one in the desk area had seen him, and that Joe and Bobby were dawdling by a cardboard display near the rear tellers station. He reached into his briefcase and pulled out his .45 then let the spray can drop to the floor. The man at the front desk looked up at the noise and saw the gun. Rice shouted, "Robbery! Everybody be real quiet or you're gonna be real dead!"

For a second, everything froze. Heads darted up behind the tellers counter; the Garcias pulled out their .45s and moved into position, their briefcases held open. Then little gasps and flutters took over, and Rice saw everything go blackish red. Swallowing, he heard a scream from a woman staring at Joe Garcia's silencered piece: "Oh my Gods" were bombarding him from every corner of the bank. Swallowing what tasted like blood, he ran to Bobby, shoved his briefcase at him and said, "Three minutes. Fill it up."

Bobby flashed his shark grin and leveled his gun at the teller directly in front of him, hissing, "Feed the shark, motherfucker, or you die." The man fumbled packets of currency into the briefcase, and Bobby shoved Rice's briefcase over to the next station, growling, "You, too, bitch—you fucking too." The woman dumped in whole cash and change drawers, and coins spilled over the counter onto the floor. When both tellers backed up and showed empty drawers, then ducked to their knees, Bobby slid down to the next station, catching a shot of Joe out of the corner of his eye. Little Bro had already hit three stations and was holding a shaky bead on the tellers. Tears and sweat were pouring off his face, soaking his phony beard. His face was as red as a baby's, and his lower lip was flapping so hard his whole head shook along with it. From somewhere in the bank Duane Rice was shouting, "Where's the fucking security boss!" sounding like a stone loony. Bobby maneuvered both briefcases and his piece too in front of the last teller, going wired when he saw it was a foxy young blonde.

"Where's the guard! Where's the fucking security man!"

Bobby heard Rice's shouts, then turned to scope out the blonde. She had her three drawers open and the money stacked on the counter. Bobby scooped it into the briefcase closest to him, tickling the girl's chin with his silencer as he clamped the case shut. "You like seafood, chiquita?" he said. "You like a nice juicy shark sausage? Go fine as wine with a nice blond furburger."

Rice saw the whole bank shake in front of his eyes. His voice sounded like it wasn't his, and the people cowering at their desks looked like scary red animals. He turned around so he wouldn't see them, and saw Sharkshit Bobby talking trash to a young woman teller. He was wondering whether to stop it when Gordon Meyers walked out of a door next to the vault.

And he knew.

Rice raised his .45; Meyers saw him and turned to run. Rice squeezed off three shots. The back of Meyers's white shirt exploded into crimson just as he felt the three silencer kicks. The dinged-out ding jailer crashed into an American flag on a pole and fell with it to the floor. The bank became one gigantic blast of noise, and through all of it, Rice heard a woman's voice: "Scum! Scum! Scum!"

Bobby turned around at the blonde's final epithet, and saw a dead man on the floor and Duane Rice and his brother gesturing for him to *move*. He turned to give the girl a *Jaws* theme goodbye, and caught a wad of spittle square in the face. Wiping it off, he saw her huge open mouth and knew that whatever she said would be the truth. He jabbed his .45 at her teeth and fired twice. The shots blew off the back of her head. Bobby saw blood and brains splatter the wall behind her as she was lifted off her feet. Recoil spun him around, and then Joe was there, grabbing the two briefcases and shoving him toward the doors.

Outside, Rice was standing on the sidewalk with the third briefcase, jamming a fresh clip into his piece. When the brothers crashed through the doors all sweat, tears and head-to-toe tremors, he shoved the briefcase at

Joe and managed to get out, "Go around the corner to the car," from some-where cool inside his own shakes. The Garcias *moved*, stumble-running, the three packages of money banging against their legs. Rice was about to fol-low when a siren came out of deep nowhere, and a black-and-white with cherry lights flashing zoomed down the sidewalk straight at him.

Rice made frantic flagging motions and fell to his knees as if wounded, holding the piece inside his right jacket pocket, knowing the silencer would cut down his range to close to nothing. When the patrol car decelerated and braked, he held his ground, knowing they had to have seen him; when it did a final fishtail, he counted to ten, got to his feet and pointed his .45 at the windshield.

The cops inside were less than four feet away and about to come out the doors with shotguns when he squeezed the trigger seven times, the gun at chest level. The windshield exploded, and Rice flung himself to the ground and rolled toward the passenger door, ejecting the spent clip, jamming in another. When both doors remained shut, he stood up, saw two blood-soaked blue uniforms and gasping faces and fired seven more times, all head shots. Blood and bone shrapnel sprayed his face, and in the distance he could hear other sirens screaming.

Suddenly he felt very calm and very much in control. He ran through the bank parking lot and down the alley that paralleled Graystone Drive, then vaulted a chain link fence, coming down into a cement backyard. The driveway led him out to the street, and there were Joe and Bobby, standing by the '81 Chevy Caprice. No neighbors; no nosy kids; no eyeball witnesses.

Rice walked across front lawns to the Chevy and unlocked the driver's-side door, then the passenger's. The brothers got in the back with the brief-cases and huddled down without being told. Rice started the car and backed out, then drove slowly down Graystone to Westholme, then across Pico to the freeway. When they were headed north on the 405, the sudden screech of sirens became deafening. The fifty-foot freeway elevation gave him a per-fect view of the bank and the street in front of it. It was bumper-to-bumper cop cars spilling shotgun-toting fuzz. Choppers were starting to fly in from the east. It looked like a war zone.

Rice drove cautiously in the middle lane; the challenge of holding down panic in an unfamiliar vehicle kept his mind off the past ten minutes. Mov-ing out of the area, the cop noises subsided, except for occasional black-and-whites highballing it past in the opposite direction. Then when he hit

Wilshire, it sounded like choppers and sirens were right there inside the car, and he remembered he wasn't alone.

The copter/siren noise was the combination of Joe Garcia sobbing and wheezing, and Bobby trying to talk. Rice thought of freeway roadblocks and pulled onto the Montana Avenue exit. He turned to look at the brothers, and saw that they were still on the floor, with their arms around each other, so he couldn't tell who was who. The sight was obscene, and the dried cop blood he felt on his face made it worse. Coming down onto a peaceful, noiseless street, he scrubbed his cheeks with his sleeve and said, "Act like fucking human beings and we'll walk from this."

Bobby untangled himself from his brother and the collection of briefcases. Rice checked the rearview and saw him lean into the backseat, then help Joe up. When he saw their unglued beards, he ripped off his own and sized them up for survival balls. Joe was twitching and sitting on his hands to control his shaking; Sharkshit looked like he was two seconds from a giggling fit that would last until his lungs blew. Knowing they were punk partners at best, he said, "Take off your beards, and your jackets and shirts. We're going to ditch the car, then go to my motel and chill out. Bobby, you do your shark act and you are one dead greaser."

Bobby winced. His voice was low, nothing like a giggle. "I had to, Duane. I knew what that bitch was gonna say, and only priests can say that to me." He started mumbling in Latin, then grabbed one of the briefcases off the floor. His garbled rosaries were hitting fever pitch as he reached in and pulled out a packet of hundreds and yanked the tab.

Black ink exploded from the wads of bills, sharp jets that hit Bobby in the face and deflected off his chest to cover the back windows. A second series of sprays burst over Joe, and he threw himself on top of the briefcase and smothered the residual jets with his body. Rice pulled to the curb and screamed, "Take off your shirts and roll down the windows!" and Bobby wiped ink from his eyes and ripped off his beard and started pawing with it at the window beside him.

Leaning over into the backseat, Rice threw an awkward right fist at Bobby's face, a glancing blow that forced him to stop his scrubbing and reflexively flinch away, leaving the window handle exposed. Rice pushed himself toward it and cranked it down, just as Joe, his torso soaked jet black, lowered the opposite one. Hissing "*The back,*" Rice struggled from his suitcoat and ripped off his white shirt. He passed them to Joe, who pushed them into the back window and let them absorb ink until they were saturated.

When they were useless sopping rags, he pulled them away and let the remaining ink soak down into the top of the seat. Then he stripped to the waist and started pulling off his brother's clothes, murmuring, "Easy, Bobby. Easy. The watchdog is here."

Rice looked at the ink-streaked window and saw that it could pass for a bad "smoky tint" job; he looked at the Garcias and knew that the tagalong had bigger balls from the gate. "We're going to Hollyweird, homeboys," he said. "Just three bare-chested studs out for a ride."

A half hour later, Rice stopped in front of an abandoned welfare hotel on Cahuenga, two blocks from the Bowl Motel. He turned off the engine, got out and checked the trunk. No spare clothes, only a ratty-looking sleeping bag. He grabbed it, then shoved it through the side window at Joe Garcia, who was still baby-talking Bobby. "Wrap the briefcases up in this, and walk your brother down to my pad. Act like Chicano punks on the stroll and you won't get rousted. I'll take the money and catch up with you." He looked at the black film on their chests, then walked back to the garage that he hoped to fucking God was still deserted.

It was.

Rice cleared an entry path, kicking away mounds of empty T-bird bottles, and then walked to the car. Joe and Bobby were standing mutely beside it, the sleeping bag rolled erratically at their feet. Rice said, "Move," then backed the car into the garage and closed the rickety door on it.

Returning to the street, he started feeling good. Then he picked up the sleeping bag, and two dimes and a penny fell out of the folds and hit the pavement. Ahead of him, he saw the Garcias turn into the alley behind the motel. He tried to think of Vandy and the rescue mission, but the chump change on the ground wouldn't let him.

15

Driving out Wilshire to the West L.A. Federal Building, Lloyd knew that the street scene was somehow off, that something was missing. Passing the Winchell's Donut joint that the local cops favored, it hit him: he hadn't seen a black-and-white since Beverly Hills, and that one was B.H.P.D. Flipping on his two-way, the dispatcher told him why: "Code Four. Code Four. All patrol units at Pico and Westholme and bank area not directly involved in crowd control or house-to-house search resume normal patrol. Code Four. Code Four."

Lloyd attached his red light and turned on his siren, then hung a U-turn and sped to Pico and Westholme. "Bank" flashed "Them," and "house-to-house search" meant violence. When he was two blocks from the scene, he passed a string of patrol cars driving slowly north with their headlights on.

Feeling a wave of nausea, Lloyd floored the gas, then decelerated as Pico, a barricade of sawhorse detour signs and a streetful of nose-to-nose black-and-whites, appeared in his windshield. He braked and parked on the sidewalk, then ran the remaining block, pinning his badge to the front of his suit coat.

Two young officers with shotguns noticed him and stepped over a sawhorse, turning the muzzles of the .12 gauges downward when they saw his badge. Catching their red faces and rubber knees, Lloyd said what he already knew. "One of ours?"

The taller of the young cops answered him in a voice trying hard to be detached. "Two of ours, two dead inside the bank. No suspects in custody. It happened forty-five minutes ago. What division are you—"

Lloyd pushed the officer aside and stepped over the detour sign, then walked around the corner to Pico, elbowing his way through the most crowded crime scene he had ever witnessed. Knots of plainclothes cops were huddled together, conferring over notepads, straining to hear each other above the radio crackle put out by dozens of official vehicles; young patrolmen were standing by their units looking fierce, scared and about to burst with rage. Cherry lights were still whirling, and the sidewalk was packed with forensic technicians carrying cameras and evidence kits. Shouted conversations were competing with the radio noise, and Lloyd picked out bits and pieces and knew it was *Them*.

". . . guy inside said .45 autos, suppressors and—"

". . . this spic was talking dirty to this teller and then just fucking offed her and—"

"One woman said one white, two Mexican, another said all white. This is the—"

In the distance, Lloyd could see the top of a forensic arc light reflecting a red shimmer. He shoved past a team of paramedics on the sidewalk directly in front of the bank, steeling himself when he saw a black-and-white sitting under the light, dried blood covering the back window.

A technician was standing beside the car, dusting a bullet clip; another S.I.D. man was squatting on the hood, his camera up against the shattered windshield, snapping pictures. Lloyd knew that he had to know, and walked over.

The remains of two young men were death frozen in the front seat. Every inch of their uniform navy blue was now the maroon of congealing blood. Both bore high-caliber entry wounds on their faces, and gaping, brain-oozing holes where the backs of their heads used to be. The driver had his service revolver unholstered on the seat beside him, and the other officer had his right hand on the butt of the unit's Remington pump, his index finger on the trigger at half pull.

Wiping tears from his eyes, Lloyd stumbled through the "Official Crime Scene" rope in front of the bank's double glass doors. A technician dusting the door handles muttered, "Hey, you can't," and Lloyd grabbed him by the lapels and shoved him toward the sidewalk, then covered his hands with his coat sleeves and pushed the doors open. Inside the bank, a cordon of Detective Division brass saw him, then stepped aside, casting worried looks among themselves.

Standing on his tiptoes, Lloyd surveyed the bank's interior straining to see something other than the plainclothes officers who were eclipsing almost the entire floor space. By craning his neck he could pick out an S.I.D. team marking the outline of a woman's body behind the tellers' counter, and another team in front of the counter vacuuming for trace elements. A deputy medical examiner was scooping the woman's brains off the wall and into a plastic bag, and at the back of the bank, near the vault, Peter Kapek and a half dozen feds were talking to distraught-looking people.

Lloyd threaded a path in Kapek's direction. More snatches of conversation hit him, a woman whimpering, "The tall Mexican was so scared and sweet-looking," a young cop in uniform telling another, "The security guy was a real wacko, he used to talk this weird shit to me. Hey, that's Lloyd Hopkins—you know, 'Crazy Lloyd.'"

Hearing his name, Lloyd swiveled and looked at the officers, who turned around and backed into a crowd of plainclothesmen. Again standing on his tiptoes for sight of Kapek, he saw the crowd part and create a space. A second later two M.E. assistants carrying a sheet-covered stretcher walked through it, and when he saw blood seeping through the white cotton, he walked over and yanked the sheet off.

Lloyd ignored the stretcher bearers' shocked exclamations and stared at the corpse of a middle-aged white man. His chest and stomach bore three large cavities circumscribed by burned and shredded tissue, obvious high-velocity exit wounds.

Shot in the back.

.45-caliber quality holes.

Them.

Before he could redrape the dead man, Lloyd felt a hard tap on his shoulder. When he turned around, Captain John McManus was standing there, legs spread, hands on hips, his face beet red, working toward purple. They locked eyes, and Lloyd knew that backing down was the only way to win. He raised his hands, and was groping for crow-eating words when McManus stepped forward and breathed in his face: "You fucking necrophile. I told you you weren't to involve yourself in any homicide investigations, collateral to your liaison assignment or otherwise. You're off that assignment as of now. This is a double cop killing, and I don't want trigger-happy vigilante shit heads like you anywhere near it. One word of protest, and I'll have Braverton suspend you. You meddle in this case and I'll have your badge and file on you for obstruction of justice. Now go home and wait for my call."

Lloyd shouldered the captain aside and pushed his way out to the sidewalk. A TV mini-cam crew was now inside the barricades, interviewing a group of Community Relations brass. Someone shouted, "That's Lloyd Hopkins, get him!" and suddenly a microphone was in his face. He yanked the mike out of the man's hand and hurled it in the direction of the patrol car cradling the wasted bodies of two young men, then ran through the crowd to his own official vehicle, with no intention of going home.

Too angry to think beyond *Them*, Lloyd drove to Louie Calderon's place, slamming the wheel when he saw federal surveillance vehicles stationed across the street and in the alley near the back service entrance. Parking down the block by a mom-and-pop market, he defused his tension by gripping the wheel until the strain numbed his brain and a semblance of calm hit, allowing him to answer his own questions rationally.

Roust Calderon? Probe, poke, threaten and scare the shit out of him? No—the Buddy Bagdessarian/warrant approach was still best.

What happened at the bank?—"This spic was talking dirty to this teller and then just fucking offed her"; "The tall Mexican was so scared and sweet-looking." *Why was the man on the stretcher shot in the back? Did the Shark or the white man shoot the two cops?*

The only sane answer was insanity; the only strategy for now was to wait for Louie Calderon to leave, then trash his pad from top to bottom. The only easy question was whether or not to obey McManus.

No.

Lloyd settled in to wait, eyeing the surveillance unit parked a block in front of him. One hour, two, three, four. No movement except a stream of customers and mechanics leaving the garage. At dusk, he walked to the market and bought the evening editions of the *Times* and *Examiner*. The Pico Boulevard slaughter headlined both papers, and the *Times* featured the complete story of the first two robberies, complete with names, mention of the girlfriend angle and heavy speculation that the kidnap assaults were tied in to the stickup that had left four dead. The names of the two dead officers were omitted and the bank victims were listed as Karleen Tuggle, twenty-six, and Gordon Meyers, forty-four, a recently retired L.A. County Sheriff's deputy and the bank's "Security Chief." California Federal was offering a $50,000 reward for information leading to the capture of the killer-robbers, and the L.A. City Council was putting up an additional $25,000. Predictably, Chief Gates announced "the biggest manhunt in Los Angeles history."

It all brought tears to Lloyd's eyes. He imagined himself squeezing Likable Louie's fat neck until either his brains or three names popped out. Then he saw Calderon walk out the garage door in the flesh and get into a Dodge van at curbside. When he drove off, the fed unit was a not-too-subtle three car lengths behind.

Lloyd started getting his B&E shakes and eyed the door of the house. Then the surveillance car from the alley pulled up. The driver got out, sat down on Calderon's front steps and lit a cigarette. Lloyd hit the wheel with his palms, sending shock waves up his bad hand. Kapek, hipped by McManus to his penchant for burglary, was safeguarding the investigation from hot-dog action. Feeling wasted, powerless and unaccountably exhausted, Lloyd drove home to think.

Going through the front door, he heard coughing coming from the direction of the living room. He drew his .38, pinned himself to the entrance foyer wall and moved down it, then hit the overhead light and stepped forward, his gun arm extended and braced with his left hand. When he saw who was sitting in his favorite leather chair, he said, "Jesus Christ."

"Don't act surprised," Captain Fred Gaffaney said. "You know why I'm here."

Lloyd reholstered his .38. "No, I don't."

"Address me as 'sir.'"

Lloyd studied the witch-hunter. Gaffaney looked colder than his deep-freeze norm; drained of everything human. "What are you doing here, Captain?"

Gaffaney fingered his cross and flag lapel pin and said in the most emotionless voice Lloyd had ever heard, "My son, Officer Steven D. Gaffaney, was shot and killed in the line of duty this morning. He was twenty-two. I saw his body. I saw his brains all over the backseat of his patrol unit, and half of his scalp hanging off his head. I forced myself to look, so I wouldn't back away from coming to you."

Standing motionless in the doorway, Lloyd saw where Gaffaney was going. For a microsecond, it seemed like salvation, then he gasped against the thought and said, "I swear to you I'll find them, and if it comes down to me or them, I'll take them out. But you're thinking execution, and I'm no killer."

Gaffaney took a manila folder from his jacket pocket and laid it on the end table beside him. "Yes, you are. I know a great deal about you. In the summer of '70, when you were on loan out to Venice Vice, you befriended a young rookie who had never been with a woman. One night you borrowed a drunk wagon from Central Division and rousted a half dozen Venice hookers and brought them to the rookie's apartment. You made them a variety of offers: service the two of you, or suffer arrest for needle tracks, or outstanding warrants, or plain prostitution. They agreed to party, and you smoked marijuana with them, and fucked several of them, and the whores went away with a good deal of your money when you started feeling guilty. I have sworn depositions from three of those whores, Hopkins. I know you're trying to reconcile with your family. Think of how they'll feel when the *Big Orange Insider* runs the depositions on their front page."

Feeling the old shame settle near his heart, Lloyd said, "I've made amends to my family, and that story is ancient history—just another cheap notch on my rep. It's old stuff."

Gaffaney tapped the folder, then tapped his lapel pin. "Here's something you were probably too stoned to remember doing. After the whores left, you and that rookie had a long conversation about duty and courage. The young man doubted his own ability to kill in the line of duty, and you told him how in the Watts Riot you had killed an 'evil' fellow National Guardsman who had murdered a group of innocent blacks. I've checked your old unit's records. Your squad leader, Staff Sergeant Richard Beller, was presumed to have been killed in the riot, but his body was never found, and he was not seen skirmishing with any rioters. He was, however, on scout patrol with you on the night he disappeared. That rookie is now a lieutenant in Devonshire Division. He's a born-again Christian, and a protégé of mine. I have a sworn affidavit from him, detailing your activities that night in '70, repeating your conversation almost verbatim. Lieutenant Dayton has a brilliant memory. What's the matter, Hopkins? You're looking weak."

Transfixed by a nightmare flashback of Richard Beller's corpse, Lloyd trembled and tried to speak. His tongue and palate and brain refused to connect, and he shook even harder.

"So you see the position you're in," Gaffaney said. "I despise you, but you are the finest detective the Department has ever produced, and I need you." He pointed toward the dining room. "On your table are copies of the existing reports on the Pico-Westholme homicides. I understand the robbery is connected to two others you were working with the feds on, so that gives you an edge. I'm throwing all my clout into getting you assigned to the investigation, on your own autonomy. I'm sure I'll succeed. Whatever you need, from other reports to men for shit work, you'll get—just call me. If you don't comply, I can guarantee your crucifixion in the form of a murder indictment."

Lloyd looked at his accuser and saw the faces of Richard Beller and the Hollywood Slaughterer superimposed over his mercilessly cold features. He tried to speak, but his brain was still jelly.

Gaffaney got up and walked past him to the front door. When his hand was on the latch, he said, "Get them and I'll have mercy. But they are not to be arrested. Kill them or bring them to me."

16

Now it was clockwork in a hurricane, staying icy in a heat wave determined to fry them to Cinder City. At 7:00, Rice gave the Garcias another check for survival balls. Bobby was quiet, sitting in a chair by the dresser, reading the Gideon Bible that came with the room. Joe was hanging drum-tight way inside himself, alternately staring at the walls and the non-inked 16K on the bed. Showered and dressed in Rice's own clothes, the tagalong looked like he had the juice to hold, the oldies but goodies he'd been softly humming for hours supplying him with the guts not to rabbit. At 7:10, for the second time that day, Rice said, "Now, Bobby, you stay here. Joe and I are going to pick up my old lady. When we get back, we'll split the money and split up. Sit still and be cool."

Bobby looked up from his Bible and made a weird gesture Rice figured was Catholic. Joe took his eyes from the stacks of money, and the tune he was humming jumped up three octaves. Rice recognized it as "Blueberry Hill," and said, "Come on, watchdog. Let's move."

They cruised down Highland in the Trans Am, then hung a right turn on Franklin and headed west toward the Mount Olympus development. Joe reached over to flip on the radio, and Rice touched his hand and said, "No. We'll buy a paper at the airport. *When we're free and clear.* Right now, you don't want to know."

Joe swallowed and returned to his humming. Rice openly scrutinized him. It looked like he was groping for words to go with the music.

At Fairfax, Rice swung over to the Strip and stopped at a stand of pay phones in a Texaco parking lot. Noting a newspaper rack beside the booths, he slipped in a quarter and nickel and forced himself to read the front page of the *Times*.

The headline screamed, "Four Killed in West L.A. Bank Stickup!" and the subheading read, "Robbery Linked to Two Others." Rice scanned the paragraphs that detailed their first two kidnap-heists, complete with the names of the victims and suspect descriptions provided by Christine Confrey, the bitch he'd saved from Sharkshit Bobby. Words jumped at him: "Largest manhunt in L.A. history"; "Stolen car by freeway off-ramp presumed to be approach vehicle, but no fingerprints discovered"; "$75,000 offered in combined reward money."

The bombshell was on page two; an artist's sketch of *him*, also courtesy of Chrissy Confrey. The resemblance was about thee-quarters accurate, and Rice balled the paper up, then stepped into the booth and called Rhonda the Fox's home number.

"Hello?"

Rice breathed out in relief. "It's Duane. You want to get paid, with a little bonus for some extra info?"

"Have you found her?"

"Just about. We're flying to New York in a few days. I need the names of some music people—solid people, no cocaine sleazebags. Do you know people who know people there?"

After a long moment of silence, Rhonda said, "Sure. But listen, I'm booked straight through until tomorrow night late. Can you meet me outside Silver Foxes tomorrow night at twelve?"

"No sooner than that?"

"I have to ask around, and that takes time."

Rice said, "I'll be there," and hung up and walked back to the car. Joe swallowed a burst of song lyrics as he got in and peeled rubber up Fairfax toward the Hollywood Hills. When they were just north of Franklin, he pulled the Trans Am into a large vacant lot, wracking the undercarriage. Killing the headlights, he eased off the gas and let the car glide to a halt behind a long scrub hedge.

Turning off the ignition, Rice said, "Wait here," then got out and waded through the hedge. The Mount Olympus access road was right in front of him, and directly across it he could see Stan Klein's house, with no lights on and no Porsche in the driveway or on the street. Returning to the car, he unholstered his .45 and put it in the glove compartment, pulling out a pushbutton switchblade to replace it. "In and out, watchdog," he said. "You've got one job and one job only. Don't let me kill him."

They waited.

Rice sat perfectly still and stared at the access road, waiting for lights to show in number 14; Joe made music in his head. The night cooled and a light drizzle hit the windshield. Then, just after 1:00 A.M., the lights in the house went on.

Rice nudged Joe and handed him the knife, then pointed through the windshield at their target. Joe got out of the car and walked through the hedge, rubber-kneed, his hands in his jacket pockets to kill his tremors. Rice caught up with him. They crossed the blacktop, then Rice bolted up the steps and rang the buzzer.

Voices echoed within the house; Rice heard Vandy's, and knew from the tone that she was tired and cranky. Joe stood beside him, his eyes wide and panicky. Then the door was thrown open, and Stan Klein was standing there, flashing a shit-eating grin betrayed by tics around his temples. "Disco Duane and friend," he said. "When you get out?"

Rice sized Klein up. Red nose from too much coke, useless muscles from too much iron pumping, bullshit dope bravado fueling him for the confrontation. Stan Man shrugged, then faked a sigh. "I don't think she wants to see you, man."

Voice steady, Rice said, "She doesn't know what she wants. Go get her."

Klein sniffed back a noseful of mucus and pointed at Joe. "Who's this . . . Tonto? The strong silent sidekick? What's shakin', Kemo Sabe?"

Through the half-open door, Rice saw the stick skinny legs walking down a wrought-iron staircase. He moved straight toward the sight, pushing Klein backward. Joe was right behind him, sliding past Klein just as he muttered, "Hey, you can't—"

Her.

Rice saw Vandy at the foot of the staircase, wearing a pink crewneck and kelly green cords. She looked emaciated, but her face was pure waiflike beauty. Her voice was just a shadow of her old vibrato growl: "I don't want to go with you, Duane."

Rice stood still, afraid to move or say the wrong thing. Joe trembled with his hands in his pockets. Stan Klein walked over to an end table by the staircase and scooped up a mound of coke with a single-edged razor blade. Squatting, he snorted it, then laughed. "You heard the lady. She doesn't want to go with you."

Prepared to see red and hold it down, Rice moved his eyes back and forth from Vandy to Klein and *smelled* the bank before it all went haywire. Vandy nibbling her cuticles; Klein doing another snootful of coke. Vandy looking like the wasted little girls in concentration camp pictures. Then Joe Garcia's scared rabbit squeak: "Duane, he's got a gun."

Klein was standing by a row of Pac-Man machines near the living room entranceway, licking coke off his fingers and leveling a small automatic at Rice. "Come here, Annie," he said.

Vandy walked to Klein in jerky little-girl steps. He threw his left arm around her and nuzzled her cheek without relinquishing his bead on Rice. Keeping one eye on Joe, he said, "You were fucking comic relief for the whole crowd. Everybody used you. If you weren't such a boss car thief, we would have laughed you out of L.A. The biggest laugh was you making contacts to boost Annie's career, gonna make her a million-dollar rock video star. Dig this on your way to the door with Pancho: I'm gonna make Annie a rock vid star. She's gonna be the queen of porn vid first, then move up. I'm producing a flick with her and this guy I gotta pay by the inch, and I'm talking heavy double digits. Annie knows what's good for her career, and she's gonna do it, 'cause she knows I'm not a dumb shit dreamer like you."

No red, but the haywire stench ate at Rice's nostrils and made his eyes burn. "You ratted me off on my G.T.A. bust, motherfucker."

Klein bit at Vandy's ear, then looked directly at Rice and said, "No, Duaney-boy, I didn't. Annie did. She got busted for prostitution and talked her way out of a drug rehab by snitching you off. Romantic, huh?"

Now the red.

Rice made a slow, deliberate beeline toward the woman he loved and her destroyer. Vandy screamed; Klein squeezed the trigger. The gun jammed, and he pulled back the slide and ejected the chambered round, then slid in another and fired. The shot went wide, tearing into the wall by the staircase. Rice kept walking. Joe pinned himself to the Pac-Man machine farthest from Klein, and stared at the man he was supposed to watchdog, who *just kept walking.* Klein fired again; the shot hit the wall directly above Rice's head. He kept walking and was within point-blank range of his objective when Klein put the gun to Vandy's head, took a step backward with her and muttered, "No no no no no."

Rice halted; Joe fed himself a bomb-burst of music, pulled the switchblade from his pocket and jumped knife first, pushing the button just as Klein wheeled and aimed at him.

The pistol jammed; Vandy dropped to the floor. Joe caught Klein flush in the stomach and ripped upward with both hands. Blood spurted from his mouth, and Rice reached for the gun. Joe saw him aim it at Vandy and the dying man, and knew he was fixing to blow away the whole fucking world. He got to his feet and grabbed a portable TV from the top of the Pac-Man beside him. He swung it forward, and Rice turned and stepped into the blow, catching the plastic and glass missile head-on. He crumpled across Stan Klein's body, and Joe and Vandy ran.

17

Only repeated readings of the Pico-Westholme homicide files kept his mind off Watts in the summer of '65, and even then, the facts that were being imprinted in his mind stuck as self-accusation rather than indicators pointing to *Them*. Karleen Tuggle, Gordon Meyers, Officer Steven Gaffaney and Officer Paul Loweth were killed by .45 gunshots, the two patrolmen and Meyers by rounds fired from the same gun, Tuggle by shots from a different piece—solid ballistics confirmation. Three for the white man; one for the Shark.

And *he* had killed Richard Beller with the same type weapon.

Eyewitness accounts were hysterical, but cross-checking them allowed him to come up with a reconstruction: the robbers enter the bank, the white man shoots shaving cream on the surveillance camera. This means that unless the lens is cleared in two minutes, the silent alarm will go off. The Mexicans hit the tellers stations, the Shark goes wacko at the sight of Karleen Tuggle, talks trash to her, she reacts and he blows her away. The white man is screaming for the "Security Boss." Gordon Meyers appears, then turns tail and runs, and he shoots him in the back.

The basics were covered: no eyewitnesses outside the bank; the '78 Malibu found by the freeway ramp, covered with glove prints, was reported stolen later that day by its owner, a rent-a-cop at a Burger King in Hollywood. Going on the assumption that the robbers lived in the Hollywood area, house-to-house checks were being initiated, the officers carrying the artist's sketch of the white man. Approach vehicle covered.

The escape vehicle was most likely an '81 Chevy Caprice belonging to a family around the corner from the bank. Neighbors reported it stolen three hours after the robbery. It was now the hottest car on the L.A. County Hot Sheet, and the object of an all-points bulletin. Lloyd shuddered. Any man seen driving that car was dead meat, and back in '59 he had paid for most of his Stanford tuition by clouting Chevys.

Them.

Me.

Looking out the window at his neglected front lawn, Lloyd thought of the new *Him*, Gordon Meyers. A team of L.A.P.D. dicks were checking out his personnel record for K.A.s and possible vengeance motives, and Gaffaney had included with his paperwork a hastily compiled addendum report on the man. As dawn crept up, signifying another sleepless night, Lloyd read the report for the fifth time.

Gordon Michael Meyers, D.O.B. 1/15/40, L.A. Graduated high school in '58, joined sheriff's department in '64, during a manpower shortage wherein they lowered their entrance requirements to recruit men.

After the mandatory eighteen-month jail training, assigned to Lenox Station. Assessed as being too ineffectual for street duty, reassigned as night jailer at county jail facility for nonviolent emotionally disturbed prisoners. Kept that assignment for seventeen and a half years, until his retirement. Unmarried, parents retired in Arizona. Address: 411 Seaglade, Redondo Beach.

The phone rang.

Lloyd jerked back in his chair; the shrill noise registered as a gunshot. Realizing it wasn't, he picked up the receiver and said, "Yes?"

The seething voice on the line was McManus's: "You're back on the investigation. Two heavy hitters pulled strings. Don't fuck up."

Lloyd hung up. A hideous thought crossed his mind: the condemned killer was being let out on parole. Getting to his feet and stretching, he ran mental itineraries: review the case with Kapek? No—this was *his*. Roust Calderon? No—Judge Penzler would be back in twenty-four hours to sign his warrant, and with Buddy Bagdessarian assisting they could squeeze Likable Louie to perfection. It was time to find out why Gordon Meyers was shot in the back. Another hideous thought made him wince. The .45 he had killed Richard Beller with was in his desk drawer, oiled, dum-dum loaded and encased in a shoulder rig.

Them.

Me.

Me or them.

Us.

Lloyd strapped on the weapon that had stood him through his baptism of fire, then went out to quash his murder indictment.

On Sepulveda southbound to Redondo Beach, he spotted a tail two car lengths in back of him. Decelerating and weaving into the slow lane, he saw that it was a Metro Division unmarked unit, distinguished from his own Matador by an olive-drab paint job and a giant whip antenna. Slowing to a crawl, he let the car come up on his bumper. When the driver applied the brakes, he stared in his rearview, fuming when he saw two classic Metro hot dogs in the front seat—burly, crew-cut white men in their mid-thirties wearing identical navy windbreakers: Gaffaney's or McManus's insurance against possible fuckups.

Lloyd gave the cops the finger and hung a hard right through a liquor store parking lot, fishtailing into the alley behind it. Seeing no cars or pedestrians, he punched the gas until the alley ended and angled off into a quiet residential street. He took the street at ninety, then slowed and zigzagged in a random pattern until he was within sight of the Redondo Beach Pier. Parking by a chowder stand, he looked around for the Metro unit. It was nowhere in sight. Exhilarated by the speed, Lloyd drove slowly to 411 Seaglade.

It was a garage apartment in the shadow of the pier. Lloyd parked and surveyed the front house. There was no car in the driveway, and the old white wood frame stood quiet in the early morning sunlight. No media vehicles were anywhere to be seen, and by squinting he could tell that there was no "Crime Scene" notice tacked to the door of 411. Knowing that MacManus's "two heavy hitters" were Gaffaney and in all likelihood the Big Chief himself, he grabbed an evidence kit from the backseat, walked up the driveway and kicked the door in.

The burst of sunlight illuminated a dreary living room, spotlessly clean, but featuring mismatched sofa, chairs, coffee table and bookshelves. Lloyd stood in the doorway and made repeated eyeball circuits of the room, picking up a profusion of small details that spelled *loner*: expensive TV, the only wall adornments photographs of Meyers himself, alone in his sheriff's uniform and standing by himself holding a fishing reel and string of trout, no magazines or ashtrays or portable bar for guests.

Lloyd shut the door and walked into a small dining room, catching a first anomaly: all the living room furniture was squared off at right angles; here the table and chairs were haphazardly arranged. The kitchen was more loner confirmation: nothing but frozen dinners in the refrigerator, plates and dishes for one in the sink, a dozen bottles of cheap bourbon in the cupboard.

The bedroom was off to the side of the kitchen. Lloyd flicked on a wall light and tingled. Everything in the small rectangular space was immaculately clean and tidy, from the G.I. made-up bed to the perfectly aligned end table with an alarm clock dead in its middle. But the dresser had been pulled out, and the three scrapbooks stacked across it had been replaced unevenly, one upside down. The pad had been crawled.

Lloyd retraced his steps to the front door, opened his evidence kit and took out a vial of fingerprint powder and a print brush. Removing surgical rubber gloves from the kit, he put them on and limbered his fingers with a series of stretching exercises. Then he went to work to find out just how solitary Gordon Meyers was, and if the pad crawler knew his stuff.

He discovered that Meyers was a stone loner, and the crawler was a pro.

For two solid hours Lloyd dusted print-sustaining surfaces and compared fingerprint points under a magnifying glass. Concentrating on doors, door-knobs and doorjambs, he found overlap smudges and viable latents for thumb and index finger, all "grab" prints likely to have been made by a per-son walking through the apartment, opening and closing doors behind them. There were also smooth glove prints on the same surfaces, and on the living room bookshelves and the dust covers of the books there. All the left and right thumb and index prints matched to the tune of ten comparison points, and there were no conflicting latents to be found. Meyers and the man who searched his apartment.

For what?

Lloyd looked under the furniture, behind the books. Nothing. He checked the kitchen and dining room; nothing but cooking and eating utensils. The desk in Meyers's bedroom was nothing but a tidy or tidily re-arranged collection of bankbooks, pens, pencils, paycheck stubs and I.R.S. forms, and his closet held nothing but L.A.S.D. uniforms and cheap civil-ian clothes.

Which left the scrapbooks.

Lloyd dusted the spines and held his magnifying glass and penlight on them to assess the results. Seeing smudged latents and what looked to be glove streaks, he began a page-by-page scrutiny of the books.

The first two books contained photographs of Gordon Meyers posing with various trophy fish, neatly mounted to the black paper in gummed edge-holders. Lloyd dusted three snapshots at random and got pristine glossy surfaces—no latents; no glove prints.

The third scrapbook was cop memorabilia—candid group shots of sheriff's deputies in uniform and Meyers himself with jail inmates in blue denim. Lloyd leafed through the book, going cold when he came to a page of snap-shots with the corners poking out of their edge-holders, going colder when he saw that the opposite page held two empty photo squares.

Thinking, *check the back for writing, just like the crawler did,* Lloyd fumbled at the snapshot immediately in front of him. When his gloves made the task too unwieldy, he went *ice* cold, then dusted the crookedly replaced photos, coming away with a perfect left thumbprint on a snap of Meyers and another deputy. Holding his magnifying glass over it, he recalled comparison points from the left thumbs assumed to be Meyers's. This print was markedly dif-ferent in whorls and ridges. Lloyd replaced the scrapbook, put the snapshot in an evidence envelope, packed up his kit and got the hell out of the tidy loner apartment.

Forty minutes later, Lloyd was at Parker Center, handing the powdered snapshot to Officer Artie Cranfield of S.I.D., saying, "Feed to the central source computer, the one with the D.M.V. and armed forces input. I'll be up in my office. If you score, get me a printout from R&I."

Artie laughed. "You're very authoritative today, Lloyd."

Lloyd's laugh was humorless. "I'm authorized on this, the big man himself. It's the cop killings, so please fucking hurry."

Artie took off at a jog, and Lloyd busied himself arranging the surveillance reports on Louie Calderon that littered his desk. Thoughts of calling Peter Kapek for an interagency confab crossed his mind, then he saw a memo propped up against his phone: Sgt. Hopkins—meet or call S.A. Kapek at downtown Fed bldg.—12/14—0940. He was debating whether to call or roll when Artie returned, breathless, and handed him a manila folder. "I ran the print. He's one of ours, Lloyd."

Lloyd shivered and thought: *Gaffaney*, then read through the L.A.P.D. personnel file, holding a hand over the full-face and profile snaps that were clipped to the first page.

The file detailed the twelve-year police career of Metropolitan Division sergeant Wallace Dean Collins, age thirty-four. His record was impressive: Class A fitness reports and a number of citations for "Meritorious Service." Lloyd scanned the list of Collins's "special assignments." Surveillance detail, narco, vice decoy, then a transfer to Metro on the recommendation of Captain Frederick Gaffaney. Since his rookie days, Collins had partnered with Sergeant Kenneth R. Lohmann of Central Division, and there was an addendum memo from the Central personnel officer stating that Lohmann was also flagged for Metro duty—on the next available opening.

Lloyd took his hand from the snapshot and smiled. Collins was the driver of the car tailing him down Sepulveda. Looking at the fidgeting Artie Cranfield, he said, "How'd you get the file so fast?"

Artie shrugged. "I told the clerk at Personnel Records you had special clearance from Braverton and up. Why?"

Lloyd handed the file back. "Just curious. Take this back to Records, hold on to the photo and be very quiet about this, okay?"

"Quiet as the grave," Artie said.

*   *   *

Lloyd drove to the downtown Federal Building, thinking of angles to cut-throat Gaffaney and kill the murder indictment now being held over his head. As he pulled to the curb at Sixth and Union, the Metro unit sidled to a stop two car lengths in back of him, Collins at the wheel.

Getting out and slamming the door, Lloyd's thoughts moved from black-mail to a double suicide scene to blow Gaffaney's career along with his own. Then curiosity about Collins crawling Gordon Meyers's pad took over, and he ran upstairs to Kapek's office, rapped on the door and said in his most commanding tone, "Come on, G-man. We're going cruising."

"Where to?"

"A hot-dog rendezvous."

They drove east through downtown L.A., Lloyd silent, with one eye on the road and the other on the Metro unit riding their tail behind a slow-moving Cadillac. Kapek fingered his acne scars and stared at Lloyd, finally breaking the tense quiet. "I've been forcing myself to concentrate on the first two robberies exclusively, and I think I may have a hypothetical con-nection between Hawley and Eggers."

Lloyd's mind jerked away from the plan he was hatching. "What?"

"Listen: I checked out both men's bank accounts and got something weird. They both withdrew similar large amounts of cash, on the same dates—October seventeenth and November first. Two five-hundred-dollar withdrawals for Hawley, two six-hundred-buck shots for Eggers. Non se-quitur stuff—both guys are strictly check writers. These withdrawals were from their individual accounts—not the joint accounts they share with their wives. What do you think?"

Lloyd whistled, then said, "Vice. I've already put in *my* Vice query, so you call the squad commanders and have them shake down their snitches for specific info. What happened on those dates? Bookies taking heavy action? Cockfights, dogfights? I don't buy Eggers or Hawley as dopers, but I could see Sally and Chrissy doing a few snootfuls of blow, with their sugar daddys footing the bill. By the way, how did the families react to the girlfriend bit? Any feedback on that?"

Kapek breathed out sadly. "Hawley's wife moved out. Eggers lost his job, because he lied to us about Confrey, and because the big boss at Security Pa-cific freaked when he heard about the dead cops and blamed Eggers. Eggers's wife is still up at Arrowhead, and he went up there to work it out. Both Haw-ley and Eggers are refusing to talk further to us, under attorney's orders."

Lloyd said, "Shit. I wrote out a memo requesting that they be held as material witnesses to avoid that, then all hell broke loose. By the way, we're being tailed. There's a Metro unit in back of us."

Kapek looked in the rearview. "Is that what this is all about? And what's 'Metro'?"

Passing out of downtown into the East L.A. industrial district, Lloyd said, "Metro is an L.A.P.D. special crimes unit, a diversified attack force. Gang fights in Watts? Send in Metro. Too much dope in schools? Metro shakes down bubble-gummers on their lunch hour. The unit is effective, but it's full of right-wing wackos. And what this is all about is me being watchdogged. We're going to the L.A. River and park. Follow me and do what I tell you."

Now Kapek was silent. Lloyd turned off Alameda and skirted the Brew 102 Brewery, then took the Water and Power Department road to the embankment that overlooked the bone-dry "river." The tail car remained fifty yards in back of them, and Lloyd slowed and parked at the embankment's edge. Checking the rearview a last time, he said, "I'm hoping they'll think we're meeting a snitch. Come on."

They walked down the concrete slope sideways, plaster debris crackling beneath their feet. When they reached the riverbed, Lloyd got his bearings and saw that the old maintenance shack was still there and still mounted on a cinderblock foundation to keep it from washing away during flood season. He pointed Kapek toward it, and they trudged over through an obstacle course of empty wine bottles and beer cans. When they were standing in the shade of the shack's corrugated tin door, Lloyd tilted his head sideways and caught sight of the two Metro cops peering over the edge of the embankment. "Stand here," he said. "Keep looking in the direction I take off in, and keep looking at your watch like you're expecting someone."

Kapek nodded, looking befuddled and slightly angry. Lloyd walked around the edge of the shack, then climbed the embankment on its opposite side, coming onto level ground behind a line of abandoned cars. Squatting low, he moved down the row to the end, then stood up, seeing nothing but a short patch of pavement between himself and the Metro unit, with Collins and his partner fifty yards away, still holding surveillance on Kapek.

Lloyd sprinted to the car and opened the driver's-side door. The two cops turned around at the noise and started running. Lloyd flipped open the glove compartment—nothing—then noticed an attaché case on the floorboard, "Sgt. K. R. Lohmann" stenciled on the front. He opened it and tore through blank report forms and plastic evidence bags, and was about to give up when his hands brushed a bag that held two glossy photographs. He fumbled the bag into his inside jacket pocket and backed out of the car just as Collins loomed in front of him.

With the open door between them, Collins halted, then approached on tiptoes. Lloyd saw his partner ten yards in back of him, looking scared. When Collins moved into a cautious streetfighter's stance, Lloyd slammed the door into his legs, knocking him backward onto the ground.

Collins got to his feet and started swinging blindly; Lloyd sidestepped the blows and brought him to his knees with a left to the solar plexus. Collins sucked air and held his stomach; Lloyd balled his right fist. The old pain was still there, so he swung a short left uppercut instead. Collins grabbed his nose and fell prone, his legs twitching. Lloyd stood over him and hissed, "Tell Captain Fred I don't need a backup."

The other cop was trembling beside the car. Lloyd stepped toward him, and he backed away. Then Peter Kapek walked over, stationing himself squarely between them. Shaking his head, he looked at Lloyd and said, "Don't you get tired of walking all over people? Aren't you a little old for this kind of shit?"

18

At first he thought it was an awful new kind of rage that took over his whole body, making him ache from head to toe and vomit and see double. Then he thought it was something even stranger—a defense mechanism put out by his brain to keep the truth from driving him where everything was bright red and skunk-stenched. A tagalong *puto* cold-cocked him and took off with his woman, and if he freaked out and went crazy he was stone fucking dead, because he was the most wanted man in L.A., bullet bait for every cop who breathed.

But confronting the truth and driving the Trans Am skillfully through the hottest part of town did nothing to kill the revolt inside his body, and he couldn't tell if he was *in* a hallucination or *was* the hallucination.

At dawn he'd awakened, sprawled across Stan Klein's body. It all came back, and he got to his feet, reeling, stumbling and puking, and ran outside to the car. Driving away, he started seeing double and pulled over behind the scrub hedge and passed out. When he came to, it was better, and he drove into downtown Hollywood on side streets. Then it got brutal.

Passing the Burger King on Highland, he saw cops handing out pieces of paper to customers; other cops were knocking on doors on Selma and De Longpre and the little cul-de-sacs north of the Boulevard. Cruising by the park two blocks from the Bowl Motel, he saw more cops distributing more paper, this time to the winos who used the park as a crash pad. The motel, Sharkshit Bobby and the money was right there, free of cops, but with the *feel* of a giant booby trap. Looking up at the palm trees that bordered the place, he started to see triple, then thought he saw snipers with elephant guns hiding inside the fronds. Attack dogs started to growl everywhere, then the sound became the whir of helicopter rotors.

When he saw a German shepherd behind the wheel of a Volkswagen, something snapped, and he laughed out loud and rubbed the blood-crusted bruise that covered the left side of his face. He drove to a pay phone and called Louie Calderon at the bootleg number, and Louie screamed that the fuzz had him pegged as the gun dealer, and there was a twenty-four-hour tail on his ass. He hadn't given up any names, but the heat was huge and Crazy Lloyd Hopkins himself had hassled him.

He'd hung up and made another circuit of Highland. More cops on the street; a group of plainclothesmen house-to-housing the block where he'd stashed the '81 Caprice. He was about to make a dash for Sharkshit and the money when he noticed a scattering of paper in the gutter. He pulled to the curb, got out and picked up the first sheet he came to. It was the sketch of himself he'd seen in the newspapers, with "White Male, Age 25–33, 5'10"–6'1", 150–180 lbs." written below it.

The Bowl Motel gave him a brief come-hither look, then blew up in his mind. Bobby had probably rabbited with the money or the cops were waiting there, trigger-happy and pumped up for glory. All he had left was Vandy.

Getting back in the Trans Am, it all came together.

Concussion.

Meet Rhonda at Silver Foxes at midnight, get *her* to make the run to the motel for the money. Promise her a big cut or nothing at all. Vandy was probably hiding out with her cocaine sleazebag friends. Force Rhonda to help find her.

Rice looked at his watch. 1:14, twelve hours since the cold-cock. A wave of nausea hit him, producing stomach cramps that shot up into his head and made his vision blur. Through the pain he got the most frightening idea of the whole horror-show past month:

Control the concussion so you can survive to get Vandy and a shot at the money and kill Joe Garcia.

Rice drove back to Stan Klein's villa and walked in the unlocked front door like he owned the place. Giving only a cursory glance to Stan Man's body and the dried lake of blood beside it, he ran upstairs to the bathroom, opened the medicine cabinet and read labels. Darvon, Placidil, Dexedrine, Percodan. He remembered a thousand Soledad bull sessions about dope and dry-swallowed two perks and three dexies. He thought of his boozehound parents walking out the door and never returning and almost retched, then walked into the bedroom and fell down on the bed. The soft surface made him think of Vandy, and when the drugs kicked in, easing his pain and juicing him with a new shaky energy, he wondered if she was worth killing for.

19

Lloyd turned on the light in his cubicle and saw that the papers on his desk had been sifted through. He looked for an inanimate object to hit, then remembered Kapek's "Aren't you a little old for this kind of shit?" and the junior G-man's disgusted goodbye when he dropped him off. Only Fred Gaffaney was worth violence, and he was much too potent to fuck with. Calmed by hatred of the Jesus freak, he took the plastic evidence baggie from his pocket and studied the two photographs inside.

The snapshots were of Gordon Meyers and a young man, dressed in civilian clothes, seated at what looked like a restaurant or nightclub table. Meyers beamed broadly in both, but in one photo the young man was slack-jawed, as if caught by unpleasant surprise; in the other he held an arm up to cover his face.

Lloyd studied the face, knowing that he had seen the blunt cheekbones, close-set eyes and crew cut before. Then the resemblance hit him. He ran to the switchboard for a newspaper confirmation, and got it from a black-bordered photo on the second page of the *Times*: the young man in the snapshots was the late Officer Steven Gaffaney.

Lloyd smiled; the connection felt like aiming a crucifixion spike at Jesus Fred's heart. He ran back to his cubicle and dialed Dutch Peltz's number at Hollywood Station. When Dutch answered with "Peltz, talk," Lloyd said, "No time for amenities, Dutchman. I'm on the cop killings, and I need a favor."

"Name it."

"Dave Stevenson still the commander of West L.A. Station?"

"Yes."

"You still tight with him?"

"Yes."

"Good. Will you call him and ask him about Gaffaney, the dead rookie? Anything and everything, no departmental hype, the real skinny?"

Dutch said, "Call you back in ten minutes," and hung up. Lloyd waited by the phone, ready to pounce at the first ring. In eight minutes it went off, a siren shriek. He picked it up, and Dutch started talking.

"Stevenson called Gaffaney Junior a punk kid, a pain in the ass and a dummy, unquote. He was resented by his fellow officers because he used to preach religion to them and because he used to brag about his father and how his clout would let him climb the promotion ladder in record time. The kid was also a thief. He stole clerical supplies up the ying-yang and used to rip off ammo from the armory. Interesting, huh?"

Lloyd whistled. "Yeah. Did Stevenson report any of this? Did he—"

Dutch cut in. "Yes, he did. He reported the thefts to Intelligence Division, rather than I.A.D., because that's Gaffaney Senior's bailiwick. Dave clammed up then. I just called a friend at Intelligence. He's going to check into it for me on the Q.T. If he gets something, I'll let you know. What are you fishing for, Lloyd?"

"I don't know, Dutch. Do me another favor?"

"Shoot."

"Call the manager at Cal Federal and set up an interview for me in forty-five minutes. He's probably been besieged by cops, but tell him I'm new on the investigation, with new questions for him."

"You've got it. Get them, Lloyd."

Lloyd said, "I will," and hung up, knowing the statement was aimed at Fred Gaffaney more than *Them*.

*   *   *

The California Federal manager was a middle-aged black man named Wallace Tyrell. Lloyd introduced himself in the bank's desk area, then followed him back to his private office. Closing the door behind them, Tyrell said, "Captain Peltz mentioned new questions. What are they?"

Lloyd smiled and sat down in the one visitor's chair in the room. "Tell me about Gordon Meyers."

Positioning himself carefully in the swivel rocker behind his desk, Tyrell said, "That isn't a new question."

"Tell me anyway."

"As you wish. Meyers was only with the bank for a little over two weeks. I hired him because he was a retired police officer with a satisfactory record and because he accepted a low salary offer. Aside from that, I had him pegged as a garrulous, good-natured man, one with a fatherly interest in the young policemen in the area. He—"

Lloyd held up a hand. "Slow and easy on this, Mr. Tyrell. It's very important."

"As you wish. Meyers used to buttonhole the local officers at the coffee shop next door, apparently to trade war stories. I saw him doing it several times. It was obvious to me that the officers considered him a nuisance. Also, Meyers approached several policemen who had accounts here. Basically, he impressed me as a lonely, slightly desperate type of man."

"Yet you had no thoughts of firing him?"

"No. Hiring one man to be head of security saves money and avoids having an old pensioner with a gun hanging around, reminding customers of possible bank robberies. Meyers adequately handled vault and safe-deposit-box security *and* served as a guard—without a uniform. It was extremely cost-effective. As I said before, these aren't new questions you're asking me."

Staring hard at Tyrell, Lloyd said, "How's this for new? Were there any shortages of cash or safety-box valuables during the time Meyers worked here?"

Tyrell sighed and said, "That is a new question. Yes, two customers mentioned small amounts of jewelry missing from their boxes. That happens sometimes, people are forgetful of their transactions, but rarely twice in one week. If it happened again, I was going to call the police."

"Did you suspect Meyers?"

"He was the only one *to* suspect. He was vault custodian; part of his job was to insert the signature key when the customer inserted their key—our boxes are double-locked. He could have made wax impressions of some of the bottom locks—his application résumé said he worked as a locksmith before he joined the Sheriff's Department. Also, this is a busy time for safety-box transactions—people withdrawing jewelry for Christmas parties and cashing in bonds. If Meyers was very careful, he would have had ample opportunity to pilfer."

"Have you told any of the other investigating officers this?"

"No. It didn't seem germane to the issue."

Lloyd stood up and shook hands with the bank manager. "Thank you, Mr. Tyrell. I like your style."

"I work at it," Tyrell said.

Driving away from the bank, recent memories tumbled in Lloyd's mind. During the pandemonium following the Pico-Westholme bloodbath, he had heard one young patrolman tell another: "The security guy was a real wacko. He used to talk this weird shit to me." The cops had backed away when he noticed them, but their faces were still in his memory vault, now part of the blurred, but clearing focus of the Gaffaney offshoot of the case. Checking his dashboard clock, he saw that it was 3:40, twenty minutes until daywatch ended. Focusing only on those faces, he drove to the West L.A. Station to make them talk.

His timing was perfect.

The station parking lot was a flurry of activity, black-and-whites going in and out, patrolmen walking back and forth, carrying report notebooks and standard-issue shotguns. Standing by the locker room door, Lloyd scanned faces, drawing puzzled return looks from the incoming officers. The flurry was dying out when he saw the two from the bank approach with their gear.

Lloyd walked over to them, making a snap decision to play it straight but hard. When they saw him, the patrolmen averted their eyes almost in unison and continued on toward the locker room door. Lloyd cleared his throat as they passed him, then called out, "Come here, Officers."

The two young men turned around. Lloyd matched their faces to their name tags. The tall redheaded cop named Corcoran was the one who had made the remark at the bank; the other, a youth with glasses named Thompson, was the one he'd been talking to. Nodding at them, Lloyd said, "I'm on the bank homicides, gentlemen. Corcoran, you said, quote, 'The security guy was a real wacko. He used to talk this weird shit to me.' You told that to Thompson here. You can elaborate on the statement to me, or a team of I.A.D. bulls. Which would you prefer?"

Corcoran flushed, then answered, "No contest, Sergeant. I was gonna tell the squad room dicks, but it slipped my mind." He looked at Thompson. "Wasn't I, Tommy? You remember me telling you?"

"Th-that's right," Thompson stammered. "R-really, Sarge."

Lloyd said, "Talk. Omit nothing pertaining to the security man."

Corcoran spoke. "Tommy and I sort of had lunch with him twice, last week. He came over to our table, flashed his retirement badge from the Sheriff's and sat down, sort of uninvited. He started asking these weird questions. Should prostitution and weed be legalized? Didn't we think cops made the best whoremasters, because they knew the whore psyche so good? Didn't we think that the county could cut costs by legalizing weed and getting inmates up at Wayside to harvest it? Stone wacko. I th—"

Thompson cut in. "I couldn't believe this clown made twenty years as a cop. He came on like he was from outer space. But I knew he was leading up to something. Anyway, the second time he crashes our lunch, he tries to act real cool and asks us if we know any fences 'who work good with us.' Unbelievable! Like he thinks policemen and fences are good buddies."

Feeling his blurred focus gain another notch of clarity, Lloyd said, "Tell me about Steven Gaffaney. Don't be afraid to be candid."

A look passed between the partners, then Corcoran said, "Nobody on the daywatch could stand him. He was a religious crackpot and a freebie scrounger, always hitting the halfer restaurants and pocketing the check, leaving a quarter tip. I heard rumors that he stole stuff from the station and that his old man, some heavy-hitter captain, bribed instructors at the Academy to pass him through. Wh—"

Lloyd interrupted. "What's the source of that last rumor?"

Corcoran stared at the ground. "I heard the squad room lieutenant talking to Captain Stevenson. The skipper shushed him."

"How did Gaffaney and his partner get along?" Lloyd asked.

"Paul Loweth couldn't stand him," Thompson said. "When they got assigned together, Paul requested another partner, you know, because of a personality conflict. They even took separate code sevens, because Paul couldn't stand eating with Gaffaney."

Lloyd said, "Here's the crunch question. Did you ever see Gordon Meyers and Gaffaney together?"

Both officers nodded their heads affirmatively, and Corcoran said, "About four or five days before the killings I saw Meyers and Gaffaney at the coffee shop next to the bank, talking like old buddies. I didn't hear what they were talking about; Tommy and I sat down at the counter so the wacko wouldn't hassle us."

Bowing with a flourish, Lloyd said, "Thank you, gentlemen," then ran for his Matador and drove to 411 Seaglade.

Still no car in the driveway; still no activity around the front house; still no "Crime Scene" notice on the door of the garage apartment. Again Lloyd kicked the door in, this time splintering the wood around the lock. Knowing that the pad had already stood two professional prowlings, he went straight for the kitchen and opened the drawers until he found a large, saw-edged steak knife. Then he walked into the bedroom, upended the mattress and looked for telltale slits or stitchings. Finding a long seam of catgut near the headboard, he dug the knife in and ripped out stuffing until his blade hit a sharp object.

Lloyd withdrew the knife and stuck in his hand, touching a flat metal surface. His fingers pried it loose, and he pulled it out.

It was a fishing tackle box, rectangular-shaped, about two inches deep and unlocked. Lloyd lifted up the top. Inside were a half dozen Dieboldt "Security" keys, balls of molding wax, loose colored gemstones and a rolled sheaf of papers. Unrolling them and turning on the lamp by the bed, he smiled. No more blur—the Gaffaney offshoot of the case was now crystal clear.

The pages were an official L.A.P.D. form—a West L.A. Division daywatch car plan list, the names of the officers, their sector and unit numbers in one column, their assignment dates in another. The list detailed November–December 1984, and beside sector G-4, the names "T. Corcoran/J. Thompson" were crossed off, while the name "S. Gaffaney" bore exclamation points followed by question marks.

Lloyd stood up and put the form in his pocket, wondering why the old pursuit high wasn't there. Long moments passed before the reason came to him: Gaffaney Junior probably didn't have time to receive the stolen jewelry, or flat out resisted the temptation. The two nightclub snapshots were probably evidence of Meyers's second go-around at recruiting him. The kid was already pegged as a thief within the Department, second-generation kleptomania was not blackmail parity with first-generation murder, and the Gaffaney offshoot was probably coincidental to *Them*.

Them.

Lloyd thought of Louie Calderon, and of Judge Penzler, still luxuriating at Lake Tahoe. He thought of the blank warrants in his desk at Parker Center, and of the signatures he had forged on stolen payroll checks during col-

lege. Forgery to kill a murder indictment was easy parity, even more justified as a means to *Them*. One thought stuck in Lloyd's mind all the way to
the Center: *Who were they?*

20

D_{usk.}

Joe Garcia looked at Anne Atwater Vanderlinden and wondered for the
three thousandth time who she was. Crouched in the Griffith Park hide-
away he'd discovered in high school, he watched her chain-smoke and stare
at the lights popping on all over the L.A. Basin. She'd run with him, away
from the lover he'd killed and the old lover chasing her, no tears, no show
of fear until she ran out of cigarettes and threw a tantrum in front of a liquor
store. Guts, shallowness or dope exhaustion?

She'd fallen asleep in his arms, and holding her made him feel strong,
even though he knew he was a dead man. Was it her, or would any woman
have done it for him?

They'd slept and talked on and off all day, and he filled her in on Bobby
and the money, but not on the bank and dead cops. She took it in with a
shrug, looking like a bored rich girl with no connection to dead men and
blood money. Stupid, insensitive or just burned out?

Her weird little speeches didn't make figuring her out any easier. During
the day she'd wake up, say things like "Duane and Stan had the same
karma," or "Stan was a pragmatist, Duane just thought he was," or "Duane
didn't understand my music, so it was easy to split from him," then doze off
again. After a fifteen-hour crash course in closeness, all *he* knew was that
she didn't know they were up someplace worse than the creek with *nada*.

Anne pointed to the lights going on in the Capital Records Tower. "Stan
was going to set me up with a producer there. Have you ever been in jail?"

"Yeah."

"I knew it. It's your clothes. You're wearing the kind of clothes Duane
would wear if he was trying to fit in someplace he didn't belong."

Seeing a picture of himself drenched in ink, Joe said, "These are Duane's threads. You know we have to get out of here. We can't stay here forever."

"I know that. Clothes should reflect a person's early environment, then, as they put out karma, they transform what they wear. What did you wear when you were growing up? You know, prep like me, or mod, surfer, what?"

Joe watched Anne light a cigarette, then exhale and sniff the air like it could get her high in place of coke. He said, "This isn't the time to be talk-ing fashion. We've got no car and no money, and a crazy man on our ass. I can't go by my pad or the motel, because *he'll* be there. But we have to move, and *I* have to eat."

Anne said, "I've got friends who can help us, and I can make money. Just answer my question."

"How? Peddling your pussy?"

"Don't say that! I can give sex and not sacrifice my karma! Don't say that!"

Joe put a hand on her arm and said, "Sssh. I'm sorry, but I am in *deep trouble*."

"Then answer my question."

Joe sighed. "I grew up dressing like a ridiculous Mexican gangster. Plaid Sir Guy shirts buttoned to the top when it was ninety-five degrees, bell-bottom khakis that dragged the ground, spit-shined navy shoes and an honor farm watch cap. It was a joke, and it had nothing to do with karma."

"Everything does."

"I killed a man last night. Aren't you scared?"

Anne sniffed the air. "I took a Dilaudid Black Beauty speedball just be-fore it got bad with Stan and Duane, and I'm starting to crash. In about an hour I'll be *real* scared. You act like a tough guy, but you talk like you went to college. You're sort of a *phony*."

Only Bobby knew that about him.

Joe put his arms around Anne and whispered, "It's because of this song I can't write, and Bobby and Sir Guys and khakis and what I have to do, but I can't do any more. Does that make sense to you?"

Anne dry-sobbed into his chest. "No no no no no."

Joe whispered back, "You're just pretending not to know. You're a musician, so I know you know. Listen. I'll tell you exactly what we're going to do. We're going to walk down the Observatory Road to Vermont, then steal some rich preppy car. Then we're going to hit up these friends of yours and get some money and get the hell out of town. Say yes if you think we can do it."

Anne made a choking sound and nodded her head up and down. Joe looked out at the L.A. skyline and knew for the first time in his life that it was his—because now he could leave it behind.

21

Lloyd pulled up across from Likable Louie's One-Stop Pit Stop. Seeing no fed units, he grabbed his forged search warrant and Ithaca pump, ran across the street and knocked on the door of the built-on house. A feeling of being close grabbed him, and he flicked off the safety and jacked a shell into the chamber.

The door was opened cautiously, held to the frame by a long chain. A Mexican woman peered through the crack and said, "Luis not here. Police took him."

Lloyd saw copwise smarts. "You mean federal officers?" he said. "F.B.I.?"

"Luis hip to men watching him. These L.A. cops, green car, big antenna."

Lloyd shuddered. Metro had glommed the Calderon info. "When?" he asked.

"Half hour. I call lawyer."

Lloyd ran back to his car and lead-footed it the two miles to Rampart Station, hoping to find Lieutenant Buddy Bagdessarian or another detective familiar with Calderon. Parking in the lot, he saw no black-and-whites, only civilian cars, and knew that the station contingent was skeletal—probably because every available unit was aiding Hollywood Division in the cop-killer canvassing. Then he spotted an olive-drab Metro wagon parked crossways in the watch commander's space. The feeling of being close got claustrophobic, and he ran into the station full-tilt.

There was a single officer on duty at the front desk. Lloyd eased his stride and approached slowly, knowing that the early evening station scene was way too quiet, way *off*. The desk officer grimaced when he saw him coming. He moved toward the intercom phone on the wall behind him, then changed his mind and mashed his hands together. Lloyd reached the desk and saw a cross and flag pin attached next to the man's badge. The abomination made his head reel. He was about to rip the insignia from the officer's chest when a muffled noise stopped him and made him perk his ears to identify it.

There was a short moment of silence, then the noise again. This time Lloyd knew it was a scream. He ran down a long corridor toward the echo, past the booking area and drunk tank to a half-open storage room door. Behind the door the screams melded with a barrage of other noises: retching, garbled obscenities, loud thuds. Lloyd forced himself to count to ten, an old strategy to resurrect cool. Then a brass-knuckled fist arced across the open door space, followed by a burst of blood. At seven, he attacked.

Collins and Lohmann looked up as the door crashed open; Louie Calderon, handcuffed behind his back to a chair, spat blood and flailed at the Metro cops with his legs. Lloyd moved straight in, both fists cocked and aimed shoulder-high. With no swinging room, he hurled jerky shots, catching Lohmann in the neck, Collins a glancing blow in the chest. Calderon toppled his chair to the floor; Collins tripped over him, missing a wide roundhouse right at Lloyd's head. Lloyd grabbed his wrist as the blow grazed his shoulder, bringing his knee up flush into Collins's abdomen. Louie Calderon moaned beneath the tangle of feet, and Lohmann lunged at Lloyd with two brass-coiled fists, his momentum sending them both back into the door. Then hands grabbed Lloyd from behind and pulled him out of the room, Lohmann still on top of him, trying to extricate himself. When the knuckle wielder got untangled, Lloyd had a clear shot. He kicked Lohmann in the face and felt his nose crack.

Lloyd was hurled into the holding cell across the corridor. When the cross-and-flag officer got the door secured, he stood up, reached through the bars and tore off his badge. The polished oval hit the floor, and the officer picked it up, looked at Lloyd and hissed, "Satan."

Lloyd laughed in his face, then spat in his face. Collins yelled, "Get back to the fucking desk!" and the cross-and-flag man half-walked, half-ran down the corridor and out of sight. Lloyd watched Collins help his partner to his feet. Lohmann was blowing cartilage and bloody mucus out of both nostrils, spitting the overflow on the floor. Collins made him tilt his head backward; then, with one arm around his shoulders, he walked him toward the front of the station.

Louie Calderon was still on the storage room floor, twisted sideways in his chair. Lloyd watched him gasp and let out little sobs. His own breathing was almost back to normal when Collins returned, picked up the chair and placed a finger under Likable Louie's chin. "You're going to give me three names," he said. "A federal officer saw your little boy with a tranq gun. We know you're the dealer."

Calderon pulled his chin free. "Your mother's the dealer," he slurred. "She deals AIDS at a lesbian bar."

Collins hit him in the stomach, knocking the chair back to the floor. Calderon retched for breath, then started hyperventilating, thrashing with his feet, heaving with his shoulders. The chair buckled off the floor as he squirmed, and one by one the wooden slats on the backing snapped. Collins stood over Calderon until he got his wind and started shrieking, "Pig, pig, pig." Then he knelt beside him and said, "The three names."

Calderon took a long gasp of air and said, "Your mother, your partner's mother and Crazy Lloyd's mother. *Chinga su madres todos*. Lesbian pig three-way with niggers. *Puto! Puto! Puto!*"

Collins said, "Pig is a no-no," stuck his right thumb and forefinger behind Calderon's ear and squeezed the carotid artery. *"The three names."*

Lloyd squinted and saw Calderon's face start turning purple. He squeezed the bars, pushing harder and harder into them. It felt like he was the first part of a chain of pressure moving straight through the bars to the hot dog and his victim, and if he let up, he would never get to *Them*. Then, when Calderon's face looked like a plum about to burst, he saw what he was doing and screamed, "No!"

Startled, Collins withdrew the hold. He looked over at Lloyd, and Lloyd saw his own eyes burning into him. Knowing it couldn't be, he held his hands up in front of his face. Seeing nothing, he felt all his senses go into his ears and pick up whispers:

"The names. I'll maim you for life if you don't give them to me."

"No. No. Fuck you. No. Don't. Please don't."

"Think of your family. Think of your wife at Tehachapi, where she'll be on dope charges if you don't tell me."

"No. No. No. Please, please. No."

"The three names. Think of your kids in a cut-rate board-and-care home. Have you watched the news lately? Lot of sexual abuse in those places. *Give me the three names.*"

"No. No. No."

"No? No? 'Yes,' or I get a dykey woman officer to skin search your wife for the narcotic substances that I know she'll find."

"No. No. N—"

"Tell me, Luis."

"No. They'll hurt me."

"They won't hurt you, but I will."

"No."

"Don't say no to me, say yes to me, or I'll hurt your family."

"Yes. Yes. Duane Rice. Bobby Garcia. Joe Garcia."

Them.

Lloyd closed his eyes and flashbacked: The "Duane/Rhonda" message on Calderon's bootleg message list; Christine Confrey's puzzled reaction to the mug shots of Duane Richard Rice, allegedly serving a year in county jail for G.T.A. He pressed himself into the bars, the better to see and listen.

Collins was squatting beside Calderon, unlocking the handcuffs that bound him to the chair. "There's a lot of Bobby and Joe Garcias," he said. "Be more specific about them."

Likable Louie fumbled himself away from the chair, slowly stretching his arms and kneading his gouged wrists. "Bobby 'Boogaloo' Garcia, the ex-boxer. His brother Joe." His voice was filled with the self-disgust of the freshly turned snitch. Lloyd held his eyes shut to give the man back some of his dignity. He kept them shut until he felt a tap on his shoulder.

Collins was standing directly in front of the cell. Lloyd saw that his eyes were brown, not gray like his own, but that they were still somehow identical. "I'll have the desk officer let you out in a little while," he said. "But stay out of this, it's ours."

Lloyd couldn't think of anything to say. He stared at Collins as he walked back to the storage room and helped Calderon over to the holding cell next to his. Still too numb to talk, he heard the door being unlocked and locked again, followed by footsteps moving away from the blood-spattered corridor. Then, from beyond the periphery of his vision, Louie Calderon said, "Don't let them kill the kid. Bobby and Duane are hope-to-die trash, but the kid was just too weak to say no. Don't let them kill him."

22

Midway down Vermont to Los Feliz, Joe Garcia realized he didn't know how to steal a car. He'd heard nine million raps on hot-wiring and drilling steering columns, and that was it. Anne Vanderlinden walked beside him, talking gibberish about karma and the ritzy houses they were passing. Her voice was getting more and more feverish, and when streetlamp light caught her eyes, they glowed wide and loony.

Then Joe caught a blast of Bob Seger and the Silver Bullet Band and weaving headlights. He grabbed Anne just as a yellow Corvette cut a sharp left turn and screeched to a stop in the driveway next to them. A young man got out of the car and stumbled across the lawn and through the front door of a large Tudor house. Joe left Anne on the sidewalk and checked out the 'Vette. The keys were in the ignition. He looked at the house and saw window lights going on, then off. Now or never.

He walked back to Anne and shoved her toward the car. She got in the passenger side and started burrowing in the glove compartment. Joe slipped behind the wheel, trembling when he saw the shifter on the floor and realized that he didn't know how to drive a stick. Muttering "Fuck it," he remembered the way Bobby used to drive his old VW and watched Anne open up a prescription bottle and start shoving pills in her mouth. He found neutral; he depressed the clutch; he hit the ignition. Bob Seger boogied. Joe slammed the shifter into reverse and inched out of the driveway. Anne giggled, "Drive to the Strip and we'll call my friends!" and Joe ground his way through the gears, stalling the car twice, but finally working clutch and gearshift to the point where he could keep them going. The moment on the hillside came back, ten times as strong, and they fishtailed toward Hollywood.

23

Two-way radio crackle in the distance; helicopter searchlights swooping the motel at irregular intervals. Duane and Joe gone over twenty-four hours, probably dead. Twice the radio had screeched, "'81 Chevrolet Caprice."

Bobby "Boogaloo" Garcia knew they were coming for him. His hours of Bible reading and prayers had reaped *nada*. He was going to die alone, excommunicated, away from God and his brother, two .45 automatics and 16 grand in cash his only companions.

No one to mourn him;

No one to talk to on the night he finally figured it all out;

No chance to pay back his victims and slide into heaven on last-minute good deeds and acts of contrition;

No one to grant absolution for his sins.

At first, when he got it all down in his head, it made him feel peaceful. Then the choppers kept buzzing and flashing their lights, pissing off the old juiceheads boozing in the parking lot, who started jabbering and throwing their empty T-bird bottles at the wall. That made him mad, made him feel like going out defiant, even when he knew that defiance was his most heavy-duty sin. That was the funniest part of it. Half of him wanted to admit it and go out clean; the other half wanted to go out righteously defiant, because that's what he was for thirty-four years, and if he reversed his act now, it meant that he never existed at all.

Bullhorns barking from up the block; copter lights flooding the sky every five minutes; the winos wailing like nigger banshees. Finally Bobby decided to cover his bets. He pulled up his chair to directly in front of the door and placed the Bible on the right armrest, then loaded both .45s and unscrewed the silencers for better range. Sliding shells into both chambers, he sat down with the guns in his lap. When they kicked in the door, he'd know how to play it.

24

Three minutes after his cell door was opened by a station trustee, Lloyd was in a phone booth on Rampart and Temple, turning out his pockets for change.

His first call was to the Central Jail Records night line, where an information clerk told him that Duane Richard Rice, white male, D.O.B. 8/16/56, 6'0", 170, light brown hair, blue eyes, had been released on a sentence modification on November 30, after serving six months of a one-year sentence for grand theft auto. He had one previous conviction, for vehicular manslaughter, and had put in three years of a five-year sentence at the California Youth Authority Facility at Soledad. He was now on both state parole and county probation, and his last known address was 1164 South Barrington, West Los Angeles. Pressing, Lloyd asked the clerk what module Rice was housed in at the Main County Jail. After a moment spent checking other records, she came back on the line and said, "Twenty-seven hundred."

The Ding Tank—Gordon Meyers connection.

But *why?*

Lloyd called the Los Angeles County Probation Department and got an operator who put him through to a series of clerks, who finally put him through to the county's chief probation officer at home. The chief made a series of calls herself and buzzed Lloyd back at his pay phone with the word: Duane Richard Rice had not reported to his P.O. after his release from jail and had vacated his condo on South Barrington. He was now technically a parole and probation absconder, and a bench warrant for his arrest had been issued.

Hanging up, Lloyd tried to recall the phone numbers from Louie Calderon's message book. After a minute, they came to him: Rhonda, 654-8996; Silver Foxes, 658-4371.

He dialed Rhonda's number and got the beginning of a recorded message, then hung up and called Bell Telephone and made his demands. A supervisor gave him the information he wanted: Rhonda Morrell, 961 North Vista, West Hollywood; Silver Foxes, 1420 North Gardner. Lloyd smiled as he wrote it down. The addresses were only a few blocks apart. With his .45 unholstered on the seat beside him, he drove to West Hollywood.

961 North Vista was a modern building, with two stories of apartments around a cement courtyard. The directory by the front gate listed R. *Morrell* in Unit 20. Lloyd studied the numerical scheme and judged Rhonda's apartment to be on the first story, dead center. He walked over, the .45 pressed to his leg.

No lights were on, but he pressed the buzzer beneath the taped-on *Morrell* anyway, then stepped to the side. A full minute passed with no sounds issuing in response to his ring. No Rhonda.

Lloyd walked around to the parking space in the back of the building. The slot for Unit 20 was empty. Feeling itchy but *close*, he drove the three blocks to Silver Foxes.

Pulling up and surveying the lavender Spanish-style, Lloyd was surprised to see no neon beacons or other accoutrements of sleaze, only a quiet four-flat with lights coming from the left downstairs side. Again holding the .45 to his leg, he walked over to the lights and rang the bell next to the smiling fox emblem. Pressing himself against the wall beside the doorway, he held the gun next to his chest, prepared to wheel and fire.

Silence, then a whiney male voice muttering, "Oh shit," then footsteps approaching the door. When he heard inside locks being unlatched, Lloyd stepped out and leveled the .45 at midpoint in the doorway.

The door swung open, and a muscle-bound young man in a tight tank top stood there, frozen by the gun held only inches from him. "Police officer," Lloyd said. "Walk backward inside, turn around and place your hands on the wall above your head, then step back and spread your legs."

Biting his lip, the young man complied. Lloyd followed him into a stark white room and nudged the door shut with his toe, pressing the .45 to the back of his neck, frisking him with his left hand. The youth moaned when Lloyd brushed the insides of his thighs. Finding no concealed weaponry, Lloyd said, "How many other rooms?"

"Just the bathroom, sweetie. There's nobody here but us chickens. Are you a chicken hawk?"

Lloyd gave the room a quick once-over, catching tube furniture, white Plasticine desk, white walls hung with pictures of rock and rollers. "No banter," he said. "Go over and open the bathroom door, then come back here."

The young man walked over to the bathroom door and pushed it open, then returned and sat down on the white desk, one foot on the floor, one leg dangling in Lloyd's direction. "Like I said, 'No one here but us chickens.' My name's Tim. What's yours?"

Lloyd reholstered his .45 and said, "Son, I am the last person in the world you want to get cute with tonight. *The last.* I'm going to ask you some simple straight questions, and I want simple straight answers. Do you understand?"

Tim smiled coyly and tapped his heel against the desk. "Shoot, baby."

"First, do you know a man named Duane Rice? Late twenties, six feet, one-seventy, light brown hair, blue eyes?"

"No, but he sounds cute. Is he your lover?"

Lloyd backhanded the young man, knocking him off the desk. He smiled and wiped a trickle of blood from his nose. Lloyd said, "I don't want to hurt you, but please Jesus God don't fuck with me. Not tonight."

Tim stood up. "Say 'pretty please' and I'll be a good Boy Scout and cooperate."

Penny and Janice moved through Lloyd's mind in precaution reflex, then Jesus Fred Gaffaney and Collins eclipsed them. He pushed Tim across the room and held him to the wall with a hand on his neck. "Pretty please talk, motherfucker, before I trash your worthless ass."

Tim made gurgling sounds until Lloyd released him and stepped back. Smiling, he rubbed his neck and sighed. "Rough play is one thing, hurting is another. You said 'pretty please,' so I'll be a good Scout and be nice. What do you want to know?"

The singsong words settled on Lloyd like fallout, and he wondered if this night would ever be over. "One of your whores," he said. "Rhonda Morrell. I picked up on one of her phone messages from Duane Rice. He was supposed to call her at home or here last night. The message mentioned someone named Stan Klein. What do you know about this?"

Tim moved to the desk and opened drawers, then pulled out a white Naugahyde binder and leafed through it. Holding the binder open, he said, "That's Rhonda. Isn't she foxy?"

Lloyd looked at the nude photographs. Rhonda Morrell was a beautiful brunet. He memorized her face, holding his eyes from the rest of her body. "Tell me about her. And about Rice and Klein."

Tim snapped the binder shut. "What's to tell? Rhonda is a real brain fox, wants to be a stockbroker. She's very much in demand with our clients. Rice and Klein I don't know about, although the way you described Rice, he sounds like this guy who came by last week, this guy Rhonda's got some kind of nonsex scene going with, you know, for money. Rhonda's a real money fox."

The "Wants $" in Calderon's message book popped into Lloyd's head. "Tell me about him—and Rhonda."

Tim wrapped his arms around himself. "Last week a man came in, looking for a fox. He didn't seem like Silver Foxes caliber, but I liked his style, so I fixed him up with Rhonda. He gave me a name, but I knew it was phony. Later on, Rhonda tells me she's helping the guy look for his girlfriend, for big bucks. In fact, she called this afternoon and told me she's supposed to meet him here tonight at midnight. She wanted me to hold him in case she's late."

Lloyd fingered the gun he had killed with, then looked at the clock on the wall. 10:49. In August of 1965 he had gone one-on-one with a .45-caliber killer; now he was coming full circle back to that point, to pay his dues for the event that had formed him. Shivering, he said, "Tim, do you believe in God?"

Tim shrugged. "I've never given it much thought."

"You should. He's a tricky bastard; you might dig him. Go home. I'm going to wait for Rhonda and her friend."

"Is this legal?"

"No. Go home. I'm sorry I hit you."

"I'm not," Tim said, and walked out the door.

Lloyd waited for ten minutes, then went out to his car and turned on his two-way. He listened for twenty minutes. The air was flooded with calls directing Hollywood Division units to the area near the Hollywood Bowl, but there was no mention of the hottest trio in L.A. History—Duane Rice, Bobby and Joe Garcia. Gaffaney and his hot dogs were sitting on the information. It was coming down to their outlaw vendetta, and his own. And when Rice fell into his hands at midnight, would he be able to press his advantage and take him out in cold blood?

Lloyd walked back to the Silver Foxes office to await Rhonda Morrell and then the moment. He sat down in an uncomfortable white chair and stared at the pictures on the white walls, unable to identify any of the rock and rollers by name. Checking the clock repeatedly, he hoped that Rhonda would be late, so he could take a post outside and back-shoot Duane Rice as he walked up to the door. God as an ironic bastard stuck in his mind.

Taking out the Pico-Westholme cop killer would be considered the zenith of his career, not the desperately selfish survival tactic that it was.

At 11:42 there was a rapping on the door. Lloyd took out his .45 and tip-toed over and opened the door, startling Rhonda Morrell, who saw the gun and opened her mouth to scream. Lloyd got her in a headlock with his free arm and pulled her inside, stifling her attempts to make noise. She bit at his jacket sleeve, and he kicked the door shut and whispered, "L.A.P.D. I'm here for Duane Rice, not you. I just want to ask you a few questions, then get you the hell out of here before he shows up. Now, I'm going to let you go, but you have to promise not to scream. Okay?"

Rhonda quit squirming and biting. Lloyd released her, and she twisted around and stood with her back to him, fluffing out her Afro. Turning back, she said in a perfectly composed voice, "He owes me a lot of money. If you arrest him, he won't be able to pay me."

Lloyd blurted, "Jesus," then mustered his thoughts and said, "There's a lot of reward money being offered for his capture. You talk to me, *fast*, and I'll see that you get it."

Rhonda smiled. "How much money?"

"Over seventy thousand," Lloyd said, stealing a glance at his watch. "Tim told me you're helping Rice look for his girlfriend. Tell me about that, and tell me about Stan Klein."

"You know a lot about it already."

"I don't know a fucking thing! Tell me, goddammit!"

Rhonda looked at the clock and said, "I guess this is trading up. Rice has a coke-whore girlfriend. I've been helping him look for her. I found out that she's been living with a sleazy entrepreneurial type, Stan Klein. I got—"

"What's the girlfriend's name?"

"Anne Vanderlinden. Duane called me Monday night, and we made a date to meet here at midnight. He said he and Vandy were flying to New York in a few days, and he needed the names of some music people. Apparently Vandy is a singer, and he wants to help her career. He promised me a bonus for that, and—"

"That was the last time you spoke to him?"

"No! He called me this afternoon, at home, to confirm our date. He sounded spacey, and he said that Vandy had left Stan Klein's place last night, with a *puto* Mexican, whatever that is. Now he's promising me the moon if I help him find her again. He also said we have to pick up some money."

Lloyd stared at the clock, his mind suddenly blank. Rhonda fidgeted, plucking at her hair. Finally she pointed to the gun in Lloyd's hand. "Why have you got that out? Is Duane dangerous?"

Lloyd laughed. "Yeah, he's dangerous."

"I think he's basically sweet, with some rough edges. If he's so dangerous, where are all the other cops?"

"Never mind. You've got to get out of here."

"Wait. I read the papers today. They said there's seventy-five K in reward money out for the person who killed those people at the bank. You don't think Duane did that? He might be a thief, but he's not vicious."

Lloyd grabbed Rhonda's arm and pulled her toward the door. "Go home," he hissed. "*Get out of here now.*"

"What about my money? How do I know I'll get it?" She paused, then looked in Lloyd's eyes and gasped, "You're going to kill him because he's a cop killer. I've read about that kind of thing. You can't fool me."

"*Get the fuck out now, goddamn you.*"

There were footsteps on the walkway outside. Rhonda screamed, "Duane, run!" Lloyd froze, then threw himself prone when three shots blew the front picture window to bits. He grabbed Rhonda's legs and yanked her to the floor, then rolled to the demolished window and fired twice blindly, hoping to draw a return volley.

Two muzzle bursts lit up the lawn; the shots ricocheted around the white walls, ripping out jagged crisscrosses of wood. Lloyd aimed at the flashes of red and squeezed off five rounds, then ejected the spent clip and slipped in a fresh one. He took a deep breath of cordite, chambered the top round and charged out the window.

No dead man on the grass; Rhonda's screams echoing behind him. Lloyd ran up Gardner to Sunset. Rounding the corner, he heard a shot, and a plate-glass window two doors down exploded. Then he saw a crowd of people on the sidewalk scatter into doorways and out on the street. And there *he* was.

Lloyd watched the man weave through shrieking pedestrians, then dart past parked cars and start sprinting east on Sunset, out of his firing range. He sprinted full-out himself, closing the gap until he saw Rice stick his gun in the passenger window of a car stopped for the light at the next intersection. Then he ran and aimed at the same time, knots of late-night strollers making scared and startled sounds as they got out of his way. The running posture was awkward and cut down his speed, but he almost had a clear shot when Rice got in the car, and it took off against the light.

Then he heard approaching sirens, and it jolted him away from the escap-

ing car and back to his own jeopardy. Rice would probably ditch the escape
vehicle within blocks. "Shots fired" and the location would hit the air *huge*
and goose Jesus Fred and his hot dogs into the area in force. Lloyd ran back
to Silver Foxes and found Rhonda on the front lawn. He forced her into his
car, but when he pulled out, he didn't know where they were going. He only
knew he was terrified.

Rice knew that he had to ditch the car, or keep the car and kill the
driver. Digging the barrel of his .45 harder into the old man's neck, he said,
"Hang a left at the next corner and park."

The man obeyed, turning onto Formosa, double-parking. Grasping the
wheel, he shut his eyes and began weeping. Rice snapped to a new plan: tie
Pops up and leave him somewhere, take his money and roll. "You got rope
in the trunk, motherfucker?"

The man nodded yes, and Rice grabbed the key from the ignition and
walked back to the trunk. He was about to open it when the driver bolted and
started running toward Sunset. He was almost there when a black-and-white
pulled to the curb on the opposite side of the street two doors up from the car.

Pops *down* from him; the fuzz thirty yards *up*. Rice got back in the car,
this time behind the wheel. His head throbbed, burned and crackled, but
he got a message through all of it: *be calm*. He turned on the engine and put
the Fairlane in drive, then started to accelerate. Then he heard the old man
screaming, "Police! Police!" *behind* him; then the cop car *in front* of him
turned on its cherry lights.

Time stood still, then zoomed back to Doheny Drive and the first time
he had dope in his veins. Rice punched the gas just as the driver of the patrol car got out with his gun drawn. Caught in blinding headlight glare, he
stood transfixed. Rice smashed the nose of his three-hundred horsepower
battering ram into him at thirty-six miles per hour, catching him flush. The
impact ripped off the grille and a chunk of the fender; the windshield went
red, just like before. Rice drove blind, his foot held to the floor until wind
whipped the crimson curtain from in front of his eyes, and real vision made
him stop the car and get out and run.

25

Bobby heard the radio voices stop screeching about the '81 Chevy and the house-to-house searches that were zeroing in on him, and start barking, "Man down, Sunset and Formosa, man down! Man down!" Within seconds sirens were wailing *away from him,* and the choppers took off, leaving the Bowl Motel in darkness and silence. Knowing it was a stay of execution straight from God, he packed all the money into a supermarket bag and walked out the door, leaving the .45s and Bible behind on the chair.

Outside, the street was deserted and still, with no cars moving either way on Highland. Walking south, Bobby saw why: sawhorse roadblocks hung with flashing lights were stationed at all intersections, shutting off northbound traffic. Turning around, he could pick out other lighted blockades a block up, just past the motel. As he stared at the cordon, a group of plainclothes cops with shotguns entered the courtyard. God had shot him a split-second salvation.

Stepping over the sawhorse at the corner of Franklin, Bobby saw the church and sent up a prayer for it to be Catholic. His prayer was answered when the white adobe building was caught by headlights coming off a side street: "Saint Anselm's Catholic Church" in large black letters.

A light was burning in the window of the white adobe bungalow adjoining the church. Bobby ran to the beacon and rang the bell.

The man who opened the door was young, dressed in black clerical trousers and a polo shirt. Bobby grimaced when he saw the alligator on his chest and his new-wave haircut. Not Mexican and not Irish-looking; probably a social activist type. "Are you a priest?" he asked.

The man looked Bobby up and down. He stuck his hands in his pockets, and Bobby knew he was digging for chump change. "I don't want no handout," he said. "Money's the one thing I got big. I want to make a confession. You hear confessions?"

"Yes, weekday afternoons," the priest said. He reached into his front pocket, pulled out a pair of glasses and put them on. Bobby stood under his gaze, watching him pick up on his ink-stained arms and face and Duane Rice's shirt that hung on him like a tent. "Please, Father. Please."

The priest nodded and moved past Bobby onto the sidewalk, making beckoning motions. Bobby followed him over to the church. Unlocking the door, the priest turned on a light and walked inside. Bobby waited by the door and murmured Hail Marys, then bolted up the steps and anointed himself with holy water from the font by the back pew. As he genuflected toward the altar and made the sign of the Cross, the shopping bag slipped out of his arms. A wad of twenties dropped to the floor, and he stuffed them into his pockets and walked to the scrim of velvet curtains that separated the confessional booths from the church proper.

The priest was in the first booth. Bobby pulled the drapes aside, dropped the bag and knelt in front of the partition that shielded him from his confessor. The screen was slid open, and Bobby could see the priest's lips move as he said, "Are you ready to make your confession?"

Bobby cleared his throat and said, "Bless me, Father. My last confession was about five or six years ago, except I heard some confessions when I worked this religious scam. I faked being a priest, but I always tried to be fair with the suck—I mean the people I scammed. What I mean—"

Bobby leaned his head against the partition. When he saw that his lips were almost touching the lips of his confessor, he gasped and brought himself back into a ramrod-straight posture. Muttering Hail Marys under his breath, he got down what he wanted to say in the right order. When he heard the priest cough, he pressed his palms together and lowered his head, then began.

"I am guilty of many mortal sins. I worked this phone scam where I impersonated priests and ripped off money in God's name, and I pulled burglaries, and I fired off lots of low blows when I was a fighter. Sometimes I rubbed resin on my gloves between rounds, so I could fuck—so I would waste the guy's eyes when I went head-hunting. I robbed a bank, and I raped a woman, and I pulled evil sex shit on another woman, and I shot a woman and killed her, and—"

Bobby stopped when he heard the priest chanting Hail Marys. Slamming the partition with his palms, he shouted, "You listen to me, motherfucker! This is my fucking confession, not yours!"

Silence answered the outburst. Then the priest said, "Finish your confession and I'll tell you your penance."

The sternness in the kiddie-confessor's voice gave Bobby the juice to say *it*, the big stuff he finally figured out. "I got a brother," he said. "Younger than me. He's weak 'cause I made him weak. I committed a heinous mortal sin with him when we was kids, and I been trying to atone for it by looking after him ever since, when what I should have done was cut him loose years ago, so he could get balls on his own. I always felt guilty about hating him, 'cause I knew that riding herd on his ass was killin' *me*, too. See, I always figured that he *knew* what I did, but he was afraid to say it, 'cause of what it would make us. Then, dig, tonight I figured out that he just didn't remember, 'cause it was so long ago, which means that all this time I sp—"

The priest interrupted, his voice impatient and severe, like a confessor's voice should be. "Don't interpret. Tell me the sin."

Bobby said *it*, sounding to himself like an old TV judge handing down a life sentence. "When we was kids, I used to tie Little Bro up so I could go out and play. I came back one day and saw that he'd wet himself 'cause he couldn't get up. The whole bed was wet, and I got righteously turned on and pulled down his pants and touched him."

"And that is your heinous mortal sin? After all the other acts you confessed?"

Now Bobby heard *disgust*. "Don't *you* interpret, Father. They're my sins. *Mine*."

"Say the act of contrition and I'll give you your penance," the priest whispered.

Bobby bowed his head and forced the second part of his sentence out in an Anglo accent, like the old Irish sisters had taught him. "O my God, I am heartily sorry for having offended thee. I detest all my sins because I dread the loss of heaven and the pain of hell. But most of all because I have offended thee, O God, who are all good and deserving of all my love. I firmly resolve with the help of thy grace to confess my sins, do penance and amend my life. Amen. Well, Father?"

"I grant you absolution," the priest said. "Your penance is good deeds for the rest of your life. Begin soon, you have much to atone for. Go and sin no more."

Bobby heard his confessor slide through the curtains and walk out of the church. He gave him enough time to make it back to the rectory, then got to his feet and picked up the shopping bag, smiling at the weight. "Begin soon" rang in his ears. On wobbly legs, he obeyed.

The poor box was on the side wall near the rear pews, ironclad, but too small to hold sixteen K in penance bucks. Bobby started shoving cash in the slot anyway, big fistfuls of c-notes and twenties. Bills slipped out of his hands as he worked, and he was wondering whether to leave the whole bag by the altar when he heard strained breathing behind him. Looking over his shoulder, he saw Duane Rice standing just outside the door. His high school yearbook prophecy crossed his mind: "*Most likely not to survive*," and suddenly Duane-o looked more like a priest than the *puto* with the alligator fag shirt.

Bobby dropped the bag and fell to his knees; Rice screwed the silencer onto his .45 and walked over. He picked up the bag and placed the gun to the Sharkman's temple; Bobby knew that *defiant* was the way to go splitsville. He got in a righteous giggle and "Duhn-duhn-duhn-duhn" before Rice blew his brains out.

26

Joe sat in a booth in Ben Frank's Coffee Shop, forcing himself to eat a cheeseburger platter. Through the tinted plate-glass window he watched Anne talk into a pay phone in the parking lot. He tried to read her lips, but she was too far away, and distant siren blare from the east kept distracting him. The food that he figured would calm him down didn't; the 'Vette, ditched on a side street two blocks away, had his prints all over the wheel and dashboard. The copter lights and sirens made the Hollywood/Strip border area feel like a war zone. The thrill of mastering the stick shift in a stolen car was dead, and Anne had now fed a dozen quarters to the phone, trying to connect with her "good music friends" who would "help them out." The black pimps at the next table were talking about a shootout on Gardner and barricades and cops with shotguns up by the Hollywood Bowl. One of them kept repeating, "Righteous fucking heat," and Joe knew he was digging it because the heat wasn't directed at him. Every word, every bit of noise, from the war sounds to waitresses clanking dishes, brought back Stan Klein's face just as he stuck in the knife. That was bad, but he knew it was only a delayed reaction, something like shock. What made it terrible was his music turning on him, "And death was a thrill on Suicide Hill" bopping in his brain along with pictures of the man he killed.

Joe felt his insides start to turn over. He jumped up, bumping the table, knocking his food on the floor. The pimps laughed when french fries flew onto a passing customer's legs, and Joe ran to the bathroom and vomited his meal into the sink. Holding the wall with one hand, he turned on the faucet and doused his head with cold water. His stomach heaved, and his chest expanded and contracted with short blasts of breath. He looked at himself in the mirror, then turned away when he saw Bobby just like *he* always looked after getting his ass kicked at the Olympic. Standing upright, he gave himself another dousing, then wiped his face with a paper towel and walked back into the restaurant.

A busboy was cleaning up the spillage by his table; the pimps snickered at him. Joe sidestepped the mess and ran out the door, the cashier yelling, "What about your check!" On the sidewalk, he looked for Anne. She wasn't by the pay phone, and she wasn't in the parking lot. Then he saw her across the street, upstaging a group of hookers with a pelvis-grinding boogie aimed at passing cars.

Joe started to jaywalk across Sunset; a Mercedes stretch limo pulled up in front of Anne, and she got in. The stretch hung an immediate right turn, and Joe ran, rounding the corner just in time to see it park halfway down the block. Walking over, he heard male sex grunts shooting out of the backseat. Then a disco tune smothered the groans, and the chauffeur got out and stood by the car, trying to look cool about the whole thing. With anger blotting out all traces of Stan Klein's death mask, Joe retreated to a dark front lawn to play watchdog.

The limo wobbled on its suspension for half an hour, the musical accompaniment going from disco to reggae. Joe moved back and forth between pins-and-needles alertness and nodding-out sleepiness. Total exhaustion was dropping over him when a door slammed, and Anne began skipping up to the Strip. When she passed him, Joe said, "You really rocked that stretch. Any bitch that can rock a Benz fender to fender has got to be a pro."

Anne squinted into the darkness. When Joe walked up to her, she said, "I told you I could give sex and not sacrifice my karma, and if you give sex for money you might as well do a good job. And I wasn't leaving you; I was coming back to B.F.'s."

Joe snickered, imitating the pimps at the coffee shop. "That's because you need a man to tell you what to do. Okay, I'll tell you what we're gonna do. How much did that scumbag in the Benz give you?"

"A C-note."

"Groovy. We're gonna use about seventy of it to check into that motel next to B.F.'s. You check us in, I'll follow you back. Dig?"

Anne did a nervous foot dance. "Now you're starting to *talk* like a tough guy—"

"People change."

"All right, but that trick just told me about this all-night open-house party at an exec producer's place. I used to trick regularly with the guy when I worked outcall. He's a video heavy, and he really liked me. I can get some money there, I know I can."

Joe shook his head. "First we're getting a flop. Come on."

Without a word, Anne led the way back to the Strip. Joe saw that she looked dejected, but was secretly glad he'd taken charge. From the rear of the Ben Frank's parking lot he watched her hit the motel office, pay the night clerk and glom a key, then walk around to the street and into the courtyard. When the clerk sighed and returned to his paperback, he followed.

She was waiting for him in the doorway of a downstairs unit, one hip cocked, one elbow resting on the doorjamb, looking like an evil little girl born to fuck. She smiled and shifted her weight; her preppy shirt fell away and revealed huge dark hollows across her stomach. Joe moved toward her to smash the pose and make her real.

Anne resisted the soft kisses on her neck and the softer hands that tried to stop her hips from gyrating. Holding herself rock still, she said, "Whores don't respond to kindness, whores rut."

Joe said, "Hush," slid his hands under her shirt and traced soft circles on her back. Anne sighed, then caught herself and said, "Whores don't make love, whores do the dirty dog deed." Her own wordplay made her giggle and press her hands to her mouth, and Joe bit at her neck until she started to squeal uncontrollably. An upstairs voice called out, "Go, lovebirds, go!" and Anne began to cry. Joe didn't know what the tears meant, so he picked her up and carried her to the bed. Applause and catcalls rained down as he shut and bolted the door. When he turned around, Anne was naked and he was crying himself.

27

The smell of decomposing flesh hit him the second he walked in the door.

Lloyd turned to Rhonda Morrell and said, "Wait here," then shot a look at an arched entrance hall crowded with video equipment. Drawing his .45, he walked in the direction of the stench.

It was a dead man who matched Rhonda's description of Stan Klein. He was lying in the middle of a large living room filled with electrical equipment—V.C.R.s, TVs, computer terminals and video games. His corpse was drained of blood, the handle of a switchblade was extending from his stomach, and the carpet beneath him was caked thick with dried blood. A small caliber automatic was in his right hand. The knife wound spelled death by stabbing: the smell and body drainage indicated that the murder had taken place at least twenty-four hours prior. Lloyd held a handkerchief to his face and knew that this night would never be over.

He walked to Rhonda, still standing by the door. "Go identify the body. Try not to get hysterical."

"Is that what that awful smell is?"

"Smart girl."

"Am I under arrest?"

"I'm holding you as a material witness. Give me shit and I'll fabricate a felony to keep you off your back for years. You almost got me killed. Be grateful that I'm a sensitive cop."

Rhonda gave Lloyd a slow once-over. "You look spooky. Really weirded out. When can I go home?"

"Later. Go identify the stiff."

Rhonda walked into the living room and let out a ladylike shriek; Lloyd found a phone in the entrance hall and dialed Hollywood Station. Dutch

Peltz answered, "L.A.P.D.," and Lloyd could tell from his hollow tone that he was scared.

"It's Lloyd, Dutch. What is it?"

"*It's* fucking all coming down crazy," Dutch said. "There was a shootout on Sunset and Gardner. Both perpetrators got away, and one of them commandeered a car, then ran down one of my men with it. He died at Central Receiving. The killer escaped on foot, and the man whose car he commandeered I.D.'s him from the eyewitness sketch of the white bank robber. Two of my men raided his pad half an hour ago—the Bowl Motel on Highland. No one was there, but they found two .45 autos. Then, and I still can't believe it, there was a body found *inside a fucking church* three blocks from the motel and a half mile from the spot where the officer was hit and run. He was twenty-six, Lloyd. He had a wife and four kids and he's fucking dead!"

The news of the two dead men and Dutch's grief squeezed out Lloyd's last remaining calm. The night came down on him from all sides, and he started to weave on his feet, death stench assailing him from the living room, mass insanity over the phone line. Finally Dutch's "Lloyd! Lloyd! Lloyd, goddammit, are you there!" registered, and he was able to answer: "I don't know where the fuck I am. Listen, have any A.P.B.s been issued?"

"No. The white man signed into the motel under an obvious alias—John Smith."

Lloyd marshaled his thoughts, deciding not to add Stan Klein to the list of the night's dead. "Dutch, Fred Gaffaney and at least two of his Metro freaks are in this big, which is why no A.P.B.s have hit the air. They know, and I know, the names of the three robbers. They—"

"What!"

"Just listen, goddammit! I was one of the perps at the shootout on Gardner. I thought I could take out the white man myself. I blew it, and he got away."

"What!"

"Don't grief me on that, goddamn you! It was the only way to do it. Have you I.D.'d the stiff at the church?"

His voice more hollow than Lloyd had ever heard it, Dutch said, "Everywhere you go there's nothing but shit. The dead man is Robert Ramon Garcia, male Mexican, age thirty-four. Is he one of the three?"

"Yes."

"Give me the two other names."

Lloyd signed his own murder indictment. "The white man is Duane

Richard Rice, D.O.B. 8/16/56. The other Mexican is Joe Garcia, the dead man's brother. It's crazy out here, Dutch."

"I know it is. Largely due to you. Every single one of my men is on the streets, along with half the Rampart and Wilshire nightwatches. I've got two reservists running the station with me."

"You feel like helping me, or you feel like pouting?"

"I'll forget you said that. What do you need?"

"First, what did you get from Intelligence Division on Gaffaney?"

"Gaffaney's in deep shit in the Department," Dutch said. "Intelligence has him nailed as having bribed school officials to doctor up his son's records so he could secure an appointment to the academy. Apparently the kid was a long-time petty thief with a lot of crazy religious beliefs. Also, Gaffaney is building up a huge interdepartmental power base—right-wing hot dogs from Metro, I.A.D. and various uniformed divisions. To what end, I don't know."

Lloyd let the information settle on him, then said, "I need a favor."

"You always need favors. I forgot to mention that right when all hell started breaking loose a guy came to the station looking for you, said he had info on the first two bank robberies. He read about you, and about the rewards, and he wants to talk. I was about to tell him to split, then one of my squad room dicks told me he had two armed robbery convictions. I've got him in a holding tank. Ask your favors quick: I want to broadcast those names."

"I want complete paper on the three names, plus Anne Vanderlinden, W.F., twenties," Lloyd said. "R&I, parole and probation department files, jail records. You've got the juice to shake the right people out of bed to get them, and you can send one of your reservists to make the run, then deliver them to my pad."

Now Dutch's voice was incredulous. "Don't you want to be on the street for this?"

Lloyd said, "No. It feels like I'm inches away from the biggest fuckup I've ever pulled, and if I hit the bricks I'll go nutso. This whole mess is so full of weird angles that if I don't figure them out I won't survive, and I just want to think. Hold that guy for me, I'll be at the station in fifteen minutes."

"What do you mean, 'you won't survive'?"

"No. Don't ask again."

Lloyd hung up and looked around for Rhonda. He found her smoking a cigarette by an open window, and said, "Come on. Don't mention Stan Klein to anybody, and you may still make a few bucks out of this."

"What are you talking about?"

"Survival."

"Whose survival?"

"That's the funny thing. I don't know."

Outside Hollywood Station, Lloyd handcuffed Rhonda to the steering column and said, "I'll be no more than half an hour. While I'm gone, think about Rice and his girlfriend, and where she'd go if she were scared."

"I think better without handcuffs."

"Too bad, I don't trust you, and with Rice on the loose you're in danger."

"That's a laugh. He didn't drag me all over town and handcuff me."

Lloyd slammed the car door and walked into the station. A uniformed reserve officer noticed him immediately, handed him a sheaf of papers and said, "Captain Peltz said to tell you that he's busy, but he sent the other reservist to get your paperwork. Here's a memo and the stats on that clown who wants to talk to you. He's in a holding cell."

Lloyd nodded and read the memo first:

To: Det. Sgt. L. Hopkins, Rob/Hom
From: Det. Lt. E. Hopper, West Valley Vice

Sergeant—Regarding your inquiry as to vice activities of R. Hawley and J. Eggers, informers have reported that both men are long-time heavy gamblers known to utilize Valley area bookies. Hawley said to sporadically pay debts through "percentage arrangement" with blank bank checks (assumed by informant to be stolen). Different informant states that Eggers has also paid debts with blank check lots—"past six weeks or so."

Hope this helps—Hopper.

Feeling *the* connection breathing down his neck, Lloyd turned to a rap sheet in Dutch's handwriting.

Shondell Tyrone McCarver, M.N., 11/29/48. A.k.a. "Soul," a.k.a. "Daddy Soul," a.k.a. "Sweet Daddy Soul," a.k.a. "Soul King," a.k.a. "Sweet King of Soul." Conv: Poss. Dang. Drugs—(2)—6/12/68, 1/27/71. Armed Rbry —(2)—9/8/73, 7/31/77. Paroled 5/16/83—clean since—D.P.

Shaking his head, he looked at the officer and said, "Bad nigger?"

The reservist said, "More the jive type."

"Good. Crank the door in sixty seconds, then lock it again."

The officer about-faced and walked to the electrical panel, and Lloyd strode through the muster room to the jail area. Passing the framed photographs of Hollywood Division officers killed in the line of duty, he pictured another frame beside them and the station hung with black bunting. He knew he was pumping himself up with anger to fuel his interrogation, and that it wasn't working—at 2:00 A.M. on the longest night of his life, all he could drum up were the motions.

Except for some babbling from the drunk tank, the jail was quiet. Lloyd saw his man lying on the bottom bunk of a cell on the misdemeanor side of the catwalk. The door clanged open a second later, and the man shook himself awake and smiled. "I'm Sweet Daddy Soul, the patriarch of rock and roll," he said.

Lloyd stepped inside, and the door creaked shut behind him. Sizing up the man, he saw a good-natured jivehound who thought he was dangerous and might even be. "Not tonight, McCarver."

Shondell McCarver smoothed the lapels of his mohair suitcoat. "Another time, perhaps?"

Lloyd sat on the commode and took out a pen and notepad. "No. You said you've got information, and you've got a heist jacket, so I'll listen to you. But catch my interest quick."

"You know I want that reward money."

"You and everybody else. Talk."

"Some brothers I know said you was always good for some rapport."

"Cut the shit and get to it."

McCarver crossed his ankles and laced his fingers behind his head. "Guess they was wrong. How's this for starters: bet you don't know how the guys who pulled them kidnap heists snapped to the two girlfriends. That safe to say?"

Lloyd's exhaustion dropped; his head buzzed with the coming of a second mental wind. "You've got my interest. Keep talking."

"The heists was my idea," Shondell McCarver said. "Up till about two weeks ago I had a bouncer job going, a temporary gig every other week or so, two hundred scoots a night, working for these people of the Eye-talian persuasion.

"The basic scene was this setup trying to re-create the sporting houses back in the old days, you know, like in New Orleans. For a C-note admission you get complimentary coke within reason, high-class whores, a shot at a few semi-pro ladies, crap game, high-stakes poker, old Ali fights on big-screen TV, fuck films, nude swimming, sauna. What—"

"Where?" Lloyd said.

"I'm getting to that," McCarver said, drawing out the words teasingly. "The spot was a big house in Topanga Canyon. The two bank guys, Hawley and Eggers, brought their chicks to the parties. They—"

"How often were they held?"

"Every two weeks or so. Anyway, there was these mirrored bedrooms, you know, for romance. They was all rigged for sound, and one of my jobs was to listen for good info, like stock tips and the like. That's where I heard Hawley and Eggers talking to their bitches, and where I figured out Hawley was pilfering from his tellers boxes. Still got your interest, Mr. Po-liceman?"

Lloyd remembered Peter Kapek's mention of Hawley's and Eggers's large cash withdrawals. "Were parties thrown on October seventeenth and November first?"

McCarver laughed. "Sure were. I got a righteous memory for dates. How you know that?"

"Never mind, just keep talking."

"Anyhow, I heard Hawley run down his scam to his bitch. He told her that Greenbacks were left overnight at the tellers cages and—"

Lloyd interrupted: "Did you know that Greenbacks is a brand name of traveler's check?"

Slapping his knee, McCarver said, "Ain't that a riot? Shit. I read that in the paper, and it made me fuckin' glad I never got to utilize my plan. Anyhow, I think he's talkin' *cash*. He tells the bitch that he goes to the bank early on certain mornings, gloms the Greenbacks from the teller drawers, runs a transaction with a duplicate bankbook belonging to some senile old cooze with big bucks, doctors tally slips so that it balances out and looks like a cash withdrawal—to the cooze, who of course is Hawley boy.

"See, Hawley is scared, 'cause the scam only works if the cooze don't get hip to the missing bucks, and he's heard the old girl's relatives is about to have her declared noncompas mental and grab the fuckin' scoots. So Hawley is pouring his soul out to his bimbo, and, unbefuckingknowst to him—me."

Lloyd looked up from his notepad. "What about Eggers?"

McCarver said, "I'm getting to that. Anyhow, I concocted the plan that ultimately got utilized by them guys you're looking for. I staked out Hawley for days, watched him glom them Greenbacks, thinkin' they was cash, watched him do his number with the tally slips and bankbook and computer. I'm thinkin', 'Too bad there's only one of these scamsters,' when this bookie workin' the house tells me about Eggers bein' way behind on his vig. So I think, 'Gifts in a manger' and nudge the bookie to nudge Eggers into the scam that Hawley pulls. Then I start tailing Eggers, and damned if he didn't start pulling the same tricks. You dig?"

Lloyd said, "I dig. But you never saw Eggers with cash in his hands, right?"

"Right. His hands was out of sight when he did his rippin'. I just assumed that since he followed Hawley's procedure, it had to be cash."

"And it was about six weeks ago that you told the bookie to nudge Eggers?"

"Yeah. How'd you know that?"

"Never mind, keep going."

"Anyhow, I never told the Eye-talians about any of this, and I cased the kidnap part of the deal real good—the bitches' cribs, the managers' cribs, the whole shot. Then I got me a partner, then he decided to take off a liquor store and got busted. You follow so far?"

"I'm ahead of you," Lloyd said. "Wrap it up."

McCarver lit a cigarette, coughed and said, "Homeboy's a righteous partner. A little on the impetuous side, but solid. Except that he's a fat-mouth motherfucker, which ain't as bad as being a snitch, but still ain't good. When I read about my plan gettin' utilized, I called Homeboy at Folsom, got through 'cause he got this cush orderly job. I said, 'Who the fuck you shoot your fat motherfuckin' mouth off to?' He says, 'Who, me?' I says, 'Yeah, you, motherfucker, 'cause whoever you blabbed to utilized my plan, plus one other, and killed four people, includin' two cops, and there is seventy thou in reward bucks on that motherfucker's ass.'

"So . . . Homeboy tells me he talked to two paddy dudes in the High-Power Tank at the New County—Frank Ottens and Chick Geyer. I figure, righteous, those are cop killer motherfuckers. Then I back off and think, 'What if those dudes blabbed to someone else, and righteous third- or fourth- or fuckin' fifth-hand info was responsible for the utilization of my plan?' So I call the jail, and they tell me Ottens and Geyer is still in High-Power fighting their beefs. So, big man, you find out who Ottens and Geyer blabbed to, and you find your fuckin' cop killer. Now, is that a righteous tip or a righteous tip?"

Lloyd stood up and stretched. What would have cracked the case twenty-four hours before was now stale bread. The High-Power Tank adjoined the

Ding Tank, where Duane Rice was incarcerated until two weeks ago. Gordon
Meyers was the night jailer there, and he had incurred Rice's wrath as a member of the overall robbery scheme or for some other reason—stale bread also,
because Meyers was dead, and Rice was unlikely to live through the night.
Everyone involved in the twisted mess was dead or marked for death, including himself. Thinking inexplicably of Louie Calderon's "The kid was just too
scared to say no. Don't let them kill him," Lloyd looked at McCarver and said,
"A righteously too late tip, but I'll give you some righteous advice: walk real
soft around cops, because nothing's going to be the same with us anymore."

McCarver said, "What the fuck," and Lloyd walked out to his car and
handcuffed witness. A crew of reservists were hanging black bunting on the
front doors of the station as he drove away.

Pulling into his driveway a half hour later, Lloyd saw a stack of L.A. County
interagency records sleeves beside his kitchen door. Killing the engine, he said
to Rhonda, "You're staying with me until Rice is kill—I mean captured."

Rhonda rubbed her wrists. "What if I don't like the accommodations?
You also mentioned money a while back."

Lloyd got out of the car and pointed to the door. "Later. I've got some
reading to do. You sit tight while I do it, then we'll talk."

The records sleeves were thick and heavy with paper. Picking them up,
Lloyd felt comforted by the bulk of the cop data. He unlocked the door,
flicked on the light and motioned Rhonda inside. "Make yourself at home,
anywhere downstairs."

"What about upstairs?"

"It's sealed off."

"Why?"

"Never mind."

"You're weird."

"Just sit tight, all right?"

Rhonda shrugged and started opening and closing the kitchen cabinets.
Lloyd carried the sleeves into the living room and arrayed them on the coffee table, noting that the paperwork came from the L.A. County Department of Corrections, L.A. County Probation Department, County Parole
Bureau and California State Adult Authority. The pages were not broken
down by the names of his four suspects, and he had to first collate them into
stacks—one for Duane Rice, one each for the Garcia brothers, one for
Anne Vanderlinden. That accomplished, he broke them down by agency,

with R&I rap sheets on top. Then, with the sounds of Rhonda's kitchen puttering barely denting his concentration, he sat back to read and think and scheme, hoping to pull cold facts into some kind of salvation.

Duane Richard Rice, quadruple cop killer, grew up in the Hawaiian Gardens Housing Project, graduated Bell High School, had a 136 I.Q. The first of his two arrests was for vehicular manslaughter. While working as a mechanic at a Beverly Hills sports car dealership, he lost control of a car he was test-driving and killed two pedestrians. He ran from the scene on foot, but turned himself in to the Beverly Hills police later that same night. Since Rice possessed no criminal record and no drugs or alcohol were involved, the judge offered a five-year prison sentence, then suspended it on the proviso that he perform one thousand hours of public service. Rice shouted obscenities at the judge, who retracted the suspension and sentenced him to five years in the California Youth Authority Facility at Soledad.

While at Soledad, Rice refused to participate in group or individual therapy, studied martial arts and worked in the facility's auto shop. He was not a disciplinary problem, he formed no discernible "close prison ties." He was not a member of the Aryan Brotherhood or other institutional race gangs and abstained from homosexual liaisons. Judged to be a "potential achiever, with high intelligence and the potential for developing into a highly motivated young adult," he was paroled after serving three years of his sentence.

Rice's parole officer considered him "withdrawn" and "potentially volatile," but was impressed with his hard work as foreman at a Midas Muffler franchise and his "complete eschewing of the criminal lifestyle." Thus, when Rice was subsequently arrested on one count of grand theft auto, the officer did not cite him for a parole violation, mentioning in a letter to the judge that "I believe this offender to be acting under psychological duress, deriving from his relationship with the woman with whom he was cohabitating."

Rice received a year in the county jail, was sent to the Malibu Fire Camp and evinced spectacular bravery during the Agoura brushfires. His parole officer and the judge who tried his case granted him a sentence reduction as a result of this "adjustment," and he was given three years' formal county probation and released from custody.

Lloyd put the Rice records aside, and turned to the paper on the girlfriend.

Vanderlinden, Anne Atwater, white female, D.O.B. 4/21/58, Grosse Pointe, Michigan, had a file containing a scant three pages. She had been arrested twice for possession of marijuana, receiving small fines and suspended sentences, and three times for prostitution. She was given two years' formal probation following her second conviction, and bought her way out of a probation violation on her third arrest by informing on a "suspected auto thief" to L.A.P.D. detectives. Shaking his head sadly, Lloyd checked the date of Anne Vanderlinden's dismissed charge against the date of Duane Rice's G.T.A. bust. Three days from the former to the latter; Vandy had snitched off the man who loved her.

The two remaining stacks of paper read like a travelogue on eerie fraternal bonding, with even eerier informational gaps. Robert Garcia, known during his losing boxing career as Bobby "Boogaloo" Garcia, the "Barrio Bleeder," had been a fight manager, the owner of a coin laundromat and a hot-dog stand, while his brother Joseph had his occupations listed as "asst. fight manager," "asst. laundry operator" and "fry cook." The brothers had been arrested only once, together, for one count of burglary, although they were suspected of having perpetrated others. Once convicted, they were sentenced to nine months' county time together, and served it together, at Wayside Honor Rancho. At Wayside, the brothers' antithetical personalities rang out loud and clear. Lloyd read through a half dozen reports by correctional officers and learned that Robert Garcia was disciplined for attempting to bribe jailers into placing his brother in the "soft" tank where youthful inmates who might be subject to sexual abuse were housed, and, that once those bribes were rebuffed, he assaulted two prisoners who spoke jokingly of Joe as "prime butthole." Released from the disciplinary tank after ten days' confinement, the Barrio Bleeder then beat up his own brother, telling a psychiatrist that he did it "so Little Bro would get a little bit tougher." When Bobby was again placed in solitary, Joe set his mattress on fire so that *he* would be placed on the disciplinary tier, within shouting distance of the brother who protected and abused him.

Those facts were eerie, but the absence of facts on the brothers' last five years was even stranger. Based on Christine Confrey's description and R&I stats, the late Robert Garcia was obviously the "Shark," yet he had no arrests for sex offenses, nor was a penchant for sexual deviation mentioned anywhere in his file. Both he and his brother were placed on formal probation after their kick-out from Wayside, and reported dutifully until their probationary term was concluded. Yet there was no mention of employment for either man. Only one fact made sense: listed as the Garcias' "known associate" was Luis Calderon. Lloyd thought the burgeoning fed investigation into Calderon right before the bank slaughter sent everything topsy-turvy. The connection was there, just waiting to be made.

But it wasn't, because there was a correctness, a sense of inevitability about this spiral of death. Lloyd shivered with the thought, then took the mental ball and ran with it, wrapping up the odds and ends of the case into a tight but anticlimactic package.

After killing the officer with the commandeered car, Rice traveled by foot to the vicinity of the Bowl Motel, came across Bobby Garcia on the street, where he could not safely take him out, then followed him to the church and killed him. Why? The reason was meaningless. Joe Garcia, the "tall," "sweet-looking" Mexican who bank witnesses said "didn't shoot anyone" was also the "*puto*" Mexican that Rice told Rhonda took off with his girlfriend from Stan Klein's pad. The only loose strand in the fabric was Klein. Rice was there to grab his woman, presumably armed with a silencered .45. Yet Klein was killed with a knife. Joe Garcia was there, too, but he did not read, sound, feel, or in any way play as a killer.

Again, Louie Calderon's words echoed: "Don't let them kill him." Lloyd put down the paperwork and called out, "Rhonda, come here."

Rhonda walked in. "Time to talk money?" she said.

Nodding, Lloyd watched her sit down in Janice's favorite left-behind chair. "That's right. Questions and answers, but first there's this: if other police officers question you, you don't mention Stan Klein's name, or anything about this "*puto* Mexican" you told me about. Got it?"

"Got it, but why?"

"I'm not sure, it's just an ace in the hole I'm working with."

"What are you talking about?"

"Never mind. First question: when Rice called you today, did he mention this Mexican guy by name, or anything else about him, or where he thought he and Anne Vanderlinden might have gone?"

"That's easy: no, no and no. All he said was 'This *puto* Mexican took off with Vandy and you've got to help me find them."

"All right. You said Rice wanted you to pick up some money. Did he say where?"

"No."

"He just assumed that since you and Anne worked outcall together—"

"We didn't work Silver Foxes together. I've never met her. It's just that we move in some of the same circles, and know some of the same people, and we've both tricked with a lot of music industry biggies. Besides, Vandy isn't working Silver Foxes now. She quit two months ago, in October."

"How are you so sure of the date?"

"Well . . . I got Duane the information about Vandy and Stan Klein on my lonesome, and I thought if he paid for that, then maybe he'd pay me for a list of all the clients Vandy tricked with regularly, so last week, when I was in the office, I looked at her old file and made a list. I was going to sell it to Duane tonight, you know . . ."

"Exploit his jealousy?"

"I wouldn't call it that."

"Do you think if she were scared and broke she'd run to any of the men on the list?"

"I'd make book on it. There's one guy, a producer, who used to use Vandy for theme parties, paid her top dollar. He's a really good bet."

"How much for your silence and the list?"

Rhonda took a piece of paper from her bodice. "Duane's bought and paid for, right? I mean, you guys are going to kill him sooner or later, right?"

"Smart girl. How much?"

"An even thousand?"

Lloyd got his checkbook from the dining room table and wrote Rhonda Morrell a check for one thousand dollars. When he handed it to her, she smiled nervously and said, "Still want me to stick around?"

Lloyd looked away from the smile. "Get out," he said.

The door was opened and shut quietly, and high heels tapped toward the street. Lloyd picked up the piece of paper that Rhonda had left, saw a list of four names, addresses and phone numbers, then looked at *his* phone. He was reaching for it when an internal voice said "*Think*" and made him stop. Obeying, he sat down in Janice's chair, still warm from the Silver Fox.

He was doomed, because he could not kill Duane Rice in cold blood. Rice was doomed from all sides, and Jesus Fred Gaffaney was doomed within the Department. He would undoubtedly offer up his evidence on the Watts riot killing as a tactic to save himself—a legendary L.A.P.D. detective as youthful murderer was prime media meat, and the Department would pay heavily to stonewall the revelation. If the high brass capitulated, they would be looking to save face by every means possible, and *he* would be dismissed without the early pension deal now being offered, while Jesus Fred himself would keep his captaincy and get shunted to some safe, shit-hole outpost where a new generation of witch-hunters would keep him under wraps until his retirement or death. If Gaffaney went public with his information, as civilian or policeman, the grand jury would either indict him or not indict him, but either way, Janice and the girls would know, and his local celebrity would be exploited to full advantage.

Lloyd thought of the other victims: the families of the dead cops, Hawley and Eggers and their disintegrating marriages; Sally Issler and Chrissy Confrey, dropped like hot rocks amidst desperate declarations of future fidelity. The bank teller and her loved ones, and the shitload of harmless street people who were going to be bait for thousands of cops in an impotent rage, because three of their own got taken out, and there was nothing they could do about it.

Feeling *buried*, Lloyd thought of Watts and the fatuous idealism that had carried him through the riot and into the Job. He had convinced himself that he wanted to protect innocence, when he really wanted to crawl through sewers in search of adventure; he had sold himself a bill of goods about the just rule of law, when he really wanted to revel in the darkness he pretended to despise, with his family and women as safety buffers when the dark ate him up.

To take the edge of failure off his admissions, Lloyd tried to bring to mind the most tangible evidence of his success—the faces of innocents spared grief as a result of his hard-charger actions. None came, and he knew it was because their well-being was only a rationalization for his desire to plunder.

The last admission shined a spotlight on the survival plan that was forming in his mind all night. Lloyd laughed out loud when he realized he couldn't figure it out for one simple reason—he thought *he* was the one he wanted to save. Knowing now that he wasn't, he picked up the phone and punched a painfully familiar number.

"Hollywood Station, Captain Peltz speaking."

Dutch's voice was stretched thin, but it was not the grief-stricken voice of two hours before. Trying to sound panicky and apologetic, Lloyd said, "Dutchman, we're in deep shit."

"One of your rare dumb statements, Lloyd. What do you want?"

"Any response on the A.P.B.s yet?"

"No, but there's roadblocks and chopper patrols all over Hollywood, and we've got Rice's vehicle, a '78 Trans Am, purchased five days ago. It was parked a block from where you guys shot it out. If he's still in the area, he's dead meat. Did you get—"

"I gave you a wrong name, Dutch. Joe Garcia wasn't in on the heists or the killings. I can't go into it, but the third man is a guy named Klein. He's dead. Rice killed him yesterday."

Dutch's hollow voice returned in force: "Oh, Jesus God, *no*."

"Oh, Jesus God, *yes*. And listen: Gaffaney and his freaks had his name and package for hours before the bulletin was issued, and they don't give a fuck if he's innocent or—"

"Lloyd, all the stats on the robbers say one white man, two Mex—"

"Goddammit, listen! Rice is the white man, Bobby Garcia is Mexican, Klein, the other dead man, is tall and Latin-looking. And he's dead. All we've got is Rice on the loose, and he's a pro car thief and probably out of the area."

"How sure are you of all this?"

Lloyd tried to sound quietly outraged. "I'm the best, Dutch. We both know it, and I know Joe Garcia is innocent. Do you want to help me, or do you want one of your men to gun him down?"

A long silence came over the line. Lloyd imagined Dutch weighing the odds of innocent lives intersecting with trigger-happy cops. Finally he said, "Goddamn you, what do you want?"

A wrench hit Lloyd's stomach; he knew it came from manipulating his best friend with an outright lie. "Garcia is most likely running with Rice's girlfriend," he said. "A blonde white woman in her mid-twenties. Gaffaney's hot dogs don't know about her, because I just found out about her myself. The Garcia brothers have got no family, and the one K.A. in their file is a gun dealer already in custody. I'm assuming they'll run to *her* friends. I've got a list of names and addresses of four likelies. I want surveillances on the four pads, experienced officers. Tell them to apprehend Garcia and the woman without force."

Another long silence, then Dutch's voice, cold and all business: "I'll implement it. I'll direct four unmarked units to the pads and have them hold tight until 0800, then I'll bring in a fresh shift when the daywatch comes on. We're talking *obvious* unmarked cars, though. There's no time to have the men come to the station for their civilian wheels. And I want a full report on this guy Klein—fast."

Lloyd picked up Rhonda's list and read it off slowly. "Marty Cutler, 1843 Gretna Green, Brentwood; Roll Your Own Productions, 4811 Altera Drive, Benedict Canyon. That has to be a house—it's all residential down there. Another no name address—Plastic Fantastic Rock and Roll, 2184 Hillcrest Drive, Trousdale Estates—that's also all residential. The last one is Tucker Wilson, 403 Mabery, Santa Monica Canyon. Got it?"

"Got it. These are all fat city addresses. Wh—"

"Rice's girlfriend is a class outcall hooker. These are former customers of hers. My source put an asterisk after the Trousdale address, and she said some 'exec producer' was an especially good bet. You take it from there."

"I will. What are you going to do?"

Lloyd said, "Figure out a way to cover a lot of asses," and hung up, looking at the door in front of him and the phone by his right hand. He knew that the door meant a trip to Stan Klein's house, wiping it free of possible Joe Garcia prints, then firing his .45 into Klein's body and retrieving the spent rounds. If the stiff moldered for a few more days, then the M.E. who performed the autopsy would not be able to determine whether the knife and gunshot wounds had occurred concurrently. The .45 quality holes and slugs straight through the body and floor to the probable dirt foundation would, when unfound, be attributed to the gun of Duane Richard Rice. It was an evidential starting point, and if maggots ate away Klein's face, a death picture could not be shown to the bank eyewitnesses. There might be no other Klein photos available, and Joe Garcia's picture, most likely a six-year-old mugshot from his burglary bust, might not be recognized. If he could plea-bargain Louie Calderon into changing his testimony and make sure Joe Garcia got out of town without being busted or standing in a lineup, "Little Bro" might survive.

Still looking at the door, Lloyd knew that it meant ending the night earning McManus's "necrophile" tag, desecrating a corpse, then crawling in the dirt. It *had* to be done, but the more he stared at the door, the more it loomed as an ironclad barrier.

So he picked up the phone, hoping his wife's lover wouldn't be roused from sleep and answer. His hands trembled as he tapped the numbers, and when he got a tone he was sobbing.

After the third ring, a recorded message came on. "Hi, this is Janice Hopkins. The girls and I have taken our act on the road, but we should be returning before Christmas." There was a slight pause, then Penny's voice: "'The woods are lovely, dark and deep.' Leave a message at the beep."

Unable to speak through his tears, Lloyd hung up and called the number again and again, until the repetition of the message lulled him past weeping, and he fell asleep with the phone in his hands.

28

With the bag of money clutched to his chest, Rice beat a footpath to Silver Foxes and the Trans Am, stumbling through dark backyards, scaling fences and rolling into a camouflage ball every time a chopper light came anywhere near him. Roadblocks on Sunset to his north and Fountain to his south fenced him in, and as he crouched low and sprinted across one residential street after another, he could see cars being searched on the wide expressways.

But here, in a womb of old houses with backyards and apartment buildings connected by block-long cement walls, he was invisible and safe. The cops expected him to be on wheels. In the three hours since blundering into Sharkshit Bobby and blowing him away he'd stuck to the dark like a night animal, working his way deeper into the danger zone, taking shelter in shadows and rest breaks every three blocks. His head still ached from the cold-cock and his vision shimmied when light hit his eyes, but the perk/dexie speedballs he'd eaten just before the one-on-one with the cop kept the pain down and juice in his system. He could still function, and when he got to his car, he could still drive.

And he could still think.

Coming out of a long driveway, Rice turned his brain into a map and calculated two blocks to Silver Foxes. If his luck was holding, his registration papers wouldn't have hit the D.M.V. computer, the fuzz wouldn't know the Trans Am was his, and the outcall office window he'd blown to bits would give him a shot at some kind of file on Vandy—and the rock sleazos she might have run to. If the office was under guard, he was still armed for pig with the .45.

The map thinking gave him a new jolt of juice. Getting itchy to *be* there, he loosened his grip on the bag in order to regrip it for a straight run at his target. When it felt lighter to his touch, he checked the bottom and saw a big hole. Sticking his hand in, he saw that more than half the money had fallen out.

Catching himself about to scream, Rice clutched the bag with all his strength and beelined, running across the street and sidewalk, back through another driveway and yard. Ignoring a copter light scanning only three houses away, he hurtled an ivy-covered chain fence and ran out to the street. He was about to keep going when a flash of lavender dented his wobbly vision and registered as *home*.

Rice let his eyes trawl Gardner Avenue for danger signs. There was no one on either side of the street, and no cop cars, marked or unmarked. Squinting at the whore building, he saw a black tarpaulin covering the demolished front window. Flipping an imaginary brain switch marked "caution," he placed the money bag on the ground and memorized its location, then took the .45 from his waistband. Catching his breath, he walked to Silver Foxes.

There were no lights on in the four-flat. Rice checked the luminous dial of his watch, saw that it was 3:40 and did a mental run-through: the whoremasters hobnobbing with the fuzz after the shooting, getting workmen to do a quick fix-up job until the window could be repaired properly, getting rid of the incriminating shit, then getting out. The thought of no files brought him to the point of screaming, and he ran to the tarpaulin, grabbed the right-side fastenings with both hands and pulled.

The tarp came loose and crashed to the lawn. Rice stepped in the window, found the wall light and turned it on.

The dispatch room was a bullet-wasted ruin, big chunks of white wall ripped out, the plastic desk dinged and cracked from ricochets. Remembering a Rolodex, Rice scanned the room unsuccessfully for it, then went through the desk drawers. Finding nothing but blank paper and rolls of film, he stood up to think and saw an old-fashioned filing cabinet just inside the bathroom door.

All three drawers were locked. Standing to one side, Rice closed the door on the barrel of his .45, so that just the silencer was inside the bathroom. He fired seven times at the cabinet, and soft plops went off like muffled thunder. The last shots reverberated off the metal surface and tore the door in half; through muzzle smoke he could see the cabinet on its side spilling manila folders.

Digging into them, Rice saw names typed on side tabs, and that the files had spilled out in close to alphabetical order. Tearing through the R's, S's and T's, he felt his bowels loosen. Then "Vanderlinden, Annie" was in his hands, and he didn't know if it was good or bad, so he turned off the light and ran with it out to the Trans Am.

But it wasn't there.

Land mines, booby traps, snipers and werewolf-faced dogs flashed through his mind, and he hit the ground like soldiers in the million old movies he'd seen on TV. Eating curb grass instead of dirt, he waited for machine-gun ack-ack and managed to slide Vandy's file into his pants along with his .45. When no attack came, he did a squat run over to the money bag and picked it up, then walked slowly toward the Fountain Avenue road-block—the eye of his hurricane.

Staying in the shadows of front porches and shrubbery, he saw the cordon setup come into focus: north-south traffic on Gardner was blocked off, with two cops standing at the ready to pass innocent cars through and fire on ones that rabbited. East-west traffic on Fountain was being inspected the same way, but only at stoplights. Since the nearest lights were three blocks away on the east and two on the west, all he had to do was get south of Fountain, steal a car and *roll*.

Rice eyed the barricade and cops twenty yards away. The roadblocks had probably been set up right after he plowed the pig on Formosa. They were figuring him for a car thief and had zipped the area up tight as a drum. If they found Bobby Sharkshit, a block off the Boulevard, they were probably knocking down doors up there. Sunset and Fountain were sealed, and probably Hollywood and Franklin. They would not have the men to hit the streets further south, and they probably figured he couldn't have made it that far anyway.

Rice swallowed and secured his only three possessions: the gun, the file and the paper bag of money. Feeling them bonded to him, he lowered himself to the ground and rolled off the corner house lawn to the sidewalk and into the street, a dark, pavement-eating dervish. Catching sight of the cops with their backs to him, he kept rolling, gravel digging into his cheeks and shredding the bag until a trail of cash drifted in his wake. He rolled until he hit the opposite sidewalk, then elbowed his way over the curb and rolled until soft grass kissed his gouged face. When he finally felt safe enough to stand up, he was on the beautiful front lawn of a beautiful little house, mid-way down a beautiful little block, with no barricade at its southern intersection and plenty of beautiful cars parked within stealing distance.

29

On the doorstep of the big house, Anne smoothed Joe's shirt front and said, "You look like a *real* street person. I'll tell my friends you're a producer, that you're scouting Chicano groups in the Barrio. Just listen to the music, and you'll have a good time."

Punk rock boomed inside. Joe took a long look at the spectacular view: the Strip winding to the east, Beverly Hills below them, glow from swimming pools the only light. "I don't want to have a good time," he said. "We're down to twenty scoots, and we need a traveling stake. Just remember that."

Anne said, "You got it, tough guy," and put out her cigarette on an Astroturf mat embossed with "If You Don't Rock, Don't Knock." She took a deep breath, then started in on her signature boogie and pushed the door open.

Following a pace behind, Joe thought he'd been transported back to Lincoln Heights in the sixties, when the vatos and the hippies were waging war, and one side of North Broadway was bodegas and poolrooms, the other side a twenty-four-hour-a-day light show/love-in/dope-in. While Anne bebopped into the scene, he hung back and eyeballed for details to prove that it was '84, not '68, and he wasn't having a shock-induced acid flashback.

The whole downstairs was a pressed-together mass of people in costume—men in full-drape zoot suits and Nazi uniforms, women in gangster moll dresses and Girl Scout outfits. Groups of gangsters and molls slam-danced into Nazis and scouts, while colored lights blipped from the ceiling and different rock videos flashed on screens hung to the four walls. The refrain "Go down go down go down go down" blasted from quadrophonic speakers, and Joe felt his head reel as he scoped out Godzilla attacking Tokyo and Marlon Brando tooling on a Harley hog while caped musicians genuflected into his exhaust. The other screens were out of focus, but he could catch people in weird makeup fucking and sucking. A conga line of gangsters were facing off against a trio of goose-stepping Nazis, who were kicking molls and scouts out of their way in the direction of a circle of amyl nitrate sniffers. And preppy Anne cut a path through all of it, screeching, "Where's Mel? Where's Mel?"

Knowing she was stone '84, Joe stood on his tiptoes and followed her bobbing pink sweater, keeping his head down as he pushed past partyers, hoping they wouldn't see his face reflected in the lights and know how scared he was. At the far side of the room he saw Anne break free and talk to a guy in a butler's outfit, who pointed her down the hall. Slipping out of the crowd himself, he caught a glimpse of Anne entering a darkly lit room.

Joe walked toward the door. When he was just outside it, he heard Anne pleading: "Just two hundred, Mel. My squeeze and I have to leave L.A."

"You'll blow it on blow, Annie," a coarse male voice said. "And I thought you were with Stan K. I know for a fact he ain't hurting—I bought some vids off him last week."

"Stan and I broke up, Mel. It was sort of . . . quick. My new guy and I *have* to leave. You remember Duane?"

"Sure. Disco Duane the discount car king. Your squeeze before Klein before your current bimbo. You see a pattern there, sweetie?"

"Mel, he's crazy, and he's after me!"

"I don't blame him; you're a class act. Third class, but class nonetheless. Sweetie, if I give you money you'll just get coked and be broke again quicksville. There's complimentary outside. Have some."

Anne screeched, "I popped some strange stuff I found, and it's still on! I don't need blow, I need money!"

Mel laughed. "You've got to earn it."

"I know," Anne said. "I know."

Joe walked away from the door, wondering why he felt betrayed—Anne was a one-hour stand at best. Retreating toward the back of the house, the reason grabbed him by the balls. She's your witness. She saw you kill a man and steal a car and drive a stick shift. She doesn't know about you being dominated by Bobby. She thinks you're as bad-ass as Duane Rice.

Coming to a small room next to the kitchen, Joe looked in and saw a guy watching TV with the sound off. The guy was strumming an electric guitar while chortling at a beer ad, and Joe got another whiff of the bad old sixties. Then double stone '84 hit the TV, and he knew it was hallucinogenic.

Bobby was on the screen, wearing gloves and trunks, crouched in his "Boogaloo" stance. Joe ran to the TV and fumbled the volume dial; the guy put down the guitar and blurted, "Hey, man, I want it that way!" Joe got the sound on just as Bobby the boxer dissolved into a shot of paramedics carrying a sheet-covered stretcher out of a church.

". . . and Garcia is the second person to be murdered in the Hollywood area tonight. His body was discovered inside a Catholic church on Las Palmas and Franklin, half a mile from the spot where an L.A.P.D. officer was hit and run by a man in a stolen car. Police spokesmen have said that there may be a link to Monday's West L.A. bank robbery that left four dead. Meanwhile, a massive—"

The TV blipped to another beer ad—"This one's for you, no matter what you're doing and you"—and Joe saw that the guitar guy had hit a remote-control button. "This one's for you!" rang out nonhallucinogenically, and he knew it was Bobby's epitaph. He grabbed the guitar from the guy's lap and stalked with it back to the party.

Gangsters, molls, Nazis and scouts were arranged in a circle in the middle of the living room. The video screens were blank, and the strobes were replaced by normal lighting. Mel's coarse voice rose from inside the circle. "Ladies and jelly beans, Little Annie Vandy, dirty, raunchy, coked-out and randy, does the too-hep dance of the dirty prep!"

Holding the guitar by the neck, Joe used the business end as a prod and poked his way into the circle. Anne was there, attempting to gyrate and pull off her sweater at the same time. Her eyes were glazed, and her whole body twitched. Mel, standing beside her in tennis whites, was snapping his fingers.

"This one's for you!" and the shot of Bobby in his leopardskin trunks gave Joe the necessary guts. He roundhoused the guitar at Mel's head, knocking him into a line of zoot suiters and Nazis, then swung an overhand shot that grazed helmets and snap-brim fedoras before catching the host in the neck. Mel hit the floor, and the partygoers separated and moved backward. Joe saw that they weren't frightened or shocked, but that they were digging it, and that Anne was running for the door.

Holding the guitar/weapon by the tuning pegs, he stuck it out at arm's length and spun around and around on a tiny foot axis, moving into the crowd, assailing them with glancing blows that set off a chain reaction of shrieks, squeals and bursts of applause. As the partygoers gave him more and more space, the applause became thunderous. Joe felt a queasy vertigo, and realized that the sleazebags loved him.

Screaming "Bobby!" he hurled the guitar into the middle of them and ran out the door. Reeling across the lawn toward a speck of pink down the street, he thought he saw an unmarked fuzz car parked in the shadows. Feeling invulnerable, he flipped it the bird and ran until his preppy partner was only a few feet away. Slowing to a walk, he caught up with her and tapped her shoulder. When she turned and looked at him with Twilight Zone eyes, he gasped, "I ain't no fucking musician. I ain't no fucking rock and roll fool."

30

Sunlight on his face forced Lloyd awake. The telephone fell from his lap, and he bent over to pick it up. Remembering Dutch's promised surveillance deployment, he put the receiver to his ear and started to call the Hollywood Station number. Then three little clicks came over the line instead of a dial tone, and the phone fell from his hands.

Bugged.

Gaffaney.

Lloyd ran outside and looked up and down the block. There were no vans on the street, and no other vehicles large enough to hold a mobile bugging apparatus. The tap was stationary and had to originate in a nearby dwelling.

Eye trawling, Lloyd saw his familiar landscape of two-story houses and apartment buildings turn menacing. His own small Colonial seemed suddenly vulnerable, surrounded by potential monsters. Then the most likely monster caught his attention and made him wince: the old Spanish-style building next door, recently converted to condos.

Lloyd ran into the entrance vestibule and checked the mailboxes. Only one unit—7—was without a name. He walked down the hallway, feeling his rage escalating as the numbers increased, hoping for a flimsy door and another shot at Sergeant Wallace D. Collins. Finding a solid doorway with a Mickey Mouse lock, he took a credit card from his wallet, slipped it into the runner crack and jiggled the knob. The door opened, and he entered a musty apartment furnished with only a desk holding electrical equipment.

Calling out "Collins," Lloyd reached for his .45, then flinched at the simple reflex and what it meant. When no sounds answered his call, he moved to the desk and examined the setup.

It was a simple tapper to outside wires hookup, with a tape recorder attached to record calls. A red light glowed on the panel by the "Remote Receiver" button, and a green light and the number 12 flashed on and off under the switch marked "Messages Received." Shuddering, Lloyd pushed the "Rewind" button and watched the tape spool spin. When it stopped, he hit "Play." "Hollywood Station, Captain Peltz speaking" filled the empty room, bouncing off the walls like a deadpan death decree.

Lloyd pushed the "Off" button. Gaffaney and his freaks had word on the surveillances and had listened to him sob to the inanimate voices of his wife and favorite daughter, and there was nothing he could do to turn it around.

Turning off the recorder and pulling the plug on the bugging device made the powerless feeling worse. Lloyd walked home. The phone was ringing, and he picked up the receiver like it was something about to explode.

"Yes?"

"Dutch, Lloyd."

"And?"

"And you owe me a report, and that outcall place on Gardner was broken into last night. The files were gone through, and there's fresh large-caliber gunshot holes in the walls, and they had to have come from a silencered piece, because two of my men were stationed at a roadblock half a block away. A Ford LTD was reported stolen on the adjoining block, and there's no reports from the first surveillance shift. I just dispatched day-watch units to relieve them, so that's covered. *And—*"

Lloyd hung up. Listening to Dutch's angry litany had been like watching two trains heading toward each other on the same track, both on locked-in automatic pilot. All he could do now was patrol the wreckage and hope for survivors.

31

Rice steered the LTD through the winding roads of Trousdale Estates. His vision was going blurry again, and he had to hold Vandy's file up to right in front of his eyes in order to read the address. Driving with one hand, he remembered his first three possibilities—big dark houses with fuzzmobiles parked across the street. If he hadn't given each pad a slow-around-the-block circuit, he'd be dead. This approach had to be just as cautious.

By squinting until tears came into his eyes, he was able to pick out Hillcrest. He tried to make his brain into a map like he did in Hollywood, then flashed that that only worked when you had some idea where you were. Slowing to a crawl, he squinted for street signs. There weren't any; Trousdale was strictly for people who knew where they were going. He was about to scrounge the glove compartment for a street atlas when an unmarked Matador passed him in the opposite direction.

So Plastic Fantastic had to be nearby. Rice drove slowly, watching the Matador hazily disappear in his rearview mirror. Straining to read house numbers was futile, making the blurring worse and causing head pounding and stomach cramps on top of it. Pulling to the curb, he got out and walked.

His legs were wobbly, but he was able to move in a straight line. Thinking in a straight line was harder, and he kept wondering why the cop car had split, giving him a clean shot. Finally he gave up thinking and kept walking. The front lawns he was passing looked soft and cushiony, and every time the green shined through his tear blur he started to yawn. Reaching into his shirt pocket for the last of the speed, he saw that he'd already swallowed it, and snapped that squinting at addresses from the sidewalk was no better than from the car, and twice as dangerous. He was about to go back to the LTD when strangely dressed people started walking across an especially beautiful stretch of grass. He cut over to meet them, and they slid past him in a jet stream that reminded him of taillights on a freeway at night.

He grabbed at their shadows and spoke to what he could see of their faces: "Vandy Vanderlinden, you know her? You seen her?" He said it a dozen times, and got nothing but hoots and catcalls in return. Then the people were gone, and there was green grass in all directions. Rice heard breathing in front of him, and rubbed his eyes so he could see who he was talking to.

The absence of tears gave him back most of his sight, and his eyes honed in on two big men in windbreakers. When he saw that they were aiming shotguns at him, he reached for the .45. The butts of their weapons crashed into his head just as he remembered he'd left his piece in the car.

He was on the main drag of Hawaiian Garbage, running red lights on a dare, trying to break his old night record of nine straight. Everything was dark red and very fast, and he knew he could go on forever. Everything was also very warm, getting warmer as the string of reds extended. Then everything went cold, and his eyes were forced open and someone was wiping water from his face. He knew he was standing, that he was being held upright. His old 20/20 snapped in on scrub bushes, dirt and a cement embankment that stank of chemicals. He knew immediately that he was at Suicide Hill.

A fuzz type in a cheapo suit stepped in front of him, blotting out his view of the terrain. The grip on his arms tightened. Rice saw a weird lapel pin on the fuzz type's jacket and a .357 Python in his right hand, and knew he was going to die. He tried to think up a suitable wisecrack, but "She was a stone heartbreaker" came out instead. *And I loved her* was about to come out, but three slugs from the magnum hit him first.

32

Lloyd waited in the third-floor attorney room of the Main County Jail. He had a perjury script in his jacket pocket, Stan Klein's rap sheet in one hand, Louie Calderon's arrest report in the other. Klein had two convictions for possession of marijuana back in the early seventies, and Likable Louie had been booked for assault on a police officer. So far, the survivor patrol was surviving—at least on the basis of planning strategies and circumstantial facts. And the more he looked at Klein's mug shot, the more he resembled Joe Garcia.

A jailer ushered Calderon into the room and pointed him toward the chair across the table from Lloyd. His face was bruised and stitched from the Metro beating, but he walked steadily, and his soft brown eyes were clear. He looked like a man capable of making smart snap decisions.

Lloyd stood up and stuck out his hand; Calderon sat down without grasping it. "What do you want?" he said.

Lloyd slid Stan Klein's mug shot over to him. "I want to save Joe Garcia's ass from the gas chamber and help you beat your assault beef. Do you know this man?"

Calderon glanced at the snapshot and shook his head. "No. Who is he?"

"He's the third member of the robbery gang. His name is Stan Klein, a.k.a. 'Stan Man.' He's taking the fall for Joe Garcia, and he's a longtime known associate of yours. *Comprende*, homeboy?"

Calderon narrowed his eyes. "He gonna lie down for a frame?"

Drawing a finger across his throat, Lloyd said, "He's dead. Have you made a statement to anyone here or back at Rampart?"

"No. I just kicked loose with the names. You should know—you were there. If this joker Klein is eighty-six, how you gonna make him for the heists? And what the fuck do you *want?*"

Savoring Likable Louie's wariness, Lloyd said, "Rice killed Klein. Bobby Garcia is dead, shot by Rice last night. Joe and Rice are still out there. Rice won't last much longer, but Joe's got a chance. Here's the pitch: I give you a little fact sheet on Klein, you memorize it. You shut your mouth until you get word that Rice is dead. I know he's a smart guy, but the heat is huge, and no cop is going to let him see due process. When he's dead, you talk to the D.A.'s investigators, who are going to start hounding your ass as soon as I submit my report to them. You tell them that you sold the hardware to Rice, and that he told you that he was forming a gang—him, Bobby Garcia and Klein. Got it?"

Calderon leaned forward. "What's in it for *me*, and what's in it for *you?*"

Leaning forward himself, Lloyd said, "Louie, there's a lot of dead people out there, and most of them are cops, and you supplied the guns that killed them. You're dead and buried. The feds have got your number, the regular L.A.P.D. and the freak cops have got it, I've got it. Bobby's dead, and Rice is as good as dead, and the D.A. is going to look for someone to crucify on this thing, and it's going to be you."

Pale now, Calderon plucked at his stitches until blood trickled out. When he saw what he was doing, he stopped and stammered, "Y-y-yeah, b-b-but what do you *want?*"

Lloyd said, "To see you and Joe get out of this alive. Here's the rest of the pitch. I've got a little scenario for you to memorize before you talk to the D.A. How you fingered Joe Garcia because he stiffed you on some burglary goods, stuff like that. You play it right, and the D.A. and his boys will buy your story. And I go to the D.A. and tell him how those Metro bulls beat the confession out of you, and I clean all the incriminating shit out of your pad, and I get Nate Steiner to defend you if you go to trial, which you probably won't, because the D.A. will not want me to testify in court against other officers. I'd lay three to one that if you cooperate with me, you'll walk."

Calderon slammed the tabletop with clenched fists. "Hopkins, nobody does something like that for nothing. What do you fucking *want!*"

Smiling, Lloyd took the survival script from his pocket and laid it on the table. "I don't want anything. If you're as smart as I think you are, you'll believe me."

He stood up and stuck out his hand, and this time Calderon grasped it and said, "Crazy Lloyd Hopkins, Jesus Christ."

Lloyd laughed. "I'm no savior. One more thing: have you got any idea where Joe would run to if he figured the heat was off?"

Likable Louie thought for a moment, then said, "The guitar shop on Temple and Beaudry. He's sort of an amateur musician, and sooner or later he'll show up there." He put the two pieces of paper in his shirt pocket and added, "Memorize, then flush."

Lloyd buzzed for the jailer to return. On his way out the door, he pointed a cocked-gun finger at Calderon and said, "Support your local police."

Now the shit work.

Lloyd drove to the Western Costume Company and purchased a high-quality black wig and full beard, then drove to Stan Klein's Mount Olympus villa. A fresh morning newspaper indicated that the pad was untampered with since last night's prowling with Rhonda. Steeling himself with a deep breath and a handkerchief around his nose, he picked the lock and walked in. The smell was awful, but not overpowering. Lloyd gave the corpse a cursory glance, then donned gloves and went to work.

First he found the central heating and turned the temperature up to eighty-five, then he stripped to the waist and wiped all the downstairs touch and grab surfaces, visualizing the Klein/Rice/Garcia/Vanderlinden confrontation all the while, finally deciding that musician Joe never made it to the upper floor. The heat and the increased odor of decomposition it created were oppressive, and he gave up his wiping after a peremptory run-through, leaving the video gadgets surrounding Klein's body alone.

With potential Garcia latents in all probability eliminated, Lloyd tossed the house for photographs of Stan Klein. Drenched in sweat, he opened drawers and tore through dressers; checked the bureaus in all three bedrooms. The upstairs yielded a half dozen Polaroids that looked recent, and the living room two framed portrait photos. Lloyd placed them by the banister, then took a pen and notebook paper from his jacket and jogged up to the master bedroom to write.

With the door shut and the air-conditioning on full, he wrote for three hours, detailing his investigation of the first two robbery/kidnaps, and Captain John McManus's assigning of him to the Pico-Westholme robbery/homicides. This account was factual. The rest of the report comprised a companion piece to his script for Louie Calderon, and stated how Calderon, under physical duress, gave the names Duane Rice, Bobby Garcia and Joe Garcia to Sergeants W.D. Collins and K.R. Lohmann, later partially recanting his statement to him, stating truthfully that Stanley Klein was the "third man," and that he had named Joe Garcia for revenge on an old criminal grievance. Omitting mention of Rhonda Morrell, he concluded by stating that he had discovered Stan Klein's body, and that a scrap of paper beside the corpse led him to Silver Foxes and his still unaccounted-for shootout with Duane Rice. Attributing his delay in reporting the body to a desire to "remain mobile and assist in the active investigation," Lloyd signed his name and badge number, then sent up a prayer for lackluster forensic technicians to aid him in his lies.

The smell was now unbearable.

Lloyd turned off the air-conditioning and heat, then went downstairs and put on his shirt and jacket. Seeing that the body had bloated at the stomach and that the cheeks had rotted through to the gums, he tossed the wig and mustache at the pile of video tapes, then found a plugged-in stereo and turned on the FM full blast. The noise covered the three desecrated gunshots with ease, and he forced himself to look at the damage. As he hoped, the entry wounds got lost in the overall decomposition. Knowing he couldn't bear to crawl under the house for the expended rounds, Lloyd turned off the music and sent up another prayer—this one a general mercy plea. Then he got out, hyperventilating when fresh, sane air hit his lungs.

Now the loose ends.

Lloyd drove to Hollywood Station. In the parking lot, he put the report in an envelope and wrote *Captain Arthur F. Peltz* on the front, then left it with the desk officer, who told him that there was no word on the whereabouts of Duane Richard Rice, and that the dragnet was still in full force.

The funereal air of the station was claustrophobic. From a street pay phone, Lloyd called the office of Nathan Steiner, Attorney at Law, and asked for a ballpark figure on a murder one defense. Steiner's head clerk said 40K minimum. Hanging up, Lloyd figured that with a "police discount" he could swing it.

Now the scary part.

Lloyd fed all the change in his pockets to the phone and dialed Janice's Frisco number, grateful that the voices he would be speaking to wouldn't be able to answer back. Holding his breath, he heard, "Hi, this is Janice Hopkins. The girls and I have taken our act on the road, but we should be returning before Christmas," and "The woods are lovely, dark and deep. Leave a message at the beep."

The beep went off. Lloyd let out his breath and said, "Take your act south before I do something crazy. You're all I've got left." Then he drove home and walked upstairs to the bedroom he had kept inviolate since his wife left him two years before. There, on a dust-covered bed, he fell asleep to wait for survival or oblivion.

33

Eight hours after executing his only son's executioner, Captain Fred Gaffaney sat down in his study and began the writing of his last will and testament.

The execution weapon rested on the desk beside him, and he breathed cordite residue as he put to paper his bequest: cash amounting to slightly over twenty thousand dollars, the house, its furnishings and his two cars to the Church of Jesus Christ, Christian. The magnum loomed at the corner of his vision, and he tried to recall Bible passages that dictated suicide excluding heaven and meeting the Savior. Verses came and went, but none stuck, and the .357 was still there. Finally he gave up trying and accepted the fact. Only Catholics bought suicide as an exclusionary sin, and they could not justify it with Biblical references. It was an acceptable out for a warrior Christian with nowhere else to go.

Looking over his words, Gaffaney saw that they took up only one yellow legal page. He had written accident reports ten times that long, and he didn't want to pull the trigger on a note of brevity. He thought he could perform the execution as a ritual that affirmed the rule of law, but when Lohmann and Collins tossed Duane Rice's body into its sewage bed grave, he knew that he had violated everything he believed in, and that that apostasy demanded the death sentence. Knowing also that the condemned deserved reflection before their sentence was carried out, he allowed himself the mercy of returning to Suicide Hill in the fall of '61.

He was a rookie then, working daywatch patrol out of East Valley Division, twenty-six years old, with a wife and baby son. His beat included the Sepulveda V.A. Hospital, and half his duty time was spent ferrying sad old soldier boozehounds from the wine bars on Victory Boulevard back to their domiciles, the other half writing traffic citations. It was boring police work for a young man who knew only one thing about himself—that he was ambitious.

There was an old wino who kept escaping the domicile to get bombed on white port and pass out religious tracts to the teenaged gangsters who inhabited Suicide Hill at night. The local officers respected him, because he refused to accept welfare and stuck the V.A. with the full tab for his room and board. He was a tall, Germanic-looking man with haunting blue eyes, and the tracts he distributed emphasized a warrior Jesus Christ, who loved his followers fiercely and exhorted them to strike down evil wherever they saw it.

The wino was a brilliant storyteller, and the gangsters liked to get him juiced and incite him to tall tales. He always obliged, and he always weaved sermons into his stories, ending them with a handing out of leaflets emblazoned with a cross and a flag.

To Officer Fred Gaffaney, Irish Catholic atheist, the wino was a pathetic crackpot. He grudgingly followed the implicit division edict of never busting him for "plain drunk," but he would not listen to his stories for a second. Thus, when the wino approached him one afternoon with a feverish account of a bunch of Demon Dog members out to kill him, he turned a deaf ear, gave him fifty cents for a jug and told him to get back to the domicile.

A week later, the wino's body was found, scattered all over Suicide Hill. He had been drawn and quartered. The investigating detectives reconstructed his death as being caused by four motorcycles taking off simultaneously, each with one of his limbs tied to the rear axle. The M.E. reconstructed that he had been decapitated after his death, and Officer Fred Gaffaney reconstructed himself as a coward and did not come forward with his information on the Demon Dogs, because it would hinder his career.

The anonymous tip on the Dogs that he sent to Robbery/Homicide Division two torturous weeks after the killing did not lead them to the slayers or ease his conscience. The wino's blue eyes singed him in his sleep. Booze and illegally procured sleeping pills didn't help, and he could not talk about it to a single human being.

So he sought out God.

Returning to the old Catholic fold helped, but he could not take his wino/victim with him to the confessional. Liquor in concert with the Church helped a little more, but the blue eyes and "The Dogs got a contract out on me, Officer Fred, and you gotta help me!" were always a half step away, ready to pounce just when he thought everything was going to be all right.

The Job helped most of all, but still did not provide a panacea. He *served*, working long overtime hours, writing laborious reports on the most minor occurrences, afraid that any parcel of information left unreported would lead to spiritual catastrophe and death. A few superior officers regarded him as fanatical, but most considered him a model of police meticulousness. Spurred by constant encouragement, he climbed the ladder.

He became a sergeant and was assigned to the Detective Division, then passed the lieutenant's exam and went to Robbery/Homicide. The Church, the wino, and cross and flag nightmares simmered on his soul's back burner, pushed there by ambitiousness and a barrage of rationalizations—his drive for power was atonement; his stern rule over lax, libertine underlings was a sword thrust that would move the blue-eyed specter himself; encouraging of his son to become a policeman was evidence that the atonement would pass to a second generation of Gaffaneys. His wife's death of cancer gave a weight of grief to the guilt procession, and when he buried her, he felt that the sad old storyteller had finally been put to rest.

Then he met Lloyd Hopkins, and the out-of-control hot dog blew everything to hell.

He had, of course, been hearing about him for years, taking in accounts of his exploits with amazement and disgust, but never considering him worth knowing from the standpoints of career advancement or Robbery/Homicide efficacy. Then, assigned as supervisor of his sector, Thad Braverton gave him the word: "Hopkins is the best. Give him carte blanche."

The undercutting of his authority had rankled, but Crazy Lloyd's actions made it pall by comparison. Hopkins's life was one giant sword swipe at real and imagined evil; the terror and guilt and rage that burned in his eyes were laser beam incisions into that part of him where "Suicide Hill '61" was engraved like gang graffiti. He had to fight what Hopkins was, so he tracked down the cross and flag leaflets and was born again.

It worked.

He carried the wino's message; took comfort in its call to duty. He studied the Bible and prayed, and found fellow officers who believed as he did. They followed him, and when he passed the captain's exam and was flagged for the I.A.D. exec position, he knew that nothing could stop him from achieving a spellbinding selfhood preordained by God and a martyred madman twenty years dead.

Then Hopkins took out the "Hollywood Slaughterer." The boldness of his measures inspired awe among the men of the born-again officer corps, and had Hopkins walked into one of their prayer meetings, they would have genuflected before him as if the sex-crazed lunatic were Christ himself. His solving of the Havilland/Goff homicides a year later again brought the men to their figurative knees. He became a rival spiritual patriarch who was dangerous precisely because he did not covet spiritual power, and the means to his destruction had to be divinely sought and given.

Hours and hours were spent praying. He spoke to God of his hatred for Hopkins, and got small comfort. His strategy to upgrade his son's school records and gain his admission to the Academy worked, and Steven graduated and was assigned to West L.A. Division. Prayer and the appointment of a second-generation Gaffaney to the Department helped diffuse Hopkins's hold on his mind, as did the building up of the interdepartmental dirt files. Then his prayers were rewarded, and promptly backfired.

Lamar Dayton, a Devonshire Division lieutenant and long-time born-again, joined the corps and told him of whoremaster Hopkins and his Watts baptism of fire. Circumstantial verification of National Guard records made the final message ring clear: Hopkins, not himself, was the divinely gifted policeman/warrior, and what drove him was not God, but awful self-willed needs and desires—all mortal in nature.

Gaffaney stood up and looked at the clock above his desk. His stay of execution ruminations had consumed an hour, and were still not one hundred percent conclusive. He thought of things to be grateful for: he and Steven had been close in the days before his death, and Steve had confided that he had resisted the retired deputy's fencing imprecations, turning over a new leaf. That was comforting, as was the fact that he had not compounded his self-hatred by letting Hopkins perform the execution.

"Hopkins" and "Execution" filled in the missing percentage points, and extended the stay of sentence to the indeterminate near future. Gaffaney looked at the magnum and suddenly knew why he had stolen his death weapon from an L.A.P.D. source. Only Lloyd Hopkins would be crazy enough and bold enough to follow the gun to its source and back to him, regardless of the consequences and devil take the hindmost. He had taken the magnum from a Wilshire Division evidence room in full view of a half dozen officers because he wanted to sacrifice himself to the man he most admired and envied.

Thinking of "Suicide Hill '61" and mercy, Gaffaney carried his three armfuls of files into the bathroom and dumped them in the tub, then walked downstairs and grabbed a bottle of bourbon off the bar. Returning upstairs with it, he doused the pile of paper and dropped a match on top. His hold on scores of men went up in flames, and he waited until all the data was obliterated before turning on the shower. The fire hissed, sizzled and died, and Gaffaney walked back to the den to wait for his executioner.

34

Awakening from eight hours of dreamless sleep, Lloyd rolled off the dusty bed and walked to the window to see if it was night or day.

Creeping sunlight from the eastern horizon told him it was dawn, and the paperboy hurling the *Times* at the front door told him that it was neither survival nor oblivion, simply time to get on with it. After shaving, showering and dressing in his favorite sport coat/slacks combo, Lloyd sat at the dining room table and wrote out a declaration that two weeks before he would have considered incomprehensible.

Gentlemen:

This letter constitutes my formal resignation from the Los Angeles Police Department. It is tendered with regret, but not under a state of emotional duress. The reasons for my resignation are threefold: I wish to devote a good deal of time to my family; I have incurred the enmity of several high-ranking officers; and events of the recent past have convinced me that my effectiveness as a homicide investigator is drastically diminished. It is my wish to be assigned to either clerking or nonfield supervisory duties until my twenty-year anniversary comes up next October. I am grateful for the Department's offer of early retirement with full pension, but feel it would be dishonorable to accept it without serving the required twenty years.

Respectfully, Lloyd W. Hopkins

Bracing himself for the outside world, Lloyd put the resignation letter in his pocket and walked to the door, hoping the *Times* would carry news of one man's death and another man's safe passage. Throwing the door open, the headline beamed up at him: "'Suicide Hill' Suicide Ends Four-Day Murder Spree."

Leaning into the doorway, Lloyd let the subheading of "Cop Killer–Robber Takes Own Life at Fabled Youth Gang Meeting Ground" sink in. Then, with his brain screaming first "Gaffaney," then "No!" he read the entire account:

Los Angeles, December 15

The Los Angeles Police Department announced today that the greatest manhunt in L.A. History has ended with the suicide of multiple murderer Duane Richard Rice, the mastermind behind Monday's West Los Angeles bank robbery that left four dead.

Rice, twenty-eight, a career criminal with convictions for vehicular manslaughter and grand theft auto, is believed also to be responsible for Tuesday night's hit-and-run murder of L.A.P.D. officer Edward Qualter and the fatal shootings of the gang's two other members, Robert Garcia and Stanley Klein, bringing the total of his victims to seven.

At a late night press conference at Parker Center, L.A.P.D. chief of detectives Thad Braverton explained how the cooperation of an anonymous associate of the gang gave police the means to reconstruct the reign of terror:

"It was a classic case of a falling out among thieves," the chief said. "Rice, Garcia and Klein were the perpetrators of two well-planned robbery/hostage forays in the Valley the week preceding the Pico-Westholme bank robbery, which we view now as having been undertaken by Rice partially out of a desire for revenge—one of the bank employees, Gordon Meyers, a former Los Angeles County deputy sheriff, was his jailer during a recent incarceration."

Braverton went on: "We do not know precisely *why* Rice wanted re-venge, but *that* he did is a safe assumption. Our witness in custody is the man who sold the robbery gang their guns, and he, a long-term as-sociate of the three men, states that distrust ran deep among them. The other men also possess criminal records—Garcia for burglary, Klein for possession of narcotics. Klein was also heavily involved in video pornography. Circumstantially, we believe that Rice shot and killed both Garcia and Klein, his motive being a desire to keep their share of the money from the Pico-Westholme robbery. There is also an evidential corroboration for this—our chief ballistics officer, Arthur Cranfield, has examined the .45-caliber slugs taken from the bodies of Garcia, Klein and Rice, and he states *conclusively* that they came from the Colt army-issue .45 found in Duane Rice's hand when patrolmen discovered his body lying in the Sepulveda Wash."

Lloyd scanned the rest of the article, a hyperbolic spiel about tragedy, law and order, and the forthcoming L.A.P.D. funerals. The total picture bom-barded him as a patchwork of victory and defeat, survival and denial. His report to Dutch, the forensic subterfuge at Stan Klein's pad and Louie Calderon's testimony had been, if not actually believed, accepted in the spirit of letting sleeping dogs lie. But the Duane Rice "suicide" was prepos-terous. On Tuesday night Dutch had said that two .45s were recovered at the Bowl Motel, while his own gun had supplied the Stan Klein "death" shots. If Rice had been killed with his own piece, which was doubtful, because he never would have relinquished it—he didn't pull the trigger himself.

Lloyd felt a queasy rage overtake him. Rice had deserved to die; he had contemplated his cold-blooded murder himself. And the man who most likely killed him held a death sentence over his own head. Running red lights and siren to Parker Center, he couldn't believe he was crazy enough to take the both of them out in one fell swoop.

The Central Crime Lab was bustling with technicians. Lloyd found Artie Cranfield in his usual workday posture, hunched over a double-plated ballistics microscope. Knowing that nothing short of an air raid would force Artie's head up, he said, "Tell me the real dope on Klein and Rice. What's Braverton stonewalling?"

Artie came up smiling. "Hello, Lloyd. Would you repeat that?"

Lloyd smiled and cleared his throat; Artie said, "Not here," and pointed to his office. Lloyd walked in, and five minutes later Artie joined him. Shutting the door, he said, "Straight business?"

Nodding affirmatively, Lloyd said, "A bunch of fixes are in. I found Klein's body, D.O.A. knifing. I fired three shots from my .45 into his stiff, so I know that 'same gun' stuff in the papers is bullshit. Did you process the evidence on Rice?"

Artie gave his four walls a furtive look, then said, "I was there at the autopsy. The M.E. handed me three spent .357s, dug them out of Rice's chest. The rear of the jackets were nicked, right where the firing pin would make contact. Very distinctive, and very familiar. I checked ballistics bulletins going back eighteen months. Bingo! Matchup to an old unsolved in Wilshire Division, street shooting, gun found and held by the Wilshire dicks, you know, to lean on possible shooters with."

Taking the stats in, Lloyd got the feel of a wild card or big wrong move. "Your conclusions, Artie?"

"Do I look dumb? One of our guys zapped the cop-killing cocksucker. Anyway, I called John McManus and told him what I found, and he said, 'Keep it zipped, Officer.' A half hour later Big Thad shows up, hands me three .45 spents and says, 'Garcia, Klein, Rice, case closed. *Capice?*' Since I intend to collect my pension, I said, 'Yes, sir.' So you keep it zipped. *Capice*, Lloydy?"

A Technicolor movie of Louie Calderon guzzling beer and Joe Garcia strumming a guitar surrounded by hula girls passed through Lloyd's mind's eye. He resisted an impulse to grab Artie in a bear hug, then said, "Do I look dumb?"

"No," Artie said, "just slaphappy."

"Well put. I need a favor."

"You always need favors."

"Well put. I've got a long stakeout coming up. Processed any speed lately?"

"Black beauties?"

"Music to my ears. I've got a phone call to make. I'll see you in five minutes."

While Artie made the speed run, Lloyd called Wilshire Detectives. His old friend Pete Ehrlich's answer to his question made wild card/big wrong move a *big* understatement:

At 9:30 Wednesday morning, Captain Fred Gaffaney appeared in the Wilshire squad room, looking uncharacteristically nervous. He cracked several uncharacteristic dirty jokes with officers on duty there, then demanded the key to the evidence room, got it, and rummaged through the lockers until he found a .357 Python, sealed in an evidence bag that also contained a dozen loose shells. Offering no explanation for his actions, he spurned Ehrlich's condolences for the loss of his son and walked out of the squad room, shaking from head to foot.

When Artie returned with five biphetamine capsules, Lloyd had gotten *his* shaking under control. After dropping his resignation letter off with Thad Braverton's secretary, he drove to Temple and Beaudry. Finding an ace stakeout spot across from the guitar shop, he swallowed a black beauty and settled in to await his hand-picked survivor. Soon an amphetamine symphony was ringing in his head:

Gaffaney.

Hopkins.

Two killers doing the doomsday tango.

35

"U n-fucking-real!"

Joe balled up the newspaper, took a bead on the bright blue sky and hurled the missile of good news straight at the sun. Street passersby turned to stare at him, and he shouted, "I got a fucking guardian angel!" and let the ball fall into his hands. Running with it like a halfback with a hot short pass, he headed straight for the motel and Anne.

She was sitting up in bed, smoking, when he came through the door and smoothed the headline out on the sheet in front of her. "Read it," he said. "Bad news and good news, but mostly righteously *good!*"

Anne put out her cigarette and read the front page; Joe sat on the edge of the bed, wondering how the fuzz had got it so wrong and why Rice offed himself there. Watching Anne read, his old song obsession did a brief boogie reprise: "... and death was a thrill on Suicide Hill."

Anne turned to the second page, and Joe got curious about how she'd react to the story on her old boyfriend and his death. He'd had her on decreasing coke use for two days now, and she was probably as close to being a normal woman as she ever would be. Would she have the soul to grieve for the crazy motherfucker?

Putting down the newspaper, Anne lit another cigarette and said, "Wow, I thought Duane was just a car thief. I think that stuff about Stan being a bank robber is phony, though. I think we were together on Monday when that bank was robbed."

Joe couldn't tell if she was being cagey or straight. "You were probably stoned," he said. "He probably split for the heist, then came back."

Anne shrugged and blew smoke rings, then said, "Wrong, baby, but who cares? Also, the paper says Duane *shot* Stan. That's wrong. I was there. Duane stabbed him."

Joe tingled at her mistaken certainty—it meant he could ditch her with a free mind. "Cops screw up sometimes," he said. "Or they work things around to fit the evidence they got. Sweetie, what do you want to *do*?"

"You mean in general? And about us?"

"Right."

Anne blew a string of perfect rings and said, "I like you as a boyfriend, but you're too uptight about dope, and too macho. When we first got together, you weren't so bad, but the more I get to know you, the more stern you get, like you think violence and manhood are synonymous or something. But basically, I want to be with you, and I want to get back into music. I think we're a wave. We last as long as we last."

Joe bent over and cupped her breasts. "What about Rice? He righteously loved you."

Anne caressed the hands caressing her. "He was a stone loser. And you know what's sad? Karmically he betrayed himself, because he said suicide was for cowards. That's sad. How much of Mel's money have we got left?"

Thinking R.I.P. Duane Rice, Joe said, "We're almost broke, but I've got a buddy holding a guitar of mine, and we can get at least three bills for it. So let's move."

"Is it okay to be out on the streets?"

"I think so. We got some kind of weird guardian angel, and I want to see if the old neighborhood still looks the same."

36

At twilight, just when the long stint of surveillance was starting to drive him batshit, his survivor walked up to the guitar shop window, a skinny blonde woman in tow. From a distance they looked like a down-at-the-heels couple—modest dreamers in rumpled clothes peering into the glass in search of a dream fix. Letting them enter the shop, Lloyd hoped they wouldn't do anything to blow the impression.

When they walked back out a minute later, he was there on the sidewalk, waiting. Joe Garcia looked into his eyes and knew; Anne Atwater Vanderlinden looked at Joe and got the picture secondhand. Lloyd stepped back toward the curb and put up his hands in surrender. "Peace, homeboy," he said. "I'm on your side."

Anne moved to Joe's side as he stared at Lloyd; the tense three-way silence stretched until Lloyd put down his hands, and Joe said, "What do you want?"

"People keep asking me that," Lloyd said, "and it's getting old. You read the papers today?"

Joe put an arm around Anne. She nuzzled into his chest and said, "Maybe he's the guard—"

"He's a fucking cop!" Joe blurted. Seeing a woman pushing a baby carriage past them, he lowered his voice. "Crazy Lloyd Hopkins, big fucking deal. You don't scare me, man."

Lloyd smiled. Garcia looked like a thirty-year-old teenager trying to impress a high school chick and get a date for the Junior Prom. Given what he'd been through in the past two weeks, the impression was astounding.

The silence hit again, broken this time by Joe's broad smirk. Smirking back, Lloyd hooked a finger at the strangest armed robber he'd ever seen. Joe walked over, and Lloyd draped an arm around his shoulder and whispered,

"Don't be a dumb taco bender. Let Klein take the fall and get the fuck out of L.A. before something goes wrong. And don't ask me what I want again, or I may have to kick your ass."

Joe twisted free. "I killed Stan Klein, man. I righteously killed him."

The proud statement hit Lloyd between the eyes as truth, and he started sensing juice behind the ancient teenager's bravado. "I believe you. Tell your old lady we're going for a little ride."

The last of the mechanics were leaving when they pulled up across the street from Likable Louie's One-Stop Pit Stop. Lloyd let them finish locking up and gave them time to get down to Sunset, then took a crowbar from the trunk, ran over and pried the garage door open. Flicking on the overhead lights, the first thing he saw was a low-rider perfection.

It was a mint-condition '54 Chevy ragger, candy-apple sapphire blue, canary yellow top, continental kit, tuck-and-roll upholstery. Lloyd checked the dashboard and grinned. The key was in the ignition.

"Bonaroo, man! Fine as fucking wine!"

Lloyd turned around and saw Joe stroking the Chevy's rear fender skirts. Anne Vanderlinden stood behind him, smoking a cigarette and eyeing a tool bin loaded with portable TVs. Tapping Joe's shoulder, Lloyd said, "Are you legit with the greaser act, or are you just trying to impress me?"

Joe started polishing the car with his sleeve. "I don't know. I *righteously* don't know."

"What *do* you know?"

"That I righteously know what I don't want to be. Listen, I got a question."

"Shoot, but nothing about what's going down. All you need to know is get the hell out. There's loose ends all over the place."

Joe fingered the Chevy's pinstriping. "Why'd Rice kill himself at Suicide Hill? What was he thinking of?"

Lloyd shrugged. "I don't know."

Anne was by the tool bin, fiddling with the dials of the TV sets. Joe could tell that she was dope-itchy, looking for something to do with her hands. Moving his eyes back and forth between his maybe girlfriend and his guardian angel, he said, "Hopkins, what's with that place? I mean, you're a cop, you must have heard the stories. It started out with this dude Fritz Hill, right? Back in the forties? He was a righteous hardball and the Hill was named after him?"

Lloyd looked out at the street, getting nervous because he was a civilian now, with no official sanctions for breaking and entering. "I think most of the story is bullshit," he said. "What I've heard is that back in the fifties and sixties there was an old snitch who used to hang out by the Sepulveda Wash. He pretended to be a religious loony, so the local cops and the punks who partied there would think he was harmless. He ratted off shitloads of gangsters to the juvie dicks downtown, and he got a snitch jacket and got snuffed. He was a German guy, and his name was Fritz something. What's the matter, homeboy? You look sad."

"Not sad," Joe said. "Relieved, maybe."

"The keys are in the ignition. Can you drive a stick?"

"Can niggers dance?"

"Only to soul music. Grab some of those TVs and split."

Joe loaded the trunk and backseat with portable Sonys. Anne stood and watched, chain-smoking and shivering. When the Chevy was filled to capacity, he led her over to the passenger's-side door and lovingly eased her in, then returned to Lloyd. Sticking out his hand jailhouse style, he said, "Thanks. And tell Louie I'll pay him off someday."

Lloyd corrected the shake in mid-grasp. "My pleasure. And don't worry about Louie, he owes me. Where are you going?"

"I don't know."

Lloyd smiled and said, "Go there fast," then dropped Joe's hand and watched him walk to his chariot. The strangest armed robber of all time hit the gas with a flourish and crunched the Chevy's gears backing out of the garage, sideswiping parked cars as he headed south on Tomahawk Street. Lloyd turned off the light and shut the door, brushing B&E splinters from his hands. When he got to his Matador, he had a clear view of Sunset. The Chevy was fishtailing it eastbound, and Anne Atwater Vanderlinden was standing under a streetlamp, dancing with her thumb out.

Tango time.

Lloyd took an inventory of his person, punching the seat when he saw that he had forgotten both his newly resurrected .45 and his standard .38 snub nose. The only piece in the car was the .12 gauge mounted to the dash, and it was too obtrusive—overkill all the way. He had to go to the house first and grab a weapon; to show up unarmed for the dance would be suicidal.

He drove home slowly, the amphetamine keeping him hyper-alert, fear of the confrontation making him dawdle in the slow lane. Turning onto his block, he began composing epitaphs for himself and Jesus Fred. Then he saw the moving van in his driveway, its headlights illuminating Janice's Persian carpet, rolled up against the side door. Antiques were arranged on the lawn like welcome beacons, along with piles of Penny's books.

Mine.

Home.

Yes.

Lloyd gasped and punched the accelerator. The homecoming dissolved like a mirage, and new bursts of death prose kept it pushed down to where it couldn't maim him; couldn't destroy his resolve. Then, with miles of obituaries behind him, he pulled up in front of Captain Frederick T. Gaffaney's house and let it hurt, letting his old hot-dog persona take over from there.

Mine.

Home.

Him or me.

Lloyd grabbed the shotgun and flipped off the safety, then pumped in a shell and walked over to the house. The downstairs was dark, but dim lights glowed from behind curtained windows on the second floor. Giving the door handle a test jiggle, Lloyd felt it click and give. He pushed the door open and moved inside.

The smell of stale cigarette smoke and whiskey filled the living room. Lloyd padded forward in the darkness, the odor getting stronger as a staircase came into shadowy view. Tiptoeing up it, he heard coughing, and when he got to the second-floor landing, he saw diffused light glinting off empty liquor bottles strewn across the hallway. Holding the Ithaca at port arms, he pressed himself to the wall back first and scissor-walked toward the light source.

It was a bathroom, giving off a different odor—that of charred paper. Stepping in, Lloyd saw that the smell emanated from the soggy mounds of blackened folders that filled the bathtub. Poking the barrel of his shotgun at the top of the pile, a layer of soot crumbled, and he was able to pick out the stenciled words: *Confidential-Need to Know Basis*. A cross and flag logo was imprinted below it.

A sudden burst of coughing forced Lloyd to wheel and aim. Seeing nothing but the bathroom walls, he traced the racking sound down the hall to a half-open door with total dark behind it. He raised his right foot to kick; the door flew open and harsh light blinded him. He threw the

Ithaca up into firing position, and when his vision cleared, he saw that he was muzzle to muzzle with Fred Gaffaney and a cocked magnum.

"Freeze, asshole."

Lloyd didn't recognize the voice, and could hardly recognize the man it belonged to. This was a high-ranking witch-hunter of booze breath, slept-in clothes and frazzled nerve ends; a born-again with a three-day beard and a shaky finger on a trigger at half pull. A doomsday apparition.

"Freeze, asshole."

The second warning came across as hideous self-parody. Lloyd lowered his shotgun, and Gaffaney eased down the hammer of the .357. The two weapons fell to rest at their bearers' sides simultaneously, and Lloyd said, "What are we going to do about this, Captain?"

Stepping back into the study, Gaffaney waved his gun at the framed L.A.P.D. group shots on the walls. "I'm not a captain anymore, Sergeant," he said, his voice regaining its authority. "I resigned this morning. You outrank me. I did it to make it easy for you."

Lloyd propped the Ithaca up against the doorjamb, keeping it within grabbing range. "I'm not a sergeant anymore. I asked to top out my twenty, but they'll never go for it. We're both civilians. That make it easier for *you?*"

Gaffaney looked at a picture of his wife pinning lieutenant's bars to his collar. "My resignation was accepted, yours was shelved. Braverton told me this afternoon. He wants you around. He wants you around because he loves you."

Lloyd kept his eyes on the magnum that Gaffaney dangled by a finger. "Captain, we're both down the—"

"Don't call me that, goddamn you!"

"We're both down the river! We killed men in cold blood, and the Department has got the fix in on yours, and you've got the fix in on mine, and all I want to do is seal the jackets on both deals and go home to my family. That's as easy as I can make it."

Gaffaney's raw-nerved features went lax; his voice went blank. "You didn't come to arrest me?"

The evidence room charade clicked in as a deliberate big wrong move. Lloyd let his fingers brush the .12 gauge. "I thought I could do it, but I can't. How about it? Your indictment for mine, then I get out of here before something crazy happens."

Gaffaney started shaking his head. His arms shook involuntarily, as if his entire body were trying to shout his denial. The .357 dropped to the floor just as he found his voice. "No. No. No. No. No, no, no, no—"

Lloyd made a grab for the magnum. He got it in his hands before Gaffaney could make a move, and had the cylinder emptied just as the string of no's trailed into a weirdly lucid monotone. ". . . I didn't come this far for you to betray me."

Lloyd slipped the shells into his pocket and tossed the revolver back on the floor, then picked up the Ithaca and ejected the round in the chamber. When the carpet was littered with neutralized weaponry, he said, "Why me?"

The witch-hunter's monotone took on resonance. "Because I was good, but you're the best. Because you were a punk civilian when you killed that man in Watts, while I was a high-ranking police officer when I committed murder. Because the Department will never let me be prosecuted, because justice in this affair must be total." Gaffaney paused, then said, "Because I love you."

Lloyd moved backward until he bumped the wall. "You're insane if you think I'm going to kill you. I'd let you hang me for Richard Beller before I'd do that."

With a ghastly smile as segue, Fred Gaffaney said, "We both learned the gift of sacrifice late, Lloyd. That happens with selfish men like ourselves. I'm only sorry that our sacrifices have to conflict. Now tell me in light of this if I'm insane:

"From the tap on your phone I surmised that you wanted to frame a dead man for Joe Garcia's part in the robberies and killings. I held on to the information. Then this afternoon, when I read the paper and saw what you had gotten away with, I sent Sergeants Collins and Lohmann to check up on Klein. He was involved in the filming of pornographic movies on the dates of the three robberies, in full view of a dozen witnesses. He cannot be connected in any way to Luis Calderon, and a friend of mine in S.I.D. said that he died of knife wounds. He has in his possession a switchblade whose edges perfectly match a biopsied section of Klein's abdomen. The handle has Joe Garcia's thumbprint on it."

"No," Lloyd said in his own doomsday drone. "No, no, no, no, no."

Gaffaney said, "Yes," and started ticking off points. "Klein's alibi witnesses won't come forth, for fear of their involvement in porno coming to light, but questioning the Pico-Westholme eyewitnesses with Klein's and Joe Garcia's mug-shots should get some interesting feedback, and

Calderon could never get by a persistent grand jury. Collins and Lohmann have Duane Rice's .45, taken from the car he was in when they apprehended him. That will contradict Braverton's fix. Had enough?"

"You filthy cocksucker," Lloyd hissed.

Gaffaney spoke softly, as a loving parent would to a child. "I know your guilt, and I know you have to expiate it, and I know Garcia is convenient for that. But if we don't follow through on the investigation, then it means as policemen we mean nothing."

Lloyd imitated Gaffaney's lucid lunatic whisper. "Captain, between us we've been hot dogging for over forty years. Joe Garcia is a drop in the bucket compared to all the railroad jobs we've pulled, *all the laws we've broken*. You're giving me a song and dance about the law to pump me up to kill you? *You are stone fucking insane*."

Running his fingers over the wall photos, Fred Gaffaney said, "I heard a human interest story on the radio today. A bunch of high school kids found some of the robbery money strewn throughout their neighborhood, some inked, some not. They didn't turn it over to the proper authorities, of course; they descended on the Strip and tried to spend it as fast as they could. An off-duty sheriff's deputy saw a boy trying to change an inked twenty and got him to talk, but by the time a search team was dispatched to the area where the money was found, not a single dollar bill could be located. You see the kind of world we live in?"

Lloyd picked up the .357 and began loading it. "It's a pretty lackluster parable, Captain. Tell it to Collins and Lohmann. It'll get them jazzed up to do some serious ass-kicking. Have you gone forward with your information on Garcia? Anyone beside you and your boys know?"

"No, not yet."

"Why did you burn your files?"

"I'm not a policeman anymore. I don't deserve to lead, and none of my followers are capable of leading. Th . . . that's finished."

Snapping the cylinder, Lloyd said, "I did what I could. Garcia's got wheels and a head start, more than he would have had without me. You got anything to say?"

Gaffaney frowned. "Rice said, 'She was a stone heartbreaker.' What do you think he meant?"

"I don't know, Captain. For the record, you did the right thing. He killed your son."

Gaffaney reached out and touched Lloyd's arm; Lloyd batted his hand away and said, "What do *you* have to say?"

"Nothing," Gaffaney said. "I have nothing."

Lloyd placed the gun in the hands of his old enemy. "Then go out like a soldier, but don't take anyone else with you."

"You won't?"

Lloyd said no and walked down the hall to the bathroom. He was clenching the edge of the tub, staring at the cross and flag logo, when he heard the shot. His hands jerked up, ripping out jagged chunks of porcelain, and then there was a second shot, and another and still another. He ran back to the study and found Gaffaney on his knees, holding the gun and an armful of framed photographs to his chest. He was muttering, "I've got nothing. I've got nothing."

Lloyd helped him to his feet. The mementos he was grasping made the embrace cumbersome, but he was able to get his arms around the sobbing man anyway. The simple act felt like mercy for all their lost ones, all their stone heartbreakers.